from
SARATOV
to
SAN FRANCISCO
FIVE GENERATIONS OF ONE FAMILY'S
STAY IN SOUTH AFRICA

AARON DI DERTSEYLER

TABLE OF CONTENTS

PROLOGUE

FROM SARATOV TO SAN FRANCISCO

The Saga of a five-generation Jewish Family: From Maimon, who left Russia in 1878 as a penniless illiterate on a boat to East London, to Mia, his great granddaughter, jetting off to San Francisco 140 years later in Book II

INTRODUCTION

Dear Reader,

In order to ensure the story's continuity, I considered it necessary from time to time to change the order in which certain events took place, and doing so has resulted in some anachronisms. Readers should remember that From Saratov to San Francisco is an historical novel, and does not pretend to represent history as it took place.

Period-specific words that might not be appropriate today have occasionally been used, and I would ask readers to judge them in the light of the 1878-1948 period in which the story takes place.

The novel is a work of fiction based on actual events. Incidents, locales, and conversations have loosely been recreated from memory, discussions, and photographs.

In order to maintain anonymity, the names of many individuals, places, identifying characteristics and other details, occupations, and places of residence have changed.

My heartfelt thanks to Penny Hochfeld, who "midwifed" this project, and also to Roy Robins, who edited the story with sensitivity and understanding, both for the Sokolovski family, and also for me.

Should any readers wish to compliment me on this story, they should feel free to do so at my email address below.

Finally, if you enjoyed "Book I," you will be happy to learn that Morrie and his siblings, their spouses, children, and grandchildren will be back in "Book II," which covers the years 1948 to 2018.

Best wishes,
Aaron di Dertseyler
aaron@fromsaratovtosanfrancisco.com

BOOK 1

1878 - 1948

CHAPTER 1
GOODBYE RUSSIA

Huddled together against the biting wind that blew in from the Russian steppes, the Sokolovski family clasped their chests and stamped their feet in a futile effort to keep warm. Poorly clothed, their fingers and toes, like their hearts, numb. Near the end of Saratov's[1] deserted railway platform, they stood in silence, because there was nothing more to say.

Anshul had never believed it would come to this. To break out of the seemingly inevitable cycle of grinding poverty his family had suffered for generations, he had left Poland as a young man and headed east, through Belarus into Russia, eventually arriving at Saratov, a small town on the Volga River. There he chanced upon, and fell in love with, Gittel Borovnik, the daughter of a wine merchant. Six months later they were married. Working day and night, even on the Sabbath, and saving every rouble he could, Anshul was able to buy a small piece of land and, when he had put aside enough to pay for the necessary timber, build a house on it.

To that house he brought his bride, and she, in turn, delivered him four children. Their firstborn, a son, did not live long enough to be named. A year later they were blessed with another son, Zelig, who grew to love the Torah[2] more than his parents. Then Kaylah, the daughter Anshul had secretly prayed for, his multifaceted diamond. Kaylah was not a star, she was a galaxy. Clever beyond her years, kind

---

1   *Saratov is a little town on the bank of the Volga River. In 1897 it had 1460 Jews. When Anshul arrived forty years earlier there were possibly half this number.*

2   *The five books of Moses*

1

and considerate, and a fighter for what was right. Anshul mused that if the Mashiach[3] could be a woman, perhaps … And then there was Maimonides.

Tall and thin – everyone in Saratov was thin – eighteen-year-old Maimonides was leaving. Leaving on his own. Leaving the only place in the world he had ever known. Leaving his father, mother, sister, and brother, and a life best forgotten.

At his feet, a battered leather suitcase with a few secondhand clothes that his mother had bought at the weekly market. In his pocket, a carefully knotted handkerchief containing seventeen roubles. And sewn into the lining of his threadbare coat, three gold sovereigns. He also had a rail ticket to Kiev, another from there to Warsaw, and a third from the Polish capital to Hamburg. And most importantly of all, a steamship ticket to America.

Many young men had set out like he was doing, arrived in America, worked hard, and sent money back to "the old country," so that their parents and siblings could join them. But those young men could read and write. Maimonides could do neither. Not because he did not try. But because God decided he would never be able to, no matter how many hundreds of hours he and his teachers tried to get the letters and numbers into his head. And so, he was being sent away.

Anshul was a man of few words, and even those deserted him now. Zelig had blessed his brother in their humble wooden home, not because he wanted to but because he knew his father could not.

Kaylah bit her lip, fighting back the tears. Her little brother, barely an inch taller than she was, whom she had looked after and shielded from the bullies at school, was now leaving. Leaving the love and support of his family. Leaving through Europe by train, and then across the sea to America. As he could neither read nor write, learning English or French or German was out of the question, because they were taught from books. What chance did he have?

But Maimonides could learn languages by just listening. There was a girl from Kiev in his class who, like him, was good at mathematics, and from her he learned Ukrainian. How would he survive? Logic and common sense told Kaylah he would not. God had not looked after him up till now, so why would He do so on the trip? And in America? How was he even going to get to America? She knew her brother had no future in Saratov, but at least here he had her to look out for him. Round and round those thoughts spun in her head like the water wheel in Mr. Harris's flour mill.

All Gittel's feelings about Maimonides had drained away in the weeks since she and Anshul had come to their fateful decision. Actually, it wasn't *their* decision, it was hers. Anshul, physically strong and morally upright, was an intellectual pygmy. Unable to debate pros and cons rationally, he had ceded the decisions relating to their son's future to his wife.

It was her fault, she knew, if Maimonides failed, and surely he would. But some thing (she did not know what) told Gittel it was the right decision. It was not God who told her, she didn't believe in Him. How could she, when He had stood by and watched His children being slaughtered in one pogrom after another? She stood impassively, waiting for the train that would change her son's life, and, by extension, their whole family's as well.

Out of the misty gray came the big iron machine, belching black smoke and white steam. They had all seen trains in the distance, but now they felt one through the soles of their shoes. It was hundreds of yards away, and then, in seconds, it was screeching to a stop next to them. Though he would never admit it, Anshul was scared. What if it jumped off the rails like an untamed horse? But it did not. Doors opened, people got out of the train's rooms and jumped down onto the platform. Other people climbed up into the rooms.

"Go, go," Kayla said nervously, pushing Maimonides up the two steps and into one of the train's half-filled rooms. He turned, his face ashen-white with fear. Kayla had seen his fear before. When pogroms started. Then her brother seized up. He could not talk. He could not move.

Doors slammed. A piercing whistle sounded and the train lurched forward. Maimonides stumbled onto the wooden bench and looked out of the window. While other people waved, the Sokolovskis stood motionless. They just looked. Leaning out of the window, Maimonides stared at his disappearing family, and they at him. And then they were gone.

Gittel turned on her heel and strode down the platform. When Kaylah caught up with her mother, she saw the tears – tears Gittel had fought back for weeks. Like a water tank overflowing, they cascaded down her cheeks. Neither woman said anything. Twenty yards behind

3

the men followed, each absorbing in their own way what had just happened. It took all of them longer, much longer than they expected, to come to terms with what they had done. None of them had said, "No, Maimonides, you should stay. We will look after you." They all bore responsibility, to a greater or lesser extent, for casting Maimonides off into a world in which he had no chance of surviving.

A dumpy woman in her fifties brushed past Maimonides and closed the window; and, in doing so, cut him off from the world he had known. It also shut out the freezing Siberian air, its place taken by the smell of boiled, sour cabbage soup. Ah, the shchi that his bobba[4] used to give him on his way home from those terrible days at school. Not only soup, but also love and folk tales when he was young, and comforting words of wisdom when he was older.

Maimonides looked around. Everything in the small room was made of wood: the floor, the two benches opposite each other, the walls, and the ceiling. Light came in through three windows: one in the door, and the other two next to it at one end of the benches.

As the train gathered speed, Maimonides clasped his family's small suitcase to his chest, as if it might be torn from his clutches if he didn't, all the while looking out of the window in wonderment. Already the train was running faster than any horse could, or at least any horse he had seen in Saratov. He recognized the fields the train rushed by, but soon there were forests and rivers he had never seen. Saratov was gone, now replaced by hills with vines growing on their slopes, and…

"You going to America."

A tired voice jolted Maimonides back to where he was, in the little wooden room on the train. It was a statement, not a question, from the plump babushka[5] on the bench opposite.

She looked about 60 years old, he thought, but was probably younger, years of physical hardship having taken their toll. Her stubby hands had two missing fingers and her swollen feet barely fitted into her once black, now badly scuffed, gray leather shoes. This was the price she had paid for thousands of hours standing in the fish market. Together with a large basket on one side of her and a nebbish[6] little man on the other, she occupied the whole bench. The two of them fitted

---

4   Grandmother
5   A Russian old woman or grandmother
6   A recently arrived immigrant, commonly used in the United States

in rather well, Maimonides thought, like bookends.

"I'm Frieda" the voice announced, "and this," she glanced at the shrivelled-up man alongside her, "is Lieb."

Maimonides could not suppress a smile. Lieb was the name for a lion, and this poor fellow looked like a pussycat. Hunched up, as if expecting a blow he could hopefully deflect, Lieb behaved as though he was trying to look invisible. Out of proportion with the rest of his body, his head was big, almost bald, with wisps of yellow hair that looked like withering stalks of wheat in a dried-up field. Maimonides couldn't see the color of his eyes as they constantly looked down. His big ears anchored a pair of heavy-framed glasses, and his face was the saddest Maimonides had ever seen.

"You think that's funny, our names?" Frieda barked.

"No, of course not," Maimonides blurted out, at a loss to explain the reason for his mirth. "I'm Maimonides," he said, still smiling, offering his hand to Frieda, who looked at it in disdain.

"Lieb, shake hands with this greener,"[7] she instructed the poor fellow who, Maimonides realized, must be her husband. "He doesn't know it is not right to touch a married woman," Frieda added, thereby establishing herself as a religiously observant person, and Maimonides as an uneducated, overgrown boy.

The overgrown boy did as he was told, and almost crushed the bones of the nebbish's hand in the process.

The lion reclaimed his right hand, stuffed it into a pocket of his coat, where it cuddled up with the left one, as if they were comforting each other. The black threadbare coat was at least two sizes too big for Lieb, and made him appear even smaller than he was.

Although you wouldn't know it now, Lieb had once been "The Tiger of Tirgoviste," the Greco-Roman wrestling champion of Eastern Russia, the only man who had ever beaten the mighty Amir from Azerbaijan. The man whose door was knocked on by every shadchan[8] in the town, until that fateful Tuesday evening.

In their one-roomed wooden house his sister was giving birth to her first child. Forewarned by a neighbor that the Cossacks were coming, and only too familiar with the sporadic outbursts of anti-Jewish

---

7   *A person, usually a man, who is regarded as pitifully ineffective, timid, or submissive*

8   *Matchmaker*

violence, the Jews barricaded themselves in their homes. With his sister's husband away bidding farewell to his mother who was dying of tuberculosis, Lieb was designated to fight off the Cossacks. Brave Lieb, who had defeated the mighty Amir.

Except that Lieb was not brave, he was petrified of the Cossacks. Instead of barricading the house, he hid in the cupboard. The Cossacks burst in just as the midwife was cutting the cord. One of them snatched the baby from her and kicked it to a fellow Cossack, who kicked it back. His sister was screaming hysterically for her baby, the midwife cowering under the only table; and in the cupboard, Lieb was shaking uncontrollably. After a while, one of the Cossacks tired of Lieb's sister's screaming.

"You want your baby. Here it is," he said as he smashed it down on her mother's head. Then, looking around and seeing there was nothing to steal, they left.

All this was told by the midwife. Lieb's traumatized sister never spoke again, except to herself and in a language no one could understand. His conquest of Amir forgotten, Lieb was shunned by everyone in the town, except the young boys who threw stones at him and taunted him and called him a pakhden.[9]

The Tiger of Tirgoviste became a recluse who lived in a shed at the edge of the woods. There he stayed for almost thirty years, until one day he helped a man load logs onto his wagon. He did so again the next day, and the day after that as well. And so the timber merchant took pity on Lieb and told him to get on the wagon. They traveled for two days until they came to the village where the man lived with his wife. After a few years, the man died, and Lieb married his widow, Frieda.

"Are your relations in New York?" Frieda asked, being more nosey than curious.

Maimonides nodded positively and smiled at his inquisitor.

"What a boychik," Frieda replied, softening. "Do you want something to eat?" Not waiting for a reply, she opened her basket and pulled out a little blue-checked cloth, which she carefully spread, revealing five hard-boiled eggs and four small apples.

Maimonides shook his head, but that did not deter Frieda. "Take an egg," she instructed him, "or an apple." Seeing he wasn't going to do either, Frieda added to nobody in particular, "He's upset at leaving

---

9   *Coward*

6

his family. That is why he doesn't eat." Carefully rewrapping the food and closing the basket, she assured him, "Don't worry, you are in good hands."

Not sure if this meant that Frieda was adopting him, Maimonides waited for further information.

"Your boat, *every* boat, belongs to our landsman. Not actually *our* landsman, because he is German. His parents came from Denmark," Frieda added, as if that would explain everything. Then taking a deep breath she announced, "Albert Ballin," which meant absolutely nothing to Maimonides.

"You don't know Albert Ballin?" she asked incredulously. "Herr Albert Ballin?"

Maimonides looked at her blankly.

"Let me tell you, Herr Albert Ballin is Jewish, and he is the largest shipowner in the world. In the world," she repeated slowly, in case Maimonides had missed it first time round. "He has boats going to China, and Africa, and places you never heard of – and America, of course. They don't only take people, they take goods as well," Frieda added authoritatively, as if Albert were her son.

"His company is called HAPAG. It is an abbreviation. Its full name is Hamburg-Amerikanische Packetfahrt-Actien-Gesellschaft," she concluded proudly. Maimonides did not know if the pride stemmed from Herr Ballin being Jewish, or Frieda having successfully got her tongue around those five German words.

"You must have something to eat," Frieda said, as if absorbing such important knowledge needed to be followed by food. Without waiting for a response, she took one of the apples from her basket and handed it to Maimonides. Realizing he now had no option, Maimonides took the apple, thanked her, and bit into it. Frieda looked on triumphantly, mission accomplished.

Now that they were on the same side, so to speak, Maimonides thought he might be able to benefit from this unofficial adoption. Noticing that Frieda was not reading or sleeping, he decided it was a good time to raise a subject he had been contemplating for many miles. He realized that he needed someone to show him the ropes in America, and here already, just over an hour into his journey, he had such a person.

Feeling happier than he had for the past few weeks, Maimonides asked, "Are you going to America?"

Frieda did not answer, continuing to look into the far distance, even though she was facing the room's wall just a few feet away. "What? What did you say?" Frieda blurted out, as if woken from a sleep, though she was wide awake.

"I was just asking, are you going to America?"

Frieda shook her head. After a while, feeling that she owed Maimonides some clarification, she said, "Just to Hamburg. That's all."

"That's all?" he asked, wondering how the pieces of this puzzle were going to fit together.

For the first time Lieb, the pussycat, opened his mouth. "We are going to fetch our granddaughter. She is arriving next week. From America," he said in a hoarse whisper. Maimonides wondered if his voice had been damaged in an attack by marauding Cossacks, or if Lieb just didn't want to draw attention to himself.

Realizing that this put the kibosh on whatever hopes Maimonides had of finding someone to show him the ropes, he was ready to drop the subject, when Lieb added, "She has trachoma. That is why they are sending her back."

Reminded of this, tears rolled down Frieda's cheeks, followed by loud, uncontrolled sobbing.

"Feigie is our daughter's youngest," Lieb explained. "All the others were allowed in, but not Feigie. She was refused."

"How old is she?" Maimonides asked.

"Just six."

Not knowing what to say, Maimonides sat in silence. While Frieda continued sobbing, Lieb picked up one of her overstuffed hands and patted it tenderly. After a while she spoke.

"Why did he do this?" Frieda asked, expecting an answer but obviously not from Lieb or Maimonides.

Maimonides did not know who "he" was, but shortly learned.

"Why is He punishing Feigie? What did that little angel do to deserve this? She who is better than all of them put together. And now? She will live like an orphan. And who will marry an orphan, especially one with no dowry?"

Frieda started sobbing again, Lieb resumed patting her hand, and Maimonides looked out of the window at the ever-changing scenery, realizing for the first time that if life was tough for him in Saratov, it wasn't going to be any easier in America.

As the train chugged on, through towns he had never heard of, with names he couldn't read, Maimonides cast his mind back, first over the last few weeks, then months, and finally years, to his very first memories.

He was at nursery school, called cheder. Just three years old, sitting on a bench with Velvel on his one side, and Chaskel on the other; the three of them sharing a well-worn page of elementary Yiddish that had served generations of children before them. His benchmates read the page carefully, but try as hard as he could, the words did not come out. Maimonides could see the letters, but not say them. That earned him many blows from the teacher, accompanied by shouts of "behaimeh chamoole."[10]

Kaylah found him crying in the corner of the playground and took him home. Hearing what happened, his mother stormed off to the school, confronted the teacher, and in front of the class, beat him mercilessly with a stick she had picked up for that purpose. Leaving the teacher cowering under his desk, she shouted "Chap en a messa meshina,"[11] and then went to the head teacher and told him what had happened.

That set off a heretofore unprecedented chain of events. Maimonides remembered many adults coming to their little house, mainly to congratulate Gittel, culminating in the arrival of the rabbi, who, as Kaylah remarked afterwards, "arrived like a lion, and left like a lamb."

Maimonides stayed home for the rest of that year; when he went back to school, it was to teacher Malka's class. Teacher Malka understood his problem and never beat him. His reminiscences were interrupted by the train screeching to a stop alongside a platform teeming with vendors selling bialys.[12] Passengers who did not take notice of the vendors had their windows loudly banged on.

"Where are we?" Maimonides asked, as if finding himself in a bad dream.

"Voronezh," Frieda replied, pointing to the sign on the platform. "Can't you read?"

"Would you and Lieb like a bialy?" Maimonides replied, wanting to get as far away as possible from any question relating to his reading ability (or lack thereof).

"From these ganovim?[13] Never! Do you know what they charge?"

---

10   *Dull-witted numbskull*
11   *"May you suffer an ugly fate"*
12   *A flat bread roll topped with chopped onions*
13   *Thieves*

Before Maimonides had a chance to reply, Frieda made it clear to the vendors that unless they moved on, both their lives and those of their families would be in grave danger.

The locomotive let out a piercing shriek and jolted forward, which was the cue for Frieda to open her basket and mine it once again. Bypassing the eggs and apples she came up with a handful of syrniki.[14]

"Take, take," she instructed. They looked so good that Maimonides took two. Frieda thrust another one into his cupped hands. Their smell opened a window into his mind whose vista Maimonides had long forgotten. One summer, when he was six, his whole family had gone to the forest for a picnic. It was the only time they ever did this. His father found a glade surrounded by birch trees, and his mother put two large plates on the emerald-colored grass: one of syrniki, the other of peaches and plums. There were also large bottles of lemonade that she had made.

The children ran around playing tag and hide-and-seek, and then threw off their clothes and jumped into a pond where they splashed each other. Exhausted, the three of them lay down in the shade of the tall trees, and their father told them folk tales written by the famous Russian author Alexander Nikolayevich Afanasyev. Kaylah loved hearing the Hansel and Gretel story, and so her mother told them that one as well. As the sun dipped behind the trees, tired and smiling, the family made their way home.

That was the happiest day of Maimonides' life.

Remembering that wonderful day, Maimonides dozed off. A few hours later he woke up in terror. It was pitch-dark. He did not know where he was. Slowly, it all came back to him. The clickety-click noise was the train, and he was on his way to America. Scared and frightened of what lay ahead of him, Maimonides stretched out and fell into a fitful sleep.

---

14   *Small blinis made of cottage cheese*

CHAPTER 2

MORE COSSACKS

"Wake up! Wake up!" Frieda shouted, shaking Maimonides. "Here is Kiev."

Maimonides blinked and sat up. The train was moving slowly, no longer through forests and fields, but past cheek-by-jowl, large buildings. Frieda and Lieb were standing at the door of their room, which Maimonides remembered Frieda told him was called a "compartment." The train stopped and the couple climbed down onto the platform. Frieda turned to Maimonides, who was still on the train, taking in sounds he had never heard and sights he had never seen.

"Greener, come on!" Frieda instructed. "We have to get the Warsaw train. Follow me."

Maimonides followed Lieb, who was struggling to keep up with his wife while gripping her heavy basket as if his life depended on it (possibly it did, Maimonides thought). Weaving between what seemed to Maimonides like thousands of people, the harried and the hurried scurried after their leader, who took them first to the station's central concourse, and then to another platform, where their train was waiting.

Frieda found an empty compartment, bundled the two men into it, and then followed, like a mother hen making sure that neither of her chicks were left behind. Seating herself once again between the food basket on one side and Lieb on the other, Frieda breathed a sigh of achievement.

"And where would you be without me?" she asked no one in particular, and then answered her question. "On another platform, or in another train. Going to Moscow."

"Thank you..." Maimonides stammered, composing in his mind a suitable sentence of appreciation.

Before he did so, Frieda said. "Don't thank me. Thank the Almighty, who sent me to make sure you get to Hamburg. What a job he has given me." She seemed to feel that as one of the Chosen People, this was her designated task.

The door opened and two Cossack soldiers got in, one obviously an officer and the other a younger private. Both were carrying no-longer full bottles of vodka. Sitting on the bench alongside them, Maimonides turned white as a sheet.

Two years ago, similarly dressed Cossacks had raged through Saratov looking for Jews. Of course, it was not the first time this had happened. Twice before Anshul and Gittel had fought off Cossacks, once with boiling water and the other time with boiling oil. The second time, Kaylah and Maimonides were shoved under the bed and instructed not to utter a word. Terrified, they clutched each other. Zelig, not home, was studying with the rabbi. Poised, as if waiting for the starter gun, Anshul and Gittel were ready to counter-attack with five pots of boiling water.

"Open up!" a Cossack roared so loudly that the children, now shaking with fear, thought he was already in their house. Standing behind the door, Gittel swung it open and, in a co-ordinated movement, Anshul threw the entire contents of the pot into the first Cossack's face. Screaming in agony, he backed off to have his place taken by another, who got the second pot of boiling water before he could cross the Sokolovski's threshold.

The remaining Cossacks, waiting for spoils of the looting, ran away as fast as their inebriated legs could carry them. A wave of relief broke over their little house. Anshul took a bottle of vodka from the kitchen cupboard, poured two tumblers full, and swallowed one as if it was water. Gittel gulped the other one down.

"Can we come out now?" Maimonides' little voice croaked.

"It's alright now," Gittel answered quietly.

Kaylah collapsed into Gittel's arms, sobbing with relief. Maimonides sat down dazed, realizing how close they had all come to being killed. That is what happened to the Stossel family a few months before. Anshul half-filled his glass with vodka, handed it to Maimonides, who swallowed the alcohol like it was lemonade. Neither said a word. Then Zelig walked in the door and, seeing the family were safe and unharmed, burst into tears.

The train jerked forward, which reminded the Cossacks that there was vodka to be drunk. Each took a swig and sat down on the bench next to Maimonides. Frieda was reading a book, as Lieb had been before he fell asleep. Maimonides took his book and pretended to read it. After a few minutes, the officer pointed at large houses the train was passing, and said in Ukrainian, "Those are Jews' houses."

"How do you know?" the young private asked.

"Because only Jews have money to buy big houses. That is the problem," the officer added authoritatively.

"What problem?"

"I'll explain it," the officer continued, happy to have an audience for his monetary knowledge. "A country has only got so much money. In our country most of it is in the hands of the Jews. If there were less Jews, there would be more money for us Ukrainians."

"What can we do about it?" the private asked, expecting an economic solution.

"Kill them."

Maimonides' heart started racing, fearing what was coming next.

That explained, the officer went hard at his bottle. Feeling the need to do the same, the private followed suit.

"How many Jews have you killed?" the young man asked in awe.

Maimonides stiffened, his heart now beating like a bass drum.

"Not enough. I don't get much chance these days," the officer said, finishing the vodka. Then looking at Frieda and Lieb, he added, "We could kill these two."

Blood drained from Maimonides' face.

"They are Jews? How can you tell?" the private asked, finishing his bottle.

"I know these things. They smell different. They look different. They are Jews," the older man answered what he considered an elementary question.

Maimonides heart was now pounding so loudly that he was afraid the Cossacks could hear it.

"You are going to kill them?" the private asked in wonderment.

"I'll throw them out of the window, all three of them," was the offhand answer he received.

Nonchalantly, Maimonides turned another page in the book on his lap, while sweat wet his shirt, thankfully hidden by the thin, black, many-owned jacket he had inherited. His heart now pounding in his head, Maimonides was petrified, as scared as he had been under the bed clinging to Kaylah.

"The fat woman, too? Can you lift her up?" the private asked, getting to the practicality of the job at hand.

"Maybe not. I will just throw the little fellow out. You can help me with this good-for-nothing," he said, inclining his head to Maimonides. "We can do it when we go over the bridge near Zhitomir."

"Do you think they know what we are saying?" the private asked, sufficiently sober to realize they might get some opposition.

"If they knew what we were saying, they would be shitting themselves. Do you smell any shit?" the officer responded, as if their fellow passengers were non-people.

They both laughed, each taking another swig of vodka.

"The young one might fight back," the private said.

"No, he won't. He is a Jew. They are all cowards," the officer replied as if this closed the subject once and for all. Like the calm before a storm, Maimonides' panic attack melted away, re placed by cold-steel resolve. He knew what to do. He had overheard two older boys at school discussing how to fight back when goyim attacked them on their way home. A knee in the testicles followed by an uppercut to the nose. That is how Maimonides had dealt with the bully at school who teased him for being stupid. An aching crotch and a broken nose squirting blood like a fountain ensured no one ever insulted him again. Maimonides was like a stalking tiger, ready to pounce.

"To three Jews less," the officer said, raising his now almost empty bottle.

"And more money for us," the young man added, his concerns having evaporated in a haze of vodka.

That decided, they swallowed what was left in their respective bottles.

"How long till we get to the bridge?" the private asked, now very much on board with the plan.

"At least an hour. Take it easy. I'm going to nap," the officer announced confidently, as if a battle plan had just been agreed with the chief of staff.

The vodka sent them both into an alcoholic slumber, and then a deep sleep.

A little while later the train made its first stop. The Cossacks were snoring, dead to the world. Wordlessly, Maimonides got up with his suitcase, opened the door, and stepped down onto the platform. Frieda followed, as did Lieb. Quickly, they found an empty compartment and settled into it.

"You speak Ukrainian?" Frieda asked.

Maimonides nodded.

"Me too," Frieda sighed, relieved at having overcome another hurdle that the Almighty had put in her path.

CHAPTER 3

ONTO HAMBURG

The rest of the journey passed uneventfully. No other passengers entered their compartment. As the sun set, Frieda went back to her basket and dug out some pirozhki[15] the previously offered apples, and a large bottle of some unidentifiable juice that the three of them shared. With full stomachs they dozed off, as comfortably as they could on the hard wooden benches. The following morning they changed trains in Warsaw, boarding one for Hamburg. The sun shone brightly on a new day. Ukraine and the Cossacks were yesterday's problem and happily forgotten. Maimonides and Frieda were in Germany, both excited about getting to Hamburg for specifically different reasons. Lieb showed no emotion one way or the other.

"Where will you be going with Feigie?" Maimonides asked.

"Back home, to Kyakhovo," Frieda said resignedly. "Where else?"

"England. Why don't you go to England?" Maimonides replied, realizing that from Hamburg they were more than halfway to England from Kyakhovo.

"And what will I do there? Visit the Queen?" Frieda shot back, keen to end this conversation.

"What will you do in Kyakhovo?" Maimonides asked.

For the first time Frieda was lost for words.

"I'll tell you what you'll do," Maimonides said, now taking a dominant position in the conversation. "Wait for letters from America that will break your heart, and wait for pogroms that will kill you – you and Feigie and Lieb."

---

15   *Fried yeast leavened buns with sweet or savory fillings*

"How will we get to England? We've got no money," Frieda responded, now definitely on the back foot.

"Give the railroad company your tickets back to Kya-wherever, and use the money to buy steamship tickets to England," Maimonides said, as if this was the most obvious thing to do.

"I don't know anybody in England."

"There are Jews in England from Russia. Do you think they will leave you to sleep in the street?"

"What about my house in Kyakhovo?" Frieda asked, falling back on the time-honored Jewish response, "I don't have much, but what I do have, I don't want to give up."

"The Cossacks are going to burn it down, with you in it if you are there," Maimonides told her from almost personal experience.

"You don't understand."

"No, I don't. Please explain," said Maimonides, now getting agitated.

"You are young. You can do these things."

"Old people, not that you are so old, can also do 'these things.' You are strong, and you look healthy."

"I am tired. Don't tell me to sleep. It is not that kind of tired."

"What kind of tired is it?" Maimonides asked gently.

Frieda looked at the greener, who just three days ago didn't know where to put his feet, and now he was telling her what to do.

"It is a long story."

"I have got time."

"She has had a hard life," Lieb interjected protectively.

Maimonides waited to hear about it, but hard lives for Jews in Russia usually meant terrible things, and he didn't need reminding about them.

"I am her third husband," Lieb continued. "Moishe, the first one, was beaten to death in front of her. Why? For taking seven peaches from a farmer's orchard. Not for himself. For Frieda and the children."

"I don't need to know this," Maimonides said quietly.

"Yes, you do. Then you will understand. Itzik, who she married later, was thrown over a high bridge onto the ice. That night Frieda and her brother went with a sledge to collect the body. They were too late. Wolves had eaten it."

For a few miles they rode on in silence. Lieb hadn't said anything about Frieda's children, and Maimonides felt it was insensitive to ask about them. The question of Feigie's future really bothered him. Her parents and siblings were in America, where they were probably building new lives for themselves, and their daughter/sister was stuck in the old world, sure to suffer one way or another. It wasn't his business, Maimonides knew, but in a way, it was, because he was the only person who could save Feigie from going back to Kyakhovo. So he persevered.

"There are Russian Jews in Manchester," Maimonides said gently.

Frieda and Lieb were either reading or pretending to read, their noses stuck in books. A past master at this form of pretence, Maimonides sensed that their minds were grappling with this new option he had suggested.

"I know a family there," Maimonides lied, "who would help you find your feet. Get settled in."

Frieda looked up from her book, sniffing the bait but not taking it.

"The father has a shop selling fried fish and chips wrapped in newspaper. It is what the English people eat." Maimonides had learned this from a visiting rabbi who lived in Manchester. "They have their own house with three bedrooms: one for the parents and one for their sons and one for their daughters."

"What daughters?" Frieda asked.

"A six-year-old girl called Rochel and an older one whose name I forget," Maimonides said, thinking, May God forgive me for this. "Also, two boys who help out in the shop."

"What is their family name?" Frieda asked.

"Rivkin. They are a well-known family in Manchester." Maimonides answered quickly, wanting to be sure that Frieda swallowed the bait.

Frieda closed her book, digesting this information. For ten minutes she said nothing.

"How would I find them?" Frieda asked, not at all happy with this alternative that she was being given.

"Go to the synagogue and ask for the 'fish-and-chips Rivkins.'"

Maimonides could see from Frieda's furrowed brow that she was wrestling with this problem. Eventually she said, "It won't work. We will go back to Kyakhovo."

Containing his disappointment, Maimonides said as dispassionately as he could, "That's a pity, because Feigie could learn English, and when her eyes are well again, join her parents in America."

Whether Frieda took this on board or not, Maimonides didn't know. Giving no hint one way or another, she opened her book and continued reading.

Unwilling to risk antagonizing Frieda for the sake of a little girl he had never met, and unable to read as Frieda and Lieb were doing, Maimonides returned to his own private world.

Coming to the end of the first part of his journey, Maimonides reflected on the last three days. What would his parents think of his behavior? What would Kaylah think? She would be proud of him, he thought. He left Saratov as a nervous boy, and 72 hours later was arriving in Hamburg as a young man. That is quite an achievement, he felt.

Looking down at his battered suitcase brought him back to earth. He hadn't left the trains, except for brief stops at Kiev and Warsaw, so who was he kidding? He was still the illiterate boy from Saratov. But what about the Cossacks? He didn't fight them, but he was ready to. And the fish-and-chips Rivkins? How easily and convincingly he had lied, surprising himself in the process. Maimonides didn't feel bad about it, which bothered him a bit. He lied to stop the girl going back to her bobba's no-hope shtetl, and so it was OK. Or was it? Maimonides wasn't sure. But it was done, and even if she didn't get to America, England was surely better than Russia. And who knows, there may even be a Rivkin family in Manchester. And if there was, perhaps they had a fish and chips shop. That made Maimonides feel better, but not much. It bothered him that he had lied to Frieda, who was a good woman. Anyway, she probably wouldn't go to England, so Maimonides decided not to torment himself unnecessarily.

The train slowed, and the change in the clickety-click tempo woke Frieda and Lieb. Looking out of the window, Frieda announced Hamburg was but a few minutes away.

"We'll go to England," she added as offhandedly as she could.

"Good! Good!" Maimonides replied, surprised, feeling some acknowledgement was needed, and that jumping up and kissing her wasn't it.

"Why good?" Frieda asked piercingly, letting slip that leaving Russia and her house, even temporarily, had been a traumatic and questionable decision.

"Because you can tell Chaim Rivkin that I haven't forgotten the five roubles he owes me. He is their firstborn, a bit older than me."

Maimonides was pleased with the way in which he perpetuated the lie, proud that he had carried it off so convincingly, and just a little uncomfortable with what he was doing.

The train stopped at Hamburg station, disgorging all its passengers and their assorted baggage onto the platform. Maimonides stood facing Frieda, not sure what to do. A hug or even a handshake was verboten,[16] but he needed some physical contact. So he shook Liebe's hand limply, and then turned to Frieda. For the first time in the three days they had spent together, she looked at him as a mother would her son. Then she threw her arms around him, buried her face in his neck, all the while muttering, "Schmulik, Schmulik."

Maimonides looked to Lieb for an explanation, and unexpectedly got one.

"Her son. Her only son. He was crushed by a carriage wheel."

Frieda released Maimonides, kissed him gently on the forehead, tousled his hair, and said "Goodbye." Then she walked away without a backward glance; Lieb following as an obedient puppy would.

Maimonides joined a crowd that was like a human river, flowing to the exit of the station and then into a large building with "Hamburg-America Line" written in gigantic letters, bigger letters than Maimonides had ever seen – it was just a pity he couldn't read the words they spelled. Inside men inspected the travelers' tickets and directed them to lines that had formed leading to tables behind which sat uniformed agents. Maimonides joined the line to which he was directed. In front of him was a gray-bearded, tall, elderly rabbi dressed in black from head to toe. At his feet was a big spherical box probably containing his hat, and in his hand was a small black battered suitcase.

"Excuse me, Rabbi. Could you please tell me what these three large words say?" Maimonides asked, adding, "I have lost my glasses."

The rabbi looked at the ticket Maimonides was holding, and in a soft but strong voice replied "America" and "East London."

"Thank you, Rabbi. Thank you," Maimonides muttered appreciatively, re placing the ticket carefully in the breast pocket of his jacket.

CHAPTER 4

DESTINATION EAST LONDON

What happened next was all a blur, or so it seemed when Maimonides looked back on the next fateful hour.

His ticket was stamped with a number by the agent at the table, and he was told to join a growing crowd of people on the quay. After about thirty minutes a big iron ship docked next to the crowd, a gangway attached to it was lowered to the ground, and people of all ages slowly climbed up the wooden steps onto the ship. There, a sailor inspected each of their tickets and directed its holder this way or that. Maimonides followed a family of eight down into a large, poorly lit room.

When his eyes grew accustomed to the light, and no longer overwhelmed by the noise of parents shouting at their inquisitive and disappearing children, he saw the room consisted of about 200 beds, each with a pillow, sheet, and blanket placed on a thin blue-striped mattress. His ticket number was "850," and with great difficulty he made his way to the bed that had these numbers written on a piece of paper attached to its steel frame.

His neighbor on one side was a man of about thirty who introduced himself as Shmuel; on the other was a shy girl of about his age. Noticing that the passengers were putting their cases under their beds, Maimonides did the same with his. Half an hour later, when the room was full, he heard three loud blasts on the ship's horn and strong vibrations under his feet.

"Come up on deck," Shmuel said, heading for a staircase, "and say goodbye to Europe."

Maimonides followed him and reached the deck in time to see the quay moving slowly away from the ship, or so it seemed. A few passengers waved, but most just looked in silence at the receding continent that had given Jews so much heartache and pain for centuries.

"Next stop Africa," Shmuel announced, more to himself than anyone else.

"That's not right," Maimonides told him, feeling good that for once he knew more than his fellow traveler. "We are going to London."

"If that is what you think, you are on the wrong boat," Shmuel said as the ocean liner, now helped by two tugs, nosed her way out of the harbor.

"No, I am not! Look at my ticket. It says 'East London.' That is where the docks are, and it also says 'America,' which is where we get off the boat," Maimonides told him confidently.

"Your ticket says 'East London' because that is the end of the voyage. And *America* is the name of the boat," Shmuel explained, as if talking to a six-year-old.

"And this 'East London' is in Africa?" Maimonides asked, hoping against hope that he had misunderstood what Shmuel had told him.

"That's right. It is where the Africans live." Seeing Maimonides' eyes glaze over, Shmuel added, "You know, the black people."

Maimonides stumbled away in a daze, sat down on a coil of rope, and burst into tears. After a few minutes his thoughts, which had run wild like chickens in a coop chased by a fox, began to fall into place. His father, the blithering idiot, the fool, the imbecile, was all he could think of. He was to blame for Maimonides' plight. He thought he had bought a ticket to America, and was sold one to Africa. Why didn't he give it to his wife to check? She could read. Or to Zelig or Kaylah, for that matter? No, Anshul was too proud. What a fool he was, more stupid even than the rabbi's daughter who gets lost between the classroom and the toilet.

And Maimonides's mother? Why didn't she check the ticket? Maybe she did. Maybe she wanted him to go to a place that nobody had heard of, or ever came back from. Her son, the cause of embarrassment, and maybe shame as well, the only adult Jew in Saratov who could neither read nor write.

And his brother, Zelig? Clever enough, to be sure, spending all his days and even some nights learning with the rabbi. Learning what? Learning what Hillel said to Shamai 2,000 years ago. Did it matter? Did it put bread on the table? No, it did not. Zelig took bread off the table. He, who could read and write, was wasting his life. And Kaylah? Even she was against him in the end. He hated them. He hated them all. They could all go to hell, and in fact he hoped they did.

Maimonides jumped to his feet, rushed to the boat's rail, and vomited over the side. When there was nothing left in his stomach, he shuffled back to the coiled rope and collapsed onto it like a sack of potatoes.

There he sat holding his head in his hands.

After a while, the girl from the bed next to his handed Maimonides a glass of water. When he didn't take it, she put it between his feet. A little while later a bell rang, which informed the passengers that dinner was being served, following which all those on deck disappeared down the staircases. All except Maimonides and the girl, that is, who now sat quietly next to him.

Again, she handed him the glass, which Maimonides now took; but instead of drinking its contents, he hurled it with all his might against a nearby lifeboat, smashing it into a million pieces. Quietly, the girl got up and brought him another glass of water.

"Drink it," she said gently. "You will feel better."

"I'd feel better if I was dead," Maimonides replied, really believing it.

The girl took Maimonides' hand while he sobbed quietly. After a while he stopped crying.

Then she stood up, still holding his hand, and led him down into the big dormitory room and to his bed.

"Lie down now," she said quietly.

Maimonides did so, and she covered him with his blanket. Then she squeezed his hand, put it under the blanket, and disappeared.

Physically and emotionally exhausted, Maimonides felt as though all the blood had drained out of his now deadweight body. If only his thoughts could be marshalled into some sort of order, but they couldn't be. Against the pain and hurt caused by his family was the gentle kindness of this girl. The more he tried to focus on the girl, the more his anger welled up against his family. In this troubled state he eventually fell asleep.

Fourteen hours later he opened his eyes. The dormitory was largely desert ed, but on the bed alongside his sat the girl reading a book; next to her, a plate containing three slices of white bread covered with prune jam, and a cup of black coffee.

"You feeling better?" she asked in the gentle voice Maimonides remembered from the previous evening. He also remembered his anger.

Still simmering, the increased distance from his parents in no way diminished the loathing he felt for them. Countering these feelings was a kind of warmth, an emotion he didn't remember ever feeling before. It had to be for this girl, there was nobody else in his life. "You feeling better?" told him that someone cared, maybe not much, but in his state even a little made him feel better.

"What time is it?" he replied, noticing the daylight coming in the port holes and down the staircase.

"Ten o'clock," she told him quietly.

Maimonides quickly sat up, as if still on a train pulling into a station.

"You don't have to get up. The captain is doing a good job steering the ship, and the engines are working fine."

Maimonides smiled. "What's your name?"

"Ayna."

"You Jewish?" he asked her, never having heard of a girl with that name before.

Ayna laughed, not at Maimonides but at the question. "It is a Ladino word."

Maimonides looked at this girl, who was not like any of the ones he had known in Saratov. She was pretty, with short dark black curly hair. Her skin wasn't white like all the Jews he knew, but the color of lightly cooked latkes.[17] She was about fifteen or sixteen years old, he thought. She moved in a graceful way, but most of all, he was captivated by her inquisitive eyes.

"Something wrong?" she asked, quickly wiping around her mouth in case any jam remained from breakfast.

"No."

"Why are you looking at me like that?" she asked quizzically.

"Because you are pretty," Maimonides replied, not really knowing what else to say.

Ayna blushed. "You'd better eat your breakfast," she said, standing up. "I am going up on deck." And before Maimonides could think of a clever reply, she was gone.

Left alone, the pain of yesterday evening returned, not as intensely, but it came back all the same. His anger at his family burned deep. Let them burn in hell, or stay in Saratov, which might, in fact, be worse. Pogroms were a case of when, not if. There was never enough food. Or

---

17   *Fried grated potatoes*

wood to keep their house even halfway warm in the winter.

What little money his father, the fool, earned had to clothe and feed them, and often there wasn't even enough to do either. One day the rabbi came round collecting money for the poor. "We give money to the poor every day," Maimonides had told the old, white-bearded man, adding "I will show you how we do it." He took two roubles out of the kufsa[18] with his right hand, and then put them into his left one. "That is giving to the really poor," Maimonides explained. No one, except Kaylah, thought it was funny, and it earned him a slap on the head from his father after the rabbi had left.

However bad Africa was, Maimonides decided, it was surely better than Saratov. With that halfway-happy thought in his mind, he ate the bread and followed it with the now cold coffee. Then he washed, dressed, and went up on deck. There he found Ayna reading, covered by a blanket.

"What's the book?"

"*Commentary on the Aphorisms of Hippocrates.*"

"Fine author. Very clever man," Maimonides shot back, remembering being told by the rabbi it was what he should have been reading.

"I bet you don't know who wrote it," Ayna said, hiding the book under her blanket.

"I won't take your money. It is Maimonides," he said, smiling.

Amazed, she said, "How on earth did you know that? Nobody does."

By way of reply Maimonides smiled.

"What is your name?" Ayna asked, wanting to learn more about this enigma now towering over her.

"Maimonides."

They both burst out laughing.

"I'll lend it to you when I am finished. Then Maimonides Two can give a response to Maimonides One. It is in Italian."

"You speak Italian?" he asked, never having met anyone who did.

By way of reply he got an energetic, affirmative nod.

"And other languages?"

Another nod, this time smiling.

"Which ones?"

"Greek, Spanish, Portuguese, Romanian, English, and Ladino, if you call it a language."

18 *Receptacle for charitable donations*

"Ladino?"

"You Ashkenazi Jews have Yiddish, we have Ladino," Ayna replied, as if every soul on the planet knew this.

"*We?* Who is *we?*" This girl has more surprises than a magician's top hat, Maimonides thought, remembering seeing a visiting illusionist in Saratov many years before.

"You people think Jews only come from Poland and Russia and a few other cold-weather countries."

"Don't they?" Are there really any other Jews? Maimonides thought. Were there Chinese Jews? These must be the lost tribes. Why didn't the Saratov rabbi know about this? These thoughts flashed through Maimonides' head while he waited for Ayna's reply.

"Of course not. Sephardic Jews live in all the countries on the Mediterranean."

All this was a lot for Maimonides to take in. This girl, who didn't even look Jewish, certainly seemed to be. He had more questions for her.

"And Hebrew? Do you also speak it?"

"Not very well. I can read it, though, like you."

This was a road Maimonides really didn't want to go down, so he cut into a side street.

"Will you teach me English? And Ladino?" He really wanted to learn English, and who better to teach him than someone as quick-witted and attractive as Ayna? As for Ladino, it might be interesting.

"I could, but we haven't got any books," Ayna answered reluctantly; the idea of spending more time with this boy was appealing.

"I don't need books. I learned Ukrainian without them," he answered, hoping that she wouldn't be put off by this conventional problem.

"In how long?" Ayna asked, now intrigued by Maimonides, the first Ashkenazi man under the age of 50 she had ever spoken to.

"About a month. We have six weeks till we get to East London, so I can easily learn them. If you will teach me, that is."

Ayna first thought Maimonides was joking, but he was so confident about learning the two languages that maybe ... Nonsense, she thought, revising her opinion. No one could learn two languages without books in just a few weeks. He was a nice boy – in fact, a really nice boy – but a show-off. She would put him in his place.

"OK," she said. "Which one do you want to learn first?"

"Let's do both at the same time."

That convinced Ayna. This self-opinionated know-all. She would show him.

"When shall we start?"

"Right now, teacher."

It was good that Maimonides didn't know anyone on the boat, because every morning and afternoon needed to be spent with his teacher. Thankfully, Ayna was also traveling alone, and though Maimonides didn't realize it at the time, she was happy to have something to take her mind off the life she had left behind.

Ayna quickly realized that Maimonides could learn two languages simultaneously, and that his mind was like a sponge, taking in and never forgetting anything and everything she told him. Ayna also found that she liked in a special way this genius from the middle of nowhere.

It happened one hot afternoon, when they were sitting in the shade of the big lifeboat and Maimonides had just repeated, word for word, Shakespeare's Sonnet 18. The one that begins, "Shall I compare thee to a summer's day?" That he was able to repeat it, having heard it just once, was amazing in itself, but that he repeated it with such sincerity and feeling while looking tenderly at her brought a lump to Ayna's throat.

She picked up his hand, kissed the back of it, and plucked up the courage that she was afraid she did not have, to ask him the question whose answer she desperately wanted.

"That's enough Shakespeare for now," Ayna told him, stretching out on her back with her head on Maimonides' thigh. As if to help him through the next few minutes that she suspected might be heartbreakingly painful, she took one of his hands and held it tenderly. "Can you tell me what happened?"

Maimonides had known for days this question was coming and had a few answers ready. He was afraid he would not know which one to use, but now, in the moment, it seemed all so clear.

Ayna was on his side, so he did not have to hold anything back, and he didn't. He started at the beginning, at the school desk with Velvel and Chatzkel, and twenty minutes later finished with the glass he smashed against the lifeboat. From time to time Ayna wiped away her tears, but as soon as she had done so, she took Maimonides' hand again, towards the end clasping it to her racing heart.

Propped up against the lifeboat, Maimonides felt as though a massive stone had been lifted off his chest – and Ayna felt that one had been placed on hers. This boy, who had suffered so much, could be helped, should be helped, and God had put her in the place to do so. She would read to him, not only Shakespeare but also English translations of Voltaire and Schiller and Sholom Aleichem that he would relate to. And teach him math, too. She would be his book of multiplication tables and do long division sums with him.

In the time it took her to arrange these thoughts, the stone disappeared and she felt like a young girl again, as happy as she had been as a six-year-old splashing in the warm Mediterranean with her parents. Jumping to her feet, smiling broadly, in one movement she pulled Maimonides up, kissed him on the cheek, and said, "Let's go for a walk."

Maimonides tried to understand this girl, who, in so many ways, was un like any woman he had ever come across. He had just told her his life story, which wasn't a fairy tale by any stretch of the imagination, and while he hadn't given any thought as to what emotion it might elicit in her, he certainly didn't expect it to be elation. It was totally illogical. All he could think of was the morning prayer in the Siddur [19] that includes the sentence, "Thank you God for not making me a woman."

In the shade of the lifeboat, they did not notice the towering clouds that now blotted out the sun. The sea that had been calm all day was suddenly covered with white caps, and a gusting wind ruffled their clothes. All the signs of a thunderstorm, Ayna thought as she led Maimonides by the hand to the foot of a staircase. Looking up, they saw a well-dressed middle-aged man facing them halfway down, followed a few steps behind by an elegantly attired lady.

---

19   *Prayer book*

CHAPTER 5

CRASH LANDING!

A blinding flash of lightning and a simultaneously deafening clap of thunder were immediately followed by the middle-aged man flying down the stairs headfirst. Maimonides could have stepped aside, but instead he positioned himself to catch the man, which he did, resulting in both of them crashing to the wooden deck.

"Lesuj! Are you all right?" the lady asked anxiously, having safely followed her fallen husband down the stairs.

"I am fine," he mumbled, while disentangling himself from Maimonides and stumbling to his feet.

Maimonides remained flat on his back.

"Get up! Get up!" Ayna screamed hysterically, bending over Maimonides, who was writhing in agony. "What's wrong? Speak to me! Please speak to me?"

With great difficulty Maimonides shuffled to his feet, his right arm hanging limply by his side.

"Look what you have done," Ayna screamed at the man, pointing at Maimonides' collar bone protruding from his skin.

"I am sorry. I am so sorry," the man repeated apologetically, straightening his expensive jacket.

Taking Maimonides' arm gently, the lady said quietly, "We are going to the doctor," and set off obviously knowing the way.

Behind them Ayna and his assailant followed, with the latter saying repeatedly, "I am so really sorry. I am so sorry."

By now the four of them were in the 1st-class section, where they passed a bar steward.

"Anything I can get for you, Mr. Vagalparot?"

"Double brandy with water," the man answered as they walked by, "and bring it to the doctor's surgery."

Down two staircases and along what seemed to Maimonides like unending passages, they eventually arrived at the doctor's rooms. Ignoring whatever protocol existed the lady marched in.

"Good afternoon, Mrs. Vagalparot –" the nurse started, only to be interrupted.

"Is the doctor in?" the lady asked authoritatively.

When the nurse nodded affirmatively, the lady took Maimonides by his good arm and shepherded him through the door, closing it behind her.

The man and Ayna sat down in silence. He opened his mouth to say something, but was interrupted by a knock on the door, and the entry of the waiter with a tray on which stood a glass of brandy and a small jug of water. The man poured the water into the glass and handed it to Ayna. "Drink it."

Used to obeying instructions from people a generation older than her, Ayna drank it as if the glass contained only water. She had barely put the glass down when out of the doctor's room came the lady.

"He is going to be alright," she announced, sitting down. She extended her hand to Ayna and said, "I am Raizel Vagalparot." Turning her head to the man, she added, "And this is my husband, Lesuj."

Ayna shook Raizel's hand weakly, as if in a daze. It was as if she, too, had befallen some terrible accident.

"And what is the young lady's name?" Raizel asked.

"Ayna Carasso," Ayna said, blinking as the brandy started to have an effect.

Mr. Vagalparot, who had seemed comatose up till then, sprang into life. "From Salonika?" he asked animatedly. Ayna nodded affirmatively. "What a wonderful family. I am honored to meet you."

Not knowing what she was supposed to do or say in response, Ayna's dilemma was solved by the white-coated doctor emerging from his surgery, followed by an ashen-faced Maimonides, his arm bent at the elbow and firmly strapped to his chest.

"Oh my God!" Ayna gasped. "What have you done to him?"

"It's a broken collar bone," the elderly doctor said. "It was a clean break and will heal in about three to four weeks."

His nurse cleared her throat and said to no one and everyone, "That will be one guinea." Lesuj took out his wallet and withdrew one pound and one shilling, which he handed to her.

"How are you?" Ayna asked Maimonides anxiously. Before he could answer, the doctor did.

"I gave him an injection to dull the pain. Make sure he gets a good meal tonight. Come and see me in a week's time." And then, as if he had almost forgotten, the doctor said, "And do not remove those bandages. Not to eat, or to sleep, or to bathe."

Mrs. Vagalparot thanked the doctor, ushered the three of them out of his rooms, and closed the door behind them.

"Such a good doctor," she said. "Now you two, Ayna and ..."

"Maimonides," Ayna filled in.

"You must join us for dinner tonight. Seven o'clock in the restaurant. Table twenty-eight. You will come, won't you?" Raizel added, more as a confirmation than a question.

Ayna looked at Maimonides for a lead. Getting none – indeed, Maimonides had not spoken since his fall – she replied, "Thank you. We would love to." Turning to Mr. Vagalparot, she said, "Thank you for paying the doctor."

They had arrived at the top of the fateful stairs, where the 1st-class passengers took their constitutional walks in the morning and the steerage horde was forbidden to ascend.

"Do be careful going down now," Raizel called out. Having watched Ayna and Maimonides safely navigate the stairs, she said, "See you at seven" as she waved goodbye.

Ayna guided Maimonides back to the dormitory, past the rows of empty beds, till she came to theirs, where she gently helped him lie down.

"Why did you do it?" Ayna asked angrily. "You could have been killed."

Feeling a bit woozy and not wanting to get into an argument, Maimonides said nothing.

"Can you still talk? Well, what do you have to say for yourself?"

By way of an answer, Maimonides smiled, sighed, said, "Let me sleep a little," and closed his eyes.

Ayna sat on her bed, absorbing what had happened in the last twenty minutes. Most importantly, Maimonides seemed to be OK, or would be before they reached Africa. The old couple, who she thought were in their 50s, seemed really nice and had kindly invited them to dinner. Whatever the food was, it would surely be better than the stewed liver with potatoes and black bread that was to be served to the steerage passengers that night.

Three hours later found Maimonides and Ayna at the top of the fateful stairs, persuading the security guard that they were expected for dinner in the 1st-class saloon. Ayna had put on a clean white shirt that she had spent half an hour ironing while Maimonides was sleeping and a black skirt she was keeping in her suitcase – she wasn't sure what for. Additionally, she had tied her hair in a chignon. Maimonides, who could not even tie his own shoelaces, was in his day clothes.

Directed to the dining saloon, they found themselves in a room grander than either of them had ever seen. Taking in the splendor of it, they almost missed the Vagalparots, who waved at them.

"How is your shoulder?" Lesuj asked, directing Maimonides to a chair next to his.

Before Maimonides could answer, Raizel turned to Ayna and said, "You look so beautiful this evening."

Ayna blushed and said "Thank you," as a black-coated waiter placed open menus in front of each of them. Realizing at once this was going to be a major problem for Maimonides, Ayna glanced at her menu, and then confidently handed it back to the waiter.

"Have you decided, so quickly?" Lesuj asked.

"Yes," Ayna responded with a smile, "I am going to have whatever you recommend."

"So am I," Maimonides said.

Lesuj ordered tomato soup, steak and vegetables, and a pavlova for dessert. Ayna watched carefully which spoon the Vagalparots chose, and used the same, as did Maimonides. Being rich and Ashkenazi, she saw, let you live in a completely different world. Not even her Salonika uncles, who had more money than anyone else in the Jewish community, had waiters push their chairs in for them and open their napkin and put it on their laps.

To break the ice, Raizel said, "We are from Paris now. Before that we lived in Prague, where Lesuj's father was a jeweller. Now Lesuj is a diamond merchant. We are going to Kimberley, for the diamonds."

"What are your plans?" Lesuj asked quietly.

"I am being met by my uncle and aunt," Ayna said. "They have a bakery, I think also in Kimberley, where I am going to work."

"Do you know the name of the bakery?" Raizel asked inquisitively.

"No, but my aunt says they make the best bourekas in the whole of Africa."

"I am sure they do," Raizel said. Turning to Maimonides, she asked, "And you?"

"I have no plans," Maimonides responded in as matter-of-fact a voice as he could muster.

"Then you must come and work for me," Lesuj replied, relieved to be able to discharge so quickly the debt he felt he owed Maimonides for possibly saving his life. "My company is called Compagnie Afrique du Sud de Diamant."

Ayna could not believe what she had just heard. In the whole of Africa, the second largest continent on earth, she and Maimonides were going to live in the same town. God, who had been so horrible to her up till now, had seen the error of His ways, and was now making up for the bad things that had happened to her. She made a mental note to thank Him in her prayers before going to sleep that night.

"You must dine with us tomorrow night. It is Shabbes. Can you come at seven again?" Raizel asked considerately, suspecting that their alternative dinner on the ship was worse.

"That is very kind of you," Ayna said, "We would love to."

The four of them got up from the table, politely said goodnight, and made their way to their respective bedrooms. On the way, Ayna and Maimonides stopped and sat down on deck chairs secured to the 1st-class deck, the security guard having long retired for the night.

"So what did you think?" Ayna asked excitedly.

"I know how the poor live, and I have seen how the rich live, and rich is better."

That was not the answer Ayna wanted to hear. Instead of saying how exciting it was that they would be in Kimberley together, she said, "What nice people. What really nice people."

Maimonides let that pass, and then, a bit hesitantly, brought up something that had been on his mind all evening. "How am I going to get undressed?" He added, in case Ayna had forgotten, "With only one hand?"

"I'll undress you. Not your shirt, because of the dressing, but the rest," she informed him as if this was as normal as cleaning one's teeth.

"Really?" Maimonides asked, not because he had not heard clearly, but to buy a little time – for exactly what he was not sure.

"Yes, really," he was firmly told.

If he had not realized it before, this brief exchange brought home to Maimonides that Ayna wanted to be far more involved in his life than he had up till now appreciated. He was not annoyed about it, but it was something new, and from the first girl who had ever cared about him, totally unexpected and not altogether bad.

CHAPTER 6

ANOTHER JOB OFFER

The following day the *America* steamed into the tropics, where it was extremely hot and particularly humid. Almost daily thundershowers cooled the passengers down temporarily, but an hour later the mercury was over 100 again. The ship's captain did what little he could to address their discomfort by twice daily (around noon and four in the afternoon) instructing the crew to open the fire hoses and let the children, and any adults who wanted to, run in and out of the cascading water. Many did so, the adults fully dressed, the older children in their underwear, and the younger ones as naked as the day they were born.

Groups of passengers sprung up, some studying religious texts, others attending literacy courses in half-a-dozen languages – Tolstoy's *War and Peace* in the original Russian drew the biggest crowd – and never-ending political debates passed many an hour. The two big questions the politicos argued endlessly about were for how much longer the corrupt Ottoman Empire and out-of-touch tzarist monarchy would survive, and what would happen in Palestine after the caliphate's demise.

Under their lifeboat the teacher and her pupil continued studying diligently. Maimonides had made great inroads into English literature, largely because of the ship's library being well-stocked with a wide variety of classical books. Ayna was particularly excited about introducing Maimonides to works by William Thackeray and Mark Twain.

One morning, while waiting for Maimonides to join her in their "class room," Ayna was approached by a clean-shaven fellow steerage passenger in his mid-forties. "Good morning, miss. I am looking for your friend. The one with the broken arm. Do you know where I might find him?"

"I am not sure where he is," Ayna lied. "Why do you want him?"

"I have a business proposition he might be interested in. I'll come back later."

"Why don't you tell me, and I will pass it on to him?"

"That would be extremely kind. My brother and I are going to open a gun-and-tobacco shop in Queenstown – that is about 120 miles from where we land – and we are looking for a young man to take in as a junior partner. We will pay him £100 a month and give him twenty percent of the profits. It really is a very fair offer."

"It certainly is. I will tell him when he comes back."

"Thank you so very much," the man said, tipping his hat. "I will wait to hear from him. Good day."

Maimonides arrived just as the man was leaving. He asked Ayna, "Who is that fellow? What does he want?"

"He is looking for slave labor. Someone to work in his Queenstown shop for £1 a month, including board and lodging, if you can call sleeping on the counter in the shop lodging. They have a lot of thefts at night, he said, and this person would also act as a night watchman."

"All that for £1 a month?"

"I didn't think it would be of interest, but as it is your decision, I didn't tell him that."

"I will do so," Maimonides said, getting up, looking for the man he had seen a moment ago. He did not get terribly far before hearing a loud "Ouch!" from Ayna, who was clasping her ankle.

"What happened?" Maimonides asked, rushing back.

"I turned my ankle. Would you please get me some ice?"

"Sure," Maimonides said, heading for the bar in the 1st-class area that he walked past every day.

No sooner had he gone than Ayna jumped to her feet and ran to the group of about nine men who were chatting, and found the one who had offered Maimonides a job.

"I told him about your kind offer," Ayna informed him, "but he said, 'thanks but no thanks.' He wants to go to Kimberley where the diamonds are."

Obviously disappointed, the man said, "Alright. If he changes his mind, he should let me know. I'm Louis."

Ayna nodded, racing back to their lifeboat. She arrived just before Maimonides with his napkin full of ice that he placed on her ankle. "How is that now?" he asked solicitously.

"Much better. It is helping a lot," Ayna replied, greatly relieved that she had seen off the possibility of Maimonides not coming to Kimberley.

As Ayna hobbled out of the dining room after a lunch of leftover meat and gravy with potatoes and black bread, she said, "No lessons this afternoon," in a voice that brooked no disagreement.

"Why not?" Maimonides enquired disappointedly; he had been particularly looking forward to his dose of Dickens.

"Because Shabbes is coming in."

"So?" The voyage so far had encompassed two Friday nights, and except for the Rabbi's browbeating them to join services (which they had both refused to do), the holy Sabbath had passed unmarked.

"We need to get ready," Ayna said. "Do you know what that means?"

Maimonides knew very well what that meant, and he told her. "It means lots of cooking, with bad-mannered people snapping at each other."

"That is not what is supposed to happen," Ayna said, aiming for a gentle landing.

"Well, that is what happens in my parents' house."

"This Shabbes will be different," Ayna said softly, trying again.

"I know. We are on a boat," Maimonides remarked.

"We are going to get into Shabbes peacefully. No rushing. No raised voices. I am going to lie down."

"You feel OK?" Maimonides asked, suspecting Ayna was diplomatically ill.

"Just uncomfortably hot, and a bit of a tummy pain. It's nothing, really."

"I'm going up on deck," he replied, happy to dodge what he suspected was a looming contretemps. "See you later."

In fact, it was not an illness but a tsunami of guilt that had overwhelmed Ayna. She knew she had no right to deny Maimonides the Queenstown opportunity, but in a way she was looking after his interests because the possibilities with Mr. Vagalparot were surely so much more promising. But were they really? Talk was cheap, she knew.

What happened if Lesuj did not have a job for Maimonides, or if the Frenchman died? And, anyway, even if he did have a job for him, what would Maimonides be paid? Certainly not £100 a month, let alone a share of Mr. Vagalparot's business.

Ayna knew she had stolen Maimonides' opportunity, and she was feeling terrible about it. In some way she had to make it up to him. But how? She was teaching him already, and since his accident, she was washing his clothes, too. What else could she do to make him happy? And then she remembered juntos. Benjamin said he liked it, so Maimonides would like it, too. With that problem solved, Ayna dozed off, not entirely happy with her solution, but feeling a little better.

Maimonides had been leaning on the ship's rail for about five minutes – reflecting on his time on the train, in Hamburg, and now on the boat – when a middle-aged man joined him.

"Louis Kravitski," the man said, offering his hand, which Maimonides shook firmly, replying with his name.

"I'm sorry you don't want to work with my brother and me," Louis said. "I think we would make a good team."

Maimonides saw no purpose in getting involved in a negotiation about a job going nowhere in some little town. Preferring to reflect on his land-and-sea trip so far, he said nothing.

"I can understand your preferring Kimberley," Louis persisted, "though I wonder how long it will take before you earn £100 a month there. And a share in the company's profits."

Maimonides' brain started spinning like an overenergized dreidel, [20] realizing at once what had happened. That little vixen, he thought, smiling to himself.

"You may be right, but there is more money in Kimberley than in Queenstown," Maimonides said.

"I can't argue with that. Anyway, let me know if you change your mind."

Maimonides watched Louis amble off. Pushing the train ride and the boat trip to the back of his mind, he concentrated on Ayna front and center.

And all this time he thought she was just being nice and helpful. She had those attributes, he could not dispute that. But to get involved in his career choices, wasn't that a bit over the top? Maybe it was, and maybe it was not. If Kaylah had been here, she would probably have also done that, he reasoned, which meant that Ayna was just looking out for him. But something did not add up. Kaylah would have told

20   *A four-sided spinning top, played during the Jewish festival of Channukah*

him honestly of Louis' offer, they would have discussed it, and concluded that, on balance, his chances would be better in Kimberley.

That was settled then, but there was something else troubling him. Teachers needed to be paid. While Ayna thought he only had a few roubles, there were the three gold sovereigns sewn into his jacket. He felt strongly that he should give them to Ayna, but he was sure he would need them in Africa. Was that right? Maimonides needed all the pieces to fit together, like the wooden houses his father built, and there were some here that did not fit. Slightly troubled by this, he made his way back to the dormitory to find Ayna fully dressed, her hair combed out and lying loosely on her shoulders.

"How do I look?"

No matter what he thought – and he was not sure what he did think – Ayna was very pretty, and he told her so. This time she did not blush, just smiled.

CHAPTER 7

JUNTOS

"Let's go up for dinner, it's almost seven," Ayna said. Taking Maimonides' hand and threading their way between the beds, they were soon out on deck. There, she straightened his jacket and brushed a few flecks of dirt off his trousers, before resuming their walk to the 1st-class dining room. Making their way to the Vagalparots, Ayna noticed that each table had, in addition to last night's cutlery and glasses, a platted white challah loaf, [21] four small wine glasses, and a decanter of red wine.

"Good Shabbes," Raizel said warmly.

"Good Shabbes," Lesuj repeated the greeting, looking at his watch.

Suspecting they were a little late (neither Ayna nor Maimonides had watches, having to rely on the big clock in the dormitory), Ayna apologized.

"Don't worry, it's not important," Raizel said lightly; and then in a more serious voice, "Lesuj is now going to say kiddush."

Lesuj withdrew two kippot[22] from a pocket of his immaculately ironed black jacket, one of which he handed Maimonides. From another pocket he produced a little prayer book, from which Lesuj started reading in Hebrew the evening Sabbath prayer. Halfway through he stopped for the four of them to drink a little wine. Lesuj and Raizel shared a cup, while Ayna and Maimonides had one each. And then more prayers, followed by a slice of the challah dipped in salt. The service over, Ayna sat down, and then quickly stood again, noticing that both the Vagalparots were still on their feet.

---

21   *White bread traditionally eaten during the Friday night meal*

22   *Smallish circular skullcap*

"Lesuj is going to bless us," Raizel announced gravely. Instead of one family blessing, as Maimonides was used to, Lesuj blessed first his wife, then Maimonides, and finally Ayna. In each case he recited the same blessing: "May God bless you and keep you. May God shine His light on you and be gracious to you. May God turn His face toward you and grant you peace."

Lesuj and Raizel kissed, said "Good Shabbes" to one another, and then did the same to Ayna and Maimonides. Happily adopting the custom, Ayna kissed Maimonides, wishing him "Good Shabbes" as well.

"This is how we did it in France, and this is how we are going to do it in Africa," Lesuj announced, obviously feeling an explanation was needed.

"And that is how we just did it on the ocean," Raizel added, lightening things up.

"Smoked salmon and Sole Véronique and the Grand Marnier soufflé," Lesuj instructed the waiter after a cursory glance at the menu.

Ayna and Maimonides waited for Raizel, who said she would have the same, with the younger generation following suit. Lesuj added a bottle of French wine to their dinner order.

"I have an announcement to make," Lesuj said gravely.

"This is not religious," Raizel interjected, smiling. "It is just that we have some good news. Well, I hope you will think it is good news. We do."

Maimonides looked at Ayna sideways, wondering if she was involved in this development, but she seemed as curious as he was. On top of everything else, maybe she was also an extremely good actress.

"We are going to adopt you," Lesuj announced.

"We would like to adopt you – not legally, of course – if you would like us to. Your parents are, of course, your real parents, but they are in Europe. We, Lesuj and I, would like to be your African parents." Having got this rehearsed speech off her chest, Raizel smiled warmly.

Tears welled up in Ayna's eyes; not having a handkerchief, she got up from the table and rushed to the lady's room. Raizel quickly followed her, leaving the two men at the table.

"That really is a great honor," Maimonides replied. "I don't quite know what else to say."

"'I will think about it' is one thing you could say. And 'Thank you' is another."

Maimonides said both, which he realized was what Lesuj had expected.

"We have one daughter, Lena, but she is in Paris and we will soon be in Africa, so we would like to borrow you and Ayna while we are all in our new home, on a new continent. You do not have to do anything, and I am not sure what documents Raizel and I need to sign. We have never adopted children before."

In the ladies' room Raizel dabbed Ayna's eyes, and then her own.

"I am so happy," Raizel gushed. "You can't know how much. I have three sisters, all younger, all with children, some with their own babies, and Lesuj and I have just one, Hélène, and she isn't even married."

"That is sad," Ayna commiserated.

"It is worse than sad. Whenever we are together, my sisters talk only of babies. And when they have grandchildren, it will be worse. Maybe one day you will give us grandchildren." After saying this, Raizel broke into tears again.

Ayna had never had to console an elder person before, and did not know what to do, so she put her arms round Raizel's shoulders and told her, "We will do our best." Which only brought on more tears, first Raizel's and then Ayna's. Eventually, they composed themselves, patched up each other's makeup, and rejoined the men in time to hear Lesuj say, "I have told Maimonides we have only Hélène."

To which Raizel added, "And I told Ayna we would be her pretend parents, and she and Maimonides would be our pretend children."

In the absence of a legal document, which Lesuj knew would normally govern such arrangements, what Raizel suggested seemed fine. Somewhat relieved to have that out of the way, Lesuj proposed a toast, "To our new family," to which the four of them drank. The smoked salmon arrived and was eaten. But when the sole appeared, Lesuj looked at it as if it was a piece of old seaweed, before calling the waiter across.

"This is supposed to be Sole Véronique," he announced stiffly. "It isn't."

"I will call the chef," the waiter said defensively while backpedaling, before almost running to the kitchen. Moments later he returned with the white-hatted head of the kitchen responsible for all dishes.

"Where are the grapes? Sole Véronique has grapes, and this dish has none," Lesuj pointed out firmly.

"Sir, we are in the middle of the ocean, and no grapes are growing here."

"Then don't call it Sole Véronique," Lesuj spluttered.

Apologizing, the chef started removing Lesuj's plate, only to be remonstrated with again.

"I didn't say the fish was no good, just that it was misrepresented."

Ayna and Maimonides witnessed this dressing-down speechlessly, and were even more surprised when Lesuj turned to Ayna and said, in the gentlest of voices, as if nothing at all had just happened, "What are you looking forward to in Africa?"

"To seeing my aunt again," Ayna replied. "She is coming to East London to meet me. My uncle is staying in Kimberley to look after the shop."

"And you, Maimonides?" Lesuj asked, hoping for a deeper response.

"To learning the diamond business and working with you, sir."

From the smile on Lesuj's face, it was clear that Maimonides had chosen the right answer out of millions of possible responses.

"What wonderful children we have," Raizel exclaimed, laughing, "family-minded and hard-working."

The rest of the meal was spent chatting about life on the ship, and when Lesuj proposed another toast, "To our family," Ayna realized it was time to say goodnight.

The four of them left the table, each lost in their own thoughts. Lesuj looking forward to having an energetic, hard-working colleague in the office, Raizel regretting that they hadn't adopted children before now, Maimonides appreciating what good fortune could come from a broken collar bone, and Ayna looking forward to juntos.

"So what do you think?" she asked Maimonides when they were back in the dormitory.

"I am not sure. I didn't know one could have two sets of parents."

"If you could choose your parents, would you have chosen the Vagalparots?" Before he had a chance to answer, Ayna added, "I would have."

Ayna had never brought up the subject of her parents, and except for some oblique comments she had made from time to time, Maimonides had no idea about her family. If she wanted to tell him about them, she would have, he decided, and it seemed that she might do so now. Suspecting that Ayna needed a bit of encouragement, he said, "Why is that?"

Maimonides was not ready, and certainly had not expected, what followed. Ayna launched into a tirade against her whole family, each one of whom, it seemed, was responsible for some aspect of her misfortune. Along the way, Maimonides learned that her mother had died during her birth, that her father – a weak man – had remarried a woman who despised Ayna, and whose children from her previous marriage were ill- mannered, generally badly behaved, and frankly stupid. Like a volcano that had erupted its contents, Ayna then took a deep breath, gathered her toiletries, and hurried off to clean her teeth. A few minutes later she returned, all smiles, kissed Maimonides on the forehead, and then lay down on her bed, seemingly without a care in the world.

Maimonides, free of his restricting bandages for the first time in weeks, lay on top of his bed in a pair of loose shorts, his palms clasped behind his head, and his elbows extended to help him keep cool. Among the many things he realized he needed to learn about were women. Kaylah was a bit bitchy every month, but only for a day or two, and then she was back to normal. Reflecting on this, he dozed off into a deep sleep.

Maimonides awoke the next morning, remembering that something very unusual, and pleasant, had happened to him, but not sure what it was. To his surprise he was under his sheet, and not on top of it, as he had been sleeping since they entered the tropics. Turning over he saw Ayna, in her usual neck-to-ankle, arm-covering nightdress, facing him, sitting on the edge of the bed, her legs swinging gently backwards and forwards.

"Good morning. Did you sleep well?" she asked innocently.

"Yes, I had a very funny dream, though," Maimonides replied, trying to make sense of what happened, or what he thought had happened.

"A nightmare?" Ayna responded, seemingly curious but not really.

"No. Actually the opposite," Maimonides responded, struggling to marshal his undisciplined thoughts.

"You must tell me about it," Ayna said, skipping off to the lady's room with her day clothes under her arm.

About to get up as well, Maimonides realized he wasn't wearing underwear. He looked under the sheet and his shorts were not there. Dropping his head, he peered under his bed, and saw his shorts lying under Ayna's. Fortunately, there were no women around, so he manoeuvred himself into a shirt and shorts, grabbed his wash things, and made for the men's showers.

They met at breakfast, sitting opposite each other at the end of a long, deserted table, two slices of buttered white bread and a cup of black coffee in front of each of them. Ayna seemed particularly happy,

Maimonides thought, thankful that the memory of her dysfunctional family was apparently no longer an issue, at least not today.

"This dream I had… it was …"

"It wasn't a dream," Ayna interrupted authoritatively, respreading the butter on her slice of bread.

"You mean you lay naked on top of me in the night?" he asked incredulously.

"Yes," she said calmly, now eating the buttered slice.

"Why did you do that?" Maimonides asked, not actually believing what he was hearing.

"Because I wanted to," Ayna responded matter-of-factly.

"That is the reason. You just wanted to?"

"Because juntos is nice," she said, as if any justification for her action was needed.

"Who is juntos?"

"It is a Spanish word. It means 'in together,'" Ayna explained, now stirring some sugar into her coffee.

"In bed together?"

"No. I put your thing into my pelvis," she said, drinking the sweet black liquid that tasted like tea and coffee mixed together.

"Do you often do this?" Maimonides asked, now totally mystified.

"No. Only with Benjamin, and now with you." The coffee finished, Ayna pushed the cup and her plate away.

"Who is Benjamin?" The plot thickened.

"My girlfriend's brother. He put it into her, and he also put it into me," Ayna answered picking up a dog-eared copy of *The Luck of Barry Lyndon*.

"Recently?" Did all girls do this, he wondered? Did Kaylah?

"About three months ago." She was paging through the book, finding the interrogation a bit tiresome.

"Why do you do this?" Maimonides asked, still miles from understanding what happened.

"I told you. Because it is nice. La Buena parte."

"What does that mean?" He didn't remember this as a Ladino phrase.

"The good part. At the end. Didn't you like it?"

For Ayna, what she had done last night was as normal as washing her hands. For Maimonides, it was an anatomical experience. Now the pieces started fitting together. Far from a nightmare, it had been most enjoyable.

"It was nice. Are you going to do it again?" he asked as nonchalantly as he could.

"If you like." Her head was in the book, looking for where they had left off the day before.

"Tonight?" Keeping her focussed was increasingly difficult.

"OK, I found it," she announced, closing the book with the page suitably marked.

"Can I ask you a question?" He still needed clarification on one aspect of what happened.

"After the good part, why did you lie on top of me? It was for a long time. Almost an hour. You weren't asleep."

"Because I felt segura. [23] I don't know the English word for it," Ayna said, standing up, the book and a pillow firmly clasped under her arm.

Curious, Maimonides asked, "Was it better than with Benjamin?"

"It wasn't better or worse. It was nicer. I'm going to the lifeboat. You coming up soon?"

Maimonides nodded affirmatively a second before Ayna headed for the door, leaving him staring at his untouched bread and coffee. No matter which way he looked at her, she really was a different girl. None of the girls he knew in Saratov would have left home on their own, and certainly not done this juntos thing. As for Ayna's messed-up home life, he felt sorry for her, but then it seemed she did not need anyone to feel sorry for her. Or maybe that sense of independence she projected was a mask? He certainly didn't know anyone who spoke so many languages, not even the rabbi of their synagogue, the wisest man in Saratov.

Putting all of that aside, there was still the big question for which he had no answer. Why did she want him to come to Kimberley? The job in Queenstown would earn him more money, at least to start with, and he could always take up Mr. Vagalparot's offer later. He remembered the Gabba [24] once saying, "Time answers many questions," but he could not see how it was going to answer this one.

He found Ayna under their lifeboat engrossed in *Barry Lyndon*. Looking down at her, she really was beautiful.

"Something troubling you?" Maimonides asked.

"Actually, there is. There is still another six days on this floating

---

23   *Safe or secure*
24   *Synagogue official*

village of sour-faced removedores de heces.[25] Half of them spend their time praying, and the other half arguing about the most inane things. Two yentas[26] nearly came to blows over three coat hangers this morning."

"And?" There was surely more to come.

"One of them invited me to come and cook cholent,[27] whatever that is, and when I refused, she asked me to look after her children while she did so."

"Both of which you refused." Had Ayna's family poisoned her against other people's children, Maimonides wondered?

"The food in the 1st-class dining room is good enough for me, so we don't need any cholent, and as for those brats, have you seen how badly behaved they are?"

You are not a very nice person, Maimonides thought to himself, but instead said, "And if the boot was on the other foot?"

"My children would have good manners and be courteous," she shot back.

"You have that all worked out?" Maimonides said, constraining himself.

"Yes, I have," Ayna replied, beginning to tire of his questions.

"The father and the gender, too?" Maimonides was nearly done.

"Not the gender. I am sure doctors are working on that."

"Who is the father then?" This was the bombshell question Maimonides casually tossed into the dynamite store.

As the conversation progressed, Ayna had become more and more uncomfortable, and this was the question she did not want to answer, so instead she picked up the *Tom Sawyer* book, and started paging through it, looking for the marker identifying where they had left off reading.

"He has just whitewashed the fence," Maimonides reminded her, which bought an "I know," and a playful hit-on-the-head with the book.

---

25   *Faeces removers*

26   *A female gossip or busybody*

27   *Slowly baked meat and vegetable dish often cooked on Friday and eaten on Saturday*

CHAPTER 8

EN ROUTE TO EAST LONDON

Now that the ship was out of the tropics, and the weather cooler, frayed tempers were repaired and the passengers once again settled into a routine that restored peace, if not harmony, among them. Maimonides and Ayna were eating both lunch and dinner with the Vagalparots, the enjoyment of which increased by the day as Lesuj's initial formality drained away and was replaced by an infectious bonhomie. Raizel explained at great length – and if it wasn't at great length, that is how it felt to Maimonides – how she and Lesuj had met, how she was courted, culminating with a wedding of 400 people at the Hotel Adlon in Berlin. Ayna understood that getting married at the Hotel Adlon was a very prestigious thing to do, and made the necessary "Oh"s and "Ah"s.

Lesuj, for his part, kept his own counsel, except on one occasion when he mentioned to Maimonides that in Kimberley he would not only be dealing in diamonds but participating in mining ventures as well. Also, that he had two young men working for him, Alfred Beit and Julius Werner, and that Maimonides would do well to learn as much as he could from them.

With the ship approaching Cape Town – in fact, when she was still two days away – the pulse of the passengers seemed to increase. More clothes had to be washed, adults' and children's hair cut, and generally it appeared that everyone was expected to smarten up. This made no sense to Maimonides as, with the exception of two sick men who would be tendered ashore, nothing changed onboard.

The ship duly arrived under Table Mountain at six in the morning, anchored in the bay, the ship's tender taking the sick men ashore and returning with fresh fruit, vegetables, and kosher killed chickens and beef. Three hours after dropping anchor the *America* was on its way again.

The change of diet affected the 1st- and steerage-class passengers differently. The highlight of the lower-deck passengers was their introduction to bananas. Once they had learned this exotic fruit first had to be peeled, there was no holding them back. Someone jocularly spread the word that this oddly shaped fruit had aphrodisiac properties, with the result that the mothers on board made sure that they squirreled away more bananas than their children could eat in a month.

With the ship's departure from Cape Town's anchorage, and Table Mountain receding in the distance, a feeling of expectation among the passengers reached almost fever pitch. It was four weeks since they last had sighted a bit of Africa, which the captain announced was Pointe des Almadies in Senegal. He might as well have said it was a crater on the moon for the interest it generated, all the passengers having their sights firmly set on East London.

"Why East London?" Maimonides asked at lunch one day.

Lesuj, a fountain of knowledge on so many subjects, had the answer to this question as well.

"The Hamburg-Africa Line has a contract to pick up a battalion of soldiers from East London before the end of the month, and take them back to England. To do so, the ship could not spend time in Cape Town and Port Elizabeth, as she would normally do. That is why we are heading straight to East London. And that is the reason the fares were so cheap."

"Cheap?" Maimonides asked, mystified.

"No one normally wants to go to East London, so to get passengers to fill the boat, Hamburg-Africa are charging virtually nothing. Cheaper than to Cape Town or Port Elizabeth, even less than a ticket to New York."

Another piece of the puzzle fell into place, raising the level of contempt that Maimonides felt for his father.

"Is that a lot of soldiers?" Ayna asked, not knowing anything about military matters.

"Usually between 400 and 800," the oracle answered, happy to be able to spread his knowledge around.

"Why do they need so many soldiers in East London?" Ayna's interest was now piqued.

"They don't anymore. The Xhosa – that's one of the black tribes – fought bravely for 100 years, but in the end they surrendered."

"They fought for 100 years?" Maimonides said. "Is that right?"

"Yes. In that time there were nine Kaffir Wars. The British had the guns, and the blacks didn't, so the outcome was inevitable."

"Were many fighters killed?" Maimonides asked, relieved to hear that he was not exchanging a European warzone for an African one.

"Let's talk about something pleasant," Raizel interjected, thoroughly bored by the military matters.

Just then the waiter put a slice of Malakoff cake in front of each of them.

"To think that Russian chefs could produce something as tasty as this," Raizel commented, daintily forking a piece into her mouth.

"They weren't Russian chefs," her husband corrected her. "They were French chefs employed by the tzarist royal family."

The remainder of the meal was eaten in silence.

Under their lifeboat on their final afternoon, Maimonides dozed while Ayna read one of Jane Austen's books to herself, Maimonides having made it quite clear that his quota of English literary ladies was full to overflowing.

"Did the voyage turn out the way you expected?" she asked, closing *Northanger Abbey* and placing it carefully on a cushion.

"Actually better," he replied, deciding it was time to entrench himself in Ayna's good books.

"Why is that?" she asked, hoping to hear the answer she so wanted.

"Because I met you." No harm done with that answer.

"Really?" Ayna purred.

"And the Vagalparots," Maimonides added, not sure, and a bit apprehensive, where this was going.

One of the things Ayna had learned about Maimonides was that, if it wasn't absolutely necessary, he shouldn't be rushed into decisions; and so she decided that the big question she had to ask him could be left till the following morning, their last on the boat, just before they disembarked.

A few hours later the *America* arrived off East London, where a pilot came aboard to guide the ship up the Buffalo River to her designated berth. All this happened as the sun was setting, and was watched by most of the passengers who crowded the deck, rushing from one side to the other to be sure not to miss anything exciting.

When the boat was securely tied to the big iron bollards on the quay, and there was nothing more to see, the passengers made their way to their dining rooms: those in the first-class saloon to enjoy roast pheasant and crêpes Suzette, while the remainder below deck were treated to boiled beef with carrots and onions followed by ice cream. In both classes, the atmosphere was festive, each passenger with a different set of expectations. A few hours later, they reluctantly made their way to bed, most too excited to sleep.

Captain Jackson was proud of his ship, the officers, and men whose welfare he considered his personal responsibility. To a man (no women worked on naval or commercial vessels in the 1800s) they reciprocated his concerns, and carried out every one of his orders as if it was the will of the Almighty himself. Included in these instructions was to ensure that the ship was safely victualled.

Accordingly, Captain Jackson and his officers made it their business to inspect every box of food that came aboard, with the result that ships under his command were amongst the few that could report never having had a food-poisoning outbreak. Sadly, that record was about to be broken, as the early hours of the following morning saw passengers from both classes making frequent visits to their toilets. By the time the sun hit the *America*, almost a hundred passengers were sick enough to be taken straight to the hospital. Among them was Maimonides.

Suffering from nausea, abdominal cramps, and vomiting, Maimonides' raging temperature confirmed that, like scores of other passengers, he was suffering from dysentery. Insisting that the sick passengers be discharged first, the Port Health Authority arranged a fleet of horse-drawn ambulances to transport them directly to the recently built Frere Hospital, where they were quickly admitted and taken to the wards. Realizing he was in good hands, Maimonides did as he was told, which consisted mainly of drinking litres of salty-tasting liquids. Around noon he fell into a deep sleep.

CHAPTER 9

ONE DETERMINED LADY

Most of the sick were taken ashore on stretchers carried by strong black men, which in itself was a cause of wonderment, as those from central Europe had never seen people of color. After that, the healthy passengers disembarked alphabetically. Ayna Carasso was amongst the first off the boat, where tearfully she met up with her waiting aunt, Amada Marcos. About thirty minutes later they were joined by the Vagalparots. The introductions made, Ayna came quickly to the point.

"I have to go and see Maimonides in hospital," she exclaimed, adding for her aunt, "That is the boy I met on the boat."

Overhearing this a port official butted in: "Excuse me, miss, but if he is one of the sick passengers from the *America*, that won't be possible. They are all being put into quarantine."

"For how long is that?" Ayna asked anxiously. Before the official could reply, she said, "I must see him. I must. I must."

Amada took Ayna by the arm, gently led her away to a quiet corner of the immigration hall, and said, "We are going to the hotel now. There we will settle in, and if the quarantine is lifted before we leave, you can see this boy. If not, the two of you can meet up in Kimberley."

"I will see him again!' Ayna cried hysterically. "You promise me that? Please promise me that?"

"I promise," Amada assured Ayna. "Now let's say goodbye to your friends, who have a train to catch, and then we will go to the hotel."

As their further presence was of little benefit to Ayna or Amada, Lesuj and Raizel took their leave, and headed off to the Cape Eastern Line's station to catch the noon train to Kimberley.

Twelve hours later Maimonides woke, not knowing where he was.

From the absence of the boat's rolling motion, he realized that he was no longer on the ship. In the corner of the room a solitary candle flickered, lighting up a pictureless white wall. Then Maimonides remembered he was in hospital, in Africa, thousands of miles from his family, not knowing anyone, and probably dying. If he was supposed to die, he may as well have stayed in Saratov. Cossacks, pogroms, the biting cold – he didn't have to come all the way here, to Africa, to die. In the depths of despair and feeling totally abandoned, tears rolled down his cheeks.

He blamed his father, the cheapskate, for this mess he was in. Not only was Anshul mean, but he was stupid as well. If it wasn't for that dumb donkey, Maimonides would be in New York this very moment, eating borscht with his cousin Yossel. Instead, he was dying in Africa. His mother would miss him, and Kaylah, too, of course. Nobody else in Saratov. Frieda also, with her nonsense talk of the task God had given her to make sure he got to Hamburg safely. She would miss him, if she ever learned he was dead, that is. And Ayna, the enigma of a girl, who was so clever in some ways, but so strange in others.

Then there was God, who got him into this mess. First, making it impossible for him to read or write, then bringing him to Africa to die. Just as well he didn't believe those folk stories and didn't waste his time praying like his putz [28] brother. The anger at his father and God was soon replaced by depression, and the realization of the many things he would never do again. Laugh and joke with Kaylah, juntos with Ayna, and having those wonderful books read to him. Feeling that his body and limbs were heavy and sinking into the bed, Maimonides realized he was dying, so he closed his eyes as he had seen done to victims of pogroms, ready for whatever God, or whoever, had in store for him.

Maimonides woke up in heaven. The sun was streaming into a room and leaning over him were two women wearing white coats. One was Ayna, but he didn't know the other one. Older than Ayna, about thirty, he thought, she had a kind face. The only other person he had ever met with a kind face was his teacher Malka. It wasn't actually her face that was kind, he knew, it was her mind. To think he had only met one kind person in his life – apart from Kaylah, that was – was really sad. Perhaps this woman, who Ayna knew, would be the second. He hoped so,

28 *A stupid or worthless person*

and that Ayna would introduce her to him. Ayna wasn't dead, so this couldn't be heaven – then where was it? Better keep quiet Maimonides decided, till all this became clearer.

"How are you feeling?" Ayna asked tenderly.

"Where am I?" Maimonides mumbled, struggling to get the words out.

"In Frere Hospital, recovering from a bad bout of dysentery," she said quietly.

Thankful that he wasn't dead, Maimonides asked, "Who is that lady?"

"That is Amada, my aunt. The one who owns the bakery in Kimberley. You remember," Ayna said slowly as if speaking to a child.

Then it all came back to Maimonides: the boat, the Vagalparots, his ill ness, and, of course, the polyglot Ayna.

"I am very glad to meet you," Amada said, joining the conversation. "The doctor said you can leave the hospital tomorrow, provided you remain nearby for the next three weeks, in case you get a relapse. Ayna and I are staying at Deals Hotel, and you are very welcome to join us." Expecting Maimonides not to have any money, she added, "As my guest, of course."

"Thank you so very much," Maimonides said, struggling to sit up in the bed.

Just then a nurse stuck her head round the door and said, "Visiting time over." Ayna kissed Maimonides on the back of his hand; then she and Amada tip toed out of the ward.

Maimonides had never been in a hospital before – in fact, none of his family had – and whatever a Russian hospital was like, he didn't think it was as nice and clean as this one. Perhaps Africa wouldn't be so bad after all. This thought was interrupted by a knock on the door. In walked a middle-aged black man wearing navy blue shorts with a red ribbon sewn at the hem of both legs, and a navy blue short-sleeved shirt, again with a red-ribboned hem on the sleeves. Complementing this peculiar outfit were thick fabric kneepads attached by leather straps to his sturdy black legs.

"Afternoon, Baas," the black man said cordially. "I have come to polish the floor."

Maimonides hadn't noticed the floor before, but now that his attention was drawn to it, he saw it was dark shiny red. He also noticed that though still weak, his recently experienced headache no longer sent shooting pains into his head. He was getting better, which meant he wasn't going to die, which he at once realized was both good and bad. Good – well, good because, even with all his problems, it was probably better to be alive. And bad because of where he was, and what hardships the future surely had in store for him.

"I think you have come to the wrong room. This floor has been polished already, and my name is Maimonides."

"I know that, Baas," the man said, dropping to his knees, and starting to polish the floor energetically. "I can read. I saw it outside your door."

"What is your name?" Maimonides asked, feeling an obligation to be social.

"Thandiwe, but they call me Thomas."

Obviously in Africa people have two names, Maimonides realized: given names and used names.

Maimonides watched fascinated, never having seen anyone so committed to any job, let alone polishing a floor that was already shiny bright. After about fifteen minutes, the now perspiring man stood up, collected his tins of polish and assorted cloths, and disappeared, saying, "Goodbye, Baas."

"Goodbye, Thomas," Maimonides called after him, his voice still weak.

America is different from Saratov, so I should expect Africa to be different, too, Maimonides reasoned. They both had black people, he knew, so in that way they are the same. Further reflections were interrupted by a white-coated lady who bustled into the room.

"Open up," she said, which could only have meant his mouth; so he did, and she put a glass pencil under his tongue. "Close," she instructed, while picking up his wrist and looking at her watch. Maimonides had so many questions, but he waited for her to finish her watch inspection. After about a minute, she took the pencil out of his mouth, looked at it, and wrote something on a pad hanging at the foot of his bed.

"Doctor, will I be able to leave tomorrow?" he asked apologetically, not wishing to disturb her.

"I am not the doctor," she answered brusquely, breezing out of his room. The whole visit, Maimonides thought, took about two minutes. If she wasn't the doctor, who was she? A policewoman? Unlikely. She didn't look like one, though Maimonides accepted he didn't know what African policewomen looked like. Nobody religious, he was quite sure of that. Maybe a health inspector, though probably not. She didn't ask for money like he had been told the health inspectors in Russia did.

Before his imagination had time to explore further possibilities, a man came in. Also dressed in a white coat, this man was gentle and kind and asked how Maimonides was feeling. "A bit weak, but otherwise fine," Maimonides replied. Then the doctor listened to Maimonides' heart through an instrument which had two tubes going into his ears, and did the same thing on his back. After that, he pushed Maimonides' stomach here and there and asked if it hurt. Finally, he picked up the pad that the woman had written on, glanced at it, and said, "You can go home tomorrow," as he walked out. If he was a real doctor, why didn't he ask for money? And if he wasn't, who was he? Ayna's aunt probably knew – she had lived in South Africa some years – and he would ask her in the morning.

For his first day in Africa, all this was quite exciting, Maimonides thought.

A few minutes later there was another knock on the door; without waiting for a reply, a black woman came into his room carrying a tray of food. "Good evening, Baas," she said, putting it on a wooden table that fitted neatly over his knees. "Tonight it is soup and steak and ice cream. I hope you like it." Then she hurried out to deliver other meals.

Maimonides had a dilemma. He was hungry, but he didn't have money to pay for the dinner. There were the gold sovereigns in his jacket, but where was the jacket? It was in his case under bed number "850." That is where it was!

Maimon regretted he wasn't dead. He couldn't read and he couldn't write and he had no money. In America it would be different. He had Yossel. In Africa he had nobody. Ayna and Amada had no money. Lesuj had money, but rich people didn't give it to poor people. He should have died from the sickness he caught on the boat, that would have been better, he realized. Then his stomach reminded him that he hadn't eaten for at least two days. If he ate the food knowing he couldn't pay for it, that was stealing, he knew. After staring at it for a minute or so, hunger got the better of honesty, and he tucked into the meal until there were three clean plates in front of him.

Ready to face the music, he didn't expect whoever took the empty plates away to do so without asking for money. But the same lady who brought the food did just that. Somebody else is coming for that, Maimonides thought, having decided that he would apologize. Instead of a money collector, the non-doctor came in, did the glass pencil and wrist-holding thing again, then gave him a pill and a glass of water. Then she stood watching him till he had swallowed the pill, after which she closed the curtains, said goodnight, and disappeared. It wasn't long before Maimonides had dozed off into a world of convoluted dreams.

The next morning the hot African sun shone brightly as Ayna and Amada walked down a long, cobbled street from Deals Hotel to the Frere Hospital. Amada was taking in the sights, sounds, and smells of this port city she had not previously visited, and Ayna's mind was working flat-out on a domestic matter.

"Would Uncle Vitali give me away?" Ayna asked suddenly. It was the first time she had spoken in a long while. Ayna stopped outside of a storefront, and looked in the window without really looking in it.

"Of course not. You aren't a bunch of flowers," her cousin replied, knowing exactly what Ayna meant. She took Ayna's hand and gently pushed her forward. But Ayna would not budge.

"When I get married," she explained impatiently.

"If you and we are in the same town, and your father isn't available, I am sure he would give you away, yes," Amada replied offhandedly.

"My father is not available," Ayna replied, as if such an obvious question needed to be answered at all.

"How can you be so sure?" Amada answered quickly, now appreciating that perhaps Ayna's question was not entirely academic.

"Because he is not in Kimberley," Ayna said and slowly moved away from the storefront. But she was still not really concentrating, or not really concentrating on anything but her own thoughts.

That was not the answer Amada was expecting. "You are getting married in Kimberley?" she asked, needing to know if this was an imminent or a long-term plan.

"In about nine weeks," Ayna said impatiently.

Now Amada had a particularly good idea where all this was coming from. "Are you pregnant?" she demanded, needing to know whether she and Vitali would have one or two extra mouths to feed.

"No!" Ayna answered; she hadn't expected her tone to be so harsh. "I don't even know how to make a baby."

"Then why the urgency?" Amada asked, realizing, with no small amount of relief, that this was merely a case of infatuation that she would have to deal with.

"Because I love him."

"The marriageable age here is sixteen," Amada said, hoping this would end the conversation, at least for a few months.

"I can wait 59 days, till my birthday. That will give us time to buy my trousseau."

"Who is the 'us'?" an amazed Amada asked. "Have you got money to do so?"

"No, but the banks have. They lend it out," Ayna said indignantly, expecting Amada to know this already.

Not wishing to get into the subject of security for any such loan, Amada changed tack slightly.

"Have you told your husband-to-be?"

"Not yet." The words came out as simply as the request to buy a loaf of bread.

Any further discussion was interrupted by their arrival at the hospital, where they soon found Maimonides, fully dressed, sitting on the edge of his bed, his suitcase on the floor beside him.

"They gave me the pajamas," he said proudly, not adding that they were the first pair he had ever owned.

"My jacket," he murmured, "I left it in the boat."

"It was put in your suitcase," Ayna said, "and moved with you to the hospital."

Maimonides felt a great relief, closed his eyes for a moment, said a silent prayer.

"Have you completely recovered? Are you OK?" she asked anxiously.

Maimonides was spared a medical interrogation by the return of Amada, carrying his suitcase.

"The horse-cart is waiting to take us back to the hotel," Amada informed him. In the cart, Amada brought Ayna and Maimonides up to date on developments.

"As you have to stay close to the hospital for three weeks," Amada said, addressing Maimonides, "and as I need to get back to the bakery, Ayna and I are catching the train tomorrow morning, and you can follow next month."

This caught Ayna completely off-guard.

"I've paid for board and lodging for you for the next two weeks," Amada continued. "For the third week, Mrs. Penshaw, that is Adelaide, says if you do light work around the hotel, she won't charge anything."

"I'll stay with him," Ayna interjected quickly.

"I don't have enough money for two rooms," Amada said firmly, not wanting to encourage Ayna's infatuation.

"We could share a room," Ayna pointed out hopefully.

"Absolutely not!" her aunt retorted, Ayna's marriage plans still fresh in her mind. Bumping back to the hotel on East London's potholed roads, Maimonides reflected on the last twenty-four hours. They were the most momentous of his life, he decided. First of all he nearly died. Then Ayna's aunt told him that she had paid for him to stay at the hotel for two weeks. She didn't look rich – not like Lesuj and his wife, at least – and as she wasn't paying for his third week's stay at the hotel, she probably wasn't. Why did she do it? he wondered. She didn't know him, so it couldn't be because she liked him. It could only be because of Ayna, he realized, which raised two problems.

First of all, his feelings toward Ayna were ambivalent. He was truly grateful to her for what she had taught him on the boat, but she wasn't a nice person and that bothered him. It probably shouldn't have, but it did. And then there was Amada's generosity. Two weeks' stay at the hotel must cost a lot of money, and he felt a bit awkward about accepting this gift, if it was a gift. And if it wasn't, how and when would he ever repay it? No matter which way he looked at it, it was really kind and generous of Amada, and he had to thank her for it. All that remained, therefore, was to find the right moment to do so. This resolved, Maimonides took a deep breath and wondered how he would spend the next three weeks.

At the hotel's entrance a distinguished black man in his 50s, dressed the way a doorman in one of London's better hotels would be, helped the women out of the carriage and took Maimonides' case.

"I am Luzuko," he said, smiling broadly. "Welcome to Deals."

The three of them walked up the wooden steps into the grand Victorian building. At the reception desk a tall, slightly built, plain woman in her thirties awaited them.

"This is Adelaide Penshaw," Amada said, "who runs the hotel with her husband, Colonel Penshaw."

Ayna didn't know why, but she took an instant dislike to the woman. Maimonides noticed that while Adelaide Penshaw wasn't pretty, her flowing ginger hair helped make her attractive in an unconventional way. Then Colonel Penshaw appeared. In his late 50s, the colonel walked with a slight limp, the result of an assegai [29] wound that earned him an honorable discharge from the army, with a pension sufficient to run the hotel. His elderly father had provided the money to buy it.

The hotel's running expenses were largely covered by takings from the bar, and while the colonel didn't measure the tots himself, his complexion indicated that he often sampled the wares his establishment was selling. Though there were no horses in sight, he wore military boots that he periodically slapped with a lethal-looking riding crop.

The introductions complete, Adelaide showed Maimonides to his room, where he unpacked his meagre belongings, while the girls left to do some shopping. Maimonides stood in the middle of the room on a carpet that he didn't notice was threadbare. Never in his wildest dreams had he ever imagined that he would be staying in a room like this.

The room was almost as big as his parents' whole house, and it certainly had more furniture. Apart from the bed, with clean, ironed white sheets on it, there was a cupboard with a full-length mirror attached to its front, a chest of drawers, a washstand with a white porcelain hand basin, a small chest containing a night bowl, a desk and chair, and finally a coat-and-hatstand.

Maimonides sat on the bed, then lay down on it, not that he was tired, but because it was there, and it was his for three whole weeks. He lay there, staring at the ceiling, which he now noticed was made from beautifully pressed iron. He didn't think there was a house in the whole of Saratov as luxurious as this. If only Kaylah was here with him to enjoy it. If only his parents could see their failure-of-a-son living like a king. Then and there he decided he would have a house filled with rooms like this. With that happy thought, he dozed off.

Over lunch in the hotel, Ayna proudly showed off the clothes her aunt had bought for her: two blouses, a skirt, and a pair of shoes. They were in such contrast to Maimonides' well-worn shirt and trousers, and scuffed shoes that he was careful to hide under the table. To his amazement, Amada insisted on kitting him out as well, and that afternoon they went to the general dealer, out of whose shop Maimonides walked feeling like a thousand roubles. They had been served by a man who introduced himself as Moses Abraham, and who acted as if he was the owner of the shop. If he had that shop in Saratov, Maimonides reasoned, he would make so much money he wouldn't know what to do with it all.

---

29   *A slender iron-tipped hardwood spear used by Southern African people*

They arrived back at the hotel in time for tea. That was another new experience in store for Ayna and Maimonides. Amada told them about the English Tea, and explained how to eat cucumber finger sandwiches, and the good-mannered way of putting jam and clotted cream on scones.

Coming out on the boat, Maimonides had overheard much talk about the famous British Empire. He knew it had just fought, and won, a 100-year war against the black people, and he was keen learn as much about its culture as he possibly could. It seemed this tea ceremony was one aspect of it.

Back in their room Amada waited for Ayna to finish trying on her new clothes before broaching the subject that was on both of their minds.

"How long have you known Maimonides?"

"Forty-six days."

"That is not a very long time to decide to marry someone," Amada said, realizing this was going to be a long battle.

"He is my basherte. Do you know what that means?" This was a Yiddish word that Ayna had picked up, which Sephardic people didn't use.

"It means your destiny. Maybe his basherter is someone else. Someone he hasn't met yet," Amada pointed out, proud of her Yiddish knowledge.

"That's impossible," Ayna said defiantly.

"Really? Has God told you?" Amada asked seriously.

Ayna changed tack. "Will you tell me how to make a baby?"

"There is time for that when we get back to Kimberley," Amada replied, dodging a question she really wasn't ready for.

"There won't be time then. There will be the bakery, and your house to run, and Vitali to look after. Please tell me now?"

Amada knew Ayna was right, and having established that no one had ever explained this to her young niece, she did so. As Amada got more and more into how women's bodies worked, Ayna became quieter, more attentive. When Amada was finished and asked Ayna if she had any questions, she was told, "No. None at all." Then the young girl got up, saying, "I am going to say goodnight to Maimonides. Don't wait up for me."

"I won't have to. If you are not back in five minutes, I will come and fetch you."

Ayna tossed her head like a petulant filly, walked out of the door, and closed it firmly. Amada looked at her watch.

A few minutes later Ayna was back, behaving as though butter wouldn't melt in her mouth. Ayna was soon asleep; Amada not. Ayna was infatuated with the boy, that was clear, but then what? Was the absence of her parents throwing her into his arms, and if so, should Amada and Vitali take on the role of surrogate parents? And if she and Vitali did take on that role, what would that involve? They couldn't afford to put money aside for her dowry. And they wanted to start a family, which they had delayed till their financial situation was brighter. Was that being selfish? All these thoughts raced round in Amada's mind; and when she realized that there was no solution to these many questions, at least tonight, she allowed herself to doze off.

The next morning the three of them met for another Maimonides introduction – this time to an English Breakfast. As Mr. Abrahams had enough goods in his store to fit out all Saratov, so the breakfast served to Maimonides was enough food for his entire family for a day, with some left over. Maybe Africa won't be such a bad place after all, Maimonides thought, finishing his third piece of toast.

Maimonides hadn't given much thought to the morning's impending farewells, considerably less thought, in fact, than Amada and Ayna had given it. From his point of view, it was a non-event. A kiss on the lips from Ayna, one on the cheek from Amada, "See you in Kimberley" farewells, and they were off in the hotel's horse-cart to the station.

CHAPTER 10

MUCH TO LEARN

Maimonides' reflection on the two women who had just left was interrupted by Adelaide calling out, "Looking for something to do?" While Maimonides was considering the question, she said, "Come and rub down the horses with me." He had never rubbed down a horse in his life, and, in fact, had never got that close to a horse, but as he had nothing better to do, why not?

"With pleasure," he said, expecting a lesson on what to do.

Ten minutes later he was quite proud of his rubdown. The chestnut horse he had been working on looked a lot better than it had before he started, and Adelaide seemed impressed.

"Good job. Want to come for a ride?" she said smiling, enhancing the invitation.

"I never have," Maimonides replied, looking at the horse that had suddenly become much bigger.

"It's not hard. I'll show you," she said as she saddled up the brown horse and helped Maimonides up onto him. Then she did the same for the larger black one that she had been working on, only this time it was she who straddled the horse.

"It is quite simple," she said. "There are four gaits. Walking, trotting, cantering, and galloping. Except for trotting, when you go up and down, you just sit there and let the horse do the work."

While what Adelaide had said was basically correct, it wasn't as simple as that. But Maimonides coped, which meant he hadn't fallen off once on their forty-minute ride, and he was quite proud of himself for that. After dismounting and looping the reins over a tree stump as Adelaide had done, he lay on the cool grass under a massive tree next to her.

"I come here quite often. It reminds me of home," Adelaide said wistfully.

"This is not your home?"

"My goodness not. I'm from Wymondham in Norfolk. That is in England. But the green grass and river here is a little bit like our village."

Maimonides realized that, for the first time in his eighteen years, he was talking to someone who wasn't Jewish.

"What are you doing here?"

"It is a long story," Adelaide said in a voice that Maimonides picked up at once wasn't a happy one.

"Please tell me," he said quickly, eager to look through this window into a world that, up until now, he hardly knew existed.

"I am one of five daughters. My father is a clergyman, and clergymen never have much money, so he sent us overseas to find husbands. Victoria and Emma went to India, Clementine and Arabella to Canada, and I came here."

"And you found one."

"Legally yes, but ..." The words slipped out in a small, sad, remorseful voice – and then stopped, just like that.

"But?" Maimonides prompted.

"The man is a beast. Drunk most of the time. But at least he doesn't want sex," she said, relieved to be getting it off her chest.

"Never?" Maimonides didn't know what "sex" was, but having overheard some of the older boys at school talking about it, he gathered it was something nice.

"We did it on our wedding night, but then he bungled it. Why am I telling you this?" Not embarrassed, but surprised at herself, she answered her own question, almost to herself: "Because I have no one else to tell."

Maimonides felt the loneliness of a woman as far away from her home, physically and emotionally, as he was from his, and for the first time since he saw his family disappearing in the distance at Saratov station, the façade of self-confidence he created around him drained away. As an infant mammal turns to an older female when distressed, so Maimonides rolled over and hugged Adelaide, his face buried in her neck. Some seconds later, realizing what he had done, Maimonides relaxed his grip, only to find that Adelaide was holding him tightly. Slowly, he drew himself away.

"I am sorry," Maimonides blurted out. "I shouldn't have done that."

Adelaide rolled over on her side, put her arms around Maimonides, and said, "Hold me. Please hold me."

Tears ran down Adelaide's cheeks. What Maimonides didn't know was that he was holding a woman bereft of love of any kind, who, for the first time in many years, or perhaps ever, was being embraced by a man who wasn't her father. A big smile spread over her face as she slowly relinquished her grip, wiping the tears away.

Pushing herself into a sitting position, Adelaide said with heartfelt sincerity, "Thank you. Thank you so very much."

Maimonides was mystified by his own feelings, a mixture of sadness and of happiness, which was overlaid by embarrassment. The only escape he could think of was to change the subject.

"Can I ask you a question?" he said, not taking his eyes off Adelaide.

Expecting to be asked about her inner feelings, and what those were for Maimonides, she braced herself mentally, and said "Of course" in as non-panicked a way as she could.

"What is a clergyman?"

"A priest," she said, relieved at the arbitrary, impersonal nature of the question. "A rabbi for Christians."

"Our rabbis don't have any money, either," he said consolingly, hoping it would make her feel a little better.

"I would have liked children, but the way things are going ... no chance. Time to go back," she said, mounting her horse. Maimonides followed suit, if somewhat less gracefully.

Riding back to the hotel, Maimonides reflected on what happened under the trees. Up till now any question he had about girls he could refer to Kaylah about, but with Adelaide he was not so sure. She wasn't a girl, she was a woman, and Kaylah could not be expected to know about older women. Thinking about it more, It wasn't Adelaide's actions that bothered him, but his own. For the first time he realized how deeply he missed Kaylah, his parents, and even Zelig. It was as if a void opened up in his chest, a void he accepted would be there for a very long time.

Back at the hotel they stabled their steeds, hung up the saddles and bridles, and rubbed their horses down.

"We should do it again," Adelaide said, walking back into the hotel.

"That would be nice," Maimonides replied, heading to his room, wondering what exactly Adelaide had in mind.

With the exception of Sundays, when the Penshaws went to church, Maimonides' rides with Adelaide were a daily event. The most pleasant resting spot for them and their horses was at the mouth of the Nahoon River, where they found a grassy spot under a big wild fig tree. There, Adelaide learned about survival in a shtetl, and Maimonides about life in a poor little Norfolk village. One particularly hot day, instead of lying on the grass as they always did, to Maimonides' amazement Adelaide threw off all of her clothes and ran into the river. Not waiting for an invitation, Maimonides did the same. They splashed about together laughing, and after about five minutes Adelaide walked out and lay on her back on the grass. Looking up at Maimonides, who had followed her, she said just two words: "Kiss me."

Maimonides lay down on the cool green grass and kissed her first on the lips and then on her breasts. Now fully aroused, his tongue sought hers and found it willing, and the next thing he knew he was on top of Adelaide and she had put him inside her. After the thrusting was over, smiling like a cat that had just finished the cream, Adelaide said, "You don't have to worry."

"Why should I worry?" Maimonides asked, wondering if he was about to be told of an English custom to which he had not yet been introduced.

"Because it's safe. We won't have a baby. In a few days it might not be safe, but today is fine."

The way Maimonides took in such important information as this made Adelaide realize that he had no more idea about impregnation than of flying to the moon. For a split-second she considered telling him the facts of life, and then decided against it.

"I was thinking what the colonel would do if he found out about us," Maimonides told her, remembering the Cossacks and their murderous whips.

It seemed that this possibility hadn't crossed Adelaide's mind. "He hasn't had an easy life," she said, as if explaining the violent behavior that would surely follow a disclosure about what had just happened between her and this young man who was really still a boy.

"Neither have I, but I don't carry a whip around, frightening the life out of everyone I come into contact with," Maimonides said.

"You weren't sent to boarding school and whipped there," Adelaide replied.

"Was he?" Maimonides asked, amazed.

"The boarding school, for sure; the caning, most probably. It is one of the English's more barbaric customs, and is what the empire is proudly built on. It is not surprising that they produce such warped human beings."

"That happens to English children?" Maimonides asked incredulously. His parents had slapped him once or twice, but never caned him.

"To a lot of them. The colonel is probably very bitter because of the English primogeniture system that has the eldest son inheriting all the money. The second son joins the army, the third son goes into law, and the fourth son, the church."

"That is why your father is so poor," Maimonides deduced.

"One of the reasons. The other is that our county, Norfolk, that used to be extraordinarily rich, is now extremely poor."

This was a lot for Maimonides to take in. He reflected on how different the social structure in which he grew up was from the one that produced Adelaide, on the one hand, and the colonel, on the other. His mind came back to a question that had been troubling him. Were there any Jewish people in Norfolk, he asked, and if so, did they suffer from pogroms? Of all the various answers he had been anticipating, none of them was the one he received.

"I have only met two Jewish people. You and Moses Abraham from the general dealer's store. What is a pogrom?"

Maimonides' explanation of a pogrom was met with disbelief.

"How can this take place in the 1880s?" she asked incredulously. "I can imagine it happening in the Middle Ages, but not today, and certainly not in England."

Maimonides wanted to know if English people also hated Jews, but as Adelaide didn't know any Jews, she wasn't the one to ask. If there were no Jews living in this Norfolk, he reasoned, then some Jews should indeed settle there. As he couldn't write, he wasn't able to tell the rabbi in Saratov. He could get someone to write the letter for him, but the rabbi probably wouldn't believe Maimonides, who should be in America but instead was in Africa. What would he know about England?

One morning after breakfast, Luzuko approached Maimonides furtively and said, more as a plea than a question, "Can I speak to you, Baas?"

Apart from Thomas and the food lady in the hospital, Luzuko was the only black person to whom Maimonides had spoken. He was in Africa,

Maimonides knew, but he wouldn't have thought so, he reflected, from the relatively few blacks with whom he had come in to contact.

Maimonides had expected the blacks to be dressed in animal skins, but those in the hospital and also at the hotel wore the same clothes as white workers doing the same jobs.

Luzuko was different. He had a uniform. From his black shiny shoes to his brown beaver-skin top hat, he looked every inch the part of how Maimonides thought the doorman of a London hotel would look, except, of course, that he was black. Also his coat, while long at the back was short at the front, which Maimonides realized was because the tailor didn't have enough cloth to make both sides the same length. This was not surprising as Luzuko was well over six foot tall, and very imposing.

Whilst he was always smiling, for the first time Maimonides noticed he was serious and not his usual over-confident self.

"Of course," Maimonides answered, wondering what on earth he knew that might interest this long-standing hotel employee.

"In your room, please?" Luzuko said with a degree of urgency.

Maimonides nodded and the two of them walked quickly down the long wooden passage to his room at its end. There Maimonides unlocked the solid mahogany door and they went in – Luzuko closing it quietly behind them.

"I would like master to please do me a favor." Again, a plea, not a question.

"If I can, I will," Maimonides said, perplexed, realizing that he was the master in this context, but not knowing what he had done to deserve the title. For the next five minutes Luzuko detailed why he should get a transfer from his doorman position to that of an office worker, which Maimonides noted, promising to take up his cause with the colonel.

This he had the opportunity of doing sooner than expected, as to his surprise a few minutes later Adelaide invited him to join her and the colonel for lunch.

It was the first time that she had done so, and he wondered why. Surely it wasn't his thrusting, and if it wasn't that, what else might it be? Maimonides usually had a sandwich in the bar during his lunch break, and joining Adelaide and the colonel in the dining room meant that he didn't have to listen, yet again, to the litany of unending complaints voiced by the six out-of-work white men who came there every day. Where they got the money to pay for their sandwiches and beer he never knew, and didn't consider it was his business to ask.

It was like sitting at lunch on the boat with Lesuj and Raizel, with white tablecloths and lots of silver knives and forks and spoons. And though he was reluctant to admit it, even to himself, it was nicer without Ayna.

"Luzuko asked if he can work in the office?" Maimonides jumped in before the soup arrived, unaware of British etiquette that held serious subjects could not be raised before coffee was served.

"Why would a kaffir want to do that?" the colonel asked, sounding mystified.

"Because he could earn more money, I suppose," Adelaide said, realizing that Luzuko might need some support in his quest for a promotion.

"You keep out of this. English people don't understand blacks," the colonel retorted, annoyed at his wife's intervention.

Adelaide cleared her throat.

"English people who haven't fought against them, that is," the colonel continued. "He probably can't even read or write."

"He says he can. And also add up pounds, shillings, and pence. And do 'take-away' sums, too," Maimonides advised, hoping that Luzuko could, in fact, do all of this, as he hadn't tested him.

"How on earth did he learn that?" the colonel asked between mouthfuls of soup, annoyed that the enjoyment of his lunch was being spoilt by this unnecessary conversation that he wanted to see the end of, at short order.

"At a mission school," Maimonides explained, as it was what he had been told.

"Believe me, those missionaries will be the death of us. The next thing you know the blacks will be wanting to vote. The answer is no," the colonel decreed, closing the subject, and putting down his soup spoon on a now empty plate.

With nobody else to carry on the fight for the man who pleaded for his help, Maimonides ignored the colonel's "no" and pushed on. "Luzuko also said that every day the milk deliveries are short," Maimonides continued. "They invoice for two full churns – he signs the delivery notes for the churns, not for what is inside – but they are only three-quarters full."

"I am sure Christopher doesn't know about this. It must be his delivery boy," the colonel said, explaining this problem away.

"His man said that Mr. Fleming instructs him to send them not full," Maimonides responded, with an even-more-devastating disclosure available should he need to use it.

"Christopher is the chairman of the club," the colonel said, inferring that no gentleman, let alone the chairman of his club, would do such a thing.

"What club is that?" Maimonides enquired innocently.

"The Queens Club. All the officers belong. And a few other people. The bank manager, the principal of the school, church leaders, and so on."

His question answered, Maimon realized that he had lost the battle and that the subject was now truly closed. Except it wasn't.

"So, either Luzuko gets the bookkeeper's job, or we pay for milk we don't get," Adelaide pointed out helpfully.

"Oh, alright, you tell him what to do," the colonel said, wishing to be done with this whole matter and having lost his appetite. "I am going to the bar to check some of their figures." He stood up, slapped his boot with his well-worn whip, and headed for the room where he spent most of every day.

CHAPTER 11

THE NON-ANGEL ANGEL

After another of their morning trysts on the grass, Adelaide got to her feet and said, "We need to get back soon, the Nagmaal starts tonight."

"The what?" Maimonides asked, increasingly realizing that there was a world beyond Saratov, the inhabitants of which he had no idea about.

"A sort of communion for the Afrikaans church. It happens every three or four months. Thank God for them: they fill the hotel and almost drink us dry," Adelaide explained, straightening her skirt and pulling on her riding boots.

Preparations at the hotel were in full swing. All the rooms that hadn't been occupied since the last Nagmaal were dusted, and the bar stocked to the rafters. In the early afternoon guests started arriving, some on horseback, and others in their ox-wagons.

The next few days were helter-skelter. The hotel was full, and Maimonides' time was spent directing women guests to the laundry and their husbands to the bar; sending messages to the blacksmith to shoe one or another of the farmer's horses that hadn't been shod since the last Nagmaal; stopping young boys from chasing chickens around the coop; and generally making himself useful. The hotel, and even the town, had a buzz about it; and on a visit to the gunsmith, Maimonides noticed that Mr. Abrahams' shop was filled with customers who had come for the Nagmaal.

Walking from the hotel to the stables to saddle up a horse for one of the guests, he saw her. Sitting on a low wall, dressed in a white dress that covered her arms and went down to her ankles, was the most beautiful girl/woman he had ever seen. Of medium height, her blonde hair was done up, not in a ponytail that a girl would have, or in a bun worn by older women, but arranged to show her graceful neck and porcelain-white skin. To his amazement she was reading a Hebrew prayer book. For a split-second Maimonides thought that she might be an angel, but then he realized she wasn't.

The book was upside down. Slowly walking over to the non-angel, he gently took the book from her, turned it the right way around, and handed it back. She looked up, her clear blue laughing eyes taking in Maimonides' smiling face. Leaning back, she said, "You read Hebrew?"

Her voice had a silky quality, and she spoke in an accent Maimonides had not heard before.

"No," he replied softly.

"Then how did you know …?"

"I'm Jewish," he cut in, hoping this would put an end to her line of enquiry.

"But you don't read Hebrew. Do you speak it?" she asked, mystified by this contradiction.

"No. I speak other languages." Maybe she does too, he thought.

"I don't understand," the non-angel said, now waiting for an explanation. That was a road Maimon didn't want to go down, so he changed direction.

"What's your name?" he asked in a way that showed her answer was important to him.

"Elize" came out quickly. Then she said, "What's yours?"

"Maimonides, but everyone calls me Maimon." Nobody called him "Maimon," but it was less of a mouthful than "Maimonides."

He felt like a chrysalis that has just come out of its cocoon. Saratov and Ayna were from his dark past. Suddenly he was in the sunlight. It was bright and it was exciting and in place of Russia's Maimonides was Africa's Maimon.

Maimon wasn't the only one who was awakening into a new world.

Living in a farming world where people spoke Dutch and were called Dirk or Hendrik or Johann, Elize suddenly realized that this man, this Maimon, was quite different. It was as if he came from another planet.

"That's a Greek name. Are you a Greek Jew?"

Maimon smiled, unexpectedly enjoying Elize's probing questions. "No. It is just the person I was named after."

"Your father?"

Maimon burst out laughing. "No. Maimon lived hundreds of years ago."

"In the Bible?" she asked, still mystified. "I don't remember that name."

"Do you always ask so many questions?" Maimon replied, not angry, just surprised at the interrogation.

"I'm sorry," Elize said, immediately backing off.

That wasn't what Maimon was hoping for. He was enjoying engaging with this girl.

"How old are you?" he asked, getting back to his real interest, this girl who was like no other he had ever met.

"Sixteen, and you?" Elize shot back, happy that the conversation was still a living thing.

"Eighteen," Maimon replied confidently, knowing it was the "right age" to be the boyfriend of a sixteen-year-old girl.

"And your mother didn't teach you to read?" Elize asked, not understanding how anyone, least of all a Jewish person, who was supposed to know the Bible, couldn't read.

Maimon was at a crossroads. When this question came up, he usually ducked it. In fact, he had ducked it so many times, it came second nature to him. But somehow this time was different. Elize was different. She wasn't being judgemental. Just naively curious. So Maimon told her about his affliction.

"My brain won't let me read," he said. "Or write." For a split-second Maimon was afraid that this might have scared off this exciting girl, but he needn't have been. Elize took his hand and gave it a little squeeze, as if to say "that's OK." Then her curiosity kicked in again.

"How do you learn things?"

"I listen. God gave me two ears and they work very well," Maimon re plied quickly, hoping that this humorous remark explaining his disability wouldn't frighten Elize away.

"That's all? You just listen?" Elize said, not believing what she had just heard.

"I don't have an option," Maimon replied, smiling, trying to lighten things up.

Elize wasn't letting go. "You learn languages by just listening? How many do you speak?"

"Five and a half," he said, now feeling that he was more than holding his own in this exchange, that there was no way she was going to judge him now.

"How can you speak half a language?" she asked, intrigued by this man/ boy who was smiling at her.

"Not very well." They both laughed.

"What is the half?" she asked, enjoying this interchange.

"Ladino. It's what Jews who live in Mediterranean countries speak."

"And the other five?"

"Russian, Ukrainian, Bulgarian, English, and Yiddish."

Elize was absorbing this when the church bell rang, jolting her back to reality.

"I've got to go. I'll be back at four. Will you?" Elize looked up plaintively at this new stranger in her life. "Please?" she added.

Maimon nodded, at which she jumped off the wall, smile still fixed to her face, and ran into the hotel.

One minute she was there – the next … gone.

A bit like a whirlwind, Maimon thought, as he made his way to the stables, but a nice whirlwind.

Maimon changed his lunch break to four-to-five that day, and spent the afternoon looking at the big grandfather clock in the hotel lobby that seemed to be working in slow motion. Eventually, it started chiming the long-awaited four long *bongs*. Before it got to the fourth chime, Maimon had jumped over the stable door into the outdoor passage next to the chicken run.

There, sitting on the wall, as if posing to have her portrait painted, was the non-angel angel.

"You've got a very clever namesake," she said. "A philosopher and an astronomer and even a doctor. The Predekant told me."

That's what Maimon liked about her. Straight to the point. "What else did he tell you?" he asked jocularly.

"That Jews are the Chosen People. The People of the Book."

"Not me," he said without rancor.

"I told him that also, and he said that we don't always understand why God does certain things, but it is always for a reason. Can I ask you a personal question?"

Maimon smiled.

"I'll take that for a yes." Then she said seriously, "Are your parents alive and do they live in Jerusalem?"

"Yes and no. Now it's my turn. Where do you live and is it far from here?" This wasn't idle curiosity; he really wanted to know.

"On a farm called Olifanstberg near Brandfort. It's in the Orange Free State. We took ten days in the ox-wagon to get here, so not too far away." And then, the question she really wanted an answer to: "Will you come and visit me?"

Of all the questions Maimon was expecting, that wasn't one of them. His heart started beating so loudly in his chest that he thought Elize could hear it, but she didn't say anything so he realized she couldn't.

"I haven't got an ox-wagon."

"You don't need one. The smouses [30] come in Cape carts. Just some donkeys and a cart with two wheels."

"I don't have enough money to buy one," he said sadly.

"Then save up until you do." No problem was insurmountable in Elize's mind.

"It might take a long time," he said, now seriously honest.

"I can wait."

This was a really big statement, Maimon realized.

This machine-gun exchange that took less than a minute was both light-hearted and deadly serious. Elize was a girl who knew what she wanted – Maimon liked that, and he especially liked that she wanted to see him again.

"You hardly know anything about me," he said.

"I know you are very clever," she said with a big smile.

"And I know you are very beautiful." It just slipped out.

"Imagine we had a baby," blushing, Elize continued light-heartedly, "and it had your brains and my looks."

"And what would happen if it had my looks and your brains?" Maimon countered.

They both fell about laughing, as if it was the funniest joke in the world. Just then a stout middle-aged woman emerged from the stable door leading into the hotel.

"Looks like I missed a good joke," she said, smiling. "Elize, come inside and help me pack. You know we are leaving early tomorrow."

It was as though a bright sunny day had suddenly become covered with heavy dark gray clouds. Elize swallowed, and blinked, and then pulled herself together.

"Maimon, this is my mother, Mrs. du Toit."

---

30   *An itinerant Jewish pedlar*

Maimon lifted the brim of the cloth cap he was wearing and muttered respectfully, "Very glad to meet you, madam."

Realizing that she had blundered into something, her mother quickly said, "Come in five minutes. That will be alright," before disappearing back into the hotel.

As if woken from a happy dream into a bad one, they just looked at one another. Then Elize did something she had not done in her life before. She kissed a man who was neither her father nor her brother, straight on the lips.

For almost five seconds they stood as if locked together; then Elize drew back and said eight words that Maimon would remember for the rest of his life.

"You will come and see me, won't you?"

Too choked up to speak, Maimon nodded, then Elize kissed him again on the lips, and quickly ran inside so that Maimon could not see her crying.

CHAPTER 12

SAVED BY …

The rest of the afternoon and evening, Maimon walked round in a daze, mostly restocking the bar from the wine cellar in the basement under the hotel and saddling up horses for farmers who were returning home. At around ten o'clock the barman verbally signed him off for the night, and Maimon went upstairs to his room, flopped down on his bed, and, reflecting on the day's happenings, fell asleep.

The next thing he knew a candle was moving round his room as if powered by some magic force – until it came over to his bed and stopped. It was then that he saw it was carried by Adelaide, in her night dress that was unbuttoned from her neck all the way down to her ankles. After placing the candle on his bedside table, she opened his shirt and stroked his chest

Then, to their joint horror, the door flew open and the colonel burst in. Drunk or sober – Maimon could not tell, what happened next occurred with such frantic speed – he was furious. Crashing his whip down repeatedly, first on Adelaide and then on Maimon, and then back to Adelaide, he shouted in rage.

"You whore! You ungrateful bitch. A whipping is what you deserve," he screamed, caning her repeatedly on her back and then on her exposed buttocks as she lay cringing in the corner of the room. "I took you when no one else would. An ugly spinster. This is the thanks I get," he shouted over and over, now kicking her with his heavy army boots.

Turning to Maimonides, who was cowering under the table, he screamed, "Get out of my hotel, you filthy Jew. Get out, get out, go. And never come back. Never ever again."

Maimonides ran out the door of the room, down the corridor, and out the front door as if a pack of dogs were after him, and didn't stop until he came to Moses Abrahams' store. There he sat on the shop's front steps, getting his breath back.

After a while he tried to put together what had just happened. Why had Adelaide come to see him in the middle of the night? She had never done so before. On the grass the previous day, she had said they would be in peril if the colonel caught them together, so why had she taken this risk? This conflict of logic went round and round in his head, till he dozed off sitting on the steps, his head resting on his knees. At seven o'clock he was woken by Mr. Abrahams shaking his arm.

"Get up, Maimon. Come inside."

Opening his eyes Maimon saw a turkey just inches from his face. Not a real turkey, but a human one. Moses was a short man, a few inches over five foot, and with Maimon sitting on the store's steps, their heads were level with one another. With a large beak nose and three double chins that looked like a human gizzard, he reminded Maimon of the turkeys in Saratov's market. His ears, so big that they looked like they had been meant for someone else, had bushes of black hair growing out of them.

"Get up."

Half-awake he stumbled to his feet, and through squinting eyes saw not only Mr. Abrahams but his wife, too. Taking him by the arm, Mrs. Abrahams guided him to the back of the shop, where Moses sometimes rested after lunch, and sat him on the big chaise longue. Putting a pot of coffee on the stove, she asked, "Why are you here? What happened?"

While relating the events of the just-past night, Maimon noticed how physically different Moses and his wife were. Rochel was tall, with a slight figure and small hands and feet. Standing next to her Moses looked like a dwarf. He might be small but he had the biggest hands that Maimon had ever seen and what were surely strong enough to wring the neck of a lamb or baby goat. One thing they did have in common was big chests. Maimon had never seen a woman with such big breasts, and found himself staring at them while telling his story.

The Abrahams listened in silence till Maimon was finished, at which point Mrs. Abrahams said, "The mumzer.[31] Fransn zol esn zayn layb."[32]

---

31   *A person born of a forbidden relationship or of incest*

32   *"Venereal disease should consume his body"*

"My wife has a litany of curses, one for each day of the month," Moses explained. "Rochel will take you home and give you some clothes."

"Thank you so very much," Maimon said, suddenly remembering the gold sovereigns in his jacket left hanging in his room. He couldn't go back to fetch them, he knew, but who could he get to do so for him?

"Finish your coffee," Mrs. Abrahams instructed, standing up, making it clear that she was ready to leave. Maimon did as he was told.

While he was devouring his breakfast at the Abrahams' house, Maimon listened to Rochel's tale, which was, if nothing else, unusual. She came from an impoverished family in Lithuania, and thanks to the efforts of an energetic shadkhn,[33] miraculously, it seemed, a Prince Charming was found for her.

On paper it was a fairy tale. Moses sent a picture of himself in front of the impressive shop he owned, together with money for her fare and enough left over to buy a wardrobe of clothes. He already had a fully furnished house, complete with sets of bed and table linen. Her wedding was small, though traditional, and a photographer took pictures for her family back home.

That night, back at his, now *their*, house, Moses dropped a bombshell. He had no wish to consummate their marriage; in fact, as he explained it, he was unable to do so. He was able, though, and had a great desire, to sleep with black women, and this is what he had been doing, and would continue to do. He accepted that Rochel might want to have children, and if she found a man in East London who would father them, that was fine. He just requested that she be discreet about it. For his part, he would bring them up as if they were his own children. That is what had happened.

Maimon's introduction to the big wide world had many surprises, and this was truly one of them.

"There is something else I need to tell you."

Maimon braced himself, wondering what more there could be that he hadn't already learned.

"Moses is going to offer to pay for a fully stocked cart and six donkeys, so that you can go out on the road and make some money for yourself."

"That is very kind of him," Maimon said, fearing there was a catch to this generosity.

---

33   *Marriage broker*

"It isn't. He prices the goods at much higher levels than he sells them in his shop, and you could buy a team of trek oxen and an ox-wagon for what he charges you for his donkeys and an old Cape cart."

"How do you know this?"

"Because it is what he has done to three greeners who came through here in the last few years."

"Why does he do this?" Maimon asked, curious to know what was behind this generosity.

Rochel shrugged. "I don't know. Maybe it is because he wants to keep me away from you young stallions," she said, smiling.

Maimon didn't know if this was an invitation or not, and while thrusting with Rochel would give him a chance to really see her magnificent breasts, he decided to pass up on it. Instead, his mind was focussing on whether anything like this went on in Saratov. After a moment's reflection, he realized it couldn't, because there were no black girls there. Anyway, everybody was working so hard to put bread on the table, they wouldn't have time for this sort of thing.

That night at dinner Moses magnanimously offered Maimon a team of donkeys and a fully stocked cart and goods. Maimon graciously accepted this most generous offer, adding that he would first need to learn the business at the feet of the master, with which Moses fully agreed.

The next morning when Moses and Maimon arrived to open the store, they found Luzuko awaiting them with a box containing Maimon's few clothes, as well as a message from the colonel. It was that if he ever clapped his eyes on Maimon again, he would finish the job he started the night be-fore. Adelaide was in hospital, Luzuko added, blind in one eye from a kick in the face, and with broken bones from the colonel's boots.

While Maimon's first reaction was relief at having his jacket, and its sewn-in sovereigns, back, his mind quickly turned to Adelaide. His feelings for her were not like those he had for Elize, nor were they like the ones he had for his sister or his mother. When they lay together on the grass either after thrusting or on the days she said they couldn't do it, he somehow felt safe. Thinking about it alone in his room one night, Maimon didn't know what he felt safe from when they held each other, but it did give him a feeling of security that he didn't understand. She was a good person and he felt sorry for her, even more sorry than he had felt for the girl in his school who couldn't speak properly. One of the teachers said she had a cleft palate and nothing could be done about it, just like nothing could be done about the fact that he could neither read nor write.

Unfortunately, he couldn't visit Adelaide in hospital as doing so would risk him being attacked by the colonel and end up with broken bones or even worse injuries. That meant he wouldn't see her again, Maimon realized, which made him feel more sad than he expected.

"It probably wouldn't be wise to visit her there," Moses pointed out, with which Luzuko respectfully agreed, adding, as though it was necessary, "Because of the colonel."

Maimon spent the next few weeks learning the advantages of the paraffin lamp Moses sold in great numbers to farmers; as well as the benefits of different medicines, which between them could cure just about any ailment known to man. When confronted as to whether they actually had any healing powers at all, Moses ducked the question, with the platitude that it was all in the hands of the Almighty.

Maimon had hoped to delay his departure till after the next Nagmaal, but short of breaking his leg, which he was loath to do, this was not possible. One market day Moses bought a cart and six donkeys, Maimon later learned for £20, though they were invoiced to him for £50. Over the next few days, the cart was stocked with various dry goods, which Maimon quickly found out were no longer saleable in the store. His departure was announced for next Sunday morning, when, to Maimon's surprise, Luzuko and Rochel turned up to wish him goodbye and good luck. Rochel's farewell was a particularly passionate kiss, which Maimon suspected might have had a message for Moses hidden in it.

The donkeys thankfully were in good condition and enabled Maimon to reach the first farmhouse on his route well before sunset. The less good news was that a smous had visited that farmer the week before and satisfied all his needs. The farmer and his wife kindly offered Maimon a plate of food and a bed for the night, which he gratefully accepted. At the next farm, the story was the same, and by the time Maimon heard a similar tale from the third farmer, he realized that he had been set up, not only with unsaleable goods, but sent to customers who had no need for any merchandise at all.

On the fourth morning Maimon set off, his heart in his boots. The farmer who had kindly fed him and his donkeys, and provided all of them with shelter, had also suggested a possible customer he might try: the next name on Moses' poisoned- chalice list.

As his donkeys trotted along the dirt farm road, Maimon looked up at the big African sky and wondered why the Almighty, or whoever, was punishing him. In the middle of Africa, not knowing where he was, or where he was going, Maimon summed up his position.

At best he would return to East London with a few of his goods sold, and some pounds to reduce his £75 debt to Moses. From the reaction of the three farmers to his wares, he realized this was unlikely to happen. More likely he would run out of farmers to peddle his wares to, and would then die of starvation, possibly on a dirt road not unlike this one. He would let the donkeys go, poor animals, to feed and fend for themselves. With the seven bullets and the gun Rochel had insisted he take along, he could probably kill enough animals to live on for a week or so. And then? Starve. No matter which way Maimon looked at it, this was appeared to be his destiny.

If only he had died in the hospital. If only his dumb father had paid more attention to the steamship ticket he bought. If only God had given him a father with a modicum of intelligence. On the subject of God, if only He hadn't made him illiterate. If only God hadn't let him be born, that would have been better. Much better. God and his father deserved to be in hell. Both of them.

The realization of his situation tipped Maimon into deep depression. Perhaps he should shoot himself. If he decided to do so, he needn't think about the terrible things that were going to happen to him. He would be spared so much suffering. Death by shooting or starvation, those were his choices. Mulling over these options he looked up again at the big African sky, then down at the veld,[34] hills, and mountains. It was a far better place to die than in Saratov. No doubt about that. And once you were dead, did it make any difference if there were or were not people to say Kaddish[35] for you? Not really. In fact no one would know what had happened to him. All that would be left would be his skull because it was too big to be eaten. That settled, he took in the magnificent African scenery as it unfolded before him, the donkey's hooves beating a rhythmic sound on the now stony road.

Towards the end of the afternoon the donkeys suddenly stopped, and refused to move, despite being encouraged by a whip Maimon had become quite proficient at using. Then he saw why. Standing not 50 yards away

---

34 *South African countryside*

35 *Prayer said by mourners*

was a large male leopard. Maimon reached for the gun the last farmer told him always to have at arm's length. It was a Martini-Henry rifle that Rochel had bought from one of the English soldiers when he was drunk. There was one bullet in it already, which he fired at the leopard, hitting it in the back leg. Ignoring his bleeding foot, the leopard snarled menacingly. Using the six remaining bullets, Maimon shot the leopard again and again.

Even though the leopard was dead, the donkeys were braying hysterically. Then Maimon saw why. The donkeys, Maimon, and his cart were sur rounded by a cackle of hyenas. Maimon counted fourteen in all. Three alpha females tore into the dead leopard while the other eleven circled Maimon and the donkeys. The donkeys took fright and bolted, knocking Maimon to the ground, the wagon clattering behind them. When the dust settled it revealed a stark picture. Eleven hyenas rounding on a terrified young man holding a gun by the barrel, its bullets all spent, ready to fight to his last drop of blood.

For a man about to be eaten while still alive, Maimon's mind was unexpectedly clear. He thought of his parents in their wooden house, and his sister leaning over its stable door laughing. Of Frieda and her crazy mission from God to get him to Hamburg. Of his brother always praying. He thought of Ayna and Adelaide, and then of Elize, the only person he really wanted to see again. Her laughing eyes, beautiful neck and porcelain white skin together with her quickfire questions. He would like to grant her wish to see him again, but sadly that wasn't going to happen. It was no use praying because God didn't care about him.

The hyena circle tightened, now only four yards in circumference, the foul-smelling rancid paste from the sweat glands under their tails making him nauseous. Widening his stance, ready to swing his rifle at the closest hyena, Maimonides knew he was going to die. His last thought was that he hoped it would be over quickly.

CHAPTER 13

AN AFRICAN FARM

Maimon heard a whip-crack and the hyena nearest him fell to the ground, its head smashed open. Then another whip-crack and the second large hyena let out a mournful cry and slumped to the grass. The other hyenas slunk away, leaving Maimon and two corpses staining the grass red.

As he tried to marshal his thoughts that were flying in a million directions, a new smell assailed Maimon. For a second or two he couldn't place it, and then he did. Gunpowder. He recognized it being from the Cossacks! Maimon froze in fear.

"Wie is jy?"[36] he heard from over his shoulder. Turning round he saw not a Cossack, but a man about forty years old, astride a big black horse. Dressed in khaki, and wearing a light-green faded felt hat, the man held the horse's leather reins loosely in one hand, and a rifle in the other. He didn't look like a Cossack.

"Who is you?" the man on the horse said, astonished by what he had seen. Realizing that the man on the ground was in shock, he withdrew his feet from the stirrups and slid to the ground all in one movement. "I am Piet." He extended his hand, which Maimon shook, grateful that this strange man wasn't a Cossack.

"Maimon," he replied, looking at this man who had saved his life. "Thank you. Thank you so very much. For the hyenas. Thank you. Thank you."

"Come then, get on behind me," Piet said, helping the shaken Maimon up on the big horse. Piet handed Maimon his gun, and the two

---

36   *"Who are you?"*

of them cantered through the re-formed hyena ring that had assembled to eat their two clan members.

After riding for about twenty minutes, they arrived at an isolated farmhouse, the front part of which was set in the shade of a giant wild fig tree. Maimon slid off the back of the horse and Piet dismounted. Hearing the horse's hooves, Piet's wife and daughter came out of the kitchen to find the answer to the mystery of the shots they had heard.

For a second or two Elize and Maimon just stood staring at each other, then Elize flew into his welcoming arms. Watched by a mystified Piet, they held each other tight, neither of them really believing what fate had delivered. While Maimon was getting his head around what had happened in the last thirty minutes, Elize was muttering over and over, "Die Here se wil. Die Here se wil."[37] Finally, to be sure it really was Maimon her father had ridden in with, Elize released her vice-like grip and stood back. "Ek kan dit nie glo nie!"[38] she said in disbelief. Then taking Maimon's hand, she led him up the steps into the farmhouse, leaving Magda to explain to her perplexed husband what was going on.

A short while later they assembled for dinner. Piet said a prayer thanking God for the food they were about to eat. Over roast Karoo lamb and mielies,[39] Maimon told the du Toit family about Moses' £75 loan to pay for four donkeys and a Cape cart filled with items from his store. Unknowingly, he had strayed from Moses' planned route and ended up in the veld not far from the du Toit's farm. When Maimon had finished his story there was silence, each of the family taking in what they had heard, and analyzing it from their specific point of view. The silence was broken by Elize, who said emphatically, "Dis die Here se wil."

She was followed by Piet, who said in a serious voice usually reserved for church matters, "Ons moet praat. Ons drie."[40] Hearing which, Elize took Maimon up to her brother's room, and returned to her parents, who remained sitting at the kitchen table.

It took the family over an hour to thrash out an agreement relating to Maimon's unexpected intrusion into their ordered lives. In the end they accommodated all their varying requirements.

---

37 "It is God's will"

38 "I can't believe it"

39 Corn on the cob

40 "We must talk. The three of us."

Magda's requirements were the simplest: whatever Maimon did, it must make her husband and daughter happy. Piet's were the most straight forward: Maimon was to be given the choice of working on the farm with him or leaving in the morning. This work would be helping with sheep shearing and the cattle dips, as well as fixing the fences and going hunting with Piet when necessary.

Elize's requirements were more complex, particularly as she was unable to articulate them clearly. Firstly, she wanted Maimon to be pleasant to her parents. Secondly, she wanted the opportunity of getting to know him better, and to do so without being spied on by her parents. Finally, she was adamant that whatever was to be said to Maimon, her mother should be the one to say it.

Next morning Maimon woke early, washed, dressed, and went down to the kitchen, where he was shortly joined first by Piet and then a little later by Magda and Elize. Piet made the coffee while the women cut thick slices of homemade bread which they served with farm butter and wild fig jam. After a morning prayer they sat down, and over breakfast Magda explained the options to Maimon.

In a soft and gentle but firm voice, she told Maimon that if he stayed he would have to work for his board and lodging, and this meant shadowing Piet on the farm, and doing whatever Piet required. It would not be easy, she pointed out, but it would give him an opportunity of learning how to manage a farm, something that might be useful in the future. This, she added, was until her son returned from Agricultural College, at which point Maimon's position would be reviewed.

Maimon listened to Magda intently without saying anything, while Elize scrutinized his face for an indication as to which way Maimon was leaning. She needn't have worried. As soon as Magda had finished, Maimon turned to Piet and said, "I would be honored to work with you, sir, and only hope that I live up to your expectations."

"We will see," Piet responded sternly.

The next eight weeks were the most enjoyable of Maimon's life. Not having to worry about Cossacks and pogroms and an alcoholic colonel out to kill him, Maimon put his heart into the job, often getting Piet's horse saddled up for him before their early breakfast. His father had told him that any job worth doing, was worth doing properly, and Maimon applied this adage to all his tasks. To start with, he wasn't very good at sheep shearing, but he persevered, working long after Piet told him it was enough for the day.

He became good at driving the cattle into dip-tanks to rid them of ticks and mites. Sheep shearing gave him cramps in his hands, while corralling the animals he found exhilarating. Corralling the cattle gave him a feeling of power, a sensation he had not experienced before. Pushing sixty bulls, cows, and heifers this way and that, whichever way he decided, made Maimon feel a real man, a man that he wanted to be for Elize. Over the weeks he became tanned, which Elize said made him even more handsome, and his arms and legs much stronger than they had been in Saratov. Most of all he was in a job that required no reading or writing, and so there was no pressure on him in this respect.

On Sunday morning the family went to church, and while they were away Maimon and Johannes prepared lunch, which really meant carrying out Magda's instructions.

Shortly after Piet was born, his father had found a little piccanin[41] wandering in the veld, too far away from any kraal from where he might have strayed. The natives working on his family's farm denied any knowledge of the little boy, so Piet's parents adopted him – not legally, of course; one couldn't adopt a native child in those days – and brought him up with Piet.

Piet didn't have a brother, and told his parents that if they had a little baby boy, he should be called Johannes, and so when it became apparent that no brother would be forthcoming, Piet named his best friend Johannes. The little black and white boys became "boeties,"[42] and when Piet and Magda married, it was not surprising that Johannes help the young couple in their new home.

Both Maimon and Johannes were "outsiders," albeit for different reasons, and so it was not surprising that they gravitated to one another. It would be difficult to find two people with less in common, their gender apart, but these men from the planet's different hemispheres forged a friendship nonetheless.

After the meal they sat under the wild fig tree, and Maimon told them about life in Saratov. Elize was full of questions, Magda had a few, and Piet only wanted to know why Maimon didn't go to his Jewish church very often when he lived at home. As Piet and Magda were Elize's parents, and as he had entrusted her with his big secret, he felt it was only right that he confide in them as well. Magda understood when

41   A small African child
42   Brothers (or close friends)

Elize told her what the Predekant had said, but Piet couldn't get into his head that someone who applied himself couldn't overcome this disability.

On the question of the Jewish religion, fortunately Piet didn't question Maimon too deeply. It was easier for Maimon to explain, and for Piet to understand, the three foot festivals (Passover, Pentecost, and Tabernacles) than to get into deep philosophical questions on the Mishnah.[43] From time to time, Maimon was asked to say grace before meals, which he did by reciting prayers in Hebrew that he had learned by heart at school.

On the days when Maimon had worked with the sheep or cattle he would bath before supper, and afterwards would sit with Elize on the swinging bench-seat that Piet had attached to the big fig tree. There she asked him detailed questions about his life at home, his relationships with his parents and siblings, and his hopes for the future.

Relieved to hear he had no intention of traveling back to Russia, Elize was less sanguine about the possibility of his going to Kimberley. It was not that she didn't accept that his career prospects were so much better there than as a farm hand in the Orange Free State; but she was not convinced that he would be able to fend off Ayna, who seemed single-minded in her pursuit of him.

Maimon had told Elize (in far greater detail) and her family about his travels from the time he left Saratov to the day Piet saved his life, but he left out of both versions Ayna's juntos activity and his thrusting with Adelaide.

As surprised as Elize had been to learn about life in Saratov, so was Maimon when she told him about growing up on a farm in the Orange Free State. Elize and her brother were home-schooled until they were eight years old, at which point they went to a farm school four miles away. There, in addition to Bible Studies, they were taught history and geography as well as two languages, arithmetic, and natural science.

"What are your hopes, your aspirations?" Maimon asked. "What do you want to do in life?"

Elize wanted to marry Maimon, but she realized this wasn't the time to tell him. Instead, she explained how in Afrikaner society the oldest son inherited the family farm, and the daughter was expected to marry

---

43   An authoritative collection of exegetical material embodying the oral tradition of Jewish law and forming the first part of the Talmud

a son who inherited his family farm. When Maimon said this seemed a reasonable state of affairs, Elize exploded.

The Good Lord had not put her on planet earth to be a baby factory for the Afrikaner nation, she told him. There were countries to visit, ballets to see, operas to hear, theaters to attend, interesting people to meet, and books to read, none of which could be done as a huisvrou[44] stuck in Africa, Elize made clear.

"So how are you going to achieve this?" Maimon asked jocularly but with serious intent.

Questions can be answered by words or by actions; sometimes words are more powerful, other times actions are.

Elize took Maimon's head in her hands, and kissed him first gently, and then with increasing passion, until her breath was hot on his neck. Maimon wanted to have Elize, not as he had enjoyed Ayna or serviced Adelaide, but somehow to give her his very being. So many times, in these past weeks he had looked at her lovingly, wondering if he would ever have the opportunity of showing her, as a man, the feelings he had for her. Afraid of offending her, or frightening her, Maimon had restrained himself, but now was the right moment.

Maimon took off his shirt and dropped his trousers. While he was doing this, Elize had removed her blouse, as well as her skirt and broeks,[45] and now stood before him in the pale moonlight, looking up expectantly. Entwining her arms around his neck, and thrusting her body up against his, Elize kissed Maimon passionately, feeling his hardness against her thighs.

"Take me now. Please do it?" she gasped.

They both sunk down into the thick grass, Elize on her back, her legs astride expectantly.

"This might hurt," Maimon explained considerately.

"I know. I know. Please do it," Elize pleaded.

Maimon was slow and careful until they were both wholly together. Then he kissed her tenderly on her lips and cheeks, and next to her nose, as he started rocking back and forward. Elize's eyes widened as she gripped Maimon, as if she was somehow afraid that if she didn't he would disappear. Soon her pain gave way to a wave of inner warmth, and then that was overtaken by a wonderful feeling she had never felt

---

44   *A housewife*

45   *Below-the-waist undergarments worn by females*

94

before, which got stronger and stronger and stronger until she thought she would melt with happiness.

After a while Elize relaxed and Maimon stopped rocking, and the two of them held each other as if afraid the wonderful feeling would be undone if they let go. A few minutes later Maimon kissed Elize gently on her lips and then slowly withdrew.

Lying on his back and looking up at the millions of stars that shone brightly in the African sky, Maimon was trying to understand why this juntos was so much more enjoyable than the ones with Ayna and Adelaide, when the silence was punctured by a question that came out of nowhere.

"Do you love me?" Elize asked, not in a way to spoil the moment, but to enhance it.

Appreciating at once that this was an important question that couldn't be fobbed off with a jocular rejoinder, Maimon looked for an honest reply. The problem was that he didn't know if he loved Elize. He really enjoyed the time he spent with her, much more than he had with Ayna, but did that mean he loved her?

"Well?" Elize answered nervously, realizing that Maimon's silence meant it wasn't a straight "yes," and maybe worse, a "no."

If loving a person meant you would rather be with them than with anyone else, then he did love her, Maimon reasoned. Relieved that he had come to the right answer honestly, he smiled widely.

"'The very instant that I saw you, did my heart fly to your service,'" Maimon told her tenderly.

"What!" Elize exclaimed, now almost sure that she had lost Maimon to Ayna.

"Shakespeare. *The Tempest*. Ferdinand to Miranda," Maimon explained.

Now beside herself, Elize beseeched him: "Maimon, do you love me? Do you?"

"With all my heart, I do. And with the rest of my body as well," he added, lest there be any doubt.

"Then say so, just say so," Elize cried out.

"I, Maimonides Sokolovski, do love thee, Elize du Toit, with all my heart and all my soul," he said as seriously as he could.

Elize pulled him to her, so that they were as close as they had been before, before saying. "Thank you. Thank you, Maimon." After a moment she added, "Why didn't you just say, 'I love you?'"

"Because I am different, and you deserve a Shakespearian quote."

"You learned that on the boat, I suppose?" Elize asked, not able to get Ayna out of her mind.

"Yes, I did. From someone whose name I forget," Maimon replied, annoyed at Ayna's intrusion into this wonderful moment of theirs.

"So will I," Elize remarked, cross with herself for bringing his old girlfriend up at this time. Then giving Maimon an affectionate kiss, she start ed getting dressed.

Walking back to the house, hand in hand, Elize asked, "Can we go and visit Shakespeare's wife's house?"

"Alright," Maimon replied, having a good idea where this was leading.

"*Alright.* Just *alright?* Do you even know where it is?" Elize said, not sure if Maimon was taking her question seriously.

"It is in Stratford-upon-Avon, in England," he answered as if it had been the easiest question in the world.

"You will take me to England?" Elize asked, wanting to make sure she had heard correctly.

"If you want to go," Maimon said, confirming the commitment he had just made.

Elize threw her arms round Maimon's neck and kissed him passionately. Drawing away, she said, "What a wonderful, different man you are!"

"I thought Karel from the next farm had already asked you," Maimon responded.

"He did. But as he doesn't speak Bulgarian, I said "Thanks, but no thanks."

"Well, you can't win them all. He got the Jukskei[46] Cup, and I get to take you to England. That's life," Maimon said philosophically.

"I suppose so," Elize agreed as they approached the farmhouse giggling.

It was the rainy season, which meant thunderstorms in the late afternoon and at night. Piet and Maimon started work at six in the morning and finished at three, which gave Elize and Maimon the opportunity of spending daylight time together. One time they went down to the river to swim and afterwards "did love," as Elize called it, in the shade under the big mopane tree.

---

46   *A folk sport whose object is to knock down a target peg by throwing pins at it*

They went horseback riding together, Elize on a filly that she had been given as a present for her twelfth birthday, and Maimon on the big stallion that he used for cattle and sheep herding. Most of the time they just enjoyed being together: Elize dreaming of visiting the capitals of Europe, and Maimon pointing out that they would first have to live in Kimberley for him to make enough money to afford such a trip.

One of the things that Maimon liked about farm work was that it was so varied. Some jobs he found extremely difficult, like sheep shearing; others enjoyable, like herding the sheep and cattle on horseback; and one or two outright fun, like putting an end to the baboons eating the du Toit's pumpkins.

One morning he and Piet collected some limestone rocks and put them in a big pot covered with water over a hot fire. After an hour or so the pot had some white liquid boiling, which Piet told Maimon was lime. Then they put the fire out, and while the lime liquid was cooling, the two men harvested all the ripe pumpkins, except three large ones into which they drilled holes just big enough for a baboon's hand.

Piet explained that it was the pips that the baboons liked. Sure enough, an hour after he and Maimon had left the field, three baboons, who had been watching them from beyond the farm's boundary, came down to eat the pips. When their hands had grasped the pips, they made a fist which was too big to take out of the pumpkin. Then Piet and Maimon each took a bucket of lime and threw it over the biggest baboon. This done, Piet chopped open the pumpkins allowing the three baboons to escape. The big white and doubtless frightened baboon ran back to the troop, which, in terror of this white monstrosity, bolted for the hills, with their white brother in hot pursuit. The last time this happened, Piet explained, the baboons didn't come back for two years.

One evening, after a particularly hard day's work, the four of them were relaxing round a fire over which they had cooked lamb chops and steak, followed by cold watermelon. Maimon felt it was the right time to make the little speech he had prepared. Getting to his feet he began, "Oom Piet and Tannie Magda," Elize having told him these were respectful words to use when addressing older people, "I do not have the words to express the thanks due to you, Oom Piet, for saving me from the hyenas, nor the words to adequately thank you and Tannie Magda for giving me a roof over my head and food on your table. One day – I don't know when or how – I will repay you for these good deeds. Among the Jewish people, it is the custom for the man to ask the father of the girl he loves for permission to marry his daughter."

Elize not knowing this was coming, grasped her cheeks and muttered, "My Here."

"I, sir, who do not have the means to support Elize, hereby ask your blessing, over the marriage of your daughter and me, sometime in the future when we are adults and I have enough money to support her in the manner she deserves."

Elize and Magda had tears running down their cheeks, while Piet looked at this man mature beyond his years. He saved this boy's life and this is the thanks he gets. He can't read and he can't write and he is not going to inherit a farm. Not only is he Jewish, he doesn't go to the Jewish church. In a way, he was worse than an Englishman asking to marry Elize. Piet glowered at this boy who was causing so much trouble, thinking how much better it would have been had he not ridden out to investigate the shots they heard months ago.

"We were both brought up under different religions," Maimon continued, "but Elize and I believe in the same God, and it is this God who is witness to my promise to look after her in sickness and in health, in good times and bad times, when we are young and strong, in middle age, and when we are old and frail. Finally, sir, if you are angry, do not direct your anger at Elize, as she knew nothing of this."

For a moment no one moved. Then Elize got up from her chair, wiped her tears away with the back of her hand, and walked over to Maimon, who was still standing. Burying her face in Maimon's shoulder, she burst out crying.

Magda got up from her chair and walked to her husband, whose cheek she kissed. Taking Piet's hand in hers, she walked slowly back to the house, Piet in tow.

"Why didn't you tell me?" Elize asked, wiping away her tears. "Why didn't you say you were going to do this?"

"Because you would have told me to wait for the right moment," Maimon said, "and the right moment might never have come." Pausing to give Elize some time to reflect on his answer, Maimon added, "I didn't think it was a bad moment."

"You really want to marry me?" Elize said, looking up at Maimon, as if the last five minutes had been a dream.

"Forever can never be long enough for me to feel –" he started to say before being interrupted.

"Maimon! Why can't you just say 'yes' or 'no'? That is all I want," Elize demanded.

"Because you deserve more than a 'yes,' and certainly not a 'no.' But if it is just a simple 'yes' you want," Maimon hesitated for a couple of seconds, "then yes, I do want to marry you."

Elize threw her arms around Maimon and kissed him passionately. Pulling away she murmured, "And what more do you want to tell me?"

"That if you want any chance of it happening, you had better get inside and help your mother persuade your father to agree to my request," Maimon said.

"What!" Elize exclaimed, hoping for some paeans of love.

"You heard me. Right now, your father is giving all the reasons under the sun why you shouldn't marry me. You are not going to change his mind kissing me under the stars."

"Why are you always right?" Elize said in a jocularly annoyed voice. Then, realizing the wisdom of his words, she kissed him on the cheek and ran inside.

The next morning Maimon was down for breakfast early, where he made the coffee and waited for the decision. He had never been in court, but he imagined the way he felt was like an accused man would, waiting for the jury's verdict.

Elize was down next, her eyes red from constant crying, betraying the jury's decision. She acknowledged Maimon with a nod, and poured herself a mug of coffee, which she clasped for its warmth. Instead of sitting at the table, she went and stood in the furthest corner of the kitchen.

Magda appeared a few minutes later, nodded to Maimon, and went to Elize, whom she lovingly hugged.

Not a word was said before Piet appeared, and when he did, it was the women he addressed, "Sit down. I have got something to say."

Magda and Elize did as they were told, joining Maimon at the old worn yellowwood kitchen table.

"You know my feelings," he said to Magda, who looked at him wondering what else he could say, so much of the night having been spent debating the pros and cons of Maimon's request; and to Elize. who stared into the wide leaves that made up the table. "Last night I had a dream." Elize looked at him for the first time. "Willem and I were on one bank of a wide river, and you two and Maimon were on the other."

Piet stopped for a mouthful of coffee, and Elize looked away, wondering what additional torture her father intended to inflict on her.

"A boat came, and Willem and I got on it. But instead of going across to your side, the boat sailed down the river, with you three getting smaller and smaller till I could no longer see you."

Piet stopped to let the meaning of his dream sink in. There was a long silence, until he finally said, "You don't have to be Joseph to interpret my dream." He sat down as he was not sure if his knees would support him for much longer. Magda went across to Piet, kissed him on the top of his head, which she then drew to her ample bosom. Piet pushed her away and turned to Maimon.

"Last night you promised to look after Elize through thick and thin."

"Yes, sir," Maimon confirmed.

"Would you also look after Magda if I was no longer here?"

"Of course, sir," Maimon responded automatically, as in his community this was always done.

"Then you can marry her," Piet announced, as if a great stone had been lifted from his chest.

Elize walked across the room, gave her father a thank-you kiss, and went to join Maimon, who was standing near the door. There, she kissed him on the cheek, held his hand, and waited for further developments.

Magda sat down next to Piet, and taking his two hands in hers, said, "It wasn't a good dream."

"No, it wasn't," Piet said. "There are hard times ahead."

Maimon put his arm around Elize, steering her out of the kitchen that he felt should be left to Piet and Magda.

The hard times were soon upon them. First the rinderpest[47] that came from German South West Africa and decimated Piet's cattle herd, and then a drought, which meant that there was less grazing for the animals that were left. But that wasn't the worst of it.

Willem had returned from agricultural college and taken an instant dislike to Maimon. They were different in so many ways. Willem was well over six foot tall, had broad shoulders and legs like tree trunks. Under his closely cropped yellow hair was a big square face that encompassed steely gray-blue eyes and a fleshy mouth encroached upon by a bushy moustache and an untamed beard.

Apart from when they were helping Piet, the only time he and

---

47   An infectious viral disease of cattle and many other species of even-toed
      ungulates

Maimon spent together was at dinner when again their differences were highlighted. While Maimon was happy with a two or three lamb chops and some vegetables, Willem ate six or more and a large plate of mielie pap.[48] Annoyed that there was no beer on the farm, most nights he drunk the peach brandy that his mother and sister made each April. Usually Magda would join him for a glass – she, too, liked to drink, perhaps more than she should. Maimon didn't particularly like any kind of alcohol.

Sadly, Maimon observed, Willem seemed angry with the world, and almost everything in it.

Nothing Maimon did was good enough, and when Piet pointed out that Maimon had done this or that job well, it merely infuriated Willem. Matters came to a head one night when Willem was to say grace before supper. Standing behind his chair, he said, "Here, los ons asseblief van hierdie Jood. Amen."[49]

"This Jew, as you call him, does more work in a day than you do in a week," Elize said scathingly.

"You only say this because he is fucking you," Willem said with icy sarcasm.

Before Piet had a chance to reprimand his son, Elize slapped him hard across the face, and ran from the room crying. Maimon excused himself from the table and followed Elize up to her room.

When Elize had quietened down, Maimon persuaded her that killing Willem would not solve the problem, but in fact compound it. Then they discussed the issue as mature adults, which they were not yet.

Maimon pointed out that there was not enough room at the farm for him and Willem, and that it was natural – even if he was Elize's husband, which he wasn't – for him to leave. This brought on a renewed longing by Elize to kill her brother. All night Maimon and Elize discussed, debated, and argued the subject; and when dawn broke it was Elize who reluctantly agreed that Maimon leaving was the best solution for her family.

Furthermore, Elize agreed that no good could be served by Maimon delaying his departure, and so that morning instead of going out with Piet to mend some fences broken by elephants, Maimon told his future father-in-law that remaining under the same roof as Willem wasn't an

---

48   *A traditional South African porridge made from maize*

49   *Good Lord, please get rid of this Jew for us*

option, and so he would like to leave for Kimberley as soon as possible. Piet reluctantly agreed, shook Maimon firmly by the hand, wished him good luck and God speed. Talking of God, Piet said, the Almighty would decide when and where they would meet again. After giving Maimon the horse he had worked with the past few months, Piet rode off. Willem made sure to avoid Maimon that morning, before following his father on his fence-mending task.

Magda packed a hamper of food that she called "padkos"[50] for Maimon, which she gave him before saying goodbye. She told Maimon how sorry she was to see him leave, but that she understood his decision.

When the time came for Maimon to say goodbye to Elize, she changed her mind on the wisdom of him going. Why couldn't he stay? If anyone had to leave, Elize argued, it should be Willem. Quietly and unemotionally, Maimon reminded Elize of their last night's marathon debate, and the decision they had reluctantly reached. In tears again, Elize begged him to stay, offering to kill her brother in order to make this possible. Again, Maimon pointed out that this wouldn't solve the problem. Finally, after promising to come back as soon as he could, Maimon kissed a now emotionally exhausted Elize gently on the lips, mounted the horse that was already fitted with his saddlebags, and cantered off to Kimberley.

---

50   *Food consumed on a journey*

CHAPTER 14

KIMBERLEY

Kimberley, 110 miles distant, was too far to reach in one day, so Maimon found a friendly farmer between Dealesville and Boshof who kindly put him up for the night. To pay for his bed and board, Maimon unpicked the lining of his jacket, and retrieved one of the gold sovereigns his mother had sewn into it. Lying on his straw-filled mattress after a sumptuous dinner, Maimon speculated on what tomorrow and Kimberley had in store.

Maimon rose early, fed his horse, and had a breakfast of cooked oats and sour milk, followed by the strongest coffee he had ever tasted. Anxious to get on his way he passed up the offer of eggs and bacon that the farmer's wife implored him to have, possibly because of the little money she would get from its sale. Not many of her guests paid for a night's boarding with a gold sovereign.

It was still a good morning's ride to Kimberley, the first sign of which was not the booming mining town Maimon expected to see in the distance, but an increasingly bad, and then terrible, smell. Half a mile later he came on its cause: the carcasses of rotting pack animals halfway up a hill. It was only later in Kimberley that he learned they were exhausted oxen, mules, and donkeys unable to take one step further. Usually, the wagon driver put the unfortunate animal out of its misery, sometimes not; in either event, they were an unexpected meal for a pride of lions that lived nearby.

Holding his breath and encouraging his horse with a crop he had persuaded last night's farmer to sell him, Maimon rode past five carcasses before he was clear of the terrible odor; but still there was no sight of the mining town he expected.

Kimberley was largely Colesberg Kopje – originally a kopje,[51] but now an ever-deepening hole in the ground. Narrow roads led across this vast abyss, connecting the sides with one another. Gingerly, Maimon rode up to the edge, dismounted, and looked down at the network of ropes that covered the hole like intricately woven spiders' webs. All the while, carts, horses, and men traversed roads, some hardly wide enough for a two-wheeled Cape cart. The giddy height, the noise of thousands of men toiling in the sweltering heat, some white but mostly black, took Maimon's breath away. After he remounted his horse and headed back to the road that led into town, Maimon hoped that whatever job Mr. Vagalparot had in mind for him, it wasn't working in that gigantic manmade hole.

Main Street was lined with general dealer's stores, jewellers, watch-makers, hotels, saloons, billiard rooms, doctors' surgeries, diamond dealers, and so-called chemist shops. Maimon had copied the first two words of Mr. Vagalparot's company's name on a piece of paper, memorized them. As he rode through the town, he kept his eye open for "Compagnie Afrique." From a distance he saw a fine stone building, and when he was closer, the words that he had memorized.

Suddenly fear gripped Maimon. What if Mr. Vagalparot wasn't there? What if he wasn't even in Kimberley? What if he hadn't told anyone in his office about the job he had offered Maimon? What if he had changed his mind?

By this time Maimon had arrived outside Mr. Vagalparot's office, tied up his horse and was standing, scared stiff, in the shade of the building, undecided whether to enter the large wooden door, or get back on his horse and ride away. Making the decision for him, a man came through the door and held it open for Maimon to enter, which he did.

The office was a large room with six desks, four of which were occupied with men who were writing in the largest books Maimon had ever seen. Later he was told they were called "ledger books." Looking up, one of the men saw Maimon and asked, "Can I help you?"

"I am looking for Mr. Vagalparot," Maimon said nervously.

"Who shall I tell Mr. Vagalparot is calling?" the man replied patiently.

"Maimon. Maimon Sokolovski."

---

51   *An outcrop, often of stones, that can reach hundreds of feet high*

The man got up and disappeared through a door at the back of the office, and after what seemed an age (but was really only a minute or two), returned and said, "Mr. Vagalparot will see you now." Noticing that Maimon was standing still, the man added, "His office is the one at the back. Through the glass-framed door."

Maimon mumbled "Thank you," walked down to the door, knocked on it, and was relieved to hear "Come in" in a voice he recognized.

Maimon opened the door to see Mr. Vagalparot sitting at a large wooden desk with his back to the door.

"Sit down," Mr. Vagalparot said, just loud enough for Maimon to hear. "I will be with you in a minute."

It was a different, more formal, less friendly Mr. Vagalparot to the one Maimon remembered, and a chill ran through his body. An exceedingly long minute later, Mr. Vagalparot swung round on his rotating chair and said, "You are too late."

The blood drained from Maimon's face. He had waited too long to come to Kimberley, he realized. Mr. Vagalparot hadn't given Maimon a date by when he should present himself for the job, but it was reasonable that he shouldn't spend months on a farm before doing so.

"Too late for what, sir?" Maimon stammered, hoping to rescue something from this precarious position.

"Too late to see your child. Your son." Mr. Vagalparot said. Seeing the bewildered look on Maimon's face, he added, "You didn't know Ayna was pregnant?"

If anything, this confused Maimon even more. "Pregnant. What is that?"

For a split-second Mr. Vagalparot thought Maimon was acting dumb, but he quickly realized from the unfakably bewildered look on the young man's face that this wasn't the case, and as a result he had some explaining to do.

"Do you love Ayna?" Mr. Vagalparot started.

"No, sir, I don't," Maimon answered honestly.

This is going to be difficult, Mr. Vagalparot realized. "Do you know how babies are made?"

"No, sir," Maimon replied, slightly embarrassedly.

Mr. Vagalparot cleared his throat, ahead of embarking on an anatomical explanation to which he was not looking forward.

"Between men's legs is an organ called a 'penis,' which is usually soft but gets hard when ... when ..."

"I understand that part, sir," Maimon interjected, noticing that Mr. Vagalparot was struggling a little and eager to help him along.

"And when it is hard and is put into the vagina … the hole where women's legs separate … some liquid shoots out into the woman. Sometimes, that liquid fertilizes an egg in the woman, and a baby starts growing. When that happens, it is called a woman being pregnant. After nine months a baby comes out."

Mr. Vagalparot noticed that while he was giving this explanation, Maimon's face varied between looks of fear and elation.

"Ayna said that you put your penis into her vagina. Is that correct?"

"Yes, sir," Maimon answered, not quite believing that he was a father. Then he added, "Sir, where is that baby now?"

"That baby is a boy called Eli, who is in Barberton with Ayna. Her aunt and uncle sold the bakery and moved there to open another one."

Giving Maimon a little while to digest this totally unexpected news, Mr. Vagalparot continued. "I assume you still want a job with my company."

Maimon nodded enthusiastically.

"Good. You will start off working with Mr. Julius Wernher as his assistant. I will introduce you to him shortly. For this I will pay you £15 a month, £5 of which I will send to Ayna for you, to look after her and Eli. I imagine you need somewhere to stay."

Maimon nodded once more.

"I will write a note to Harry Isaacs, who owns the London Hotel, asking him to give you a nice room at a fair price. You may have seen the hotel on your way into town."

"Thank you, sir. Thank you so very much," Maimon gushed. "And how is Mrs. Vagalparot?"

"She is in good health, thank you," Mr. Vagalparot said, opening the door of his office and motioning Maimon to follow him.

Sitting at a desk in the middle of the room was a smartly dressed man in his mid-twenties, of medium height, with a beard that gave him a distinguished look. This was evidently Mr. Wernher, which Mr. Vagalparot shortly confirmed.

After the introductions, during which Maimon explained that "Maimon" was what he now preferred to be called, he was told by Mr. Wernher to be at the office at seven o'clock the following morning. Maimon thanked him, and before he knew it, found himself out on the street again.

Maimon needed to collect his thoughts. In ten minutes, he had become a father and got a job. Many people had neither. He also had a place to stay, in what surely was at least a halfway decent hotel – Mr. Vagalparot was unlikely to sanction an indecent one). Yes, Maimon thought as he gently cantered back to the London Hotel that he remembered noticing on his way into town. It had been an amazing morning, truly amazing.

Unlike most other buildings in Kimberley, the hotel was made of brick, and, Maimon thought, was probably called what it was because it was fine enough to stand in London. He handed the reins of his horse to a young native whose job, it seemed, was to look after guests' horses, and walked up a few steps into a hotel that was even grander than the one in East London. A smartly dressed native escorted him to the reception desk, where Maimon handed the woman behind the desk Mr. Vagalparot's letter to Mr. Isaacs. A minute or so later, a formally dressed, shortish man in his thirties seemingly bounced out of his office and up to Maimon.

"Ah, Mr Sokolovski, so glad to meet you," the man gushed. "The name is Harry Isaacs." He thrust an arm out that Maimon shook energetically. "David here will show you to your room." After which, he bounced back to his office. Probably because of Mr. Vagalparot's note, Maimon was shown to a room far grander than the one he had occupied in East London, which, on reflection, was understandable, because, after all, this was Kimberley.

Maimon flopped on the bed, his mind going to Ayna and their son. He would like to see the baby, but if he went to Barberton, he knew what would happen. Ayna, no doubt aided by her relations, would pressurize him to marry her, which was the very last thing in the world he wanted to do. Even if he didn't love Elize – and he certainly did – he didn't love Ayna, so that was the end of that discussion, except he knew it probably wasn't. Mrs. Vagalparot, surely happy at having just acquired a grandson, would undoubtedly want to see Maimon married to Ayna; and if he didn't do so, Maimon worried she might cause problems for him at her husband's office. Reflecting on this possible problem, suddenly wide awake, Maimon's thoughts went back to the boat and the time he spent with Ayna.

Ayna was pretty and clever, but she was devious and not a nice person. He first realized this when she scolded him for trying to catch Mr. Vagalparot. Then there was her refusing the financially attractive

Queenstown job on his behalf without first discussing it with him. Her attitude to the mother who wanted some babysitting help he first thought was disappointing, but on reflection he decided was unforgivable. On top of all of this was her seducing him at a time when she knew she would fall pregnant. He would rather spend the rest of his life single, Maimon decided, than to be married to Ayna.

His further thoughts were interrupted by two loud knocks on his and other guests' doors, with a man shouting 'Dinner Aand Ete,[52] Dinner Aand Ete."

Maimon got up, straightened his clothes, and went in search of the dining room, which was much less smart than the one on the boat, or even at Deals Hotel in East London. He was shown to a table and handed a menu. Maimon glanced at it, and then informed the waiter he had forgotten his glasses and would appreciate being told what was being served. Soup, steak, and ice cream was the answer, and Maimon chose all three.

A minute or so later the man who took his order brought the soup, which gave Maimon a chance to verify his suspicion. Before the waiter left Maimon said, looking up at him from his chair, "Can I ask you a question?"

"Yes, sir," the waiter said. "I am certainly not clever enough to answer it."

"You are a white man in a brown skin. How did you do that?"

For a couple of seconds, the waiter was nonplussed; then a broad smile crossed his face. "I am from India. I am not born here like the black people you see in the street. We are not many, only about 60 or 70 in all of Kimberley."

"Thank you," Maimon muttered, keen to start his soup before it got cold.

"My name is Arjun Patel," the waiter said; seeing Maimon had no further interest in his genetic make-up, he respectfully withdrew back to the kitchen.

Amazing, Maimon thought, as he finished his soup. Not only people from Europe came to benefit from the diamonds, but also Indians. Maybe Chinese, too, and even Japanese, he speculated, making a mental note to ask Mr. Wernher about this in the morning.

After he had finished his dinner, which comprised more food than

---

his whole family sat down to on a Friday night, Maimon headed back to his room. Not that he wasn't interested in exploring Kimberley after dark, but he had to be at the French company's office at seven in the morning, so he had better get an early night, he reasoned.

Before dropping off to sleep, Maimon's thoughts turned once again to his son, this time speculating how his parents and Kaylah would take the news that they had a grandson and a nephew, respectively. Anshul and Gittel would insist that he marry Ayna, that was as certain as the rabbi's white beard. But Kaylah? He wasn't so sure. Anyway, they would never meet Ayna, which on balance he thought was sad. Did they have bar mitzvahs in Africa, Maimon wondered, and then, confident in the knowledge that this wasn't something he had to worry about for at least twelve years, he dropped off to sleep.

Next morning, when it was still dark, found Maimon at the French company's offices at 6:50. Expecting to be the first person there, he was surprised to find lights on in the building. Tying up his horse, he knocked on the big wooden door; and not waiting for an answer, he pushed it open to find Mr. Wernher working on schedules in a big ledger book. Pulling over a chair next to his, Mr. Wernher gestured at Maimon to come and sit down.

"Good morning, Maimon. I didn't want to say so in front of Mr. Vagalparot last night as he is quite formal, but call me Julius."

"Good morning and thank you," Maimon responded, quite deferentially.

"I want you to look at these figures," Julius said, pointing at some numbers towards the top of the page.

Maimon took a deep breath and explained his problem. If doing so was going to cost him his job, so be it. Maimon made sure to add that he had a phenomenal memory.

Wondering what kind of a schlemiel[53] Lesuj had given him, Julius accepted that he had to go through the motions with this youngster – and so he did.

"Our business is two-fold," Julius said slowly. "On the one hand, we buy rough diamonds from the miners, and sell them to whoever will pay us a fair price. The miners call us, and everybody who does this work, koppie-wallopers.[54] Our other activity is doing the mining our-

---

53   *Fool*

54   *A man who visits the miners to buy diamonds*

selves." For a moment Maimon's face went white. Observing his reaction, Julius added, "Mr. Vagalparot and I don't dig the stones out of the ground ourselves, we pay laborers to do it for us. Here are the important figures you need to remember."

Maimon concentrated hard, realizing that his job depended on it.

"Labor costs £2/5/0 a day, and we need a party of fifteen men, those fifteen consisting of five miners and ten natives. Additionally, we need to pay for removing the dirt, which means carts, horses, and wear-and-tear on ropes and tackle, which comes to £1,200 a year."

"So that means," Maimon said, "if you allow £125 for unexpected costs, the company needs £2,000 a year to keep a claim operative, not counting any rent that needs to be paid for the claim."

"How do you get to that?" Julius asked mystified.

"Based on 300 working days a year, using your figure of £2/5/0 a day, for fifteen workers comes to £675, and adding that to the £1,200 a year for horses, carts, and so on, works out to £1,875, which, plus the £125 for unexpected costs, brings the total to £2,000."

Knowing this figure to be correct, Julius hid his amazement at the fact that Maimon had not only done these calculations in his head but had worked out the total only seconds after he had given Maimon the figures. Thankfully, this overgrown boy is not the schmendrick[55] I expected, Julius thought happily.

"Let's go and buy some diamonds," Julius said, heading for the door. Outside his and Maimon's horses were being tended by a native. Maimon noticed that Julius gave the native one or two coins, and he made a mental note to do so as well when he was able to.

Maimon let Julius set the pace, which, at a fast walk, enabled almost everyone they came across to greet his boss. Between the "Good mornings" and "Goeie mores,"[56] Maimon waited to get a word in. When he could he asked, "How many people live in Kimberley?"

"We think about 13,000. Ten thousand natives, 2,000 white men who work on the mines, and the 1,000 balance are people who do jobs in hotels, saloons, and entertainment."

"Are the blacks all from the same country?" Maimon asked, remembering the Indian man in the hotel.

"They are from different tribes, not countries," Julius explained

---

55   A foolish or ineffectual person
56   "Good morning"

patiently. "Most are Zulus, who are highly intelligent. There are also lots of hard-working Basutos. Natives working on the mines are also from other tribes, but unfortunately I don't know much about them."

They rode in silence for a while, both Maimon and Julius looking to their left and right, each of them observing the activity from different perspectives. After a while Julius said, "We are coming to some Cornishmen soon. Four brothers who work hard but haven't had the best of luck."

"*Cornishmen?* Is that another tribe?" Maimon asked, wanting to make the best use of his time with Julius, who obviously knew so much about Kimberley, having lived in the mining town for over a year.

"Goodness, no," Julius replied, laughing. "Cornwall is in England, and they are men who used to mine tin near their home."

A few minutes later they came round a large pile of dirt to find four big, bearded men sitting on large rocks eating breakfast.

"Yerr too late for breakfast, Mr. Julius," one of the brothers called out in jest.

"It is Spingo[57] I am after," Julius replied.

"Aren't we all?" one of the brothers shot back.

"We do have some stones," another brother said quietly, and all of a sudden the conversation lost its frivolity and became serious. Out of his pocket, the oldest-looking brother took a small cigarette tin and handed it to Julius, who opened it carefully, examined the diamonds, and then passed the tin to Maimon, who did his best to look at them as professionally as he could. Having done so he handed the tin back to the oldest brother.

An earnest discussion took place between Julius and the brothers, which resulted in Julius buying three of the five stones in the tin. From his saddlebag Julius took out a portable scale, on which he weighed the diamonds individually, then did some calculations on a piece of paper, and finally counted out £780, which he handed the oldest brother.

"From any other Kopje-walloper we would count it ourselves," one of the Cornishmen said to Maimon, "but from Mr. Julius we know that isn't necessary."

The business done they were soon on their way. At each stop Julius forewarned Maimon of the reception they were likely to receive; his

---

57   *Beers brewed in the brewery of the Blue Anchor Inn in Helston in Cornwall, England*

appraisals were always accurate, and in every case respectful. And at each stop, Maimon's esteem for his new colleague grew. The Germans were hard-working and organized, and in their heads fixed prices for every stone. Julius didn't try to change their minds, he told them what he was pre pared to pay, there was no bargaining, that was that. From some of the German miners he bought stones; from others, nothing.

With the Americans, quite a few of whom originally hailed from Ireland, it was different. Julius warned Maimon that for them it was a big game, and if one wanted their stones one had to play along. After many theatricals, and swearing on their mother's lives, and if what they said was not the truth, they should be thrown over the Cliffs of Moher, some stones were bought. Riding away Julius chuckled, pointing out that there was the world of difference between the truth and the whole truth, something that Maimon remembered for many years to come.

Between their negotiations, Maimon felt they took their lives in their hands as they navigated from one digging to another. Most of the heavy work was done by the natives, who, Maimon learned, toiled from first light to just before dusk. Some spent their whole day digging, others pushed wheelbarrows across ridges that Maimon felt a goat would think twice about crossing.

Some natives stood on the summit of pillars 60 feet in height, and not broader than those a man could stride. They worked with crowbars and picks, with as much concern for the danger they faced as would be the case were they in the middle of a five-acre field.

If it was a very deep claim, the bottom was reached by going down a ladder made of chains and rope, to a ledge about 50 feet below the surface. From that ledge there were ladders of wood that went down from ledge to ledge, until the bottom was reached. At the bottom there was gravel in which the diamonds were found.

All the while it was getting hotter and hotter, with the sun almost directly overhead, something that Maimon didn't remember ever happening in Saratov. For this reason he was relieved to hear Julius say, "That's enough for one morning. Let's go to the club for lunch."

Maimon didn't know what or where the club was, but as he had done all morning, he respectfully followed Julius, now riding alongside of him as the wider path permitted.

"Every miner we bought from this morning was working a legitimate claim. We only buy diamonds from them, or from licensed dealers." Julius paused as they came upon a path that permitted only single-file riding.

When it widened some yards later, he continued.

"Buying any other diamonds, which are often stolen, is illegal. That is called Illicit Diamond Buying, and people caught doing it go to jail." Julius paused again, this time to let what he had just said sink into Maimon's consciousness, then added, "For a very long time."

Maimon didn't often think of his father, and when he did his thoughts were usually not good or kind. But one thing he had to say for his father was that he was honest. Even when it cost him money. Maimon remembered his mother berating his father for giving to the orphanage some timber he found that had fallen off another merchant's cart, rather than sell it in the market; he regretted not standing up for his father in the ensuing argument.

They arrived at a single-story brick building. After dismounting, Maimon followed Julius inside, and shortly thereafter to the bar, which, with the exception of the ceiling, was made of rich-looking dark brown wood.

"Two gin and tonics, please, Dinesh," Julius said to a man in a starched white jacket, who Maimon now knew was from India. Turning round Julius saw someone he recognized.

"Ah, Louis Cohen. There is a man who knows about IDB," Julius said, walking over to him and shaking his hand warmly. "Meet my young friend, Maimon…" Julius hesitated before hearing "Sokolovski" from Maimon behind him. "Sokolovski," Julius added, quickly but brightly, "Maimon Sokolovski. Maimon has just arrived in our fair city, and I was telling him about the evils of Illicit Diamond Buying. From what I remember, you have as good an understanding of how it works as any man hammering stones on the breakwater in Cape Town."[58]

As one of the most voluble raconteurs in Kimberley, Louis never waited for a second invitation, and started right off.

"It is important that everyone, and particularly the sons of Abraham, understand the evils of the wrong end of the diamond market. As we are both here and enjoying Julius' gin and tonicss, I will tell you."

Louis described the process that went through four stages. First the stone was stolen by a "raw and naked kaffir," who was not infrequently paid with small gilt medals made in imitation of the British sovereign sterling and inscribed with silly words like "gone to Hannover." Then

---

58 *The Breakwater in Cape Town was built largely with convict labor, including those   convicted of Illicit Diamond Buying*

the stone was sold to the well-dressed tout, usually a Cape boy, a native of St. Helena (another name for a colored person), who, in turn, passed it on to the eager debased white man, often an ignorant Polish or Litvak Jew, unable to read or write English. He, in turn, disposed of it with the greatest facility to one of the licensed diamond dealers who had a keen scent for bargains.

"Time for lunch," Louis said, almost expecting applause for his mini-thesis on the evils that await the uneducated in this darkest part of Africa. "I am sure Virat can find us a table for three."

They were shown to a table by another Indian man in a starched white jacket and black pants, who placed open menus in front of each of them. Maimon was concerned about being embarrassed, but as he soon found out, he needn't have been.

"I can recommend the smoked salmon, Karoo lamb, and Eton Mess," Julius said, pre-empting any discussion.

Maimon said, "That sounds good. I will have the same."

Louis then sounded forth on the fact that last time he ordered guinea fowl at the club it came with shot in it – Julius winked at Maimon – and that Eton Mess could not be made at altitude without adjusting the temperature of the oven. Eventually, he ordered roast beef and York-shire pudding, with plum and gooseberry crumble to follow. The orders placed, Julius asked Louis a question which Maimon felt had more to it than appeared at face-value.

"I hear you and Barney have dissolved your partnership. The word around the diggings is that both of you made more money than you could ever spend on women and horses, so why waste any more time handeling with the miners."

On the way back to the office, Julius told Maimon it was because Barney was bringing in more than four times as much money as Louis was. This disproportionate share of the profits Barney likened to being rolled over. Maimon didn't understand what that meant and decided to wait for a more opportune time to find out.

"Ah, Barney," Louis said, "doing business with a Barnato is not like having tea and scones at Brown's Hotel in London."

The rest of the lunch Julius and Louis spent gossiping about people Maimon had never heard of: Alfred and Otto Beit, Sir David Harris, Hermann Ekstein, and Sir Joseph Robinson, who they both agreed was a bit of a dog, whatever that meant. Most of the time was spent discussing Cecil Rhodes, who Maimon realized must be a particularly important person.

Back at the office Maimon met Alfred Beit, who Julius congratulated on an extraordinarily successful property deal. Later, Maimon learned that he had bought a piece of land on which he built twelve corrugated iron offices, almost all of which he rented out. Later he sold the property, and the buildings on it, at a considerable profit.

Julius told Alfred about their morning's endeavors, and when given the opportunity, Maimon chipped in with details not only on the stones they had bought, but also those Julius had decided not to purchase. Maimon would have stayed there all night, but at six o'clock both Julius and Alfred left, and so did he. Riding back to the hotel, Maimon passed a saloon and was tempted to stop in for a drink, but not knowing what time supper was served at the hotel, Maimon decided to leave it for another day.

It was just as well, for dinner was only being offered for another thirty minutes; and so he went straight to the dining room, where he was shown to a table by his waiter of the previous evening. Having ordered what Arjun recommended, Maimon leaned back in his chair and reflected on what he had learned in the last twelve hours.

Somewhat to his surprise, a good-looking buxom red-haired woman, whom he thought to be about twenty-five years old, sat down at his table, and almost immediately one of the waiters put glasses containing what looked like a double helping of whiskey in front of each of them.

"Kathleen O'Brien," she said, holding out her hand, which Maimon shook, "Glad to meet you." Then lifting her glass, she added "Slainte."[59]

Maimon lifted his glass and replied "Slainte," without having any idea what it meant.

"Mr. Maimonides Sokolovski," she was careful to pronounce both words correctly, "I know who you are."

They both smiled, and Maimon said, "Just call me Maimon."

"Thank you. Because I work at the hotel, I know you are paying £5 a month, which is a lot of money which could be spent on Bushmills."

Maimon frowned.

"Irish whiskey," she said, pointing at the glass in front of him. "And so I think you should come and stay at our boarding house. My husband Padraig and I charge £3 a month. We also do your washing, and if you are sick, look after you."

---

59   *Used to express friendly greetings by one drinker to another*

Maimon didn't know what to say, so he kept quiet, which Kathleen took to mean her price was too high, and so she said, "£2/10/0, but I can't go a penny lower than that."

"Let me think about it," Maimon said, "and I will tell you tomorrow."

With that Kathleen stood up, finished her whiskey, put the glass back on the table, and said, "Don't worry about paying for the drink. It comes with Mr. Isaacs' compliments."

They said good night, and as Kathleen left, Arjun put a plate of hot mulligatawny in front of Maimon. Sipping the soup, Maimon felt something wasn't right. Mr. Isaacs paid this O'Brien woman, and not only did she give Maimon his whiskey, but also tried to steal one of his customers. That wasn't his problem, Maimon told himself as he slowly made his way upstairs to his room. There, fully dressed, he collapsed on his bed and fell fast asleep.

The week flew by, the highlight of which was Julius doubling Maimon's salary to £30 a month, on the understanding that £10 of each check went to Ayna. Over lunch at the Kimberly Club one day, Alfred asked Maimon to tell him frankly what the situation was with regard to Ayna, because he didn't want to spend months training him, only for Maimon to disappear off to Barberton. Maimon explained that the baby was an unnecessary complication as he wanted nothing to do with Ayna, which obviously was not now possible. Maimon added that there was another girl in the picture, but she was a long-term project, to put it in business terms, and neither he nor Julius should have any concerns that his focus would not be 100% on the business.

Before Maimon knew it, Saturday lunchtime rolled around, which was the end of the French company's working week. This was when he packed his meagre belongings and rode off to the O'Brien's guesthouse. Unlike the Kimberley hotel, the building was made of corrugated iron, which Maimon was to learn was boiling hot in summer and freezing cold in winter. His room was small and sparsely furnished, and upon seeing it Maimon made a mental note never to rent a room again without first inspecting it.

On the flip side, Padraig and Kathleen were very warm and friendly, even after Maimon had told them that he was spoken for, and thus did not have any interest in Kathleen's younger sister. That night, while Padraig was writing letters, Maimon and Kathleen sat on a swinging couch on the stoep[60]of their house. After exchanging a few pleasantries, Kathleen said, "Why don't Jewish people have their own country?"

"How do you know I am Jewish?" Maimon asked naively.

"Because all the clever people in Kimberley are," she said, before repeating "Why don't you?"

Maimon pondered the question. "I don't really know," he finally said. "Every year at Passover we say, 'Next Year in Jerusalem,' but nobody ever goes. People from other towns might go, but no one from our village ever went."

"I'll tell you why," Kathleen said confidently, "because you don't want to enough."

"That's not entirely fair. From the pictures I have seen, all Palestine is either rocky fields or desert. How could a man make a living there?"

"If a million Jews went there, they would find a way. They are clever."

"If a million Jews went to Palestine, 900,000 would starve to death."

"And the other 100,000?" Kathleen asked, sensing that she was about to make a breakthrough.

"They would go back to Europe. Anyway, why this interest on where Jews should live?" Maimon asked, curious where this conversation was going.

"Because of our struggle."

"*Our* struggle?" Maimon asked, now truly perplexed.

"Not your struggle, though you should have one. Our Irish struggle."

"What are you struggling for? You have a country."

"We have and we haven't. We live there but we don't own the land. The English do."

"So what's the problem?" Maimon asked, mystified.

"The problem is that we have to pay rent. The money we get from farming is just enough to buy some food. As a result, we are always poor. And then every now and then they poison us."

"They poison you? The whole nation? How do they do that?" Maimon asked intrigued.

"Haven't you heard of 'the Great Hunger,' when a million people starved to death?" Kathleen said, amazed at Maimon's ignorance.

"I am ashamed to say I haven't. In Saratov, the village I come

---

60   *A paved area adjacent to the front of a house, often covered by corrugated iron sheets*

117

from in Russia, we didn't learn about Irish history." In a flash Maimon realized they didn't learn about French or Italian or Australian or any country's history. Just Russian. "But how did they poison the whole country?" Maimon asked, trying to get his head around the logistics of the exercise.

"They poisoned the potatoes. That is our staple food. The Irish Lumper. I suppose you haven't heard about that, either. And a million people emigrated."

"Is that why you came here?" Maimon asked, finally feeling he knew the purpose of the conversation.

"No. That was forty years ago. We came here to make some money. Like you Jews. Except we are going to use our money in the Struggle."

"You are going to buy the land from the English," Maimon said, now understanding.

"No. We could never make enough money for that. We are going to use the money to buy armaments to fight them," Kathleen explained, quickly realizing that Maimon didn't understand the word "armaments," or appear to know very much about the world. "Guns and bombs and hand grenades and so on. And we would like some help from you."

Maimon liked the compliment and smiled.

"We know you haven't got any money, but we would like some advice. We got a donation from Mr. Rhodes for the Struggle. Between Mr. Wernher and Mr. Beit, who do you think is the richer?"

"You don't want to go to either. It is Mr. Lesuj Vagalparot you should ask. He is their boss." Maimon immediately realized he had said the wrong thing. He didn't know why, but in his bones he knew it. "Whoever asks him for money won't say that I told you?" Maimon asked, panicking. When no answer was forthcoming, he said, "Will they?"

"Of course not. I won't even tell the leader where I got this information. Don't worry."

This put Maimon's mind at rest, not entirely, but mostly. "Thank you," he mumbled, getting to his feet, "I need to go to bed. We start at seven in the morning."

"That is why the Jews are so rich. You are working while we are still fast asleep," Kathleen said smiling.

CHAPTER 15

A SUCCESSFUL STRATEGY

As he rode to the French company's office on Monday morning, Maimon noticed the sun glinting on the hundreds of corrugated iron roofs. In almost all of them he imagined there was some form of activity. Breakfast made and probably already eaten, dishes being washed, the house being cleaned, shops getting ready to be opened, what few children there were being sent off to school; and then he compared that with Europe, where at seven o'clock in the morning people were just getting out of bed. It wasn't just Kimberley. East London also woke up early, and now that he thought of it, in the main, both went to bed early, too. Before he had a chance to reflect on why this was so, he had arrived at the office, tied up his horse, and gone inside to find Julius getting ready for their morning's activities.

"Morning, Maimon" he said, not looking up from his notes.

"Good morning, Mr. Wernher," Maimon replied respectfully.

"Do you remember how we tell diamonds from similar pieces of quartz?"

"The specific gravity is 3.1 to 3.5,' Maimon said quickly, "and the hardness is…"

"I didn't ask you for the tests, I just asked if you remembered," Julius interrupted impatiently. From his questions and unusually brusque tone, Maimon wondered if Julius was in a bad mood, or if he was cross with him, and if he was, why? Maimon wracked his brains to think what he had said or done the previous day that might have upset Julius, but couldn't think of anything. He would just do his best, Maimon decided, hoping that it would be good enough.

"Yes, sir, I do remember."

"Good. This morning when we go to the diggings, you will look at the diamonds and tell me what we should pay for them. Then I will examine them and see how similar our figures are." Then packing up his papers and scale he said, "Let's go. The bird that flies early is never hungry."

Maimon's mind was in a whirl when they mounted their horses. He remembered what Julius had paid for every single stone they had bought the previous week, and he remembered why Julius had paid those prices; but every diamond was different, and he would have to extrapolate this knowledge and apply it ... And before he knew it, they were at the first diggings.

It was a group of Americans and not one of the diggings they had previously called upon. To their surprise, Julius, whom it was apparent they held in high regard, handed their tin to Maimon, and a pencil and a piece of paper to one of the diggers. Maimon laid the seven diamonds in a straight line on a piece of white paper, before examining each one carefully. Then he stood up and, out of Julius' earshot, said the following figures that one of the Americans then wrote down. By now all the miners had stopped what they were doing and watched with intrigue what was going on. Maimon's figures were £120, £400, £800, £600, £1200, £50, and £500.

After that, Julius carefully examined the diamonds, stood up, and called the following prices out to the miner who had written down Maimon's numbers: £130, £400, £850, £600, £1,100, no thank you, and £500. Julius looked at the piece of paper and smiled. A few of the Americans craned their necks to see the figures and then came over and slapped Maimon on the back. Julius graciously offered to buy the diamonds at the higher of his and Maimon's prices, which the Americans thought was a great deal for them and sold him the lot.

At the next digging, where the claim was owned by a crowd of excitable Italians, they did the same thing, and again Maimon's prices were almost identical to Julius.' Taken by Julius' offer to buy the stones at the higher of the two prices, the Italians sold them the entire parcel including a large yellow stone that they had both valued at £2,500.

The same procedure was undertaken at each of the ten diggings they visited that morning, and all with the same results. Their prices were virtually identical, and the miners sold Julius almost all the stones they had recovered.

Back at the office, Julius took Alfred into the meeting room and told him of their morning's activities and showed him the yellow diamond that they had bought from the Italians. Entering into the spirit of the exercise, Alfred asked Julius to write down what he thought they could get for the yellow stone, and Julius did the same. One price was £20,000 and the other was £25,000.

"Time to have a chat with the youngster," Alfred said.

"I heard you had a very successful morning," he said, having asked Maimon to join them at the round mahogany table in the middle of the room. It was the first time Maimon had been invited to do this and it made him feel as if he had been accepted into Julius' and Alfred's club. He sat down, smiling inside, only sorry his mother and father and, of course, Kaylah couldn't see this.

"It was Mr Julius who had the idea and it worked very well," Maimon said deferentially, not quite believing what was happening.

They both smiled knowingly, before Alfred said. "You really did very well, and so Julius and I will be recommending to Mr. Vagalparot that your salary be increased to £100 a month."

Maimon could hardly believe this. He couldn't read or write but was still able to do such an important job. Elize would be so proud of him if she knew. In a few years he would be able to buy a house with rooms like the one he had in Deals Hotel. For him and Elize.

Many years later, when walking out of Prime Minister General Smuts' office, having just been lent a fully crewed four-engine South African Airforce airplane for a week, Maimon realized that it was that morning in Kimberley around the mahogany table that he knew he would be a success.

"Thank you, sir," Maimon said. "And thank you, Mr. Julius, also. It really is most kind of you. If I had any money, I would ask you to join me for lunch, but I am afraid I don't."

"Fortunately, I do," Alfred said, before adding as an afterthought, "they wouldn't accept your money at the club. When you are a member, you can take both of us for lunch." Removing their hats and coats from the hatstand, Alfred and Julius led the way to the club.

The following four mornings Julius and Maimon worked the same procedure, with the result that by lunchtime on Friday, Alfred remarked that they had bought more diamonds than they had purchased in any previous week.

Late that night, Alfred and Maimon were sorting the stones when there was a loud knock on the door. They looked at each other, and then Maimon, being taller and stronger, went to see who was there. A moment later he was back.

"It is a Mr. Rhodes," Maimon told Alfred, who got up at once and went to the front door and brought the man into the office.

"Cecil, what brings you into town at this time of night?" Alfred asked.

"To find out what you are doing," Rhodes replied, easing himself into one of the round table's chairs.

After introducing Maimon, Allred leaned forward in his chair and, looking Rhodes in the eye, said, "Too many diamonds are being mined. The prices are either sky-high or rock-bottom, and that is good for no body. What I need to do is amalgamate all the diggings into one company so that the supply can be controlled."

"That is exactly what I am doing," Rhodes said, before adding a statement that demonstrated his foresight. "We should work together."

"What are you proposing?" Alfred asked.

"You and I will buy up every claim and workings."

"Including Barney Barnato's?" Alfred said, wanting to be clear he understood exactly what Rhodes was proposing.

"Every single claim, including those not presently being worked. No matter who owns them, we will buy them," Rhodes said adamantly.

"You have the money for this?" Alfred asked.

"I don't, but the French Rothschilds do," Rhodes said, more than answering that question.

"When can we meet to plan our campaign?" Beit said, keen not to lose the momentum.

"Come to my office first thing tomorrow morning. I have a map showing every single claim. We can start from there," Rhodes said, standing up.

"I will be there," Beit said, his keenness and excitement evident from the enthusiasm in this voice.

"Fine," Rhodes said, putting on his coat and hat. "Goodnight."

"Goodnight," Beit said, standing up as Rhodes walked out. As both Rhodes and Beit were standing, Maimon did so, too, and then the two of them sat down, absorbing what had just taken place. It was Alfred who spoke first.

"What you just witnessed is the beginning, in a way the birth, of the diamond industry that will keep thousands of people in steady employment. This task that Mr. Rhodes and I are committed to will not be easy.

Strong men will fight against us, but we will persevere, and we will win, and generations of white and colored and black people will have jobs because of us. There is one thing I ask of you, Maimon. That for ten years you do not speak of this meeting. Men can behave irrationally when their egos are damaged, and some will possibly be jealous, so not a word please to anyone."

"I promise, Mr Beit, not a word will spill from my lips about what I witnessed tonight." And then, to make sure he was believed, Maimon said, "On my mother's life, I promise. Not a word."

"Thank you," Alfred said. "You and I have had a long day. Time to pack up." He put his papers in the main drawer of his big wooden desk, Maimon switched off the gas lights, and Alfred locked the door. Then they walked out into the cold black night, each assimilating what had happened in the last thirty minutes.

Though he had hoped to sleep in on the one day that he didn't have to go diamond buying, Maimon woke on Saturday at six o'clock, and so dressed and went to the office, where he found Alfred sitting at his desk, upon which colorful pencils were scattered, poring over the largest piece of paper he had ever seen. On it were little squares and rectangles and a few triangular shapes, each of which Alfred was coloring in either green or red or yellow.

"The green Rhodes or we own. The red are owned by people who might not immediately see the benefit of what we discussed last night. And the yellow are claims that are not being worked at present," Alfred explained, coloring in another red triangle.

"Too many reds," Maimon remarked as Alfred finished one red rectangle and started on a red square.

"Don't worry, my boy," Alfred said, apparently not at all concerned at the number of reds springing up. "Remember, there are few things in life one cannot get for money and a kind word. I have the kind words and Rhodes has access to the money. Maimon, why don't you go outside and enjoy the lovely weather, which I think is also expected tomorrow. I will see you on Monday morning."

It was about forty minutes' walk back to his lodgings, during which time Maimon reflected on his experiences on the train, and the boat, in East London, and at the du Toit's farm, and finally in Kimberley.

His reflections were interrupted by first one, and then another, and then even more families walking to synagogue. None of them spoke to him, they didn't have to remind him of the peace that observant Jewish people seemed to be enveloped in on the Sabbath. No matter how worrying a week had just passed, that was all put in a box that would not be opened till after dark on Saturday night.

Maimon imagined his family trudging through the snow, bundled up against the cold in threadbare coats that his mother had bought at the market. "No need to spend good money on clothes you are not going to wear for half the year," she said, hiding the fact that they didn't have money to pay for anything better. Why was his coat thick and his brother's wasn't? Maimon knew why. Because he had £100 coming to him next Tuesday, an amount his brother wouldn't earn in a year, even if he was in a real job, not learning with the rabbi.

And why was this? Because he had the courage to see out the train and boat journeys, the foresight to catch Mr. Vagalparot, and the memory that had so impressed Julius Wernher and Alfred Beit. He conveniently forgot about his close shave with the hyenas, and the good luck of finding Ayna, who taught him English. Summing it up, as he rounded the corner to the O'Brien's home, Maimon realized that you had to have courage, and that is what he had, and his brother didn't.

"Top of the morning," Kathleen's younger sister, Roisin, called out to him, waving her arms energetically. She was strikingly beautiful and obviously confident, Maimon observed, not at all like her sister. What was she doing in Kimberley? he wondered.

"I made some Irish apple cake," she called out, laughing. "Come and have some with me."

Maimon jumped over the low fence, ran up the grass lawn, and dropped to one knee, from which he looked up at her pretty face and said, as seriously as he could, "Roisin, will you give me a slice of your Irish apple cake?"

"Get up, you silly fellow," she said quickly, concerned that her sister or Padraig would see them.

A few minutes later they were both sitting on the stoep, sipping coffee and eating the cake.

"You should get a job at Mr. Gillingham's Irish bakery," Maimon said in all sincerity.

"That is where I learned how to make it," Roisin admitted. "It is his recipe."

"How old are you?" Maimon asked, finishing the last piece of cake.

"I am nearly fifteen," she volunteered in the most grown-up voice she could muster.

"Can I ask you a question?" Maimon asked, not quite sure what to make of this girl who was the same age as Elize but so different from her.

"Only if it is the kind of question a young girl wouldn't be embarrassed to answer," she said with a twinkle in her eye.

"What is a clever, confident, good-looking girl like you doing in Kimberley?"

Roisin looked at Maimon, her eyes welling up with tears, before running inside, leaving him perplexed. If only Kaylah were here, she would explain why Roisin wasn't upset when he asked her how old she was, but she was when he asked her a less personal question. A few minutes later a composed Roisin reappeared.

"I am sorry," she said apologetically.

"No, it is I who am sorry," Maimon countered. "I owe you one."

"One what?" she asked, mystified.

"One anything. I embarrassed you so I owe you one. When you want one, come and ask me."

"OK. I will remember that. One anything," she said, now smiling again. Then the smile disappeared from her face. "I will tell you why I am here. Because I trust you. I trust you not to tell anyone."

"I promise," Maimon said, looking into her eyes in a way that Roisin knew he would not betray her trust.

"My stepfather raped me when I was twelve. Many times."

"Didn't you tell your mother?" Maimon asked incredulously, now knowing what this meant.

"I did, but she was afraid that if she accused him, or even just asked him to stop doing it, he would leave her."

"Oh my God," Maimon said, grasping his head in his hands. He knew that sex could be wonderful as it was with Elize, and that it could also be alright, as it was with Ayna and Adelaide, but he never thought it could be hurtful and traumatic, as it had been with this poor girl. "What did you do?"

"I ran away."

"Where did you run to?"

"I stopped the first horse-and-cart that came along and asked the farmer driving it to take me as far away from that place as he could. Fortunately, he was a kind man and he took me to his home, where he and his wife looked after me. They didn't have any children of their own. We agreed I couldn't go back home, and I informed them the only other close relation I had in the world was my sister, far away in South Africa.

"Listen to what this farmer and his wife did for me: They gave me enough money to buy a steamship ticket from Dublin to Liverpool, and another one from Liverpool to Durban, and then also for the cost of a stagecoach seat from there to Kimberly."

"That is amazing," Maimon said, having difficulty believing that strangers could be so charitable.

"What is amazing is that they gave me £285, telling me to use the extra I didn't need for traveling to spend on my bottom drawer."

"For a cupboard you are going to buy? For a wardrobe? So much money?" Maimon asked bewildered.

"No, you silly thing," Roisin said laughing. "That is for linen for my first house, and some dresses for me. In England they call it a 'dowry.'"

"You Irish people are truly wonderful," Maimon remarked, still getting over the farmer's generosity.

"We Irish people are not wonderful," Roisin said very firmly.

"I am sorry. I forgot about your stepfather," Maimon said humbly.

"There is a man coming to lunch today. All hail fellow and well met. If you ask him what he does for a living, he will tell you he is in finance. His 'finance' is robbing the couriers, taking diamonds down to the coast. And then tomorrow he goes to church, and says all his 'Hail Marys,' and you know what is worse? Everybody, including the priest, knows about this, but nobody has got the courage to confront him, or go to the police, not that I know what good that would do. And I am in that group of Irish who does nothing," she said, disgusted with herself as much as she was with her people.

While they were chatting, a few people had arrived at the O'Brien's home and were standing in the garden around a fire on which meat would shortly be cooked. Ahead of the food they were drinking beer, Irish whiskey, and for some adventurous souls, vodka of dubious origin.

"Roisin, bring Maimon down here, so I can give him a drink and introduce him to our friends," Padraig called out in his lilting Irish brogue, evident after a few Bushmills.

Roisin took Maimon by the hand and pulled him willingly down a few steps into the garden, where Kathleen introduced him to their seven guests. Doing so interrupted the conversation, for which Maimon apologized.

"I was just saying," the man just introduced to him as Liam Murphy continued, "the Jews are buying up all the claims and soon we will be out of work."

"I thought Rhodes was behind it," one of the guests said.

"Yes, I heard that, too," Liam said. "He is probably fronting for Barnato and Vagalparot and the others. Anyway, I heard a good joke yesterday. Do you know why the Jews have big noses?"

There was a silence, during which the other guests and Padraig looked on curiously.

"Because air is free," Liam said, downing another whiskey.

Maimon stiffened. Roisin gripped his arm, afraid that he was going to take a swing at Liam.

"Mr. Murphy," I am Jewish, and I find that offensive," Maimon said, containing his anger with difficulty.

"Liam, that was offensive. You owe Maimon an apology," Padraig said, embarrassed by the way Maimon had been spoken to.

"I won't apologize," Liam began, "but I will salute you, Padraig. For centuries, the Jews have been taking money off us Irish. By having this boarder," he said, pointing to Maimon, "you are redressing this by taking some money back from them."

Maimon turned on his heel, heading back into the house, with Roisin a step behind him. Liam called out, "Don't fuck her. She is underage."

Maimon headed up to his room and was about to slam the door behind him, when he saw Roisin would be hurt if he did so. Throwing himself down on the bed, he punched the pillow over and over in anger. Roisin sat quietly on the chair. When he stopped, she said quietly, "They only do it out of jealousy. Your brains are not bigger than ours, you just work harder. Also, you drink less. We have Bushmills whiskey and Guinness, the Scots have all their whiskys, the English their beers, the French their wines, and so on."

Maimon turned onto his back, clasping the pillow to his chest. After about five minutes Roisin said quietly, "Please tell me about your girlfriend?"

Maimon looked across at her quizzically. "Why should I do that?"

"Because I think it would make you feel better."

"Me telling you about my girlfriend will make me feel better?" Maimon said, not sure if she was serious.

"Yes. Why don't we try it?"

Maimon whose anger had been replaced by his love for Elize was intrigued.

"Alright. But on one condition. That you don't tell anyone about her."

"I promise," Roisin said in a manner that made Maimon believe her, and so told her. From the beginning, when he met Elize at the hotel in East London, to when he said goodbye to her the day he rode away from her parent's farm.

"Do you write to her often?" Roisin asked tenderly.

Maimon explained why he didn't, and also that he had often thought about dictating a letter for someone else to write; but in each case had decided against it because his love was for Elize, and he didn't want anyone to come in between them, even a letter-writer. He added that he didn't expect her to understand that.

"But I do understand," Roisin protested, "and you shouldn't let anyone come between you and Elize."

Maimon lay on the bed, feeling happy that Roisin had understood his position. Then, to his surprise, she said, "Would you give me her name and address?"

"Why do you want that?" he asked, mystified.

"So I can write and tell Elize how much you love her."

"You don't even know her."

"If I was Elize I would treasure that letter for the rest of my life."

Maimon thought for a minute, and then said, "Alright."

A moment later there was a knock on the door and Padraig came in. Before he said anything, which was a good ten seconds, Maimon and Roisin saw how uncomfortable he was.

"I am really sorry," Padraig began. "The man was drunk, but that is no excuse. He is an asshole. I sent him home after his outburst, but I was the host and I want you to know that none of us share those views."

"That's alright," Maimon said. "We don't need to spend any more time discussing it."

"Thank you. There is a whole lot of food left. Why don't you and Roisin come down and eat some of it. Otherwise, I will have to, all week."

The next few months passed quietly for Maimon. He and Julius went out almost every day, and as the rising sun began to glint on Kimberly's ever-growing number of corrugated iron roofs, Julius would say that the market was up ten percent, or the demand for yellow stones had fallen away. The miners insisted on he and Julius maintaining their double act, which worked well. The pair of them were able to pick the eyes out of the available stones, and the French company must have made good money from their purchases, because they soon raised Maimon's salary to £250 a month. Maimon saved as much of that as he could, and worked out that after about two and a half years, he would have enough money to buy a house, and marry Elize.

Alfred Beit's and Cecil Rhodes' claims purchases were continuing apace, and when they got control of Barney Barnato's Kimberley Central Mining Company, the job was pretty much done. They put all the claims into a company they called De Beers, named after Arnoldus and Nikolaas De Beer, two brothers who owned the farm on which the Colesberg Kopje was situated.

There was, however, a group of Ukrainians who had four claims, for which they wanted £20,000, that Rhodes and Beit agreed were not worth a penny more than £17,000. One afternoon Maimon saw Alfred Beit in the office and asked him for permission to negotiate the purchase of the Shevchenko's claims for £17,000.

"What makes you think that they will sell their claims to you when they wouldn't sell them to Mr. Rhodes?" Alfred Beit asked.

"I speak Ukrainian," Maimon replied, suppressing a smile as he knew that would not get him a discount of £3,000.

"Here are the sale contracts," Alfred said, taking them out of his satchel. "Not a penny more than £17,000."

"Not a penny more," Maimon repeated, having an idea how he might be able to bridge the gap.

An hour later Maimon was back. "Signed contract?" Alfred Beit asked.

"Yes, sir," Maimon responded, handing it back to Alfred.

"But this is for £20,000. Where is the extra £3,000?" Alfred asked, not worried but curious to know how Maimon had bridged the gap.

Maimon took £3,000 out of his satchel and handed it to Alfred.

"And all that for speaking Ukrainian?" Alfred asked quizzically.

"Speaking Polish also helped," Maimon said, smiling, both of them knowing that it hadn't and didn't.

"I give up," Alfred said, now intrigued how Maimon had put the deal together.

"The brothers agreed each of them had to get £5,000. I said that we would pay £20,000 if they threw in the six pink diamonds they have been trying to sell for the past five months. They quickly agreed to that, so we all signed the contract, and I took it and the six pinks."

"To?" Alfred asked.

"To Stransky, whom I knew had a customer for pinks. So I sold him all six for £5,000." Maimon took out a further £2,000 and handed them to Alfred.

"Well done, Maimon," Alfred said appreciatively, calculating his share of the profits on Stransky's pinks. If they wanted to keep Maimon, Alfred realized, they would have to make him a partner sooner than later, and he made a mental note to discuss this with Lesuj and Julius.

The following day Maimon was given a £2,000 bonus, and the house for the future Mr. and Mrs. Sokolovski was looking more in focus.

If there was one reason why De Beers was formed, it was to prevent an oversupply of diamonds pushing the price of the commodity down, and now, in the company's early days, they faced just such a risk. Whether credit for devising the masterstroke that prevented this happening was due to Beit or to Rhodes, Maimon didn't know and couldn't ask, but it was Rhodes who carried it out.

Sales of De Beers diamonds in those days were done by offering carefully put-together parcels of roughly equal value to each of the dealers at set prices. This was done virtually single-handedly by a man called Brink, with whom Maimon had become friendly. On this occasion the diamonds were displayed in the De Beers boardroom, where each parcel was placed on a single large piece of white paper. Even though he wasn't associated with any of the dealers, Maimon was invited to attend by Sir David Harris, who represented the Barnato brothers at these "sights."

Mr. Rhodes left the room to allow the dealers to discuss the parcels, and eventually they collectively agreed on a price of £650,000, which they had been advised would be acceptable to De Beers. On Rhodes' return they told him this, which he acknowledged. Walking back to his office, he nonchalantly lifted a corner of the paper on which the little piles of diamonds had been carefully placed, and tipped them into a wooden bucket that was positioned on the floor for the single purpose of receiving the diamonds. Maimon had never seen grown men groaning and shouting as the fourteen or so gathered in the boardroom did when they saw their allocated stones in the bucket of diamonds.

A minute or two later, Brink came over and explained the effect of what Rhodes had done. It had taken him and his team five months to sort these diamonds into twelve roughly equal parcels, and it would take him almost as long as that to do so again. The effect of this was that these diamonds were off the market for almost six months, which gave prices a chance a recover. Much later, Maimon learned that diamond prices did in fact go up, with the result that when the dealers got to sell these stones, they achieved much better prices than they would have had Rhodes not tipped them into the bucket.

Over the next few months, De Beers mopped up the few remaining independently owned claims, and Maimon's daytime life was limited to working with Brink sorting De Beers production.

He had fallen in with the Irish crowd, and it seemed every couple of weeks they had another reason to celebrate. It was usually one of the saint's birthdays, but the big one was St. Patrick's, which Maimon likened to the Jewish holy day Yom Kippur, in as much that the one brought all the Irish out and the other did similarly for the Jews. Of course, the big difference was that on Yom Kippur the Jews drunk nothing, while on St. Patrick's Day the Irish drunk anything, as long as it wasn't water. Maimon was feeling particularly happy as Roisin had received a letter from Elize, telling her how much she loved him, and that, if necessary, she would go to the end of the earth to be with him. She quoted the Book of Ruth, whose implication Roisin understood, though Maimon didn't.

.

CHAPTER 16

ONE MURDER INSTEAD OF TWO

Maimon hadn't been in The Green Man, a pub favored by many of Kimberley's Irish community, for more than thirty minutes, when he noticed Liam Murphy stumble through the door. He had obviously started celebrating much earlier in the day than many of his country-men. Seeing Conor, who was sitting next to Maimon, Liam sidled over to him and said in a stage-whisper, "Taim chun na Vagalparot sin a lam-hach anocht." Then he went to join other of his Irish mates.

After a few minutes Maimon got up and strolled over to the bar, where he waited to catch the eye of one of the girls serving drinks. Due to the throng of boisterous Irishmen, it took longer than expected, but eventually he did.

"Rosie, what does 'Taim chun na Vagalparot sin a lamhach anocht' mean?"

"What is a 'Vagalparot'?" she asked inquisitively.

"A little animal about this size," Maimon responded, holding his hands about two feet apart.

"It means, 'I am going to shoot those Vagalparot tonight,' but it is unbelievably bad grammar. Is he drunk, the man who said that?"

"It looks like it," Maimon said, dropping two shilling pieces into her hand.

"You're a darlin,'" Rosie said with a big smile. "Can I get you a drink?"

"No thanks," Maimon replied. "Not now."

Maimon walked unhurriedly over to the hat-and-coat stand, found his warm black overcoat, checked it was his by the gloves in one pocket and the balaclava in the other, and waved goodbye to Padraig. Then he opened the door of the pub and ran as fast as he could to the Vagalparot house. Liam Murphy probably had a horse, or would steal someone else's, so Maimon realized he didn't have much time to spare.

Arriving at the Vagalparot house, the first things Maimon noticed was the absence of the security guard and the fact that the big steel gates were open. Without pausing to catch his breath, Maimon ran up the winding paved drive to the front door, on which he knocked loudly.

"Who's there?" Lesuj called out.

"It is Maimon. Please open the door quickly. It is important," Maimon gasped, out of breath.

"Are you alone?" Lesuj enquired. "Yes. Yes. Please be quick."

Lesuj opened the door, Maimon pushed in and slammed it behind him, making sure it was locked and all its bolts were shot home.

The sight that greeted Maimon was comical, and if the situation wasn't so serious he would have laughed out loud.

Lesuj was wearing a heavily patterned maroon-and-black smoking jacket that almost reached down to his knees, the right arm of which hung empty and loosely by his side. The jacket covered a pair of black, striped trousers with double-folded hems that ended about three inches above two oversized sheepskin slippers.

In stark contrast to his formality, Raizel sported an oversize white nightdress that made her look like a becalmed sailing ship. On her head was a sort of hat that Maimon remembered the du Toits called a "doek."

"What happened to you?" Maimon asked, seeing Lesuj's arm in plaster and a sling.

"He fell down and broke it," Raizel answered. "Why are you running here? What is the problem?"

"The problem is," Maimon started, looking around the entrance hall, where he saw two heavy firedogs. Picking one up, he estimated it weighed about 75 lbs.

"The problem is," he continued, now having caught his breath, "that there is a drunk Irishman on his way here to kill you."

"Why would he want to do that?" Raizel asked, more curious than concerned.

"Because you didn't give the Irish Home Rule Movement any money. The Irish say the richest man in Kimberley did, and as the second richest, you refused to."

"The Commissioner of Police told me that having done so, Rhodes would never get a knighthood," Lesuj explained.

Just then they heard horse's hooves cantering up the drive, and only seconds later "Open up! OPEN UP!" was bellowed in a strong Irish brogue.

Lesuj and Raizel were rooted to the spot in fear.

"Open up, or I will set your house alight and burn you alive in it" came the fearful but, to Maimon, familiar voice.

Lesuj shuffled to the door, and while he was doing so Maimon grabbed one of the firedogs, put it on his shoulder, and then hid in the corner of the room behind thick double velvet curtains. As he only had one arm to work with, it took Lesuj longer than usual to unlock the door and slide the steel bolts open. Liam Murphy pushed his way into the room, brandishing a Smith & Wesson large-frame revolver.

"So you are the famous Mr. Vagalparot," Liam spat out.

"What do you want?" Lesuj asked in a stronger voice than Maimon expected.

"I wanted some money for the Struggle, but you wouldn't give me any. You wouldn't even see me."

"I will go and get some now," Lesuj responded, and disappeared down a long a dark passage.

"Two weeks ago, I would just have taken the money," Liam said to a quaking Raizel, "but your husband has put me to a lot of trouble. So now I am going to take the money and I am going to shoot him."

"You wouldn't do that," Raizel said, but from her voice it was clear she believed he really would.

"He won't be the first man I have shot," Liam explained. "Actually, the fourth. The others were in the last Boer War. Did you know there was an Irish brigade in that war?"

Before Raizel had a chance to answer Liam's question, Lesuj reappeared with a carpet bag holdall.

"Here you are," Lesuj said, throwing the bag at Liam's feet. "There is £10,000 in the bag. Take it and be gone."

"I will take it, and I will be gone, but not before I have shot you," Liam told Lesuj calmly.

"Don't shoot him! Please don't shoot him!" Raizel wailed.

"Shut up, you fat bitch," Liam told her. "Or I will shoot you, too."

"If you shoot me now, you won't get any more money next year," Lesuj explained logically.

"I won't get any money from you next year because I will be dead. 'Hung by the neck until dead' is the saying. But one of my brothers will pay a visit to this fat pig here, and if she doesn't give us another £10,000, we will blow your daughter's head off. Just Like I am going to blow yours off now. Say goodbye to your wife, as you are not going to see her for a year or so. In heaven or hell, wherever you two Jew blood-suckers are going."

While Liam was giving this speech, Maimon crept from behind the curtain. Raizel saw him and let out a piercing scream. Lesuj dropped to the floor. Liam fired the gun, aimed somewhere between Lesuj and Raizel, and Maimon crashed the base of the heavy firedog down on Liam's head with all the strength he could muster. Almost in slow motion, Liam's head split open as he slumped onto the Persian carpet.

Overcome by seeing Liam killed, Raizel collapsed on the floor sobbing. Lesuj made his way to the cocktail cabinet, where he poured three tumblers, each two-thirds full of whiskey. He handed one to Raizel, another to Maimon, and the third he drunk himself as if it was a glass of water.

Maimon, mesmerized by Liam's split open, heavily bleeding head, held the glass of whiskey as if not knowing what to do with it.

"Take this," Lesuj instructed Maimon, handing him the bag containing the £10,000 that had been offered to Liam. "Take it, and the Irishman's horse, and ride to the station. The next coach leaves for Johannesburg in fifteen minutes."

"I couldn't do that. I have just killed a man. I must go to the police," Maimon stammered.

"That is the last place you should go," Raizel told him. Having downed her whiskey, she now fully recovered her redoubtable self.

"They will catch me," Maimon said, accepting the inevitability of his position. "It is better that I hand myself in. I will stay. I have decided."

"Listen to me carefully," Lesuj said in a serious parental voice. "You are a minor and we are your adopted parents. You have a legal obligation to carry out our wishes. You will catch the eight p.m. coach to Johannesburg. When you get there, give the bag to Mr. Edward Nathan, a lawyer. Now go!"

"But what if …" Maimon began panicking.

"There is no *what if* anything," Lesuj said, his voice unusually calm. "None of your fingerprints are on the fire dog, as you had gloves on when you picked it up."

Maimon looked down at his hands to verify this.

"And there is no extradition between the Transvaal and Griqualand West."

"Alright. I will go." Deciding against taking Liam's horse, Maimon ran to the station, arriving a good five minutes before the coach's scheduled departure.

At the office he bought a single ticket to Johannesburg, wondering as he did so if he would ever come back to Kimberley. About a minute later the driver cracked his whip, which told the passengers he was about to depart. The whip-crack noise reminded Maimon of the morning Elize's father saved him from the hyenas, and climbing up into the cab, he thought of what had happened to him since then.

One of the smaller coaches on the Kimberly-Johannesburg run, this last-of-the-day carriage was fully loaded with its six passengers, all of whom were encouraged to put their bags on the roof. Five of them did. Mumbling something incoherent as his reason for keeping the carpet bag, Maimon clutched Lesuj's valise as he had the old leather one his mother had carefully packed before he left Saratov.

As the coach started bumping along Kimberly's poorly maintained roads, Maimon looked at his fellow travelers. Opposite him was a girl of about his age with a greatly distended stomach, and next to her a woman who could be her mother. Perhaps it *was* her mother, who was taking her daughter to see a Johannesburg doctor about the girl's condition. Next to them was a well-dressed businessman of about 50 years old, also clutching a bag. On his right side was a quite good-looking woman in her twenties. And on his left was an old babushka of indeterminate age, who spent the whole trip mumbling to herself. They rumbled on in the dark and in silence.

Maimon took a deep breath and considered taking a nap as it was still more than three hours before they reached the overnight scheduled farm stop. What kept him awake was the hand of the girl next to him, who had placed it firmly on his thigh. Maimon lifted it up and put it on her lap. To his surprise, her hand came right back, and this time held his. How she found it in the dark he didn't know, but she did, and she held on to it firmly. Maimon was in a quandary. He didn't want to be familiar with her, but she may be frightened, so he just left his hand hanging limply, and she held it all the way to the overnight farmhouse that they reached at about midnight.

The farmer and his wife were waiting for them with large slices of melktert, a kind of caramel tart, and koeksusters that looked and tasted like sickly sweet fried dough. And coffee, always coffee. Maimon had a slice of the caramel tart and a mug of coffee, after which, following the farmer's wife, he went up to what turned out to be a big dormitory. It had about 50 beds, and the farmer's wife made it quite clear that the two men would sleep at one end and the four women at the other. Exhausted by the day's events, and four hours of being bounced around in the coach, Maimon was soon fast asleep.

After a couple of hours Maimon jolted awake in a cold sweat. It was pitch-dark and he didn't know where he was. Near him someone was snoring. Was it the Irishman? It must be. He wasn't dead after all! When he woke up he would shoot Maimon. Maimon had to get away, wherever he was, so he rolled over. Scared half to death he was falling, and a second later landed loudly on the wooden floor. That woke the Irishman. Maimon froze in fear.

"What are you doing down there?" a man with an English accent asked half asleep.

Then Maimon remembered. The stage coach. The farmer's wife with her food and coffee. Kimberley and everything that happened that night was miles away. Maimon climbed back onto his bed, mumbled something about a nightmare, and covering himself with the heavy rough bottle-green army blanket, curled up in a fetal position. There he lay, sometimes asleep, sometimes awake, until hours later the sun's rays beamed in through the Dutch gabled dormer window. A new day, Maimon realized thankfully. A day of increasing miles away from Kimberley. Maimon stretched his cramped arms and legs. He was grateful to be alive.

The remainder of the trip was uneventful. The road varied between being more or less bumpy, the "more" part causing the mother of the girl with a swollen tummy a great deal of concern. They stopped for lunch and a change of horses at a farmhouse close to the road, where they finally introduced themselves. Maimon was sure that the mother and daughter gave false names, and the old lady mumbled hers in a way that, even after repeating it, rendered it incomprehensible. The man next to Maimon announced himself as George B. Hamilton, an industrial chemist who did freelance work for the mining industry.

A few hours later they arrived in Johannesburg, which, though younger than Kimberley, was already much larger. The coach dropped them all at the post office, and the first thing Maimon wanted to do, and needed to do, was to get rid of the carpet bag, which, when he was not holding it close to his body, had remained within arm's reach. He didn't know the address of Mr. Nathan's office, but suspected that if he walked around, he would find a lawyer's brass plate and their office would direct him to Mr. Nathan; and this is exactly what happened.

Edward Nathan was a short man, slightly built, whose eyes were continually darting from one object to another. At first Maimon found this disconcerting, but after a while he ignored it. Yes, Mr. Vagalparot had told him Maimon would be delivering a bag containing £10,000, and no, he did not intend to count it. If he knew about the genesis of the money, he gave no inkling that this was so. He did say that Mr. Wernher had asked him to give Maimon £720, which was in an envelope he handed over. This done, he pulled a piece of paper from his pocket and told Maimon he had a three-part message from Mr. Vagalparot.

"Firstly, he says 'thank you.' I imagine you know what for." Maimon nodded. "Then he says, 'One cannot find a diamond whose description is not known,' and finally that 'he is looking after his grandson and his mother.' I assume all this makes sense to you?" the lawyer asked.

Again, Maimon nodded.

"If I may be so bold as to ask, what are your plans now, Mr. Sokolovski?"

"Please call me Maimon."

"And I am Edward," the lawyer gladly responded.

"I need to visit a farm in the Orange Free State, so I have to buy a horse and the tackle for it, and also some more clothes."

"Why don't you do that this afternoon, have dinner with my wife and me, sleep at our house, and then leave in the morning?"

"I really don't want to impose myself on you," Maimon protested weakly, welcoming the offer of eating and sleeping in a Jewish home.

"No imposition at all," Edward said. "Come at seven p.m. Our house is at 10 Saratoga Avenue in Doornfontein. We have a stable for your horse at the back."

Maimon thanked Edward and set off on his quest to buy what he needed for his trip to the du Toit farm. He also bought a pouch of tobacco for Piet, some perfume for Elize, and a lace item for her mother. Thinking it would be wise, he added a bottle of brandy for Willem. While he was about it, Maimon picked up a bottle of whiskey for Edward and a large bunch of flowers for his wife. At seven o'clock sharp, Maimon tied up his horse at 10 Saratoga Avenue, and knocked on its front door.

The dinner and the chat afterwards were the most enjoyable that Maimon had had since he left home. Maimon told Edward and his wife Pauline his story since leaving Saratov, omitting any mention of Ayna and Adelaide, and the reason for his hasty departure from Kimberley. Edward Nathan, Maimon learned, came from Lithuania, as did almost all the Jews in South Africa. After Pauline retired for the night, Edward and Maimon sat up chatting about financial matters till well after midnight.

The next morning Maimon came down for breakfast, where he was greeted by a plate of two fried eggs, some baked beans, grilled tomatoes, and Wachenheimer's sausages, which Mrs. Nathan assured him were the best in Africa. This meal, with toast and coffee, meant that he would not have to eat till dinner time. Getting up from the table and thanking both Edward and Pauline, Maimon headed for the stables, where his horse had also been fed and rubbed down.

CHAPTER 17

CHECKING THE CAMPS

Maimon set off shortly after eight, and as soon as he was out of Johannesburg and its environs, he saw one farmhouse after another burned to the ground. Not only that, but their surrounding fields had also been torched. After an hour or so, and about ten burned farmsteads, Maimon came across two natives walking barefoot, with the laces of their highly polished shoes tied together and slung across their shoulders. It was the first time Maimon had seen this, but during his African travels in the years ahead, he was to come across many men walking in this manner. After greeting the natives, he asked them about the burned farmhouses, and was told this had been done by the British soldiers who had also poisoned the farms' wells. It was only the women and children who were left on the farms, as the men were away fighting.

It was one thing observing the burnt farmhouses as he rode past them, it was quite another being told what the soldiers had done to the farms and their wells.

For a long time Maimon pushed to the back of his mind the possibility that this fate might also have befallen the du Toits and their farm; but after hearing about this wanton destruction from the natives, he could no longer do so.

As he rode past more and more burnt farms, Maimon came to accept that, in all likelihood, this is what he would also find at Brandfort. Then he saw an untouched farm, and a few miles on, another one, and so maybe, just maybe …

It was now late afternoon and both Maimon and his horse were tired. At the next unburned farm Maimon came to, he slowed to a trot;

about forty yards from the homestead's front door he dismounted and dropped the reins of the bridle over an upturned tree.

Walking very slowly to the house, he heard a woman screaming, "Wat soek jy?"[61] Looking up he saw the long barrel of a gun pointing out of a window at him.

"'n plek te slaap, M'vrou. Ek het nie 'n geweer nie,"[62] Maimon shouted back.

The door slowly opened and a woman in her thirties approached Maimon, still pointing what seemed to be a shotgun at his head. Maimon lifted both hands in the air. The woman came closer. "Jy is mos 'n kerel,"[63] she said, lowering her gun. "Wat is jou naam?"[64]

"Maimon Sokolovski," he answered, hoping that it would not be taken for an English name, which it certainly wasn't.

The woman took a close look at Maimon, and realizing he was not English, muttered, "Kom binne."[65]

Maimon followed the woman, whose name he learned was Marie, into the house, which was very basically furnished. Over the next three hours, Maimon got a plate of meat stew over pap and gravy, together with an apology that while this was what the natives ate, it was all she had left. Maimon also got her tragic story. Away from Russia and its pogroms, Maimon had forgotten that life, even in South Africa, was not all smooth-sailing.

Marie told Maimon that her husband's family had been allocated this farm in the Great Trek, and three generations had worked to turn it from barren veld into the developed property it was today. Her husband, Frik, had joined one of the northern Orange Free State commandos, and she had not seen him for five months. She was afraid he had been killed in a skirmish with the British.

When the soldiers came to their farm, her son, little Danie, who was not yet a year old, was sick with fever. Marie pleaded with the soldiers for some medicine, as she had none left; in reply, one of the soldiers grabbed Danie by the ankles and put his head in a bucket of water. When Marie saw he was drowning, she ran and grabbed him back, but it

---

61   "What are you looking for?"

62   "A place to sleep, missus. I don't have a gun."

63   "You are just a guy."

64   "What is your name?"

65   "Come in"

was too late. He was already dead. On hearing of this, the commanding officer was furious. He made the man who drowned little Danie dig a grave for him, and after he was buried, he was also ordered to fashion a cross for the freshly dug grave. Then he told Marie that she had suffered enough, and so they were not going to burn her farm.

At about nine o'clock they went up to bed, Marie emotionally exhausted and Maimon very tired after a long day in the saddle. There was only one bed, quite a big one, and when Maimon saw which side Marie got into, he went round and lay on the other. Sometime in the night Maimon felt her snuggling up to him. He was not sure what to expect, but it soon became clear that she just wanted another person to hold her tight, and that is what Maimon did for much of the night. In the morning, a little embarrassedly, she thanked him for doing so.

To see Maimon on his way, Marie gave him some corn bread and a little jam. Before leaving he asked for an axe, with which he chopped some firewood that she would not be strong enough to manage. Marie was so grateful for this gesture that she took both Maimon's hands and kissed them, which embarrassed him. Making sure that his horse had also eaten, Maimon threw on its saddle, tightened the girth strap, and quickly attached its bridle, which he was now adept at doing. Then he mounted the horse, waved Marie goodbye, and cantered off.

The day was largely as the one before, mostly burnt-down farm-houses and crops, with occasional untouched homesteads surrounded by green fields. As he got closer to Brandfort, Maimon's emotions swung widely. One minute he was in the dumps, expecting to find another destroyed house and scorched-earth policy enforced, and then the next minute he felt euphoric, against all the odds of gratefully finding Elize and Magda safe and sound.

At long last Maimon saw the big fig tree in the distance, and he felt like he was coming home – to a home that he loved, not to his Saratov home that he had decided he would never, ever go back to.

And then his worst fears were realized. The house where he had spent so many happy hours was no longer. The fields just black stubble. There was nothing to stay for. Maimon was turning his now stationary horse to trot away from this desolate place, when he heard a voice call out, "Baas Maimon." And then again, coming from the direction of the fig tree, though a little weaker, "Baas Maimon."

Maimon turned round and there, sitting on a stump next to the giant tree, was Johannes, the family's old and trusted manservant. He dismounted and slowly walked over to the big fig tree to see the man he knew so well. Maimon sat down quietly next to him.

"How are you, my friend?" Maimon asked concerned.

"I am alright, Baas." And then after a minute or so, "It was bad, Baas. It was very bad."

Maimon waited to hear how bad it was, but Johannes had to be coaxed. "What happened? To Mrs. Magda and Miss Elize?"

Maimon wanted to know, and if it was bad news he didn't want to know, what had happened to Elize. Sitting on a dead wooden log Maimon realized for the first time how much he loved this girl, this woman, for whom he had saved every penny he could. So that they could be together again, but if she was dead … His heart was thumping in his chest, in his head, in his ears.

"They got taken away but they was living."

Maimon smiled, with relief, with thanks, with happiness, the jury had found him not guilty. She wasn't at the farm but she was alive. He would find her. They would be together again. He would rent a house in Johannesburg, he didn't have to buy one. Suddenly he felt warm all over. Not warm from the sun, but warm inside his body. In his arms and his legs and even his chest. Maimon closed his eyes, took a deep breath, and did something he had never done before. He thanked God.

"And Baas Piet and Willem?" Maimon asked, imagining what was coming.

"The British shot them. There," he said, pointing to an oleander bush next to the house, "in front of the Madam and Miss Elize."

"Do you know why they did that?" Maimon asked, as if a reason would bring back the man he respected, and the overgrown boy he loathed.

"It was war, Baas Maimon. It was war."

They both sat in silence, and then Maimon got up and walked slowly to the well.

"It is poisoned," Johannes called after him.

Maimon came back and sat on the stump next to Johannes, saying, more to himself, than to his old friend, "Why? Why?"

Johannes did not know whether he was expected to answer or not.

"Because it is war," he said again, this time his voice little more than a whisper. "They killed the men, took the women away, and poisoned the well so we blacks would die of thirst."

Up to that moment, Maimon had viewed the war as a sort of theoretical subject. It was between the British and the Boers, of which he was neither. Therefore, he was uninvolved and indifferent, or so he thought. He did not think this now. In just one sentence, Johannes had brought home to him its horror. Tears ran down his face and he started sobbing, first gently, and then uncontrollably.

Maimon now realized that Piet had been a father figure to him. After he got permission to marry Elize, they worked together like Maimon believed fathers did with their sons. His father had never even hinted that he would like Maimon to work with him in the lumber business, so his relationship with Piet was something new and special and a combination of satisfying and rewarding.

That was gone, forever, just like Kimberley, for him, was gone forever, and all he had left were memories. Memories of his wonderful months at the farm before Willem returned, and his all-too-brief commercial career with Julius and Alfred. But he did have Elize, and that he hung onto like it was *America's* strong steel anchor chain. He just had to climb up it, which he would do, link by link, because waiting on the deck in the sun, would be Elize.

Maimon stopped crying, and said humbly, "Please show me where Baas Piet and Willem are buried."

Johannes got up and slowly walked round the side of the house, where two mounds of sand lay side by side, each with a rough-hewn wooden cross stuck near the head, one a little larger than the other.

"I made those crosses," Johannes volunteered. "I know they were Christians." And then added as an afterthought, "Do you think Madam Magda and Miss Elize will be cross with me?"

Maimon smiled. "No, they won't be." Then taking two £5 notes out of his pocket, he said, "One is from the Madam and Miss Elize, and the other is from me."

For the first time, Maimon looked Johannes in the eye. Up till that moment he had not felt strong enough to do so, and when he did, he saw the friendly face that had weathered over fifty summers and winters. Johannes looked at Maimon, not able to comprehend the madness of these white men. If I can't, Maimon thought to himself, what chance does Johannes have?

Maimon walked slowly down to the river. Either the British hadn't poisoned it, or the poison had been washed away, because upstream he saw some impala drinking. Cupping the clear cold water in his hands, Maimon slowly drank it. Then he picked up two smooth river stones, one slightly larger than the other, and walked back to the graves, carefully placing the larger one on Piet's grave and the smaller one on Willem's.

There was nothing to keep Maimon at what was now a desolate place, except for the memories to which he was desperately clasping lest they slip away. Then he remembered the brandy in his saddlebag. Calling Johannes to join him, the old and young man, each of whom having witnessed so much sadness, sat under the fig tree and, as the sun sunk lower in the sky, shared the golden liquid. Sometime after sunset, when the crickets were having a party and the bullfrogs a convention, Maimon and Johannes finished the bottle, and then both passed out.

The morning sun has no respect for hangovers, especially for those sufferers who are sleeping on east-facing slopes. Maimon stumbled to his feet, not quite sure, for a moment, where he was. Then remembering, he needed to get away from this place as quickly as he could. Maimon saddled his horse, and leaving Johannes in the arms of the African Morpheus, set out for Brandfort.

For reasons he did not know, or care about, Brandfort had been designated the British capital of the Orange Free State for the duration of the war. Accordingly, it was bristling with British military personnel. Ravenously hungry, Maimon made his way to the Masonic Hotel, where he marched straight into the dining room, sat down at the first unoccupied table he saw, and ordered a "full house" breakfast that he remembered from Deals Hotel in East London. Traditionally, this was two fried eggs, grilled sausage, liver, bacon, kidney, grilled tomato, and hot baked beans. To his pleasant surprise, the Masonic was maintaining the tradition. Then Maimon booked himself a room, making sure that it had a deep bath, in which he lay for a long time, alternately remembering, and trying to forget, yesterday's encounter with Johannes.

After a while, the ridged skin on his fingers reminded Maimon how long he had been in the bath, so he washed, dressed, and went downstairs to find out where the Brandfort concentration camp was located. With explicit directions from the concierge, who, it seemed, had been asked this question before, Maimon quickly found himself at the administrative office, or more accurately, the administrative tent, of this camp. To his surprise, they had no record of Mrs. M and Miss E. du Toit. Maimon was so adamant that they were there that he accepted the major's invitation to walk around the camp to see for himself if this was, in fact, the case.

Half an hour later Maimon was back, deeply depressed, not only because he had not found Magda and Elize, but because of the terrible conditions in which the woman and children were living. Their tents were overcrowded, the food insufficient, and the pots from which it was served those used by natives. Very politely, Maimon pointed this out to the major, who, in double-quick time, told Maimon this was none of his business and that he should bugger off. This was not an expression that Maimon had heard before, but he understood exactly what the major had in mind.

If Elize and Magda were not at the Brandfort concentration camp, then they were at another one, Maimon realized. And so, with a lighter heart, he headed for Bethulie, the next closest camp. They were not there, either, and so Maimon set about visiting the other four camps in the Orange Free State. When he exhausted all six, Maimon turned north to the Transvaal camps. One by one, Maimon worked his way through those six. After the third one, the realization dawned on Maimon that the reason he had not found Elize and Magda was because they were dead. With just the Irene and Johannesburg camps left to search, Maimon's head told him what had happened, but his heart refused to accept that they had died.

A day later, when he had thoroughly searched the camp outside Pretoria, and finally the one in Johannesburg as well, Maimon accepted what he had feared was inevitable when he crossed the Vaal River two weeks earlier. Before getting back on his horse, he took Elize's perfume out of his saddlebag and gave it to one of the young girls in the camp, and the crochet-work items to her mother, who blessed him.

Back in Johannesburg Maimon booked into The Hights Hotel, took a bath, and went round to his lawyer's office. When Edward saw Maimon in his waiting room, he did not have to ask what happened.

"Come in, young man," Edward said as cheerily as he could, watching Maimon get to his feet in slow motion, before following the lawyer into his office, where, ashen-faced, he slouched in the chair on the other side of Edward's desk.

"Did you find her?" Edward asked, knowing the answer. Maimon shook his head. "That's good," Edward said as positively as he could.

"Good?" Maimon asked, not sure that he had heard correctly. His voice, like everything else about him, was flat, joyless, colorless.

"That you did not find her grave, either, means that she might be alive."

Of all the possibilities Maimon had considered, this one had escaped his mental list, as remote as it was.

"There is that possibility," Maimon conceded, not sure whether he wanted to hang on to another string of hope that would surely break, as all the others had before it.

"I expect your options are Saratov, Kimberley, and Johannesburg. Or is there one I have missed?" Edward asked, trying to get Maimon thinking positively.

"That is about it," Maimon agreed wearily, becoming resigned to a directionless life. With neither Elize nor Julius and Alfred … his mind wandered back to the du Toit's farm, not as he knew it but as it was now.

"I expect, and hope, Russia is out," Edward said, "which leaves Johannesburg and Kimberley. Johannesburg is growing, and Kimberly isn't, so it seems this is the place to be."

Maimon nodded in agreement.

"Any idea what you would like to do?" Edward asked, trying to pry out something that together they might build on, trying, above all else, to lighten the mood (an almost impossible task, he quickly realized).

"Not really," Maimon said. Realizing that this was the end of the conversation, that Edward had helped as much as he could, Maimon got up, saying, "Please give my best wishes to Mrs. Nathan," before shaking Edward's hand and heading for the door.

"Let's keep in touch," Edward said to a departing Maimon, who raised his hand in acknowledgement.

CHAPTER 18

SKUNKELOWITZ & WIESELOVSKI

Maimon spent the next two weeks wandering the streets of Johannesburg, coming back in the late afternoon, looking more tired than he was as he had not eaten since leaving the hotel in the morning. The Indian manager, Dilip, responsible for everything in the hotel except the bar, was concerned that one of his guests was so miserable, and to cheer Maimon up offered him a girl, black or white, and when Maimon graciously refused, offered him a boy, black or white. Maimon shook his head, and then asked, "Can you get me an Indian girl?"

Dilip hesitated and Maimon smiled broadly, saying, "Got you!"

They both burst out laughing and Maimon realized that this was the first time he had laughed since arriving in Johannesburg. Would there ever be a second time? he wondered.

The following afternoon Maimon was wandering round Jeppe, a suburb east of Johannesburg, when he noticed something unusual. A horse-and- cart belonging to Skunkelowitz & Wieselovski and loaded with about twenty bags of what looked like agricultural produce had stopped on an empty lot; a few minutes later, a horse and unmarked transporter pulled up alongside. In less than a minute, the driver of the S&L cart had thrown three filled bags onto the unmarked cart, the driver of which threw three seemingly identical bags onto the S&W one. Understanding the possible implications of what he had witnessed, Maimon sprinted after the S&W cart and jumped onto it. The stone-faced coachman turned round immediately, feeling the extra 170 lbs that his tired horse was now required to pull.

"What are you doing?" he shouted at Maimon.

"Hitching a ride to see Mr. Skunkelowitz," Maimon shouted back.

"I have got three more deliveries before I get back to the warehouse. It will be about an hour."

"That is alright," Maimon replied, "I am in no hurry."

Maimon sat on the bags, making sure that the three swapped ones were not dropped off at any of their customers. Eventually the driver, his unexpected passenger, and some assorted bags arrived back at S&W's Carr Street premises. This was about 4:30.

"Mr. Skunkelowitz's office is up there," the driver told Maimon, pointing to a glass window on the second floor of quite an impressive building for Newtown.

"Please tell him I am here," Maimon asked, not expecting a co-operative response. He was not disappointed.

"That is not my job," the driver shouted back. "My job is to drive this cart, without passengers, so get off it."

"Only when Mr. Skunkelowitz is standing right there," Maimon said, pointing to a spot next to the cart, "will I get off. Till then here I stay."

This altercation had drawn the attention of a few S&W employees, one of whom told Maimon not to worry as he would fetch the boss. Maimon thanked him most politely, keeping his position on top of the dozen or so remaining bags.

A few minutes later an unkempt, overweight, angry-looking man of about 5'5" walked down the outside steps of the company's offices towards the cart, around which about fifteen S&W workers had now gathered.

"Who the fuck is this monkey on your cart?" the boss said aggressively to its driver.

"I don't know, Mr. S. He jumped on in Jeppe and would not get off. Said he had an appointment with you."

"I have got no appointment with no fucking monkey. Call security to get him thrown out. And by *thrown*, I mean thrown over that fence," he said, pointing to a six-foot concrete slab wall.

Realizing it was time to take the initiative, Maimon said, "Mr. Skunkelowitz, sir. This driver of yours has been stealing your beans."

"Really?" said Mr. S, now interested to see how this was going to play out.

"Yes, really, and before I prove it to you, it might be wise for your security to make sure he doesn't jump over that fence you had allocated to me." Pointing at one of the swapped bags, he asked innocently, "Do you know what is in that bag?"

"Brown assorted beans, not that it is any fucking business of yours," the boss replied, now getting tired of this whole stunt.

Maimon heaved one of the swapped bags off the cart and onto the concrete floor, and the noise it made certainly was not that of beans. Before anyone moved, Maimon called out, "Don't move. I have two others of the same quality."

At which point he threw the two other swapped bags onto the floor of the company's loading area, which, upon landing, made the same noise as the first bag.

Mr Skunkelowitz had a pen knife out in a second, and ripped open first one bag, which was filled with stones, and then the second, and finally the third, all of which revealed the same contents.

"Security, take Brutus and find out who else is involved in stealing my beans. When you have that information, slaan hom dood.[66] Monkey-man, come to my office; the rest of you get back to work," Skunkelowitz ordered.

"My name is Maimon Sokolovski," Maimon called out.

"Monkey-man Maimon, come down and do not waste my time."

"Fuckface Skunkelowitz," Maimon called out authoritatively,

The boss turned around in amazement, as no one had ever spoken to him like that.

"Either you speak to me respectfully," Maimon said, "or I bugger off and your whole store ends up looking like a quarry."

"Mr. Sokolovski, would you be so kind as to move your fucking ass off those bean bags and come up to my office?"

"With the greatest of pleasure, Mr. Skunkelowitz," Maimon said, jumping off the cart and joining the boss walking back to the office block.

Sol was a small man in all senses of the word. In addition, he was mean-spirited and a bully. In the office he bullied his much taller partner, Lev, and in the factory everyone he came across. "When you sign their paycheck , that's what you can do," he had told Lev when the subject of his unpleasant behavior had been raised. Sol had married Fruma, old man Zevcheski's only child, and she was a match for him when it came to meanness. Her only checks that bounced were those made out to a charity. But Sol did get half of Zalman Zevcheski's business, and that was something not to be sneezed at.

66   *"Kill him"*

151

The other half was owned by Lev, a tall, thin, stooped, quiet man, a trained bookkeeper and the son of Zalman Zevcheski's original partner. Sol was sure Lev squirrelled money out of the business. How else could his wife have so much jewelry and be so much better dressed than Sol's? Her figure was one reason, and his friendship with Barney Barnato was the other. Lev was gentle, kind, considerate, and a thief. Sadly, he and his wife could not have any children, and so it was Zelda, Sol's daughter and the apple of his jaundiced eye, who would inherit the S&W empire for whatever it was worth. Unfortunately, she also inherited some of her father's less attractive character traits.

Once in the building, little Skunkelowitz suggested that they get on first-name terms, so it was "Sol" and "Lev" and "Maimon." Over a cup of tea Maimon explained what had happened and suggested that he come to the company's premises the following day to see if he could identify any other weak spots in their operation. This agreed, they parted in a civilized manner.

The following day Maimon talked himself into S&W's premises, past the so-called security guard, and then spent the morning mooching around the plant, storehouse, receiving and despatch areas, and cash-management department. At noon he told the man on duty at the security gate to call Baas Sol, and when he showed some reluctance to do so, a £5 note changed his mind. Maimon then went and sat on the grass bank opposite the factory gates. A few minutes later Sol appeared and was told by Maimon to come and sit next to him. Having learned the previous evening that Maimon was not a man to be trifled with, Sol did as instructed. Surreptitiously, Maimon took £6,000 from his pocket and handed it to Sol.

"From your cash department. Would you like me to tell you now how you are being ripped off, or shall we go up to the office so that Lev can also hear?"

They went up to the company's executive suite, which reminded Maimon of the Ukrainian's diamond mining office, except for the rats.

"First of all," Maimon began, "when wagons come into your premises they are weighed. The driver and his mate stand on the scale, so you are paying for about 300 lbs of produce you do not receive. When the bags are unloaded, about ten percent are put on one side, and later in the morning taken away. I found them piled up next to the natives' toilets. Maybe they are supposed to be there, but if not, you might look into this. Then I thought you dealt only in agricultural produce, and so I was surprised to see two forty-four-gallon drums rolled out of the gate, I suspect filled full of paraffin. And lastly, your cash department needs tightening up, for, as Sol will tell you, I snitched £6,000 from under their noses."

For one of the very few times in their lives, the owners and managers of the esteemed produce-dealing company, Skunkelowitz & Wieselovski, were speechless.

"Now we need to discuss the next step," Maimon told them.

"And what might that be, Mr. Know-All?" Lev asked. Being responsible for the accounts and cash, he was feeling particularly uncomfortable with the £6,000 that was lying on the table in front of them.

"The next step is that you hire me as your General Manager," Maimon said, remembering being told that the head of De Beers was called the "General Manager."

"Mr. Sokolvensky …" Sol began.

"Sokolovski," Maimon corrected him.

"Whatever. Who are you? Do you have references? What experience do you have in running an empire like ours?" Sol asked.

"We have already discussed who I am. As for a reference, feel free to contact Mr. Edward Nathan. If you need an introduction to Mr. Nathan, I will be happy to provide one."

"We know Edward," Lev interjected. "What about the experience question?"

"Working with Julius Wernher and Alfred Beit in Kimberley I gained a tremendous amount of experience," Maimon said confidently.

"*With* or *for* these gentlemen?" Sol asked shrewdly. "And by the way, pisher,[67] how old are you?"

"You heard correctly, and I am twenty-five," Maimon lied, and then said, "We need to discuss my remuneration," a word he remembered learning from Ayna on the boat.

"That's pay," Lev explained to Sol.

"I know," Sol told him, irritated.

"One thousand pounds a month, with special conditions for running your empire," Maimon pointed out to the speechless partners.

"We don't even take home that much," Lev said to Sol's annoyance.

"What conditions?" Sol barked, doubtful that whatever this pisher had in mind would be acceptable to Lev, let alone to him.

---

67   *A young, inexperienced, presumptuous person*

"For three months I don't get paid a penny until I have saved you £5,000 and no matter how much over this amount I save the company, I don't take home more than £3,000."

Sol and Lev looked at one another trying to see the "catch" in this proposal, neither finding one.

"What else?" Sol asked, knowing there was always another angle. No one ever put all their cards on the table to start with.

"The profits on any new business I bring the company also counts towards this £5,000 hurdle," Maimon added.

"What else?" Sol said, just in case Maimon still had something else to concede.

"You should both kiss my ass, for this deal of the century I am giving you," Maimon said, grinning.

Both Sol and Lev smiled, knowing they were on to a good thing, and before Maimon changed his mind, Sol made sure that the three of them shook hands, thereby cementing their agreement.

Maimon said, "You are looking at your company's General Manager. Make sure to tell the staff that tomorrow morning."

"With pleasure" Sol said happily, as giving Maimon a title wouldn't cost him or Lev anything.

"A General Manager has total control, which means no interference from either of you on matters big or small," Maimon said.

"Pisher, where do you live? In case we need to come and find you," Sol asked.

"Schmuck,[68] in the Hights Hotel. Room 211," Maimon replied. "If there isn't anything else, I will see you in the morning."

On his way back to the hotel, Maimon stopped in at Mr. Nathan's office to bring him up to date with his career developments. After doing so he asked, "What do you think?"

"You should know that you are getting into bed with two of the most slippery men in Johannesburg. People say when you shake hands with Sol, you should count your fingers afterwards."

"They may be slippery, but they don't know much about running a business."

"Do you?" Edward asked mischievously, hardly believing the metamorphosis he was witnessing.

"There is a saying in English," Maimon told him, "'a blind man

---

68   *A stupid, foolish, or unlikable person*

can't see anything, but a man with one eye can, and that is why he is an emperor.'"

"That is close enough," Edward said, amused. "What do you want me to do now?"

"Tell them I worked *with* Alfred and Julius. Not *for* them." Maimon got up to shake Edward's hand, and that's when the lawyer realized that he had another Barney Barnato as a client.

By the time Sol and Lev arrived at the office at nine the following morning, Maimon had shaken hands with all forty-five members of the staff, knew their names and what they did. He spent the rest of the day walking around the plant, talking to the natives and to the white people; and by four in the afternoon he knew the S&W operation inside out. Twice during the day he wanted information from women employees, and on each occasion was told that "they were with Mr. Sol," which explained the chaise longue in one of the office back rooms. For an hour Maimon drilled Lev on the company's financial position, which, taking all things into account, was remarkably healthy. As the partners were about to leave for the day, Maimon caught their attention.

"As I unearthed yesterday, there are major security leaks in a number of areas. To rectify this position, I will be employing a small Zulu impi, who will be moving into the empty storeroom until we are able to build separate accommodation for them. I expect this should take a week or two. I know that room is needed to store kaffir corn, but that crop doesn't come in till April or May, so we will not be under any time pressure." Taking Sol aside, Maimon said quietly, "Tomorrow the chaise longue goes."

"But that is not company business," Sol protested.

"Which is why it should not be on these premises, even though I suspect the company paid for it. Would you like me to send it to your house, or should I give it to a deserving poor person?"

"A poor person would be fine," Sol muttered, keen to be finished with this subject, and having had enough of Maimon, and in fact the business, for the day.

Over the weeks and months ahead, S&W came to be known as an efficient company that paid their bills on time, and as a result were successful in tenders, which had not been the case in the past.

Maimon was a breath of fresh air sweeping through Newtown, the area where Johannesburg's abattoir was situated, and where the grain brokers and traders had their premises. Modern thinking was unknown to their competitors, and, as a result, S&W were the first company to build a flour mill in the Orange Free State. They hadn't actually built the mill yet, the plant and equipment was still on the high seas, having been shipped from England. But the way Maimon spoke, anyone would think that the factory was up and running and producing record output. This worked to Maimon's advantage in an unexpected way.

A delegation representing the Jewish community was assembled to present a petition to President Kruger in Pretoria, in an endeavor to persuade him to increase the land he had allocated to build a large synagogue in Johannesburg. As Maimon was the only executive among the delegation who spoke fluent Dutch – which he had learned on the du Toit farm – he was the obvious choice to present the community's case. Because of this, he found himself on a rickety wagon in the company of Johannesburg's senior Jewish businessmen and professionals, whom, apart from Edward Nathan, he had not met before.

Eventually they arrived at the President's house, and were shown into a waiting room, where, after about ten or fifteen minutes, the man himself arrived. Without his black top hat he was already a tall man, and the hat added about a foot to make him an even more imposing figure. After the member of the diamond industry thanked the president for making time to see the delegation, Maimon was given the task of trying to get the president to change his mind on land allocation to the Jewish community.

The president had offered the Jewish community a property half the size of the stands allocated to the various churches, because, in his eyes, the Jews only believed in half of the Bible. Maimon slowly got to his feet, addressed the president in respectful terms, and then, to everyone's surprise, told the president about the twelve concentration camps in the Transvaal and Orange Free State he had recently visited. He named every one of them and impressed upon the president that, as a human being, he was ashamed to see women and children kept in the conditions he had witnessed. At the end of forty days, he came back to Johannesburg, Maimon continued, and at the end of forty days Moses came down with two tablets containing ten commandments. These two tablets, on which the moral foundations of the civilized world were built, were surely enough reason for the Jewish community to be granted two lots on which to build their synagogue. Had applause been appropriate, it would have been resounding, but it was not, so Maimon sat down in silence.

The President took a long time to answer, and when he did, in his reply he did not just repeat his refusal, but quoted from the Old Testament justifying his decision. Then the member of the delegation representing the gold-mining industry thanked the President for his time and the twelve Jewish men slowly filed out of his Church Street house. While standing outside waiting for their carriages, one of the President's clerks buttonholed Maimon and asked whether it would be possible for him to see the President next Thursday at noon. It would be an honor, Maimon assured him.

CHAPTER 19

THE BANK'S MISTAKE

Maimon had continued staying at The Hights Hotel for several reasons, not least of which was the fact that it was closer to Newtown than Doornfontein, where most of the better-off Jews lived.

At eleven o'clock one Wednesday night, there was a knock on his hotel room door, and to his amazement, Zelda Skunkelowitz, Sol's daughter, walked in.

It was summer, and so he was surprised that she was wearing a coat. Beneath it were just two pieces of loose-fitting silk underwear: one partially covering her breasts, and the other legless shorts to more-or-less cover her lower privates. About medium height, with long flowing dark brown hair and a spotless complexion, she was attractive, and unlike many other Jewish girls of her age, not overweight.

He had seen Zelda around the office from time to time, but had not paid particular attention to her. Zelda kissed Maimon passionately, at the same time removing his shirt and trousers, and then his underwear as well. Had Elize been alive, Maimon would not have kissed Zelda back, let alone allowed her to remove his clothes, but what the hell, he thought, and submitted.

Two hours later, unsteady on her feet, Zelda reclaimed her underwear, the top part of which was on one of the lights, kissed Maimon, who was lying exhausted on the bed, said, "Goodnight, stallion," and slipped quietly out of the door. Maimon wasn't sure if that was a compliment, but frankly he couldn't care, as he had learned so much in the last two hours that if it was an insult, he didn't mind.

The next morning Sol sought Maimon out, finding him in the bean-sorting shed.

"I need to talk to you," Sol said in a conspiratorial manner, pulling Maimon out of the shed into the blazing sunlight. As they both blinked to accustom their eyes to the light, Sol blurted out, "You should marry Zelda." Even though he had not considered it, Sol's suggestion was not altogether a surprise.

"Isn't it usually the young couple who discuss and decide these things?" Maimon asked, playing for time.

"Zelda and I have decided," Sol replied without the slightest embarrassment. "I will give you £40,000, a furnished house, and the business. Lev, you know, has no children, so I will buy him out."

Maimon wondered if Sol's negotiation with Lev was as brazen-faced as this one was.

"I need some time to think about this," Maimon answered honestly.

"You'd better hurry up. Zelda has her eye on a lovely house in Siemert Road. And you know they don't come up very often."

Neither do men who are prepared to marry your daughter, Maimon thought, instead telling Sol, "I will come back to you in a few days."

How different it was with Piet du Toit, Maimon thought as he walked back into the shed, and then how different Elize was from Zelda.

Maimon went to see his only friend in Johannesburg, Edward Nathan.

"I love Elize dead or alive," Maimon said, "and I will till my last breath of air. What should I do?"

"Perhaps the question you should be asking yourself is, 'Do I want to live alone for the rest of my life?'" Edward pointed out.

"I don't want to live alone, no, I don't."

"Then the question is another one. Would you be more unhappy living alone, or living with Zelda and possibly your children?"

Maimon hesitated before answering. There was Ayna and his son, he knew, but he would rather live alone than with them. Maybe when his son was older they could get together, but that would only be after he was no longer under her influence, and knowing Ayna as he did this was about twenty years away.

"Possibly, just possibly, living alone."

"Then there you have it," the legal mind pointed out.

"I guess so," Maimon said, getting up to go, more in the tone of a man headed for the gallows than one facing what should be the happiest day of his life.

"Just one thing," Edward said, "be sure to have the £40,000 in your bank account before you set a foot in the synagogue."

"Thank you, Edward, wise words indeed," Maimon said, leaving the law office for the heat and dust of Commissioner Street.

Maimon left early for his appointment with the President. It was just after four in the morning when he mounted his horse and set off for Halfway House, where he would have breakfast, change horses, and then head on to Pretoria. He let the horse walk up to the top of the Witwatersrand, canter down the other side, and then on the flat grassy highveld, gallop on to the hotel.

The air was cool and Maimon remonstrated with himself why he did not ride more often. Mile after mile they rode, fifteen in all, until Maimon saw the ribbon of smoke from the hotel's kitchen. The "farmer's breakfast," not that he imagined a farmer ever had one as he was served that morning, did not let him down. Refreshed, he was soon on his way to the famous single-story house in Church Street. Maimon was a few minutes early and had a chance to cool down before the time it had been agreed that the President would see him.

Calm and composed, and hopefully ready to respond maturely to whatever the president had in mind, Maimon banged the heavy iron knocker on the unremarkable house's white-painted front door. It was quickly opened by one of the Dutch clerks the president employed. Maimon had been told that they were specially recruited in Holland, as there was a dearth of literate Transvaal resident Afrikaners to do the president's clerical work.

Shown into a room whose shutters were closed to keep out the summer heat, it took Maimon's eyes a minute or so to accustom themselves to the semi-darkness. When they did, he saw the president sitting at a big wooden desk, reading a document with the help of a small desk light and a large magnifying glass.

After a minute or so the giant of a man looked up, motioned Maimon to sit down, and bent his head ever closer to the paper being examined. The room was filled with heavy Victorian furniture Maimon noticed, mainly leather covered armchairs around a low table on which rested three well-polished brass ashtrays. A little while later the big man put down his reading aid, leaned back in his chair, and looking directly at Maimon, said, "Why did you go to all those camps?"

"I was looking for my fiancée, Mr. President."

"And you didn't find her?"

"No, sir, unfortunately not."

"We have lost many fine people," the President said before pausing.

"The British wanted to have a war and there was nothing we could do." This was followed by another lengthy pause. "Mr. Sokolovski, will you promise me something?"

"If I can, Mr. President."

"If you find your fiancée, will you bring her to see me?"

"Nothing will give me greater pleasure," Maimon replied with a sincerity that was felt by not only the President, but also by his two clerks in the room.

"Good. Now to business. We need a bakery here in Pretoria. By the time the bread comes from Johannesburg it is hard and stale. The problem is that we do not have sufficient money to purchase one. I hear that you are building a flour mill in the Orange Free State. Can you build one for us here?"

"I can, Mr. President, with no money required from your country. To do so I will have to charge cost plus 60% on the bread loaves for thirty years, but yes, I can most definitely do so." Maimon paused for a moment to let the good news soak in. "I will also need to be sure that no other bread factory is allowed in Pretoria during this period."

"Thirty years is a long time, Mr. Sokolovski," the president said, looking Maimon straight in the eye.

"If the time is shorter, then the price of bread needs to increase. It is your decision, Mr. President."

"We will leave it as it is. Cost plus 60% for thirty years. My people will draw up the contract, and you and I can sign it in an hour's time."

"That is fine, Mr. President, I will wait."

Maimon waited, and in just under an hour, two copies of the document were brought for him to sign. These he did, handing one back to the clerk, who then said, "The President would like to know the name of your fiancé, please?"

"Elize du Toit."

"I will tell the President, and I too hope you will find her."

"Thank you, sir," Maimon said shaking his hand.

Back in Johannesburg Maimon found Charles Fletcher waiting to see him. Chuck, as he insisted on being called, was an American from Georgia, USA, and had answered an advertisement that Maimon had placed in *The Albany Herald* looking for a supplier of peanut-butter-making machines.

"Welcome to Africa. Sit down," Maimon said, gesturing Chuck to a chair. "Did you have an interesting trip?"

"A wonderous interesting trip, sir," the American began. Dressed in blue denim trousers that were worn by Californian gold miners, a checked shirt, and brown leather boots, Maimon thought he looked like a typical American. "Coming through the Orange Free State I saw a thousand acres of sunflowers and thought, sir, that if you also wanted an oil-crushing machine, my company can supply that, too. The most effective peanut-butter plant makes ten tons a day, and the cheapest-per-ton sunflower-oil producer turns out 500 tons a day of oil. That is working twenty-four hours a day for both machines."

Unlike the American diamond diggers Maimon remembered from Kimberley, this man spoke with a pleasant drawl he hadn't heard before.

"What would be the cost of both machines on a turnkey basis?" Maimon asked.

"You mean, we install the machines and make sure they work to your satisfaction?"

"And we only pay you then for them," Maimon made clear.

"We do many contracts on this basis, sir, so that will be no problem. If you give me a couple of hours to work on the pricing, we can finalize the contracts today."

"Fine," said Maimon. "Just one thing. Call me Maimon, like everybody else does."

Maimon wandered into Sol's office and sat down in the chair opposite him.

"Well, Maimon?" Sol asked anxiously. "Do we have a deal?"

"We do, with two adjustments. I get the £40,000 before the wedding, and all the other stuff, the house, the furniture, and so on goes to Zelda."

"Fine," said Sol, who had expected this to be a long, drawn-out negotiation. Maimon pulled an official-looking paper out of his pocket and put it in front of Sol.

"What is this?" Sol asked with feigned indignation.

"Our contract for the £40,000, the house, and so on. You just have to sign on page two."

"But we are gentlemen, we don't need contracts between us," Sol protested.

"We are not gentlemen, and we do need a contract between us, and unless you sign it here and now, no wedding," Maimon replied calmly, getting up to fetch one of the clerks to witness their signatures.

A few minutes later Maimon and Sol each had signed, witnessed contracts in their pockets.

The wedding was scheduled to take place three months hence, not earlier because the hall Zelda wanted for the reception was under construction and would only be finished at that time. During this period, the house in Siemert Road was bought and furnished, the caterer's contract finalized, the flowers ordered, six plump bridesmaids were appointed, and their dresses made, as was Zelda's own.

There was a major altercation between Zelda's mother and the dressmaker over the mother-of-the-bride's dress, which threatened to cancel the wedding. Maimon knew this would not happen, and so refused to get caught up in the hysteria surrounding this issue. But he did keep an eye on his bank account, which showed no sign of the contractual £40,000, the absence of which he mentioned to Sol both verbally and in writing.

At six o'clock on the Friday evening two days before the nuptials, Maimon told Zelda that the wedding was off, as he had just come from the bank and the contractual money had not been received. Understandably, Zelda became hysterical, which resulted in Sol promising to bring proof of the transfer the following morning. This he did, in the form of Mai mon's bank account statement showing a £40,000 credit as well as a letter from the manager confirming this transfer.

Not convinced that the bank statement and letter were genuine, and doubting that the transfer was, Maimon told Sol that this was not acceptable. If he wanted the wedding to go ahead the following day, he needed the bank manager personally to confirm that the requisite funds had been transferred. This resulted in more hysterics from Zelda, and more promises from Sol, and the presence of the bank manager and Sol at The Hights Hotel at eleven o'clock on the morning of the wedding. Hamish McDonald, the manager of Barclays Bank (Dominion, Colonial, and Overseas), not only confirmed that the documents were genuine, but, with some reluctance, swore it over a Christian Bible that Maimon had borrowed from St. Mary's Cathedral earlier that morning. Ultimately, Maimon relented and the wedding went ahead as planned.

The ceremony was scheduled to take place in the Park Synagogue at four pm. In fact, it started at 5:35, which didn't thrill Maimon, but didn't upset him, either, the £40,000 going a long way to keeping him calm. After the ceremony, 400 guests made their way in carts that got horribly jammed up to the Diamond Cutters Hall, where glasses of champagne, whiskey, brandy, gin, and vodka were offered to the arriving, perspiring guests. It took well over an hour for all of the invitees to travel the half a mile from the spiritual home of Johannesburg's Jewish community to its secular one, and during these 75 minutes the guests who had successfully made "the crossing" celebrated this achievement by making a considerable dent in Mr. Skunkelowitz's liquor stocks.

Two hours late, the bride and groom entered, followed by six bridesmaids and eight pole holders. Some food was served and then the speeches began. Not only were these long, but many – Maimon gave up counting at number nine, his being the last on the card. A little unsteadily he eventually got to his feet, waiting for the catcalls to stop, before starting.

"Distinguished Ladies and Gentlemen, religious leaders, and others." At this point there was an outbreak of catcalls. "It seems there are more 'others' than expected," Maimon added off-script.

"If it wasn't for Zelda's family and mine, we wouldn't be here tonight, so that is what I will speak about. Zelda's father and mine are quite different. My father is extremely hard-working and honest, Zelda's is extremely hard-working. My mother is slim and slight. If Zelda's mother was denied food for a month, not only would she look better, but one could feed a Zulu impi for six weeks on her uneaten food." Slight, embarrassed laughter. "As for my beautiful bride, what can I say? She is such a friendly person, not only with our community, but with the goyim[69] as well. She knows the whole Johannesburg polo team, and recently made the acquaintance of the visiting Argentinian horse-riders as well."

Zelda blushed, clasped her head in her hands, and the guests who had been deadly quiet now started sniggering.

"And now, to give you something to think about, I will end my speech with a quotation from Rabbi Menachem Mendel of Kotzk. Please listen carefully. 'If I am I because you are you, and you are you because I am I, then I am not I and you are not you. But if I am I because I am I, and you are you because you are you, then I am I and you are you.' Thank you and goodnight."

As Maimon reclaimed his seat next to Zelda, few people clapped, but most of the guests turned to their neighbors and asked if they thought Maimon was drunk, or possibly mildly insane. The majority thought he had been in the sun too much, something people born in Europe suffered from.

---

69   *A non-Jewish person*

"What was that all about?" Zelda demanded.

"Bartolome Cambiaso or Rabbi Mendel?"

"You are impossible," Zelda almost spat out, getting up from the table and walking briskly away.

Although Maimon waited another hour or so, disappearing Zelda was the last Skunkelowitz he saw that night. When there were very few guests remaining, Maimon excused himself and took a carriage to The Hights Hotel, where he had retained his room. Mentally and physically exhausted, and having eaten nothing and drunk much, Maimon collapsed on his bed. As the room attendant hadn't been told not to do so, she knocked on Maimon's door at six am the following morning as usual, and as his body was used to getting up at that time, Maimon roused himself and had a cold shower.

But instead of going to the office, he made his way to Barclays Bank to check his account. Not entirely to his surprise, there was no sign of the £40,000; but entirely to his surprise, he was told that the manager, Hamish McDonald, had left twenty-four hours earlier on the train to Durban, where he was picking up the mail ship today for Southampton.

Maimon contained himself in the bank's offices, but once outside he exploded like an erupting volcano. The one person he wanted to discuss this with was Edward, and by the time he reached the lawyer's office the volcano's eruptions had reduced to about a million tons of magma every second.

Edward listened to the whole story, and then said, "From your wedding speech, I suspected there was trouble afoot, but I didn't think it was this. Listen to me carefully: run as fast as you can to Jeppe Station, and then at the same speed back to your hotel. Take a bath, change your clothes, and come back to see me."

"But Edward …" Maimon protested.

"No buts. Do as I say, and I will be waiting for you in about an hour and a half. Now off you go."

Maimon did as he was told, and it was a much calmer young man who presented himself back at the lawyer's reception just over an hour later.

"You feeling better?" Edward asked, and before waiting for a reply said, "Sit down," gesturing Maimon to one of the big leather armchairs in his office.

"There is a book called *The Art of War* written by a Chinese general, Sun Tzu, about 1,500 years ago. There is much wisdom in this book, and one of its pearls is his advice about fighting battles. He points out that battle should be fought when you want to, how you want to, and where you want to. You may not appreciate it at the moment, but you have a number of poison-tipped arrows in your quiver, and what you need to do is to decide when to shoot them, and at whom. Should you wish, I will be happy to fight the battle alongside you."

"That is very kind of you, Edward," Maimon said, really appreciating his offer.

"Fine. There are two things you need to do. The first is to drop by at Alfred Beit's office on the way back to yours, and tell Alfred the whole story from the day you jumped on the delivery cart, to what happened at the bank. And the second is to go back to S&W's offices as if nothing untoward happened to you over the weekend. Then come and see me on Friday morning."

"Thank you so much," Maimon mumbled, wondering what Edward was going to do in five working days.

It wasn't easy for Maimon to suppress his feelings back at the company, but he made a supreme and successful effort to do so. Also having a strong suspicion that Zelda was in on the £40,000 theft, his feelings for her were not those of a recently married husband, but he never mentioned the subject to Sol, Lev, or anyone in the Skunkelowitz family.

A week or so after the wedding, Zelda started suffering from nausea and frequently vomited up whatever meal she had just eaten. At first Maimon was worried about this, but as Zelda wasn't, he didn't pay too much attention to this illness which stopped after a couple of months. This nausea did limit their social life somewhat, which suited Maimon as he was able to stay at the company's office till eight o'clock most evenings, which he would not have been able to do were they invited to, or hosting, a dinner party.

As keen as Maimon was to shoot the first of his arrows, both Alfred and Edward cautioned him against doing so, which restraint Maimon carried out with increasing ease as Zelda had recently told him she was pregnant. She added that, according to the doctor, it was a big baby that might well be born prematurely.

Maimon had taken out of the Johannesburg Public Library a book entitled *The A- to-Z of Bread Making: From the Wheat Mill to the Customer* by Joseph Rank that he carried around with him, telling whomever he was with that he had left his glasses at home, and asking him or her to read a page or two to him.

During the day Maimon made a serious effort to keep in touch with Johannesburg's commercial life. As he was a sociable fellow, hardly a day went by when he wasn't invited to lunch at one of the banks, or by a stockbroker, or by one of the transport companies seeking S&L's business.

Maimon found the bank lunches particularly interesting, as he invariably met one or two people whose commercial activities were outside those of an agricultural produce trader. These were usually jolly affairs, but one of them unfortunately was not. James Charrington, a redheaded fellow who made ploughs and similar farm equipment, had come straight from the cemetery, having buried his six-year-old daughter, Olivia, who had died as a result of a horse-riding accident.

There were some problems with the peanut butter factory being built in the Orange Free State that required Maimon's presence, but he kept postponing his visit to the site as he didn't want to be away when the baby was born. The doctor had warned Zelda that it might come early, which Maimon reminded himself of every day, when there was another message from his office near the construction site requesting his presence. Zelda and Maimon had moved into a hotel close to the hospital, which was most fortuitous as, after breakfast one morning, Zelda's waters broke, and shortly thereafter her contractions began.

Together they walked the short distance to the hospital, where Maimon kissed Zelda and wished her good luck before the nurses took her away. Maimon had been told that it could be twelve hours before the baby was born, and so he settled down in the waiting room for what he expected would be the whole day. Unable to read but fixed to the spot, Maimon used opportunities like these to think about growing up in Saratov, the happy times he had spent with his parents, few as they were, and the fun he and Kaylah had had playing in the forest.

Lost in thought as he was, Maimon didn't at first hear the nurse say, "Mr. Sokolovski, Mr. Sokolovski, it is a girl. All fingers and toes are where they should be, so nothing to worry about."

"Thank you," Maimon said, "when can I see her?"

"In just a few minutes, and your wife as well. We will call you."

Maimon got to his feet, ready for the call as if it was a track race, subconsciously expecting the ready, steady, and then the noise of a pistol being fired. It wasn't long before the nurse returned and gestured Maimon to follow her, which he did down long corridors, and finally into a private room, where Zelda was holding a white bundle of swaddling clothes out of which a head stuck. Amazingly, the head was covered in bright ginger hair.

"Isn't she beautiful?" Zelda purred.

Maimon hadn't seen many newborn babies, and to his mind none of them were beautiful, but he knew this wasn't the time to tell Zelda his view on the subject.

"Let's call her Olivia," Zelda suggested, kissing the baby's head.

"But we agreed on Joanna," Maimon reminded her.

"I want my baby to be called Olivia. Look at her. She is an Olivia," Zelda said in an uncompromising manner that Maimon knew from the wed ding arrangements was one from which she could rarely be moved. Then the penny dropped. It wasn't his baby at all, it was James Charrington's. Maimon's blood started to boil, and he knew that whatever he said, he would probably live to regret, so he didn't say anything at all. He just walked out of Zelda's room, down the corridor and out into the bright light of the hospital's garden.

What he suspected was true, and sadly was without any doubt: Sol had given him a blow in the solar plexus, and Zelda a knockout uppercut to his jaw. What he needed now was to get away from Johannesburg, and specifically the Skunkelowitz family. In fact, Maimon wasn't upset, and that bothered him. Perhaps because subconsciously he knew the Skunkelowitzs were all scum. What was starting to bother him was how, in good conscience, he could ever work with Sol again. This was the thought turning over in his mind when he arrived at Edward's office.

Calmly, he told his friend what had happened, that he proposed going to the building site at Heilbron to sort out their problems, and, depending on what they were, he would be back in about a fortnight. This being the case, Edward asked Maimon to give him a power of attorney, as he might not be back for "P. Day." Maimon signed the document, but frustratingly all he could get out of Edward was that "P. Day" would be about the tenth of next month.

CHAPTER 20

SHIMON KATZ'S UNINTENDED GOOD DEED

Putting some clothes in his saddlebag, Maimon set off on the 100-mile ride that he was going to do in two days, even though he knew he could complete the journey in one. It was the same story once again. Most of the farmhouses were burnt to the ground, as were their crops, with one or two properties left untouched. This time the farmer's wife didn't threaten to shoot him, but she did demand payment for his dinner, bed, and breakfast in advance. Her husband had been captured and sent to a Prisoner of War camp in Ceylon. The British didn't torch her house as her aged parents were living in it with her at the time, and so the officer took pity on her family. Two months ago, her parents had both died, and she buried them in the little family cemetery on the farm.

As he cantered through the desolate northern Orange Free State the following day, Maimon reflected on how the ruined landscape was a metaphor for his life. He was in a loveless marriage to a woman to whom the word "fidelity" was unknown. He had a son by a woman who blatantly misled him over an important aspect of his life. Financially, he did have a few thousand pounds in the bank, but that was little recompense for the nights and weekends he had put in over the past eighteen months.

Then there was the Vagalparot's "night-time" matter, which one day might rear its dangerous head. Against this, he had a cousin in New York who surely could give him a lead or two, if nowhere else than in the diamond industry. That was a field he knew very well, and if there was anywhere in the world that people bought diamonds, it was the USA. The more he thought about it, the more it made sense. When he got back to Johannesburg, he would resign his position at S&L, say goodbye to Edward and his mining friends, and catch a train to Durban. Maimon reached this decision around two in the afternoon, just as he was arriving in Heilbron.

The problem at the plant was serious but not complex. Once solved, at Maimon's suggestion, the senior managers broke open a case of beer for sundowners a little ahead of the solar disappearance. The conversation soon veered from the elasticity of steel to chit-chat about the company.

"Did you know little Shimon Katz died?" the plant manager asked Maimon.

"Yes, I heard so," Maimon replied. "Was his pension adequate for his family?"

"He didn't have any family as far as we could find out," the chief engineer chipped in. "When we buried him, the Jewish women from the camp all came to the funeral. Even though they couldn't say some important prayer, they stayed for the whole service. Shimon was very friendly to them and used to go every Friday night to bless the kinderer, as he called the children. Now there is no one to do this."

In his present frame of mind, Maimon had no intention of getting mixed up with another group of Jewish mothers and children, just as he was extricating himself from those in the Skunkelowitz family. There was a silence that he ignored, and the conversation turned to hunting. All except Maimon, it transpired, were keen marksmen. Maimon listened for a few minutes and having no interest in killing animals for sport, said goodbye to the five managers and walked slowly to his horse. What Maimon didn't notice was that the oldest man on site had slowly followed him, and arrived just as Maimon was about to mount his horse. When Maimon did see him, he noticed that the man was walking slowly, almost uncomfortably, as though he was limping. He identified himself to Maimon as Koos.

"I know it is none of my business, Mr. Maimon, but those ladies would really appreciate it if you blessed their children, like Shimon used to. Their husbands fought with us and have been sent to Ceylon with our men. It is only my messed-up leg that stopped me going there, too," the man said, gesturing half-heartedly at his left, and shorter, leg. His speech finished, the manager looked up at Maimon, not in a pleading manner, but as an older man does to a much younger one.

You are bloody right. It is none of your fucking business, Maimon thought, but he didn't say that. Instead he asked in a gentle voice, "Is the camp far from here?"

"Not at all, Mr. Maimon. Turn right out of our gate and then it is about a mile further, on your left," he said gratefully.

"Just one more thing, Mr. Maimon. We found this half-bottle of Jewish wine in Shimon's desk. It didn't seem right to give it to the ladies at the funeral, but I am sure they would appreciate it now."

"Give it to me," Maimon said, without even a hint of rancor in his voice. Koos handed it up to Maimon, who slipped it into his saddlebag.

"Thank you, Mr. Maimon, Thank you so very much. Have a safe journey home," Koos said as Maimon's horse trotted out of the gate.

It was Friday night, after all, and his parents would be walking to synagogue, and if they knew he was doing this mitzvah,[70] it would make them happy, he reasoned as his horse trotted down a quite well-made road. It wasn't even a mile to the gate of the camp, which Maimon reached with a warm heart, about to do a good deed that some people would appreciate.

Maimon handed the reins to a soldier from Lancashire or Essex or someplace thousands of miles from this desolate part of Africa, thanking him in advance for looking after it. The soldier directed Maimon to the camp headquarters, which was about 100 yards from the road, where he found what he thought was an officer but turned out to be only a sergeant. Satisfied that Maimon was not about to release all the women and children under his jurisdiction, the sergeant directed a now weary man carrying half a bottle of sweet red wine to a group of about ten women sitting in a circle. As he got closer, about thirty yards away, a middle-aged woman on the far side of the circle got to her feet. Maimon knew her, but for a moment he didn't remember where from, and then a second later he did.

IT WAS MAGDA!

Maimon stopped, not knowing what to do or say. Was he dreaming? Surely not. This woman from that time of his life when he was blissfully happy, what was she doing here? Then she said three words that proved to Maimon that it was really Magda. They were, "Elize. Kyk agter."[71]

Elize got to her feet and turned round all in one motion. For a moment, she stared at this man whom she had dreamt about, prayed for, thought of every single day since they parted; and here he was, thirty

---

70   *A good deed*

71   *"Look behind you"*

173

yards away. Then he smiled, the smile whose memory Elize had treasured for almost two years. As if chased by a lion, Elize flew to Maimon.

Afraid it was a dream he was in, Maimon blinked and stamped his foot to wake up. Whether it was or not, Elize was running towards him, so he opened his arms, into which she jumped. She felt the same and she smelt the same, and so he gripped her tightly. Then he knew. It wasn't a dream. Hardly believing it, he gripped her tighter still.

There they stood, glued together, both crying. After a minute, or maybe it was two, Maimon loosened his grip to have a look at this girl who God, or someone, had brought back into his life. Then he saw Magda out of the corner of his eye, patiently standing a few yards away, tears streaming down her cheeks. Maimon opened his arms to include Magda, and the three of them stood in a close embrace, interrupted only by a little boy's voice from somewhere down near their feet, "Mama, wat doen jy?" [72]

Maimon let go of Elize and Magda, and the three of them looked down to see a beautiful little boy staring up. With brown almond eyes, porcelain skin like Elize's, and auburn hair down to his shoulders, he looked to Maimon like a little Kaylah. Elize bent down and picked him up and said, "Maimon, dis jou pa." [73]

Maimon looked at Elize quizzically. "Seker?" [74]

"Yes, really. I thought God gave me little Maimon to remember you by. And now he has given me big Maimon, too. What have I ever done to deserve this?"

Remembering the others, Magda said, "Will you come and bless the children like Mr. Katz used to?"

"Not only that," Maimon replied. "We are going to have the full Shabbes service."

The four little boys covered their heads and Maimon recited the service from memory. The wine was sipped, and bits of bread eaten, and then the highlight of the evening, each child was blessed, and from the pockets of one of the women, four sweets emerged as if by magic.

"Do you know any Hebrew songs?" Maimon asked the children, and was happily informed yes, they all knew "Adon Olam." Happily and lustily, they sung it, and then did so again.

---

72   *"What are you doing?"*

73   *"This is your father"*

74   *"Are you sure?"*

After the song, Magda took little Maimon by the hand, telling him it was time to kiss mommy and daddy goodnight, which he dutifully did, still somewhat confused by the arrival of his daddy seemingly from nowhere.

Each of the ladies lined up to kiss Maimon goodnight, and then at last, Elize and Maimon were alone.

They looked at each other and hugged, and then kissed first tenderly and then passionately. Then they hugged again, and holding hands went to sit on a low wall. For the next four hours they spoke: mainly Maimon, who told Elize everything, and that really was everything, that had happened between the day he left her and the day he found her.

Some things they laughed at, like Maimon's family reference in his wedding speech. And other things Elize cried at, like the £40,000 Maimon had been cheated out of; not because of the money, but the fact that he had been cheated. She bristled with anger at how Zelda had lied to him, and they laughed together at the quote at the end of Maimon's speech, which Elize made him repeat twice.

At odd moments they stood up and hugged; and at others they stayed on the wall and kissed. Elize thanked Maimon three times for giving the little Irish girl her address, and cried and hugged Maimon when he asked why she never wrote to him. She wrote three letters to him, Elize told him, but was afraid to send them because she thought they were too passionate and personal, and besides she knew that it would be someone else reading them to him. She had them in the tent and would give them to him in the morning, if he promised not to show them to anyone, ever. Maimon promised.

Maimon asked why they weren't at the camp the first time he came, and they worked out that it was the day that Elize and Magda took Maimon to the doctor. Maimon explained that it was not customary to name a Jewish child after a living person, and Elize apologized and said she didn't know that. They discussed names and it came down to Adam or David or Solomon. Solomon, Elize ruled out, because that was the name of "that horrible man at the factory," and as for the other two, they decided to ask Magda what she thought.

There was a silence when Maimon was finished. Elize knew it was her turn. Maimon, seeing her anxiety, suggested that they leave it for another day, but Elize, gripping Maimon's hand, insisted on telling him her story.

Her father and Willem had ridden off on the first commando, and returned after three weeks; and then done the same again for a six-week campaign against the British. Before they were called up for the next raid, the British army came. They questioned the family, and the men said they hadn't been on commando and were prepared to swear this on the Bible. The officer made some derogatory remark about the validity of an oath sworn by a Boer on the Bible. Hearing this, Willem told the officer that one Boer was worth ten red coats. Not surprisingly, the officer took out his revolver and aimed it at Willem's head. After a few seconds, he put it back in his holster, at which point Willem said something very stupid. Elize stopped talking now, unable to continue.

Maimon knew that wasn't the end of the story, so he gently kissed the back of her hand. Elize continued slowly, her voice and body shaking softly. Willem said to the officer, "You see. You haven't got the courage to shoot me." The officer took out his revolver and shot Willem in the head. One of the soldiers pointed out to the officer that he had better kill Piet as well, as he was a witness to what happened. So the officer also shot him in the head. Then they set fire to the house and the fields, poisoned the well, and when they were sure that the house would burn properly, marched off. Johannes dug two graves and buried her father and her brother.

A week later another army unit came and took her, little Maimon, and his grandmother off to this camp. It was the first time Elize had told anyone what happened, and Maimon saw that she was emotionally exhausted. Lovingly, he picked her up and carried her to the mouth of the tent, where he put her down, kissed her goodnight, and gently nudged her into the tent. Then Maimon took a deep breath, and went in search of his horse and somewhere to sleep. He found both.

Neither Elize nor Maimon slept well, or long; and five o'clock found them both dressed and back on their little wall. Last night was about the past, this morning was to be about the future. Elize wanted to thank Koos personally, but Maimon pointed out it was Saturday, and so he wouldn't be at work. Maimon wanted to sell his horse and buy a four-wheel cart with two horses. Elize said that was OK as long as he had enough money to do so. Elize wanted to get the mailing details of the camp, so that she could send food parcels to the other women and their children, as well as clothes and shoes, and Maimon said that was fine with him. Maimon wanted to get a divorce from Zelda and marry Elize, who said that was fine with her, adding that he might have told her this in a more romantic way, and in fact wanted to know why he hadn't.

"Because I am different. You know that," he said, smiling.

"Yes, I do," Elize said smiling "That is one of the reasons I love you." She squeezed him tight again.

"Were you two lovebirds here all night?" Magda asked, sticking her head out of the tent.

"Unfortunately not," Elize said, holding Maimon's hand tightly, subconsciously afraid that he might escape if she didn't.

"Good Morning, Magda," the ever-polite Maimon said. "I am sorry I can't stay as I have got some jobs to do.

"Off you go then, young man," Magda said. "We need to get washed and dressed."

A quick kiss from Elize, and Maimon was off loping to his horse. Two hours later he returned, having swapped his one black horse and some money for two similar animals together with the necessary straps, a four-wheeled covered wagon, and a basket full of sandwiches and fruit that Elize insisted on giving to the remaining ladies.

Before the two adults and one child could be released from the camp, forms had to be signed. The problem was, no such forms existed. Maimon pointed out that he wasn't a Boer, and wasn't going to fight for them, and as the officer could see, he didn't have a gun, and, anyway, he was Russian and not English. Finally, the British army wouldn't have to feed these three people anymore, which would save them some money. The officer didn't dispute any of that, but he could not let Magda, Elize, and little Maimon go if the forms weren't signed, and as the necessary forms didn't exist, they couldn't leave.

While the debate was going on, Elize took a large piece of white paper and wrote across the top in big black capital letters, "Official Release Form," and then under it, "Permission for the British Army to release Magda du Toit, Elize du Toit, and Adam Sokolovski." Maimonides gave it to the officer, who was getting bored with this whole affair, so he happily signed it. Following this, Elize and Magda each shook the officer's hand in a very formal way. Seeing this, Adam did the same thing, which lightened the atmosphere.

Formalities completed, the four of them got on the wagon, and while the women waved goodbye to their friends, Maimon carefully steered the horses out of the camp. They hadn't gone 50 yards when Elize picked up a basket of fruit and sandwiches and, showing it to Maimon, said, "What is this?"

"A basked of fruit and sandwiches."

"Maimon, don't start that with me now."

"I knew you would give our basket to your friends, so I bought two."

Elize ruffled Maimon's hair as he got the horses into a controlled canter, too occupied to return the ruffle.

The trip back to Johannesburg was uneventful. They found unburnt houses on each of the two nights they stopped, and at each Elize couldn't wait to tell the mother and grandmother at the first house of her good fortune. This brought on further tears, which Maimon didn't mind as there was so little good news for these poor, isolated women who, in addition to everything else, were now subject to occasional attacks by natives desperate for food.

On the first night, after Adam had been put to bed and Magda was engrossed exchanging tales of woe with the widow who owned the farm, Maimon led Elize out to the stoep that had the inevitable suspended couch on it. As soon as they sat down, Elize grabbed Maimon's arm and snuggled up to him.

"We need to decide where we are going to live," Maimon said.

"I don't mind. Anywhere with you is fine for me," Elize murmured.

"I was thinking of America," Maimon told her truthfully.

"What!" Elize almost shouted, expecting to be given the choice of Johannesburg or Kimberley, or, at the very worst, Cape Town.

"There is nothing for me here, so I thought we might go and join my cousin in New York. There are surely more opportunities for me there."

"And what about Adam and my mother?"

"They would come, too."

Since Elize had been rescued, although she had not thought about it, subconsciously she expected to live in the Transvaal, the Orange Free State, or even Natal. This was her country, after all, and that is where she belonged. Starting out as a young wife in a country she knew would have challenges enough, but in another country so far away, Elize shuddered to think about it.

"What's the problem?" Maimon asked, aware from her body language that Elize was not happy about the prospect of living in America.

"I am scared," Elize confessed, gripping Maimon even tighter.

"Let's leave this for another time," Maimon said, not wanting an unhappy fiancé, and seeing that she was flustered enough already, too anxious to think anything serious through.

"This decision we need to take won't change in a day or a week or a month," Elize said.

Noticing how the concentration camp experience had matured Elize, Maimon said, "The decision won't, but things that affect the decision might, either way."

"What do you mean by that?" Elize asked.

"Things could happen that encourage me to stay here," Maimon explained.

"And things could happen that encourage us to go," Elize replied, thinking of Maimon's night at the Vagalparots.

"It depends on something Edward is working on," Maimon replied, using his lawyer as an escape hatch.

"Will you ask him as soon as we get back?"

"The very same day," Maimon promised.

Elize wasn't happy, but there wasn't anything she could do, so she put her head on Maimon's shoulder and, still holding his arm, fell into a deep sleep. Not wanting to disturb her, Maimon made himself as comfortable as he could and was soon asleep, too.

As he drove their coach-and-two into Johannesburg, Maimon reflected on the things in his life that he had never expected to do. Driving a coach into Johannesburg was one of them, but then, on further consideration, Maimon realized that for a boy from Saratov, he had done more unexpected things in his life than expected ones.

CHAPTER 21

PANIC AND PAIN DAY

Maimon drove straight to Edward's building, helped Elize, Magda, and little Adam down onto the ground, and marched proudly, he later admitted to himself, into the lawyer's office. His exchange with the clerk was a short one. He told him to tell Mr. Nathan that Maimon was waiting to see him.

A few seconds later Edward emerged from his office. This was one of the occasions where words were unnecessary. Maimon smiled at Edward, who looked at the two women and little boy, and rushed to give Maimon a hug, partly because he was so happy for his friend, and partly so no one could see the tears welling up in his eyes. With his head on Maimon's shoulder, he wiped them away. Ushering the four of them into his office, and asking the clerk with whom he was discussing a matter to come back later, Edward sat them all down, and said, "You have to tell me what happened."

And so Elize did. When she had finished, Edward said, "You have arrived on an auspicious day. You remember before we went away, I told you about P. Day?"

"Yes," Maimon said, not sure that he remembered the reference, as so much was going on in his mind that day.

"'P' stands for panic and pain," Edward continued, "and quite a few people will be panicking today."

"For example?" Maimon asked, petrified that he was in this "P" group; but for the life of him, he couldn't think that there was anything left for him to panic about.

"The director of Chartered Bank responsible for Southern Africa," Edward said with unusual excitement, as if savoring each word, "who was told over breakfast this morning by Alfred that unless the bank paid you £40,000 today, plus £80,000 damages, word of their injurious and uncommercial behavior would be all over Johannesburg today, Cape Town tomorrow, and London later in the week."

"That is a good start," Maimon said. "I understand the pain. Anyone I know panicking?"

"Messrs Skunkelowitz and Wieselovski; and Zelda, whose surname is in question."

"What is Zelda's reason?" Maimon asked, not embarrassed that Elize was present.

"She gets a divorce document on account of her infidelity. We have had a man following her to all parts of town, including those where the hewers of wood and drawers of water reside," Edward replied, having obtained the required information on Zelda's extramarital activities for his legal document.

"And those cultured gentlemen who rejoice in the names of Skunkelowitz and Wieselovski, what do they have to look forward to today?" Maimon asked, a little embarrassed that he was enjoying this so much.

"They will be discussing high finance with the banking community: Sol with the Chartered Bank about the matter of £40,000, which I understand he hasn't got, and Lev with the Nederlandsche Bank, with regard to equipment the company has paid for but not yet received, I understand from Georgia in the United States. In both cases the banks require payment in thirty days."

"You know what that means?" Maimon asked.

"I think the technical term is 'overs kadovers.'"

"Nothing else?" Maimon asked, not imagining there could be.

"That's enough for one day," Edward pointed out.

"In that case, I have a favor to ask, please," Maimon said. "Tomorrow, or as soon as possible, could Pauline please take Elize and Magda to a dress shop, and also to buy them some shoes. I will settle up with her later."

"Of course," Edward said. "I will get a message to her right away."

"I will take the ladies and this little man to the hotel, and then call on my employers. On the way back, I will come here in case you are still in the office," Maimon said, hustling the three of them out to the carriage, whose horses were waiting patiently.

Ravi and Dilip gave Maimon and his party a welcome that was fit for a winning sports team, which was made even more enthusiastic when they heard Elize was Maimon's wife. They had to stay in the President's Suite, no question about that, and the older lady would have a room next door, and the little fellow could sleep in either room, where there were spare beds. Magda looked at Elize, who smiled and said, "He is different."

Walking to their room, Maimon pulled Elize aside and said to her quietly, "Three or four dresses each, please. I don't want to see you and Magda in the same clothes every day. Also, Adam could do with some that fit."

The women were overwhelmed by the suite, which Dilip said was built for royalty, but none had come to Johannesburg yet. Little Adam ran around playing hide-and-seek with his mother, whom Maimon found hiding behind the bathroom door, where he kissed her and she wished him good luck.

Riding to the S&W premises in Newtown, Maimon thought about how his fortunes had changed in the last few weeks, and wondered what he had done to deserve this. He was met at the gate by Moses, who gave him a big smile and equal welcome, which Maimon knew he wasn't going to get in the directors' offices. For the first time, Maimon didn't knock and just walked into the office, where Sol and Lev were both looking ghostly white.

"What right have you got to come here?" Sol snarled.

"To the best of my knowledge, I am still employed by your august organization," Maimon shot back. "It is still another week till payday. How is your granddaughter Olivia, Sol?"

"Who told you your daughter's name? Zelda said it was a secret."

"She is not my daughter. She is James Charrington's."

"How dare you say that?" Sol responded, truly shocked by Maimon's statement.

"I dare say it because it is true. And, truly, her name is Miss Olivia Charrington the 2nd. Or maybe the 3rd, I don't know. Anyway, I hear Zelda has now crossed the color line, so you had better pay attention to what comes out next time."

Sol got up to strike Maimon, which Lev restrained him from doing.

"That is the most honorable thing you have done in this whole debacle," Maimon told him.

"What did I do wrong?" Lev asked, virtually dragging Sol back to his chair.

"At first I didn't think that you were in this cesspit, too. But then I realized you were, because you gave the name and address of the bank manager to Sol," Maimon said.

"I couldn't help it," Lev pleaded. "He made me do it."

"He also made you send weevilled beans to the small retailers who couldn't afford to sue you, I suppose, and kaffir corn you had made heavier by watering it to the beermakers," Maimon said.

"We paid the claims on the beans," Lev replied indignantly.

"Of course you did. By telling the poor buyers that you would give them a discount on their next order, the price of which you inflated anyway. So they were locked in and you had a guaranteed outlet for your weevilled beans. Nice business? I think it stinks, like the two of you do," Maimon said.

"I am going to get you, Maimon. There is a weak link in your squeaky-clean skin, I know that. I just don't know where it is," Sol said, not very convincingly.

"If and when you do," Maimon told him very seriously, "remember that I know you authorized the Zulu impi to kill Brutus."

With that Maimon dropped his office keys onto Sol's desk, and said, "I hope our paths never cross again."

Maimon walked out of the partners' office, down the steps to the ground floor, and glanced around. The forecourt looked the same as it had the afternoon he rode in on the bean-cart so many months before. It hadn't changed, but Maimon had. How he had grown, from an abrasive cocksure youngster who had no reason to be, to a worldly young man who had negotiated a government deal with the President of the Transvaal on the one hand, and with an American equipment supplier on the other. One day he would look back on his entrance into the Transvaal commercial world and remember the two ganovim[75] who facilitated it.

After knocking on the now familiar sandblasted glass door of Edward's office, Maimon walked through it to his inner sanctum. After shaking Maimon's hand, Edward ushered him to one of the big leather chairs, and then, sitting on the corner of his desk, said, "Maimon, you must be the only person in the world who can neither read nor write, who got £120,000 without inheriting it, and surely the only teenager to do so. For a reason best known to him, the Good Lord is smiling on you."

Maimon looked at Edward quizzically, now appreciating where the pain lay.

---

75   *Thieves*

"Listen to what happened," Edward continued. "Alfred met with a very embarrassed Horace this afternoon. After an extensive bargaining session, in the most refined manner, I am sure, Horace agreed to pay you £120,000, on the condition that you do not mention this to anyone apart from your wife. When you sign the agreement," he handed a two-page document to Maimon, "I am authorised to give you this check."

"For £120,000?" Maimon asked incredulously.

"Take a look for yourself."

Though he was itching to jump up and sign the document and then shout for joy, Maimon said as calmly as he could, "Is there any reason I shouldn't sign this?"

"Not that I can think of," the lawyer replied sagely.

Maimon signed the document with a squiggle, and said, "Thank you so very much for everything you have done for me. I do appreciate it. I will go and see Alfred in the morning."

Taking the tumbler of whiskey Edward handed him, they wished each other l'chaim,[76] Maimon slowly sipping the golden liquid and savoring the moment.

"Then there is this matter of your hotel – well, not your hotel quite yet. Max Raphaely wants to sell The Hights Hotel and move to Doorn-fontein," Edward said, not sure whether he still had Maimon's attention. After all, the news thus far had already been a lot for the young man (or anyone, for that matter) to take in. "It gives a 50% return a year, which means you get your money back after two years. If you are interested, speak to Raphaely, he is there most of the time."

"There must be a good reason Raphaely wants to sell it, which is probably a good reason why we shouldn't buy his hotel," Maimon pointed out.

"The reason is that his wife went into one of their daughter's rooms one night last week, in time to see a rat the size of a small dog scamper-ing across Clara's bed. That made Johanna's mind up, and Max is now looking for a house in Doornfontein for their whole family."

"Sounds opportune," Maimon said, slowly getting to his feet, shak-ing Edward's hand, thanking him again, and asking Edward to open an account at one of the banks and pay the check into it.

---

76   *To life*

CHAPTER 22

THE CLUB IT IS HARD TO GET INTO AND IMPOSSIBLE TO GET OUT OF

On the way back to the hotel, Maimon stopped in at Mr. E.J.P. Jorissen's office. Jorissen was President Kruger's representative in Johannesburg, and Maimon told him of his last conversation with the President, and the President's wish to see Elize should Maimon have found her. Jorissen congratulated Maimon on his good fortune, and said he would ask the President for a date and time for the meeting, which Jorissen would then put in a note addressed to Maimon at the Hights Hotel. Maimon thanked him and continued his slow walk back to the hotel.

Two conundrums went through Maimon's mind, one replacing the other before either could be resolved. The one was that just a week ago, riding to Heilbron, he was ready to throw in the towel and go to New York; and now he was rich, both in personal and material assets, beyond his wildest expectations. Why did it happen?

And the other was that the money he had received, which he hadn't earned, was more than the whole of Saratov worked for in ten years, and he felt uncomfortable about that. And even as these two conundrums circled and clashed with him, he felt the deep and certain warmth of his affection – no, his love – for Elize. He wanted her in a way he never had before.

This last feeling he found most perplexing of all. He didn't know why, but he had to do love with Elize, and do it now. He tried to explain it. It couldn't have been Mr. Jorissen that triggered it, and it certainly wasn't his meeting with Sol and Lev, and he had had many discussions with Edward without creating this feeling. No matter the cause, the closer Maimon got to the hotel, the stronger it became.

Maimon hadn't decided when and how to tell Elize of their new-found riches, but when he walked into their suite, he had no chance of doing so. Elize threw herself into his arms and said "Thank you" about eight times, before Maimon could dislodge her and find out what the gratitude was for. Pauline Nathan had taken Elize and Magda to three dress shops and a shoe shop, and in just under two hours, the two of them had bought four dresses each, and four sets of underwear. Little Adam had got some new clothes as well, and much more important to him, a red ball that he spent all his time kicking around. Maimon had to sit and watch both Elize and her mother model each of their dresses and their new shoes, and so it was just before the hotel kitchen was about to close that they thought about dinner.

"Do you know they have something called 'room service'?" Elize said excitedly.

Untruthfully (but generously, not wanting to take anything away from her discovery), Maimon disclaimed any knowledge of this service.

"You order your dinner and they send it to your room. Can we have that tonight, please?" Elize asked.

Sometime later they were having a picnic in their suite, the women still bubbling over with excitement, and little Adam only agreeing to eat anything at all if his confiscated ball was given back. After the room service people had removed their dirty plates and glasses, and while Eliza was giving little Adam a bath, which was an exciting event for both of them, Magda had an opportunity to talk to Maimon.

"I know Elize and I were excited about the clothes, like two school girls, but you must understand, before this afternoon, me and my mother and my grandmother only had farm dresses. None of them were ever as pretty as the ones you bought us. And so I want you to know how much we both appreciate these clothes. Elize and I have already thanked you for bringing us here from the camp, and we will forever be grateful for that."

Magda sighed deeply, clasped her hands on her lap, and continued with some difficulty.

"What I want to know is, why did the Lord send you into our family? Elize could have met any boy at the East London Hotel. Not that she needed the hotel to meet boys. Before you came, they were like bees on a honey pot at the farm. And then Piet shooting the hyenas, and you finding us in Heilbron. The Lord must have some plan for us, but how do we know what it is?"

Magda looked at Maimon as if he was some Biblical prophet. He had rescued her and Elize and little Adam from the deprivation they faced in the camp. After the war, which would not last forever, what would have happened to them? Their burnt-down house was not habitable. Magda had thought about this a lot in the concentration camp. It was clear to her now that the Lord had sent Maimon, the question was why?

In a less religious way, the same question was bothering Maimon. He didn't know the answer, which he told Magda, adding that when the Lord was ready, He would tell Magda, and till then she should continue being the good person that she was. This seemed to give her some comfort, and after thanking Maimon again for the clothes and the shoes, Magda went to her room.

A minute or two later, Elize emerged from the bathroom with little Adam wrapped head-to-toe in a big soft hotel bath towel. Maimon snuggled and tickled him till they were all laughing, and then when he was dry, Elize put him in pajamas – another new experience. They both kissed him goodnight, and Elize put him down. In a few minutes Adam was fast asleep, clutching his ball.

Elize quietly closed the door of Adam's room, and then in front of Mai mon she did a striptease, except it wasn't a tease. First she kicked off her shoes, and then she undid the buttons of her dress that she stepped out of. Her underwear, which Maimon had never seen before, was cream-colored and shiny, and Maimon later learned were made of silk. Maimon found himself getting hard. Then Elize took off her top, and under that her brassiere, exposing her firm breasts with slightly darker nipples pointing upwards. Finally, she dropped her silk undies onto the floor.

Maimon had never seen Elize nude in broad daylight before, and he wondered at her beauty as she stood in front of him, one hand holding her hair on top of her head, exposing her graceful neck, and the other on her hip. Maimon looked at Elize as if through new eyes. What he saw was the East London angel again, this time without clothes, and just like Magda didn't know what she had done to deserve her rescue, so he didn't what he had done to deserve this angel. An illiterate Saratov Jew just a few years ago, and now in the best suite, in the best hotel, in Africa's richest city, with a woman of exquisite beauty in love with him. It defied explanation.

Smiling, she came across the room to Maimon. First, she took off his shirt, then his trousers, and finally his undershorts. Then she kissed his manliness, and after that his lips, searching for his tongue as she did so. Without saying a word, Elize went and lay on the bed on her back, her legs slightly apart. Gently Maimon lay on top of her, his head level with her breasts, whose nipples he teased with his tongue. While he was doing this, Elize's legs opened and he slipped down and did one of the things Zelda had taught him. Elize sighed, first once and then repeatedly, and when her hips started lifting and falling, Maimon moved in: slowly at first, and then all the way.

Maimon's actions became faster and deeper. Elize arched her long and graceful neck, which Maimon kissed, first on one side and then the other, as he pushed more and more. Between the sighs Elize was saying, "Yes"; and then holding her tight, Maimon exploded, before gently lying on top of her. Their sweat mingled as Elize ran her fingers through Maimon's hair.

Still connected as they were, Elize wished they could stay like this for all time. After a few minutes Maimon started again and soon the two of them were as one, rolling on the bed, first Maimon on top, and then Elize, and then Maimon again until it was over. Elize gave him two squeezes, something she never knew she could do, before Maimon withdrew, exhausted. Lying on his back, Elize kissed him gently, first on his manhood and then on his lips while he was awake, which wasn't for long.

Elize, wide awake, lay on her back, too stimulated to fall asleep. It had almost been too much and overwhelmed her, but it wasn't and it hadn't. In fact, now that she had a chance to think about it quietly, she didn't have to do anything. Maimon had come to the concentration camp, picked her up, and brought her to Johannesburg, where he had installed her in the President's Suite at the best hotel, and then had bought her a wardrobe of clothes, and what had she done in return? Nothing.

Then she thought about it a little more deeply. Maimon had only come to find her because he loved her, the light of which flame was lit in East London and flared into a bonfire at the farm. The more she thought about it, the more confused it all became. No matter which way she looked at it, Elize came to the conclusion that there was an invisible hand guiding the two of them that she couldn't understand. In fact, the dominee had said that there were some things in the Bible which were not for man on earth to understand, and maybe this was one of them. With this thought she kissed the sleeping man that God had sent her, sighed deeply, closed her eyes, and was soon asleep.

The previous afternoon, when they were buying dresses, Elize had told Pauline that she didn't want to live in the hotel, and could she possibly suggest an area where they could buy or rent their own house. Pauline, only too glad to help, promised to pick Elize and her mother up from the hotel at ten the next morning to go on a property-viewing exercise. Elize wanted to tell Maimon about this, but when she woke the following morning, he had already left the hotel.

Pauline Nathan was on time, and the three women and Adam climbed into her carriage and set off for Doornfontein, one of the only two areas Pauline told them was worth considering.

The other was Parktown, but there one had to build one's own house. They spent almost two hours looking at houses, some for sale, others not, some larger, others not, as well as a derelict house on a large piece of ground in one of the nicer parts of Doornfontein. When they had exhausted examining the houses for sale, and gone into three others that were owned by Pauline's friends, it was well past twelve and Pauline invited them to her house for lunch.

Magda's and Elize's protestations were quickly brushed aside, and before they knew it, the two adults were sitting in the parlor of Pauline's house gently sipping homemade lemonade, and little Adam was kicking his ball in the garden with one of Pauline's domestic servants.

Seemingly out of nowhere, Pauline conjured up a meal of soup, steak, and vegetables, with fresh fruit to follow. All this was served by an immaculately dressed native wearing black trousers and a white jacket, across which a bright red sash had been placed. He was so different from the natives on the farm, Elize realized; she could not imagine Johannes or any of his grown-up sons serving as this man was doing. This man, whose name was James, was the first non-farm native that she had come into contact with, and it brought home to her that there were natives and natives, and not all of them were the same.

Maimon was having a similarly interesting morning. When he arrived at Alfred's office to thank him for the assistance he had rendered in getting the money from the bank, Maimon was invited to join a meeting that was just about to start. About ten people, most of whom Maimon remembered from Kimberley, were gathered in Alfred's boardroom. He knew Alfred and Julius, of course, as well as Cecil Rhodes, whom he had met that night in Alfred's office. Also assembled was Barney Barnato, who remembered him from a diamond sale he had made. He recognized J.B. Robinson, and was also introduced to Sammy Marks and his cousin, Isaac Lewis, as well as George Albu, Hermann Eckstein, and Lionel Phillips.

It came as a shock to Maimon that he was considered if not an equal, then at least equal enough to be invited to the meeting. The topic was the formation of the Rand Club, and after a few formalities, which included confirming the purchase of an office block in Loveday Street, the meeting agreed to appoint Frank Emley as the project's architect. Hermann Eckstein proposed that all present pay £1,000 to cover expenditure to date and costs in the foreseeable future, which would accord them foundation member status of the club.

After the meeting Maimon made his way to Edward's office. He had an important question to ask him, specifically what needed to be done in order for him to marry Elize. Under the Transvaal Marriage Act, Edward told Maimon, both he and Elize needed to be twenty-one or older, and if they were not, it was necessary for them to provide parental approval documents enabling them to be wed. In Elize's case this wasn't a problem.

"What about me?" Maimon asked, seeing no way round the fact that Saratov could as well be on the moon, as easy as it surely would be to get his father to sign the necessary consent.

This problem was solved by Edward handing Maimon the required authorization, adding that it had been delivered to him by the clerk of the Magistrate's Court, where Maimon and Elize would shortly be married.

Maimon took the paper and looked at Edward for an explanation.

"The Russian government's honorary consul, Vladimir Meshennik, I have been told, can be most helpful if approached correctly."

"*Correctly?*" Maimon queried.

"Today is 'Defender of the Fatherland Day.' It seems on such days Mr. Meshennik can be moved to make humanitarian gestures in the spirit of The Internationale. Apparently, Lesuj is one of his friends, and hearing that you had found Elize, he put two and two together ..."

"And made five," Maimon finished the sentence, smiling.

Not being involved in this documentary activity, Edward changed the subject.

"You know a Jewish wedding is out of the question."

"Lesuj?" Maimon asked, wondering how far his friend's influence spread. "Am afraid not. Last week the Beth Din fired a chazen[77] for

---

77   *A cantor*

watering his garden on Saturday afternoon. Those people are still in the seventeenth century."

"When will my divorce be through?" Maimon asked, really wanting to get married this time.

"On Friday," Edward replied. "So anytime next week will be fine legally."

"Wedding days, I remember, are chosen by the bride," Maimon said. "I will find out the date and get back to you. One last thing, the Weiss diamond shop on the corner. Are they related to the diamond dealers in Kimberley?"

"Same family," Edward replied. "Are you about to give Robert a lesson in diamond-valuing?"

"Possibly," Maimon said, "very possibly."

Thirty minutes later Maimon walked out of the Weiss' Johannesburg shop with a two-carat diamond and three words ringing in the manager's ears – color, clarity, and cut – not the bullshit, bravado, and Barnato that he had used in his sales pitch to Maimon. On the way back to the hotel, Maimon passed a jeweller who set the ring while Maimon waited. He had seen enough diamonds swapped in his short career not to leave his stone with this man overnight.

Back at the hotel Adam had finished his supper and bath, and was enjoying what Elize called "quiet time." Usually, this transitional time between bath and bed was spent telling stories, but as daddy was here some rules could be broken. While Elize was hanging the towels, Maimon coached Adam on what to say when she returned.

"Will you marry daddy?" the little voice asked when Elize returned to the room.

Puzzled, she said, "If he gives me a ring, yes, I will marry him."

"She says she wants a ring," Adam told his father. Upon hearing this, Maimon took a little black box out of his pocket and gave it to Adam for his mother. The box dutifully delivered, Elize opened it, saw the ring, and shrieked so loudly her mother came rushing in, fearing some catastrophe. This was followed by more tears and more hugs.

In a few minutes calm was restored, "quiet time" commenced again. Elize took Adam to bed and told him the story of Jack and the Beanstalk.

"When will you marry, Daddy?" Adam asked Elize as she returned to the suite's sitting room.

"When his divorce is through."

"It is done. Zelda is history," Maimon told her, surprising her by his presence, standing behind his son, his hands on the child's small shoulders, as fragile as a bird's bones. Seeing father and son in this position filled her with warmth again. She felt blessed, by the ring but not only by the ring, by Maimon and her life right now. She had suffered through so much tragedy, only to be blessed with so much light and love.

Elize went and sat on the floor, her legs curled up under her. Looking up at Maimon, she began, "You have been so generous to my mother and me that I don't like asking this question."

"But," Maimon said gently,

"I am only going to get married once. Could you spare a bit more money for my mother and me to buy wedding dresses? If it is too much money, I quite understand."

"It is a Jewish custom," Maimon lied, "for the father of the bride to leave money under his daughter's pillow for her to buy such things."

Elize got up slowly and went to her bed, and under the pillow found £40. Turning round she looked at Maimon.

"Had Piet been here he would have done it," Maimon explained.

Tears welled up in both Elize's and her mother's eyes as they hugged each other again. Then Elize came and sat on Maimon's lap, and kissed him, too, and between the tears said smiling, "But he wasn't Jewish."

"Are you sure?" Maimon countered. "I thought the du Toits were an old French Huguenot Jewish family."

"They were definitely not," Elize told him, now laughing.

"Then Raguel put it there," Maimon said.

"Who is he?" Elize asked, not sure if Maimon was joking or not.

"The angel of justice and fairness. He probably felt that you and your mother had suffered enough in life and he was evening up the scales."

"Elize, you are a very lucky girl," her mother told her. "You don't know how lucky you really are."

That night after "doing love," Maimon and Elize lay naked, practicing "quiet time" of their own, simply happy in each other's presence.

"Too much money can bring sadness," Elize said. "You haven't got too much, have you?"

"I haven't got that much, but I have got enough."

"Is 'enough' a figure?" Elize asked, now curious.

"It may be to some people. I have enough to buy a house for the four of us, and to put bread on the table. I don't need more than that."

"A house in Johannesburg or New York?" Elize asked, having been afraid to bring up this subject since they had arrived in Johannesburg.

"Probably both," Maimon replied honestly. "But right now I am happy in Johannesburg."

With the one thing that Elize was worried about now swept out of the door and blown away, she felt a combination of great relief and overwhelming love for this man who had taken over her life. Like the female vervet monkeys she remembered at the farm sprawling over their mates, Elize climbed on top of Maimon, her legs on his legs, her arms on his arms and her body wholly on his.

"Don't move," she said to Maimon, who was lying on his back enjoying the cool breeze coming in the window. Sitting astride him, Elize kissed her loved one on his neck and his ear, then on his face and his lips. It was at this point when Maimon captured her tongue with his and rubbed it this way than that. Feeling his hardness, she kissed him there, too, and looking up at him smiling, she opened her legs and let him slide in.

"My darling," she murmured, "I do love you so much," as it settled in its warm and moist place. Slowly Elize rocked backwards and forwards, whimpering softly while looking down at the man of her dreams.

Disobeying her instructions, Maimon licked his palms and gently rubbed Elize's nipples, which immediately hardened. Taking one breast in each hand, he squeezed them softly, and then released them and did the same again as Elize's whimpering turned to moans.

Again he squeezed her breasts, this time harder, pushing whatever was inside to the nipples, which were erect and looking for a welcoming mouth. Feeling the fire in his loins, Maimon grabbed Elize and pulled her down to him, her thighs now pressing against his, her breasts on his chest and their bodies together as they moved in unison, apart and together, again and again. Maimon tensed, his body ready to give Elize what it craved. Then she kissed him, and kissed him again and again, until they both melted, which happened at the same time. Exhausted they fell asleep, joined together and deeply in love.

About five o'clock the next morning they woke, both on their sides, Elize curled up against Maimon's similarly shaped posture.

She kissed his arm, and then laying her head on it, said, "Can I ask you a question?"

"Sure," he said, not sure what was coming.

"Your penis and little Adam's are different. Something is missing on yours. Did you have an accident?"

"No accident. I, and all Jewish men, are circumcised, which means that a little piece of skin on our penises is cut off."

"Why do you do that? It must be very painful."

"We do it because of a deal. It is called a 'covenant' that God made with Abraham. According to the Bible, Abraham said he would circumcise all the men, and, in turn, God promised to look after all the Jewish people. We honor our side of the undertaking, but God doesn't always honor his."

"How can you say this?" Elize protested. "Look how he brought you and me together."

"And look how he permits so many pogroms to take place."

"He must be busy on other things," Elize said defensively. "Anyway, we need to get Adam circumcised. Who does it? A rabbi or a doctor?"

This wasn't the time to tell Elize that, even though he had a Jewish father, Adam was not Jewish, as the religious line passed through the mother.

"Let me make some enquiries," Maimon said, hoping that his friend Edward could help on this matter.

"I have a question for you," Maimon said, greeting Edward. "And I have one for you," Edward unexpectedly replied.

"Mine is more important. Adam needs to be brissed.[78]"

"You are right, it is more important," Edward said, rubbing his beardless chin, a new habit of his. "On balance I would take him to the hospital."

"Because?"

"Because the hospital is more hygienic," Edward answered sagely. "The mohel[79] doesn't issue a bris certificate, so in twenty years' time, who knows?"

"Who knows what?" Maimon asked mystified.

"The story of the talking dog," Edward replied, smiling.

"The talking dog?" Maimon said, bemused.

"The Cossacks," Edward began, "led by an officer on his horse, were visiting a pogrom in some defenceless Jewish shtetl. Leading the

78 Circumcision
79 The religious official conducting a circumcision.

pogrom was an officer, and perched on the pummel of the his saddle was a little dog, to whom a Jew, while dodging the lashes of the officer's whip, was calling up.

"'Hello, little dog. Are you thirsty, little dog, or maybe hungry?' the Jew said, taking a few whip blows while doing so. 'Are you crazy, Jew?' the officer said stopping his attack, 'Dogs don't talk'. 'Your dog might not,' the Jew replied, 'but I had one that did. Nothing intellectual. Just the weather and some gossip now and then.'

"The officer blew his whistle signalling the pogrom's end, handed his dog to the Jew, and said, 'I will be back on this day next year and if my dog isn't talking your wife and daughters will be raped, you and your sons will be sodomized, and then all of you will be burnt alive.' Then he galloped away. Rochel, the Jew Abe's wife was white with fear. ' Dogs don't talk. You have never had a dog. Next year we will all be raped and killed. What have you done!' 'Rochel,' Abe said quietly. 'Next year the officer might be dead, we might be in Omsk or Tomsk or maybe Minsk or Pinsk.'"

"What is your question?" Maimon asked.

"Do you want to buy the Hights Hotel?" Edward asked, his tone now serious.

"Not really. Elize wants to live in Doornfontein, and I have an appointment with Herbert Baker about a house I propose building in Parktown." Then, after a pause, Maimon said, "Unless there is an angle?"

"Sit down, young man." Maimon did as he was told.

"Raphaely wants £2,000 for it, and we can probably knock him down to £1,700 or £1,800."

"*We?*" Maimon asked, getting interested.

"I thought we could do it in partnership. Eighty, twenty. My twenty. We are getting the hotel for nothing," Edward said, and, as if for emphasis, stroked his chin again.

"Then why the £1,700?" Maimon asked, now totally confused.

"That is what we pay for the land. Two city blocks in the middle of Johannesburg will be worth thousands after the war. We can borrow the money we need from the bank, the interest cost of which will be paid for by the income from the bar, and the poor souls who sleep there."

"And the rich souls who drop in for thirty minutes' companionship in the afternoon," Maimon reminded him.

"Them too. I will get the best offer I can from Raphaely, as well as confirmation that the bank will lend us 75% of the purchase price, for our meeting tomorrow morning. One other thing. If you haven't already done so, you had better buy a wedding ring. Just a gold band."

"Can't I use the diamond ring I just bought?" Maimon asked, having conveniently forgotten everything relating to his bad experience with Zelda.

"Am afraid not. And you are going to need someone to give Elize to you. Remember Sol did that for Zelda."

The memory of that terrible evening flashed through Maimon's mind, and particularly the image of him and four male pole holders standing under the chupa, as if waiting for the executioner's rope to be tightened around his neck. He had tried for a long time not to think of these images at all, and yet they were, unbidden and awful to contemplate. Maimon found he was sweating at just the memory of it.

Seeing that Maimon looked a bit disorientated, Edward said, "I will do that for you, if you like."

"Please, yes please," Maimon responded, hastening to delete anything relating to that terrible night from his memory.

Back at the hotel, if last week's mannequin parade was exciting, this evening's was heart-stopping. Elize was wearing a full-length white wedding dress, tight at the waist, demure at the top, with a wide skirt that itself took many yards of fabric to make. When Maimon entered the room, Elize was dancing round and round, one hand holding her hair above her head, and the other parallel to the floor like a graceful ballet dancer. Seeing Maimon, she dropped to her knees in front of him, one hand pointing up, and the other on the floor to stop her falling from giddiness.

Maimon took the hand of her raised arm and said, "Arise Mrs. Sokolovski" which Elize did as gracefully as she could. "Your wedding dress?" Maimon asked, not knowing what to expect following his talk with Edward.

"Of course not," Elize replied. "The lady in the dress shop lent it to me for tonight, so you could see what I would look like at a high-society wedding."

Another so called high-society wedding was the very last thing Maimon wanted; indeed, he was still trying to erase the memory of the last one from his highly retentive mind.

"You don't look like a high-society bride," Maimon told Elize, "but like a fairy princess."

Tired from all of her dancing, Elize flopped down on a chair, not as any fairy princess would do.

"My mother and I decided we don't need special wedding dresses; the ones we bought last week will be fine. Then we – or you, if you want to – can give the money to people who are much poorer than us."

That is just about everybody in Africa, Maimon thought to himself, but instead said, "That is a really good idea. Let's think about it a little more." He remembered the kufsa and the rouble and kopek coins, and how he was chastised for making fun of charity when the rabbi came to call. For the first time since he left home, Maimon wondered if he would ever go back. It was just a flashing thought, but somewhere in his head, deep down, that thought existed.

In bed later that night, when Maimon was examining the drawing of a flour mill for the umpteenth time, Elize said, "When I was trying on wedding dresses this afternoon there were two other girls also doing so."

"It is good to meet other people," Maimon said, understanding that he was expected to be part of the conversation.

"They were both Christian girls marrying Jewish men. Do you know what they said?"

"No, I don't know," Maimon said keeping his end of the conversation going.

"That Jewish men are better lovers than Christian men."

"Really," Maimon answered rotely, trying to work out what powered the rollers in the mill.

"I don't have a basis of comparison, but they said with Christian men it was usually 'bang, bang, thank you, ma'am.'"

"Really," Maimon said, realizing that the power was coming from the fly wheel.

"Maimon! Are you listening?" an exasperated Elize said, taking the magazine from him and flinging it to the far-corner of the room.

"Of course I am. I am just feeling a bit guilty," he answered defensively.

"And why is that?" Elize said, not sure what was coming.

"Because I never say thank you. I will make a determined effort to do so in future." And then, after a short pause, "Shouldn't you also be saying thank you?" While Elize was working out how to answer that, Maimon said, "What else did they say?"

"That Jewish men make good husbands. They spend less time drinking in the pub, and as they are rarely drunk, they don't beat their wives."

"We don't have to be drunk to beat our wives. Didn't they say anything bad about us?" Maimon said, realizing his *Wheat Millers* magazine was gone for the night.

"They said the food was too much and often too heavy. Kugel[80] and cholent[81].were mentioned often. When we move into our house, I will make them for you."

"I wouldn't do that if I were you," Maimon said as seriously as he could.

"Why not?" Elize asked in surprise.

"Because I will beat you, or divorce you, or do both. That stuff is good in Russia when it is freezing cold and you have nothing else to eat."

"When we get to our house you will have to say Eishet Chayil,"[82] she continued, as if she had not heard him.

"What!" This really took Maimon's full attention. "Who told you that?"

"Rabbi Hertz. You should meet him. He is a really nice person."

Running from behind made Maimon uncomfortable. Somehow, he had to catch up, and in doing so he said as offhandedly as he could, "Where on earth did you come across him?"

"In his office, of course," Elize said as if it was the stupidest question in the world. "I see him every Tuesday and Thursday afternoons."

"Why?" Maimon said, now having a good idea where this conversation was going.

"Because I am learning Hebrew and doing a Jewish conversion course."

"Don't you think you should have told me?" Maimon said, taken aback.

"I am telling you now," Elize replied, surprised Maimon wasn't pleased at this development.

"Do you know what you are letting yourself in for?" Maimon asked, to find out the depth of her commitment.

"Nine to twelve months of study, according to the rabbi."

"What about the persecution, the pogroms, being hounded from here-to-there for centuries? Not having a country of our own?" Maimon asked antagonistically.

---

80 *A baked pudding or casserole most commonly made from noodles or potatoes*

81 *Jewish stew usually simmered overnight for twelve hours, or more often made with beef and vegetables*

82 *Prayer praising the woman of the house*

"What is it with you people?" Elize asked, getting annoyed.

"*You people?*" Maimon asked, which was a saying he would hear many times in the years ahead.

"Every other religion would welcome people who wanted to join. It was the same with the rabbi. I don't get it. You are the People of the Book, the Chosen People, the moral leaders of the world, there are not many of you, and when one person wants to join you, you play hard-to-get. Are you crazy?"

"Yes, we are. If you want to join a club of crazies, I will help you. But be aware of what you are getting yourself into," Maimon said.

"Thank you," Elize said, thinking that one of the reasons Jews had survived for all these thousands of years was because they were a bit nuts.

"Welcome to the club, which is hard to get into and impossible to get out of," Maimon said with a smile.

Elize gave him a hug and a kiss and another hug and then said, "I want you to teach me Yiddish, please."

"You are not even Jewish, and already you are crazy. What is it with you, woman?"

"When we go and visit your parents, I want to be able to speak to them," Elize explained.

This was now going way faster than Maimon wanted. Alfred had once said to him, "Control what you need to control," and this part of his life was definitely in this category, but he was losing control. Seeing that Maimon was far from enthusiastic, Elize added, "When we go to visit Shakespeare's wife's home. You promised."

"I will take you to her house, and anyone else's house in England you want to visit – but Russia, no. It is a wild place, even getting there is dangerous, and then getting out is dangerous. Absolutely not."

"More dangerous than the British army?" Elize asked seriously.

"Way more dangerous. I know what happened at your farm, and I can't imagine how horrific it must have been for you and your mother – but Russia, no. Subject closed." And, as far as Maimon was concerned, it was.

Realizing that she was not going to make any progress on this now, Elize smiled, kissed Maimon, and moved on.

Walking to Edward's office down Market Street the following morning, Maimon took in some unusual sights, or at least sights unusual to

him. He didn't often come this way, and so the Litvaks[83] hawking secondhand clothes, either wholesale to the Indians, or at slightly higher
prices to the natives, was new to him. He was particularly amused by
the hawkers shouting to one another in Yiddish, warning that this native
was a shop-lifter, or that one was a schlemiel, and generally at how
good-humored the Litvaks were.

How fortunate he was to have come into the Transvaal's economy
through the diamond business, he realized, and so was spared the secondhand clothes trade. Which got him thinking about Yiddish and
Elize's request to learn this mongrel language. Also, the Litvak's Yiddish was different from the Pole's Yiddish or from Russian Yiddish.

He was right, of course, to object to going back to Russia. Not only
was life in Russia bad enough on its own – cruel, cold – but he remembered the Cossacks on the train, and what they would have done to him,
Frieda, and her husband given half the chance. But there was another
reason that he did not want to return, one he hardly admitted to himself.
Guilt. Guilt that he hadn't sent his family money. These Litvaks, with
much less than he had, sent money every week. That is why there were
so many of them.

Maimon wasn't sure why he hadn't sent any back, but he was honest
enough to admit it was a conscious decision not to do so. Did he still
resent his parents for sending him away? For getting rid of him? Or was
there another reason? Before he had a chance to dig deeper into his subconscious, Maimon arrived at his destination.

"We got it for £1,700!" greeted Maimon as he stepped into Edward's
office. Maimon just had a chance to get in a "Well done" before Edward
continued proudly, "And the bank will lend us £1,200, and the insurance will give us all risks cover, so we are about to become hoteliers."

"You did all the work," Maimon said, slightly embarrassed.

"And you are putting up most of the money," Edward countered.

Which is how Maimon came to own most of the Hights Hotel. Elize
wasn't interested in this prime property purchase. Every waking minute
of every day of hers was taken up with her imminent meeting with the
President and his wife. The meeting was scheduled for the following
Wednesday morning, and Elize insisted on their arriving in Pretoria on
the Tuesday afternoon, so that she would be clean and fresh the following morning. Maimon was nonplussed by the fact that Elize could talk

---

83   *Jews of Lithuanian extraction*

of nothing else, until that Paul Kruger wasn't Maimon's president, or indeed his, but it was *her* president.

Maimon remembered one of the psalms he hadn't learned at cheder, which started with "Put not your faith in Princes" or something like that, and as far as he was concerned, the same went for presidents. President Kruger would probably die before he did, and then he would have to deal with another president.

Thankfully, the two-day trip was uneventful, and they arrived in Pretoria in good time for Elize to bathe and change for dinner. She slept fitfully and, too excited to eat breakfast, was dressed at eight o'clock for their ten a.m. meeting. Maimon, who had met the President twice before was very relaxed, which was just as well as Elize was a bundle of nerves. They arrived a few minutes early and were shown in to what Elize told Maimon was the "voorkamer."[84]

A few minutes later, President Kruger came in, and introduced Maimon and Elize to his wife, Gezina. The President was charm itself, and insisted that Elize tell him and his wife how Maimon had found her.

Elize explained that not only had Maimon found her, but her mother as well; she then went into the story, not missing a single detail. The President listened attentively, and when Elize was finished, he said that the Lord works in mysterious ways. He also said that he had some business to discuss with Maimon, and it would be a good idea if the ladies went next door, and maybe Elize could tell Mrs. Kruger how she had met such a handsome young man. Elize blushed, got up, and followed Mrs. Kruger to the adjacent room.

"It is important for me to listen to such stories," he told Maimon. "I am so caught up with politics, and the crops, and the price of cattle, that I sometimes forget that it is Elize and her sisters who are the backbone of our country. Now listen to me."

Although he could hear the President clearly, Maimon pulled his chair a little closer to the colossuses of the man, and for the first time noticed the absence of one of his thumbs. Maimon had been told that as a younger man the President had been hunting rhinoceroses along the Steelpoort River, when the elephant gun he was carrying exploded in his hands and blew off most of his left thumb.

"Maimon," the President said, "the mining industry uses a lot of steel, all of which is imported from Europe. We need a steel factory in

84   *The front room, especially of a Cape Dutch house, or farmhouse*

the Transvaal, and I would like you to build one for us. You and Sammy Marks are very capable businessmen. But Sammy has got so much on his plate right now, so I think it is better that you build it."

Already Maimon was building a wheat mill and bakery that he knew nothing about, so why not a steel factory as well? If the President believed he was the man for the job, who was he, Maimon Sokolovski, to tell him this wasn't the case?

"I would be honored, Mr President" Maimon responded.

Before he could ask any questions about the size of the plant, and by when it should be completed, the President got to his feet and said, "Fine. Come and see me in two weeks with the contract," while ushering Maimon into the room where his wife and Elize were drinking coffee.

"You should hear the story about the hyenas," Gezina said to her husband, who courteously replied that this should be left for another day, as he was so short of good stories that he didn't want to hear them all at once. Maimon and Elize said goodbye to the President and his wife, and half an hour after entering their one-story house in Church Street, they were out on the dusty road again.

"I will never forget this day as long as I live," Elize told Maimon. "You are the most amazing man." She gripped his upper arm as she had before.

Maimon smiled. If the President thought he was up to building factories, and Elize thought he was amazing, he must be. Quite a difference from the "can't read" and "can't write" boy who left Saratov just a few years ago. With that thought in his mind, Maimon steered Elize back to the hotel to pick up their bags en route to the coach station for their ride back to Johannesburg.

The next couple of weeks were the busiest in his life. On the way back from Pretoria, Maimon stopped at the public library and took out a book on steelmaking that Elize and Magda together read to him, twice – in case he missed anything the first time, he told them.

That took him back to Pretoria to see the President, with an arm full of papers and a packet of Dutch chocolate from Elize for Mrs. Kruger. Negotiations involving the proposed steel mill, as Maimon now knew such a factory was called, were much more complex and complicated than had been the case for the flour mill and bakery. This was because the steel mill need ed coal as well as iron ore, both of which had to be secured before any progress could be made. The President bought in a very clever man about his age called Jan Smuts, who was given the job of finalizing the contracts with Maimon. Fortunately, the two men took a liking to one another, and agreed to meet again when Maimon had bought reserves of coal and iron ore. Seeing Maimon out, Smuts suggested Maimon look in the Southern Transvaal for coal. As for iron ore, Smuts said he had heard there were outcrops in the west of the country, but he hadn't seen any himself.

Back in Johannesburg, Maimon walked into their hotel suite to find Elize teaching Adam the Aleph Bet, and Magda hassling the laundry staff to make sure they had clean clothes for Shabbes.[85]

"Lessons over," Maimon said, picking Adam up and throwing him in the air, which caused the little boy to scream with excitement. After four or five such throws, Maimon threw him onto the bed.

"Now it is Mommy's turn," he told Adam.

Kissing Maimon warmly, Elize said, "Mummy is too big for this," which did not deter Adam from saying repeatedly, "Mummy's turn, mummy's turn, mummy's turn."

"Magda, we need to go out for thirty minutes," Maimon said. "Can you please look after Adam?"

With Piet and Willem murdered, and Elize about to be married, Adam was the center of Magda's universe, and she relished any opportunity to spend time with him. A smile was all Maimon needed to know that it was no problem.

"Where are we going?" Elize asked as Maimon ushered her out of their suite.

"There is a little market in Commissioner Street, and walking past it I noticed that some of the Litvaks are selling bits and pieces, amongst which I saw a pair of lovely silver candlesticks. I would have bought them, but this is something that husbands and wives do together, so ..."

"Let's hurry," Elize replied, as if these were the last silver candlesticks in the world.

In the market area Elize immediately spotted them, about 16" high and brightly polished. Picking them up, Elize realized how heavy they were, which made her think they were made of pure silver. It was then that she looked at the seller. Not much older than Maimon, he was dressed in a jacket and trousers, no shirt, as threadbare clothes as one would expect a native to wear. He was also painfully thin.

---

85   *The Sabbath*

"What is your name?" Maimon asked quietly, to be told "Moshe" in the same tone.

"Moshe, what do you want for these candlesticks?" Maimon asked him.

Looking down at the candlesticks, and then up at Maimon, he said "£10."

"Is your wife in Lithuania?" Maimon asked, noticing the wedding ring on his finger.

"Yes, sir. Also, my parents and my brother and sister."

"May I ask him a question?" Elize said, looking up at Maimon, who nodded in approval. "Do you possibly have a Havdalah[86] set?"

From under the table, and wrapped in a cloth that was once white but after years of use was a gray piece of fabric, the man carefully unwrapped a beautiful silver three-piece Havdalah set. "That is £15," Moshe said, not expecting a sale as the value was about a third of this figure.

Elize picked up each piece one by one, and carefully examined it, before replacing it on the gray cloth. Then pulling Maimon aside she said, "The candlesticks are a lot of money, I know, but if we are going to have Kiddush,[87] we should also have Havdalah. Perhaps we could ask the man to put the Havdalah set on one side, and we can save up, and when we have enough money, we can buy them," Elize suggested.

Maimon took Elize by the arm and together they walked back to the silver seller.

"Moshe, we would also like the Havdalah set," Maimon said. "Please wrap them up with the candlesticks."

Moshe did so very carefully, using what seemed like a ream of newspaper before handing the parcel to Elize. Maimon took a £50 note out of his wallet and handed it to Moshe. Neither man said anything, they just looked at one another, and then tears rolled out of Moshe's eyes. Maimon nodded at Moshe and said, "Sholem Aleichem,"[88] to which Moshe replied, "Aleichem Sholem."

Taking the parcel from Elize and steering her back to the hotel, Maimon's thoughts were thousands of miles away in Saratov.

"We should give them back," Elize told Maimon. "Did you see how emotional he was to see them go?"

---

86   *Prayer said at the conclusion of the Sabbath*
87   *Prayer said at the commencement of the Sabbath*
88   *"Peace to you."*

Maimon didn't reply, just continued walking, his eyes focusing on sights he had blocked out since the day he said goodbye to Kaylah, his parents and Zelig. Over the past months Maimon had realized that, no matter how long he lived in Africa or America or wherever, there was a piece of Saratov in him that would be there till he died. His parent's house, Kaylah, Zelig and the day they picnicked in the forest.

Those were the good things. The bad things were also seared into his memory. Cheder and the pogroms of course, and his fight with the school bully that everyone expected him to lose. They were all so against him, Maimon remembered, that he felt guilty breaking the boys nose.

Maimon didn't say a word till they were back at the hotel. He obviously felt bad, Elize realized, for buying this poor man's family heirlooms.

Magda and Adam were having the most wonderful time. Noticing Maimon and Elize leave the hotel, unordered, Dilip brought up to their suite a coffee, a slice of the hotel's special cake of the day for Magda, and a bowl of ice cream covered with chocolate sauce for Adam. The reason Dilip gave Magda for bringing up these goodies, was to say thank you to Maimon for financing his son's studies to be a doctor at Edinburgh University.

Magda decided to let Adam eat the desert by himself, and while the tea spoon he was using got most of the ice cream into his mouth, a good part also covered his face, pajama top, and some even got in his hair. Seeing his parents and eating ice cream and chocolate sauce, Adam was in heaven.

CHAPTER 23

THE IRON MOUNTAIN

Edward had much to tell Maimon. First of all, the sunflower oil-crushing machinery and peanut-butter-manufacturing plant that Lev had paid for came up for sale at an auction, and as Maimon was the only man in the Transvaal who knew anything about this equipment, Edward bought the whole lot for £500. The auctioneer said S&L had paid £14,000 for these two lots, so he assumed this was OK with Maimon.

Maimon thanked him and said it certainly was.

"There is another matter," Edward told him. "Have you heard of the Central Diamond Mining Company?"

"I know, of course. of Kimberley Central, Barney's company, but Central Diamond, I don't think so," Maimon said.

"Hardly anyone does. It was one of Barney's holding companies. It had a lot of Kimberley Central shares that have now been distributed, and an iron mountain called Thabazimbi out in the northwest somewhere."

Neither of them spoke, and then Edward said, "'There is a tide in the affairs of man, which, taken at the flood, leads on to fortune.' It is Shakespeare, not me. Do you want to hear the rest of the quotation?"

Maimon nodded.

"'Omitted all the voyage of their life is bound in shallows and in miseries.' The auction is this afternoon. I have registered you as a bidder and found out two other people have also registered. Both have German names, but I haven't heard of either of them."

"What will it go for?" Maimon asked, realizing that in the scale of an iron mountain, his £120,000 was puny.

"I don't know. There is no precedent, and nobody needs an iron mountain except you. There is no reserve price, so the highest bidder gets it, no matter how high, or how low, the price is."

"Where and when is the auction?"

"At three o' clock this afternoon, in the Chamber of Mines boardroom."

"I'll be there."

"So will I," Edward said.

Maimon spent the next hour wandering round Johannesburg, trying to decide how much to spend on the iron mountain. Initially, he thought £50,000, but for a mountain that surely wasn't enough. On the other hand, no one else was going to give him £120,000, and if he only had £10,000 or £20,000 left, that might prevent him joining mining syndicates in the future. Not forgetting that he had to finance the peanut butter plant and the oil mill, and goodness knows what the steel plant would cost, Maimon remembered he would also need coal for the steel mill. No matter where he looked, all Maimon saw were lots of holes needing to be filled with money.

At a few minutes to three, Maimon walked into the Chamber of Mines boardroom to find a sea of faces, and with the exception of Edward's, he recognized none of them. At three o' clock sharp, the auctioneer started his gabble, telling the assembled gathering what a unique opportunity this was, and how close the deposit was to the railway line connecting the mine to the Transvaal gold fields. The more attractive the auctioneer made the asset, the more despondent Maimon became. When the preamble was finally over, the auction itself began.

"Do I hear £100,000?" the auctioneer asked, and as he didn't, he enquired at £50,000. No one was interested at that level, either, so he dropped first to £30,000, and then to £20,000, and then to £10,000. "Sadly, we have no buyers here this afternoon, so I will have to wrap this up," the auctioneer said, closing his file.

"Five thousand pounds," Maimon called out in a loud and clear voice.

"Do we have a joker in the room this afternoon?" the auctioneer asked.

His answer came in a German accent: "Six thousand pounds."

Which Maimon immediately raised to £7,000, doing so without encouragement from the auctioneer. The price went up in £1,000 increments, until it stuck at £11,000. Despite cajoling from the auctioneer, no one would go higher, which is how Maimon bought his iron mountain for £11,000.

The next day *The Diggers News* called it "the steal of the century," and J.B. Robinson sent one of his men round to see if the sale could be undone, and if not, whether he could buy the mountain from Maimon. He was unsuccessful on both counts.

Back in his lawyer's office they drank some of the aged Scottish whiskey that Edward had been keeping for a special occasion, both of them agreeing that the mountain purchase certainly qualified. Maimon pointed out that anyone who owned an iron mountain should have his own office, with which Edward agreed, though he wasn't happy with Maimon hiring one of his accountants, Kris Skot, to manage it.

His whiskey downed, Maimon had an irresistible urge to be with Elize. At a fast walk he was at the hotel in fifteen minutes, and in their suite, where he found Elize alone. Locking the door behind him, Maimon tore off his shirt, and then Elize's blouse and brassiere. Kissing her passionately first on her mouth, then on her neck and breasts, and back on her mouth, he pulled off her undergarments, lifted her onto the table, and then they were together. It was not the Maimon Elize knew. He was strong and it hurt her a little, but he never said anything. Not a word.

When he was finished, he lifted Elize onto the bed, removed her skirt, and then they " did love" again. This time it was slow and deep, and it took much longer, and at the end they were both perspiring, and kissing each other over and over, and Maimon was squeezing her breasts, and Elize was digging her nails into Maimon's back, and then the fireworks, and then it was over. Not a word had been said by either of them.

"What was that all about?" Elize asked, rolling onto her back, her legs still apart.

"I just bought an iron mountain," Maimon said by way of explanation.

"Would you please buy another one tomorrow?" she asked, smiling. Maimon was too tired to answer.

Maimon had to make two trips that he could combine into one. He needed to secure coal for his steel mill, and peanuts and sunflower seeds for his crushing plants. He had heard that there was an extremely successful coal miner in the southern part of Transvaal by the name of "Cracker" Biermann, and Maimon went to visit him.

Mr. Biermann was famous for his frequently used four-letter words to illustrate his points, and while keen to sell Maimon his coal, queried whether it was coking coal or steam coal that was required. Maimon didn't know, was honest enough to say so, and was told to "Get the fuck out of here, and don't come back till you know what the fuck you need for Oom Paul's steel factory.'"

Other people might have been upset by this response – Maimon wasn't, and on turning to leave was told to "Sit the fuck down so we can have a drink together." A drink turned into a bottle. The following morning found Maimon fast asleep on the floor of Mr. Biermann's office, with his host nowhere in sight. One of Mr. Biermann's natives brought Maimon a cup of black coffee and a plate of eggs, baked beans, boerewors,[89] bacon, and grilled tomato, all of which Maimon gratefully ate and felt better for doing so.

His horse had been fed and stabled, and was in better shape than it's rider, as Maimon trotted down the road to Leon Hirsch's farm. Jewish like Biermann, Leon couldn't have been more different. He introduced Maimon to his wife, Shoshana, and twin girls, Rifka and Leah, who were about the same age as Adam. It transpired that Shoshana Hirsch, nee Susannah du Preez, had been converted to Judaism by Rabbi Hertz, and would very much like to meet Elize.

The business part of his trip was quickly concluded when Leon told Maimon that most contracts with farmers weren't worth the paper they were written on, and that he would get as many peanuts and sunflowers as he needed as long as he paid market prices for them. Leon had to be in Johannesburg the following week, and it was agreed that the Hirschs would spend the Sabbath with the Sokolovskis at the hotel. Maimon slept in a bed, as opposed to the floor the night before, and while his breakfast was wholesome, it didn't have bacon. Refreshed, Maimon set off for home.

On his arrival Maimon was told that his wedding was set for Friday afternoon, and that it would be a good idea if he bought a new suit for the occasion. For the first time he felt bad that his parents would not be present, as neither would Piet. That night when Adam was asleep, he told Elize and Magda, "Piet saved my life, which I will never forget." He concentrated now solely on Elize. "More than that, not only did we work well together, but he gave me permission to marry you." Turning to Magda, he said, "Can you tell me about him, please?"

"He was a good man," Magda began, her hands folded in her lap, as was her habit when she had something important to say. "He didn't have an easy life. The house that that he grew up in was not a happy one. His

---

89   *Farmer's sausage*

father had a drink problem, and used to beat Piet's mother when he was drunk. Piet tried to shield her, and so he got beaten, too. One day he beat her so much she lost a baby, and after that she never fell pregnant again. Later he was killed in a shooting accident. Piet waited for his sisters to get married before we did."

Magda stopped and smiled. "We were happy in the beginning. And then first came the drought, and after that the rinderpest. Willem was not an easy baby. He used to cry a lot, which upset Piet. When he was older, he behaved very badly. Piet said I never had time for him because I was always looking after Willem. And then Elize was born. She was an easy baby, like Adam is, and Piet loved her so much. She used to go and sit on his lap in the evenings, and he would tell her stories that he made up, about dragons and princesses. If only he could have seen her in that white wedding dress…" Magda stopped to compose herself, and then said, "Perhaps he can."

First Elize and then Maimon gave Magda a hug.

"Tell me about your family, please," Maimon asked Magda, whose hands were back on her lap.

Magda looked at Elize, who said, "It is alright. Maimon is our family."

"My father, Denys, was a dreamer. He was so clever and could do so many things. He wrote poetry and told stories and was a philosopher. He didn't agree with the church. He wasn't a dopper,[90] and said the church had God all wrong. He didn't think it was right that natives shouldn't come to church. That caused a big problem for the dominee. My mother was the same. I was told that at their wedding Oupa said her feet were firmly planted in the clouds. They were so happy together, and so was I growing up. My next sister, Lucinda, was like my parents. She was an artist, and went off to France with a man. My youngest sister was an angel, like Elize, but she died young, from one of the diseases going around. I think Oupa gave my parents money, because my father didn't work, or do any work that brought an income. We were not rich, but there was always food on the table."

Magda paused for a moment, and then continued, "I have had two lives, BM and AM. I don't know why the Lord sent us Maimon, but there is a reason, a good reason, I am sure. I just wish He would tell us what it is."

---

90   *The most conservative of the three Afrikaans Protestant churches*

Maimon went and sat in front of Magda, took her hands in his, and said, "On the boat from Hamburg, the wrong boat I got on –"

"How can you say that!" Elize shot in. "What right have you got to do so! If you got on the wrong boat, where would Dilip's, or Tulip's, or whatever-his-name-is son be now? On the way to Edinburgh? Certainly not! And those ladies and children in the Heilbron camp with new dresses and shoes! What would they be wearing? And Adam! He wouldn't exist! And you have the gall to say you got on the wrong boat! How dare you!"

Maimon had stood up to defend his position when Elize began her tirade, but now he saw facing him a woman with fire in her eyes, who was pleading not for herself, but for those who had no voice to do so. Getting on his haunches in front of Magda, he said to her, "I am eternally grateful for two things. Firstly, that you gave birth to the wonderful woman who has agreed to become my wife. And secondly, that the good Lord, in His wisdom, put her right in front of me, so that even an idiot like me could not have missed her." After a pause, he added, "The good Lord, possibly not in His wisdom, gave me a sense of humour appreciated by few others."

Elize turned to her mother, and said, "He does this to me all the time, and it drives me mad."

To which Magda responded, "None of us is perfect. Not even you, my daughter."

Not being able to read or write, Maimon had learned of necessity to make mental to-do lists, and this was one of those occasions. In order of doing them: he had to tighten the security at the hotel. Now that he owned it, or almost all of it, he had to be sure that his two managers were not feeding their families out of the kitchen, or that Ravi didn't have a thriving retail liquor business on the side. Then he had to get married; and after that see the President about the steel mill; and finally get on a boat for Europe.

Later that evening they were lying in bed, Elize painting her nails and Maimon looking at drawings of a steel-making blast furnace.

"Have you thought about a honeymoon?" Maimon asked in a matter-of- fact way, wondering what temperature was required to melt his iron ore.

"Not really," Elize lied.

"I have," Maimon said, studying a drawing of the furnace's inlet air ducts.

"What are your thoughts?" Elize said, painting one of her knuckles in excitement.

"I am not sure," Maimon replied. "Either a weekend in Nylstroom, or a trip to London and Stratford-upon-Avon."

"Nylstroom has an advantage," Elize pointed out, now joining in the fun. "It is a lot closer than London. Pity they are having a war there."

"London it is then. Have you seen these ceramic bricks?" he said, showing Elize a picture of the furnace's refractory lining. "It is amazing how efficient they are."

Elize grabbed the book Maimon was reading and threw it as far away as she could. Then she kissed him passionately.

"When do we leave?" Elize asked.

"Next year," Maimon replied. Then, seeing Elize's disappointment, "Next Jewish year."

He didn't see the pillow that came crashing down on his head.

Next morning found Maimon in Edward's office, discussing their security issue at the hotel.

"There are two issues," Edward said. "Cooking the books and stealing the stock. I have an answer to the first one, but not the second."

"What is your answer to the first one?" Maimon asked, having an idea how to handle the second.

"Ravi and Dilip are Hindus. They are hated by the Ishmaelites, another tribe in India. If we employ two Ishmaelites and promise them ten percent of all the money they save us, the stove that has been cooking the books will disappear. I don't know what to do about physical theft, though."

Remembering the Zulu impis, Maimon suggested they employ a team of them who be given the monetary value equal to ten percent of any stock they found leaving the premises. Having no Zulu impi experience, Edward was happy to accept Maimon's suggestion.

Half an hour later, Maimon was explaining these new developments to Ravi and Dilip, both of whom protested their honesty and told Maimon that employing the Ishmaelites and Zulus was a complete waste of money. A month later, having the figures read out to him by Edward, Maimon found that the annual salaries of the eight extra employees was about twenty percent of the money they had already saved the two new hotel owners.

This task completed in less than a morning, Maimon had time, with a full day's ride, to reach Pretoria before nightfall, which enabled him to be fresh for his Tuesday-morning meetings. Compared to the wheat and flour contract discussions, the steel ones proved extremely difficult. Jan Smuts was as sharp as a bag of razorblades, and twice Maimon was on the point of calling off the negotiations. Only the fact that he owned the iron mountain kept him at the negotiating table, something he suspected Jan Smuts knew.

In the end they agreed on terms which made no sense to Maimon. He would supply steel to the Transvaal Republic for fifteen years at cost plus 72.5%, after which the plant would belong to the government, with Maimon having the first option to buy it back. What Maimon realized, and he suspected Jan Smuts didn't, is that all machinery needs to be regularly maintained and serviced; and if Maimon knew that after fifteen years the plant wouldn't be his, he would run it into the ground during the last twenty-four months of the contract. Fifteen years was a long time, Maimon thought, as he and Jan Smuts signed the contract.

For sentimental reasons, Maimon said he would like the President to also sign, which he not only did, but additionally came out to find out about Elize's health. It was the last time they were to meet, which perhaps the President realized, as he said to Maimon, "Look after our country. I am relying on you and Sammy to do so."

On the way back to Johannesburg, Maimon overnighted at Halfway House, so that he arrived back in Johannesburg on Wednesday afternoon. Had he known that wedding fever had broken out, he would have delayed his return until Friday morning – but it was too late for that, and as his contribution he agreed with everything Elize said, and to everything she wanted. That helped keep the temperature down to what it was on the surface of the sun, but in due course Friday afternoon arrived, as did Elize and her mother, both of whom looked stunning.

The wedding itself was not like any of the ones Maimon had attended in Saratov. No drinking glass was broken,[91] no drunk Charedim[92] danced and sang, and not only was there not too much food, there was no food at all. This was to be expected in the magistrate's office where the contract was signed. Edward walked Elize into the office, where Maimon was waiting for her, and while all brides are beautiful, Elize was especially so. A hairdresser had tied her hair with flowers at the top of her head,

91   At the conclusion of a Jewish wedding ceremony, a drinking glass is stamped on
      by the bridegroom
92   Ultra-orthodox members of the Jewish community

which, from an engineering point of view, Maimon conceded was quite a feat.

The small party, which included Leon and Shoshana, who happened to be in town, then went back to the hotel, where, much to Maimon's surprise, they were joined for drinks by Hermann Ekstein, Alfred Beit and his brother Otto, Julius Wernher, Isaac Lewis, and George Albu. Even Barney Barnato popped in for a few minutes, during which time an outsider would have thought it was his wedding.

Maimon made a brief speech, leaving out the rabbinical quote he had included in his last wedding address, largely because Elize promised to divorce him if he did so.

Edward said a few words, and Barney Barnato said many, all of which were humorous. Then the uninvited guests left, and the rest sat down to a four-course dinner, which took longer that Maimon would have liked – its length due to the production of the wedding cake, the third version of which was wheeled out with candles lit and sparklers blazing.

Later that night Leon and Maimon sat down together, making good in roads into a bottle of whiskey on the table between them.

"You should come to my meeting with Meir tomorrow morning. He is helping me buy some land in Palestine," Leon told him.

"Why on earth are you doing that? From what I hear, it is all stones – and what isn't stones is swamps."

"Because it will be a country, *our* country, this century, and it won't be a nebbish country, either," Leon told Maimon confidently.

"I know we have been praying for it for 2,000 years, but why should it happen in this century?" Maimon asked, constraining himself from making fun of his relatively new friend.

"I have been in touch with Max Nordau and his friend Theodor Herzl," Leon told him, as if that would answer any further questions Maimon might have. Maimon did have one or two more.

"Isn't Palestine part of the Ottoman Empire?" he asked; and then he couldn't stop himself, adding, "Is Joshua going to come back and blow his horns?"

"You are a young man. You have to look to the future," Leon told him.

"And what does that mean?" Maimon answered, losing interest in the subject.

"This country is finished." Leon told him.

"Finished?" Maimon asked, pushing the alcohol haze clouding his mind to one side.

"The natives are going to run it, and they are not trained to do so, and they will mess it up," Leon explained.

"And the Boers are going to hand it over?" Maimon asked, waiting for the answer to this question.

"How many Boers are there in the Transvaal and the Orange Free State? I don't know, but let's say 100,000, certainly less than 200,000. And how many natives? Probably a million, if not more."

"That is the answer to my question?" Maimon asked.

Leon smiled as if talking to a child. "It took the British ten years to win the Kaffir Wars, and they had guns and the natives didn't."

"And the Boers are going to hand over their two countries that they have fought first the animals, then the natives, and finally the British for?" Maimon asked, not sure if his friend was mad or farsighted.

"If they are smart, they will; otherwise there will be a lot of blood spilt, and I don't want my children or grandchildren to be here for it," Leon explained.

"And what about the gold and diamonds?" Maimon asked, feeling that if Leon's theories were far-fetched, they were in fact logical.

"Either they will be exhausted by then, or the natives will take them," Leon said, reverting to his childlike-explanation tone.

"And the Cape Province and Natal?" Maimon asked, feeling he was pulling a rabbit out of the hat.

"Too many natives," Leon explained patiently. "The Zulus in Natal and the Xhosa in the Cape Province."

"And that is why you are leaving the country?" Maimon asked, now seeing the logic of it.

"Largely. But it is why you should come to my meeting with Meir tomorrow morning. Nine o'clock here in the bar," Leon said, pouring the last tots into his glass and Maimon's.

Maimon went up to his room, where he found Elize in the most alluring night attire, her hair still up in the construction that Maimon had admired earlier.

Seeing him hang the "DO NOT DISTURB" note on the door, Elize undid the three uppermost buttons on the top half of the piece of clothing she was wearing, whose name Maimon did not know.

"We need to talk," Maimon told Elize, taking off his shirt and tie and slipping out of his trousers. Kicking off his shoes and throwing his socks after them, Maimon lay down next to Elize.

"We can talk later," Elize told him, caressing, and alternatively kissing, his chest.

"Later we will be too tired," Maimon told her.

"I hope so," Elize said dreamily.

Maimon got up from the bed and went and sat in a chair.

"Elize, listen to me," Maimon instructed her in a voice that she knew was serious. "Why did the British win the Kaffir Wars? I want just one answer." When one wasn't forthcoming, he told her, "Because the British had guns and the natives didn't. And why are we living safely here in the Transvaal? Because the Boers – and, in a small way, the police – have guns, and the natives don't."

"What is your point?" Elize asked, annoyed they were having to discuss this on their wedding night.

"When the natives get guns, then we will have to leave."

Unable to imagine that the natives in the Transvaal and Orange Free State would ever have guns, Elize said, "Fine. Now come to bed."

Moving from his chair, Maimon said, "I have a meeting with a man from Palestine at nine tomorrow morning here in the hotel. I would like you to attend it."

This was the first business meeting at which Maimon had ever asked her to join him, and Elize thought it was because she was now married to him.

"With pleasure," she replied. "What is the subject?"

"A property investment," Maimon told her, undoing the rest of the buttons on Elize's top.

CHAPTER 24

BUYING SAND DUNES

To Elize's surprise, Leon was also at the meeting but not Shashona. A few minutes later, Meir, the man from Palestine, arrived and Leon introduced him to Maimon and Elize. Stockily built, in his forties, Meir wore an open-necked shirt, shorts, and sandals, which surprised Elize as she thought people who attended business meetings were more formally dressed. Meier gave Leon some papers to sign, which he did, handing half of them back to Meir, who put them in his briefcase. Turning to Maimon, Meier said in Yiddish, "Dos iz a sexi meydl,"[93] to which Elize replied, "Danken dir."[94]

Embarrassed, Meir immediately switched to English.

"You are looking for a large holding, I understand," Meier said to Maimon. "The only large piece I have left is two hectares for £100,000 at Zichron Ya'akov."

"Thank you, Meir," Maimon said, getting to his feet. "If my wife and I are going to pay New York prices, we would rather buy in New York." Elize smiled at Meir, to whom she had taken an instant dislike, and stood up as well.

"No need to rush away," Meir said hastily, "There is another wonderful property, on the seashore, eighteen miles long, from Tel Aviv to Netanya that I can highly recommend," Meier told Maimon.

"Not exactly on the seashore. I understand that is not for sale," Maimon replied.

"That is correct, sir," Meier replied, impressed (albeit annoyed) by the

---

93 *That is a sexy girl*
94 *Thank you*

young man's knowledge. "From the high water mark no property can be sold for 70 yards, but after that, it is yours. Eight hundred yards wide and eighteen miles long. That is irreplaceable."

"And the price, Meier?" Maimon asked.

"It could be yours for £20,000."

"The price is preposterous for some miles of sand dunes, but I need to discuss with my wife if we want these sand flies or not," Maimon said, getting to his feet and helping Elize to hers, and then escorting her to the end of the otherwise deserted bar.

"I have no idea what that beach is worth," Elize was quick to tell Maimon.

"I don't, either, but it is important that they see us in earnest conversation. How would you compare last night's doing love with last week's?" Maimon asked Elize calmly, with a mischievous expression on his face.

"I don't keep a record of enjoyment in bed with you," she told him earnestly.

"Perhaps you should, then I can compare it with Zelda's chart." Maimon knew that would set Elize off, and it immediately did.

"Calm down," Maimon told Elize, shepherding his wife back to the anxious Meier.

"I am sorry that my wife says there are enough sand flies in Kommetjie.[95] She doesn't need to go to Palestine to get bitten by more."

"But we have no sand flies in Palestine," Meier protested.

"I told her that, but she is adamant," Maimon told Meier. "She would be interested in three acres in the German Quarter in Jerusalem, in which case she said I could buy my sand dunes."

"Whose money is it, exactly?" Meier asked, this new information being contrary to what Leon had told him.

"It is the Almighty's," Maimon explained to Meier, "and he said it would be alright to spend £5,000 on these two pieces of land."

"He told you this himself?" Meier asked, now getting quite aggravated.

"In a dream last night." Maimon replied, not upset that it was Meir who was now on the back foot.

By way of a reply Meir said, "Mr. ..."

"Sokolovski," Maimon informed him.

---

95   *A seaside resort near Cape Town infested with sand flies*

"Mr. Sokolovski, I have negotiated with Jews in Paris and London and New York, but you are the smartest I have come across. You can have those properties for £5,000, provided you, or your children, or your grandchildren spend at least six months a year in one of them for any five years out of ten. If they don't, we get them both back and we keep your money."

"You are not such a slouch yourself, Meir," Maimon said, shaking his hand firmly. "What did you say your family name was?"

"Dizengoff," he was told.

Walking back to their room, Elize said, squeezing Maimon's hand, "You are a genius. An absolute genius."

"Where did you learn that Yiddish?" Maimon asked her, curious to know.

"Shoshana has a book of it that she lent me. It isn't a very difficult language," she told Maimon.

"As long as you don't have to read it. By the way, let me have a look at your chart when you have a minute?" Maimon asked, confident that it would set Elize off again. It didn't, but it did earn him a spank on the bottom.

CHAPTER 25

THE FIRE

The next few weeks were busy, but not frenetic, with Maimon attending to various business matters, and Elize furnishing the house they had rented in Doornfontein, as well as researching what there was for Adam to do during their absence. As a result of the war, the hotel's bar sales were down by about half, but Maimon and Edward could survive on that, and the arrival of the British troops in Johannesburg reminded everyone that the war was not going to last forever. Fortunately, many of the British soldiers drank heavily, and more than a few of the rooms were occupied by British officers, sometimes together with their pre-war daytime occupants, and at other times without them. Then disaster struck.

One night three soldiers got into a fight, during which they knocked over a paraffin lamp that set some curtains alight. With other soldiers (and some civilians) either joining in the fight or watching it, nobody noticed the rapidly spreading fire. When they did, the fire department was alerted, but by the time their wagon arrived, most of the building was ablaze. Old hands agreed it was the biggest fire Johannesburg had ever seen, and even with their modern high-power hoses, the fire department could not prevent the fire engulfing the whole hotel.

Maimon was reading a story to Adam when Paulina, the native that Elize employed to help her in the house, knocked on the door. Unusually she came in without being asked to. Quickly she said, "Master, there is a very big fire in the city."

Maimon looked out of the window, and even from as far away as Doornfontein, he could see the flames licking up. Kissing Adam goodnight, he asked Alpheus, his Man Friday, to saddle his horse, while he told Elize, who was comparing one fabric with another for their living room curtains, that he was going into town and would be back later.

Riding up Bree Street, Maimon saw that the fire was not only very big, but was quite close to their hotel. He spurred his horse on until, turning into Eloff Street, his worst fears were realized. It was the Hights Hotel that was burning fiercely.

Maimon stood watching the blaze, with the same feeling in the pit of his stomach that he had felt the morning he rode away from Elize's parents' farm. In a daze he spent the next hour watching the blaze from one vantage point or another. At one stage he heard the gas cylinders explode, and at another saw the bar, with all its spirits, burn spectacularly. The hotel that had been his home was now just a pile of ashes, with the odd metal rod sticking out here and there. It was then Maimon felt an arm round his shoulder.

"There is nothing more to do here. Come to my office in the morning, and then we will go and see the insurance company."

It was Edward Nathan, who then led a dazed Maimon back to their horses that they had left in President Street.

"I know it is tough, but after all it was only a building," Edward reassured Maimon. "Another, better one can be put up in its place with the £2,000 we will get from the insurance company."

Two thousand pounds was a new figure for Maimon. Everything always started with a one. They bought the hotel for £1700. They borrowed £1,200 pounds. Where did the two come from?

"Why £2,000?" Maimon asked, never having heard that figure.

"I added in £300 for loss of profits while a new hotel was being built."

"You knew it was going to burn down?" Maimon asked incredulously.

"Of course not. But one day it would need to be replaced, and this is as good a time as ever. The builders don't have much work, and business is generally slow. When the war is over, Johannesburg will be booming, and having the hotel ready will be a bonanza."

They agreed on a time to meet in the morning; then Edward wished Maimon good night and peeled off to his house in Siemert Road.

The more Maimon thought about it, the more of what Edward had said made sense, so that by the time he arrived at their rental house, he was positively jubilant.

"Good news," he told Elize "the hotel burnt down."

"Our hotel, The Hights?" Elize asked fearfully.

"That's the one."

"I am sorry, but I must be very stupid. You and Edward bought a hotel. It burns down and you two are happy. Why is that?"

"Because Edward insured it for loss of profits. If the hotel isn't there, and we can't make profits on it, the insurance company will pay us out," Maimon explained.

"Really?" Elize asked, not believing this was actually going to happen and now feeling thoroughly ignorant about the ways of the business world. "Apparently so, according to Edward."

"I bet you they won't pay. I want them to, of course, but they never will," Elize said confidently.

"I'll take that bet," Maimon answered. "What are the odds?"

"If I win, you can give me one of Zelda's lessons," Elize answered mischievously.

"And if I win?" Maimon replied, interested to hear what Elize would come up with.

"I will wash your feet, like they used to do in the Bible."

The next morning, after a good night's sleep, Maimon was feeling happily confident that he and Edward would soon own the most modern hotel in Africa. In fact, walking up President Street to the offices of South Britannic Assurance Company, he felt better than he had for months.

Judging by the speed at which they were shown into the manager's office, Edward was obviously an important client of the assurance company. Behind the biggest, and surely the heaviest, desk that Maimon had ever seen, sat an Englishman not dissimilar to the manager of Prestige Mills, whose name Maimon had temporarily forgotten. Of average height, with a well-waxed moustache, a bright red bow tie, and a stomach that arrived wherever he was going some time before the rest of him, sat Mr. Campbell-Hawthorn.

"Terribly sorry to hear about the hotel, old man." he said, addressing Maimon, who had never been called "old man" before but realized it must be an English custom.

"It was really fortunate that no one was killed or even hurt," Edward remarked, thinking that the only hurt would be borne by the shareholders of the South Britannic Assurance Company. Taking the policy out of his pocket, Edward added, "If we could have the check today, that would be appreciated."

"I am afraid there won't be a check today, or any other day, old fellow," the Englishman said almost offhandedly.

"Why is that?" Edward asked, not believing what he had heard.

"Because I was told that the fire was a result of a fight by three British soldiers."

Maimon sat astounded and speechless, his head turning between the Englishman and Edward.

"What difference would that make?" Edward asked incredulously.

"A very great difference" the Englishman said, "because it was an act of war. Acts of War are excluded from the policy. If you look at clause 23.7, section 7b, you will find this is the case."

"Mr. Campbell-Hawthorn, you are not going to tell me that you consider a fight by three off-duty soldiers at ten o'clock at night an act of war?" Edward asked in a tone of biting sarcasm.

"Not only do I do so, but so did our Johannesburg claims department, and so, I am sure, will our Claims Committee in London, when they read my report," the Englishman replied as if he was discussing the declaration by the captain of a cricket team.

Edward put the policy back in his pocket, and standing up said scathingly, "I suspect my client's religion might have been a factor your company considered."

"Off the record, I won't deny that that might have been one of the aspects we took into account," the insurance man conceded. "Out of my hands. Entirely out of my hands."

Edward and Maimon stood up, refused to shake the Englishman's proffered hand, and walking across the Persian carpet to the door of his office, and heard "Sorry, old chap" as they exited into the company's general office, where about ten white male clerks were quietly working.

Out on the street Maimon and Edward looked at each other in silence. Eventually it was Edward who spoke. "I really am sorry, so very, very sorry." Then taking Maimon by the arm, Edward led him away from the building. "There is a way that you can get your money from these mumzerim, and much more in addition," Edward said, and in the next few minutes explained to Maimon how this might be done.

"Fine," Maimon declared, "Let's call it Operation Den of Thieves."

"So be it," Edward said. "ODOT, for short."

Back at the hotel Maimon told Elize, "It is good news and bad news."

"I won the bet and get a Zelda lesson."

"How did you know that?" Maimon asked, thinking that no one could have told her about the meeting.

"Because that is the only 'good news, bad news' outcome. Now tell me, teacher, when do I get the lesson?"

CHAPTER 26

ONE BIG GREEN AND TWO BIGGER
WHITE LIZARDS

The remaining item on Maimon's mental "to do" list was a visit to Europe to meet the wheat-mill magnate, Arthur Rank, and the steel-maker Henry Bessemer. As neither of these get-togethers were urgent, Maimon decided to first go and see the iron mountain he had bought.

It was spring, before the summer heat beat down and the rains set in. The grass was low so hunting for the pot would be easy, and Maimon organized the trip down to the last pillow and pineapple. Half-a-dozen mounted natives carried everything they could possibly need except firewood, Maimon having organized what could best be described as a luxurious adventure.

Elize asked to come along, which initially Maimon refused. Then she said Magda would look after Adam, and if he loved her, he would find a place for her. Three days later, the two of them set out riding ahead of the column. Maimon said it reminded him of the cartoons he saw of African explorers, followed by a line of bearers with luggage and pots and pans on their heads. Elize, a little embarrassed by the comparison, said everybody was riding a horse and no one had anything on their heads, except Maimon, who was wearing a veld hat. Maimon let it go.

Their first night was spent at the Halfway House Hotel, where, by coincidence, Jan and Issie Smuts were also dining. Maimon introduced Elize to the famous Boer general and his wife, little did either of the men realize when, and under what circumstances, they would meet again.

Taking it leisurely, they slept at The European Hotel in Pretoria the next night, when Elize said the city would always give her a thrill because of her meeting with the President and his wife.

The following night, near Nylstroom (named by the early Boer trekkers who thought they had discovered the source of the river Nile), Maimon got a taste of what organized camping had in store for them. No sooner was the spot chosen than a big fire lit, allegedly to keep the lions away. Two canvas folding chairs were put some yards away from it, where Maimon was brought a whiskey and ice. Elize ordered a gin and tonic – her very first, it transpired – after which a discussion took place with the barman whether it was legal to serve spirits to an underage woman outside municipal limits. The three of them agreed it was. Seeing how Elize behaved for the rest of the evening, the two men felt that her next drink should be left for a year or so.

The cook shoveled some red-hot cinders from the fire, and behind Maimon and Elize, cooked some boerewors, lamb chops, tomatoes, and mielie samp, the last of which Elize was happy with, and Maimon less so. Fresh apples and pears ended the meal.

The mixed smells of the bush, combined with smoke from the fire cooking the supper, was new to Maimon. The fires he made on his trip from East London to the du Toit's farm were small and extinguished as soon as his food showed signs of being partially cooked. Together with Elize he watched the sparks dance up and then disappear.

Contrary to his expectations, he liked being in the veld with the wide range of natural smells. They hadn't seen a lot of game but that wasn't important. Here he was away from Sol, the insurance company manager who wouldn't pay him out; J.B. Robinson, who was still trying to nullify his Thabazimbi purchase; Jan Smuts, who might want to cancel his government contracts; and the police, always the police, who Maimon knew might pounce any day. As long as Mr. or Mrs. Vagalparot was alive, there was a chance this would happen. Here he was free of these worries, all of them. As if a load had been lifted from his shoulders, Maimon reached across to hold Elize's hand, which gripped his tightly.

"Don't you love it here?" Maimon asked, the only nearby noise being the natives quietly chatting over their supper. In the far distance a lion roared.

"No, I am scared," Elize replied, the tone of her voice confirming the meaning of those three words.

"Scared of what?" Maimon asked, wondering what there was to be scared of.

"The animals," Elize answered.

"You are a farm girl. You lived among the animals. That is how you grew up," Maimon reminded her.

"Except for some field mice in the house, the only animals I ever saw were dead ones. Those that my father and Willem had shot out hunting, and which they brought home to braai or to make into biltong,"[96] Elize explained. "Please look after me?"

"Of course I will," Maimon reassured her.

"Can we go to bed now?" Elize asked plaintively.

"We?" Maimon said, now understanding how petrified she was. "Yes. Will you come with me? Please. Now."

"With pleasure," Maimon said, rising to his feet, Elize not letting go of his hand.

Only in bed, with Elize gripping tightly onto Maimon during every one of her waking minutes, did he realize the depth of her fear.

On their second night in the bush, the natives erected the tents on the bank of one of the rivers that hadn't dried up in the winter, which afforded Maimon and Elize wonderful sightings of the animals as they made their way down to the water. Most of the time, Maimon sat in the folding canvas chair and Elize stood behind him, her hands firmly planted on his shoulders. It was such a beautiful spot that they decided to delay their departure to eleven o'clock the following morning. Maimon expected a steady stream of animals would come down to the water the following day, and he was not disappointed.

When the heat of the day drove all the animals away from the river, looking for shade, and the caravan was saddled up ready to go, Maimon told the natives to wait under an acacia tree about 75 yards from the river. Taking Elize by the hand, he led her down to the rocks on the river bank, where he took off all his clothes.

"What on earth are you doing?" Elize asked, remembering he was Russian and half-expecting some form of weird behavior that she hadn't yet witnessed.

---

96   *Dried cured meat usually from wild antelope*

"Kaalgat[97] swimming," Maimon answered, remembering one of the words he had learned at the du Toit's farm that he hadn't had much opportunity to use since then.

"I sent the natives away so they can't see us, and put two towels on the thorn bush over there. There are no crocks or hippos here, so come in," he said and jumped into the pool.

"I can't swim," Elize protested, a little envious of Maimon, who was standing chest-deep in the water, looking much cooler than she was feeling.

"You don't have to," Maimon called up. "I will save you."

That was all the encouragement Elize needed before stripping off her clothes and executing the most inelegant water entry probably ever seen in Africa up to that time. It was aimed into Maimon's arms, more or less accurately, with him ducking out of the way at the last moment.

"I can see how cold it is." Elize said, looking down.

"It conforms with Einstein's fifth law of thermodynamics," Maimon explained.

They splashed about for ten minutes, and then got out and sunned themselves on the rocks like big white lizards.

"You told me Einstein only had four laws of thermodynamics. When did he invent the fifth one?" Elize said, soaking up the warming rays of the sun.

"Last year. It's formulae is $tA(ot)D \propto tH(ot)M$. Allegedly he worked it out in bed one night."

"Do you think he enjoys doing these calculations?" Elize asked seriously.

"I am sure he does," Maimon replied, smiling to himself.

When dry, they dressed.

Arriving in time to see the iron mountain with the late-afternoon sun glinting on its ferrous rocks, they both agreed it was spectacular. It was as if God, or whoever, had stuck this giant arm of iron in the ground, waiting for man to come and mine it.

Maimon and Elize viewed the mountain of iron ore differently. To Elize it was one of God's wonders, created millions of years ago when the planet was mostly volcanoes. Maimon saw it commercially. Realizing that in order to bring the mine into production, it would be necessary to develop an infrastructure incorporating a power supply and

97   *Naked*

232

sufficient water, both to work the mine and also to supply the inhabitants of the town he would have to build to house both the white workers and also the natives. The town would need not only power and running water, but also a school and a hospital, and probably other requirements he hadn't thought of. All this would cost a lot of money, more than he had. One way or another he needed a partner with deep pockets.

The weather on the trip back to Johannesburg was hotter than on the way out, and so they broke camp every morning at five a.m., and usually arrived at their next overnight resting place at about three in the afternoon. The natives erected the tents on arrival, and Maimon and Elize flopped down on their camp beds, exhausted after nine hours in the saddle.

One such afternoon, Elize squeezed Maimon's arm to wake him.

"There is a crocodile about to eat us!" her voice betraying how petrified she was. Maimon knew whatever had frightened Elize, it certainly wasn't a crocodile. Looking over the edge of his bed, he saw a giant monitor lizard sunning itself on a rock outside their tent.

Having done a good job of calming Elize down, mainly by pointing out the size of the lizard – about three feet compared to her 5'6" – and that it posed no threat to either of them as it didn't eat people, Maimon looked up and saw a poisonous boomslang[98] in the rigging of their tent. With Elize's eyes firmly fixed on the lizard, Maimon slowly got off the bed, exited through the back of the tent, returning with a long fork-ended stick. Now for the hardest part, which, he realized, was to persuade Elize to get off her bed so that if the snake fell, it didn't do so on her.

It wasn't easy, but mentioning the snake did the trick. Seconds later the snake was coiled round the stick, which Maimon threw into the large donga[99] behind their tent. During this activity, the lizard disappeared, and Elize developed an acute thirst for a gin and tonic. Maimon had a double whiskey, in the absence of ice, "straight- up" as the Americans termed it.

The longer they spent in the bush, the more relaxed Elize became about the wildlife. To Maimon's pleasant surprise, Elize wanted to get a better view of a kudu family that were 80 yards away, and stopped to take in the beauty of an impala herd that were grazing all around them.

---

98   *Snake*

99   *A dry gully formed by the action of running water*

She did have to be told that black rhinos didn't always have a good attitude to people and should not be approached, neither on foot nor on horseback.

There was a matter that had been troubling Elize since they left Johannesburg, and unable to resolve it herself, she asked Maimon for his opinion.

"Leon said that one day the natives will all have guns and that they would shoot all the whites. Do you believe that?" Elize asked.

"That wasn't quite the way he put it. What he said, and I agree with, is that the Boers took the land from the natives, and one day the Boers will have to give it back to them."

"First of all, I think you are both mad. Secondly the Boers are much better marksmen than the natives," Elize pointed out.

"You may be right on both points, but don't overlook that there are millions more natives than there are white people," Maimon explained.

"And what will happen to the whites, the ones that don't get killed in the fight?" Elize asked.

"They will live under the natives, like they live under us now; or they will leave."

"Leave? Where will they go?" Elize asked, not believing what she was hearing.

"Wherever things are better. We Jews have been doing it for generations," Maimon explained quietly.

"I am not going anywhere," Elize announced firmly. "I was born here. My parents were born here. Where would I go? Unlike you, I don't speak a dozen languages."

"I don't think you will have to go anywhere, and maybe not your children, either, but your grandchildren probably will," Maimon told her.

"I won't be around to see that, I am happy to say," Elize said, sounding somewhat relieved.

"It will be a different world. People will fly to London for the weekend. Man will go to the moon. Doctors will swap your old heart for a new one. Many people will live to be a 100," Maimon told her, warming to the subject.

"And we will live under the natives," Elize reminded Maimon, to which he nodded affirmatively. "You are mad. Completely mad."

On their return, Elize cross-examined her mother on what she had done with Adam every waking hour she and Maimon had been away.

Maimon suggested giving Adam the impala and buffalo heads the natives had shot for the pot, which Elize vetoed.

CHAPTER 27

MID-ATLANTIC RICE CONTRACT

The week they spent in Johannesburg before catching the train to Cape Town was extremely busy. Elize was buying summer clothes, not only for Magda and Adam but also for herself, as Maimon had told her that for about seven-to-ten days it would be unbearably hot on the ship.

Maimon had some meetings with Edward, who said that their ODOT project was on track, and while it was only in its embryonic stage, he was confident it would grow significantly. Alfred gave Maimon letters of introduction to Rothschild's London office, and also to Baring Brothers, another prestigious London merchant bank.

Before they knew it, the four of them were on the platform next to the train that was to take Elize on the greatest adventure of her life. While Maimon and Adam walked up the platform to look at the locomotive, Elize gave her mother last-minute instructions. Adam declined the offer to stand in the cab next to the train driver – after all, he was only three years old; but he did peek into the firebox and asked if it wasn't going to make the train burn down. Then back to their compartment, final hugs and kisses, a blast on the train's whistle, and it slowly pulled out of the station, with waves from Elize and Magda and wonderment from Adam.

The train stopped at Jeppe Station, and then speeded up for its fast-as-possible run to Bloemfontein. Looking at Elize, her nose glued to the window, taking in sights so new to her, Maimon's mind went back to his last train journey. In less than five years he had come from abject poverty to an undreamt-of degree of wealth. Here he was, in a first-class compartment, exclusively for him and Elize, with padded seats, and under the middle window, a basin with hot and cold water. Above them, two bunks which were later made into beds with sheets, blankets, and pillows.

If only Frieda could see this, Maimon wished, it would have vindicated her "God's wish."

"Aren't you excited?" Elize asked like a school child on her first excursion. Before waiting for an answer, she added, waving her hands expansively, "Thank you so much for all of this."

Maimon smiled, hoping this trip he was giving his wife would go a little way to reversing the debit entries he had accrued in Frieda's "God's wish" book. Before leaving they had had little time to talk about the trip. Elize knew they were going to London and to see Ann Hathaway's house, and that Maimon would be spending some time in the English "countryside," as she called it, visiting factories.

There was also the question of going to see his parents, who lived "next door to London," Elize pointed out, having looked at a map of Europe on a two-page atlas spread. In her mind there was no question at all. Trekkers, as her family were, usually looked after their parents, and in the wedding-dress shop she heard the girls next door say that Jewish people also do so.

She couldn't understand why there was even a question about it in Maimon's mind. Maimon had told Elize about the wrong-ticket episode – for which she was extremely grateful – but not how furious he was that his father had done this to him. The fact that tickets on the *America* to East London were so much cheaper than those to any other destination reinforced in Maimon's mind that this had not been a mistake. Then there was something else. Since he learned about the sperm going into a woman's body to make a baby, he realized that his problem was because of something in his father's sperm. His father didn't read or write, and so it was his fault that Maimon couldn't, either.

Dinner in the saloon car – as they learned a restaurant on a train is called – was even smarter than on the ship with the Vagalparots, which Maimon did not mention to Elize. Lots of knives and forks and spoons on each side, as well as some in front of Elize, completely flummoxed her. Following Maimon's example and working from the out inwards, it didn't seem so daunting. When the waiter brought the wine list, Maimon suggested a bottle of champagne, which elicited an unexpected response from Elize.

"That is a wonderful idea."

"Something to celebrate?" Maimon asked, a little mystified.

Elize took Maimon's hand that was on the table, squeezed it, and said, "I am pregnant," and then, in case he didn't know what that meant, "I am having a baby."

Even though he had fathered two babies already, this was the first time he was told about it before the child was born, and not knowing what was customarily said in this circumstance, Maimon blurted out, "That is wonderful," and stood up and walked round the table to give Elize a kiss.

Maimon had never knowingly been in the presence of a pregnant woman, especially one for whose condition he was responsible, and so was unaware whether to wrap Elize in cotton wool, or keep her in a bath of warm water twelve hours a day, or …

Fortunately, there was a doctor on the train who said that Elize should carry on as normal, pointing out that native woman continued working in the fields until their waters broke. Maimon was on the point of telling the doctor that Elize should not be compared with a native woman, a reaction Elize had anticipated, so she put one of her hands on his, preventing this from happening. Back in the compartment Elize pointed out that she had already had a baby, and so knew what to do. She also explained that Maimon didn't have to worry about anything for another seven months.

The boat was leaving late that afternoon, in time for Maimon to deliver a message to Sir Percy Fitzpatrick from Julius Wernher, and still check in before the gangway was raised. Waiting in line before boarding, Maimon suddenly heard, "Maimon, Maimon. Come over here."

Looking behind him he saw Cecil Rhodes.

"You must meet First Viscount Milner," Rhodes said. "He and his wife Violet Georgina are sailing with you." Maimon and Milner shook hands firmly, and then Rhodes said to Milner, "This man here is one of the few Transvaal industrialists not in the mining business. He is making steel and bread for the Burghers."

Milner said, "Call me Alfred," to which Maimon reciprocated with "Maimon."

Elize had another good surprise for Maimon, but realized this wasn't the time to give it to him.

That night the ship, handling the Cape Rollers[100] quite well, was rocking those in their beds from side to side.

"You didn't tell me about this," Elize said frightened.

"Didn't I?" Maimon asked, knowing full well that he hadn't. This was

---

100   *Ocean swells off the south coast of the Cape Colony*

a conscious decision, as he had suspected that if he did so, they would have got in to a conversation about ships sinking, which would result in Elize excusing herself from the trip. "It is nothing really," he said. "Actually, it is quite fun," he added, as Elize rolled onto him. "It should be fine from tomorrow night for about two weeks."

"And then?" Elize asked in a frightened little girl's voice.

"Then we come to the Bay of Biscay off France, which is sometimes calm and other times not, but let's enjoy the trip till then," he said, rolling over to Elize and kissing her.

They both slept till seven in the morning, when they were woken by their cabin steward with a tray of tea and a plate of biscuits. "Would Madam like me to draw a bath for her?" the steward asked.

"Yes, please," Maimon answered. "And for you, sir?"

"No, thank you," Maimon responded.

When the steward had disappeared into Elize's bathroom, Elize said to Maimon in a hoarse whisper, "I don't want a bath."

"Yes, you do," he told her quietly.

"Do I smell?" Elize asked, a little embarrassed.

"No," Maimon said firmly but softly.

The cabin steward returned and said, "That is done, sir, madam."

As soon as he had left the suite, Maimon bounded out of bed, saying to Elize, "Come and see this." To her amazement the bath water was flowing from one end of the bath to the other.

"It looks good for one, but more fun for two," Elize said, stripping. "Come on, lazybones."

The bath wasn't built for two, and so there were lots of knocked knees and elbows, but as Elize remarked, it was more fun together. They made their way down for breakfast leisurely, where they were shown to their table.

After breakfast they toured the ship, Maimon having got permission for them to go into the now empty steerage area. It was the same as the boat Maimon had sailed to East London on, and it wasn't. This boat's dormitory and dining hall had a similar layout to that of the *America*, but without people it was sterile. No shouting and arguing, and no davening.[101] No human smells, perspiration and halitosis, and at mealtimes, no unpleasant food smells. For Maimon it was a visit to the past, to his past, that he would never forget. To Elize it was like a visit to the zoo,

---

101 *Praying*

"That's nice, now let's go home."

Maimon couldn't blame her, but he did expect some empathy, and there was none. He knew it wasn't her fault, but, wrongly, he felt let down. There was nothing more to see, so they went back to the 1st-class decks, where the sun shone, the air was clean, and white-jacketed stewards waited upon their every need.

Their daily routine followed a similar pattern. After breakfast each morning Maimon chatted with the Viscount, and Elize lay in the sun. Then lunch and a siesta, a Spanish word meaning an afternoon nap, Maimon explained. Elize slept most afternoons, which she told Maimon she also did when pregnant with Adam.

Late one afternoon, when Elize was having one of her extended siestas, Maimon went up on deck, where he saw the Viscount looking at the distant horizon. Noticing Maimon he called him over.

"Cecil said you are not in the mining business. Is that right?" It was more than just a question in passing.

Though they had been on the boat together for over a week, this was the first time that Maimon and the most powerful man in South Africa were in each other's personal space. It didn't seem to bother Milner, but Maimon felt uncomfortable and moved a foot or two away. Almost bald with piercing steel-gray eyes and a big, well-trimmed moustache, Milner exuded power.

"I was in Kimberley," Maimon said, "but that was over three years ago. Since then I have been largely a spectator."

"The Chamber of Mines have a problem," Milner informed him. "When the war[102] started and most of the gold mines closed down, the natives went home. Now the mine owners want to start up again, but without labor that is not possible. The Chamber want permission to import 70,000 coolies. What do you think I should do?"

"I think you should permit it subject to two conditions," Maimon said. "Firstly, it should be for a specified time, one or two years, or whatever meets the Chamber's requirements. There needs to be a non-negotiable condition that every single coolie goes home after their contract expires. We have enough different racial and tribal groups already, without introducing another one."

"And secondly?" the Viscount asked.

"Before any coolie gets on one of the Chamber's boats, he should

---

102   Second Boer War

prove to their agent that he can lift 70 lbs, or whatever amount the Chamber decides."

"Good thoughts," the Viscount replied.

"One last thing," Maimon added. "If the Chamber are asking for 70,000, they probably want 60,000 or 65,000. You might want to consider that."

"Now I have one last thing," the Viscount said, smiling. "You are Jewish. Right"?

"Correct," said Maimon, wondering where on earth this question was leading.

"There is this fellow Herzl campaigning for a Jewish homeland. Have you heard about him?"

"No, sir, I haven't."

"It is important that the Jewish people have their own homeland. Every other nation – well, almost all of them – do, and there is no reason why you people should not have yours as well. When I get back to London, I will speak to Arthur Balfour about it."

"Thank you, sir. I look forward to buying you a drink in Jerusalem," Maimon replied sincerely.

"I look forward to that, too; but first we have to get the Ottomans out. From our intelligence I understand that all we have to do is to give them a push and they will fall over."

"Like the walls of Jericho?" Maimon asked.

"More easily, I am told. I am keeping you from your wife, which is not right of me. I think you should get back to her," the Viscount said with a smile.

Maimon excused himself, but instead of going back to their suite, went up to the cable office, where he dictated the following wire which he instructed should be sent right away. It was to his office.

SEE EKSTEINN AT CHAMBER MINES IMMEDIATELY ADVISING HIM THAT AS I WAS INSTRUMENTAL IN PERSUADING MILNER TO APPROVE THE IMPORT OF ABOUT 65,000 COOLIES I WOULD APPRECIATE CHAMBER BUYING TEN THOUSAND TONS RICE FROM MAIMCOM TO FEED THEM STOP CABLE OUTCOME SOONEST REGARDS

Having been promised that his message would be despatched without delay, Maimon went back to their suite, where he found Elize lying naked on her back on their bed under the ceiling rotating fan which was switched on to maximum speed. Thirty minutes later they were both lying naked on the bed under the fan, hotter than they had been earlier.

The *Dunnottar Castle* made good headway through the tropics, and just when Elize thought the good weather would last forever, it didn't. Anticipating their 1st-class passengers' requirements, the shipping line provided autumn and winter clothing of various sizes in their suite, which Elize said was very generous of them. Maimon tried to explain that it wasn't the shipping line that paid for them, but that he had, which Elize appeared unable to comprehend.

Around this time Maimon received a number of cables, and whenever this happened Elize was very anxious to learn if any of them mentioned Adam, which Maimon assured her was not the case. "No news is good news," he told her, which Elize reluctantly accepted, He did get two cables that made him particularly happy. One was from his office:

RICE CONTRACT OBTAINED EKSTEIN GRATEFUL FOR YOUR ASSISTANCE REGARDS

The other one was from Edward:

ODOT PROGRESSING NICELY EXPECT TO HAVE MORE NEWS FOR LONDON

Traversing the Bay of Biscay was achieved at a good speed, and through seas whose swells did not exceed three feet, with the result that they arrived at Southampton almost a day earlier than scheduled. From the organization awaiting their arrival one would think it was bang on schedule. Customs and Immigration were a mere formality, and it was not long before they were comfortably seated, again in a 1st-class compartment, this time in the boat train to London, thoughtfully chartered by the shipping line and paid for by Maimon and the other passengers.

Maimon looked out of the window and was surprised with what he saw. The farm fields were much smaller than those in South Africa, and the farmers all wore suit jackets and trousers as well as ties, as if they were going to church. This was the case all the way up to London, which took quite a few hours.

On arrival at Charing Cross Station, they saw a number of representatives from different hotels holding boards bearing the names of their establishments. Elize quickly spotted the Claridge's Hotel man, and she and Maimon identified themselves, resulting in they and their luggage being put in a carriage to the hotel just a few minutes later.

Claridge's, where royalty stayed when they came to London, provided Maimon and Elize with one of their better suites, where, apart from the welcoming flowers and boxes of chocolates and biscuits, there was a note that Elize read from the head concierge, advising that he was holding two tickets for *Madame Butterfly* at Covent Garden Opera House that night. Should Maimon require them, the note continued, the concierge would be happy to deliver the tickets to Maimon's suite. After discussing the offer briefly with Elize, Maimon told the chief concierge that he would like the seats, as well as a dress consultant to accompany Elize to obtain London-suitable clothes. This was arranged in minutes.

Maimon spent the afternoon in Charing Cross Road bookshops, looking for publications on bakery machines and steel plants. They both returned to the hotel at the same time: Maimon with three books, and Elize with three suitcases containing clothes from Derry & Toms, Marshall & Snelgrove, and Bourne & Hollingsworth.

Up in their suite Maimon was subjected to a mannequin show, with each dress more beautiful than its predecessor.

"I am so grateful for everything you have done for my mother and me, and there is so little I can do for you. Here is a present from me to both of us," Elize said, handing Maimon a sealed envelope.

"From you to both of us?" Maimon repeated, tying to work out what it could be. After a minute or so, he gave up and opened it to find a certificate from Rabbi Hertz, which Elize explained confirmed her conversion to Judaism in accordance with the rabbinical orthodox authority.

Maimon whistled.

"Most days when you were at the office, I went to Rabbi Hertz for lessons. Last week I had three exams: in religion, in history, and in Hebrew. Shalom, Maimon. Ma shlomcha?"[103]

"Tov,"[104] he answered. "We can speak to one another and Adam won't understand."

"And when we go to Saratov, there will be no snide remarks about the shiksa[105] traveling with you."

Here it was again. Maimon had put this subject to the back of his mind to be addressed when it needed to be, and he was now reminded that that moment was getting closer.

"Let's talk about that later," Maimon said, ducking it again, but sensing also that he was running out of both time and diversionary tactics.

---

103 *"Greetings, Maimon. How are you?"*

104 *"Good"*

105 *A non-Jewish woman*

"No. Let's talk about it now," Elize said firmly. And then, softening her voice, "What is the problem?"

What is the problem, indeed? That I hate my father, not for one reason but for a good number of them. And my sponging brother, who lives off other people who haven't got enough food for themselves. And my mother, who could have checked my steamship ticket – and is even worse than I imagine if she did. No, Maimon thought, I am not going back there.

"They are many, and complex," he answered.

"They are also your parents, without both of whom you would not be here, and *here* happens to be in the most expensive suite in London." Elize paused and then said in a voice he had never heard from her before, "Maimon, you have an obligation to them."

He hadn't thought of it that way. Perhaps he should have sent them some money. Alright, he should have sent them some money, which he could still do. That could solve the problem, but he knew it wouldn't. For the first time in his life he hated himself, and what made it worse was that it was Elize who caused it, and so he hated her, too. Unable to understand how he could love and hate a woman at the same time frustrated him even more. Maimon closed his eyes, sighed deeply, opened them, and looked out of the window, at nothing. Time in Saratov would be like standing paralyzed under an ice-cold shower. That's what it would be like. Only worse.

Elize broke the silence and, in the same tone she had just used, said, "I want to meet them."

Then and there Maimon knew he had lost, and so he replied as jovially as he could, "I also want to see them again."

Elize flew across the room and hugged Maimon, gave him a kiss, and said, "Thank you."

Maimon's operatic knowledge was thanks to a man called Searelle, who, together with some singers, had stayed at his hotel for just under two months. No sooner had Mr. Searelle arrived in Johannesburg than he bought a vacant stand on the corner of Eloff and Commissioner Streets, and on it built a rather grand building which he called "Theater Royal."

When Maimon asked Mr. Searelle who the royalty was, the impresario had just smiled and said, "Come tonight and see." Curious, Maimon had arrived at seven, bought a ticket, and soon learned that opera was actors singing, instead of talking. After the orchestra played a nice tune, actors came on stage, and sang in Italian one night, and German another. Not speaking either of those languages, at a break in the performances, when the orchestra had disappeared, probably for a drink, Maimon asked his next door neighbor what the singing was all about. Maimon liked the Italian music and saw each of the four operas, Mr. Searelle's company produced learning their stories from his next-door neighbor for the evening.

On the way to the opera house, Maimon told Elize the *Madame Butterfly* story. An American ship went to Japan, and an officer called Pinkerton falls in love with a Japanese girl and makes her pregnant. Three years later the officer returns, now married to someone else, to collect his child; after which, the little boy's mother commits suicide.

"That is terrible," Elize said, shocked.

"It is only an opera," Maimon reminded her, and then added, "and it is life."

Elize had never been to a theater before, let alone an opera, was amazed at the grandeur of the opera house, and that all the women were so smartly dressed. Similarly, the men wore black suits with white shirts and black bow ties. Even though the opera was sung in Italian, from Maimon's explanation Elize knew exactly what was going on.

There was a thirty-minute interval for a scene change, in which time they walked around, Elize marvelling at the dresses and Maimon seeing where half of De Beers' production last year had ended up. As Maimon had explained, the second half was taken up with the mother stabbing herself to death. This upset Elize so much that she burst into tears, and so Maimon helped her out of the opera house before the curtain calls. She cried in the coach, and all the way back to the hotel; where, in their suite, she burst into tears again. In vain Maimon tried to comfort her. But in the morning it seemed all was forgotten, because Elize bounded out of bed, excited that it was the start of their Ann Hathaway cottage day. Not to rush the excursion, Maimon had agreed that they would sleep in Stratford, returning to London the following day. At breakfast, a hotel messenger handed Maimon a cable that he put in his pocket.

CHAPTER 28

ADAM LOST … AND FOUND

On the way back to his suite Maimon asked the concierge to read the cable to him and then told him to cancel their Stratford bookings.

A minute or so later, Elize joined Maimon in their suite, and before she had a chance to sit down, he handed her the cable. Elize read it, and then her legs collapsed under her. Not wanting to believe its contents, she read it again, aloud this time, as if doing so would wind the clock back twenty-four hours. Of course it didn't.

REGRET ADAM MISSING MAGDA FOUND DRUNK ON POST OFFICE STEPS NOW IN POLICE CUSTODY POLICE STATIONS HOSPITALS BORDER POSTS ALERTED ALL DOING EVERYTHING POSSIBLE CABLING DEVELOPMENTS TOMORROW REGARDS

"No! No! No!" she cried, sobbing uncontrollably.

"Yes! Yes! Yes!" he shouted at her, the first time in his life that he had ever done so.

Elize looked up from the floor in horror, white with fear. If she was expecting support, she wasn't getting any.

"You want to know 'yes' what?" Maimon continued shouting, "Yes you knew your mother was a drunkard. When we came back from Thabazimbi, you knew it. And what did you do? Nothing. Look around this suite," Maimon roared, waving his arms.

"Look at it. What I am paying for one night would have been more than enough to employ three natives, on eight-hour shifts for six weeks, to look after Adam while we are away, and then send them to Lourenço Marques for a month's holiday. And you knew about her problem and you didn't tell me. Why? Why? Go on, answer me that." Maimon looked down at Elize, even more angry than he had been on the *America* when he learned he was going to Africa.

"Go on. Tell me why. Tell me! Tell me now," he shouted furiously.

Elize was quivering on the floor, looking up in abject fear at this man who she loved, her husband, who she would do anything for, anything. She would even kill their child for him, and then she realized that maybe she had.

Shrieking and sobbing like a demented person, Elize pounded the carpet. Then physically and emotionally exhausted, she lay on the floor like a limp rag doll.

Maimon left her there for a full five minutes, the time it took for him to collect his thoughts. When he had done so, in a normal voice, he said, "Elize, get up." She always did what he told her to do, and so she staggered to her feet, looking like mad Ophelia from *Hamlet*. "Sit in that chair," he said pointing to the closest one. Again, she obeyed him.

"Now listen carefully." Elize nodded wordlessly. "Either Adam will be found, or he won't," Maimon said.

What Maimon didn't say was that if he wasn't found, it may be because he had been trafficked to one of the Arab countries to spend the rest of his life as a eunuch.

"Oh, please God! Let someone find him. Please, please, please?" Elize cried out in desperation.

Elize's momentary hope that he might be found alive was suddenly overtaken by the horrendous alternative.

"They might find him dead!" she wailed, bursting into hysterical tears.

Maimon had already realized this possibility, having been told about "witch doctors" and their insatiable demand for children's organs.

"They might find Adam alive," he said optimistically, not believing this was going to happen.

Elize knew she had done something terribly wrong and now she had to pay for it. Getting to her feet she took off her underwear and lay over the arm of a settee, her bare bottom in the air.

"What are you doing, woman?" Maimon asked, bewildered by his wife's bizarre response.

"When we did something bad at school, we got beaten" she replied. "So you should beat me till the blood runs out."

For the first time Maimon realized that he was not dealing with an adult, but an overgrown schoolgirl. Maybe it was his fault for not inter-vening when he saw her remonstrating with her mother. Elize probably did so to protect Magda, as Kaylah would have done to protect their mother. As for not telling Maimon about Magda's problem, perhaps it was unfair to expect her to behave like an adult, as she wasn't one.

And then it struck Maimon. Tomorrow he might have, or would have, a demented, hysterical woman to deal with, and no idea how to handle her. Overwhelmed by the prospect of what surely lay ahead, Maimon collapsed onto the nearest chair and grasped his head in his hands. To lose their child would be tragic, and he had already steeled himself for this eventuality, but to lose his wife as well, in her case to lunacy, needed more strength than he had. Maybe he would also fall apart. It was just too much, too bad, for him to get his head around. Gripping his hands powerfully as if doing so would give him strength, Maimon looked at the woman he loved fearful that she was not strong enough to bear tomorrow's burden. Then he stood up.

"Get dressed," he told her quietly "and go and lie down next door."

Silently she did as she was told, keeping her eyes on her feet so as not to look at the man she loved so much, whom she had let down more badly than anyone could ever imagine.

A few minutes later Maimon stood up, took a deep breath, went next door, and sat on the bed next to Elize. Neither of them spoke.

"When are you going to beat me?" Elize asked finally, really wanting to know.

This girl had made a bad mistake and it was likely that she would pay a terrible price for it. How beating her would help anything, or stop her ever doing it again, Maimon could not imagine. So he took her hand in his and said, "Tomorrow morning it all will be clearer. You are going to rest in this bed till then, and depending on what we learn from Johannesburg … well, we will see."

"Why are you not going to beat me?" Elize asked, not sure she correctly understood what Maimon had said.

"That wouldn't help bring Adam back, would it?" Maimon said gently.

"But I did something terrible. Maybe I murdered our son. Should I not be punished for that?" Elize asked, looking into Maimon's eyes for some understanding of what he meant and why.

"If Adam does not come back, you will remember today and tomorrow for the rest of your life. Is that not punishment enough?" Maimon asked quietly.

"If you won't punish me, God will," Elize told Maimon, remembering that the Dominee had said that sinners, of which she was now one, are not capable of doing works that satisfy God's justice.

"God doesn't punish people. Didn't Rabbi Hertz teach you that?" Maimon asked confidently, having no idea if this was true or not.

Elize nodded and smiled weakly, the first time she had done so since reading the cable.

Maimon put a glass of water on the table next to Elize, kissed her on the forehead, went out, and closed the door quietly.

Downstairs he asked the concierge for directions to the nearest synagogue, and it was there he spent the next hour. On the way back to the hotel Maimon brought a bunch of red roses from a street seller, replaced the hotel flowers with them, and put the freshest ones on the table next to Elize, who was fast asleep. Then he kissed her gently on the forehead and went off to the British Library. There he looked at the drawings in all the books they had on steelmaking and wheat-milling. When the library closed at six, he wearily made his way back to the hotel, where he found Elize still in bed, but awake and looking into the far distance.

Fearing the worst, he said, "A penny for your thoughts."

Elize looked up at him and said, "When we get back to Johannesburg, I am going to the farms in the area of my parents' one, and I am going to tell all the farmer's daughters to find Jewish husbands."

"When we get back to Johannesburg, your time will be fully taken up buying curtains and carpets and furniture for our new house, and also getting ready for the baby," Maimon reminded her, still speaking softly, as though she herself was a small child.

"Have you eaten anything since I left?" Maimon asked. When Elize shook her head, he pulled on a fancy rope in the bedroom, and a minute later a lady in a black dress and a white starched apron appeared, took their order, and disappeared.

"What did you do today?" Elize asked, hoping for something, anything, positive.

"First I went to the synagogue …"

"I also prayed," Elize interrupted him. "Do you think God was listening to our prayers? I prayed harder than I have in my whole life."

Elize was just an overgrown schoolgirl, Maimon was reminded, and tomorrow she would have to be handled very delicately, he realized. He would have to be careful not to shout at her again.

"If the news is good that will be wonderful; but if it isn't, we should be ready for it." he said gently

"I don't want to think about that," Elize said defensively, pushing the worst possible outcome to the furthest recess of her mind.

Maimon realized that he was not going to make any progress before the morning, so they chatted about what they were going to see in England before they moved onto Russia. Ann Hathaway's cottage was nowhere mentioned. Any chance Maimon had of getting out of the Russian leg of the trip was finally dashed when Elize crawled out of bed and opened the largest of the three cases from Marshall & Snelgrove, to reveal six heavy, fur-lined winter coats.

"One each for you and me, your parents, and your sister and brother. I took a chance on the sizes, but as the girl in the shop said, rather too big than too small." Elize paused, waiting for Maimon to say something, anything, maybe "Thank you." When he didn't, she continued. "It is important that I know something about your family before we arrive. This is a good time to tell me."

As far as Maimon was concerned, no time was a good time, though he did accept that he would have to tell Elize about his childhood before they arrived in Saratov.

"When I left, my parents, sister, and brother all lived in one small wooden house. The whole house was the size of the living room on your farm. My brother and sister have probably married in the meantime, so if that happened, they will be living elsewhere." Maimon stopped, not sure how to continue and not wanting to speak at all, and Elize was sensitive enough to let him do so in his own time.

He didn't know why, especially as he wasn't at all religious, but suddenly Maimon felt that he and Elize were like the two wooden scrolls connected to the parchment on which the five books of Moses were written. Right now the Torah was all on his side, and heavy, and he had to hold it up. One day, if he was sick, or old, or poor, or all three, which was unlikely, Elize would have the heavy side. Funny, he thought, I am not at all religious, and in a way it is the bible that is holding us together. He didn't tell Elize this, as the last thing he wanted was a religious discussion, but he did think it was symbolic of their situation. Instead he got back to their poverty.

"Our family are very poor; in fact, everyone in Saratov is very poor."

"My family were also very poor, so I know what that is like," Elize reassured him.

Maimon smiled to himself, accepting that some clarification was required.

"When I say poor," he continued, "I mean poor like native poor. As poor as the poorest native you have come across."

"White people are not poor like natives," Elize told him confidently, again exposing her youth and naivety.

"In Saratov they are."

Elize couldn't get her head round this.

"Poor means lots of things, including not having enough food," Maimon told her.

Elize knew poor families, poorer than her family. But they always had enough food. This was completely different from what she expected.

"So we should take them some food," Elize volunteered, as always working on a practical solution. Maimon had already set these wheels in motion, which was a subject he was coming to later.

"My sister, Kaylah …"

"What a lovely name," Elize interrupted.

"My sister Kaylah is probably married. She is beautiful and very clever. She and I were extremely close."

That was where he would like to have left it, but he knew this was not possible.

"My brother, Zelig, studies all day, and many nights," Maimon added.

"He must be either very clever or very stupid," Elize observed.

"Actually, he is neither. He studies holy books with the Rabbi."

This didn't make sense to Elize, but it wasn't important, so she left it for the time being.

"My father is a lumberman, and my mother a housewife." Maimon had said what needed to be said, nothing more.

Elize, on the other hand, suspected that there was more behind the stark facts she had heard, but she realized also that this was not the time to push for these details, so she moved on.

"Do you think it is a boy or a girl?"

"Absolutely one or the other," Maimon replied at once, happy to change the subject.

The rest of the evening was spent chatting about their new house, the color of the baby-to-be's room, how deep the pool should be, and the fact that both of them needed to take swimming lessons. Before he dozed off Maimon wondered what his family would think about his house having a swimming pool. Not even Ezra Samsonitsky, the richest man in Saratov, had one. He knew Ezra, who was a good man, and not at all envious, but then there was nothing for him to be envious of.

Maimon dozed off first, Elize almost two hours later.

Maimon had instructed the hotel to slip under the door of their sitting room any communications that came for him. Just after eight the next morning, when Elize was still asleep, he slid out of bed and saw the envelope. The envelope that would tell him whether his son was alive and well, or lost forever.

He tore it open, looking at the letters in vain. This thankless effort was interrupted by a gentle knock on the door. If Maimon hadn't been in the sitting room, he would not have heard it. Forgetting it was by arrangement, Maimon opened it to find the young rabbi he had met at the synagogue the previous day.

Wordlessly beckoning him to enter, Maimon closed the door quietly behind him, and with shaking hands, he handed the cable to the rabbi, who read it. From the look on his face, Maimon needn't have asked, but he did anyway.

"He's dead?"

The rabbi nodded.

Maimon stumbled to the closest chair, collapsed into it, and with tears running down his cheeks, started sobbing.

This woke Elize, who rushed into the sitting room, saw Maimon, and screamed, "No, no, no," throwing herself onto Maimon's heaving shoulders.

There they sat, in a heap, sharing their grief. Elize looked at Maimon for some comfort, but there was none, so she rubbed her tear-stained face against Maimon's, as animals sometimes do.

After a while Maimon got up and looked round for the rabbi, who had quietly slipped out of the room when Elize entered. He found him on a chair outside their suite reading a prayer book.

"Isn't it too late?" Maimon asked sarcastically.

"They are not for Adam, but for you and Elize. Tehilim, or Psalms, in English."

"I am sorry," Maimon said hastily. "This is not a good time."

"Would you like me to come back at all?"

"Yes, yes, please do so," Maimon said plaintively, "in two hours."

"Yes, of course," the rabbi said, standing up and waiting for an indication if Maimon wanted to shake his hand, or give him a hug, and getting neither, added, "See you later" as he disappeared down the stairs.

Back in the sitting room, Maimon found Elize staring at the wire and seeing him she read it aloud.

ADAMS BODY FOUND HEALTH AND RELIGIOUS AUTHOR-
ITIES WILL NOT PERMIT DELAYING FUNERAL TILL YOUR
RETURN ADAM BEING BURRIED THIS AFTERNOON ALL HERE
SEND SINCEREST CONDOLENCES ON YOUR TRAGIC LOSS
REGARDS

"Why did God do this to us?" Elize asked. "Are we such bad people?"

"Maybe by some people's standards we are. I haven't taken half my money and given it to poor natives," Maimon told her.

"Neither have Lionel Phillips, nor Hermann Ekstein, nor Lesuj Vagalparot, nor a whole lot of other people much richer than you, and they haven't had their son murdered."

None of them have alcoholic mothers-in-law, Maimon thought.

"The rabbi is coming in two hours. Ask him," Maimon told her, in no mood for philosophical questions for which he had no answers.

They both got their feet, and in slow motion walked to their separate bathrooms.

An hour later they were back in the living room, dressed, still operating as if under water. Maimon ordered two black coffees, which were delivered with toast, butter, and marmalade. While they were drinking their coffee in silence, there was a knock on the door. It was the manager of the hotel expressing his condolences and asking whether they would like a black silk ribbon attached to the outside of their suite door. Maimon looked at Elize, who shook her head. The manager said, "I understand," and withdrew quietly.

After the agreed two hours the rabbi returned. Shaking Maimon's and Elize's hand's he quietly wished them "long life." Seeing that neither of them were familiar with this phrase, he explained it's significance. Then he sat in one of the chairs and waited until he had their attention.

The last thing Elize wanted was a sermon about the all-knowing God whose actions we have no right to question, so she readied herself for what she hoped would be no more than thirty minutes of an unnecessary lecture she had heard before. Maybe this rabbi, who looked about half the age of her ministers, might be different, though probably not.

Maimon, having already abandoned what little faith he had in the Almighty, readied his mind to go over the workings of a Bessemer furnace.

"At times like this," the rabbi began, "we ask ourselves why? Why has God taken from us a child who had never committed a sin in his life? What had he done to deserve the end of a life which had so much promise?

"We believe," the rabbi continued, "that we are all put on earth with a soul. Some people with souls that need a lot of repentance; others with souls that are nearly perfect. Adam did not have a bad thought in his head, and all he probably had to do was to show the two of you the love that little children have. When he did that his soul was pure and God called him back."

Elize looked at the rabbi, and smiled the kind of smile that angels have, the same smile that Maimon saw when she was sitting on the wall in East London.

"He was pure with an unblemished soul," Elize said to herself as much as to anyone else.

Maimon also smiled and thought, What a load of absolute rubbish. If that was true, Sol and Lev would both live to 150. Instead, he went over to Elize, sat down next to her, held her hand, and then kissed it.

Seeing the reaction his mini-sermon had had on the young couple, particularly Elize, the rabbi wisely said nothing more.

"Maimon said you were saying some prayers for us," Elize said in a soft gentle voice. "What were they?"

"Psalms. I have some books with me, and we can recite them together if you like," the rabbi said quietly.

Elize said she would like that very much, and she and the rabbi spent the next forty-five minutes reading together many psalms. Elize got particular comfort from Psalm 23, which she asked the rabbi if they could recite together twice.

The rabbi mentioned to Maimon that services were at six that evening, and if he wanted to say Kaddish that would be the time to come. Elize remembered that prayer from Shimon Katz's funeral, and that she had asked the reverend conducting the funeral to explain it to her. It was, she told the rabbi, from what she could remember, a reaffirmation of one's faith in God, which the rabbi confirmed was the case.

On his way out the rabbi said to Elize, "Except for the sermon, the service is in Hebrew."

"That is alright," she replied. "I speak Ivrit."

Elize went and sat next to Maimon, mentally and emotionally a different person to the one she had been an hour before. How wonderful, Maimon thought, to have that strength of faith.

"Adam is with God and the angels" Elize said, and from the tone of her voice Maimon realized that, for her, the worst of the storm was over. There might be rough seas ahead, but they were through the dangerous part.

They spent the rest of the day in their suite, reaffirming their love for one another and drawing on each other's inner strengths. They didn't do love, but there were times when they held each other very tight, and there were times when they just sat together on the couch and gently stroked their loved one's leg or arm or tummy.

The synagogue was about half a mile from the hotel, and Elize insisted that they each put on their new coats to walk there, thus signifying their new lives now that Adam was with the angels. That was fine, and in fact very good to think, Maimon accepted, if you could, in fact, think it. For his part, he would like to take Magda and impale her on a wooden stake two feet up her anus, somewhere in the veld, and leave her there, hopefully alive, for the animals to eat. That was until he thought of a more punishing death for her.

Elize had been told that, unlike in church, men and women sat separately in synagogue, and while she would have liked to sit next to Maimon, this was a Jewish custom that she respected. There were many customs that she liked, and she knew that she could not pick and choose. She said Kaddish when Maimon did towards the end of the service, and after it finished some of the members invited the two of them home for supper, which they graciously declined.

They walked back to the hotel slowly, arm in arm, Elize wondering what the new baby would be like, and Maimon trying to think of a more painful death for his mother-in-law. Dinner was eaten quietly in their suite, each of them coming to terms with life after the absence of the focus on whom their lives had revolved. Emotionally exhausted they crashed into bed after dinner and fell asleep in each other's arms.

Next morning, they discussed how, when, and where Adam should be mourned. Elize said that in the Dutch Reformed Church that had until recently been her spiritual home, the deceased was largely remembered before he or she was buried, which had to be within six days of their death. Maimon explained that, in the Jewish religion, the first step after burial was for the mourners to sit on low chairs for a week and for their friends and relations to pay condolence calls on them. They looked at each other, their hearts breaking. Then Maimon said holding Elize's hands,

"When we get back to Johannesburg, we will visit the cemetery, and then decide how we will mourn Adam. Till then we will put this at the back of the wagon, so securely tied that even an earthquake won't disturb it." That sat as well with Elize as any proposal she could think of, so she smiled weakly, which Maimon understood was her way of reluctantly saying yes.

CHAPTER 29
UNEXPECTED GOLD REFINING INCOME

This vitally important subject taken care of, they were both emotionally free to address other matters, the most pressing of which was how much longer they were to stay in England. Maimon explained that he needed two days, one each to visit J. Arthur Rank in Yorkshire, the manufacturer of wheat-milling machines, and the other to call on Sir Henry Bessemer, who had invented a cheap way of making steel. Fortunately, Sir Henry lived in London. They agreed that Elize would accompany Maimon to both meetings to record what was said. This turned out to be a masterstroke, because not only did Elize charm both gentlemen, but when they heard why she was present, they called in their secretaries to do so.

Both meetings went very well, which Elize took as a sign that their future would be bright. J. Arthur Rank lived in Yorkshire, and it was so beautiful in that part of England that they decided to stay for a few nights in the Dales. The people were so friendly, even if Maimon and Elize couldn't always understand what they were saying. They slept in cottages, and it was wonderful to get a feel of England that was not London. London reminded Elize of their tragedy, and while she accepted that they would have to go back there, she made Maimon promise that they would never stay at Claridge's Hotel again.

J. Arthur Rank pointed out to Maimon the importance of having good engineers to operate his facilities, and that the best pool of qualified technical people was in Scotland. As a result of this comment, and as Scotland was not far from Yorkshire, Maimon, and Elize took a train to Glasgow, where the office of the Scottish Institute of Engineers was located. Hearing the couple's accents, which were so different to those of the Scots, a tall man with a long face, made longer by the white beard on his chin, came out of an adjacent office.

"And what have we here?" he asked in a voice so deep that it seemed to have started in his boots.

"This is Mr. and Mrs. Sokolovski from Johannesburg. They are looking for engineers to run their steel plant," the man at the reception desk explained.

"James Howden," the tall man said, extending his hand first to Elize, and then to Maimon. "Come into my office and tell me about your steel plant."

Maimon explained that he had bought the plant on a turnkey basis from Henry Bessemer, and that when it was up and running, the people who had commissioned it would go back to England.

"Ah, Henry," Howden said. "A good man. He has even more patents than I have. For steel-mill operators you have come to the right place. You will need a team, and if you like I can put one together for you."

"I would be most grateful," Maimon responded, kicking himself for not having thought of this before.

"From Johannesburg," James said, "do you know anything about gold production?"

"Not very much, but my good friends Julius Wernher and Alfred Beit and others certainly do."

"Good. Meet me at the club at seven this evening. McDonald, on the way out, will give you the address." Getting to his feet, Howden added, "Now I have work to do."

A minute later Maimon and Elize found themselves back on the street and looking at one another. It reminded Maimon of the day he got his first job from Lesuj Vagalparot in Kimberley. Less than a mile away a steel mill was scamming off dross, and on the Clyde River they counted five steel ships in various stages of construction. The noise of rivets being hammered into steel plates on all the boats was nothing either of them had ever heard before. Added to this, coal was being dumped into silos and then carried by conveyer belts into hoppers for releasing, mixed with iron ore, into the next blast furnace requiring topping up.

They found a hotel on George Square, where Elize spent the rest of the day relaxing and reflecting how far she had come, not only in miles from their Brandfort farm. How lucky she was to have met Maimon, and how she should thank God for giving him to her. If it wasn't for him, she would be another "plaas vrou"[106] making boere biskuits and feeding chickens. Standing at the window and looking out at all the activity, she told herself that none of the girls in her class even knew this world existed. It wasn't their fault, of course, but there were two or three girls – Sarie and Aletta, in particular – who would have given their smartest dress to be popped down next to her here in Glasgow.

Remembering her school friends, Elize moved away from the window and looked at herself in the cupboard's full-length mirror. She had changed and surely they had as well. She wondered how, especially Sarie, who somehow made sure to always come round when Tjol was visiting. Elize remembered how, at first, Sarie used to bump into Tjol, and then, smiling, apologize, and later hold his hand or leg under the kitchen yellowwood table. She couldn't blame Sarie. Tjol was over six foot and very handsome. He also played in the Orange Free State Schools under-nineteen rugby team, which annoyed Willem who couldn't even get in to his school's first team. At midnight one New Year's Eve at the Olivier's farm they kissed properly, and after that were inseparable. Elize wondered if they "did love"? For both their sake's she hoped so.

How Elize wished she could have shared some of her experiences with them. Not all of her experiences, of course. Going to the Jewish synagogue on Saturday for services. *The Pirates of Penzance* at the theater. And the hotel accommodation everywhere they went. Even this room in Glasgow, with hot and cold running water, a big deep bath, and a toilet inside, just for them. She hoped they wouldn't be jealous. Sarie wouldn't, Aletta she wasn't so sure.

Maimon spent the time wandering round the industrial part of the city. The shipyards were of particular interest as he had never seen a ship being built before. As there were five in different stages of construction, he appreciated what a complex undertaking it was. There was no control as who could and couldn't go aboard, and so he climbed up ladders on to all five.

Later on, he found two steel mills where he spent most of his time, watching molten steel being poured into ingot moulds, and when still red-hot, giant cranes lifting the moulds off the ingots, which were then rolled either into flat plates for ships, or long beams for construction. When there was nothing left for Maimon to see, he made his way back to the hotel.

The collar and cuffs of his shirt were black with the soot from the air,

---

106   *A farm wife*

and when Maimon had a bath he found his hair had also collected a great deal of dirt. Wondering how much of this black stuff he had breathed into his lungs, Maimon made a mental note to ensure that somehow the air in his steel mill would be cleaner.

Maimon and Elize were at the Institute of Engineers Club a few minutes before seven, where they found James Howden had already arrived. He led them to their table, which Maimon noted was laid for six people. A minute later the other three arrived and were introduced as John McArthur and two brothers, Robert and William Forest. Drinks were ordered and menus were placed in front of each of them. Elize studied hers and Maimon pretended to study his. Being the only lady, Elize's order was expected first, and tactfully she said that she would follow their host, as did Maimon, which is how they came to eat haggis[107] for the first, and probably only, time in their lives. It was preceded by smoked Scottish salmon and was followed by bread and butter pudding. Then James Howden spoke.

"It is an English custom that business is not discussed before the main-course plates have been removed, but as none of us are English, let's get down to it."

Nobody disagreed so he continued.

"These three gentlemen here have invented and patented a cyanide gold extraction process, the bottom line of which is that they can get more gold out of gold-bearing ore than out of the chemistry currently being utilized."

In a deep voice Robert Forest continued, "This can be proven by taking ore that has been processed as is presently done, and then extracting gold from the residue."

"You need someone who is au fait with the industry, and specifically the owners of the mines, to organize this experiment; and then, when proved, to set up legal agreements committing the mines to pay you so much per ounce of gold thus produced," Maimon told his hosts.

"That is specifically it," John McArthur replied. "Are you up to such a task?"

"Absolutely," Maimon replied confidently. "I know the mine owners from my days in Kimberley, when I worked most closely with Julius Wernher and Albert Beit, and also Lesuj Vagalparot before he went back to Paris. I believe the man most open to this proposal will be Herman Ekstein

---

107   A Scottish dish consisting of sheep's or calf's offal mixed with suet, oatmeal, and
        seasoning, and boiled in a bag traditionally made from the animal's stomach

of the Corner House Group, together with whom I and others founded the Rand Club."

If there was every any doubt in James Howden's mind as to Maimon's suitability for the job, his Rand Club involvement erased it.

"When could you do this?" William Forest enquired.

"As soon as we have signed the agreements, which I hope will be tomorrow morning, I can get a letter off to Herman asking him to erect the necessary plant, for which you need to give me detailed drawings. Allowing for the post, and the fact that I will be going to the continent shortly, I would expect the plant to be ready to be put into operation on my return to Johannesburg."

"When will that be?" John asked.

"Probably in about five weeks' time. I wouldn't think the plant would be commissioned by then," Maimon pointed out.

"That sounds about right" Robert said. "The drawings are ready. The process works in California and Australia, so there is no reason why it shouldn't in the Transvaal as well."

"What do you propose to pay me?" Maimon asked, suspecting that what the inventors had in mind was only going to be a pittance.

"Our contract states that the mines pay us ten percent of the value of the additional gold processed, and our thinking is to pay you twenty percent of that amount," John said, looking straight at Maimon, who held his stare.

No mention of California or Australia, Maimon noted, so they were prob ably paid more.

"I was thinking of around thirty-three percent," Maimon responded. "I expect my duties will include ensuring that the process is utilized correctly, and furthermore that the mines pay you the amounts due within thirty days of the end of their month. You wouldn't want your money lying in the National Bank, when it could be earning interest here in Scotland."

Unknown to Maimon, Scottish people have an attitude towards money bordering on affection, and the idea of their money earning interest in Johannesburg when it could be doing so in Scotland, was anathema to them.

"We are paying our Australian agent twenty-five percent, and our American one thirty percent, so I think 27.5% would be a good place to end up on," William pointed out.

Since they had not excused themselves to consider his proposal,

Maimon realized this indicated that his thirty-three percent was not more than they had previously agreed among themselves.

"I make it my business not to look into other people's pockets," Maimon said quietly, thus pushing the American and Australian figures off the table.

"You are not an easy person to do business with," Robert said, uncomfortable that Maimon had not moved an inch.

"Easy or not, I am fair. I am being no easier with you than I will be with the miners." And, after a pause that an acting school would be proud of, Maimon added, "It has been my experience in life that one gets what one pays for."

The brothers looked at one another, and then at James, who reached across the table and shook Maimon's hand. Maimon shook the brothers' hands as well.

"Tell me," James asked, now that the business of the evening was done, "how old are you?"

"Twenty-five," Maimon lied with the straight face that he had cultivated months ago.

Next morning Maimon met with the lawyers, and they went over the contracts, line-by-line, first his with the license-holders, and then theirs with the miners. With one exception they agreed on all points, the stand-out one being the life of his contract. The license period had started at ten years, then moved up to twenty, and stuck at thirty. Maimon insisted it be on the life of the licenses. When one of the lawyers said that this could be 100 years, Maimon pointed out that two years had already elapsed and so the maximum was 98. The lawyers excused themselves, and came back with 50 years that, under duress, they moved to 60.

Maimon excused himself and said he was going for a walk and would come back for their decision. They expected him to return in ten or fifteen minutes; instead, it was almost two hours before Maimon walked back into their office and innocently looked at the lead lawyer, who showed every indication that he had been concerned Maimon might not come back at all. Both contracts were then read to Maimon, who had the graciousness not to comment that the "life of the licenses" clause had been inserted as he required.

CHAPTER 30

A TALE OF TWO CITIES

In the train back to London Elize and Maimon were each lost in their own thoughts. Elize was worrying that Maimon's family might not like her, and Maimon was worrying about … a hundred things. Would his parents feel angry because he had neglected them all these years? Would Zelig and Kaylah even speak to him when they saw how rich he was? Honor thy mother and father. He hadn't honored them, he had deserted them, and it wasn't because he couldn't help. Maybe God punished him for this desertion by taking Adam's life He hadn't thought this before, and it scared him.

Maimon looked across at Elize, serenely gazing out of the window at the beautiful English countryside. God wouldn't punish Elize for him deserting his parents. Surely, He wouldn't? He wasn't that irrational, or hateful – or was He? But then, who knows? God allows all the pogroms to take place, and the victims were no more guilty that Elize. A cold shiver ran down Maimon's back. Maybe they were both responsible for Adam's death? He for abandoning his parents, and Elize for hiding her mother's alcoholism from him.

This thought sat uncomfortably with Maimon for some miles; he was unable to get it out of his head. Thankfully Elize did it for him. Suddenly turning she said, "We need to buy them some food as well. Do you know where we can get Jewish food?"

Once again Elize had saved him, and she didn't even know it.

"You mean kosher food. The rabbi said he would drop a list of kosher shops off at the hotel while we are away. Those shops will be closed tomorrow, so we can go on Sunday morning."

"Then we can thank him when we go to services tomorrow morning,"

Elize said. Happy to be able to kill two birds with one stone, she once again looked out at the passing emerald-green countryside.

"As well as what?" he asked.

"The coats," Elize replied, without taking her head away from three cows in a field with more grass to eat than they knew what to do with. In the Orange Free State that field would feed about eighty or ninety cows as well as some sheep.

Some more green pastures slid by before Elize added, "If it is as cold as you say, we should buy boots as well. For them and for us." That settled, she went back to her pastoral gazing.

How his parents and siblings felt was one thing. How Maimon was going to handle it was another. By crying? He hoped not. It depended on them. His family surely wouldn't make a scene at the station. More miles flew past, and the green fields gave way to red-brick factories with tall chimneys belching jet-black smoke. If his family were happy to see him, or were even neutral about it, that would be fine. The presents should go some way to mollify any ill-feeling they had. That was the best he could do. As for the thought that he was partially responsible for Adam's death, that was complete nonsense. More miles of green fields reappeared. Maybe it wasn't nonsense. More miles. Yes, it certainly was.

The train puffed into the majestic King's Cross station, probably the most magnificent in the world, Maimon decided. They were taking the overnight train-boat-train to Paris on Monday. Maybe Paris had an even grander station? Probably not he decided, looking up at over a thousand steel girders criss-crossing each other, hundreds of feet up in the air. His steel company would be making beams like that, Maimon decided, a feeling of achievement coursing through his veins. Elize also looked up at the roof, and the beautiful artistic way in which the steel poles had been placed to enable light to shine through the glass panes above them.

Back at the hotel Elize had a favor to ask.

"Could we please move out of the hotel tonight – in fact now?" she pleaded.

It took a bit of organization, but an hour later found them ensconced in a no-less-grand suite in the Savoy Hotel. The recommendation to move there was that of Claridges's manager, who felt they might enjoy one of the Gilbert and Sullivan musicals playing in the hotel's theater. While Maimon was organizing tickets for the evening's show, Elize made sure that two candles, a glass of red wine, some bread, and salt were delivered to their room. To her surprise the bread was supplied under a white silk handkerchief which had "Shabbat Shalom"[108] in Hebrew letters embroidered into it.

"If it wasn't for Shabbat you wouldn't have found us," Elize reminded Maimon before any "Is this necessary?" comment came her way. They didn't rush the prayers, and then walked down to the theater where *The Pirates of Penzance* was being performed. It wasn't like Italian opera, Elize pointed out – thankfully, Maimon thought. It was an operetta, he explained. Much lighter, it finished the day on a happier note, and they walked upstairs holding hands, both feeling that life was slowly getting back to normal. Still, Maimon doubted it ever would, which he didn't tell Elize, who was probably thinking the same thing.

Elize was more at ease in the synagogue the following morning than Maimon. She could follow the service and liked the tunes, which were nothing like any she had heard before. Maimon had heard them, hundreds of times, on each occasion keenly waiting for the one that closed the service, "Adon Olam."

When that song was reached Elize, winked at him across the aisle, remembering their singing it together with the ladies and children in the concentration camp. For a different reason he winked back.

None of the congregants invited them home for lunch, so they walked slowly back to the hotel, through Piccadilly Circus and Leicester Square, "people watching," as Elize called it. The first thing she noticed was that there were no black people. It wasn't good or bad, just a fact. At home, except in their bedroom at night, there was always a native about somewhere. Another difference, Elize pointed out, was that all the men wore ties and jackets, and were dressed as if they were going to church or a funeral. Even some of the little boys. They passed a man selling chestnuts that he had freshly roasted on a fire in a steel box at his feet, and Maimon bought a bag each for Elize and himself. The chestnuts cost a penny a bag, and Maimon gave the chestnut man a sixpence, telling him to keep the change. It seemed nobody else did this, Maimon remarked, as the chestnut griller behaved as though it was Christmas.

Christmas. Elize hadn't thought of it before, but now that she was Jewish, they couldn't celebrate the birth of a man, although also Jewish, who had caused so many of her husband's co-religionists to be murdered.

That, unfortunately, was a fact, she realized. Perhaps there were Jewish holidays when people exchanged gifts. She really hoped so, remembering the excitement on Christmas morning when as children they opened their presents. For the girls it was usually a pretty dress, and for the boys, once they were old enough, a gun. Maimon was so generous, she reminded her- self, their children wouldn't be short of anything, and it didn't make any difference if gifts came at Christmas or Passover or whenever.

They spent the afternoon lazing about their suite before having a light snack and attending another Gilbert and Sullivan production – *The Mikado*. Maimon wasn't surprised to hear Elize say that it was so much nicer than *Madame Butterfly*.

Next morning found them in London's East End, and another scene completely foreign to Elize. She couldn't believe that everyone, absolutely everyone, they saw was Jewish.

"Is it like this in Palestine?" she shouted into Maimon's ear. "I hope not," he said, and they both laughed.

Everyone spoke Yiddish, except Elize, who was not yet fluent, and so she clung to Maimon's arm like a leech. From what she could make out, everything, absolutely everything, was bargained for, which initially she thought was quite fun, until she realized that the store owner and prospective purchaser were both deadly serious. As they were going to Par is, which also had a Jewish Quarter, they decided not to buy any food- stuffs in London, instead stocking up on warm woollen socks, fur-lined boots, gatkes, which Elize learned were long-legged warm woollen broeks,[109] leather jackets, scarves, plus a suitcase big enough to hold all of their purchases. Riding back to the hotel Elize was overwhelmed by a variety of sensations. She had seen more Jews that morning than were in the Transvaal, she told Maimon, who agreed.

"How many Jews are there in the world?" Elize asked, trying to get her new people in perspective.

"I don't know. About six million, I suppose," Maimon guessed.

"That is much more than the Afrikaners," Elize said, as much to herself as to Maimon.

"If you are right," she continued, "about the natives taking over, then the Jews can go to Palestine."

---

109 *Waist-to-toe woollen underwear*

"That's right," Maimon added, happy to keep his end of the conversation up without much effort.

"And where will the Afrikaners go?" Elize asked.

"God knows, and He is not telling," Maimon replied.

"I am serious!" Elize responded, her tone confirming her words.

Maimon didn't know, either, and any further comment would surely get him into hot water, so he said nothing.

"There will be millions of Afrikaners by the time that happens," Elize pointed out, hoping this additional information would elicit a response. It didn't. After a minute or two, Elize added, "It will be a serious problem."

"Not in our lifetime, or that of our baby's," Maimon said, patting Elize's tummy.

"Yes," Elize agreed. "But it will be a serious problem one day."

Fortunately, at that moment the coach arrived back at their hotel, and Maimon was spared any further interrogation about the future of the Afrikaner Nation.

One of the many things that Maimon loved about Elize was her anticipated excitement about what lay ahead. Tomorrow it was boarding a train in London and getting off it in Paris twenty-four hours later, some of which time the train – or, rather, their Pullman Coach, Maimon told her – would go on a boat traversing the English Channel. Sadly, Elize reflected, she had no one to write to about this. Maimon replied that she could write to him.

"I will," she replied happily.

"And I will keep every one of your letters," Maimon replied, neither of them dreaming that these letters would be their great-granddaughter's most treasured possessions, flying to America with her over 100 years later.

It was exciting, even Maimon had to admit. Before leaving the hotel, they made reservations for their return. A suite for them and three extra double rooms that they both hoped would be needed. Their trip to Paris was uneventful, and as their train pulled into the Gare du Nord, Elize said, "Isn't it amazing! London yesterday and Paris today."

"Charles Dickens wrote a wonderful book, *A Tale of Two Cities* about London and Paris. I will ask the hotel to get you a copy in English," Maimon said, reminded of Ayna reading it to him under their lifeboat on sultry tropical afternoons.

"One day, I don't know when, I will tell you something that you don't already know," Elize said, smiling. "And thank you in anticipation for the book."

Maimon smiled, too. He hadn't thought about it before, but now that Elize mentioned it, he had picked up quite a bit of knowledge in his short life, which, considering he couldn't read, was a significant achievement, he told himself.

"Don't look so smug," Elize told him, anticipating what Maimon was thinking. "You don't know everything."

"I don't know the compression ratios of the cylinders in the engine pulling this train," he admitted.

Their conversation was cut short by a porter who removed their baggage and put it next to the door they would use to get down onto the platform. Maimon wondered why the platforms were always so much lower than the train doors. Surely it couldn't be so expensive to build higher platforms, he reasoned.

In just over thirty minutes they were safely ensconced in their suite in the George V hotel. Maimon arranged for tickets for the Folies Bergère and The Lido for the two nights they would be in Paris; and after Maimon had an incoming cable read to him, they took a carriage up to Montmartre. There they strolled about looking at artists painting portraits and landscapes.

Down one of the alleys they saw a sign that Elize said was Association Les Nabi's. They didn't know what it meant, but the door was open and so they went inside. It turned out to be a gallery with various painters' works displayed for sale. Elize liked a painting by Edgar Degas, while Maimon was particularly taken with the work of Henri Matisse and couldn't decide which of two of his works he preferred. The pictures were not expensive, but they both agreed it was impractical to take them to Saratov, and as they had no plans to return to Paris, they decided not to buy them.

Down another alley they found a coffee shop just as it started to rain, so they went inside. It turned out to be a pâtisserie which made the most wonderful cakes either of them had ever tasted. The rain stopped and they continued strolling, which brought them to the bottom of the hill, where they caught a carriage back to the hotel. There they found the Charles Dickens book Maimon had requested.

Later that evening they went to the Folies Bergère to see a musical performed in a beautiful, though not very big, old opera house building. The dancing was performed with split-second precision, and, when the final curtain was lowered, neither Elize nor Maimon could believe two hours had passed. They strolled back to the hotel, arm in arm, like the lovers they were, each one more grateful for the other than words could express.

As different as Paris was from London, so were English breakfasts from French ones. Not having eaten the night before, Maimon was ravenous. Instead of eggs and toast, he had to make do with some light brown rolls called croissants which were mainly filled with air. There were other sweet breads, but nothing suitable for a hungry man. Elize, following the example of French ladies in the dining room, ate what was served as daintily as she could.

An hour later found them in the Marais area, where aristocrats lived before the French Revolution. After that Jews moved in and today had what Maimon and Elize agreed were the most wonderful food shops they had ever seen. There were also outdoor stalls that sold very thin pancakes called crêpes, some of which were filled with savory fillings and others with alcohol and/or chocolate. Maimon had five, and that kept him going till lunchtime.

The suitcase they bought was soon filled with sides of salted beef, as well as a good quantity of pastrami. While French soft cheeses were delicious, they decided that it would be more prudent to take only harder ones to Russia; and so they filled the empty spaces in their suitcase with what Maimon called "bricks" of Parmigiano, pecorino, and manchego. Even Elize was hungry by now, and so they slipped into the nearest restaurant, where Maimon introduced Elize to matza ball soup. When he did not recognize any of the other items on the menu that Elize read out to him, he asked the waiter for suggestions, and was rewarded with pastrami beef on rye bread followed by New York cheesecake.

Walking back to the hotel they marvelled at beautiful architecture in every street, which Maimon said was all designed by Baron Haussmann, who wasn't a baron at all.

"How do you know this stuff?" Elize asked incredulously, and not for the first time.

"I overheard the concierge at the hotel telling another guest this morning," he said, smiling.

"I am going to catch you out, I promise I will," Elize replied making a mental note to keep her eyes open for something, anything, that Maimon might not know.

CHAPTER 31

TO SARATOV ...

They left the next morning on the train to Warsaw, in a French Wagon- Lits coach which was not anything like the trains that he and Frieda had traveled in, en route to Hamburg. Elize had her nose buried in *A Tale of Two Cities*.

Reflecting on the last years of his life, Maimon regretted not having made a greater effort, or any effort at all, to keep in touch with his family. It was only after he and Elize had been in Johannesburg for some time that, through her, he began corresponding with his parents. Over the years he agonised why this was the case. The easy answer was his illiteracy, but he knew that was not the real reason.

Was he afraid that his family would try and use his wealth to draw him back to Saratov? Would he be able to withstand the strength of that magnet? Maimon thought so, but he couldn't be sure. Or was it because he knew there would be bad news from home, there always was, with inevitable pogroms and the dire financial situation of the whole Jewish community? Or was it because, now a grown adult, he still could not read or write, which even five-year-old Jewish children could do. As the snow-covered fields of Eastern Europe slipped by, he reflected on the fact that it probably was a little bit of all these factors, and possibly one or two others as well, that had played on his subconscious mind.

The train pulled into Warsaw station, and from here on he knew the ropes. Maimon had never forgotten Frieda, and from time to time wondered what had happened to her. He hoped that she had gone to Manchester, and that there was a Rivkin family, and that they had looked after her. She would have realized that he had lied to her, but she would have forgiven him. And Feigie? Did she get to America?

He hoped so, even though he had never met her.

Porters were waiting to meet the well-dressed passengers in the 1st-class coach from Paris, and to make a few zloty from their acquaintances. Unlike the time he had followed Frieda, Maimon and Elize traipsed after Szymon, who saw them safely onto the train to Kiev. Maimon had reserved a compartment for their exclusive use, but he was under no illusion that he was now in a part of the world where might is right. It was on the Kiev-to-Warsaw train that he had encountered the Cossacks, and while he no longer had nightmares about them, he would never forget that officer and soldier and what they planned to do with him. While Elize reburied herself in Charles Dickens, Maimon moved uncomfortably in his seat.

As the train hissed steam and pulled out of the station, she glanced up from her book, smiled at Maimon, got up and gave him a kiss, and then settled down again with Charles Dickens.

Maimon looked across at the woman of his life without whom … It didn't bear thinking of what, or where, he would be without her. With all the hardship she had suffered, primarily losing Adam, and also seeing her father and brother shot dead just yards away from where she stood, she still maintained a wonderful disposition. How she handled the reunion with her mother, which would be a major psychological hurdle, was yet to be seen, but that was down the road, and Maimon was not going to remind her of it.

Elize's reaction to all the misfortune that had befallen her certainly wasn't logical, and Maimon could only account for it by her belief in God. Not the Christian God she grew up with, or the Jewish God she now embraced, but God, the same God she had told him, that looked after us all. Maimon had a problem with the "looked after us all" part, but what counted was the strength it gave Elize. Had God organized his meeting with Elize at the East London hotel, or was it pure coincidence? It all depended whether you believed in God or not, Maimon decided, and with that thought sitting uncomfortably in his mind, he dropped off to sleep.

The train's screeching brakes and Elize rubbing his shoulder woke Maimon with a start.

"We are in Kiev," she told him. "Time to change trains."

Maimon smiled to himself. The last time he was on a train pulling into this station he was a "greener," and here was his wife who had never been to the Ukraine before, behaving like an old hand. Remembering his Ukrainian, Maimon told the porter which train they needed, and not too long after they were in the Russian compartment of the coach heading further east.

The compartment was 1st-class, and had Maimon not been worried about leaving Elize alone, he would have walked down the platform and looked into a couple of 3rd-class coaches that he and Frieda, and of course, Lieb, had ridden in all those years ago. About thirty minutes late, the train finally left Kiev on the last leg of their journey. Having thought through the various welcomes he might receive, and deciding that he had already given this matter a great deal of thought without making any progress, Maimon stretched uncomfortably and dozed off.

Leaving Dr. Manette for a while, Elize gazed at the unfolding landscape that passed by her window. Much of it was covered in snow, something she had only seen in pictures, but here and there the snow had melted, leaving patches of green grass. So unlike our winter, Elize thought, where everything is brown, and every day you can play after school in the bright highveld sun. What a wonderful youth she had had till that horrible, terrible day when the soldiers came and killed her father and Willem. If it wasn't for little Adam, she would have drunk poisoned water from the well, as three of their natives had done.

Focussing on the meeting with Maimon's parents, brother, and sister, she felt confident. A year ago, before she was Jewish, it would have been different. But now she knew about all the festivals, about keeping kosher, the grace-after-meals prayer, and quite a few songs. Of course, they could always catch her out, but she hoped that they weren't those kind of people.

Importantly, she and Maimon had agreed not to mention Ayna's child; and as far as Adam was concerned, that was totally off-limits. Maimon would simply say that they had lost a little boy and did not want to discuss it. Anybody who brought it up would be reminded of their wishes. Through the letters that were written by Maimon's mother, Elize felt that she had got to know Maimon's family; but had she really? Would they like her? Before her imagination had a chance of going off in who-knows-which direction, the train slowed down and shuddered to a stop. Elize took a deep breath and told herself she was ready, ready for quite what she did not know, but she had said her prayers and the Good Lord would see her through.

The motion change woke Maimon, who stared out of the window and saw, appearing out of the mist, the station he remembered so well.

For a split-second he thought it was a nightmare. Then Elize smiled at him, and thankfully he realized it wasn't. The train didn't stop at Saratov for very long when it was on time, and certainly didn't when it was running half an hour late, so Maimon opened their compartment door and, one after another, tossed their cases onto the platform. Then he helped Elize down and followed himself.

Waiting alongside the pile of cases, with the widest smile he had ever seen, was Kaylah, and next to her Zelig, looking no less happy. While Maimon and Kaylah were locked together, Zelig helped Elize over the cases, and introduced himself. Elize knew she shouldn't kiss Zelig, or even hug him, but he had held her hand that had stopped her falling, which was probably alright for a sister-in-law.

Maimon let Kaylah go and then looked down the platform for his parents. There were three uniformed railway employees and an old couple, but no sign of Anshul and Gittel. He was just about to ask Kaylah about them when he recognized the woman on the platform. It was his mother, old and stooped, as she had never been. And the man? Not his father, surely. His father was a foot taller than his mother, but this man was bent over and shorter than she was. It couldn't be… but it was. It was then that tears rolled down Maimon's cheeks. He left two big strong people and came back to …

Zelig gave him a bear hug and on releasing Maimon, looked him in the face and said, "Thank you so very much for coming back."

What had happened to his parents? He left them young and healthy, and now in just a few years, they were old and frail. A million thoughts cascaded through his mind as he clasped them tighter and tighter, and then, with one on each arm, he slowly walked down the platform.

Elize watched this scene like an actor waiting for her cue to come on stage. But none came. Instead, she looked at Zelig and Kaylah, whose clothes were little better than the rags she and her mother had worn in the concentration camp, and which contrasted – like black and white – with her and Maimon's thick coats and high boots.

A tap on the arm by the station porter, who had just finished loading their suitcases into a waiting wagon, told Elize that she was expected to pay for his labor, and so she grabbed a fistful of roubles from her purse and handed them to Kaylah, asking her to give the man an appropriate amount.

The old people were too frail to walk the 600 yards to their home, and not wanting to leave them alone, Maimon rode with them in the wagon, while Zelig, Elize, and Kaylah walked arm-in-arm to their parent's house. Elize took the opportunity to tell them in the Yiddish that she had been studying about her little boy who had died, which, she stressed, she did not want to talk about. Zelig said that, praise to the Almighty, he and Rifka had been blessed with children – Kaylah whispered six – whom Elize said she looked forward to meeting. Kaylah did not mention having any children, of which Elize took particular note.

The eight family members sat round the heavy wooden table in their parent's basic home and spoke for four hours, interrupted only by dinner, which consisted of a root vegetable stew with a few bits of meat in it.

They spoke first in generalities, and then in excruciating detail of specific happenings.

The years since Maimon's departure had not been good ones. All had been bad, some terrible, and one traumatic. Elize, whose only contribution was helping serve the meagre dinner, listened open-mouthed to the litany of disasters that had befallen Maimon's family.

Afrikaners, she knew, had a difficult history, from the Huguenot expulsion from France, to their humiliation by the British in the Second Boer War. But compared to the Jews, their degree of suffering was in the kindergarten category. Elize had never heard the word "pogrom," and by the time she and Maimon went up to their freezing cold bedroom, that word was seared into her mind, like the cattle her father used to brand on the farm.

Despite hearing over and over of the attacks on the helpless and defenceless little Jewish community by sometimes drunk, but always violent, Cossacks, Elize could not believe how barbaric they were. She heard how Maimon's father had been beaten to a pulp while unsuccessfully trying to prevent his wife from being gangraped, after which she almost bled to death and could not walk for three weeks.

Elize had to run outside where she vomited all her supper up, after hearing from Rivka how the Cossacks had swung the two-year-old son of a family with whom they rented a farmer's barn round and round before smashing the little boy's head against a wooden post, causing it to split open like a ripe watermelon. Her mother, screaming in terror, was then raped, and when she would not stop screaming, was knocked unconscious with the butt of one of the Cossack's rifles. She did not speak for six months, and even now, three years later, said little. All the while, before and after this and all the other pogroms, her husband studied. He did not have a job and did not want one, and spent every day, except the Sabbath, studying holy books. Also sharing the barn with Zelig and Rivka was another family who had eleven children.

Kaylah looked after her parents and with her husband, Saul, ran a little timber business that put food on the table, though not much, Elize realized. This commercial activity required them to work from dawn to dusk in summer, and in winter often in the dark. Once a year, when the river thawed, Saul lumberjacked 50 logs tied together with rope forty miles downriver to a sawmill. It was dangerous work, and every year men drowned doing it, but the job earned Saul enough money to feed their two families for a few months, and to put a little aside, as well as giving some to charity. It was the job Maimon's father used to do before the Cossack attack.

Later Elize learned that Kaylah had escaped being raped by throwing a pot of boiling water in a Cossack's face, before running into the woods to hide. Saul had come back from work to find their house a pile of smoldering ashes and no sign of Kaylah. She was not in the shtetl, Saul quickly ascertained, nor were her bones among the ashes of their house. As the Cossacks rarely took Jews away, he prayed that she must be hiding in the forest. A few hours later she returned to a desperate Saul. That night they slept in her parents' house. The following morning, Saul insisted that they emigrate to America. Kaylah would have none of it, pointing out that, should they do so, who would look after her parents? They both knew that Rivka was not up to it; and so they stayed.

When there was no more wood to throw on the fire and the room grew colder and colder, all eight family members, each for different reasons, felt that they had been through enough for one night. Picking up their share of the clothes that Maimon had given them earlier, they said goodnight and disappeared into the darkness.

Unusually for Maimon, he undressed in silence before joining Elize in bed, and for the first time in their life together, instead of hugging Elize, he pulled the thin blanket up to his chin, lay on his back, and stared at the ceiling. Intertwined with his life as she was, even though they had never discussed it, Elize knew what was tormenting Maimon, and as there was nothing she could do or say to alleviate his misery, she kept quiet.

No matter which way his mind turned, the fifth commandment kept hammering in his head: "Honor your father and mother."

He hadn't honored them. He had abandoned them in the hour when they most needed him. And why did he do it? It made no difference why. The fact was that he did it. He with all his money.

Not religiously observant, Maimon did believe in God. He hadn't always, but it was surely thanks to the Almighty that he found his soulmate, and then made enough money to bring his whole family to Johannesburg – except he hadn't.

Slowly the distress he felt turned to anger, and then fury. Fury with himself for being so selfish, because even though he hated to admit it, his selfishness was the cause of everything. Exhausted, he dozed off only to dream of his father being beaten up and his mother gangraped. Like an infant seeking its mother's breast, Maimon reached out in desperation for Elize, who was always there for him, and tonight she was again. Though asleep he pulled her to him, and her smell, and her soft body, and her warmth was his security. With her he would be alright. That is how it always was.

If Maimon was tormented emotionally, Elize was physically. First, when she got into bed she was freezing cold; and the moment she warmed up, Maimon had grabbed her in his sleep. He often did that but soon let go. Last night he had not, and when she had tried to escape, his long strong arms had prevented her from doing so. The room had no curtains and so Maimon woke at first light. He kissed Elize lightly on the cheek, and then unwound his arms from around her. Elize sighed, smiled, and carried on sleeping.

Lying in bed Maimon reflected on yesterday, which, together with the day he learned of Adam's death, were unquestionably the worst of his life. Adam had left a scar on his heart that would last forever, but he had been able to move on, and while yesterday's scar was still raw, in time, it would heal, too. The past could not be undone, but the future could be made more comfortable for his parents in Johannesburg than they were here in Saratov.

Herbert Baker was building him a twelve-bedroom house with ten bathrooms and lots of what Maimon called "enjoyment rooms." There was the mandatory Billiard Room, and for the first time in Johannesburg, a house with its own theater. Outside there was a tennis court and a heated swimming pool – also unique in the "Golden City," as some called Johannesburg – for his children, and hopefully also his grandchildren.

But his first task was to get everyone to agree to leave the hell-hole that was Saratov, or, as Elize described it, "a pogrom waiting to happen." His parents would be told what to do, as they had told him when he was a child. Kaylah would come, and while he hadn't broached the subject with Saul (or anyone else), he was surely young enough to want to get out of Russia. As for Zelig and Rivka, he just didn't know.

Maimon had asked all of them to come back to his parent's house at eleven the following morning, and he was not surprised that Kaylah was there at ten. Seeing her smiling face and observing her bright, bubbly personality reminded him how much he had missed his big sister. Another price for being in Africa. After a big hug, and a kiss on the forehead which Maimon had to bend over to get, they both sat down.

"You are a lucky man," Kaylah told him. "You have the most wonderful wife. How did you find her?"

Maimon smiled, so happy that it looked as though Kaylah and Elize would get on together.

"That is a story that Elize tells better than I do. You had better ask her."

"You do want us all, don't you?" Kaylah asked, in a serious voice that Maimon had not heard for years.

The honest answer is often the best one, so Maimon said, "I have just finished building a house with twelve bedrooms. I only did it because I have the family to fill it."

Tears filled Kaylah's eyes, which she wiped away with her hands. "I always knew you would come good. I told the family so often they politely told me to 'Shut up,' and when I didn't, they impolitely told me to. My little brother, how I missed you."

They hugged again and then Maimon asked, "Will they come?"

"With a lot of gentle persuasion, Mom and Dad will. I am working on Saul, but there is problem, a financial one. As for Zelig and Rifka, which means Zelig, I just don't know."

Maimon had learned that any problem that could be solved with money wasn't a problem, so he said, "What is Saul's problem?"

"The wood he collected is ready to be floated down to the sawmill when the ice melts. That is 1,500 roubles he has worked extremely hard for."

"That can be fixed," Maimon said. But before he had a chance to move on, Kaylah interrupted.

"He won't take your money! I think he is crazy, but Saul is adamant."

"Is Itzik Yankelowitz still the biggest timber merchant in town?" Maimon asked.

"No. He died. His son Shmuel has taken over the business."

"I remember Shmuel from school. I will go and see him and sort something out. What about Zelig?" Maimon asked, suspecting this would be a greater problem.

"Like everything else, it is in the hands of the Lord – except it isn't. These Yeshiva bochers[110] don't go to the toilet without their rabbi's permission."

Maimon looked at his watch, one of the very few in Saratov, saw it was eleven, and got up to stretch his legs. In the next couple of minutes everyone arrived. After the initial pleasantries Maimon dived in.

"Thank you all for coming this morning. I know it isn't easy for any of you, and your time is precious, so I will get straight to the point. The Lord has been good to me, in fact extremely good. A rabbi once told me that money is like manure. If you leave it in a pile it smells terribly, but if you spread it about it makes things grow." This was totally untrue. Maimon had worked it out for himself.

"The money He has given me I have spent on charity, some learning, building a house with twelve bedrooms, on travel, business ventures and so on." Except for Zelig, who noted the learning, everyone else focussed on the twelve-bedroom house.

"'Who needs a house with twelve bedrooms?' the architect asked me. I told him, 'A man with a big family.' I haven't got a big family, all I have is a wife and five-nineths of a baby, so I need all of you, and your children, to fill the house." The twelve-bedroom house and the unborn baby were too much for some of the family to absorb at once, but Maimon ploughed on.

"There are many natives looking for work, men and women, and generally they are both kind and gentle. They make extremely good helpers, and I know an elderly couple who employ them on a twenty-four-hour-a-day basis, seven days a week. Each one works only eight hours, and so they are always completely fresh and wide awake."

This was another blatant lie. Maimon had never heard of natives being employed as helpers, but it wasn't a difficult job, and he was sure they could do it.

"Johannesburg is a place of opportunity – commercial and spiritual opportunity, primarily, but in many other fields as well. Please give me the opportunity to spread my money around a little, and let me pay for

110   A student in a Talmudic Academy

your travel costs to Johannesburg, and your accommodation there until you want to move out. I know this is not an easy decision to take, so there is no rush. Take your time and let me know in the next day or two. I know a day or two is not much time to make such a momentous decision, but I really would like to have all of us out of Saratov before the Cossacks come back. Oh, one last thing. Anyone who doesn't like Johannesburg can go to England or America. Or Hong Kong," Maimon added, trying to lighten up the conversation.

While those who had thought about Maimon's return expected there to be a conversation along these lines, no one had anticipated a twelve-bedroom house. He must be a millionaire, some thought; others were just blown away. Everyone came to their senses and wished Maimon and Elize Baruch Hashem[111] for the baby before leaving. One minute the room was full, the next Maimon and Elize had it to themselves.

"How do you think it went?" he asked, keen to have Elize's feelings on how things were going.

"You could have knocked them over with a hoopoe's tail feather," Elize said, never in her life having seen a room full of people so stunned. "When do you think we are going to leave?"

"Within a week, I hope. Why the question?"

"Because I want to walk around the town and get a feel of the place," Elize answered.

"That is fine. If the Cossacks come, just dive into the closest Jewish house."

"How will I know it is a Jewish house?" Elize asked.

"The same way as the Cossacks do. They are much better than those owned by the goyim."

This wasn't the answer Elize was expecting. She thought it would be the mezuzah on the door post, but that wasn't the last surprise that lay ahead of her.

That afternoon, when Maimon was discussing the timber market with his old school friend, Elize strolled around a town that was hemmed in by the river on one side and woods on the other. Maimon was right, the Jewish houses were markedly better than those of other faiths. This surely did not endear them to their Christian neighbors, she thought. Standing outside of one of the Jewish houses, a woman opened the top half of a stable door to see what this blonde shiksa wanted.

---

111 "Thank God"

"Shalom Aleichem," Elize said.

"Aleichem Sholom," the woman customarily answered, surprised at the shiksa's greeting. "What do you want?"

"A glass of water, please?"

"Come in. Quickly. Before you are seen."

Elize hurried into the house, which, like her parents-in-law's, consisted of one large, sparsely furnished room downstairs, and accommodation upstairs.

"Sit down," the woman commanded, and seconds later a battered pewter mug of water was put in front of Elize, which she partially drunk.

"What does a shiksa know about Shalom Aleichem?" the woman asked inquisitively.

"Tevye the Dairyman," Elize replied, naming the author's most famous character. "I am not a shiksa. I am from Africa."

If Elize's first statement was hard to swallow, the second was totally in- comprehensible. Then the penny dropped.

"You are little Maimon's wife," she said, jumping to her feet and giving Elize a hug. "I am Zillah," the short, fair-headed lady said. "It is wonderful that he has done so well. Perhaps now he will look after his parents."

Zillah paused to let this information sink in, and then added, "So what do you want from me?"

"To learn about the Jewish community in Saratov. What interaction you have with your Christian neighbors? Do you borrow or lend them firewood? Or medicines when one of you is sick?"

Zillah looked at Elize as if she was a child at her first day at school. "These goyim!" she spat out. "I wouldn't take their firewood if my mother was freezing to death."

"Why not?" Elize asked, amazed at the woman's response.

From the silence that ensued it seemed that no one had ever asked Zillah that question. Eventually she said, "You wouldn't understand."

"Maybe I would, and maybe I wouldn't," Elize replied. "But please tell me anyway."

"A white African Jewish woman who looks like a shiksa would never understand," closed the subject from Zillah's perspective.

Saddened, Elize finished her water, thanked Zillah, and made her way to the door that Zillah opened for her. As soon as Elize left she heard the bolts shot home, and then she made her way slowly down the street, trying to understand Zillah's reaction to her non-Jewish neighbors. The farm closest to Elize's family's belonged to the Kapeluskys, who always helped whenever they were asked. And when little Ivan was so sick that they thought he would die, her mother had taken some Boere medicines made from plants to help him get better. Why, Elize wondered, didn't the Saratov people also cooperate with one another?

Elize had come to a park that was snow-covered. Just as she turned round to head back, she saw two drunk tramps fighting over the remains of a bottle of vodka. If it wasn't so desperately sad, it would have been amusing, Elize thought, as she quickened her step back to Maimon's parents' house.

There she found Maimon and Kaylah talking to their mother.

"Absolutely not," Elize heard Gittel say as she walked in the door.

"Honestly, I cannot think of any reason to stay here," Kaylah informed her. "The weather is better in Johannesburg. It never snows, and it rains in the summer when it is warm."

Gittel just looked at her daughter, resolute and unmoved by the climatic advantages.

So Maimon pointed out, "To take a bath, which you can make eighteen inches deep, there are hot and cold water taps. It might help your arthritis."

"I don't need to lie in hot water," his mother told him. "Nobody dies of arthritis."

Maimon said, "What I have told you are good reasons. I think the most important reasons of all are the indoor toilets. No matter what the weather outside, you sit in warmth and comfort, and when you are finished, you pull on a chain and water flushes it all away."

Gittel thought for a moment, and then shook her head. Exasperated, Maimon threw his hands in the air and stood up looking at the ceiling.

Kaylah pushed a heavy wooden chair next to Gittel and said quietly, "Mother, Saul and I want to leave Saratov. If we do, there is no one to look after you and Dad. So that means we can't go. Isn't that extremely selfish of you?"

"We can get that peasant girl who lives next to the river. She can look after us."

Kaylah knew that girl was totally incapable of doing this job as did her mother. Shaking her head defiantly, a gesture she performed very much like her mother, Kahlah got up and went and stood next to Maimon.

There was nothing more to be said. Gittel was staying, and that meant that Anshul and Kaylah and Saul were as well.

Almost unnoticed, Elize, who had been standing in the corner, slipped into the chair that Kaylah had vacated. Slowly she took Gittel's hand and put it on her tummy. For half a minute she didn't say anything, then with a pleading voice, "My children need a bobba, and you are the only one they have got," Elize said, her voice breaking and eyes filling with tears, not for her, but for her and Maimon's unborn children.

Nobody said anything, so Elize reclaimed her hand, slowly stood up, and went to join Maimon and Kaylah looking at their mother.

After a minute or two, Gittel slowly got to her feet and dispensing with her stick, walked over to Elize. Putting a hand on each of her shoulders she said, "I will be their bobba."

Elize grabbed Gittel and hugged her, tears running down both their faces. Kaylah took Maimon by the hand, and pulling him into the kitchen, said, "I am not sure you deserve such a woman."

"I am not sure, either," he replied, smiling.

"Saul wants to speak to you," Kaylah continued, this time catching Maimon off-guard. "I am not sure it is good news."

They got together the following morning in Saul and Kaylah's house. The women drank tea in the kitchen, the Russian way, with a cube of sugar in their mouths, while the men discussed the issue in the other room.

"I didn't appreciate your involving Shmuel in my business," Saul began.

Maimon had bigger battles to fight, and didn't want to spend his powder on telling Saul he didn't have to sell his timber to Shmuel, so he just looked at Saul.

"If you were going to America that would be different," Saul said.

"If elephants had wings they would fly, but they haven't, and they don't," Maimon said impatiently. "I am offering you an introduction to the largest timber merchants in Africa. With the money you make there, you can go to America. Or, when we get to London, I can lend you the money to buy two steamship tickets to New York. But that would be a mistake."

"Why a mistake?" Saul asked.

"Because as important as 'what you know' is, 'who you know' is more so. You will arrive in New York, or Baltimore, or wherever, knowing nobody. When you find a timber merchant, you will be fortieth in line for a job."

"Who are the African timber merchants?"

"Montfreres."

"Goyim?"

"French Jews."

In the silence that followed Maimon realized that there was more to come. He waited for it.

"Kaylah and I would love to have children. There will be better doctors in America to help us."

"I am sure there are," Maimon agreed. "But how will you get to them, and how will you even know who they are? You land in New York and the fertility specialist is in Houston, or Chicago, or any one of the major American cities – or maybe even a minor one, like Nashville or Memphis. Come to Johannesburg, see the best doctor there, who will give you a letter of introduction to the 'go-to' American doctor, who might be in Kalamazoo, for all you know."

Saul looked at Kaylah, who was with Elize. For a moment Kaylah hesitated, and then she nodded. Saul smiled and turned to hug his wife, but he was too late. Elize had grabbed Kaylah in a bearhug, and said, "Will you be the sister I never had?"

Saul was happy to wait in line for his turn, remembering the old saying "Happy wife happy life."

Elize pulled Maimon outside into the bright and cold winter's day. "What about Zelig and Rivka?"

"Indeed, what about them?" Maimon said, having no idea how to crack that nut.

"Let's go and see them now," Elize said, and as Maimon didn't have a better idea, he agreed. It turned out not to be a good one, as what seemed like twenty-five children (but was probably half that number) running around shouting and screaming wasn't a good place to talk. Anyway, Zelig hadn't returned from morning prayers, so they agreed with Rivka to get together at four that afternoon.

Irrespective of Zelig and Rivka's decision, Elize wanted to leave the next morning. She could not get over Zillah's reaction to her suggestion that she borrow firewood from her neighbors, and could not get out of her mind that, apart from the Cossack danger, Zillah's attitude would, sooner or later, only bring further strife to Saratov's Jewish families. Elize pointed out to Maimon that she asked him for very little, and would he please agree to their catching the noon train to Kiev the following morning. There was no reason to stay one day longer than tomorrow, whether Zelig and Rivka joined them, or if they didn't.

Maimon smiled to himself, relieved that Elize now shared his view of this hell hole that his brother called home.

Lastly Elize said, "This place scares me." With his fear of Cossack attacks that, he knew from experience, could come at any time, Maimon agreed to leave on the first train out, which was scheduled to depart the following morning. This he told Saul and Kaylah, who started readying her parents for a trip of their lifetime.

At four o'clock sharp, Zelig and Rivka arrived looking as if they were going to a funeral, or had just come from one. Smiling, Maimon invited them to sit down and Elize offered them tea.

"We are not coming," Zelig said in a voice that had a reluctant over-tone to it.

"Can we talk about it?" Maimon asked his older, and much more learned, brother. Zelig nodded. "In Johannesburg there are copies of the Gemara[112] and the Talmud[113] and whatever you want, and Rabbi Hertz to learn with." That cut no ice with Zelig, so Maimon continued. "I accept that there are, not yet, as many learned scholars in Johannesburg as there are here, but if you come you will attract them. Isn't that a mitzvah in itself?"

If Maimon was getting through to either of them, there was no visible sign of his doing so. Elize, unable to contain her amazement at their lack of response, asked quietly, "Why are you not coming?"

"Because the rabbi said we will not be able to lead as kosher a life in Johannesburg as we can here," said Zelig.

Elize looked at Maimon, who explained, "As observant a life."

"But doesn't that depend on you?" Elize asked. "If you want to observe the fast of Gedaliah, you can do so as well in Johannesburg as you can here. Or am I missing something?"

"The rabbi said we shouldn't go," Zelig repeated.

Maimon turned to Rivka. "You know this place. You grew up here. It is terrible. In the spring it is a mud bath, in the summer a dust bowl. The autumn is the only nice time, but then you work your fingers to the bone to scrape together enough food and wood to see you through the winter. When one of your children gets sick, they all do, and what do you wait for? The Shabbes, when you never have enough food, and

---

112 A rabbinical commentary on the Mishna

113 The body of Jewish Civil and Ceremonial law and leg end comprising the Mishnah and the Gemara

letters from America with money to keep you from starving. Is this the life you want? The life for your children?"

Zelig and Rivka sat impassively, as if listening to a train timetable being read out.

Unable to restrain herself, Elize pleaded, "Rivka, my sister-in-law. You who have been blessed with children. With Kinderlich, on whom parents and grandparents have showered love and food for generations. They are our future. They are who we need to protect and cherish. For their sakes please come?"

Zelig and Rivka sat unmoved, so Elize fired her last shot.

"If the Cossacks come tomorrow, and set your house alight with all your family in it..." Elize didn't know how to finish the sentence, so Rivka did so for her.

"It will be God's will."

Maimon and Elize finally realized that they had no chance. As hard as they had tried, and they tried every approach they knew, their family was going to be divided, for ever. Maimon sat with his head in his hands, devastated, until after a minute or so he felt a hand on his shoulder. It was Rivka on her haunches.

"Don't be sad," she said, "It is God's will." Maimon tried to smile, but he couldn't.

They lay in bed together that night, Maimon and Elize, each with their own thoughts racing through their minds. Maimon still plagued by not having brought his parents out of this hellhole before the Cossacks came, and Elize wondering why Jews wanted to live in such terrible conditions in the first place. It was about fourteen hours until she said goodbye to Saratov, for ever, and she prayed that nothing bad happened to them before they left.

The next day they all woke early, excited about the trip that lay ahead, and Africa at the end of it. At Maimon's suggestion, his mother gave their house to Zelig and Rivka, who, for the first time in their lives, had a house of their own. Two horse-drawn carts were ordered for 11:30, but everyone was dressed and packed – not that they had much to pack, Elize observed – an hour before that. And then it happened.

There was a loud bang on the door. Their excited chatter stopped.

Cossacks! All six of them thought (even Anshul, who had a wild look in his eyes).

They looked at each other. Saul went and opened the door. On the doorstep stood the widow Grunblatski, the only resident Jewish redhead in Saratov, with her two children, one hanging onto each arm. Her eyes were red from crying. Pushing past Saul, she walked up to Maimon and said, "You don't know me. I didn't grow up here. I came from Alexandria with my husband, Francesco. I am a good woman." The woman composed herself before carrying on. "Mr. Sokolovski, these are my two children, Joshua who is nine, and Sarah who is seven. They are good children."

The widow took a deep breath before continuing. "I cannot leave this place. I have an aged mother to look after. There is no future here for the children. Will you take them to Africa, please?"

Making an unbelievable effort not to break down, the widow said, "When my mother dies, I will come and take them from you. Till then, please, please, will you look after them?" And in her final movement before collapsing on the floor sobbing, she thrust a handful of roubles into Maimon's hand.

Maimon looked at Elize, who nodded affirmatively.

Gently Maimon and Saul picked up the widow and sat her in a chair. Kaylah handed her a glass of water; Maimon put the money in her coat pocket, Elize dropped to her haunches, and taking the widow's hands in hers, said softly but firmly, "Of course, we will take them. And look after them as we would our own children, until you come and fetch them."

These were the words the widow had prayed to hear, ever since news of Maimon's and his wife's arrival swept through Saratov's closed Jewish community. And now what she was hearing she could scarcely believe.

"You will? You really will?" she asked again and again.

"Like our own children" Maimon added. "It is still over an hour before we leave, so let's talk about life in Johannesburg." Leading Sarah over to Elize, he said, "This is Elize, my wife, and she is going to have a baby. She is going to need someone to help her. Will you help her?" Sarah nodded and smiled for the first time. Turning to Joshua he said, "Would you like a horse all of your own?" The little boy couldn't believe what he was hearing. "I have stables in my house for six horses, so if you like, one can be for you." Seeing that Joshua was speechless, Maimon added, "Do you think we should call him Boris or Alexey?"

Joshua looked at his mother, who nodded, and then up to Maimon. "Boris" came out in a little voice.

Maimon walked across to Sarah, dropped to his haunches, and looking at the girl who was now on Elize's lap, said, "And would you like a pony?" Smiling, the girl nodded vigorously. "And do you think we should call her Katya or ..."

"Katya," she said, almost jumping out of her skin with excitement. Her own pony, she could not believe it.

"Katya it is," Maimon said, now standing up, just as Sarah gave Elize a kiss on the cheek.

"The house also has a swimming pool," Elize told Sarah and Joshua, who had come to listen. "I can't swim," she said, "but there is a teacher who is coming to teach all of us. Even Uncle Maimon."

Elize was so used in the Afrikaner culture for older people to be called "Oom"[114] and "Tannie"[115] that she automatically lapsed into "Uncle Maimon."

"And are you Aunty Elize?" Sarah asked. "I am," Elize said, giving Sarah a hug. All the while the widow was looking on in amazement, first at Maimon's generosity, and then at her children's acceptance of this new regime. The God she had prayed so hard to had listened to her.

Maimon was happy to have this diversion as he feared that in this last hour his mother or Saul might backslide on their decision.

Elize was over the moon. Sarah didn't replace Adam, of course, but she was a child, and ... and Elize couldn't put into words how she felt, but it was warm and fulfilling. She came with no children, Elize reflected, and would be leaving with two.

---

114   *Uncle*
115   *Aunt*

CHAPTER 32

… AND BACK

Maimon's mother, who had never before left Saratov, was torn between the sadness of saying goodbye to her friends, and the excitement of embarking on a journey to another continent. Anshul, who had never really recovered from his near-death experience, did as he was told.

Zelig and Rivka were waiting for them on the platform. They kissed Anshul and Gittel, then Saul and Kaylah, and finally they stood in front of Maimon and Elize.

For the first time since they arrived, Elize saw Rivka crying. No words, just more and more tears running down her pale white cheeks. God's will might be Zelig's but it wasn't Rivka's, Elize realized as she held her sister-in-law by the shoulders, and said, "You will come and visit us, won't you?"

Not remembering whether a married woman could touch a married man according to the rules of the strictly orthodox, Elize looked at Zelig helplessly, knowing she had lost the battle she so wanted to win for Rivka's sake, if not for his.

Defeated, Elize held out her two hands, palms upwards, for Zelig to do with what he wanted. He thought it meant "come to me," but he couldn't, even if he wanted to, and in his heart of hearts he didn't know if he did, or not. So Zelig took the safe route, he always did, and remembering his rabbi, turned and walked away. Near breaking point, silently Elize screamed at him, shooting imaginary daggers into the back of the most selfish man she had ever met.

Defeated, Elize went to Maimon, and said, "Give me all the roubles you have."

Maimon opened his wallet and took out about 5,000, which he gave to Elize, who stuffed them into the pocket of Rivka's coat, and then walked away before bursting into tears.

The train was now in earshot. Maimon hugged Zelig, kissed Rivka, and the widow who was as happy now as she was desperate an hour before.

"May God reward you for what you are doing," the woman said looking at Maimon in wonderment as a woman would at a priest in Lourdes who had just performed a life-changing miracle. Borrowing words he so hated hearing, Maimon replied, "It is God's will."

Maimon smiled, the train's whistle drowning out the widow's reply. In seconds it screeched to a stop. Elize, Joshua, and Sarah piled into one compartment, and Maimon handed their new leather cases up to Elize, who stowed them under the seats. Joshua's and Sarah's meagre belongings were tied up in an old sheet, the way most Russians traveled, and Elize made a mental note to buy them cases as well as clothes as soon as they got to London. Saul, Kaylah, and her parents climbed into the next-door compartment. Unlike Maimon's last train-ride out of Saratov, this one was in a 1st-class compartment. The whistle sounded again, and the train slowly pulled away, with the widow smiling as she waved, and her children waving back, about to embark on the most amazing adventure of their lives. Glumly, Zelig and Rivka also waved.

Maimon heaved a sigh of relief, struggling to get comfortable on the train seat. Elize smiled and handed him an envelope with his name written on the outside.

"What is this?"

"My first letter to you."

"Please read it."

Elize carefully opened the envelope and started reading.

My dearest, most wonderful Maimon,

After my prayers every morning, I ask God what I have done to deserve you. I know He organized that we meet first in East London, then on the farm, and finally at the camp. So, it wasn't a coincidence, or by accident. He must have some plan for me, and I am sure in the fullness of time, and at the right moment, He will tell me what it is.

Until then, the reason I have been put on earth is to look after you. Please don't make it difficult for me to do so.

It was brilliant the way you rescued your family, but the hardest part is still to come.

Your mother wants to talk to you – no, she didn't tell me this – and it is not going to be an easy conversation for you. I don't know what, if anything, you can do to prepare for it, maybe just knowing will help you. I am, as always, here for you, though this is a battle that you need to fight alone.

Also, you will have to go back to that terrible place to try and prise Zelig and his family out of it. Not this year or next, but sometime in the future. Only bad things can come from staying there.

It was so wonderful the way we, but it was really you, adopted Joshua and Sarah, and the horse and pony idea was brilliant. If only the Good Lord put more Maimons on this planet.

I expect Edward will bring a letter to London from my mother, and that will be a bitterly hard time for me. Please help me through what I expect will be emotionally unbelievably difficult. Already I am thinking how hard it will be for me to visit her in jail.

My darling, please look after yourself and don't take chances. I have lost you twice already and could not bear doing it again. Not only for me but for our baby, who is bigger than Adam was at this time. Maybe God is giving the world another Herbert Castens.

I must go and pack now. I feel so guilty about the wonderful clothes I have, and the terrible ones everybody in this horrible place wears. I know we brought your parents, sister, and brother coats and boots, but can I please buy them some more when we get to London? Also, Joshua and Sarah need a whole wardrobe. It won't be a lot of money but it will make them so happy.

I love you more than words can say.

Take care,
Your Elize

Maimon took back the letter, carefully folded it and replaced it in the envelope, which he put in his pocket just as the train slowed down ahead of its stop at Michurinsk. Sarah, her head on Elize's lap, was fast asleep, and Joshua was looking out of the window in wonderment. When the train had stopped, the door to their compartment opened and Gittel stepped in.

"Go next door and sit with Saul. He is doing lots of calculations. Maybe he can teach you something" she told Joshua, who scampered out of his compartment and climbed into the one occupied by Saul and Kaylah. Maimon ensured that he was safely with his sister and brother-in-law, the door of their compartment securely closed, before returning to Elize and his mother. A short while later, the train chuffed-chuffed on its way to Kiev, and Gittel sat down next to her youngest son, her hands folded on her lap. After a minute or so she said, "What happened?"

It was a very wide-ranging question, but Maimon knew where it was aimed.

Elize smiled at him.

"Nu," his mother said after a minute or so.

"It wasn't easy," Maimon started slowly.

"Life is not easy," his mother reminded him.

"Especially not when you are told you are going to America," Maimon continued, throwing down the gauntlet, ready for whatever was coming, "but your father bought you a cheap ticket on a boat to Africa, and your mother didn't think it was important enough to check it."

"We all make mistakes," his mother pointed out.

"And I was carried off the boat unconscious, on a stretcher, straight into hospital. Imagine, in a hospital, almost dying, in Africa, where no one knew me."

"You didn't die," his mother said, showing not the slightest hint of contrition.

"With no help from my family."

"So?"

"So, in a hotel, recuperating, I was whipped out of the building at three o' clock in the morning."

"You must have deserved it," his mother observed.

"Then I was nearly eaten by hyenas …"

"But you weren't," his mother said, losing her patience with Maimon's litany of near-death escapes.

"No, I wasn't, with no thanks to you. But I did work on a farm for ten months. And you know how much they paid me? Zilch. Zero. Nothing. But that wouldn't count for you, because for you it's all about your money. Actually, life isn't all about money, if you are born unable to learn to read or write. And don't tell me it's not your fault, because if it isn't yours, it is your husband's."

That knocked Gittel back and Elize winked at him encouragingly.

"And who decided to put me on a train with zero chance of succeeding? Was it the mayor of Saratov? I don't think so. Was it the ferry master? Unlikely, as the ferry doesn't run in winter. Was it your husband? Certainly not. The only decision he makes is when to go to the toilet. So it must have been Zelig, or Kaylah, or you. But it couldn't have been Zelig or Kaylah as they were minors. So it was you, you alone who sent me off, hoping I would never return."

Tears welled up in Gittel's eyes and Elize winced.

"Yes," Maimon began. "I should have sent you money, and I am sorry I didn't, but you have no idea what I have been through. No idea at all. And the good news for you is that it is a secret. My secret. If you want to make peace with me, that is fine; and if you want to have a faribble[116] that is your decision. Is there anything else you want to know?"

Gittel smiled inwardly. He didn't get this fighting spirit from Anshul. No, he got it from me. He should thank me for it, she thought.

"We all have to live with our decisions," Gittel started. "Come to terms with them if we can. If we can't, life is a living hell. I have prayed for repentance and have received some solace. Not entirely, but largely. I don't think we are ever forgiven for our major mistakes."

Maimon could have hugged his mother and said, "All is forgiven," but he didn't, because it wasn't. His tirade reminded him how he had been abandoned and cast to the hyenas, the southern hemisphere

---

116 *A dispute between two people, often known by only one of them*

equivalent of being thrown to the wolves. But this wasn't metaphorical, it was factual. He might forgive his mother in time, but not now, not today, and if she needed any proof that the conversation was over, Maimon's pulling out a magazine on electric-arc furnaces put her mind beyond any doubt.

At last Elize could go back to her tale of London and Paris without worrying that her husband needed any support. Uncomfortable in his seat, Maimon squirmed around and eventually fell asleep.

An hour or so later the train shuddered to a stop in Kiev station. With little other chances of income, porters jostled each other for business where the 1st-class coach stopped.

"Ziovyty moyi sumky," Maimon shouted to one of the porters, throwing their suitcases down to the most aggressive of them.

"Your Ukrainian is pretty good," Elize remarked, not knowing if this was in fact the case. Actually, it wasn't, because what Maimon said was, "My bags are yawning."

"Last time I was here it saved my life," Maimon said, tossing the last of the cases down. "You look after Sarah." He gestured to the young girl, who was clinging to Elize like a leech, never having seen so many people in one place in her life. "I will find Joshua."

That wasn't difficult. The little boy was gazing wide-eyed at a train pulling in on the adjacent platform. Kaylah looked after her parents, as the six adults and two children slowly followed the porter and his overloaded trolley to the necessary platform.

To Maimon it was surreal. The station looked the same and smelt the same as it did when he followed Frieda and Lieb all those years ago. How much water had passed under so many bridges since then, he thought. Where was Frieda, he wondered? Hopefully in England or America. And her granddaughter? Hopefully happily at school somewhere in the USA. Reflecting how someone you only met once could stay in your mind for so long, Maimon remembered Frieda as vividly as if she was standing beside him right now, instructing him where to go. His thoughts were interrupted by the porter, who pointed out that they had arrived at their coach; after which, Maimon pointed out that his job was only half done. The cases had to be stowed in the compartments.

This finalized and the porter paid, Maimon asked Joshua if he would like to see the locomotive. As soon as he said it, Maimon knew it was a mistake, as it would remind him of a similar inspection he had made with Adam. But it was too late. With the little boy's eyes alight with excitement, there was no getting out of it now. Holding Joshua's hand tightly, they walked slowly to the front of the train, where the locomotive was venting steam. From the cow-catcher in the front, to the coal tender behind the engine, Maimon knew it all, and as Joshua was interested, he got the full explanation.

"You are very clever, Uncle Maimon," Joshua said, having been told exactly how the locomotive works.

Walking back to their coach, Maimon was relieved it hadn't been as bad as he had feared. Adam had been overawed by the size and noise of the engine, while Joshua wanted to know how the locomotive actually worked. Thankfully, they would be moving straight into the new Parktown house, so there would be no Doornfontein memories to reopen his slowly healing wound.

"Uncle Saul is also very clever," Joshua said, looking up at Maimon as they walked together. "He calculated exactly what time we were going to arrive here, and he was only out by two minutes."

"How did he do that?" Maimon asked.

"He took the distance and worked out the average speed of the train, and then divided it out. I checked his figures, and they were correct," the little boy said proudly.

"But he didn't know the speed of the train," Maimon pointed out.

"He timed the distance it took to get from one telegraphic pole to another, then he guessed how far apart they were, and with that information he calculated it out. It was quite simple," Joshua explained excitedly. "I also checked those figures for him."

"You are a smart little boy," Maimon said, ruffling Joshua's hair, and wondering how his brother-in-law would be with pounds, shillings, and pence.

That brought them back to their coach, where Elize was waiting on the platform for Maimon. She didn't tell him, but she had decided that if he wasn't on the train, she wouldn't be, either. What she did tell him was that he had handled his mother masterfully. When Gittel came into their compartment, she thought she had all the aces, but when she left it was with her tail between her legs. Maimon complimented Elize on her English idioms.

The ride to Warsaw was uneventful, in as much as no Cossacks got into their compartments. When Maimon realized this was the case, he pulled out the revolver that he had been carrying since Paris. Elize, who had grown up with guns, watched Maimon empty its chamber and stow the gun in his suitcase, and the bullets in hers. The story of Paris and London had been given a rest, as Elize spent much of the journey relating to Sarah tales of the African Bush. That of Mrs. Warthog required repeated tellings, and Sarah could not believe that Mr. Waterbuck had a ring round his bottom from sitting on a lavatory seat that had just been painted. Eventually they both fell asleep.

Warsaw station was as Maimon remembered it. Scruffy with beggars leaning against the walls, some missing limbs and all clothed in rags. As in Kiev the porter found their train and coach which was, Maimon thankfully noted, a Pullman. All of them piled into it, immediately noticing the step-up in comfort.

They didn't have long to wait before their train pulled out of the station, when, one by one, the adults, realizing that the lawlessness of Russia and the Eastern European countries was now thankfully behind them, sighed with relief and fell fast asleep. All except Maimon, who knew Edward would be waiting for him in London, when the two of them would execute a capture of such daring that it defied belief. Elize, with Sarah once again sleeping in her lap, was having her head pushed away by Elize's ever-growing tummy. With difficulty Elize dipped from time to time, into the second half of *A Tale of Two Cities*, having conquered the first half on the train out of Saratov.

Not since they had left Johannesburg, and Maimon's business matters there that required his daily attention, had Elize noticed her husband so preoccupied. In Saratov with its challenges, and even during the showdown with his mother, he had looked relaxed. Now he was slipping in to the mould she remembered so well.

"I am worried about something," she said to Maimon, who never liked to hear those five words. "When I was five months pregnant with Adam, I was so much smaller. Do you think everything is alright?"

Relieved it wasn't anything more important, Maimon said, "When we get to London, I will arrange an appointment for you with the Queen's obstetrician."

"Do you know him?" Elize asked, ever amazed by her husband's scope of acquaintances.

"Not yet," Maimon replied, his mind reverting back to how the following day's events with Edward would hopefully pan out.

Elize couldn't but help notice how the desperately poor peasants pleading for the train's passengers to buy their food and knick-knacks in Eastern Europe gave way to better dressed salespeople selling a wider range of higher quality food from well-stocked station shops and kiosks in Germany and Holland.

Everyone awoke when their coach was shunted onto the cross-channel ferry, and once the train's wheels were securely anchored, Maimon, Saul, and Joshua went down onto the boat deck to witness the big steel doors clanging shut, the harbour staff casting off the mooring ropes, and the boat steaming out of port heading for Dover.

Looking down at Joshua, who was running this way and that, Maimon wondered who was more excited, he or his little charge. Saul was once again doing calculations, writing with an ever-shortening pencil in his little black book. When he stopped for a minute, Maimon asked him, "If you could choose any job in the world, what would it be?"

Saul scratched his head with the pencil, and said, "Something, almost anything, involving figures. Nothing to do with timber."

"I need an accountant I can trust, and I can pay much more than you can earn in a timber yard. Do you know anything about double-entry book-keeping?" Maimon asked, hoping Saul would fill one of the vital holes in his burgeoning little empire.

"Not yet," Saul replied. "But how difficult can it be? In London I will pick up some accountancy books and on the sea trip to Cape Town learn all about it. I might need a lesson or two after that, if you can find a teacher who knows the subject."

"Good idea," Maimon said, not betraying the sense of relief he felt at hopefully tying down one corner of his tent.

Before they knew it, the giant white cliffs of Dover were upon them. The Pullman passengers were instructed to get back in their compartments while the coach's wheels were released from the steel clasps securing them to the ship's deck. After a few minutes, the coaches were hooked up to a locomotive, pulled ashore, and shortly thereafter were on their way to London.

Like children who had unexpectedly been let out of school early, the adults suddenly took on new energy. Kaylah and her mother looked at the small fields, meticulously separated from one another; all seemed to be growing vegetables. Occasionally, they saw a farmer ploughing behind the biggest horses they had ever seen. They both commented, with a little surprise, how well-dressed the farmers were, all wearing suits and ties.

Gittel thought this enabled them to go straight from the fields to church. After a few hours they pulled into Charing Cross Station, where the porters were smartly dressed, efficient, and unlike those in Kiev and Warsaw, had pride in their jobs. The Savoy Hotel had despatched two coaches to collect their party from the boat train and take them on the short ride up The Strand to the hotel.

CHAPTER 33

QUEEN VICTORIA'S OBSTETRICIAN

To their party's surprise, but not to Elize's, who never knew which rabbit Maimon was going to pull out of what hat, as their coach turned in to the hotel, Maimon became a count.

"Here is Count Sokolovski," he announced in a Russian-English accent. "Where is hotel manager?"

In a matter of seconds, the manager appeared dressed in a long black jacket, pin-striped trousers, and mirror-shining patent leather shoes, a white shirt and silver tie. Having introduced himself as James Hutchinson, he asked what service the count might like him to render. Maimon told him.

"Wife here is pregnant. You see. Must have an appointment with Queen's doctor for not-yet-born babies. You tell me what time."

"Sir, I mean Count, that is not possible," Hutchinson spluttered.

"Is possible. Either you make appointment, or I wire my cousin, the tzar, who wires your queen, who makes appointment. In such happening, your job finished."

Protecting his job, hassled Hutchinson said, "Count, I work for this hotel. I don't think they would fire me if I couldn't make an appointment for your wife with Doctor St. John Storkman."

This was no problem for Maimon. "Hutchinson, I buy hotel, then make you fire."

"Count, I don't think this hotel is for sale."

"Everything for sale if price right. Also, your wife."

This was now too much for the manager, who spluttered, "Count, this is most irregular."

"Hutchinson," Maimon said, looking him in the eye, "if I give you one million pounds for your wife for three months, and then send back to you, and you keep one million. That is right price."

Drawing himself up to his full 5'6" height, the hotel manager told Maimon in a firm but still-professional voice, "I would never accept that!"

"You may not accept, but your wife, yes. For one million pounds for three months, she accept quick. Sokolovski knows women. Depending on looks, maybe for half a million also yes. Now you make appointment with doctor St. John Storkman of Queen. Come and tell me in suite. In ten minutes." After this, Maimon and his entourage swept up the wide staircase to the hotel's Victoria & Albert suite.

Elize had great difficulty containing herself while Saul and Kaylah looked on in amazement. Sure enough, in less than ten minutes Hutchinson reappeared with a written confirmation of an appointment with St John in forty-five minutes.

"Good," Maimon told him, "is doctor saint from Pope?"

"No, Count, 'St John' is not necessarily Catholic, it is his Christian name and pronounced *sin jin*."

"Ah, naughty Jin. I understand. Now carriage in ten minutes."

Hearing this, the manager backed into the suite's closed door. Opening it with his hands behind his back was challenging, but Hutchinson did it.

In the carriage on the way to the Harley Street rooms of St. John Storkman, Elize asked her amazing husband, "Is this Count thing finished, or is there more to come?"

"I quite enjoyed it," Maimon said with a smile. "I think Count Sokolovski will live for a little longer."

The carriage stopped outside the doctor's rooms, and as Maimon approached the door, it was opened by a nurse. Uncharacteristically, Maimon pushed in first, with Elize following right behind. Off the passage was a large, well-appointed waiting room, and in it a man who Maimon realized must be the famous St. John.

Extremely tall, about 6'6", with a Roman nose down which he seemed to look despairingly at mere mortals, the Queen's doctor wore a shiny black jacket that Maimon had last seen on Mr. Vagalparot. Beneath the jacket were the inevitable pinstriped trousers. gray spats and well shined black leather shoes.

"Sokolovski," Maimon said, thrusting his hand out, to be shaken by St John.

"Hotel tell me you called *Sin Jin*."

"That is correct," the doctor confirmed.

"I also sin," Maimon announced. "With cousin's daughters, Olga, Maria, Tatiana, and Anastasia, we steal Tzarina's jewelleries. Hide diamonds in garden. Tzarina very cross. German sense of humour no laughing matter." He pointed at Elize. "Here is wife, with baby."

 "I can see that," the doctor replied.

"This second baby. First baby not so big stomach. Wife worried something wrong. You examination her?"

"If you would take a seat, Count, and your wife would come with me, I can examine her."

Elize and a nurse disappeared into a room whose door the nurse quietly closed. This left Maimon with the young receptionist, a chance too good for him to miss.

"You Russian?" he asked.

"No, Count, I am English," the pretty girl told him.

"Your mother or grandmother Russian," Maimon told her. "That is why you beautiful. English girls not so beautiful. You Russian." Warming to the task, Maimon went on.

"My wife not Russian. She African. White African woman hard to find but make good wife."

Before he could expand on what makes a good wife, the door opened and the nurse invited Maimon into the examination room, where Elize was sitting on a chair looking like a cat who had lapped up a pint of cream.

"Sit down, sit down, sir… err, Count," St. John Storkman said. "I have some interesting news for you."

Maimon considered asking if this meant his wife had a rabbit in her tummy, but thought better of it.

"Count," St. John reverently continued, "I am happy to tell you that your wife is carrying twins."

"Twins is two babies?" Maimon asked, knowing very well what twins were.

"Yes, Count. Two healthy babies."

Maimon jumped to his feet, grabbed St. John by his ample sideburns, and planted a kiss on each of his cheeks.

"That was not necessary," the doctor pointed out, having been kissed for the first time by a man to whom he was not related.

"I sorry," Maimon told him, "I forget English very reservationed. In

303

Russia two babies same time is good luck. You have vodka?"

"I am afraid not," St. John said, thankful he didn't have to deal with foreigners very often.

"I send you good vodka," Maimon told him. "Give your wife, bring many babies."

Realizing that Maimon could carry on like this for another thirty minutes, Elize got up, pulled him towards the door, and thanked the doctor for his time and trouble.

"Thank you also Mr. Sin doctor," Maimon said, and then stopped before adding, "Vodka and woman best with candle," leaving Dr. Storkman to wonder if the candle was to provide light or for some other purpose.

On the way to the door, Maimon turned to Elize and, gesturing towards the receptionist, said, "Beautiful girl. Russian grandmother," before Elize yanked him out of the building. The carriage door was open waiting for them, and Maimon carefully helped Elize into it before following her up its steps. Closing the door, he said, "That is fantastic!"

"Your Russian or my twins?" Elize asked.

"Our twins, of course. That is amazing! I am so excited! Aren't you?" He took Elize's face in his hands and gently kissed her on each cheek."

"St. John –" Elize began.

"Next time I call him Jonnie," Maimon interrupted.

" – said twins are hereditary," Elize continued, now with a note of sadness in her voice. "My father was one of a twin, so that is probably why."

Reminding Maimon of Piet threw a wet blanket over this exciting news.

"I miss your father so much," he said. "Such a good man. Killed for what? A stupid war that politicians start and never fight themselves. Good people like Piet do their fighting and often pay the ultimate price."

Elize took Maimon's hand in hers and kissed it. "Piet lives on in us and our children. That is the circle of life," she told him philosophically.

"None of our children should ever have to fight wars," he said adamantly, and then, on reflection, added sadly, "Oh, if only that could be so."

To cheer him up Elize reminded Maimon that she was carrying two of his babies, and that did the trick. He stroked her tummy, smiling, as they returned to the hotel.

"Do you mind if I tell your mother and Kaylah?" Elize asked.

"As long as you tell Sarah, too," Maimon added.

CHAPTER 34

MAGDA'S LETTER

When Maimon got back from the doctor, the front desk told him that Mr Nathan was waiting to see him.

Opening the door into Edward's suite without knocking, Maimon found his lawyer sorting papers into different piles.

"Welcome to London, my friend," Maimon said, hugging Edward who was as much as a friend as he was his lawyer, before adding, "This is your fifth visit to London if I remember correctly."

"And my first one not mining-orientated. It makes a nice change," Edward said smiling. "I have been in business thirty years and never in an action anything like this like this."

"Once in a lifetime?" Maimon asked.

"Once in many lifetimes," he was told.

In a few minutes the papers were all in their right places and order, piled in the middle of the suite's dining room table.

Knowing he had to do it at some stage, and probably the sooner he got it over with the better. Addressed in green ink to 'Elize and Maimon Sokolovski,' it could only be one thing.

"From Magda?" Maimon asked.

Edward nodded. "I saw her in the Fort in Braamfontein. The police are keeping her there in a holding cell. Normally she would be offered bail, but the magistrate said that if she took to the bottle again she might be mugged, or worse. I went to see him to get him to change his mind but he wouldn't."

"How was she?" Maimon asked not entirely out of curiosity. He was angry with her, very angry, his overwhelming feeling was that she should be punished for what she had done.

"Distressed."

And so she should be, Maimon thought to himself.

"She had written a letter to you and Elize," Edward said, "and was waiting for me or one of your friends to come and see her, to pass it on to you." He took an envelope out of his pocked, addressed in green ink to "Mrs. Elize & Mr. Maimon Sokolovski," and handing it over, Edward asked, "How is Elize coping with it?"

"Badly. She cries a lot and dreads the day she has to see Magda. Because she knows it is at least a month away, she has pushed it to the back of her mind. The problem is that every now and then it pops up in the front."

"And you?" Edward asked.

Maimon didn't answer, not because his feelings were unclear. He just didn't know if he should tell his friend that he thought Magda should be hanged. His dilemma was solved by squealing and laughter they heard in the corridor.

Putting his head round the corner, Maimon saw two deliriously happy children and four smiling adults. A good time to join in, he thought, slipping the envelope in his pocket.

Joshua and Sarah were so excited they could hardly speak, so Elize and Maimon took them to a corner of their suite and quietened them down.

"Good manners is girls first," Maimon pointed out.

"I got three things," Sarah said excitedly. "Two dolls and lots of clothes. Here are the dolls," she said, thrusting them in Elize's face. "Can I go and fetch the clothes now?" she added, almost bounding out of her chair.

"No. Sit down. Now it is Joshua's turn," Elize told Sarah, who did so impatiently.

From behind his back, in slow motion, Joshua brought out a medium-sized wooden box. Putting it carefully on the table, he slid open the lid to reveal a working model of Stephenson's Rocket.

"Do you know the real Rocket can go twenty-five miles an hour?" he asked Maimon.

"I never knew that," Maimon lied. "Thank you for telling me."

Not sure how to display his appreciation, Joshua held back, but when he saw Maimon open his arms, he jumped into them. The big man and the small boy held each other tight for almost a minute, and then Joshua said,

"My mother said you were from heaven. She was right."

"We are all from heaven," Maimon reminded him.

Elize held Sarah on her lap, who held two dolls on hers, and said, "And I have also got a present from God."

The children looked on the floor for any unopened parcels, and not seeing any, looked back at Elize.

"My present, also from Uncle Maimon, is two babies in my tummy."

Sarah looked up at Elize, as if it was the icing on the cake.

"I think it would be a good idea to write to your Mummy, telling her about the trip, and what you bought today," Elize suggested.

"I will do that now," Joshua said firmly, adding in a superior manner, "Sarah can't write, she is too small."

"Then I will write what she tells me to," Elize announced. "Let's go into your bedroom to do so."

With all the excitement, they decided to have dinner in the big suite. Room service was a novelty for the ex-Saratov residents, which added to the excitement of the day. As an additional special treat, the children, and also the adults, were allowed to eat with their fingers. When the serviettes ran out, bath towels were inspanned[117] to everyone's laughter and excitement.

The fun wasn't over for Joshua and Sarah, who were to have the first truly hot baths of their lives. To make it extra special, their temporary parents made sure both baths were deep, with Maimon washing and drying Joshua in one bathroom, and Elize doing the same for Sarah in the other.

"Is this how the Queen lives?" Sarah asked Elize. Believing she was telling the truth, Elize answered the little girl, "I think so."

More excitement about their first-ever pajamas, and then different stories for each of the children, before tucking-up time. Elize saw something was bothering Sarah.

"What is it, my skat?"[118] she asked gently.

"Can I please sleep in your bed tonight? I am scared here," a little voice said.

"Of course. Uncle Maimon will carry you across."

Which he did, making one happy little girl.

"And you?" Maimon said to Joshua.

---

117 *Assembled often for labor*

118 *Treasure*

"I'm fine here," the boy replied. Truth be told, Joshua wasn't 100% fine, because some time in the middle of the night, Maimon felt some knees and elbows climbing over him. That was OK, too.

It wasn't only the children for whom a hot and deep bath was a novelty, and from having a sitting room full of excited children and adults, Maimon and Elize suddenly found themselves alone. While Maimon welcomed the newfound quiet, Elize took the last of the plates to their own kitchen, before sitting down at the round dining room table.

"You have the letter," Elize said, more as a statement than a question.

Maimon took the envelope out of his pocket and put it on the table between them, so that it faced Elize. The both looked at it for a minute or two, and then Elize opened it, removed the exercise book sheets inside, and began to read aloud.

My Loving Children,

I don't expect you to love me anymore, and I don't deserve your love anymore, but I just want you to know that I am bitterly sorry for what I did.

Sorry is an easy word to say; perhaps there is a better word in English, but I don't know it.

What I did deserves a heavy penalty. Some people are saying that I should be hung, and perhaps they are right. But the lawyer that Mr Nathan kindly found for me says I will not be executed. Instead, I will probably sit in jail for a long time. When I asked him how many years that would be, he said that depends on the jury, and also on which judge I get. Some, he said, are stricter than others. That is my punishment. I cannot blame the devil. He didn't make me drink. The blame is all mine.

Every day when I wake up here, I feel that I am being punished, and that is right. What I did was a terrible thing, and this is society's way of making me pay for it.

But when I wake up, or in the night when I cannot sleep, I think of how you are being punished for what I did. That is not fair and that is not right. I ask God why he is punishing you, but He does not answer me.

Mr Nathan says you are overseas, and that he will give you this letter in London, and so I know you cannot visit me. And when you come back, if you don't want to see me, I understand. I do not deserve any compassion.

If God was a fair God, he would have had me fall under a wagon. That would have been fair. But he did not make that happen. No, he made me do something much worse, and not only to me, but more to you.

Please don't think that I am blaming God. He did not do the terrible thing.

I do not expect you to forgive me: God knows, few people in your position would, so why should you?

That is all I have to say.

Your mother,
Magda

Tears ran down Elize's cheeks as she gasped for air. As much as Maimon wanted to comfort the only person in the world he loved, this was her issue, and she had to deal with it. If she wanted him, she would ask with her eyes, or her voice, or her arms. Instead, she just sat at the table and wept.

That gave Maimon a chance to again think about Magda and what she had done. She was right. It wasn't God's fault or the devil's. It was her fault. One hundred percent her fault, and she was being punished for it, and that was good. As to why God had punished Elize and had punished him, that just proved once again what he had long suspected. Either God didn't care, or He had other, supposedly more important, things to do – or maybe even both. Fuck God. Yes, Fuck God, who watched impassively as His people were murdered in pogroms. In fact, now that he thought of it, why did supposedly smart people like Zelig believe in God? Because they were demented, Maimon decided.

Yes, he was right. Fuck God.

Maimon ordered a double Glenlivet for himself and a gin and tonic for Elize; and as soon as they came, Elize, who was still sobbing, downed hers. Wordlessly, Elize gave Maimon his pajamas, which he put on because Sarah was sleeping with them.

Something bothered Maimon. There was someone who had also done wrong, and then he remembered. It was Edward. What right did he have to find a lawyer, that he, Maimon, would have to pay for, to defend the woman who murdered his son? Obviously, Edward wasn't thinking clearly, and he would take it up with his supposed lawyer friend in the morning. With that settled, Maimon fell asleep.

After a while Elize had no more tears, and she just stared at the letter that Maimon had pushed across to her. Elize didn't want to touch it again, as if it was a castor bean plant that would poison her. Her mother was a good woman, Elize knew that. She just had a weakness like all human beings have a weakness. After all, it was her, Elize's, weakness that didn't say to Maimon, "My mother has a problem. It is not safe to leave Adam with her." But she did not say that, and therefore she should also be in jail. But if she went to jail, what would happen to her babies? Elize could no longer fight this battle alone. Carefully, so as not to squash Sarah, Elize got into bed and hugged Maimon, and he hugged her back because she had suffered enough.

CHAPTER 35

CHANGING MANY LIVES

Maimon woke at six, his mind no longer on Magda's letter but on the morning's meeting ahead. Maimon was lucky, he had the meeting to concentrate on. Elize was less fortunate. Maimon didn't give Magda a thought, his mind fully focused on the next few hours. Quietly, he showered and dressed and went down for breakfast, where he found Edward halfway through his meal.

Pointing at his plate, Edward said, "This proves I slept less well than you did."

Maimon smiled weakly.

"You are mad with me, aren't you, for finding a decent lawyer to defend Magda?" Edward said quietly.

"Actually I am. Not only to help a woman who deserves no help, but to use my money to do so. Who do you work for, Edward?" Maimon asked sarcastically.

Edward looked across the table at the man, actually the boy, less than half of his age, whose experience of life was extremely limited and who had, in so many ways, been more fortunate than he would perhaps ever realize.

"Well, Edward who I you work for?" Maimon asked impatiently.

"Not for me."

"You are right. Not for the Maimon who is sitting across from me, but for his better self."

"And who might that be?" Maimon asked, not expecting a debate about what was or was not his better self.

"That is the man who told me that when he asked permission to marry Elize, he said he would look after her mother no matter what."

"That is not what I said," Maimon retorted.

"I wasn't there," Edward replied. "But I am sure that is what you meant."

Edward was right. That is exactly what Maimon meant when he was on his knees under the fig tree all those years ago.

"You are right, my friend, and thank you for reminding me of it," Maimon said sincerely.

"If you hadn't said that I would have walked out on you here and now."

"And left me to handle this morning's meeting all on my own?"

"Entirely on your own. But that is history now. I am going to my room to get the papers and will meet you in the lobby in five minutes."

Edward left and Maimon breathed a sigh of relief. Following minor matters do great empires begin to crumble, he remembered Ayna telling him, though he couldn't remember whom she was quoting.

They met in the hotel lobby and walked in silence to the Annual General Meeting of the South Britannic Insurance Company.

The meeting was due to start at nine a.m., and by 8:50 Maimon and Edward were comfortably seated in the front row of Butchers' Hall in Bartholomew Close in the City of London. It was an unbelievably grand hall, Maimon had to admit, and he only hoped the occasion would not overawe him. On the stage was a long table with nine chairs facing the hall, and one on the end at right angles. It was the only occupied chair, and to it went Edward, some papers in hand. A minute or two later he returned to Maimon, explaining that he had registered with the Company Secretary the two 100-share certificates in his and Maimon's names, enabling them to officially attend the meeting.

Although he had envisaged the scene a million times in his head, Maimon never realized how quick and brutal it was going to be.

Over their left shoulder, two rows back, was a tall, smartly dressed gray-haired man in a blue striped three-piece suit, a gold fob watchchain stretching from his jacket's buttonhole to a pocket in his waistcoat.

"That is the Radcliff's senior partner," Edward told Maimon. "Will we need him?" Maimon asked nervously.

"I don't know. It is really just £100 insurance," Edward whispered back. "And the other fellow?" Maimon asked, looking at the poorly dressed middle aged man who looked out of place in the magnificent Butchers Hall. His shirt was into at least it's second day of wearing, and probably its third or even fourth, with its detachable heavily starched collar that was clean on that morning. No fob watch chain, or pocket handkerchief, complemented his shiny suit of a style worn a decade earlier.

"A press hack from one of the dailies."

On closer inspection he didn't seem a threat, Maimon decided, breathing a sigh of relief.

Just then the company's board of directors filed in, nine men who seemed to be aged between 60 and 80, Maimon guessed, most with moustaches and all in ill-fitting suits. A couple were limping, and a few wore medals whose ribbons had seen better days. The animals they looked closest to were walruses, Maimon decided. One of the walruses recognized the Radcliff's senior partner.

"Hello, James," the walrus called out. "What are you doing here?"

"Just keeping an eye on my clients," the senior partner replied.

"I didn't know you had any," the walrus replied to chuckles all round.

"I see we have two visitors," the Chairman observed. And then, addressing the man at the end of the table, "Are they accredited, Chambers?"

"Yes, Mr Chairman. They each have 100 shares."

"Good, then let us proceed," The Chairman started. "The first item on the agenda is the appointment of the directors. Nominations have been received for the reappointment of the nine gentlemen at this table. All in favor raise your hands." Nine arms went up like clockwork. "All against raise your hands." Maimon and Edward raised theirs.

"Fine, motion carried. Now to the next item on the agenda," the Chairman continued.

"Not so fast, Gaston Chevrolet," Maimon called out.

"This is not a racing circuit," the Chairman said. "Perhaps the gentleman in the first row is at the wrong meeting."

"No, sir. My name is Maimon Sokolovski, and I am at the correct meeting. I require the votes for and against this motion to be counted."

"Alright," the Chairman said impatiently, "It is 200 against ..."

"No, Mr Chairman," Maimon interrupted. "It is 952,000 against."

"Really?" the Chairman said patronizingly, in a tone he reserved for foreigners. Leaving no doubt in anyone's mind that he found this quite tiresome, he said mockingly. "How does 200 shares become 952,000? Are we back in Biblical days – Ecclesiastes 11:1, if I am not mistaken?"

While the Chairman and Maimon were verbally duelling, Edward had taken the proxy votes for 951,800 shares to the Company Secretary, who verified their validity.

"Chalmers, what is the tally?" the Chairman called out.

"952,000 against Mr Chairman," Chalmers reported.

There was a deafening silence, broken by Maimon pointing to the walruses and quoting an Oliver Cromwell saying he had learned from Ayna: "Depart, I say, and let us be done with you. In the name of God, go."

The walrus near the end of the table stood up and shouted. "Fortescue, how did you let this happen?"

Maimon answered the question for him. "It isn't the chairman alone who bears the responsibility for the position in which you find yourselves. The board minutes record that all of you voted to pay only minimal dividends, despite record profits year after year. Doing so disillusioned your shareholders, who voted with their feet."

"You said this would never happen," another walrus called out.

"Oh, shut up, Algernon. You should be at Cowes, anyway. I forgot you just come to collect your fees. Never say a word and don't contribute anything."

While the bickering was going on, Maimon had gone up to the Company Secretary and doubled his salary to £2,000 a year.

"You have stolen our company," the Chairman shouted at Maimon.

"No, sir, it is you who invited me to mount the raid that resulted in my acquiring the shares I did."

"I never did such a thing," the chairman protested.

"Indirectly you did. I own a hotel in Johannesburg that was insured by South Britannic. One night three inebriated British soldiers got into a brawl. In the course of which, they knocked over a paraffin lamp, which caused a curtain to catch alight, and subsequently the hotel to burn to the ground. Your Johannesburg office refused to pay our £2,000 claim, maintaining that the fire was caused by an act of war. Three soldiers fighting among themselves an act of war? Gentlemen, refusing to pay a £2,000 claim, together with your parsimonious dividend policy, resulted in my gaining control of your company."

"Fortescue, how am I going to pay for my daughter's wedding and my son's commission? Tell me! How am I?" another walrus asked, his voice shaking with emotion. Now sobbing, he added, "Clementine will leave me. It is the poorhouse, that is where I will have to go."

The broken man sat down, still sobbing, his head in his hands. No one moved. Not one of his fellow board members, some his friends, went over and put an arm on his shoulders. Not one made a move to commiserate with the man whose life had disintegrated in front of their very eyes. For a whole minute no one moved.

Then Maimon got up, slowly walked to the stage, up the few steps onto it, and made his way to the distraught, now ex-board member. Dropping to his haunches, Maimon handed his handkerchief to the sobbing man, who took it, and then looked at Maimon before wiping his eyes. When the sobbing had stopped, Maimon said quietly, "What is your name?"

"Hubert Cuthbertson," a quaking voice answered.

"Hubert, come to the Savoy Hotel tomorrow morning at eight. I am sure we can work something out together," Maimon said, standing up and, retracing his steps, reclaiming his seat next to Edward.

In the last couple of minutes, Maimon realized they weren't walruses at all, but men, some of whose lives he had possibly, or probably, ruined. Nobody else had done so, he alone was responsible for their hardships, the magnitude of which he hoped he would never know.

Quietly and sadly, all nine shattered men filed off the stage. Maimon turned to Chalmers, and said, "Please arrange a meeting with the company's management at ten one morning this week, and let me know what day. In the meantime, it is business as usual."

Chalmers said, "Yes, sir," gathered up his papers and left the beautiful Butchers' Hall to two bewildered Jews, one South African and the other Russian, who looked at each other non-plussed.

"How the hell did you do it?" Maimon asked, incredulous at what they had achieved.

"I thought you were never going to ask," Edward replied, smiling. "The London stock exchange operates on a wholesaler basis, and the biggest wholesaler, that they call a jobber, is Durlacher. Your lawyers, Radcliff's, instructed Durlacher to buy all South Britannic shares that became available, and register them one-third each in Rothschild's and Barings' and Seligman Brothers' nominee's names, so each one has about thirty percent of the company. This should have aroused the board's suspicion, but it didn't, which proves how asleep at the wheel they were. These three merchant banks paid for the shares under a guarantee from the Nederlandshe Bank in Johannesburg, but as they knew the company's assets were closer to £20 million, they never called up the guarantees. So now you owe the three Merchant Banks about £650,000 each."

"And that was the guarantee document I signed in Johannesburg," Maimon remembered. "I owe you one," he told Edward, smiling.

"One what?"

"One house wherever in the world you want it," Maimon said. "Think about it and let me know."

"What are you going to do with the money?" Edward asked.

"Leave it in London with the Bank of England for the time being. Then see what opportunities present themselves."

"There are wonderful opportunities in Johannesburg. Why don't you bring it back?"

"Edward, you must understand," Maimon told him, "A Jew and his money should never live in the same country."

They set out walking back to the hotel, each reflecting on the past hour, which would affect so many people, mostly unknown to them, in different ways.

"Do you remember Ravi at the Hights Hotel?" Maimon asked.

"Yes."

"When I had no money, and I told him I was saving up till I had enough to go and fetch Elize, he told me there was no such number as enough."

"After repaying the loans and settling the fees, you should end up with about £18 million. Is that enough?"

They walked a further 50 yards before Maimon replied, "When I had no money, enough was important. To buy a house, feed and clothe my family, with some left over for charity. I was fortunate to reach that figure early in my life. Theoretically, I should have packed up and moved to a tropical island. I didn't, because it isn't the money from successful deals that gives me satisfaction, but competing and winning. In a way the money is a byproduct. An extremely nice one, I must admit, but a by-product nonetheless."

They walked on in silence, Edward reflecting on what Maimon had said, and thinking that this applied to many of his clients.

Maimon, elated beyond words, wondered when he should tell Elize and how she would react.

CHAPTER 36

BACKSLIDING

In the lobby they met Kaylah in tears. "We are going back. All of us."

"What!" Maimon exclaimed. Realizing the lobby wasn't the best place to discuss his family's affairs, he steered his sister to a quiet alcove where they wouldn't be overheard.

Kaylah dried her eyes, composed herself, and told Maimon what had happened. Their mother, while enjoying being in London, did not feel secure away from Saratov and said she had decided to go back.

"You know she and Dad cannot cope on their own," Kaylah continued, "so I have to go back, too. And while Saul is really excited about the job you offered him, he will not let me return on my own."

Overhearing this, Joshua, who was already showing signs of homesickness, said he wanted to go home, too, and Sarah who up till then was happy with Elize and her dolls, said she also wanted to go back.

Maimon smiled to himself; telling Elize about his business coup all of a sudden paled into insignificance compared with the crisis that he now faced. His mother was the key, and he had to turn her around, and do so in the company of the rest of the family, which now included Joshua and Sarah.

"What are we going to do?" Kaylah asked her little brother, who seemed to have a solution to every problem.

"We are going to have a meeting in our suite in ten minutes. You make sure everyone is there. I will talk to Elize," he answered with more confidence than he felt.

Maimon found Elize crying her eyes out, because with her mother in jail and Maimon's mother in Saratov, her twins would not have an Ouma.

Smiling to himself, Maimon was reminded of the "from hero to zero" saying he had heard in Kimberley from a miner who found an eight-carat stone one day, and in one of the market's doldrums periods, sold his concession for just £10 the next.

He calmed Elize, explaining that they were having a meeting in a few minutes time, and it would not look right if she came in crying.

On the way into their suite's sitting room, Maimon lifted the lids on both their toilets and purposely left the doors open in those two little rooms.

In their sitting room he found everyone seated in silence; Joshua and Sarah on the floor. Without introductory remarks he sailed right in. Looking at the adults, Maimon said, "Kaylah told me that you want to go back to Saratov, and if that is what you really want, then you must go."

The blood drained from Elize's face. How could Maimon say this? They had fought so hard to get Kaylah and Saul, and his parents as well, to come to South Africa, and now, to her horror, instead of telling all of them how wonderful Johannesburg was, he decided to use this moment to do some lavatory experiment.

Looking directly at his mother, Maimon said, "In London, before you get on a bus you have to buy a ticket. It costs one penny. If you decide not to ride, the bus company doesn't give you your penny back. When you buy tickets on a steamship from London to Johannesburg, it doesn't cost a penny. It costs hundreds of pounds. The same amount of money it would cost to buy every single house in Saratov, and still have enough left over for a Purim party."

Maimon looked away from his mother to Joshua, and getting down on his haunches, said, "Would you please go and pull the chain in the toilet and then come back here?"

Joshua did as he was told.

Looking straight at his mother, Maimon said, "That noise you heard was like flushing hundreds of pounds down the toilet, into the ocean, and lost forever. If that is what you want to do, then do it. But remember one thing: it is your son's hard-earned money that you are throwing away. Come to South Africa now with us. If after six months in Johannesburg you want to go back to Saratov, I will pay for your tickets. I will come back in ten minutes for your decision."

Maimon took Joshua by the hand and went into their bedroom. Elize followed with Sarah. They all sat on the double bed.

"I know it is hard for you," Maimon said to Joshua, "but you must remember that in a year or so, and maybe less, your mother is coming to Johannesburg to live with you and Sarah. Also, you have Boris, your own horse waiting for you, and if you don't take him, he will have to pull carts for the rest of his life, sometimes in the rain, and often he will get whipped."

Elize looked at Maimon questioningly, and anticipating what was coming, he said, "That is exactly what is going to happen. If you don't believe me, come to Newtown any day of the week."

"And what about Katya, my Pony?" Sarah asked.

"He will have to live the rest of his life in a field eating grass with no one to love him."

"There is one thing I would like to say," Elize butted in. "Both of you can sleep in our bed with us for as long as you like."

"I want to go to Katya," Sarah said, looking at Joshua. "Please come with me? Then we can ride together."

Maimon, Elize, and Sarah all looked at Joshua, who nodded OK, biting his lower lip.

"Let's have a Johannesburg hug," Elize said, pulling the children and Maimon into a giant embrace. After it was over, Maimon went next door to hear the meeting's decision.

Instead of six people there was now just one, Kaylah, and she was smiling broadly. "You were wonderful," she said. "Thank you so very much."

Maimon smiled and thought to himself, all in a day's work. He didn't say that, but instead said, "I have got to get a model train to operate. Please excuse me."

Maimon and Joshua spent the next hour assembling the model of Stephenson's Rocket, and then running it round their suite over and over, until it ran out of methylated spirits, and stopped. Maimon called room service for a refill, and was told they didn't keep methylated spirits in the hotel, but that they would send out to a shop for a bottle, which they expected to have within thirty minutes.

"Do you have room service in your house?" Joshua asked.

"Not exactly. Something nearly the same," Maimon replied, which made Joshua visibly happy.

Just then there was a loud knock on the door. "I'll race you to open it," Maimon said to Joshua, making sure to come second. It wasn't room service with the meth, but Kaylah, who wanted to know if any of them wanted to come to the Queen's house, Buckingham Palace, to see the soldiers marching up and down. Maimon and Elize chose not to go, and, for the first time since they read Magda's letter, they found themselves alone.

"How did the meeting go this morning?" Elize asked, but he did not answer. Noticing Maimon hanging a "DO NOT DISTURB" sign on the outside of the door, which he then locked, she knew.

Later, lying on the bed, Elize said, "It went well."

"Actually, it did. Very well. It went just as Edward and I planned."

"What does that mean for us?" Elize asked.

"That we will have to stay in London for another week. Also, that we have got a lot more money."

"You are such a clever man. Are you tired?"

"No," Maimon said, and so they did love again.

Afterwards, Maimon was tired. Elize got up and took an envelope from the writing desk and handed it to Maimon when he woke up. On the outside was written "Letter #2."

Maimon opened it carefully and then gave the pages to Elize to read aloud. It began,

My Dear Darling Wonderful Maimon,

I could not believe that anyone could change their minds this morning, but you did, from the oldest to the youngest. You were brilliant.

Thank you for leaving me to read, and digest, my mother's letter. You were right, again, I needed to do it myself. It was hard, extremely hard, but I knew you would be there when I needed you, and you were. Thank you. When we get back home – and what a home you are building, f rom the plans it looks like a little hotel – I will have to decide if, and when, I go and visit my mother, but that is a back of the wagon decision, as we say.

I never thought you would get me an appointment, and on the same day, to see the Queen's obstetrician. Count Sokolovski, indeed. I suspect I have not seen the last of him. I learned that in England they make you Sir and Lady So-and-So, but I would rather be Countess Sokolovski, even if the title is self-endowed. After all, how many people can say that their husband is a cousin of the Tzar!

Thank you for bringing me to London. Paris was beautiful, and much smaller, but London is really special. I know you are busy during the day, but could we go to the theater on one or two nights? I am sure you will enjoy it, and it will take your mind off business for an hour or two.

But maybe you don't want that.

One of the magazines in the hotel says that there is going to be an auction next week. I have never been to one, and it doesn't cost anything to get in. It only takes an hour or so, and it would be wonderful if we could go together, so please don't make any meetings for when that happens.

When I get home, people are going to ask what I enjoyed most about my stay in London, and no matter what we do together in the next week, it has to be my visit to the doctor you kissed.

> *For anybody who reads this letter after we are dead, it was a man Maimon kissed. Maimon doesn't kiss men, except this one, who was the Queen's doctor, whom Maimon kissed on both cheeks as a joke. I don't think Doctor Sin Gin thought it was very funny.*

> *Before you get an even greater swollen head, don't forget I know something that you don't. Remember Herbert Castens from my last letter? He was South Africa's first rugby, and I think cricket as well, national captain. In South Africa sport is especially important, so if we have sons you are going to be playing a lot of cricket and rugby. I will buy you some books about them – you have looked at enough boiler and furnace pictures for the time being.*

> *And so, my darling – who as I write this, is playing model trains with someone who is not even his son – just as you are there for me, I am for you. I don't know if you will ever need me, perhaps when we are old together, not that I can ever imagine you being old.*

> *I love you so much.*

> *Your*
> *Elize*

Maimon took the letter from Elize, folded it carefully, replaced it in its envelope, and put it together with his business papers.

Maimon and Edward met later that day to plan their business

week. They had already set up a meeting with the senior management of the insurance company, in addition to which Edward pointed out they needed to see the three merchant bankers who were financing his South Britannic purchase. Maimon said he wanted to visit the Bank of England to open an account there. The Bank of England did not open accounts for individuals, but Edward was wise enough not to tell Maimon this. Edward also wanted to pay a courtesy call on Durlachers, the jobbers through whom they had bought their insurance company shares, and Maimon said he would also like to attend that meeting. Just one last thing, Maimon added, "There is an auction of pictures on Thursday morning that I need to go to, so please don't make any meetings when that happens."

Leaving Edward to set up the appointments, Maimon went down to see his friend Mr Hutchinson. Reverting to the count's Russo-English accent, Maimon asked the hotel manager to get him a detailed catalogue of the upcoming art auction and to register him as a potential buyer. Furthermore, handing the manager a £5 note, he asked him to buy the most expensive bottle of vodka in London and to send it to Dr. St. John Storkman with his compliments. As for the change, Mr. Hutchinson should keep it.

The first bank meeting, which Edward had made with the senior partner of Baring Brothers Bank, was at ten the following morning – Maimon was to learn that no meeting with a banker could be scheduled before that time – Maimon wanted to see a senior person at the Bank of England, and Edward believed that his best chance of doing so would be by Baring's requesting it. This proved to be the case, and the Bank of England meeting was scheduled for four p.m. the following day. To lighten what Maimon soon realized was a painfully boring Baring meeting, Maimon used his Rus so-English accent and vocabulary, which seemed not to faze these bankers in the slightest.

"I give you one million pounds, which you keep in safe very safe. Good English?" Maimon enquired. Not getting an answer, he continued, "From that you take interest for loan. Keep rest carefully. Don't lend to bad people, otherwise Okhrana come and that not good for Baring family."

Maimon didn't know if the Baring blueblood he was talking to knew that the Okhrana were the feared Tzar's secret police. From the man's reply, "Don't worry old chap, that won't be necessary" Maimon suspected not, but anyway added his investment instructions.

"When market fall down, I tell you what to buy. Meantime, you keep money in safe, safe for me. Maybe extra safe to make three safes. Two safes good, three safes gooder?" Maimon asked.

"Two safes are satisfactory," one of the Eton-Oxford bluebloods told him.

"English wonderful language," Maimon proudly told the assembled company. "Two safes satisfactory, and better than one safe, worser than three safes, which not satisfactory."

Walking back to their hotel, Maimon and Edward agreed they were not at all impressed by the Baring man and his sidekick, the response of whom, Edward said, was in line with their well-known financial guideline, which was, "If in doubt, do nothing."

"On that basis they are not going to last," Maimon advised. "When in doubt, doing nothing is the worst option; but then who am I, an illiterate Jew from Saratov, to tell these British aristocrats who have been around for generations how to run their bank."

CHAPTER 37

A CONVENTIONAL AUCTION

The reason they were returning to the hotel was to meet Elize, with whom Maimon was going to the Christie's auction house. The couple had carefully looked through the sales catalogue, and Elize had fallen in love with a picture by Pierre-Auguste Renoir. It was called "Luncheon of the Boating Party," and the reason she liked it was because each of the nine visible faces told a different story. Maimon liked a much smaller picture, also by a Frenchman, Henri Matisse, entitled "Nu Bleu IV." It was of a formalised body in motion, whose limbs, even though disconnected, had a wonderful feeling of rhythm.

All the chairs were occupied before the eleven o'clock start. At the chimes of a clock in Christie's antechamber, the auctioneer began describing the first item being sold. Maimon paid particular attention to the price-calling of the auctioneer and to the psychology of the bidders, so that by the time their items came up, he was au fait with the system. Elize was so captivated taking in the atmosphere that she missed the early bidding on the picture Maimon liked.

The auctioneer started the bidding at £100, raising it in £25 increments until there were just two bidders left, at which point he increased the price by £10 at a time. The auctioneer was just about to knock the picture down for £270, when Maimon raised his paddle and called out "£300."

For a second or two, even the auctioneer was surprised by Maimon's unorthodox approach, but he quickly regained his composure, looked at the £270 bidder, who shook his head, and then knocked it down to Maimon for £300. Elize kissed Maimon and the man on his other side congratulated him.

About a half an hour later, Elize's hoped-for picture was displayed while the auctioneer sang first its praises, and then those of Monsieur Renoir. The longer he went on, the lower Elize's heart sunk. Eventually, he was finished and started the bidding at £1,000, raising it in £200 increments.

The price soon went through £2,000, and then past £3,000, with four bidders still active. At £3,400 one of the bidders dropped out, and at £3,800 another one. The remaining two battled it out till the £4,600 figure was reached. Just as the auctioneer was about to knock it down, Maimon raised his paddle and said in a loud clear voice, "Five thousand pounds."

The hall fell silent as the auctioneer looked at the now-mentally exhausted underbidder, who shook his head, and the picture was then knocked down to Maimon for £5,000. Elize kissed Maimon on the cheek, whispered "Thank you" in his ear as the room broke into applause. The man on Maimon's other side said, "Well done, old chap."

Having previously agreed to leave after the second of their pieces came up for sale, Maimon and Elize walked to the end of the row to further applause, up the passageway, where Maimon handed the paddle to one of the stewards, and out into Bond Street. There he picked Elize up, kissed her, and put her back on the pavement. "Thank you, thank you so much," Elize gushed. "You were wonderful."

"Elize's picture", as the Renoir came to be known, hung in their living room, admired and envied, for many years. In 1923 an overseas dealer who had heard about it came to their house and offered Elize £25,000 for it. She asked Maimon what she should do, and he reminded Elize that it was her picture, and therefore her decision. Elize agonized over her decision for a week and eventually agreed to sell the picture because she could not bear to have something so expensive hanging on the wall. There was one condition she made: whoever bought it should allow ordinary people to view it. The dealer assured her that it's new owner, Mr. Duncan Phillips, would definitely do so. (For those who want to see this wonderful picture, it is now hanging in The Phillips Collection in Washington, D.C.)

Maimon's picture hung in his office for decades: jocularly – or perhaps only partially so – the story went that anyone who "screwed" Maimon would have their limbs torn apart, one by one, as in the picture.

Maimon's meeting with the Rothschild Bank turned out to be a lot more business-like than the Baring one Maimon had suffered through earlier in the day. Again, Maimon said that he would be transferring a million pounds to cover the interest owed, the balance of which was to be held in his account. Furthermore, Maimon told the Rothschild people that sometime in the next twenty years, markets would crash worldwide, and when that happened, or a year or two afterwards, when only the worst was expected, he planned to buy as many buildings in Regent Street as possible. Till then his money would remain in cash. As to when to pull the trigger, he would be in touch with them.

The Rothschild team, taking careful notes, received this information expressionless, as if instructions of this nature were given by clients every day. Having done so, they told Maimon two signed copies of an *aide-mémoire* of their discussions would be delivered to his hotel in the morning, one of which they would appreciate his counter-signing and returning to their office.

One other thing, Maimon added, with regard to their French cousin's winemaking activities in Palestine, he would appreciate being given a letter of introduction to the senior people there. This, he was told, would be done with pleasure.

The following day, Maimon and Edward met with Seligman Brothers, a much smaller bank who nevertheless were members of the exclusive Accepting Houses Committee. Edward didn't remember how many banks belonged, he thought about eight in all, but importantly no more banks were being accepted into this exclusive club, even those much larger than Seligman's.

Maimon gave them the same story as he had the Rothschild team, except, having studied a map of Manhattan, the property he now had in mind was that bordering on Central Park in New York City. All buildings on Central Park South, as well as those on Central Park East and West, for one mile from their junction with Central Park South. He didn't expect Seligman's London office to do this, but if they would have a word with their American cousins, J&W Seligman, he would be most grateful.

Back at the hotel it was all excitement in the Sokolovski suite. Without telling them where they were going, Elize had taken the children to the nursery school run by the synagogue, and as Kaylah promised to behave herself, Elize said she could come, too. Sarah was in the "rabbits" class; before every activity, Sarah, bubbling over with joy, insisted on explaining that they had to hop about like rabbits.

"They told us a story about brave King David," Sarah explained. "And then we sang songs and clapped our hands. And then we did dancing, and the aunties also danced. And tomorrow we are going to do painting." What she didn't say was that during story time she kept glancing back to make sure Elize and Kaylah were still there.

Joshua was in the "lions" class. After a little coaxing, he related the morning's happenings.

"First, we sat in a big circle and the Morah, that is what they call the teacher, told us the story of Jonah and the whale. Do you know that story?" he asked Maimon, who nodded. "And then we did an experiment all about the air pressing down on us. I tried to explain it to the aunties, but they couldn't understand. We each had a little tin with some water in it, which the teacher put on the stove until the water boiled, and then he put the lids on the tins, and you know what happened?"

"Let's ask Uncle Maimon if he knows?" Elize said.

"When the tins got cold, they collapsed and got smaller," Maimon said.

"I knew Uncle Maimon would understand," Joshua told the aunties, as if it was something only men knew about. "Tomorrow we are going to do another experiment." Then turning to Elize, he said, "Can I go again tomorrow, please?" Elize's smile answered his question.

While Maimon was being told about the nursery school, Saul was having his studies interrupted by Kaylah, who was more excited than she had been for years. Kaylah explained that she only went along to keep Elize company, and instead of boring cheder[119] taught by old men, Sarah's class was taught by two girls in their twenties, and Joshua's by a man the same age. They read stories, and then the younger ones danced and sang songs while Joshua's class did the science experiment.

"It is called kindergarten. I think it is a German word," Kaylah explained. "And the children loved it and can't wait to go back tomorrow. You remember how we hated cheder? It was like the difference between black and white and color. When we get to Johannesburg, I want to be a kindergarten teacher. If they haven't got a kindergarten school there," she announced, "I will start one." Then, upon reflection, she added, "It can't be too difficult, can it?"

"When you want to do something, it gets done" Saul reminded Kaylah, who smiled and gave him a kiss.

---

119 *Religiously orientated school classes*

CHAPTER 38

COUNT SOKOLOVSKI vs THE BANK OF ENGLAND

A head of their meeting with the Bank of England, Maimon and Edward set aside a morning to discuss what to do with the insurance company. With Maimon adamant that he did not want any of his money underwriting risks over which he had no control, the discussion turned to what Edward called "monetizing the investment" and Maimon termed "selling the company." They agreed it would be best to strip the assets out of the company, and then sell South Britannic, which had a good name in the market and over 40,000 policyholders. Edward told Maimon of the various options, all of which included involving one or more London merchant banks, as well as lawyers and accountants. True to form, Maimon came up with a heretofore unheard-of way of selling the company.

Firstly, they would put advertisements in the main London, Frankfurt, and New York financial newspapers, inviting interested parties to apply to attend a meeting that Maimon called "The Sale Operation."

"TSO", as it came to be known, required all interested and accredited parties to attend a meeting in the Savoy Hotel at eleven am the following Friday; at which time and place, a representative of each potential buyer would hand Maimon a sealed envelope stating the price and conditions at which their company would like to buy South Britannic Insurance Company, it being under stood that before a transfer of the insurance company to the new buyer, its financial assets would be stripped out.

Even more revolutionary was that Edward would read aloud each of the bids submitted for all to hear. This was to minimise the possibility of any "verneukery,"[120] as Maimon called it. As they expected, the announced modus operandi drew much negative publicity in the press, fuelled, Maimon suspected, by one or more of the merchant banks, lawyers, and accountants, who, as a result of this revolutionary sale method, would forfeit substantial fee income. That wasn't his problem, Maimon reminded himself.

Edward pointed out that negative publicity was never a good thing, and it might be an idea to call in the editors of the London papers to remind them that every coin has two sides. This they did, advising the editors that if they wanted their reporters to attend the Friday meeting – which he knew they desperately did – then Maimon needed to see more balanced reporting of his activities. To restore the balance, the negative reports published to date needed to be replaced by positive ones. Their reporters access, or otherwise, to the meeting would depend on the reports Maimon looked forward to reading. (Little did they know he couldn't read!)

Walking to their Bank of England meeting that afternoon, Edward reminded Maimon that he needed to switch to Russo-English as it was that accent that he had used at the Barings meeting. In fact, before Edward had even mentioned it, Maimon was relishing the thought.

Arriving at the doors of the bank at the same time as the Baring team, Maimon asked the man they had seem in their offices earlier, "Why is circus man here at bank?" He pointed to the bank steward, who was dressed in a long, pink jacket and a top hat. Before the Baring's man could explain that he was, in fact, a bank employee, Maimon added, "Whip and lion gone. Circus man looking to find two. We should go before lion comes." At which point, Maimon hurried into the building. Edward followed, fearful of what was to come but enjoying Maimon's unconventional approach which was so different to those of all his other clients.

Down a long stone passage they walked, following the lion tamer; then up a wide stone staircase, down another stone corridor, and into a mahogany-furnished meeting room. Around the circular table were six chairs, Maimon noted.

"Good chairs," he said to the Baring's man, and to Edward; "We buy twelve for house."

"They are Thomas Chippendale's," the Baring's man helpfully responded. "He is dead."

---

120 Cheating

"Sorry he is dead. We still buy twelve," Maimon said, walking over to what looked like an Old Master painting on the wall. Edward's fears of what Maimon would say next were assuaged by the arrival of three bank officials, all identically dressed in black morning coats, pinstriped trousers, black patent leather shoes, white shirts, and silver silk ties. Thankfully Maimon did not develop his circus theory.

After introductions, for the first ten minutes or so, Maimon and Edward were subjected to a lecture on how good and sound the Bank of England was as the fallback storehouse of gold and foreign exchange reserves for the British Empire. When the senior bank man stopped for a breath, Maimon chipped in.

"Good. We come to proper bank," he said to Edward, and then to the bank men, "In Russia many banks, lots not proper."

Before giving the bank people a chance to enquire which Russian banks Maimon believed were possibly not stable, Maimon continued. "I will lend your bank fifteen million pounds for five years. We agree on interest. What is your number?"

The senior bank man thanked Maimon for his proposal, adding they did not take money from individuals, only from governments.

"I know," Maimon said. "You wrong. Is small money from Andorra better than big money from Sokolovski? And Albania, and Herzegovina, and other poof-poof countries?"

"Sir, I am sorry, but that is our policy."

Maimon looked the bank man in the eye, and in a deep voice said, "I am cousin of Tzar. Russia has gold in your bank. I will tell cousin to transfer gold to Banque du France. You know, Russia has good feeling to France, not good feeling to England." Maimon leaned back in his chair, waiting for the bank's riposte. It never came. Instead, the lead bank man whispered something in the ear of his assistant, who excused himself from the room.

"It is too low," Maimon told the remaining banker. "Your interest is too low."

"You haven't heard it," the banker pointed out. "We will pay you four percent."

"I am right. Interest too low. Federal Reserve of New York want English money to pay for British machinery." This Maimon had learned from Seligman's the day before. "They pay six percent. I will wire them."

"That might not be necessary," the banker said. "You are an

331

experienced businessman, Count. Why don't we meet in the middle, at five percent?"

Maimon did his best to look disinterested. Eventually, he said, "One percent big difference. Much money."

"We could compound the interest every 60 days," the banker offered, sweetening the deal considerably.

Maimon made an effort to look mildly interested, realizing that if he could pull this off, the insurance company deal would pale into insignificance. Pretending to be thinking, Maimon eventually said, "I am here. Bank of England is good bank, like Federal Reserve, who pay compound every thirty days. If you also compound like Federal Reserve, I will accept lower interest rate."

Leaning across to Edward, he whispered, "I have these buggers by the balls."

"It seems like it," Edward replied.

"Excuse me. I look for English word. It is 'concession.' I make big concession. My lawyer says I not smart, but I say OK. Bank of England is good bank. So OK with me."

The banker came across to shake Maimon's hand, saying, "It is a pleasure doing business with you, Count Sokolovski."

"It is pleasure also for you," Maimon replied, smiling "Please excuse my English. I not speak not too badly."

"Considering English is not your first language, you acquit yourself very well," the banker replied obsequiously.

"I am good acquit yourself," Maimon said to Edward proudly.

"Yes, you certainly are," his lawyer agreed.

Happy to get the unpleasantness of business out of the way, the banker asked, "What do you think of the British Empire, Count Sokolovski?"

"British Empire great, wonderful, but soon finished," Maimon told his shocked host.

"Finished, sir! Finished? How is that?"

"Persian Empire great and finished. Roman Empire great and finished. British Empire great, soon finished," Maimon explained.

"How soon is 'soon'? When do you believe this will come to pass?" the banker responded uncomfortably.

"Fifty years at mostest. India, Australia, Canada all gone. Also all African countries. Maybe you keep Gibraltar. Ottoman Empire, also Austrian-Hungarian: both poof. Nineteen-century top for British, twenty-century top for America."

"And the twenty-first century? The banker asked, warming to this strategic global discourse.

"Maybe China. You and me dead, so won't see."

"I have one more question. About Russia. May I ask you that?"

"Russia big place. For many questions I have no answer. But ask anyway."

"It is about the Romanoff dynasty. Will it last?"

At once the jovial count became very serious. He looked behind him to see if anyone was there. Then he said to the banker's two assistants, "You. Out." Maimon was silent until they left the room. After they had departed, he checked that no one was listening at the door. Then leaning forward, in a conspiratorial voice, Maimon said, "In twenty years, Romanoffs gone. Poof-poof. Do not say Sokolovski told you, or I poof-poof."

"And in their place? What will there be?"

"You say $64,000 question," Maimon started. "We say 200 billion rouble question. I have answer. Wait twenty second." At that moment, Maimon called Edward over and whispered, 'How do you think I am doing?'

"You are doing fine," Edward replied. "Just don't mess it up."

"In charge will be General Chaos. This new word for Sokolovski. In Russian nearly same. *Khaos*. Russians like strong man, but where is he? God knows," at which point Maimon crossed himself extravagantly, "but He not telling. Even church He not telling. I good friend of Archbishop Russian Orthodox Church."

"This has been a highly informative discussion, Count," the banker said. "I am so pleased to have had the opportunity of meeting you."

"I am also have had," Maimon replied warmly. "I hope our roads cross again under the bridge which many waters flows over."

The lion tamer was recalled to escort the two visitors out of the building, affording Maimon one last opportunity.

"You find lion?" he asked the steward. "No, sir. I did not."

"Maybe tomorrow or day before," Maimon said sagely. "I hope your lucking is good."

"Thank you, sir," the steward answered before wishing Maimon and Edward a very good afternoon.

"What a nice fellow," Maimon said to Edward. "Pity his lion is lost."

They walked in silence for about 400 yards. There, Maimon found an empty bench, sat down, and said, "Write down this figure."

Edward opened his briefcase, took out a pencil and paper, and waited. For over a minute he sat, pencil poised, before Maimon said," 40689604 five shillings and nine pence"

"What is that figure?" his friend asked.

"How much the bank of England is going to pay me after five years. Put in the commas. It is over £40.6 million."

"You worked that out in your head?" Edward asked incredulously.

"It took more time than I thought. When we get back to the hotel, please check it."

CHAPTER 39

AN UNCONVENTIONAL AUCTION

The next few days flew by. The children attended nursery school every morning, and in the afternoon Elize and Kaylah went with Sarah to what they learned in England were called "little teas." These were held at the houses of similar-aged girls to Sarah, at which three or four of them played together on rocking horses, with dolls, and in one house, even in a miniature, fully operational kitchen.

Joshua also went on "little teas," which, being for older boys, were called "get-togethers." Most of the games they played were with little lead soldiers, carefully painted in the colors of various regiments. One afternoon Saul accompanied Joshua and the other boys in the class, together with their teacher, to the Science Museum. This was undoubtedly the highlight of Joshua's time in London, and Maimon was delighted to join him on two further visits. This gave Joshua the opportunity of proudly explaining the various exhibits to "Uncle Maimon," and for Uncle Maimon to learn a lot more about science than he had known.

The school also arranged an outing for all the children to the Natural History Museum, where, apart from many stuffed animals that the children never knew existed, there was a giant replica dinosaur suspended from the ceiling. Initially, Sarah was afraid of it, but when Elize assured her it was only a play-play animal, Sarah giggled and happily touched its tail.

The fateful Friday eventually arrived – Maimon thought it never would, the clock ticking so slowly – and he was in the large conference room well before the scheduled time, waiting for the insurance company's representatives. Eight insurance companies (five English, two Scottish, and one German) had completed the necessary application forms, and Maimon had notified them all that they were accepted.

"What would happen if they changed their minds?" Maimon worried. The press speculated that the companies would submit prices in the £3-4 million range, and should a company bid £5 million they would probably secure the prize. That was fine with Maimon. Included in the cost of renting the room, the Savoy Hotel had provided tea and coffee and biscuits. Too nervous to have breakfast, unusually the biscuits were eaten by Maimon, his body craving sugar. Eventually the hall filled up.

Edward and Maimon sat at a table covered in green baize, facing rows and rows of formally dressed, white men between 50 and 70.

Maimon welcomed everyone, and then invited representatives of the approved companies to place their sealed envelopes on his table. To his immense relief, eight envelopes of various sizes were placed on the green fabric. At the back of the room, Elize, the only woman present, sat on a chair to one side. In an endeavor to add a degree of excitement to the proceedings, Maimon asked random members of the audience to select an envelope and hand it to Edward, who would then read its contents aloud. The first figure, from an English company, came in at £6 million. Looking up, Maimon saw Elize smiling. Then the two Scottish companies: one at £4.5 million and the other at £4.8 million. Each time Edward read out the figure there was applause. Then another English company at £6.5 million drew excited clapping. Halfway there, Maimon realized it was going to be alright.

Another English company at £6.2 million resulted in groans. Three envelopes remained on the table. The atmosphere was electric. To increase the tension, Maimon asked a gentleman from the back of the room to come forward and select an envelope. Edward opened it, and as he had done in all previous cases, first he read out the name of the company and then their figure. It was £6.8 million from a company in Norwich, which resulted in wild cheers. Two envelopes remained. When the room was deadly silent, Maimon pointed at a man in the front row, who came forward, picked up one of the envelopes, and handed it to Edward.

"The Amicable Society for a Perpetual Assurance Office," Edward announced to a hushed silence, and then "£7 million." The room erupted in cheering.

When silence was again restored, Edward opened the last envelope. He looked at it long and hard before reading out "Hamburger

Feuerkasse." Anyone listening for a pin to drop could have heard it, before Edward said "£7,100,000." Eighty men and one woman were stunned into silence. A single German company had beaten seven British insurance institutions. Maimon slowly got to his feet.

"Those people who read the Terms and Conditions under which South Britannic Insurance Company was offered for sale, will remember that I am not obligated to accept the highest price." A hundred and sixty-four lungs were immediately starved of oxygen. "It is important," Maimon continued, "that this jewel of British insurance remains in the hands of those who live and work in this great country, and I have therefore decided to sell the company to the Amicable Society…"

Maimon never got to finish the sentence. Wild cheering erupted. Maimon was lifted onto the shoulders of a red-faced man and carried round the room to the strains of "For he's a jolly good fellow."

Put down back at his table, Maimon was asked to pose for a flash photograph with Sir Gordon Donaldson, the chairman of the Amicable Society. Noticing Elize trying to get to Maimon, the crowd took up the chant, "Let the lady through, let the lady through." Like the Red Sea parting, a passage formed for Elize to walk through, and to cheers she was photo-flashed kissing Maimon on the cheek. Enjoying the hype and in order to prolong it, Maimon invited Sir Gordon and his team up to his suite for a glass of champagne.

Sipping vintage Moët & Chandon, Sir Gordon said, "Sir, it is people like us who created the British Empire, and it is wonderful to see the next generation building on the foundations that we have laid."

"To the British Empire," Maimon said, raising his glass, not wishing to spoil the party by telling Sir Gordon that he forecast its disintegration within 50 years.

Three bottles of champagne emptied, Sir Gordon, now a little unsteady on his feet, thanked Maimon once again, and having set up a meeting on Monday with Edward to finalise the contract and pick up a check, he led his team out the door.

"You did it. My genius. You did it," Elize said pulling Maimon into the bedroom and locking the door.

Sometime later, back in the sitting room, Maimon noticed an afternoon newspaper had been pushed under the door. Elize read the front page headline: SOUTH AFRICAN SAVES SOUTH BRITANNIC FROM GERMANS, AND GIVES UP £100,000 TO DO SO. There was a picture of Maimon being carried aloft, and a smaller one of Elize kissing him. An illiterate Russian heralded as a champion of the British Empire, Maimon mused smiling to himself, and then thought what benefit he might derive from this sacrifice. Little did he know how unexpectedly it would impact both his and Elize's lives. Elize ordered six more papers to keep as souvenirs.

CHAPTER 40

ADAM'S BIRTHDAY

To reciprocate the hospitality extended to Joshua and Sarah, Elize invited all the school children to a party in their suite that Friday afternoon. With the help of one of the teachers, Elize found a magician. While the girls played ring-a-ring-a-rosies and pass the parcel, the boys had a lot of laughs with blind man's bluff and Are you there, Moriarty? To the children's wonderment, the magician pulled a rabbit out of his black top hat, yards and yards of colored ribbon out of his arm, and to their total amazement, water squirted out of his ears when he coughed.

Immediately after the conclusion of the magician's act, the hotel staff wheeled in a chocolate cake comprising a steam engine and three coaches, which had written on the side in white chocolate, "Happy Birthday Adam."

Everyone looked at Adam Gamzumfeld and called out, "Happy birthday, Adam," in reply to which the little boy shouted, "It is not my birthday." The more he did that, the more the other children called back "Happy birthday, Adam."

Maimon looked across the room at Elize, who nodded in reply. How much more sensible, Maimon thought, to remember a loved one on their birthday, which is so often a happy occasion, than on the day they die, as in the Jewish religion.

When the noise died down, Elize called out, "As the Adam whose birthday it is today isn't here, we won't sing 'Happy Birthday.' Instead, just enjoy the cake. Anyone who wants some, line up in front of me."

For as long as they lived, Maimon and Elize always had a cake on Adam's birthday. When their children were growing up, it was often an ice cream cake; after they left home, it reverted to a sponge-type cake, and as they got older, the cakes became smaller.

The remains of the cake were wheeled away, and in its place the catering staff provided a table covered in a white cloth. On cue the children quietened down. The table was covered with about twenty little candles, which Elize carefully lit, as the little girls gravitated to them. When all the candles were burning, the girls said together, "Thank you God for finishing off the week so nicely for us, and for giving us the Sabbath that we can spend with our family."

Had God been looking down into the room then, He would have seen Maimon and Elize holding hands tenderly, Saul and Kaylah standing so closely shoulder-to-shoulder that a sheet of paper could not come between them, and Gittel giving Anshul a kiss on his bald and scarred head.

Maimon gave a truncated child-orientated version of the Sabbath evening prayer, saying that on Friday night God had finished making the world, even the stars in the sky and everything anybody could ever see.

Before eating it, everyone thanked God for giving them bread, especially as some children in faraway countries didn't even have bread. One of the little boys asked Maimon why God didn't give all the children in the world some bread to eat, to which Maimon responded that he actually didn't know.

"Maybe He is too busy looking after sick people?" the little boy postulated.

"You could be right" Maimon told the little fellow, thinking to himself "Bloody hell. God should get his priorities right and look after little children. Especially little children abandoned by their alcoholic grandmothers."

The pain had subsided somewhat, but certainly not entirely. It would never completely go away, Maimon told himself, nor should it.

The parents of the invited children waited patiently in the passage for the service to end, and then came in to collect their offspring. Elize had organized dolls as gifts for the girls and model trains for the boys, which were handed to them as they left. Sarah's three little friends, Julia, Bella, and Emma didn't want to go home. They wanted to sleep with Sarah. Their parents looked at Elize for guidance, and her warm smile told them that was alright.

With four little girls repeatedly jumping up and down on their beds under Kaylah's watchful eye, and Elize organizing a Sabbath dinner to be served in their suite, Maimon went into their bedroom and collapsed on the bed, physically and mentally exhausted. Worrying about how the insurance company's auction would go had affected Maimon more than he expected. It wasn't the money, as he had told Edward, it was that he hated losing, and bids of around two million pounds would have been bitterly disappointing.

His spur-of-the-moment decision to sell the company to Amicable had probably been the right one and might win him contracts in the future. Hopefully, the profit on those transactions would make up the £100,000 he had given away. Unlikely, Maimon thought, but possible. Then Elize came in and closed the door quietly behind her.

"I didn't know it was Adam's birthday," he said sadly.

"I never told you," Elize answered softly.

"I should have asked," Maimon said, feeling guilty.

"We all deal with tragedies differently. I am making progress, very slowly. Are you?"

"I don't know," Maimon lied. He was angrier with Magda than he had ever been with his father, even that evening on the boat when he learned he was going to Africa and not to America. Her proposed death was still under review, Maimon not having had much time to think of anything more harrowing than Magda being eaten alive by wild dogs.

They lay on the bed on their backs, both sets of eyes on the ceiling but seeing hugely different pictures. Elize was imagining being in their new house, getting the nursery ready for the twins. So different from when Adam was born. Notwithstanding Maimon's request to marry Elize, which Piet admitted seemed genuine, her father was not comfortable with his daughter giving birth without a gold ring on her finger. Willem was gloating, thinking, if not saying, You made your bed, now lie in it. Magda was trying to keep everyone happy, which was just not possible, and Elize was scared. Perhaps at seventeen her body wasn't ready to have a baby, she worried. On top of all that, they had no money. The drought was unrelenting, and the rinderpest had decimated their cattle herd. Thankfully, Adam was born with ten fingers and ten toes, even if it took a long time for him to come out. Then the British army arrived.

Maimon's thoughts were tumbling one over another, like in the pool under a high waterfall. He could not have imagined how the week could have turned out better. He had Elize, and as it is written somewhere in the Bible, his cup was running over.

But he was not at peace. Adam's murder gnawed at his very being Control what you can control, he told himself, and don't worry about the rest. Easier to say than to do, he admitted. Feeling empty and hollow, he reached across to Elize, who had dozed off. She looked so peaceful and contented. He hoped she was. He loved every part of her, from her second toe that was longer than her big toe, to her upturned nose. He was next to her shoulder. He hadn't studied it before. It too was beautiful. Porcelain white and beautifully curved. Not only was she beautiful on the outside, he didn't think she had an evil thought in her head. Maybe about her mother, but he wasn't even sure about that. Perhaps he had enough evil thoughts for both of them. He wanted her then, and there, but you do not disturb angels when they are asleep. Especially ones who had just smiled in a good dream.

Kaylah moulded herself into a big leather chair, her legs and feet tucked under her; she was in another world. It didn't often happen, but Saul knew to leave her alone when it did. God had closed her womb, and this week, for the first time in her life, He gave her a peek into the world of children.

At first it was wonderful, but as the week drew on, and she had more and more exposure to these wonderful little people, she saw what she was missing, and what she was going to miss for the rest of her life. Maybe a doctor in America could open her womb. Maybe it wasn't her fault that they couldn't have children. Maybe there was something wrong with Saul. If that was so, could it be fixed? Kaylah couldn't think how.

Elize's twins would soon be born. She hoped they wouldn't make her envious. Elize was such a wonderful person who had had such a terrible life. Not yet twenty she had watched her father and brother being shot, and heard that her mother was responsible for her only child being murdered. Kaylah thought this kind of thing only happened to Jewish families. What was God doing when all those bad things were happening? And Elize wasn't bitter, despite those tragedies. If only I could be more like her, Kaylah wished, then maybe God would give me twins, too. Unlikely she thought, very unlikely.

Like many men, Saul was uncomplicated. Immersed in figures, with his lumberjacking days behind him, he was as happy as a fox in a chicken coop. He didn't fully understand Maimon, he wasn't sure if anyone did, even Elize, but his brother-in-law seemed a fair person. Maimon had told him, "Above all, I demand honesty and loyalty. Without both of those, we have no future together." Saul had not forgotten that.

One thing bothered him, though. If Maimon was doing something he thought was wrong, should Saul tell him? He didn't expect Maimon to do wrong things, but Saul had been in business long enough to know that no successful businessman ever does everything right. Small wrong things were OK, but when does small become big? What is the cross-over line?

Realizing that he was looking for a problem that might not exist, Saul relaxed. There was the other thing, of course. The one they never spoke about. Saul prayed it was not his fault that they had no children. If the American doctor said it was his fault, what would happen? He knew how much Kaylah wanted children. Possibly more than any other woman he knew. Might she leave him? Saul loved her very much, but he didn't say so often, or at all. They were like two planets in orbit around one another, together for different reasons.

Gittel was a complex character, and as each of her children thought, more complex than necessary. By the time children are old enough to examine their parents' characters, they are set in concrete. Gittel was the boss and that was fine if she was only the boss of Anshul. But the more people bosses get to boss over, the happier they are. Zelig did his own thing, or more accurately, his rabbi's own thing.

Like her mother, Kaylah didn't tolerate anyone bossing over her, and with Maimon sent away, her mother's bossing cupboard was almost empty. One thing didn't make sense to Kaylah, which was why her mother had sent Maimon away. He was her emotional punching bag. Her "lord it over" person day and night, seven days a week.

It was probably for one of two reasons Kaylah thought, and neither of them were particularly nice. Either she sent him away to sink or swim, because there wasn't a possibility for him to make a living in Saratov. Or she didn't want him as a responsibility when she grew old. If he couldn't survive in Saratov, where he had family support, he certainly wouldn't make it elsewhere. After hearing the leopard and hyena story, Kaylah had to concede that he very nearly didn't survive at all. Perhaps being raped by the Cossacks was Gittel's punishment for being so terrible to Maimon. That, Kaylah admitted, was a terrible thought.

The rest of the family had their Shabbat dinner more or less in silence. The four little girls were too excited to eat, and at nine o'clock Kaylah said anyone who wanted a bath could have one in the morning, but now it was bedtime. Lights went out then, and about twenty minutes later she heard the last little voice saying, "Goodnight best friends."

"We are going to services," Elize said, sitting up and blinking as the morning sun streamed into their room.

"We are?" Maimon asked. "Why is that?"

"To say thank you, and to hand back the little girls," Elize told him, heading for the bathroom.

As the six adults and five children approached the synagogue, Maimon had a surprise for Elize – except it wasn't a surprise. He had been gone for too long Elize knew, and Count Sokolovski was overdue for a return visit.

"Is Jewish church?" Maimon asked the guard at the gate, who nodded affirmatively. "You don't look Jewish. What you doing in Jewish church?"

Elize pulled Maimon inside before the conversation moved to the various shades of Christianity. The service had begun, notwithstanding which a number of men came up and congratulated Maimon. Instead of thanking them in English, he did so in Russian, telling his hand shakers "Spasibo."[121]

After the service there was the customary kiddush, savory and sweet finger food, followed by soft drinks for the children and harder stuff for the adults. One of the congregants suggested they drink a toast, to which Maimon responded, "Toast for breakfast. Now vodka time. I drink vodka, you eat toast."

Fortunately for Elize, vodka was not being served, and Maimon refused the whiskey he was offered, telling the steward, "Scottish water for women and childs. Vodka for man."

To try and break the ice, another congregant asked Maimon if he had a deep knowledge of the insurance industry.

"Not deep knowledge. No. I actuarial graduate of Moscow Polytechnic. I get gold medal, first in class, but not real gold, so I give back."

Looking over his shoulder at one of the buffet tables, Maimon spied a pot of cholent. "Why you give poor man's food to rich people? In Russia, no food in week so Shabbat special treat, we eat cholent. Very unhealthy. Makes fat. Also gives heart attack. Jews die from cholent, goyim die from vodka. This I learn in Moscow Polytechnic."

Not seeing any likely conversationalists, Maimon headed for Elize and announced, "Sokolovski ready for Shabbat Schluff."

Kaylah promised to keep an eye on Sarah and Joshua, and to bring

---

121 *"Thank you"*

them back to the hotel with Saul. Their parents had already started the long walk to the Savoy.

Maimon and Elize ambled back to the hotel, holding hands, and looking in shop windows, remembering the things they had done together, and regretting the many they had not. They hadn't managed a theater, Elize pointed out, nor any German opera. There was much to be grateful for, Maimon pointed out.

While Elize and Kaylah bathed Sarah and Joshua, Maimon and Edward had their wrap-up meeting. Maimon asked Edward to come to the station the following morning, in case there were any further matters that they needed to discuss.

CHAPTER 41

BONSOIR OLD THING

The boat train left at eleven o'clock, and as this was one train they could not afford to miss, Maimon had ordered carriages for 10:15. To his surprise and relief, everyone was ready to leave at ten. The middle generation (Maimon and Elize, Saul and Kaylah) were happy to go. It was time to move on. Gittel was excited about embarking on the next leg of this amazing trip her son had organized and paid for, though she told anyone who would listen that she was too old for this kind of thing. Anshul dutifully followed her like a puppy dog, as he had done since he had been beaten almost to death by the Cossacks. The only sad ones were Joshua and Sarah, who had made really good friends in their short time here and would now have to do so in Johannesburg all over again.

On the platform they were shown to their carriage and compartments, and as they were putting their hand baggage in the racks, they heard a choir of little voices singing,

> *"Goodbye-ee! Goodbye-ee!*
> *Wipe the tear, baby dear, from your eye-ee.*
> *Tho' it's hard to part I know,*
> *Johan-nes-burg is where you have to*
> *go, Don't cry-ee, don't sigh-ee,*
> *There's a silver lining in the sky-ee! Bonsoir old thing,*
> *cheerio, chin-chin, Nah-poo, toodle-oo, goodbye-ee!"*

They all rushed outside to see the entire little school who had come to say goodbye to Joshua and Sarah. Waving paper Union Jacks, the children had been practicing for over a week this song that they sang so well.

On one side of the group was the train conductor, and on the other the train driver, and in front of them two press photographers whose cameras were flashing away.

Then Sarah saw it. The biggest teddy bear in the world, which Julia, Bella, and Emma had bought for her as a present. It was almost as big as Sarah. Holding it as best they could, the three little girls walked over to Sarah, to whom they handed it; after which the four of them had a long Johannesburg hug. When the hug was over, the only one not crying was the teddy.

Joshua's friends had bought him a boxed model of the Wright Brothers' airplane, and while none of the boys cried, there were quite a few quivering lower lips.

Over to one side Maimon saw Pauline Nathan standing quietly. Unknown to Edward, Maimon had arranged for her to arrive on the mail boat a week after he had, and the surprise was that the couple could spend some quality time together in London on Maimon's account, taking the boat back the following week.

The train's whistle blasted, and the little choir sang their goodbye song lustily once more. Sarah and Joshua had also been given flags that they waved as the train slowly pulled out of the station. After a while they couldn't hear the song anymore, but they could see twenty or so flags waving in the disappearing distance.

It was then that the children broke down, and it was about half an hour before Sarah (on Kaylah's lap) and Joshua (on Saul's) were ready to think about the exciting trip ahead.

The wonderful thing about traveling first-class Maimon was reminded, is that there are people designated to make sure that you and all your bags (and in their case two pictures as well) were all placed where they should be and unharmed by the upcoming voyage. On the ship, in their cabins, everyone except Anshul was excited. Elize told Sarah and Joshua that if they wanted to they could sleep with her and Maimon; but as their cabins had interleading doors, the children said it would not be necessary.

Dinner on the evening of departure was traditionally a buffet, and the children could not believe that they could take as much food as they wanted, and then still go back for more. To prove it, they did just that. After quick baths they were in bed and soon fast asleep: Sarah guarded by her teddy, and Joshua with his arm around the Kitty Hawk balsa-wood box.

Maimon took a shower and came to bed to find an envelope on his pillow, marked "Letter #3."

A few minutes later, Elize kissed Maimon, took the envelope from him, opened it, and began to read,

My Dear Darling Maimon,

My dream life with you continues. I expected this trip to be wonderful, but it wasn't. It was a hundred times more wonderful than I ever imagined it could be. Not because of all the countries we visited, but because I went to them with you. You are so clever, so strong, and in your presence I feel so safe. Nothing bad could ever happen to me – you would not let it. And when I am in your arms it is like what being in heaven must be like.

I was so proud of the way you handled the meeting on Friday morning. I knew you were nervous, but I was the only one who did. I could feel your heart beating in my chest when the envelopes were put on your table. I knew it was your heart, because mine doesn't make such a loud noise.

Edward told me that you were brilliant at the Bank of England. He didn't go into details, but he did say that when you told them the Tzar was one of your cousins, it opened closed doors. He also told me that you and Barney Barnato are the two smartest men in Johannesburg.

You were wonderful the way you handled what I called the family mutiny. I am only sorry that my father was not there to see it. Hopefully, looking down from where he is, he saw how you brought first your mother, and then Sarah and Joshua, round to what I am sure is the right decision.

I don't understand God, and maybe I never will, but I know that your God, and now mine, too, is an understanding and compassionate God. Rabbi Hertz told me that Jewish people should not carry money on the Sabbath, and I understand that, but I am sure he won't be cross with you for handing all

that money to the rabbi yesterday and asking him to give it to some poor Jewish people. I wasn't spying on you, I just heard you talking as I came out of the lady's bathroom.

And the little boy selling roast chestnuts because his father was drunk or asleep, or both, on the pavement. I don't think he had ever seen a £5 note in his life, and telling him to give it to his mother was so wise.

On the subject of charity, do you know what the highest form of charity is in the Jewish religion? In case you don't, it is giving a person a job. You have no idea how hard Saul has been working on the accounting books he bought in London, and he says he will be ready for the exams by the time we get to Johannesburg, so thank you for that as well.

And, of course, for that wonderful picture. I know you call it my picture, but everything of mine is yours, especially our two little babies. Last night when you were asleep one of them started to kick. I was going to wake you to feel it, but you looked so peaceful, and after the hard week you had, I did not think it was fair to do so. I am sure one, or both of them, will kick on the boat tomorrow.

And so we embark on another chapter of our life together. We left with no children and are returning home with four. We are so blessed.

I specially left Ann Hathaway's Cottage to the end because I want you to know that I never, ever want to go there. I hope that you don't, either, because I don't want to have an argument with you about it.

Back in Johannesburg I know you are going to be so busy, so please try and take it easy on the boat. I am only an arm's-length away if you need anything, and if I am not, I should be.

There is one thing that I would like you to please do for me, and that is when I am finished reading this letter, and you have put it in a safe place, please take me and hold me tight. I am so worried about what to do about my mother. I know that you, who are so wise, cannot guide me on this. It is my decision that I must reach myself. Perhaps God will help me with some suggestions.

Your grateful and ever-loving life-partner who will be with you wherever you choose to go.

Your over-happy wife,
Elize

Next morning Elize woke and saw Maimon fast asleep. She showered and dressed and, leaving Maimon, went next door and found the children cleaning their teeth and then ready for breakfast.

A family table with eight places had been reserved for their party, and there they found Saul and Kaylah. Gittel and Anshul had already eaten and were sitting on wicker cruise-style leg-extending deck chairs, looking at the Atlantic ocean that neither of them had seen before.

Breakfast was also a buffet, and Elize explained to the children that they had to eat some healthy food before tucking into the pancakes with chocolate sauce. With eyes like saucers, they walked up and down past the hot and cold stations, a counter of fresh fruit, another with cereals and breads, and then the pancakes with maple syrup and waffles with jam. Joshua started helping himself very carefully, oblivious to his sister, who had gone back to Elize.

"Can we send some of this food to my mommy? In the morning sometimes she gets so hungry she has to sit down, or she faints."

Swallowing to hold back her tears, Elize said, "We are in the middle of the ocean and food can't be sent from here. When we get to Cape Town, we can send some food from there."

Her mother looked after, the little girl went back to the buffet to choose her own breakfast.

When Joshua returned, his plate laden with all manner of food, Saul told him that the captain had stopped by at their table to introduce himself and ask if anyone in their party would like to come up to the bridge to see how the ship is steered and instructions given to the engine room. The lookalike father and son (who sadly were not) agreed to go straight up after breakfast.

Waking before Elize on their second morning at sea, Maimon lay quietly reflecting on how different this voyage was from the previous southbound one he had taken. What had happened to that fellow who with his brother was going to open a gun-and-tobacco shop in Queenstown, Maimon wondered. And then, for the first time in years, he consciously thought about Ayna.

Interestingly, Maimon observed, the passing years had not diminished his negative feelings towards her. The only tangible evidence of bad things she had done was the Queenstown job offer, and on balance, was that really so bad? Of course, she did it to serve her own purpose, but it was in his interests as well. He couldn't put his finger on it, but in his gut Maimon knew, or thought he knew, that something was amiss.

After a while he came to the conclusion that his feelings for her stemmed from the fact that he didn't trust her – feelings for which he had no objective basis, excluding the job of fer incident, of course – so instead of going round in circles, he switched to her son. It wasn't her son, it was their son, whom Maimon had no wish to see. This was illogical, he knew, and it wasn't a wavering thought: if he could avoid seeing Eli, that is what he would do.

Unable to make sense of his emotions, Maimon tried to apply scientific principles to explain his feelings. The child's blood was 50% his and 50% Ayna's, so he should have been attracted to his 50%. The fact that he had no wish to see his son must be because his dislike for Ayna's 50% was greater than his like for his own 50%. It was good to have science to fall back on, Maimon reminded himself. It wasn't always conclusive, but it was more so than his possibly illogical feelings.

Having progressed as far as he could, Maimon looked across at Elize and saw he was right up against her beautiful shoulder he had so admired.

Leaning across he kissed it, once and twice and, like a man who suddenly finds out how much he is enjoying a dish of food, over and over. Angels are not used to being kissed on the shoulder, and so Maimon's angel woke, and smiled at him. It made Mona Lisa's look like a scowl, Maimon decided, and kissed its shoulder again.

Voices from next door reminded them that their time was not entirely their own, and while Elize checked on the dressing and teeth-cleaning progress, Maimon showered and dressed. All through this activity, though, he had an uneasy feeling. Something was wrong – but what?

He couldn't say. And then he put his finger on it. There were no meetings to prepare for and attend, no discussions and negotiations on which not only the fortunes of his children and grandchildren would depend, but also those of the charities which would benefit should he be successful.

In fact, he had nothing to do. He wanted to visit the ship's engine room and have a chat with the chief engineer, but there were twelve days to do that. It was unreal, but the feeling was wonderful. While important negotiations got his adrenalin pumping, and made his whole body come alive, being on a boat was exactly the opposite, and as much as Maimon relished the former, he realized that he also enjoyed the latter. The sea was calm, the sun shone from a cloudless sky, it wasn't too hot yet, and best of all, Elize was with him. Sarah and Joshua, now old hands at the buffet business, took Maimon and led him to the dining room, and then gave him a conducted tour of what was on offer.

At their family table Kaylah said to the children, "Story time starts in ten minutes, are you coming today?"

Maimon pointed his index finger at his chest and looked at his sister quizzically.

"I'm afraid not," Kaylah said. "You are more than fourteen years old."

Maimon looked around for the under-fourteens and, with the exception of those at their table, didn't see any.

"It is two decks down. Yesterday we had 50 children. I think more will come today."

"In the dormitory?" Maimon asked, remembering the big room as if it was yesterday.

Kaylah nodded smiling, getting up, taking each of the children by the hand, and heading for the door. Maimon watched them go.

"Life isn't fair," Elize said to Maimon, who nodded in agreement.

Having done this trip before, albeit under vastly different circumstances, Maimon knew the drill and was happy to be a storytelling spectator. He also had time, which he had overlooked that he needed, to plan for the next few years. The war was over, the mines were restarting, and with average rainfall the country would do well. Post-war periods, he remembered hearing, were times of pent-up demand, often for consumer goods. He didn't think there would be much opportunity in pots and pans, but people needed to eat, and if they could eat food that he grew, or processed, all the better.

The Afrikaners and some English-speakers had taken the good farming lands in the Transvaal and Free State, and so he would have to look elsewhere. Maybe there were some farms with good soil he could buy for a reasonable price outside of Cape Town. Instead of rushing back to Johannesburg, they could spend a week or two in Franschoek, Paarl, and Stellenbosch. Yes, they would definitely do that.

He also had another thought. East of Johannesburg, where the land fell down the escarpment before the border with Mozambique, he had been told that there was a lot of good land. The problem was that it was ridden with malaria-infected mosquitoes, with the result that no white men and very few natives could live there in the summer. One day there would be a cure for malaria, or some chemical would be formulated to kill the mosquitoes, and then the land would be arable, and farming profitable. Excited by the prospect of being a landowner, Maimon went up to the Radio Officer's room and fired off a wire to his office telling them to ascertain what land was available in these two areas and at what prices.

This done, he headed for the dormitory to find out how the story-telling was coming along. Unfortunately, this was not possible, as in addition to what Maimon estimated were about 80 children, there were at least an equal number of adults, there not to keep an eye on their children, but rapturously listening themselves. He stood at the door looking in, in some cases at three generations listening to Kaylah explain how God led and fed the Jewish people in the desert for forty years. Amazed how many intelligent adults actually believed this, Maimon retreated to their suite where he found Elize struggling with a letter to her mother. This was territory he knew well to keep away from. But suddenly Elize turned to him and said, "Quickly. Come here. One of the babies is kicking."

Maimon rushed over. Elize put his hand on one side of her increasingly extended tummy, and he felt some moving parts. "Is that a knee or an elbow?" Maimon asked, remembering Joshua climbing over him in the middle of the night about a week ago.

"I don't know, silly," Elize replied, and then remembered something important she had to tell Maimon. "We need to have a talk about bringing up the babies. Mothers-in-law think they know best, and tell their son's wives what to do. I brought up Adam very well, and know what works and what doesn't, and I don't want any input from your mother."

"I am sure you won't get any," Maimon said, accepting that both women knew more than he did about this, and foresaw himself being the extremely uncomfortable meat in a sandwich between two strong-minded mothers.

"I am sure I will," Elize continued, "and here is a good example. When a child is born in Europe, it is wrapped up tight and put in a crib to sleep – which it does, usually after crying. We don't do that in Africa."

Realizing that he had a great deal to learn in the next number of months, Maimon nodded seriously.

"In Africa," Elize told him in a voice that was not to be contradicted, "we put the baby on our backs, tied with a sheet or a blanket, depending on the season, and go about our daily chores."

"And the baby likes that?" Maimon asked.

"Of course it does, because it feels the mother's heart beating, and is moved about continually, as it was in the mother's tummy. And one other thing, as I am not strong enough to carry both babies, the other one will be carried by one of the native nannies."

"If you are resting, then they will be carried by two native nannies?" Maimon asked, to be sure he understood what was going to happen.

"That's right. And one other thing" Elize went on. "At some stage solid foods, mashed up, of course, are introduced into the baby's diet. Adam liked avocado and peanut butter, not at the same time, of course, neither of which you have in Europe, so ...."

"So, I tell my mother to keep her baby raising opinions to herself," Maimon said, foreseeing a clash of wills in the not-too-distant future.

"And one other thing," Elize added, "you support me at all times, whether you think I am right or wrong."

Of all his instructions that was the easiest, Maimon decided, as it involved no technical aspects.

"Another thing," he said, reintroducing the count into the conversation. "We stay in Cape Town. Not for long time, maybe two weeks. Cape Town very beautiful. You enjoy."

"And you will be doing some business?" Elize replied, not letting Maimon get away with it entirely.

"Maybe yes, maybe no. We stay Captain Nelson Hotel. Captain gone but hotel good."

Elize put her arms round Maimon's neck, kissed him, and said, "I do love you, Count Sokolovski."

"Also, one more thing," the count said, eyeing Elize's swollen breasts.

"Absolutely not. I am much too hot."

"Hot is good, doctor tell me," Maimon said hopefully.

"Hot is good," Elize agreed, getting Maimon's hopes up, before adding, "Too hot is bad."

You can't win them all, Maimon thought, as he collapsed onto the bed, hoping it would be cooler later.

Impatient for his office's response to the wire he sent about buying up farmland in the malaria-infested Eastern Transvaal, Maimon reminded himself that it was more complicated than buying a tin of jam at OK Bazaars, and as he would not be prejudiced if he got the requisite details a day or a week later, he persuaded himself not to be impatient. As with voyages having long periods between port calls, the days at sea merged one into one another, and so it was for the Sokolovski family, who, Maimon sometimes reflected, did not appreciate how fortunate they were not to be traveling in the bowels of the ship.

Kaylah's morning story class was preceded by games for the children involving physical exercise, and was followed by a noon hosing-down enjoyed by all the children, and increasingly by some of the adults as well. Returning to his suite, and its constantly revolving ceiling fans, Maimon found an envelope that had been slipped under the door. Opening it he saw the neatly typed cable letters, and immediately looked for Elize to read it to him. He found her lying in a bath of cold water, the ship's gentle motion causing little swells that washed over all of her body except for her daily growing tummy.

"It is still too hot," Elize said as she spotted Maimon. Unexpectedly by way of reply, he handed her the cable which she read aloud.

LAND OWNED BY MANY FAMILIES ALSO GOVERNMENT FIVE ESTATE AGENTS ADVISE ALL OWNERS SELLERS WHICH PROBABLY CORRECT OUR DEEDS OFFICE RESEARCH INDICATES THIS APPROXIMATELY 10,000 HECTARES IN TOTAL PROPERTIES HAVE WILD ANIMALS ESTATE AGENTS INDICATE TEN SHILLINGS PER HECTARE SHOULD SECURE PROPERTIES ADVISE ACTION REQUIRED REGARDS

Maimon fetched a pencil from the bedroom, and Elize had already turned the paper over, ready to take down his reply.

KEEN TO BUY TOTAL TEN THOUSAND AT OR ABOUT INDICATED PRICE USE BEST THREE ESTATE AGENTS ACTING FOR SOKOFAM EDWARDS OFFICE PLUS ARCHITECT BAKERS ONE EACH WHEN DONE TRAIN TO CAPETOWN AND ASCERTAIN AVAILABLE FARMLAND FRANSCHOEK STELLENBOSCH PAARL

ADVISE DEVELOPMENTS RE GARDS

"From no farms to many farms?" Elize said, looking up at Maimon.

"Your family has farming in its blood, and so will our children. What good is it to have farming blood without farms," he said, closing the bathroom door and heading up to the ship's telegraph office.

Though she had never thought about it, logically Maimon was right, and a smile crossed Elize's face as she remembered the wonderful times she had growing up on their farm. Then the smile disappeared as a picture of their burnt-out farmhouse replaced her earlier memories. She looked at Maimon, grateful again that it was he who rescued her from the camp, he who had saved her life, and made it, in almost every way, better. A slightly bigger wave washed over her as one of the babies kicked. Looking down at her big round tummy, Elize smiled again.

They crossed the equator a few mornings later, and to mark the occasion the captain served a generous helping of ice cream to all of the passengers. Ice cream and running-through-the-fire-hoses'-water – could life ever be better than this? the children thought.

Slowly the days became less oppressively hot and were replaced by heavy mists off the Skeleton Coast of German South West Africa. The daily, ship-produced-showers ceased, and with Cape Town three days away, the atmosphere on board changed. As Maimon remembered it so well, it was as if the holiday part of the trip was over. Smart clothes were washed and ironed – by the passengers in steerage, and by the laundry service for those on the upper decks.

And then one sunny morning they all awoke to the majestic view that, once seen, is never forgotten. Cape Town nestling under Table Mountain. Remembering hearing about orographic clouds, Maimon told the children that sometimes God put a tablecloth over the mountain in the afternoon, which, if the words had not come from Uncle Maimon's mouth, they would not have believed.

An hour or so after breakfast, pushed by two small but strong tugs, the ship that had brought them safely to Cape Town gently bumped against the wharf. Gangways were lowered, and health and immigration officials in spotlessly starched white shirts and shorts, each one carrying a black leather briefcase, swarmed aboard.

The first-class passengers had been told to wait in their cabins for the officials who would call upon them. When he heard a knock on their door, Maimon expected either the health or immigration officers, or both. Instead, it was a reporter from the *Argus* (Cape Town's afternoon newspaper) and his accompanying photographer. News of Maimon having "left £100,000 pounds on the table," as the press put it, had reached South Africa, and the Argus was keen to steal a march on their competitors with an exclusive interview. The few minutes that followed could be called "exclusive" because no other press people were present, but it certainly wasn't an interview. All they wanted were pictures of Maimon, first alone, and then with Elize.

With those passengers in the more expensive cabins getting first-class treatment, the Sokolovski family were soon on their way to the Mount Nelson Hotel. In a matter of minutes, they passed through the gracious Palladian Columns that separated the hurly-burly of Orange Street from the tranquillity and manicured gardens of the hotel property.

In his welcoming speech the hotel manager, seeing Sarah and Joshua, mentioned to Elize that just down the passage was a shop that sold bathing costumes, both for little people and also for big people.

"What about very big people?" Maimon asked, looking at Elize's tummy.

On the way to their rooms, all except Gittel and Anshul excitedly examined the black swimming costumes for sale. In and out of the change rooms they hurried, until eventually five costumes lay next to the new-fangled large silver-colored cash machine. It had keys with different numbers on them, and every time they were depressed, bells rang and a drawer containing money ejected itself.

"We call it the Jewish piano," the shop assistant remarked with a smile.

Without a smile Elize looked her straight in the eye, and said, "I am Jewish, and I found what you said most offensive."

While the shop assistant offered her profound apologies, Maimon and Kaylah exchanged discreet smiles.

With Gittel and Anshul fast asleep – leaving the ship and checking in to the hotel was tiring for the older people – the rest of the family gambolled in and out of the swimming pool. Fortunately, Maimon could stand, even in the deep end, and cognisant of the fact that none of them could swim, he acted as a lifeguard, especially for the children.

Elize sat on the side of the pool, her feet underwater on the first step. Watching Sarah and Joshua, she wondered how soon she would be able to swim with her twins in their own pool. Around six o'clock, weary and hungry, they ordered supper from the Garden Restaurant; for a special treat, Maimon said anyone who wanted to could have an ice cream. Sarah and Joshua took up the offer. Then, looking up at the mountain, Sarah said excitedly, "Look! There is Uncle Maimon's tablecloth."

Uncle Maimon pointed out it wasn't his tablecloth, but God's – to which Joshua replied, "You both know about it."

After supper, the children went up for a bath with Elize and Maimon, leaving Kaylah and Saul alone at the now-deserted pool.

"A penny for your thoughts?" Kaylah said, wondering why Saul was looking so serious.

"Of all the millions of Jews in Russia," Saul said, "how many do you think have been given the opportunity that we have?"

"Two," Kaylah answered.

"Do you ever ask yourself 'Why us?'"

"I don't. I suppose I should. I have another "Why us" question that fills my wondering time."

This was the elephant in the room that they never discussed, but with an empty wine glass or two providing Dutch courage, Saul said, "Maybe it will be different here in Africa."

"Maybe it will," Kaylah replied, knowing their physical location would make absolutely no difference at all. Maybe God was unhappy with her, and His way of telling her was by closing her womb? She hadn't done anything bad that she could think of to deserve this terrible punishment so why? Why her?

Kaylah had thought about this for hours and had rationalised that even without children, life in Africa for her would be better than in Saratov. The nursery school idea was extremely exciting, and as Elize explained, one could get exceptionally good native carers for her parents, so she would no longer be burdened with looking after them day and night. Already on the boat she had noticed the difference. Whatever her mother wanted could be brought by someone else. It certainly couldn't be worse than in Saratov, and even if it was just a little bit better, that would be a great improvement on the poverty and fear with which she had grown up. Thinking about it further, if only half of what Maimon and Elize had told her was true, it would be like starting life all over again. As an adult of course, not a child, but in a much better place.

With that thought sitting happily in her mind, Kaylah looked up at Table Mountain disappearing in the dark, only it's upper rock buttresses catching the sun's last rays. Yes, tomorrow, and all her tomorrows, would be better, Kaylah thought as brown rose beetles tucked in to what little was left of her pickled fish. Wordlessly, she got to her feet, smiled at Saul and inclined her head towards the hotel building. Remembering what that meant, and how long it had been since Kaylah had transmitted that message, Saul also smiled.

CHAPTER 42

OOM KOOS EN TANNIE ELNA

Even without the boat's rocking, Maimon and Elize slept well, woke early, ordered breakfast in their suite, and were just finishing their coffee when the telephone rang. Maimon picked it up, listened for a while, and replied, "We will be down shortly." Then turning to Elize he said, "The front-desk man said there are two people to see you, but from the tone of his voice…"

"From the tone of his voice what?" Elize said, looking at Maimon to ascertain the reason he hesitated.

"Something is wrong. I am coming down with you – if you are going, that is."

"Of course I am going," Elize said. "I don't know anyone in Cape Town, so it must be a mistake."

In the lobby of the hotel, they found two tired-looking middle aged people, obviously uncomfortable in the Mount Nelson's luxurious surroundings. Their clothes, probably the smartest they possessed, had seen much better days, and were so ill-fitting that they might have been bought for other people. Their shoes, though clean, were down-at-heel. The man nervously held an old gray felt hat in his hand, and the woman gripped a cheap plastic leather handbag in hers. As well as tired, Maimon thought they looked desperately sad.

Elize stopped about eight yards from the couple and stared at them. Maimon, who had never seen these people before, stood next to her, waiting for a cue. Slowly, Elize edged forward. She knew them from somewhere, but couldn't remember where or when.

"Oom Koos?" she asked finally, hesitantly, and the man nodded. "En Tannie Elna?" Elize's voice grew now in confidence and strength and the lady smiled weakly.

Not believing this was happening, Elize walked up to the out-of-place couple and threw her arms round both of them. There the three of them wept together, in happiness at being reunited, and in sadness at the strained circumstances in which the older couple found themselves. To give them space, Maimon moved off to one side.

After a while, Elize took each of them by the arm and led them to a round table in the garden, under a big oak tree. Maimon followed at a respectable distance. The elderly couple sat down, Elize between them, holding their hands. Maimon filled the fourth chair, opposite Elize. After a while she told Maimon, "This is my uncle and aunt. My father's twin brother."

It was so long since Maimon had seen Piet that he hardly remembered what he looked like. In respect to the older couple, he got up and shook their hands, and then sat down again.

"This is my husband, Maimon" Elize said, now more composed. "Where have you been, and what are you doing in Cape Town?"

It was a long story in time and sadness, but not in words. Koos and his son had fought in that terrible battle with General Cronje at Paardeberg. Elize's cousin, Sarel, with whom she played so happily for weeks on end when their families got together, was killed. Mercifully, Cronje surrendered as they were out of ammunition and most of their horses were dead or wounded. Together with hundreds of prisoners of war, Koos was shipped to Mauritius, and Elna herded into a concentration camp. When the peace treaty was signed, Koos returned home to find that the bank had taken his farm. The British told him where to find Elna. The government offered him and other commandos jobs on the railways, and he was sent to Salt River here in Cape Town. With Elna he now lived in a one-room railway cottage. There was nothing more to say.

"What about Tjol?" Elize asked, almost afraid to do so, but desperate to know what had happened to her older cousin?

By way of reply, Koos carefully took a faded but obviously treasured newspaper cutting out of his pocket, unfolded it, and handed the flimsy paper to Elize.

It was a picture of a young couple that had appeared in *Die Transvaaler* newspaper about eighteen months before. The couple were standing in front of a large painting that the paper reported was the work of the young woman, Cynthia Kapalushnik. The man next to her was her husband, Tjol du Toit, who worked for I.W. Schlesinger, who owned all the bioscopes.[122]

"Have you been in touch with them?" Elize asked, hoping against hope that the answer would be yes, but knowing it would not be. Another silence, and then Elna said, "He was too proud."

The older man looked down at the grass, turning the hat round in his hands many times before saying, "I am not proud. I am ashamed. A father should not ask his children for money. You know that, Elize."

How different these Afrikaners were, Maimon thought. Jewish children were looked after by their parents when they were small, and when they grew up, looked after their parents when they were old.

Maimon had listened to this heart-rending story long enough. There was nothing more he could hear that was going to lighten the burden under which these two sad people lived. Elize had heard him say often enough, "Action is the only prayer that is answered," a statement with which she did not agree. She was therefore not surprised to hear Maimon clear his throat and say, "Oom Koos and Tannie Elna, I am not an Afrikaner, and I have never fought in a war, and so I can have no idea of the mental and physical hardships that you have suffered. I do know that no human being deserves to have gone through what you and your family have."

Maimon took a deep breath, hoping he would not upset Elize's uncle and aunt with what he was going to say. Elize looked at her husband, not knowing what was coming, but confident that whatever it was, she would not be ashamed of him for saying it.

"Would you please do me a favor?" Maimon asked.

Koos and Elna looked at one another, wondering what in the world they could do for this man.

"Please rebuild your brother's house, better than it was when Elize and Willem lived there. And fix up the fences, and plant crops, and buy some cattle and sheep, and build some kyas[123] for the natives. And when you have done all of that, would you please build another house, a bigger one, near the old fig tree, for Elize and her family, and Tjol and his family, to come and spend holidays there. And between the houses build stables for twelve horses."

---

122   *Cinemas*
123   *Small, handbuilt houses; in this instance, specifically, outhouses*

Koos and Elna heard very clearly what Maimon had said, but both thought that this was some kind of a joke. For confirmation they both looked at Elize, who amazingly said, "That is what he wants you to do."

"For this work I will pay you £1,000 a month. Also, I will put £1000 into what we will call the 'Farm Account' at Barclays Bank, to pay for the materials and labor you will need. You are a farmer, not a builder, and so you must contract with a builder to rebuild Piet's house, to build Elize's and Tjol's house, and also the stables. When you are ready, I will ask an architect to come and see you to discuss details of the buildings."

Then to lighten things up, Maimon said, "And I am sure Elize will say that we also need a rugby field and a cricket pitch, but as the one is played in winter and the other in summer, perhaps we can combine them?"

Appreciating that, much like a man who has just eaten a big steak has no room for dessert, these shocked people would be burdened with more details, and realizing that it was going to be very difficult for Elize to tell them her story, Maimon quietly got up and excused himself.

Waiting for Maimon to be out of sight, Elna said, "Where did you find this man?"

"At a Nagmaal in East London."

"You found a Jewish man at a Nagmaal?" Koos said, now willing to believe anything.

"It is a long story," Elize began, just as a waiter put a jug of fresh orange juice and four glasses on the table.

"The Baas says if you want anything else, you must tell me," the waiter advised.

An hour later Maimon returned to find three stunned people sitting in silence. Elize had just told them about her mother's letter from Pretoria Central Jail. He sat down and poured a glass of orange juice and waited. After a long while Koos spoke:

"When I was in the prisoner's camp on Mauritius island, I prayed to God. Not for money or gold or silver, but for another chance. I had taken the chance He had given me and broken it like a piece of pottery. We had no hope of beating the Whole British Empire. What chance did we few thousand Boers have? No chance at all, but still we followed Oom Paul like sheep to the slaughter. And not only us, but the generals as well. Why didn't they see the futility of it? Even smart men like Louis Botha and Jannie Smuts."

There was another long silence before Koos continued. "From what you said, Mr Maimon, God is giving me another chance, and as He is my witness under this oak tree, I will not break the cup again."

Then, for the first time in Maimon's presence, Elna spoke. "Elize told us you are Jewish. Tjol's wife is also Jewish. To think how we Christians have persecuted you people because of your religion, and here this morning, people who you never even knew existed, are being given another chance in life. Mr. Maimon, if you live to 100 years old, and I pray that you do, you will never know what a wonderful thing you have done this morning. I walked into your hotel like a tired old woman, and I am leaving like a sprightly young girl."

Waving down a passing waiter, Maimon ordered some sandwiches, cakes and four coffees. Then he removed a sealed white envelope from his pocket and put it in front of Koos.

"There is £200 in there. Give up your job and your cottage, and with Elna take the train to Brandfort. There, rent a house that you can live in until Piet's is finished. When you have found a place to live, please send Elize a letter with your address. Then we will be in touch. Now, if you will please excuse me, I am the on duty lifeguard."

He got up, kissed Elna, shook Koos' hand while looking at him straight in the eye, winked at Elize, and started walking off. Stopping suddenly, he turned round, and said, "Please stay for lunch. Then you can meet my family."

Maimon headed straight for the dining room, where he found their family table in shambles, proof that everyone had eaten breakfast. Grabbing some bread and cheese, he ordered a coffee, wolfed it all down, and got indigestion in the process.

Then he changed into his bathing costume and joined the family at the pool, taking over the lifeguard duties from Saul. Hours later, when they sat down for lunch at a table laid for their family under another big old oak tree, Elize, Elna, and Koos joined them, Maimon having ensured that two extra places had been set. Sadly, Maimon noticed but was not surprised by, six red eyes joined those of the swimmers (also red, but from the chlorine in the swimming pool).

The waiter who had earlier brought the orange juice, now handed Maimon a telegram. Seeing this transaction, Elize got up and followed Maimon behind another of the garden's massive old oak trees. Holding the cable behind his back with one hand, Maimon took Elize's in the other, and asked her softly, "How are you?"

By way of reply, Elize lay her head on Maimon's chest. Then she locked her wrists behind his back and squeezed him, needing the solidarity in her life that the past few hours had stripped away.

"However bad I thought it was," she began, her voice quivering, "it was, in fact, much worse. Girls I was at school with, two of my best friends, died in concentration camps. Every single one of Willem's friends was killed in one battle or another. The British scorched-earth policy has destroyed our country. There is nothing left. Nothing!" And then Elize started sobbing.

Maimon handed her his handkerchief, sat down on a tree stump, and pulled all three of them onto his lap. When Elize had dried her eyes, Maimon said, "You are, of course, right; but that was yesterday. Already the rains have started and enough mielies have been planted to feed all of the natives and many whites. The herds are recovering, calves are being born, and we are living in a bigger, stronger South Africa that would not have happened without the war.

"Yes, the war was terrible, all wars are terrible, and that is why I pray that none of our children ever have to fight one. Look at your tummy. Two new people will be born soon, who will make South Africa a better place to live in. Isn't that what we should be concentrating on? And again, in a few years' time, please God, two more children. The past is the past, and we can't do anything about it. Who knows what the future holds, so what we have is the present, and that is where we live now. God has just given you your uncle and aunt back, that is what you should be grateful for."

CHAPTER 43

A FARM IN FRANSCHOEK

Elize spent the little lecture nodding her head in agreement with everything Maimon said. He was right, he always was. Every coin has two sides, he had often told her, and she was so silly not to also look at the reverse one.

Back at the table, there were so many animated cross-conversations going on that Maimon couldn't work out who was talking to whom about what, so he grabbed a plate of fruit, whispered in Elize's ear that he was going for a nap, and excused himself. When he woke up, he found "letter #4" on his bedside table, and Elize sleeping soundly beside him. He kissed the usual shoulder and went back to sleep. With the sun setting behind Cape Town's majestic Lion's Head mountain, Maimon opened his eyes to hear Elize begin reading:

My Wonderful Special Maimon,

As you can imagine I had a terrible morning, but it was my family's story and I had to hear it. You were right to leave us, you didn't know the people and would soon have got bored. Every single one of Elna's family died, either fighting, or in Ceylon, or in the concentration camps. Her cousin had two stillbirths, and when she heard that her husband had died, she hanged herself from a beam in their kitchen.

It was Elna who saw our picture in yesterday's Cape Argus and told Koos that they should come and see us. Koos admitted he took a lot of persuading. It is not easy for poor relations to visit rich relations, and that is something we need to be aware of in Johannesburg. None of your or my relations are going to be rich, and we need to be sensitive to their feelings.

I don't know how much you enjoy making money, but I get so much pleasure seeing you give it away. It took me about ten minutes to persuade Koos and Elna that not only did you have the money, but that you would spend it on our family farm. They couldn't understand why you wanted to do it, especially as you are not going to live there. I think they are having difficulty understanding Jewish people. For example, at lunch today, everybody was talking at the same time. In the Afrikaans culture, when the elders speak everyone keeps quiet. And the questions! I hadn't noticed it before, but there are always questions flying around, and the answer to one question is often another question. And the children are not shushed but listened to. It is much more fun the Jewish way, and I must learn to dive in like everyone else does.

As you were telling my uncle and aunt of the two houses and stables, I kept thinking of my mother and if she would live to see it. Food in jails is not good, and I don't know how often the doctors come round. I am still struggling with the if, and when, of visiting her. I know I have to go, but I don't have the mental strength to do so now. There is one thing I have decided, and that is not to go before the babies are born.

Cape Town is so different from the Transvaal and Orange Free State, and though, driving from the docks, I have only seen three roads of it, I would love to spend a week alone here with you. Cape Town is old, like London in a tiny way, and I have come to the conclusion that I like old things. I overheard someone in the garden saying that a few of the farmhouses in Stellenbosch and Franschoek are over two hundred years old. When you go and look at farms here in the Cape, can I please come with you?

The babies are kicking a lot, especially in the bath. I hope they are not fighting one another. Sometimes I think they are two boys, and other times two girls, and then occasionally one of each. The London doctor told me that one day they will be able to tell before the baby comes out, what gender it is. I don't think I would like that.

It is wonderful to see you relaxing and sleeping such a lot. Joshua said there is more oxygen in the air at the sea, and that is why we sleep so well here. You probably do know that there is less oxygen in the Johannesburg air, but it doesn't seem to slow the people down. On the contrary, everybody seems to be in a hurry in Johannesburg. Was it also like that in Kimberley?

You are stirring now so I should end up, but I don't want to, because the more I write, the more I feel my love is getting into your heart. I was thinking yesterday whether I love you more during the day or at night, and came to the conclusion that they are different kinds of love. I am not talking of "doing love", that is wonderful any time of the day or night. I wish I could write poems of love to you, like Shakespeare and Shelley and Keats wrote. Thank you for introducing them to me on the boat. Either in Cape Town or Johannesburg, I want to buy a book of their sonnets, so I can read them to you.

Your ever-loving wife,
Elize

Maimon opened his arms, and instead of crashing down on top of him as she used to do, Elize let herself down slowly, so that neither the babies nor Maimon were crushed. Then they kissed like they used to do on the farm. First gently like two naïve teenagers, then one of their tongues on the other's lips, and then the other way round, and then fully together, as two people who love each other deeply do.

At dinner that night, Maimon asked who wanted to visit the penguins, who wanted to climb Table Mountain or Lion's Head, who wanted to stay at the hotel and swim in the pool, or who wanted to do something he hadn't mentioned. He then explained how voting worked, and by a show of hands by far the majority wanted to stay at the hotel. That was fine with Maimon.

Next morning Kris Skot arrived with a briefcase full of papers, including a list of wine farms available for sale and presently open for inspection. The three of them sat down and agreed that two farms in Franschoek looked the most attractive, which Maimon pointed out was probably why they were more expensive than those in Paarl and Stellenbosch.

"Let's go out today, sleep in Franschoek," Elize said. "Then we will have the whole of tomorrow to inspect the farms."

"Great idea. I will organise a horse cart and driver to leave in half an hour. You go and tell the family what we are doing, and throw some clothes in to a case for both of us. I need a few minutes more with Kris, and then we can leave."

The few minutes more Maimon needed with Kris was to tell him about the arrangements that needed to be made for the construction of a cyanide gold-extraction plant, about which he had already written to Hermann Ekstein. Hermann had replied, promising to erect the necessary buildings at his Salisbury mine; as soon as he received drawings for the machinery, Hermann advised Maimon, he would instruct his man Hennen Jennings to get them built. Maimon handed Kris the drawings, asking him to take the afternoon train back to Johannesburg and deliver them to Jennings as soon as possible. He should also tell Hermann that he had done so.

The hotel had provided a picnic basket for Maimon and Elize, and also one for the driver, as well as some names and addresses of farmers who might put them up for the night. After hurried goodbyes they were on their way, down the lower part of Table Mountain and across the Cape Flats to Stellenbosch. There they changed horses for the steep climb up Hellshoogte, then down the other side of the pass, through Pniel and onto Franschoek.

Nine hours after leaving Cape Town found them on the stoep of Francois and Marie-Claire du Plessis' beautiful Cape Dutch farmhouse, sipping chilled white wine and watching the sun disappear behind the mountains that ringed this beautiful little farming town. They spoke long into the night: Marie-Claire and Elize about their lives, which were different though similar, and Francois and Maimon about the new South Africa.

The big challenge, they agreed, was for Botha and Smuts to get English- and Afrikaans-speaking white people to come together in the United Party, which wasn't being made easy by Hertzog (with his Afrikaner nationalism and populism) continually snapping at their heels. They both felt that the combined four provinces which would make up the Union of South Africa, rich in gold and diamonds, and with good arable land and sufficient water, could turn into a little United States. There was, of course, the Native Question, for which no one had an answer; but Francois pointed out that if guns could be kept out of their hands, the situation was manageable.

Maimon didn't know what "manageable" meant in this context, and didn't ask Francois, because that was where Maimon's opinion differed from almost every other white man and woman in South Africa. In Maimon's opinion, it was the natives' country that the whites had taken away from them, and one day would have to give back. The likelihood of this happening, most South African whites felt, was about the same as the sun rising in the west.

Next morning, after more of a French breakfast (croissants, brioche, butter, jam, and coffee) than 'n boere ontbyt[124], Maimon and Elize set off, first to look at the larger of the two farms. Much of it was rows of grape vines growing on the side of a hill, and as Elize pointed out, after asking one or two searching questions, they had insufficient water for the area under cultivation.

The other farm (on the edge of the town, but sufficiently distant not to hear any of its clatter) was smaller – only about 50 acres under cultivation – built on flat land with a river meandering through it. The estate agent told them that this property had overriding riparian rights, and so even in the driest periods, water would not be a problem. Elize noted that it was close enough to town for the children to walk there to buy an ice cream; while Maimon examined the broad old floorboards for any sign of bore-beetles. He didn't find any, but Maimon realized that even if the whole house was about to collapse about their ears (which, of course, it wasn't), having stood unharmed for 230 years, he was going to buy it.

Elize had already pointed out where the children's paddling pool could be situated; not too far from the adult's swimming pool that would fit nicely between the main house and one of the guest cottages.

---

124 *A farmer's breakfast*

The property was too small to ever be a financial success, and Maimon was reminded of being told by a Transvaal farmer, "Women are the most enjoyable way of losing money, horses are the quickest, and farming is the surest."

There was only one problem: Elize had to be persuaded that they could afford the smaller of the two Franschoek farms. She had grown up in a house where money was always tight, and during the few years when it wasn't, her father had reminded them that difficult times lay just round the corner.

Sadly, Piet was usually right. As soon as Maimon mentioned numbers with noughts, he lost Elize. Noughts were for school books and homework, not for buying farms. Realizing this wasn't a battle Maimon was going to win there and then, he told the agent he would get back to him in a day or so. They headed back to the du Plessis farm, where Francois quickly picked up the difficulty. His pointing out that, unlike Paarl or Stellenbosch, there was no more land to farm, cut no ice with Elize. Neither did his telling her that the soil was much more fertile in the Franschoek valley, and because of the horse-shoe mountains around the farms, there was always sufficient rain. Then Marie-Claire asked Elize if she would rather have her children messing around on the beach with skollies[125], or safe on their own farm, knowing where they were, and with whom they were playing.

Being from the Orange Free State, Elize had never heard the word "skollie" before, and when Marie-Claire explained who skollies were, Elize's concern about buying the farm melted away like a block of ice in the midday sun. Standing at his bar with Francois, Maimon asked, "A case of what?" Nothing was necessary, Maimon was told, but next time you come, a good bottle of French cognac to share would be appreciated. Maimon had never heard of any kind of cognac, but he made a note to bring a case, not a bottle. Red wine replaced white, and rugby replaced politics, and well into the third bottle, they all agreed that South Africa was God's own country. Maimon was concerned that God might not share that view, but who was he to spoil the cool and mellow night?

Next morning Maimon and Elize left, with "Totsiens, buurman" ringing in their ears.

"Is that good or bad?" Maimon asked.

---

125   *Delinquent young men often from the colored community*

"Good," Elize said, kissing Maimon on the cheek and squeezing his hand. "It means 'Goodbye, neighbor.'"

Maimon smiled and squeezed back – happy wife, happy life.

Impatient to get back to Johannesburg – Kris had said that Lesuj Vagalparot's lawyer wanted to see him – and with no good reason to remain in Cape Town, Maimon and Elize hurried back to the city. Arriving in Cape Town mid-afternoon, they found the family where they had left them, in the swimming pool. "Last swim" orders were given, and soon the pool was deserted, just as the flush-faced sundowner brigade arrived for their "kick-off" drinks.

The excitement of another train journey ensured that everybody was dressed and packed and breakfasted in good time, and as it was downhill all the way from the hotel to the station, the horses pulling three carts hardly raised a sweat. Their compartments found, cases stowed, porters paid, train doors slammed, whistles sounded, green flags waved, and they were on their way.

Through the Cape Flats their double locomotives rushed, as if to get up speed for the high Hex River pass that lay ahead. It would have been in vain, anyway, as the train stopped in Paarl to drop off school children and to pick up some adults heading for financially green er pastures. The pass was steep, and the train slowed to a fast-walking pace, prompting Elize to say to her obviously impatient husband, "You would like to get out and push, wouldn't you?"

He loved her for so many reasons, including the way she was often inside his mind.

Maimon, impatient to get back to his office, had many things to consider, primarily the state of his house. Herbert Baker had said the building was complete, but this of course excluded curtains and carpets. Herbert had bought some temporary furniture so they would have beds to sleep in, and a table to eat off, but Elize was getting very tired in her last days of pregnancy. Her back had started hurting and shopping was the last thing on her mind.

As for Maimon, there was the gold/cyanide plant at Hermann Eckstein's mine that needed to be commissioned, lawyer Wentzel to see, the progress on the peanut butter factory and oil-crushing plant to check up on, and then just as he was leaving the hotel, a telegram arrived from another Johannesburg lawyer, Godfrey Heyman, who wished to see him. Also, he had been told that in the new South Africa, his steel and flour-milling contracts would be cancelled, which he needed to discuss with Patrick Duncan. The most urgent item needing his attention was buying a horse for Joshua and a pony for Sarah. Much to do.

Elize had her own worries, primarily relating to her mother. She had no intention of visiting the jail before the babies were born. But for how long after she was home from the hospital could she put this off?

And then there was their new house, as big as a small hotel. She had never managed a house before, and even though Maimon had not said so, she knew he expected it to run like clockwork, which was probably not possible. Elize also knew she had to tell Maimon this, but trying to find the right moment with her always-on-the-go husband was not easy. She was worried about the babies. Not for any reason. They were both kicking, but with births you never knew. What happened if she lost one, or even both of them? It would be devastating, especially after Adam.

Kaylah's concerns were easily understood. Did they have nursery schools in Johannesburg like the one at the synagogue in London? If so, would there be a teaching position for her there? And if they didn't exist, why not? Would she be able to establish a Jewish nursery school if there wasn't one already? In such a case could she find premises at an affordable rent? Were there government regulations, or religious ones, that would bar her? Kaylah thought not, but one never knew.

Saul was totally focussed on passing the accountancy exam, to the exclusion of everything else. If he failed it, would Maimon still give him a job? And in any event, when could he next sit the examinations? Should he get a coach to help him revise? And if so, where could he find one?

Joshua and Sarah had their own worries. They would know nobody at school. Was their English good enough? Was their academic level up to their age groups? Would they be teased about their accents?

Gittel was an enigma, looking unhappy but quietly enjoying all her new experiences. Maimon had promised her a steamship ticket back home, but she would have to go by herself – or with Anshul, which was worse than being on her own. So she would have to stay in Africa. Was that good or was it bad?

Just over two days later the train pulled into Johannesburg's Park Station. Maimon's coaches were waiting for them, and in minutes they were on their way to the Parktown house Herbert Baker designed, Murray Doug las had built, Maimon had paid for, and Elize dreaded having to look after. Johannesburg did its welcoming part, with a bright sunny day. Painted white, with Italian columns, the house looked like nothing any of them had seen before. Whatever the Russians expected, "the palace", as Sarah called it, took their collective breath away.

While the adults explored the house, Maimon took Joshua and Sarah by the hand and led them to the stables. Kris Skot had done his job well. Sticking his head out over the top, half-open stable door was the most beautiful horse Joshua had ever seen. At just over fourteen hands, he had a friendly brown face, and lapped up the carrots that first Maimon, and then Joshua, gave him. Next door, waiting patiently for attention, was a Shetland pony. As Sarah couldn't easily see over the stable door, Maimon lifted her up, and to her delight, the little animal nuzzled her tummy.

From a bag at his feet Maimon took two carrots, and explaining to Sarah how one had to hold a carrot in the flat of one's hand, first he fed the pony, and then Sarah did. Suddenly, Maimon noticed Joshua clinging to his trouser leg, which was becoming wet. The little boy was crying. Maimon dropped to his haunches and asked what was wrong.

"I am so happy. I don't know why I am crying. Uncle Maimon, this is the happiest day of my life. Thank you so very, very, very much."

Sarah put her arms round her brother, and said, "Please don't cry, Joshua. I don't think your horse would like that."

The only way Maimon could get the children away from the stables was to suggest that they asked Aunty Elize to come and look at Boris and Katya. At this suggestion, the children hared off to the house to spread the amazing news to everyone they saw.

Exploring the house, Elize found the kitchen, which, with the pantry that led off it, was as big as the biggest house in Saratov. Siting at the handsome yellowwood kitchen table was a native lady, about thirty years old, with the kindest face Elize had ever seen. Respectfully, she clasped her hands on her lap and looked down at them, waiting to be addressed. Elize sat down next to her and they exchanged names, and then Eva handed Elize a reference letter that recommended her in the highest possible terms.

"Will you help me with the babies?" Elize asked quietly. Eva nodded, smiling. "I am going to need other people to clean and cook, but I would like you to help me with these," Elize said, patting her tummy.

"Is he the madam's first baby?" Eva asked.

"No. My first baby died," Elize answered, surprised how easily the words came out.

"My first baby also died," Eva said compassionately.

"Do you have other children?"

"My second-born and third-born and fourth-born are with their granny in Rustenburg," Eva explained.

Just then the children burst in. "Aunty Elize! The horse and pony are here. Come quickly. Come. Come now!"

"Would you also like to see them, Eva?" Eliza asked.

"Thank you, madam. I have already done so."

Their patience at breaking point, the children pulled Elize out of the house and to the stables. If there was one thing that Elize knew about, it was horses. She rubbed their faces and patted their necks and gave them each a carrot that Maimon had thoughtfully left in a paper packet around the stable's corner.

The family met for dinner at seven, in a room which had to be the dining room, because it had a big, long table and was close to the kitchen. Another native, Margaret, who was taller and fatter than Eva, told them that she was the cook, and for dinner had prepared hot vegetable soup, Karoo lamb chops and vegetables, with fruit salad to follow. At Maimon's request, Margaret brought out an uncut pineapple, a bunch of bananas and a large pawpaw, all of which were passed around in wonderment. Then Maimon cut the skin off the pineapple, sliced the pawpaw into four equal segments, and peeled one of the bananas. At first, none of the Russians were sure about the fruits' tastes, especially of the bananas, but seeing how much Elize liked them, everybody agreed that they were very special.

Some rooms had beds in them, others didn't; but as there were more beds than people, the unfurnished nature of their house wasn't a problem to any of its occupants. Joshua and Sarah insisted on saying goodnight to their respective animals, after which they climbed into bed, the happiest children in the world.

Maimon woke in the night and saw an envelope on his bedside table with "Letter #5" written boldly in green ink. The next morning Elize read it to him.

My Dear Wonderful Husband,

Before I came to bed tonight, I went to see your parents, to make sure they were comfortable, to find out if there was anything they needed, and then to thank them for bringing you into this world. Joseph and Mary are remembered as

Jesus's parents, and Anshul and Gittel should be remembered as yours.

Before you get a swollen head, don't think you are another Jesus. You are not, and I thank God for that. He could easily have made a mistake and made you one, but fortunately He didn't.

One of the wonderful things about being your wife, is that I am always learning from you. When we arrived at "The Palace" this afternoon, you could easily have called us all together and taken us on a conducted tour of this wonderful house you have built. But you didn't. You took Joshua and Sarah to meet Boris and Katya, and the look of wonderment and excitement on their faces was worth so much more than the thousands of pounds, or whatever it cost, to build our house.

We are spending a lot of money on "The Palace" and the Franschoek farm. I know you wouldn't if we couldn't afford it, but I worry all the same.

The reason for this letter is to tell you that if we ever lose all of our money, I will take in other people's dirty clothes to wash and iron so that we can have food on the table and a roof over our heads.

I know it is not likely, but you never know, and I would like you to please remember this.

Thank you.

Your grateful and ever-loving wife,
Elize

Maimon and Elize rose early the following morning: Maimon to get to his office, and Elize to meet Lewis Michaelson, a recommended interior decorator. Lewis was to help her find furniture, curtains, and carpets, all of which he said he would be happy to have delivered to their house on approbation. He just needed to know what style Elize had in mind. This was a question Elize had never heard before, and Maimon left the two of them deep in discussion about the advantages of Georgian, as opposed to Victorian, furniture. Later, Maimon was to learn that included in Lewis' many talents was that of being a thief, after Maimon caught him stealing his money.

Back in the office, Maimon felt comfortable for the first time in many months. This was where he was in control, where he knew what was going on – and, if he didn't, he could find out in minutes, if not seconds. First things first: he needed to see Patrick Duncan. That was set up for the following Friday. The gold/arsenic plant was being commissioned and would be ready on Monday. That left the two lawyers. Normally, Maimon would have taken Edward with him to see them both, but that would possibly have meant waiting another ten days and, at that point, who knows? In both cases their need to see him might be urgent. Mr. Wentzel had contacted him first, so Maimon reciprocated that treatment.

To his surprise and relief, Mr. Wentzel called him in right away. The two men hadn't met, but both knew of the other. After a few pleasantries, the lawyer opened the documents' safe in his office, withdrew an envelope, and handed it to Maimon, who opened it, took out the contents, and gave it back, asking Mr. Wentzel to read it to him. Apologizing for overlooking the fact that Maimon did not read, he took the letter, sat behind his heavy black stinkwood desk, and began:

My Dear Maimon,

I am terribly sorry for not having kept in touch with you on a one-to-one basis.

I have followed your career with great interest, and with South Africa's future in the hands of young people like you, the country can only go from strength to strength – if the politicians leave the businessmen alone to get on and do their jobs, that is.

I am writing this letter from Paris, where my doctors tell me my heart is on its last legs, and, sadly, I don't have any evidence to refute their opinions. In fact, I suspect that by the time you receive this letter I will have shuffled off this mortal coil, as Shakespeare wrote.

We are all built differently – physically as we see, and mentally as we can't see – with results flowing from both these characteristics. Amongst mine is the difficulty of giving away any of my financial assets. My wife thinks it stems from the time when I had no money, which might well be true.

The day on the boat when you saved my life is etched on my mind, and the time has now come for me to add material thanks to the verbal ones I have already expressed.

In my will I have left 850,000 De Beers shares for you to do with as you wish.

If you don't need the money, I would not sell them, as the preeminent diamond mining company in the world, now managed by the very capable Cecil Rhodes, will surely be extremely profitable and pay consistent dividends.

While I have not been a particularly good, adopted father, my record as an adopted grandfather is somewhat better. I have covered all of Eli's financial needs up till now, and set aside sufficient money to meet any reasonable costs he might incur for his welfare and education till his twenty-first birthday. As this support should rightly have come from you, Eli and his mother believe that it has.

With renewed thanks and best wishes,
Lesuj Vagalparot

From time to time Maimon reflected on how fortunate he had been, and that on so many occasions the fortunate way his proverbial ball had bounced. The result of this was that overall he had few regrets. One regret he did have was his losing touch with Lesuj, particularly in view of the start this middle-aged European Jew had given him. Had Lesuj not offered him a job, Maimon knew he would probably be selling secondhand clothes in Commissioner Street with the Litvaks.

And then there was the money Lesuj had sent Ayna, which Maimon knew – irrespective of his feelings for this woman – he should have.

The more he thought about it, the worse Maimon felt.

While Mr Wentzel was replacing the letter in its envelope, a thought flashed through Maimon's mind. Why is it, he wondered, when you don't have money and need it, it is so hard to come by? And when you have made a bit, this sort of thing happens?

Mr Wentzel said he would keep in touch, and would contact Maimon in about six weeks regarding the re-registration of the De Beers shares into his name.

That left Godfrey Heyman. Working on the premise that what Heyman wanted to discuss with Maimon might be important enough to interrupt some other task on which he was working, Maimon headed for his office. Luck was with Maimon. After a few introductory remarks, Mr. Heyman said, "I believe you know my client, Mr. Bellingham."

The name rang a bell, but Maimon couldn't remember where from. Mr. Heyman helped him out.

"The managing director of Prestige Milling. He said you met briefly at the Hights Hotel a few years ago."

"That's absolutely right," Maimon said, remembering a man who was more interested in gins and tonics than the business of the day.

"I will come straight to the point. Mr. Bellingham would like to sell his company to you. He appreciates that you may not wish to commit the quantum of capital required to purchase it, and therefore suggests that the requisite end might be achieved through a reverse takeover mechanism."

This suggestion was something new to Maimon, which clearly showed on his face.

"Let me explain," the kindly Mr. Heyman said. "Prestige Milling will buy your agricultural industry assets, which I understand comprise a peanut butter factory, a sunflower-seed-oil-expressing plant, and a flour mill in Pretoria whose profit is underwritten by the government."

Considering than none of these assets were operational, this was a bit of a stretch, Maimon thought. He didn't say so, of course, instead just nodded in agreement.

"My client," Mr. Heyman continued, "would pay for these assets with 850,000 newly issued Prestige Milling shares. This would comprise 65% of the newly capitalised company, which you would then control. It would give you almost 2/3 ownership of the enlarged company. This, you may know, includes wheat mills at the four coastal cities, a fish-oil expressing factory at Simonstown in the Cape, a big maize mill at Randfontein, seven kaffir beer factories in the Transkei, Eastern Transvaal, and near Nylstroom, as well as a breakfast oats factory under construction at Meyerton."

Maimon knew the Prestige Group was big, but before now he had no idea that it was possibly the largest non-mining company in South Africa.

"I appreciate that this is a proposal in its nature and form that you were possibly not expecting," Mr. Heyman continued, "and so I have prepared a memorandum confirming the above and setting out some of the important details that you may wish to discuss with your legal advisors."

Maimon took the document and asked what time frame Mr. Bellingham had in mind for this transaction.

"He would like it done in thirty days," Mr. Heyman said. "But I told him forty-five or 60 days might be more realistic."

"That makes sense," Maimon agreed, pleased to be able to make a responsible contribution to a conversation whose implications he was still digesting.

They agreed to meet as soon as possible, and in any event not later than in ten days' time.

Seconds later Maimon was out in the bright Highveld sunlight, realizing for the first time in his life that it was possible to have a lucky number.

Being scientifically minded, to Maimon the idea of a lucky number was a form of alchemy, but ... could it just be a coincidence? His bed on the *America* was also number "850," he now remembered, and while he could examine what, if anything, happened 850 days after this or that event, there were more urgent matters requiring his attention, specifically getting four factories up and running. So instead of returning to the office, he rushed home to tell Elize that he would be away for six-to-seven days.

A week later, as the sun was setting, an extremely tired Maimon walked up the Parktown Hill, leading an exhausted horse that looked like it might not even make the final 300 yards. Elize met them, and recognizing that Maimon was wearing the same stained shirt that he left in, said, "Same clothes."

"Different horse," Maimon replied.

"Different smell," Elize said, smiling, now close to Maimon. "I will go and run you a bath."

"How many horses did you use, Uncle Maimon?" Joshua asked, never having seen an animal so tired as the one he handed over to Alpheus.

"That was number nine," Maimon told him. "How are your riding lessons coming along?"

"Very nicely," the little boy replied excitedly. "Can we go riding together tomorrow, please?"

By way of a reply, all Maimon could think of was the children's joke whose question he had forgotten, just remembering the answer, which was "Colonel Bumsore."

"Let's decide tomorrow," Maimon said, playing for time, his aching bones crying out for the hot bath Elize was running.

In the six nights he had been away, Maimon had worked harder than during any other week in his life, and that included for ten hours at a time in the blazing hot sun on Piet's farm. Toiling during the day and riding at night, he had spent sufficient time at each of the sites under construction to light a Mauser fuse under both the management team and the natives.

At each location, he called the total workforce together and told them he felt betrayed, and let down, by the minimal amount of work that had been done in his absence. He knew it wasn't because they couldn't do better, and he was relying on them to catch up. Catching up, he knew, meant working day and night and not taking any shortcuts. He was working seven days a week, and they had to as well. He would be back in ten days' time, when he expected to see each of their plants fully operational. If they were not, he would call in General Kitchener and his men to finish the job, informing him that our white and black Africans were not able to do so.

Twenty minutes in the steaming bath with a generous helping of "boere sout"[126] helped restore his muscles to more or less working order, and just when Maimon was feeling better, Elize made him stand up and lathered and louvered him down with Lifebuoy soap. His every pore screaming for relief, she then threw buckets of cold water all over him. Out of the bath, Elize dried Maimon back and front, and then rubbed into his body a soothing mint cream her mother had taught her to make.

---

126 *Farmer's salt*

Taking Maimon by the hand, Elize led him to the bedroom and laid him down on the cool white sheets. Normally observant, Maimon didn't remember the bed, or the comfortable mattress, and definitely not the cool white sheets. Elize and Lewis had been busy. Maimon wanted to tell her that he had noticed, and how wonderful the bed was and how cool the sheets were, but his mouth would not listen to his brain, and in seconds he was asleep. Eighteen hours later Maimon woke, feeling like a new man, and to prove it, he pulled Elize onto their temporary bed.

The gold/cyanide extraction plant had been commissioned, and ten o'clock on Monday morning was the time set for the official trial to commence. To interest other gold producers in the process, Maimon laid on pre-lunch drinks, a sumptuous lunch, post-lunch drinks, sundowner drinks, a finger supper, and post-supper drinks. Many mining engineers remembered the catering, but not the smelting, which Maimon didn't mind as long as they remembered being there.

At the end of the second day, the little kerosene smelting furnace kicked into life, and thirty minutes later a trickle of gold ran over the refractory bricks and into the ingot mould placed there to catch it. For very different reasons, neither Maimon nor Jennings had let the furnace out of their sight for the full two days, and when the gold eventually trickled out, they were both so tired they could hardly stand up. Jennings and Maimon went straight to bed, Maimon via the post office, where he dictated a brief wire to McArthur and the Forest brothers.

TRIAL 100 PERCENT SUCCESSFUL MANY MINERS IMPRESSED FULL REPORT FOLLOWS REGARDS MAIMON SOKOLOVSKI

CHAPTER 44

NEW BABIES

Early one morning, a week after Elize's twin boys were born, when both of them were gaining weight after their initial losses, they were circumcised and named at the hospital. With Kaylah's help, Maimon organized a celebratory breakfast in a room the hospital kept for such events; and later that day Elize came home with Morris and Max.

A few weeks later, Kaylah and Saul returned to the "Palace" late one afternoon. Kaylah had obviously been crying, and Saul, not a man of many words at the best of times, shocked into silence.

"Where is Elize?" Kaylah spluttered.

Maimon, the first to be alerted to the unfolding crisis, sat Kaylah and Saul down in the little ante-room next to the front door. Elize rushed in, took one look at her shattered in-laws, and said, "Oh my God. What is wrong?"

With Kaylah too overwrought to speak, Saul said, "It's Xenopus Laevis."

Instead of throwing light on the cause of Kaylah crying, the explanation confused Maimon and Elize even more.

Smiling through her tears, Kaylah said, "My visitor was late this month. It is never late, so I went to see Dr. Jacob Stanolowsky, the one who you say is so good. After examining me, we went to Mr Lancelot Hogben. He is not a doctor but a scientist, and has worked out that by injecting a woman's urine into a frog, you can tell if the woman is pregnant or not. So I peed into a bottle, and he injected some of it into two frogs, and said I should come back this afternoon. If the frogs laid eggs, it meant that I was having a baby."

Kaylah looked at Elize through her tears and nodded affirmatively.

"There were hundreds of eggs," she said as they hugged, both crying.

Ever the sceptic, Maimon said to Saul, "Do you trust this frog-fellow?"

By way of reply, Saul took out a sheet of paper and handed it to Maimon, in his excitement forgetting that Maimon couldn't read. Taking it back he read, "Thank you for your report on the pregnancy test on Mrs. X. You may be interested to know that out of one GP of many years' standing, one specialist gynaecologist, and one frog, only the frog was correct."

Speechless, they all stood up and had a Johannesburg hug. The hug released, the only one not crying asked, "Who is Xenopus Laevis?"

"The frog," Saul told Maimon.

Gittel, who had given up hope of Kaylah ever having a baby, immediately started drawing up lists of what her daughter needed to do. Observing this behavior, Elize secretly wished Kaylah "good luck" in dealing with her mother.

Never had nine months of Kaylah's life passed so slowly. The bump took so long to show that Kaylah was afraid the baby had stopped growing, but Dr. Stanolowsky listened to the baby's heart and said it was fine. Eventually Kaylah's waters broke, and a few hours later she held a wet, warm, little pink baby girl on her sweating shoulder. They named her Netanya, which means "Gift from God." A year later, God blessed them again, with another healthy baby, this time a boy, who they named "Akim," which means originating from God.

Shortly after Elize finished feeding her boys, she fell pregnant again, and nine months later Jenna and Alison burst upon the world.

CHAPTER 45

SIR PERCY FITZPATRICK

Maimon's most important meeting on his return was with Percy Fitzpatrick, a man of so many parts it was difficult to believe they were all housed in one mind. "Milner's Kindergarten," as the bureaucrats running the country were known, had been sure to get the message through to Maimon, and others who had monopolistic contracts, that those contracts would not be honored in the New South Africa. The Pretoria wheat-milling contract was central to Maimon's Prestige Milling negotiations, and somehow he had to make sure it would be honored.

Maimon thought carefully about the Fitzpatrick meeting: what he wanted to achieve, and what he was prepared to concede in order to do so. He certainly didn't want his meeting held in a government building, or in Sir Percy's offices. Instead, he suggested the Rand Club dining room for lunch, and if necessary that they continue afterwards in one of the club's private conference rooms.

Sir Percy Fitzpatrick, who regarded the Rand Club as his second home, was delighted with Maimon's suggestion, as was Maimon with Sir Percy's acceptance, as he thought his adversary might go in with his guard down. They agreed to meet at 12:30 the following Thursday, and just before leaving his office, Maimon drank a pint of milk and ate a ¼ pound of cheese.

Not having had breakfast, Sir Percy Fitzpatrick suggested they begin with a Bloody Mary, to which Maimon responded that it would be a pity to trouble the barman too often, so better to start with a double each.

"Great Idea," Sir Percy told him. This was followed by "a double screwdriver" before they got to the table. Most of lunch was spent on politics, which Maimon considered a fruitless exercise because all he ever heard was what had been written in the morning's *Diggers News*.

Over desert, his tongue now loosened, Sir Percy ventured the opinion that while Jewish people had made a considerable contribution to the development of South Africa, they had also included a number of citizens who were occupying Her Majesty's jails. Maimon pressed Sir Percy for names and dates, and even when told that his accuser couldn't remember them, Maimon persevered.

When he noticed that Fitzpatrick found this tiresome, he switched tack, pointing out that while there were many Irishmen in South Africa, only one, who was sitting at the table now, had done any good for the country. With Fitzpatrick's ego at bursting point, Maimon asked him what he knew about the Irish Brigade, who invaded and occupied Eureka City near Barberton in April 1887. Also, their constant ambushes at Elephant's Creek in the late 1880s, what did Fitzpatrick know of that? And, in particular, John "Foxy Jack" MacBride and John McLaughlin, the latter better known as "'Captain Moonlight"? And what about Charles Harding, Jack McCann, and the McKeone brothers?

Obviously discomforted by this reminder, as he was by the fact that the South African Police Force (or ZARPS, as they were called) was severely stretched and had great difficulty keeping the gangs at bay, Sir Percy suggested that they repair to their booked conference room. This they did; but as soon as they sat down, Maimon struck.

He told the no-longer-sharp politician that he had heard talk that the government was considering annulling some contracts entered into by the defeated Transvaal Government. Maimon added that he hoped his Pretoria wheat contract wasn't included in this category, as it had been drawn up and witnessed by the government's own very capable Jannie Smuts. In order to ensure that the government honored its side of the bargain, Maimon stated, he was prepared to take his case to the Supreme Court in Bloemfontein, where he would put Jannie Smuts in the witness stand. Whatever Sir Percy was expecting, it wasn't Maimon's broadside.

Adopting a more conciliatory position, Maimon continued: "We are all concerned about the unfolding unemployment situation, particularly among the defeated Boers, whose farmhouses were torched, wells poisoned, and fields set alight." The very people, Maimon reminded Sir Percy, whom the government referred to as "poor whites." Furthermore, there was no escaping the fact that they were all voters. What would happen, Maimon asked Fitzpatrick, "if, at the next election, they all voted for the emerging communist party?"

Both men knew there was no answer to this; but Maimon had a solution. The steel works that he was building on the Vaal River could use, but did not actually need, steel scrap. According to some reports, the British Army were leaving behind one million tons of broken pieces of iron and steel in one form or another. To help the government with their ever-growing "poor white" problem, he, Maimon, would be prepared to pay the government £1 a ton for any such raw material delivered to his works, provided no other steel works were permitted to be built in the country for 15 years. The government could pay the collectors £4 or £5 a ton, which would put money into the workers' pockets as well as into the economy, and would clean up the countryside at the same time.

"I ask you, Percy," Maimon concluded, "isn't that an extremely good deal for the government?"

Through his slowly clearing mind, Sir Percy could find no fault with Maimon's logic, and so when Maimon extended his arm, he had no hesitation in shaking it, thus sealing the transaction.

On the way downstairs they parted, Percy heading to the bar to have one for the road, and Maimon hastening to his office to dictate an *aide-mémoire* setting out the salient facts of his extended lunch meeting with none other than the esteemed Sir Percy Fitzpatrick.

Riding slowly up the hill, Maimon noted that while there were still important loose ends to be tied up – particularly with regard to his reverse takeover of Prestige Milling – it seemed that he was on the home straight. He would take two weeks to visit the three construction sites, and if the factories were working satisfactorily, he would have an ox killed and braaied,[127] accompanied by as much Lion Lager and kaffir beer as his workers could consume. And that is exactly what happened.

---

127 *Barbecued*

CHAPTER 46

THE FORT JAIL

As much as she was dreading it, Elize realized that she could not put off visiting her mother any longer. When the day had been fixed, Maimon told Elize that he insisted on accompanying her to the jail. This "accompanying," he made clear, did not include joining Elize in the visitor's room. What he didn't tell Elize was that this was not because he did not want to support his beloved wife, but because he feared that when he saw Magda again, he might not be able to restrain himself.

As was necessary, Elize made an appointment for two weeks ahead, and the nominated day arrived more quickly than she or Maimon expected. They rode to the jail in silence. On arrival Maimon parked his newly arrived American car, a gleaming black Hupmobile, and the policeman on duty escorted Elize to the General Reception Office. There she identified herself, and left her handbag with Maimon, taking only a small white handkerchief with her.

Maimon expected Elize to be back in about thirty minutes, but it was almost two hours before his wife, pale and shaking, returned to the General Reception Office. Maimon walked her back to his car, holding her tight against his shoulder. On the road back to Johannesburg, Elize did not utter a word, not even a thank-you when finally they arrived at home. That night Maimon found letter "#6" on his pillow. Later Elize read it to him:

> *My Dear Wonderful Maimon, who knows me better than anyone on earth and possibly even better than God.*

First of all, thank you for taking me to the jail this after-noon and bringing me home afterwards.

You alone knew how I was dreading the visit, which, unlike you, I had to undertake. You can hate Magda, but I cannot hate my mother. She is the woman who pushed me out of her womb, who suckled me, who cared for me when I was a vulnerable infant, who was there for me when I was a girl, who told me when we got back to the farm after the Nag-maal that God would bring you to me.

It was my mother who stood solidly behind me, and some-times in front of me, when I announced I was pregnant, and Willem was on the point of beating me. It was she who dis-solved my father's opposition to your asking permission to marry me, and it was my mother who sat with me for over a day and a night while I struggled to bring Adam into this world. I am sorry I lied to you, my labor wasn't two hours, it was twenty-two. I thought the baby would die, and then I thought I would die, but I prayed to God to keep us alive for you. And he did. It was my mother who gave half her meagre rations in the concentration camp to Adam, which is why he was so much healthier than all of the other camp children.

And it was my mother who made the mistake that cost Adam his life.

Yes, she effectively abandoned him, but the guilt for Adam's death is not hers alone. I share it. Adam was not killed by his grandmother, he was killed by his grandmother and his mother, and that knowledge lives with me every day, every single day of my life, and will till I join him in heaven.

I was shown into a small room with a wooden table, and single chairs on each side of it. A lady policeman stood on guard at the door, and a thin, old, haggard woman with streaky gray hair sat on one of the chairs. For a moment I thought I had been taken to the wrong room, and then I saw it was my mother. I just stood still. I could not move, and did not, until the policewoman told me to sit down. On the table was a chipped enamel jug and two enamel mugs like the natives use.

I sat down and looked at this woman, my mother, and saw a different person. After a while I put my hand on the table, and she did too, and we held hands, except it wasn't my mother's hand. It was cold and bony. She didn't look at me, just down at the table.

She said she was sorry, and I said that was all right. I didn't know if she was sorry, but she did know it wasn't all right.

I told her about the babies, which she said she knew. One of the guards had given her the news. She asked for their names, which I told her, and then she smiled, and then I cried. One mistake, just one mistake, and our boys will not have an Ouma. Is that fair? I don't know. Is it right that our boys should be punished for something their Ouma did? I don't know.

She asked about you. I said you were well. I didn't say you sent your regards, and I know she didn't expect you to. She asked if you still looked after me so well, and I told her you did.

I told her how Koos and Elna found us in Cape Town, and the wonderful thing you did to give them back their self-esteem. I told her what you wanted done to the farm, and how Koos' eyes lit up with gratitude. She said you were a good man.

We didn't discuss the upcoming trial, or that Edward had been to see her four times – the policewoman told me that – or what her sentence might be.

Hardest of all for me, and I think for my mother, too, was that neither of us knew if she would get out of jail alive.

She looked so thin. I asked her if the food was OK, and she said yes. I asked her if she wanted anything, and she said no. Then a bell rang, I looked at the policewoman, who indicated I should leave. We both stood up, and to my dying shame, I did not hug her. We both half-smiled, I said I would come back, and she said that would be nice. Two minutes later I was back in the real world with you.

Now I am ready to go to the cemetery. To see Adam's grave and to say goodbye to him.

Can we please do that tomorrow?

It is going to be harder for me than today was, and I know it is going to be very difficult for you. We will need to support each other.

In my prayers every night I thank God for giving you to me. For finding me sitting on the wall at the hotel, when I was a silly girl holding a prayer book upside down. You have never asked me why I had the Jewish prayer book, and I am not 100% sure myself. The Predekant had over eighty Afrikaans prayer books, but only one Hebrew one. Why did I take it and sit on the wall? I don't know. The only reason I can think of is that God told me to, because he wanted you to find me. I know that your belief in God is not as deep as mine, but even a little bit is good. God will be at the cemetery tomorrow to help us. I know he will.

I love you,
Elize

CHAPTER 47

ADAM'S EVOCATION

The next morning they went to the cemetery. The Jewish religion dictates that within eleven months of a death, a tombstone of the deceased needs to be unveiled, and there is a ceremony to accompany this consecration. It is customary, but not necessary, for the parents of a deceased child to be present at this service; knowing how hard it would be for Elize even without attending the ceremony, Maimon had arranged for it to be held in their absence.

They soon found a cemetery attendant who knew the grave and asked them to follow him as he walked slowly to the children's section. To Elize's horror, the children's section was bigger than the adults' one. And it wasn't just for infants, but for children up to twelve years of age. Later Maimon told her this was because many children had a low resistance to illnesses like smallpox and diphtheria.

Like the graves of the adults, those of the children were in rows, except smaller and closer together, and to Maimon they looked pathetic. And then they came to Adam's. It was all in shiny black marble. The headpiece had "Adam Sokolovski" in English and Hebrew, his birth and death dates, and a brief inscription: "Desperately missed by his loving parents Elize and Maimon."

They stood in silence, looking at it.

"If you don't like the inscription, I can change it," Maimon said quietly.

"It's fine," Maimon heard Elize whisper. And then in a stronger voice she said, "Goodbye, Adam. I will see you in heaven. I will recognize you because you will be one of the angels."

Maimon had picked up two white river-smoothed pebbles, about the size that Adam's clenched fist would have been. He put one on the black marble frame, and the other one he gave to Elize, who put it next to his. Then she looked up at her husband, as if asking what good that would do.

"When Adam looks down," Maimon told her, "he will see our stones and he will know that we have not forgotten him."

Elize looked round and noticed for the first time that all the children's graves had little stones on them: some just one or two, and others a lot.

"We will never forget you, Adam" Elize said, talking to the black marble stone, and then to Maimon, "We can go now."

Slowly they retraced their steps to the motor car on the walk that took about ten minutes.

On the way home in the car, Elize chatted about this and that. She had obtained closure, Maimon realized, something that he had not, and she was at peace with Adam and herself. Because he had had other matters on his mind, Maimon had not found a better end for Magda than being eaten alive by wild dogs. She may be thin, but she wasn't old, and he still had time to come up with alternatives. "Work in progress," they called it in the engineering world, Maimon remembered.

Elize agonised long and hard over what name she would like to give their house, and in the end, as it looked down over a copse of cedar trees, she told Maimon she wanted to name it "Cedar View". Maimon had long learned that there were battles worth fighting, and those not, and this one was definitely in the latter category. A few days later, when Elize went to the sign maker, she had a Count Sokolovski moment, and ordered a sign with "See Da View" spelled in big letters, and in a corner in a much smaller font, "aka Cedar View." When the children were old enough to read, they thought it very funny.

Some months later a letter arrived from Sarah and Joshua's mother, advising that their gran had died, and giving details of the ship bringing her to South Africa. Maimon and Elize agreed that the children should be escorted to Cape Town to meet their mother, and also that with the twins still feeding, it would be wisest for Elize and the infants to stay in Johannesburg.

Tears are usually associated with sadness, but the tears of happiness shed by Francine when she was reunited with her children during that day, and, indeed, the following day, would have alleviated many a South African drought, Maimon thought.

Elize and Maimon insisted that Francine and her children live with them in the big house, for which they built on three more bedrooms with bathrooms as well as a living room and a little kitchen. The children called it "Francine's Wing".

On his return to Johannesburg, Maimon found Elize as happy as a monkey who had just stolen someone's breakfast, and it wasn't solely because she had seen Francine again. Two of Mr Hogben's frogs had confirmed what Elize knew, and with Max and Morris still occupying their nursery, an additional room had to be added … for Jenna and Alison.

A judge had been allocated for Magda's manslaughter trial and a date set down for the case. Edward had been able to secure a meeting with the judge and had persuaded him to visit Magda in jail. To put Magda at ease, Edward had accompanied the judge, and the three of them spent thirty minutes talking about this and that, but not about the impending case. Following their jail visit, Edward told the judge that Magda would plead guilty to manslaughter, and in view of her mental and physical condition, and the fact that she had established an Alcoholics Anonymous chapter in jail, there were grounds to give her a non-custodial sentence. The judge undertook to consider Edward's request.

With the date of the case approaching, Elize visited her mother every week. Maimon never did. Magda told her proudly that they now had nine inmates attending the weekly AA meetings, and in fact the man who had worked most closely with her establishing the group, Daniel Casper, would be released shortly. While in jail his wife had sold their house, taken the money, and moved in with another man. Daniel had nowhere to go. Might it be possible for Maimon to find him a job? He was literate, had a motor car driving license, and had promised the Lord, Magda, and himself, that he would never ever touch another drop of alcohol in his life. Elize promised to speak to Maimon about Daniel.

Maimon took a liking to the tall thin man with a sad face and sent him on a refresher course of driving lessons. After he returned with a red rosette confirming that he had obtained the highest possible number of marks, Maimon offered Daniel a job as his personal chauffeur. Because of the long hours involved, the job came with accommodation at See Da View. When told this, to Maimon's great embarrassment, Daniel dropped to his knees and thanked the Lord and Maimon for this opportunity, which he assured both of them he would discharge to the best of his ability and for as long as he had a breath of air to breathe.

The appointed day for Magda's trial finally arrived. In court Elize and Maimon sat just behind Edward and his senior counsel. The thin, scared, middle-aged woman sat in the accused box, her eyes darting around looking for Elize.

Magda pleaded guilty, after which Magda's counsel requested permission to address the court, which was the judge. He told the judge what had happened and that Magda, now a broken woman, had already been in jail for ten months awaiting trial. During this time, she had established a branch of the Alcoholics Anonymous organization, and according to the records from the Fort, Magda had been an ideal prisoner.

Taking all this into account, the advocate respectfully suggested that this woman had already suffered more than enough, and that a non-custodial sentence would be appropriate. Furthermore, the advocate noted, the consulting psychologist had recommended that Mrs. du Toit spend three months in a halfway house, before moving in with her daughter, where more than adequate accommodation was available.

The lead prosecution lawyer advised the court that he had no objection to this, after which the judge closed the case, advising that sentence would be handed down the following week. And so it was, with the judge accepting Magda's lawyer's recommendations.

Elize visited her mother twice a week, during which time Magda became physically and mentally stronger, and, 92 days after the court case, Magda quietly moved into See Da View. The babies gave her a new lease of life, and she did whatever she could to help Elize and Eva with the children.

Magda hadn't been in the house a week before she told Elize that she needed to visit Adam's grave, which the two of them did a few days later. To Elize's surprise, in addition to the two stones she and Maimon had placed on Adam's tombstone, there were now nine others. When pressed Maimon admitted that he had been going to the cemetery and sitting next to the black marble plinth and weeping. Elize suggested that he talk to a psychologist, to which Maimon replied that if doing so would bring Adam back, he would make an appointment right away. The wild dogs remained in first place.

Once a year Maimon met with the management of all the Prestige Milling companies to set income and expenditure budgets. As long as they were adhered to, he left them alone. If the income was short, Maimon wanted to know why right away, and if expenditure was exceeded, and the reason was not "force majeure,"[128] Maimon usually parted company with the men running those companies. "Surprises are for birthdays," Maimon told his people; he wanted to know everything good and bad as soon as it happened.

Realizing that he was not able to devote sufficient time to both his agricultural and steel-making activities, and as the former was more personnel intensive, Maimon did a deal with Sammy Marks and Horace Wright. A new company, Union Steel, was formed in 1909 – its name taken from the about-to-be established new country, the Union of South Africa, the following year. Sammy Marks would be the controlling shareholder, and construction of its first blast furnace under his supervision began in 1911. With a guaranteed and profitable outlet for his Thabazimbi iron ore, Maimon was a comfortable minority shareholder.

As important as his businesses were to Maimon, he made quality time every week for his children. When they were infants, he sometimes skipped a day here or there, but once first the boys, and then the girls, were two, he was there for them every day. A special treat was his "snug as a bug in a rug" after-bath, drying routine, when a child was wrapped in a large bath towel, and for about thirty seconds Maimon energetically snuggled them, partly upside down, ending up with both of them crashing onto a bed. "Again! Again!" was so frequently heard from four little voices that Maimon had to ration his children to three snuggles each per night. After twelve wall-to-wall snuggles, he was ready for the drink that Elize had waiting for him every evening on their veranda overlooking the Parktown valley. No matter how hard a day Elize had had, she made sure to wear a clean dress and the lipstick that Maimon liked, for their quiet time together. This quiet time, Kaylah observed, was possible because of the help that bathed, dressed, and fed their children.

---

128   *Unforeseeable circumstances that prevent someone from fulfilling a contract*

CHAPTER 48

DOMO ARIGATOU GOZAIMASU

Maimon also made time for charity, having formed the DAG Foundation. For those who asked, "DAG" stood for "Domo Arigatou Gozaimasu," which was Japanese for 'Thank you." It was Maimon saying thank you, rather than what he expected to hear from the recipients of his largesse. In fact, so generous was Maimon that around Johannesburg people quipped that DAG stood for "Do Ask aGain."

In addition to the Jewish charities, many of whom needed DAG's assistance to stay afloat, Maimon also helped Christian, Hindu, and Muslim organizations, who looked after the poor and vulnerable people in their communities. Concerned that the diet of the natives did not possess sufficient vitamins, he set up canteens in Johannesburg as well as on the East and West Rand, where natives could get a meat, vegetable, and fruit meal for a penny. Once established, the Chamber of Mines took them over. Maimon also set up basic clinics, where natives could go if they were ill.

With hygiene poor to non-existent, the disposal of dead bodies was an ongoing challenge. For rich white people there were undertakers, the largest being AVBOB. Jokers said it stood for "Alles vrek behalwe ons besigheid."[129] Max Raphaely, from whom Maimon had bought The Hights Hotel, had started "the Chevrah Kadisha – the Jewish Helping Hand & Burial Society," which not only assumed the responsibility for burying all Jewish people according to their religious requirements, but also provided microloans, and, where these could not be repaid, grants enabling those members of the community who had fallen on

---

129 *Everything dies except our business*

hard times to purchase food and pay rent. In the society's early days, Max Raphaely was at Maimon's office so often, some people thought he worked there.

Anshul and Gittel were both old. Anshul was in an advanced state of dementia, and during the last six months of his life, did not know who or where he was. Maimon provided round-the-clock carers for him, which freed Gittel to move around the house, confident that he was in good hands. Maimon had a wheelchair made for his mother that the children loved pushing, with or without their grandmother in it. As they became bigger and stronger, he had to install a basic governor that prevented it from being pushed too fast.

One morning Gittel fell in the bathroom, broke her hip, and was rushed to hospital. There she developed pneumonia and died two days later. Anshul passed away one night three weeks after that, as a result of his multiple health problems.

As much as Kaylah and Maimon expected their parents to die, when it happened it was a greater shock than either of them expected. In accordance with Jewish custom, they were buried as soon as possible, in their case the day they died. For the next week, Kaylah and Maimon, as well as their spouses, stayed at home and sat on low chairs. During this period, known as shiva, Maimon and Saul did not shave, and prayers were held every morning and evening at See Da View, which were attended by members of their congregation. During the day friends dropped in to pay their respects, and to talk quietly to Maimon and Kaylah about their parents, and the lives they lived in Russia.

Elize was not surprised that Maimon hardly spoke to people about his parents, and that he just listened to their comforting words. She alone knew the torment he was suffering, and to try and help him letter #7 appeared on his pillow. For every one of the first six letters, Maimon couldn't wait to hear what his wife had written. Letter "7," however, lay unopened for two days before Maimon asked Elize to read it.

My ever-dearest partner in life, Maimon,

We are taught that God created us in his own image, and that he put us on earth to make things better. He didn't make us perfect, because he wanted us to improve. Improve ourselves and improve the lives of other people.

Even though I am almost as old as you, and neither of us are really old at all, God did not give me your wisdom. By making me your wife he put me in a position to learn from you, and in the years we have been together, I have learned so, so much.

It is not only from you that I have learned, but also from God. He has made me observant, not only to appreciate the flowers and the birds and all the other things He made, but also His greatest creation of all, human beings.

We all make mistakes, and you know I am the living proof of that, but God lets us make mistakes so that we can learn from them. Not only should we never make the same mistake again, but because of our mistakes, we can be better people.

Look at all the natives whose lives you have made better. Those at the iron mine and all those at your food factories. If it wasn't for you, they would be living in kaffir huts and smoking dagga. Now their children have school uniforms and books and will learn to read and write – and all that because of you. That is what you should think about.

Lastly and most importantly, never forget that your parents were proud of you, and so they should have been. You have done wonderful things in the few years you have been alive, and God willing, you will do many more in the decades ahead.

I don't know if this letter will help you, I know it should. But you are quite a different man – how grateful I am for that – and in the end it is only you who can put the past behind you and move on.

I share your pain now, let both of us move on, to a brighter, loving future together. Your partner, lover, wife and ... everything,

Elize

The Great War of 1914-18 – which resulted in about forty million men killed, wounded, gassed, buried alive in collapsed trenches, and mentally scarred – did not leave little South Africa unscathed. Most, but not all, of the country's casualties were white. On the 21st of February, 1917, the SS Mendi was struck by another ship not far from the Isle of Wight; irreparably damaged, it sank. Most of the 600 South Africans on board were black.

They all drowned.

While European men on both sides of the conflict, as well as others from the British Empire, were fighting themselves to a standstill in the trenches of Europe, the children at See Da View were no longer children. They were young adolescents, with strong bodies and strong opinions. Morris, whom everyone called "Morrie," and Max were like two capital "S" letters that fitted into one another. Morrie was the extrovert, hail fellow well met, whom everybody liked. Max was introverted, though not to an antisocial extent, and solid. He listened to all sides of an argument, and then made up his mind. No one ever criticized Max's moral position.

Not identical, they were both good-looking, academically above-average, intellectually curious, and good at ball sports. Maimon made sure they were also good sportsmen. Next to the tennis court Maimon laid down two cricket nets: in the one, Manfred Susskind, a right-hand batsman who was Jewish, taught aspiring Morrie how to bat; in the other, Bill Duff explained to Max how to bowl leg-breaks and googlies. Both Manfred and Bill played cricket for South Africa; neither Morrie nor Max did.

Jenna and Alison were similarly different. Tall, blonde, and lithe, Jenna was the belle of every ball. The girl every mother wanted for her son. Bright as a spark plug, she didn't suffer fools gladly, but would help anyone who came to her for assistance. Academically OK and an above-average sports person, she was outstanding at nothing but good at everything. Alison was the genius of the family. She matriculated at fourteen with the highest Latin and Greek marks in the Transvaal. With a light skin, brown hair and eyes, she drew to her like a magnet intellectuals of all ages. In law school she was top of her class every year, and the only question was, when she graduated would she further her studies at Oxford or at Cambridge university?

CHAPTER 49

THE APPLICANT

One day, in the autumn of 1921, a young man came to see Maimon. Unusually for those times, Maimon worked on an "open-door policy," and after a brief but very audible knock, Maimon looked up to see a smartly turned-out fellow of about twenty years old, with black hair well Brylcreemed down, light gray trousers, and a blue blazer. In his hand was a new-looking leather briefcase. He was what Edward would have called "a clean-cut young man." Maimon smiled at him, which the young man took (correctly) as an invitation to enter the "holy sanctuary," as one of the clerks called Maimon's office.

Striding towards Maimon, he stretched out his hand, shook Maimon's firmly, and said, "Ari Cole."

"Sit down, Mr Cole," Maimon said, unusually impressed by this young man's forthright manner. "What can I do for you?"

"I would like a position with your organization, please, Mr Sokolovski," the young man said without hesitation.

"We have a Personnel Department," Maimon told him, "which looks after matters of this nature for me. I think it best if you contact them."

"I do know that, Mr. Sokolovski," the young man replied. "But I think it would save your time and mine, if you and I had a brief discussion about this."

A young Maimon, the older man thought, now warming to the youngster across the desk from him.

Not discouraged, the young man took out a folder with about twenty documents in it, and handed it to Maimon, with the explanation, "These are my references, sir."

From nursery school through to the University of Cape Town, many people had good things to say about Ari Cole. Academically, he had topped his classes at school and university in every subject every year.

He had also been the captain of the university under-nineteen Rugby, Cricket, Hockey, and Swimming Teams. He spoke English, Afrikaans, High Dutch, Yiddish, and Hebrew. He had also undertaken voluntary work in the Jewish community, and had taught elementary literacy courses to adult natives in Cape Town over the weekend.

"Tell me, Mr Cole," Maimon asked, "did you enjoy all these activities?"

"Yes, sir," the young man shot back.

"Is there nothing you don't enjoy?" Maimon asked, now a bit suspicious.

"Actually, there is, sir. Mountaineering. I don't have a head for heights."

Maimon was thankful that he had a human, and not a super-human, across the desk from him.

"What position do you have in mind in my company?" Maimon asked, wondering if it was his chair, this year, that this young fellow was eyeing.

"That is, of course, your decision, sir," Mr. Cole began. "But I think my most meaningful contribution would be as your Personal Assistant."

"Why do you say that, Mr. Cole?" Maimon asked, amazed at his chutzpah.[130]

"Because Mr. Oppenheimer has one and I understand you don't, sir," Mr. Cole replied, cool as a cucumber.

"Perhaps I should speak to Mr. Oppenheimer about that," Maimon replied, trying to stay on equal footing with this confident young man. "Should I need to, where can I get hold of you?"

"I am staying with Max Raphaely. He tells me he knows you," young Ari replied.

"Please come to us for Friday night Shabbat dinner. I will tell Mrs. Sokolovski to expect you at seven."

Maimon got up, shook the young man's hand, and watched him walk to the door. If Ari Cole had any intention of telling Maimon he had already accepted the Raphaely's invitation for dinner that Friday night, that opportunity was gone.

There was only one Jew that Maimon knew in the Western Cape, and that was Charles Back, the wine farmer who owned and managed Fairview at Paarl, so Maimon shot a telegram off to him, asking Charles

---

130 *Extreme self-confidence or audacity*

for a character and community opinion on the young man who had just walked out of his office.

When Maimon got home that evening, Elize was waiting for him. Who is Ari Cole, she wanted to know?

"That is what I am trying to find out," Maimon answered. "Why are you asking me?"

"Because of this telegram from Charles Back."

"Which says …?"

"YOU HAVE A PROBLEM TWO DAUGHTERS AND ONLY ONE ARI COLE."

Over their sundowner drinks, Maimon brought Elize up to date with his day's interaction with young Ari Cole, and requested that a place should be laid for him at the Shabbat table the following evening. Also, that neither Jenna nor Alison should be told of this invitation. This was not unusual, because the Shabbat dinner that they hosted every Friday night invariably included what the girls termed a number of "waifs and strays." One or two of these waifs and strays usually had an eye on Jenna and/or Alison.

In fact, Alison was "spoken for" the following night, so to speak, because Maimon had invited Judge Kotze to join them. The Judge, who, as Chief Justice of the Transvaal Republic during the Kruger dispute, held that the courts had the right to test against the constitution, and to declare invalid resolutions and acts passed by the legislatures. Alison was looking forward to discussing this ruling with the learned judge.

Ari Cole arrived on the dot of seven, in his hand a giant bunch of flowers for Elize. Some guests were already on the terrace drinking, and Ari joined them, chatting about this and that and not discriminating on age, gender, or religion. After a few minutes he was pulled away by Joshua and Sarah to show him their steeds. It was customary for Maimon to sit at one end of the long Georgian five-pedestal mahogany table, and for Elize to take the other end. The women tended to congregate towards Elize, and the men to Maimon, with the youngsters more or less in the middle. It was therefore not surprising that Ari and Jenna found themselves seated next to one another. What was surprising, though, was that they spent the whole evening talking only to one another. During the desert course and just before "Birkot Ha Mazon"[131] was sung, Morrie called out, "Hey, Ari, because you hogged my sister the whole evening, you had better come round tomorrow afternoon and play tennis with Max and me – and Jenna, of course. That is, if you play tennis. Do you?"

"I play a little," Ari replied modestly.

"Well, then, tomorrow will be your lucky day. Max and I don't charge for lessons on the Sabbath. Are you sure you will be there?"

Ari looked at Jenna, who nodded her approval.

"Look at that," Morrie called out, laughing. "After only two hours he is already asking Jenna if he can go to the toilet."

They all laughed, and then Jenna asked why he had looked at her for the OK, to which Ari replied, "Because you are more important to me than your brother."

Jenna laughed, blushed a little, and changed the subject. When the guests departed, and those living at See Da View went up to bed, Jenna and Ari moved to the little ante-room next to the front door, and there they talked, sometimes quietly, other times animatedly, till two a.m., when Jenna suggested that Ari should get some sleep, as he had a big tennis game the following afternoon. Ari thanked Jenna for her hospitality, and Jenna told Ari to drive carefully.

At exactly 2:30 the following afternoon, Ari returned to See Da View. Togged out in whites, with a bottle of Oros in one hand, and a state-of-the-art wooden tennis racket in the other. Max and Morrie were knocking up on the tennis court, and Jenna was sitting on a bench near it. As soon as she heard Ari's car, she jumped up and ran to the tree under which Ari had just parked. Instead of walking towards Jenna, Ari stood still, staring at this woman who looked like she had just walked off a film set.

"Is everything alright?" Jenna asked anxiously, fearing that she had some spinach in her teeth, or had spilt some fruit juice on her extremely short, pleated tennis dress.

"Yes. Fine," Ari said, smiling.

Jenna didn't want to ask why he was staring at her, but she did want to know. Somehow Ari sensed this.

"You look like a Hollywood star who has just come off a film set or is going onto one," he told her.

Jenna blushed. "Do you always say things like that to girls?"

"Only when they are true. If someone deserves a compliment, surely it is better to tell them. It makes them feel good, and that makes me feel good. Let's get this tennis lesson over with," Ari said, jogging down to the court.

What a man, Jenna thought, running behind Ari, who seemed to move with the grace of a ballet dancer. Ari and Jenna won the first set 6-3, the second 6-2, and the third 6-1. A few games into the first set, the three Sokolovskis realized that Ari, on his own, could easily beat Max and Morrie together, and when they changed for the second set, Morrie apologized for being such an asshole. Ari smiled and said that was OK.

After the third set Maimon, who had been watching unobserved from his study, came down to the court and told Ari to come to his office at nine am on Monday morning. Then, just as he was leaving, he turned to his children, and asked them to have a drink with him and Elize on their veranda at six. The children looked at each other. This had never happened before. Ari, ignoring the sudden silence, slipped his tennis racquet into its double-square wooden frame and tightened the four screws to prevent it warping, stood up, said goodbye to the boys, and walked back to his car with Jenna in close attendance.

He told her how much he had enjoyed being her partner on the tennis court, at which Jenna blushed. Ari added that if she didn't have a commitment for lunch on Monday, they could get together for a quick bite. Jenna said that unfortunately she had a lecture over lunch time, but she was free for dinner. They agreed Ari would pick her up at seven. Jenna watched his car disappear down the drive, and then skipped back to her brothers.

"Where did you find him?" Max asked in a matter-of-fact way but wanting to know.

"At the dining room table last night," Jenna answered airily.

"The south wind just blew him in, I guess," Morrie said, realizing that he wasn't going to get any more information out of his sister.

As it was almost six, they closed the tennis court gate and ambled up to Maimon's veranda, where, to their surprise, their mother and Alison were waiting.

"Don't look at me," Elize said. "I know no more that you do."

A minute later Maimon emerged, offered everyone a drink, which all declined, and then took the unoccupied chair in the circle.

"You know of course" he began. "about the terrible inflation gripping Germany. There were pictures in the *Cape Times* this morning of a man with a wheelbarrow filled with banknotes that he needed to buy a loaf of bread."

To the best of their knowledge, the family had no assets in Germany, so they had no idea where this conversation was going.

"German hand tools are the best in the world," Maimon continued, "and with their currency in freefall, we should be able to buy many thousands of saws, chisels, knives, and other precision tools at knock-down prices. These we will ship to America, and hopefully sell at a considerable profit."

God bless the old man, Max thought, he doesn't miss a trick. But why the big meeting to tell us this?

"I would like the four of you to accompany you mother and me on this trip that will take in a few European countries as well as the United States, the Far East and Palestine," Maimon said. "I expect it will take about a year."

If that wasn't enough of a shock, there was more to come.

"On Monday morning I am going to ask Ari Cole to join us as a salaried employee of the Sokolovski Group."

And then the thunderclap.

"Ari will be joining us on the trip, not to give him the opportunity of developing any romantic thoughts he may have about Jenna, but for me to judge whether you two boys are capable of working with him, and vice versa."

Maimon waited a minute or two for this to sink in, and then continued.

"This is not a compulsory trip – any one of you can opt out of any part of it. Alison and I have been chatting about whether she should further her studies at Oxford or Cambridge universities, or at Harvard Law School. She might decide to attend one of these, which could preclude her joining us in Hong Kong, for example. We both agreed that Hong Kong will still be there in ten and twenty years' time.

"We leave by train for Cape Town, via Brandfort, tomorrow a week, which should give you enough time to buy a suitcase and some clothes for the trip. Any questions?"

As Maimon expected, Elize and the children needed time to digest what they had just heard, and to come to terms with its implications. It was Max who marshalled his thoughts first.

"I am sure I speak for all of us, Dad, when I say we are speechlessly grateful for this unbelievable opportunity." Max's siblings all nodded. "And I am sure that I will have many, many questions, but right now I only have one. Why?"

Maimon smiled and said, "All will be revealed."

"That's it?" Max asked.

"That's it," his father confirmed. "Now I need to discuss this with your mother, who knew as much about it ten minutes ago as you did."

Saying which, Maimon got to his feet, took Elize by the hand and led her to their suite. As soon as he closed the door she said, "Maimon! What is going on?"

"The sun is rising in the east and setting in the west," he replied calmly, which only stoked the fire more.

"Don't start that with me now! Tell me!"

"As we Jews, you and me, often answer a question with a question, here is my reply: would you like to go back to London? Would you like to visit New York and Hong Kong?"

Elize's mounting anger evaporated, and smiling she said, "Maimon Sokolovski, why didn't you tell me before?"

"For the same reason I didn't tell you I was going to ask your father's permission to marry you."

Elize's mind flashed back to that evening at the farm. In answer to her question then, Maimon had told her that she would have told him to wait for the right time, and he had replied that "The right time," whenever that was, might never come.

"So, this is the right time?" Elize asked, knowing, of course, that her husband would say it was.

"I forget his name, your boyfriend on the farm next door who won the Jukskei competition. He got the cup, and I got the girl."

Elize walked over to this man she had loved all her life, or all the important years of her life, and with tears in her eyes, kissed him, and said, "He wanted to be my boyfriend, but he wasn't."

"Whatever," Maimon told her.

A week proved more than adequate for the children and their parents to wrap up whatever needed to be finalised before their departure.

As the Sokolovski Group's office clock chimed nine on Monday morning, Maimon heard a knock on his door, and without looking up, called out, "Come in." Ari Cole strode in, and before he reached the chair opposite Maimon's desk he heard, "Sit down." Ari did as he was told, as Maimon continued to peruse one of Baedeker's atlases. After what was an uncomfortable minute for Ari, Maimon looked up.

"Good morning, Ari."

"Good morning, sir," Ari shot back.

"I am prepared to take you on as my Personal Assistant, with immediate effect, at £10,000 per annum, for a trial period of one year, with all travel costs for my account."

"Travel costs, sir?" Ari asked.

"Yes, on Sunday we leave for about a year."

The blood drained from Ari's face at the prospect of being away from Jenna for a year, or refusing Mr. Sokolovski's job in order to be with her. Ari was left in a quandary. "A year."

"Do you have a hearing problem, young man?" Maimon asked, his face back in the atlas.

"No, sir," Ari's voice replied, his head being somewhere else.

"Good," Maimon said. "Come back tomorrow morning at nine and tell me if you want the job. If you do, I would like to meet your parents when we get to Cape Town at the end of the month."

"Thank you, sir," Ari said, his mind in turmoil. "I will be back tomorrow morning." With which he got up and walked slowly out of his possible future boss's office.

Over the weekend, Maimon had conducted some research. There were rumors, even heard as far afield as Johannesburg, that the senior Cole was a gambler of note, but Maimon decided that one could not hold the sins of the father against the son. Besides, Ari Cole's own reputation was stellar.

Ari spent the whole day thinking: what did he want, and what did he want more? If he refused the job, he might develop a deep, meaningful relationship with Jenna. Or he might not, in which case he would lose both the girl and the job. And if he took the job, and Jenna fell in love with someone else, how would he feel then? Probably seeing her every week, with her husband working in the company, he couldn't take that. Round and round he went until at about five o'clock he reached the conclusion he should have come to eight hours earlier. He would ask Jenna what she thought he should do. At seven o'clock, with his heart in his boots, Ari drove his convertible slowly up the long Sokolovski garden drive.

To his surprise Jenna was waiting for him in the car park, and to his great surprise, she didn't open the door of his motor car but jumped over it; and to his greatest surprise, she took his face in her hands and kissed him, on the lips!

"Isn't it wonderful!" she said, laughing, with tears in her eyes.

Ari's mind raced, trying to make sense of Mr Sokolovski's job offer, his insoluble dilemma, and now Jenna's reaction. There was obviously a big piece of this puzzle that he was missing, but what was it?"

"You don't know, do you?" Jenna realized. "I am coming on the trip, too!"

They went out for supper to an Italian restaurant, and held hands first walking from the car to the restaurant, and then on the table, and afterwards walking back to Ari's car. Like two overgrown adolescents, which is what they really were, they spoke about London, which they could explore together, about exciting New York – there is a new dance called the Charleston, Jenna told him – about the mysterious East, and about Palestine. Back at See Da View, sitting in the car under a giant magnolia tree, Ari told Jenna that her father wanted to meet his parents when they passed through Cape Town. It was getting late, so Ari walked Jenna to the big house's front door, kissed her gently, said goodnight, and made his way back to the car. Jenna watched him go, then quietly opened the door, and slipped inside.

Next morning Ari was in Maimon's office at nine, the news of his acceptance having reached the patriarch's ears from unofficial sources.

"You need to understand a few things," Maimon started, and Ari took out a notebook. "Put that away," Maimon told him. "If you can't remember them, you are no good to me. I demand, I repeat, demand loyalty and honesty. I expect hard work, intelligent thoughts, a positive approach, teamwork with your colleagues, and if you get knocked down, then you are to spring back like in a Punch-and-Judy show. One last thing, the Good Lord gave you two ears and one mouth for a good reason, so that you listen twice as much as you talk. No one ever learned anything while talking."

"Thank you, sir," Ari said. "Would you like me to repeat that back to you?"

Maimon had learned that the older one gets, the fewer surprises there were lying in wait, and for this reason, when one came along it was all the more enjoyable. So Maimon said yes, he would like Ari to repeat his words back to him, and Ari did so, word-for-word correctly.

Maimon had worked out in his mind what information he wanted relayed to him while away, which he dictated slowly over the next twenty-five minutes to Saul and Kris. Confirming they understood exactly what was required, Maimon told them that he would be happy for each of them to take four weeks holiday while he was traveling, on the condition that when one of them was away, the other was in the office. Finally, he advised that he was raising their salaries to £40,000 a year, a considerable amount of money for Johannesburg employees at that time.

At See Da View Elize and Kaylah spent the best part of a day going over what needed to be done to keep the house, the gardens, and the staff running smoothly. Kaylah's bank account would be increased when necessary on an impress basis.

Elize and Jenna each bought a cabin trunk and filled them with new clothes in a day and a bit. The boys, Alison, and Maimon bought little; they did so because, on the one hand, they had sufficient to start with, and on the other, Maimon pointed out that wherever their travels took them, people would be happy selling them whatever clothes they needed.

Later that night, when Maimon was lying on his bed and thinking about the fun he was going to have with his children in London, and Elize was pottering about, there was a soft knock on the door. Elize and Maimon looked at each other, and Elize said, "Come in."

Through the door walked Magda, looking stronger than she had been in court, but more of a little old lady than Elize remembered. Over the years she had lost an inch or two in height, become stooped, and, understandably, lost her confidence. At See Da View she had fussed over her grandchildren, but as they got older, they needed less fussing, and wanted less fussing, and while they still showed Ouma respect, their lives had drifted more and more apart.

It was therefore no surprise to either Elize or Maimon when she asked them if it would be alright if she moved back to the farm. And if it was, she inquired, could she please go down with them on Sunday? Elize realized at once where this request had come from and smiled affirmatively. Maimon agreed in a heartbeat, happy that he would finally be seeing the last of the woman who murdered his son. Legally she hadn't murdered Adam, he knew that, but her actions enabled someone else to. Good riddance to her, yes good riddance. Magda said thank you and kissed both of them goodnight, before withdrawing as quietly as she had entered.

"You know what that is all about?" Elize asked Maimon.

He knew it wasn't only about a lift down, but the inner workings of a woman's mind still mystified Maimon after all these years, so he nodded gravely.

"It will be the first time that my mother and I will have been back to the farm since the British came and burnt our house down."

"And poisoned the well and burnt the fields," Maimon added.

"You and I will have each other, and the memories of our loving youth together," Elize began. "My mother's memories are of her husband and son being shot, the farm that they worked their whole lives to build up being destroyed, and then being carted off to the concentration camp in a kaffir wagon."

"The farm has been rebuilt, Koos has done an outstanding job, and I am sure he and Elna will make Magda very happy," Maimon said.

"Of course they will," she agreed, "but it is the memories which are important."

Here Maimon began losing Elize again, so he mumbled, "Yes, the memories," and went back to thinking about what he was going to do with the children in London. But another question from Elize snapped him back to reality.

"How long have you been thinking about this trip?"

"A couple of months," Maimon said vaguely, having a reasonable idea what was coming next.

"But you sprung it on us with just a week's notice?"

"There is old Russian saying," Count Sokolovski began. "Man with net waiting for fish. Many small fish swim in river, but man do nothing. Then big fish come. If man want big fish, man must make big effort."

Elize giggled and Maimon went back to thinking about London.

Except for the dogs, on Sunday no one was sad to see the Sokolovskis leave. The departing family were understandably excited. Meanwhile, Saul, Kaylah, and Francine were happy that they and their children now had the run of See Da View's house and garden, without feeling that they were tramping on Maimon's toes. In fact, with his recent raise, Saul had started looking at empty stands on which he could build a house for his own family.

CHAPTER 50

BACK AT THE FARM

The overnight train ride to Brandfort was what Morrie called "the slow train to nowhere," but eventually the big locomotive pulled into Brandfort's almost deserted station. Koos and Elna were there to meet them, along with three motor vehicles that Maimon had arranged. During the ride to the farm, Maimon sat next to the driver, and behind him Elize and her mother held hands. Both knew it would be traumatic, but neither knew to what degree.

In fact, it was hardly traumatic at all, because the farm Magda found was not the one she had left behind. As Maimon knew, Koos and the builder had done a magnificent job. The main house was rebuilt, slightly enlarged, but with the same rooms and similar furniture. Elize led her mother into the voorkamer, and sat down with Koos and Elna. Coffee and rusks were brought out, and when it became apparent that Magda would rather be alone with her brother-in-law and his wife, Elize quietly withdrew. Outside she saw Maimon sitting on the big rope-swing under the wild fig tree, about twenty feet from where he had asked for her hand in marriage.

Memories of that evening, when Maimon made his speech asking her father for permission to marry her, came flooding back. She could still hear him say, "We were both brought up under different religions, but Elize and I believe in the same God, and it is this God who is witness to my promise to look after her in sickness and in health, in good times and bad times, when we are young and strong, in middle age, and when we are old and frail."

How blessed she was, with Maimon and Morrie and Max and Jenna and Alison, all in good health, and on top of that, with enough money.

No rinderpest worries, and whether it rained or not, there were always enough monkey nuts to make peanut butter in Maimon's factories, and kaffir corn for him to make samp for the natives. As if pulled by the farmers' tug-of-war team, a force she could not resist even if she wanted to, which of course she didn't, Elize moved effortlessly to the man God had given her.

Seeing her walking towards him, Maimon paced out the few yards, went down on one knee, and waited for Elize's hand. Graciously, she gave it to Maimon, who kissed it and then stood up, and out of his pocket pulled a curtain ring, which he carefully put on Elize's finger. What neither of them saw was Jenna watching from the large guest house, tears running down her face.

Koos had shot a kudu, and for the last number of hours two natives had taken it in turns to constantly turn it on a spit alongside a leadwood fire. For those who didn't fancy braaied kudu, there was waterblommetjie stew and a Malay curry with saffron rice, whose recipe Elna had cut out of a magazine. There were also two deserts: Elna had baked both a large Malva pudding and a melktert that was served in slices. To drink, Koos served home-made ginger beer, Lion Lager, and kaffir beer. Although Magda abstained from alcohol, her mood was in no way dampened. On the contrary, Elize had never seen her mother so happy.

Away from the rotating kudu, the natives had built another, much bigger fire, also from leadwood, which burned slowly and gave off tremendous heat, around which chairs had been placed in a circle. With Lion Lager on tap, the stories flowed, the most unbelievable being that of Harry Wolhuter, whose shoulder was held in the jaws of a big male lion while he was dragged away. With his free hand Harry stabbed upwards into the lion's heart, killing it.

After each story, they sang a song. "Sarie Marais" was, of course, the favorite, followed by "Vat jou goed en trek Ferreira," "Daar kom die Alibama," "Januarie, Februarie, Maart…," "Suikerbossie," "Aai, Aai, die Witboskraai," and "Jan Pierewiet." Elize looked across at her mother, who, knowing all the songs, sung them as lustily as her aged lungs would allow, while clapping her hands in time with the tunes. Elize realized she had never, ever, seen her mother as happy as she was that evening.

As the fire slowly burned itself out, so one by one the guests made their way to bed. At Maimon's suggestion, Koos had designed the guest house so that it had two large bedrooms: one for the boys and the other for the girls, and as much as Maimon wanted to sleep with Elize, he retreated to the boy's dormitory, leaving the three generations of women to themselves in the big room. The next morning, while the three boys were swimming kaalgat in the river, Elize told Maimon that she and her mother had spoken till about two o clock about the old times, at the end of which Magda had said, "You can go to America. I am alright now."

At eleven o'clock the following morning, Koos organized a brief service for his brother and Willem. Their graves had been cleaned up since Johannes showed them to Maimon; each now had a tombstone with the name of the deceased and their birth and death dates. Under those figures was written "In Aksie Vermoor,"[132] which Maimon thought accurate and honest. Koos spoke of the blood that had been spilt so unnecessarily in the two Boer Wars, and of the hope that never again would shots be fired in anger within the boundaries of the Union of South Africa. Then they all recited Psalm 23: "The lord is my shepherd..." Finally, each of them put a small stone on Piet's and Willem's graves, next to the much larger ones Maimon had placed on them all those years ago.

According to the SAR&H timetable pasted on the wall of the railway station, the Cape Town train stopped briefly at Brandfort at three minutes past one, and Koos made sure his guests and their bags were on the platform at 12:45. The only sadness, felt by both the hosts and their guests, was that it would be too long before the Sokolovskis returned to Brandfort and the farm.

Settled on the train, each of them reflected on their time at the farm: Elize on her childhood, and her time there with Maimon; Maimon on the heavy work he had done with Piet, driving sheep and cattle, mending fences, and general maintenance around the farm; and their four children on the fact that what they had just witnessed was part of their heritage.

Ari viewed it all from a completely different perspective. Born and brought up in Cape Town, while he knew some of the songs from concerts he had attended, Afrikaans culture was totally foreign to him. He thought hardship and persecution only happened to Jews, and for the first time in his life, Ari realized that his people did not have a monopoly on tribulation and tragedy. The Brandfort visit had left a deep impression on him. It was Jenna who asked the question that was on all their minds.

"Dad, when we go to Europe, can we also go to Saratov?"

Like a steel animal trap snapping shut, Maimon shot back, "Absolutely not."

"Because?" Max asked quietly.

"Because it is not safe. You read about Kishinev. It could have been Saratov or any of the hundreds of towns in between."

"Kishinev is in Bessarabia," Alison pointed out helpfully.

"And Bessarabia is in Russia. If any of you want to talk to me about converting to Catholicism, I will listen to you. But visiting Saratov, never."

"What about Uncle Zelig and his family?" Morrie asked.

"I have pleaded with him to leave," Maimon said. "I send him money every month. I even sent him railway and steamship tickets, and what did he do? He returned them. Why? Because his dumb, insular, inward-looking rabbi said he and his family should stay in that pogrom-infested country."

"Isn't that a bit tough on the rabbi?" Max asked, feeling uncomfortable hearing a religious authority spoken about in this manner.

"Tough?" Maimon told his son. "It is complimentary."

Never had the children heard such pain in their father's voice, and realizing that there was no way they were going to get him to change his mind, reluctantly they dropped the subject.

Through the mielie fields of the Orange Free State and on to the Karoo the train rushed, coating the trackside in black soot, and scaring away what few wild animals remained after 100 years of indiscriminate hunting by whites. Before that, more natives lived healthily, off less game that they tracked and speared. The train stopped for thirty minutes at De Aar to rewater and replenish its coal tender, as well as for a crew change.

Walking up and down the platform to stretch their legs, the children realized they could be in another country. Not only was the scenery different from anything they had ever seen, but so were the people: not black and not white, small of stature, many with broad, almost eastern, faces. They didn't speak English, Dutch, or Afrikaans, but chattered together in a tongue that sounded to the unknowing like high-pitched squeaks and clicks. Alison said they were mainly Hottentots with some Bushmen inbreeding, or maybe the other way round. The Station Master waved a green flag, the locomotive's whistle pierced the quiet Karoo evening, the train started moving slowly, and the children made sure it didn't leave without them.

Next morning found them in the Hex River Valley, with towering mountains on either side and deciduous fruit trees crowding every square inch of land. Peaches, nectarines, apricots, and, later on, vineyards that stretched as far as the eye could see. Compared to the Transvaal and Orange Free State this was a land of plenty, a cornucopia of everything man could want. They stopped at Paarl, under the giant black pearl-looking rock that gave the town nestling below it its name. Suddenly they were between the mountains, the Hex River range behind them, and Table Mountain and Devil's Peak beckoning them to the Cape of Good Hope.

Even though Ari had specifically asked his parents not to come to the station to meet him and the Sokolovskis, they specifically did so. Ari's mother, a little overweight, was bouncy and all smiles; his father far more serious. Maimon commented on the rose in the buttonhole of Ari's father's suit, which brought forth a smile and an explanation from the older Cole.

"I have to meet visitors from overseas in Cape Town harbour from time to time, and to enable them to identify me easily, I telegraph ahead advising them to look for a man wearing a buttonholed rose in his suit jacket. Ari's father said." About a year ago, one of my onboard visitors asked if I, or one of my assistants, had sent the cable, and when I asked why, he showed me the message he had received: WELCOME TO CAPE TOWN STOP FOR EASY IDENTIFICATION LOOK FOR A MAN WITH A FLOWER IN HIS BOTTOM HOLE STOP REGARDS COLE."

The Mount Nelson Hotel, which held such fond memories for Elize, had sent three vehicles, into which the family piled, for the short ride up Adderley and Queen Victoria Streets, and then under the gracious Palladian columns to the hotel's reception area.

For the children this was a whole new world.

CHAPTER 51

KOM WEER TERUG

Not because they wished to hide it, but due to pressure of time, neither Maimon nor Elize had told their children about the wine farm they had bought. This they did a few minutes later in their suite.

"Any other surprises?" Morrie asked.

"Nothing that comes to mind," their father replied calmly, knowing full well that he would have to tell them about his London financial dealings. But there was time for that.

Maimon had arranged that they would go out to Franschoek the following morning, spend the rest of the day at the farm, sleep there, and return to Cape Town the morning after. Remembering his debt to Francois du Plessis, Maimon asked the hotel to buy him a case of French cognac, and when Maimon saw the bill, he understood why Francois had said a bottle would suffice.

Farms, in the children's eyes, were big, dry (often festooned with flies), had cows, sheep, and sometimes goats wandering around, and were generally not at all attractive. The Franschoek farm that Maimon had smothered with money was, of course, completely different. Everything was green, a small river flowed through the property twelve months a year, and the farmhouse was 200 years old. Built by the Huguenots, the walls were over three-feet thick and the floorboards, cut from yellowwood trees, about half as wide. The children fell in love with it at first sight.

Over lunch of babotie, saffron rice, sjambals, papadoms, and chutney, the children agreed that the Western Cape was not South Africa, or the other way round. Because neither Maimon nor Elize were wine drinkers, the children had not been introduced to wines in Johannesburg, and the chilled *rosé* made on the farm next door complemented the slightly spiced mince-meat dish so well that Morrie suggested the family should give serious consideration to relocating to Franschoek.

The early summer heat, copious helpings of babotie and malva pudding, plus the wine to which they were unaccustomed, resulted in four young people falling fast asleep on the lush green grass under one of the giant oak trees. That evening the staff had prepared a light supper of Cape pickled fish and salad, followed by cheese and biscuits. The cheese was made on another Franschoek farm, and the biscuits by the staff of "Kom Weer Terug,"[133] which is what the children had decided their Cape wine farm had to be called.

The conversation ranged from the philosophical to the whimsical, with Maimon and Elize taking a backseat and just listening to their children's diverse opinions and rhetorical styles, which brought Elize to thinking how different children from the same parents could be.

Alison was brilliant, which everyone knew. Only sixteen she had just completed, summa cum laude, her first university degree. Elize worried that, being a bluestocking, Alison's social life, already restricted, would disintegrate to nothing, because emotionally she was so different from the older people with whom she mixed. With an enquiring mind, and not afraid to try new things, Alison was fiercely ambitious, something that was not evident from her quiet demeanour. With a most disarming smile, Morrie had once remarked, "What Alison wants, Alison gets."

Jenna was sensitive, both personally and towards others. Somehow the underdog always found his or her way to Jenna. She was always asking Maimon for money for this or that person who had fallen on hard times. Blacks and whites, it made no difference to Jenna, and she even "adopted" a Chinese man who had lost his wife. For seven weeks Jenna's studies suffered, because her heart and her time were invested in finding Mrs Chen. Eventually she did, in Walvis Bay, over 1,000 miles away from Johannesburg – the lady having got on the wrong train at Park Station.

Max was serious and solid. He had Maimon's mathematical ability without his personality. On a one-to-one basis he was good, and even with four-to-six people, but large crowds put him off. He didn't talk often, but when he did everyone listened. Of her four children, Elize was most worried about Max. Sensitive and easily hurt, he had been

---

133   *Come back again*

sheltered under Morrie's wing all his life. That would end when one, or both of them, married. She prayed that he would find a woman who would stand by him through thick and thin.

Morrie, the life and soul of every party, had Maimon's personality. Fearless, he would argue with the devil himself if necessary. Plugged into all of his siblings, he somehow always knew where they were and what they were doing, and if he thought they needed him, he popped up totally unexpectedly. Last year he barged into one of Alison's exams, having somehow got into his head that she had forgotten to take a bottle of ink into which she needed to dip her pen. On another occasion he verbally accosted one of Jenna's lecturers because he gave his sister a bad mark, accusing him of being an anti-Semite. When he was told that the marker was Jewish, he said to his face, "Just as I thought. A self-hating Jew."

Not having slept under the big oak tree, or anywhere else, that afternoon, Maimon and Elize excused themselves around midnight, leaving their children discussing whether Jannie Smuts' beard was real or not.

CHAPTER 52

ON THE HIGH SEAS

The family left the farm early the next morning, as they needed to board the boat by three pm, ahead of its scheduled departure an hour later. Maimon had arranged that the hotel despatch their cabin trunks and other cases to the ship in the morning, and to all their surprise, the ship's crew had correctly delivered the right suitcases to their suites. Morrie found Alison leaning on the ship's mahogany wooden rail, looking up at Table Mountain, which seemed to have been there for ever, and probably had.

"What's troubling you, kid?" he asked his little (by thirty months) sister. Morrie had the uncanny knack of knowing if there was something bothering his siblings, even when their body language and vocal comments gave no hint of this.

"I am seventeen years old, strong and healthy, and my hormones are screaming out for opposite-sex interaction, and all the men I meet are thirty or older and only interested in my mind."

Just then a young officer, who looked about twenty, clad in immaculate white shorts, shirt, socks, and naval hat walked past them.

"Officer!" Morrie called out after the rapidly disappearing young fellow, who spun around and in a couple of seconds was at their sides.

"Afternoon, sir, afternoon madam," he said to Morrie and Alison, touching the peak of his hat in respect. "Is there anything I can do for you?"

Morrie explained that their family were a party of seven in the 1st-class section, and that he would really appreciate it if the captain could get someone else to steer the boat that night so this young man – who had introduced himself as Michael Christopher Colhoun – could join them for dinner.

"I am sure that won't be a problem," the young officer replied.

"What time should I meet your party, sir?"

"In that case we should tell you our names. I am Morrie Sokolovski, and this is my stepdaughter, Alison. We will be dining at eight."

"Till then, sir" Michael said, touching the peak of his hat again. And then to Alison, "I very much look forward to spending time with you, miss."

The officer was but three paces away before Morrie called him back again. "Michael, tell me something. Do you play cricket?" Morrie asked curiously.

The young officer's eyes lit up. "Actually, I do, sir. Opening bat. Scored 117 last weekend."

"Against the Blind School?" Morrie asked.

"You are right, sir. It was not appropriate for me to tell you my score without first being asked. I do apologize."

"Think nothing of it," Morrie said, as someone from the older generation might have stated, whereas both men were both about the same age.

"Thank you, sir. I do appreciate that." Then, touching his hat to both Morrie and Alison, he walked away for the third time.

"Thank you, Father," Alison said, still gazing at Table Mountain.

"Think nothing of it, my child" Morrie said, watching two tugs deftly manoeuvring their ship, the *Dunnottar Castle*, out of the harbour and into the Table Bay roadstead.

They both giggled.

"How did you know he was a cricketer?" Alison asked.

"Easy peesy," Morrie told his sister. "His initials gave it away."

MCC. That didn't sound very cricketing, Alison thought. Anyway, as her father had said a few days earlier, "All will be revealed," and hopefully it would.

A note under the doors of each of the 1st-class cabins reminded their occupants that it was customary to dress for dinner. The Sokolovski men all wore dinner jackets – white tuxedos were only sported when the ship was within the tropics – and Elize a beautifully cut full-length black silk dress that did justice to her well-maintained figure. Jenna sported a striking bright red dress, a bit more décolleté than Maimon would have liked, and Alison had on a black dress, which from the waist downwards was made from a non-see-through fabric, but the upper part constructed from intricate Bruges lace. A skimpy black brassiere covered what needed to be.

Michael Christopher turned out to be extremely good company. Frightfully English, he said all the right things at the right time, and none of the wrong things at any time. Elize sat him between Jenna and Alison, and it quickly became apparent that he only had eyes for Alison. This was fine with Ari.

Dressing for dinner, Alison had decided that her academic achievements should not be mentioned for the length of the cruise, which she told, not asked, her parents and siblings. She was simply a seventeen-year-old girl, in Standard 9A, interested in lacrosse, swimming, netball, and hockey, who was going on a trip with her family.

After dinner, when the men repaired to the smoking room for brandy and cigars, Alison suggested that she and Michael look out to see if there were any flying fish. Alison had no idea if one could see flying fish at night, or at all, but after a minute of looking at the moon's reflection in the sea, she asked Michael to kiss her.

"I am not terribly good at kissing," he told her, somewhat embarrassed.

Not counting her father and brothers, Alison had never kissed a boy in her life, but she had read a lot about it and the fact that French kissing was the most sensuous of all kissing, so that she reached up and did what the book she was reading had described.

When she was done and withdrew, Michael said, "Golly! That was capital."

So Alison did so again, and this time Michael kissed her back. For a minute or so they held hands, and then Alison told him, "I have to go now," which was totally untrue, but in the novels she read she had noticed that the heroine always left her partner wanting more after their first kiss; and while Alison would have been very happy staying out all night kissing Michael, she accepted that the authors knew more about flirting than she did.

Alison kissed him on the cheek, said goodnight, and disappeared into the bright interior of the ship where, she saw Jenna and the three boys sitting together sipping drinks.

"Come and join us," Morrie called out.

"You look like the cat who has swallowed a mouse," Max observed.

"More like the whole mouse family," Ari added, noting Alison smiling and looking away blushing. He had never seen her look so radiantly contented.

Jenna looked at her sister, trying to work out what was going on. Morrie said nothing.

"It is a bit like a movie," Jenna said, looking at their attractive and beautifully attired party. "What can we do tomorrow to follow this up?"

For the first time since Alison returned from kissing Michael, Morrie looked at her, the very smallest of smiles crossing his face.

"I am going to teach your mother to play bridge," Maimon announced.

"And I am going to teach Ari how to speak Sanskrit," Jenna announced, everyone except Ari knowing that she couldn't speak a word of it. A short while later the party broke up: the girls going to their suite, which had a large twin-bed sleeping room, as well as a sitting room and two bathrooms. The boys had a mirror image on the other side of the ship, but with one bed added, and their parents the Owner's Suite in between. On Maimon's pillow was an envelope, with a big "8" written on it, which he handed back to Elize, who began reading.

Dearest Maimon – who doesn't make the sun rise in the east and set in the west.

One minute you were a farm hand, and I was a plaas meisie,[134] and the next we were sitting as a family, you and I and our four grown-up handsome and beautiful and clever children, in a first-class dining room on a ship sailing to London. God has certainly blessed us.

You and I deserve some credit for the way they turned out. As we know getting them to where they are wasn't all plain-sailing.

There is something I am worried about, in fact very worried about. Traveling with you is what it must be like if one was royalty. We have the best of everything and that is wonderful. Our children have known no other way. You said we are going to be traveling for a year, and so it is for another 364 days that we are going to be pampered.

What will happen when our children stumble and fall? Please God those still standing will help them up, but what happens if they all fall together? They never worked

---

134   *Farm girl*

as farmhands or lived in a concentration camp. We have given them everything and made life so easy for them, and if they can't or don't get up when they fall, that will be our fault.

We gave them what we did because we wanted the best for them, but was it wise of us? I don't know.

You once called me "worry pots" and you are right. I worry about our children, which I suppose all mothers do.

If you have an answer to my problem, please tell me what it is.

Your worried and loving,
Elize

They all overslept, which Alison explained was probably due to the increased ozone at sea level, and Morrie said was due to the brandy they had drunk the night before, and Max pointed out was likely to be a combination of them both. More or less at the same time, the family arrived at the Sokolovski family table, where the conversation ranged between shuffle board challenges and which, if any, film stars were on board. After breakfast Elize's bridge lesson was to start in the card room; Alison moved to a deck chair to continue reading her book on Bentham, the father of jurisprudence, which, at Morrie's suggestion she had covered in brown paper; Ari and Jenna said they were going to chat; and Morrie and Max played chess. The morning sped by, and as agreed they met for lunch at one.

Sea voyages have a habit, especially if there are no intermediate port calls, of slipping one day almost unnoticed into another. The ship develops its own routine, as do the passengers. To Maimon's surprise, Elize became quite a good bridge player. She learned all the rules and so got her head around the bidding – playing out the tricks was more challenging, but most of the time she made her contracts. Maimon was eons ahead of Elize in the science of the game, but they enjoyed playing together, and neither of them got upset or angry if things didn't work out as they should have. Mostly they played in the morning with an older couple, had lunch with the children, and napped in the afternoon.

Before dinner they had a drink together in their suite, when they chatted about this and that and nothing in particular. They just loved being in each other's company, and sometimes just sat holding hands, looking out of their suite's porthole. After dinner they spent an hour with the children before heading to bed. Elize knew that once they got to Europe Maimon would be extremely busy, and so she was keen that he get as much rest on the boat as he could.

One night after dinner Morrie brought up the subject of the ongoing pogroms in the Ukraine, and the tens of thousands of Jewish orphans who were destitute as a result. Isaac Ochberg, a Cape Town business-man, had collected some money and was in the Ukraine rescuing these poor, destitute, and often starving children. Should we not go and help him? Morrie asked. As was the case when he brought up the subject of going to Saratov, the answer was a non-negotiable "no."

"I gave Ochberg some money, I suspect more than anyone else, for food and medicines," Maimon told Elize, his children, and Ari. "He specifically wanted to go on his own. I think the man is crazy."

"Why crazy, sir?" Ari asked.

"Because the way he is going about it he will get killed. What he should have done, or maybe still can do, is to hire about 100 White Rus-sian officers and soldiers. One hundred men will find a lot more orphans than one man. Perhaps Ochberg is on an ego trip? Or has a death wish. I don't know."

Not put off, Morrie continued, "So, let him do his thing, and we will do ours. From what I read in the Cape Town papers, there are more orphans than rescuers. Speaking Ukrainian, it will be a cakewalk for you. Then we can go on to London and New York and wherever."

Maimon took a deep breath, forcing his mind back to the terrible time he had lived through that he hoped he would never have to revisit, phys-ically or mentally, ever again. He wanted to spare his children what he had experienced, but they were adults now, and if at least Morrie, and possibly others as well, wanted to go to the Ukraine, they needed to know his story. In a few short paragraphs he told them how, if they hadn't fallen into a drunken stupor, a Ukrainian officer and his accompanying soldier would have thrown him as well as an elderly Jewish woman and her hus-band, from the train into a river of ice-blocks and melting snow.

"Look at a map," Maimon continued, "and you will see that France and the Ukraine are more or less the same size; and you think if you can go to one, it is safe to go to the other? There is a chance we will all be killed on this trip, in England or the United States in a train or motor car crash. The chances are probably one in ten million. If you go to any of those Russian countries as a Jew, the chances of being killed are about one in 10,000. Now listen very carefully. If on my watch, and you are on my watch now, any of you children, and that includes Ari, makes a serious effort to visit a Russian country, I will personally sign papers committing them to a madhouse. Not because I think you are mad, but to prevent you getting killed in eastern Europe. I understand once a person is in one of those madhouses, it is extremely difficult to ever get out of them. Have I made myself clear?"

Maimon looked at his children, and Ari, one by one, and did not withdraw his stare from them until every last one had personally agreed to Maimon's wish.

"You have no idea, and I pray, nor will you ever have any idea," Maimon added, "of what it is like to live as a Jew in those countries. It pains me to remember my years in Russia, and if you have any consideration for your father you will never, ever, ever bring up this subject again."

Morrie was the first to rise, to come over to his father to apologize for the hurt he had inadvertently caused. He kissed Maimon goodnight and headed down to his cabin, followed by Max, and then Ari and the girls. In the last twenty minutes, the children had looked, for the first time, through the window into their father's youth, and it was a frightening picture. Decades later, when they were sitting shiva for him,[135] the children clearly remembered this conversation on the boat.

Unlike Cape Town, Southampton is not a very impressive entry point into Great Britain, but what was impressive was the efficient way in which the Customs and Immigration formalities were handled, at least for the 1st-class passengers. Almost before they knew it, six Sokolovskis and a Cole were sitting in a train compartment that made the one they traveled onto Cape Town look like a 3rd-class Mongolian carriage. On arrival at London's Charing Cross Station, representatives from the Savoy Hotel ushered them into two large automobiles – their luggage following in a third vehicle. To the children this was all magic.

Waiting in the lobby of the hotel was Count Sokolovski's old friend, Mr. Hutchinson, who delivered a short speech welcoming the Count and his family and wishing them a pleasant stay.

---

135 *First seven days of mourning in a Jewish house*

"Hutchinson," the Count responded, "thank you for speeching." Then patting the front office manager's ample stomach, Maimon said, "You have been hungry, but eating is good. I see your wife gives many caloriefications." Then lowering his gaze, he added, "Your wife makes you happy?"

The front office manager ignored the question and reminded the count that he was at his family's disposal night and day for the entire duration of their stay.

Up in her parent's suite five minutes later, Jenna said, "Dad, you cannot say things like that. You just can't do it."

"It is not I of whom you speak, but the noble count whose presence in London has coincided with ours," Maimon replied sanctimoniously.

"You are impossible," Jenna answered, stomping out of the room to the slightly smaller suite she and Alison were sharing.

The children, who Maimon called "YPs" – for "young people" – in their company, and simply "children" when alone with Elize, by agreement hit the ground running, having promised to be back by eight o'clock for Friday night prayers. They were.

Maimon and Elize similarly dumped their bags, and, arm-in-arm, set out walking the streets that were like old friends. The Covent Garden flower market was only a few hundred yards up the road from their hotel, and Maimon and Elize spent the best part of an hour admiring and smelling blooms from England and the Continent.

By this time they were hungry, and were directed by one of the florists down Maiden Lane to an old – since 1798 – English restaurant called Rules. Telling the happy couple that they looked like honeymooners, the head waiter led them to the table, where they were advised The Prince of Wales had dined with his mistress, Lily Langtree. The head waiter kindly closed off the table with a heavy red velvet curtain, as the restaurant had done for the future king of England. Maimon and Elize held hands under the table, and then when the curtain was closed, tenderly kissed. At the head waiter's recommendation, they ate Whitstable oysters, Welsh lamb with English vegetables, and apple crumble for dessert.

When Maimon pulled out his wallet to pay the bill, an envelope dropped on the table. Maimon recognized it as the one given to him on arrival by his man Hutchinson. Putting £5 on the plate for their lunch, Maimon handed the envelope to Elize, who opened it, and gasped. Instead of reading it to Maimon, she put it on the table, and covered her face with her hands. When she removed them, Maimon saw the tears he feared. It wasn't bad news from home – that would have been wired; so as far as he was concerned, it couldn't be too serious, and he would wait for Elize to compose herself to hear what it was about.

Drying her tears with the serviette, she told him it was a letter …

CHAPTER 53

SURPRISE SATURDAY

Addressed to Mr. Maimonides Sokolovski care of the Savoy Hotel, the letter invited Mr. Sokolovski and two guests to attend his investiture at Buckingham Palace the following Wednesday at noon, when he would be knighted by Her Majesty, with the title of Knight Commander KCVO for services to Business and Charity. From that moment he would be known as Sir Maimonides Sokolovski, and his wife as Lady Elize Sokolovski.

As Elize continued reading, her tears turned to giggles, which turned to hiccups, which turned to coughing, which brought the head waiter with a glass of water and an enquiry if everything was alright. By way of explanation, Maimon handed him the letter, which he read quickly and said, "May I be the first to extend to you my personal, and this establishment's, hearty congratulations, sir." And then to a waiter, "Thomas, two glasses of champagne right away."

Maimon and Elize giggled down the short incline to their hotel, through the lobby, and then up to their suite. There they burst out laughing.

"Lady Sokolovski," Maimon said, bowing low.

"My lord, Knight Commander, KCVO," Elize replied, curtseying, "I await upon thy command."

"In that case," Maimon replied, "I command thee to be done with thine clothes, and to lie upon thy bed to await thy Lord's pleasure."

"And shalt I be permitted some pleasure as well?" Elize asked demurely.

"If thou art indeed a good woman, the Lord shall ensure that sufficient pleasure is available for thee as well."

Not being able to sustain this, they both fell about laughing.

"Do you mind if I tell the children?" Elize asked, which Maimon said was fine with him.

Eight o'clock bought a few knocks on the door, and five excited YPs tumbled into their parent's sitting room. Maimonides had ordered bread and red wine, and after Friday night prayers, they all went down to the Savoy Grill Room, where the children's free-flowing conversation even eclipsed the wonderful food. A few hours later they made their way up to bed.

Back in their suite Maimon asked, "Why didn't you tell them?" thinking their impending Buckingham Pal ace visit was more important than hearing about the children's escapades.

"I was waiting for the right moment," Elize explained.

The "right moment" indeed, Maimon thought to himself, grateful that he had not waited for it on the previous occasions when an important announcement needed to me made.

Next morning at breakfast they all agreed to go their own ways and to meet up in their parent's suite at four that afternoon. Maimon and Elize went to the Wallace Collection, which contained irreplaceable paintings, sculpture, furniture, porcelain, arms, and armor from the eighteenth and nineteenth centuries.

After a couple of hours, they were hungry and wandered into a pub, where they ordered two ploughman lunches, and warm beer they noticed everyone else was drinking. Having learned a great deal of English history from the exhibits they saw, Maimon and Elize agreed that that was enough culture for one day, and headed back to the hotel and the comfortable chairs of their sumptuous suite.

In drips and drabs the children arrived, all bursting to tell their parents and siblings what they had done in the previous six hours.

Max held his hand in the air, as if a child in school, until one by one the others noticed him, and kept quiet.

"Sit down. All of you. Sit down," Max said in a more serious voice than anyone could remember him using since they left Johannesburg. "I had arranged to meet a friend from Johannesburg in synagogue this morning, and, whether it was his fault or mine, I went to the wrong synagogue. Thinking it would be bad form to leave before the end, and being hungry, I went to the kiddush.[136] There I got chatting to a girl

---

136 *Light refreshments after a synagogue service*

who invited me home for lunch."

Jenna's right hand shot up and Max stopped. "Girl's name, please?"

"Serena Alfombra," Max told her before continuing. "She introduced me to her father, Alberto, who asked if I was related to that wonderful man, Maimon Sokolovski? It turns out that this wonderful man, when still a Russian teenager, bought a British insurance company for two million pounds, stripped out fifteen million pounds of cash, and then sold the residual shell for seven million pounds, thus netting a profit of twenty million pounds before interest and costs. Dad, is that true?" Max asked a room of stunned people in dead silence.

"Yes. That is more or less right," Maimon admitted.

"So, apart from your South African assets, you have £20 million in London?" Max asked.

"No," Maimon told him, "the correct figure is close to £45 million."

"Excuse me?" Max said, now intrigued. "How did £20 million become £45 million in twenty five years?"

"By Count Sokolovski promising not to tell the Tzar that he should transfer Russia's gold from the Bank of England to the Banque du France."

"And for that great favor the Bank of England agreed to pay you almost £50 million pounds?" Max asked, wondering where the key to this mystery could be found.

"Not exactly 'agreed to pay.' I lent them £15 million pounds, at five percent per annum, for twenty years."

Suddenly Max had a eureka moment. "Compounded?" he asked.

"Yes," his father told him, smiling.

That being the end of the financial report, not a word was said, so Maimon put up his hand.

"Having money is a responsibility, and while none of you will ever have to worry where your next meal is coming from, you will have to worry about a lot more important matters. Money destroys more families than it builds, and if I see that happening to us, I will give every last penny to the home for old tired donkeys, and the five of you will have to find jobs to pay the rent and put food on the table. Clear?"

All five YPs nodded sagely, and then Jenna raised her hand. Addressing Max, she said, "What did you and Serena do this afternoon, and where is she now?"

"We walked and talked. She is in the lobby now, drinking tea."

"Surprise Saturday!" Morrie said, and Alison raised her hand.

"Does anyone have any more, little surprises that we should know about?"

To the YPs amazement, Elize raised her hand.

"I knew it!" Jenna said. "Four children is not enough, we need to be six."

Elize took Maimon's hand and, smiling, gave him a kiss on the cheek.

"There you are. I told you so," Jenna said convincingly.

Elize picked up "The Letter" and handed it to Morrie, who read it, burst out laughing, and gave it to Alison, sitting next to him, who did the same, and passed it on until the whole room was convulsed.

"A Russian Jew and an Afrikaans meisie[137] at Buckingham Palace. Well, fuck me blind," Morrie said, more to himself than anyone else.

"Watch your language, young man," Maimon said admonishingly. "There are ladies in this room."

"Yes, my lord," Morrie responded respectfully.

---

137 *Afrikaans word for girl*

CHAPTER 54

SERENA ALFOMBRA

Elize told Max it wasn't right to leave Serena in the lobby and that he should bring her up to their suite. Max disappeared, and a few minutes later took off his shoe and with it banged loudly on the suite's door. Everyone inside froze. The door opened, and Max led Serena into the room in dead silence.

At about 5'7", her large mahogany-colored *Fabergé*-egg-shaped brown eyes complemented Serena's olive complexion and sensuous mouth, which was separated from her hourglass body by a strikingly graceful neck. Those were the family's first impressions, their second impressions, as she glided into the room like a mannequin – was she one? – took their collective breath away.

"My God, Max," Morrie called out, "where did you find such a beautiful woman?"

That broke the ice, and in a few minutes everybody was talking at the same time, the girls about and around Serena, telling her the Sokolovski family wasn't as mad as they first appeared, and the men discussing how they could capitalise on their soon-to-be knighted parents.

A more discreet knock on the door brought a waiter with two bottles of cold champagne. He opened one and poured eight glasses. "Congratulations, sir," he said to Maimon. "My friend at Rules told me the good news."

To Serena the Sokolovskis might not be mad, but they certainly were different. When all had champagne in their hands, Morrie said, "To Serena." And after a theatrical pause, "And to Max as well."

Everyone drank "To Serena and Max," to which Morrie added,

"And to tomorrow's fair damsel and her knight in shining armor," which Serena found a bit overwhelming until Alison handed her "The Letter."

"How wonderful!" Serena exclaimed, and spontaneously kissed both Maimon and Elize.

"The Sephardim are big kissers," Max explained. "Already Serena's father has kissed me on both cheeks."

One by one the chatterers noticed that Maimon had his hand raised, and silence eventually descended.

"This hands-in-the-air thing is new today," Max whispered to Serena.

"We are all so blessed," Maimon started, "to be here in London, together, in good health. We have two weeks before we leave for New York, and we need to make the best of these fourteen days. London is wonderful and exciting, but London is not England, and before we leave, we should see a bit of the lovely English countryside. Also, London is not only shops, it is galleries and museums and has wonderful theater and opera and ballet. I see the Maryanski Company from St. Petersburg is in town. There are some meetings we need to attend, and I will try to get them all set up for the first week, so we can go to the country in the second. At night you are free to do as you wish, within reason, but one night I would like you to accompany your mother and me to see Mr. Verdi's new opera *La Traviata*. It is being performed at Covent Garden Opera House, which in itself is worth a visit."

Realizing that Serena might have already seen this production, Maimon apologized for his presumption, and added that if she hadn't, the assumption that she might want to. Serena quickly replied that she hadn't, but would love to.

"Can I get tickets for Monday evening?" Maimon asked. When no one objected, he added, "Fine. I will ask the hotel to arrange it. Tonight, we are celebrating in an Italian restaurant. You are all welcome. We are having an early dinner because I understand there is a jazz festival in Soho, and after dinner those of us who are interested can wander from one venue to another. We need a table for … eight," Maimon calculated, observing seven hands in the air. "Let's leave at seven."

The sitting room of Maimon's suite that had witnessed so much excitement was suddenly silent, with just Maimon and Elize looking at each other.

"We are so blessed," Elize repeated, pulling Maimon onto the settee and putting her head on his shoulder.

At dinner that evening, Maimon invited Serena, as the only English person in their party, to draw up a proposed itinerary for the next couple of weeks – the only restriction being that he had to be in London on Wednesday for his investiture. Could she bring it to the Savoy the following morning for breakfast? he asked.

It all reminded Elize of the fisherman standing on the bank of the river.

After dinner, the party broke up and made their way to the sounds of the negro jazz bands. Eight bands had come to England for a week, and that night were playing at different Soho jazz clubs. Maimon and Elize had never heard jazz before and they marvelled at the musician's skill. Some on the trumpet, others on the trombone; every band had an outstanding drummer, while the tunes were held together by their pianists.

Once Elize saw they were on a collision-course to bump into Max and Serena; another time they came across Jenna and Ari dancing in the street. At about eleven o'clock, when the streets started filling up with people half their age, Maimon and Elize strolled back to the hotel, each reflecting on the last twelve hours from their own perspective.

The suggested programme Serena tabled the following morning was not short on imagination.

"In London till Thursday morning," Serena read out, when the party moved to Bath to visit the Roman ruins, with the option of "taking the waters," which some believed to be beneficial from a health point of view. That afternoon at leisure, and the following morning the party moves to the beautiful Cotswolds area for two nights. On Saturday there was a point-to-point race meeting, which Serena explained was amateur riders on working horses racing over fences. On Sunday, the train to Dover, boat to Calais, and train to Paris for three nights, returning to London on Wednesday for the museums and galleries and any last-minute shopping.

From the silence that greeted her suggestions, Serena thought she may have overdone it, but, in for a penny, in for a pound, so she gave them the balance.

"Today," Serena continued, "we take a river boat to Greenwich to examine the navigational instruments in the morning." (Go, girl, go, Morrie thought to himself, knowing Maimon's scientific interest.) "And then after lunch the same boat to Kew to see their magnificent gardens."

"That all sounds good to me. I am in," Maimon said to Serena's palpable relief. Holding one of the clean forks on the table vertically with its base on the tablecloth, Maimon added, "Forks up for any other takers."

443

Six forks joined Maimon's pointing to the ceiling.

Serena hadn't included visits to Oxford and Cambridge, which she explained to Alison was because she didn't want to interfere in her decision-making processes, but she could go up on Monday or Tuesday this week, or on Wednesday, Thursday, or Friday next. Alison squeezed her hand and said thank you.

On their trip down to Greenwich the sun shone from a cloudless sky, Jenna and Ari, like Maimon and Elize, held hands and quietly watched the scenery slide by. Max and Serena held hands, too, and talked to each other incessantly. Morrie read a Sunday paper and Alison perused some cuttings about Solomon Schechter, the Romanian-born rabbi who was a lecturer in Talmudics at Cambridge University. On arrival at Greenwich, Maimon and Max went off to inspect the navigational instruments, and the rest of the party lay on the grass, some chatting, others reading, and the rest dozing.

Born into the close Sephardic London community, Serena rarely moved out of it. Three boys had already been shortlisted for her to marry: she didn't fancy, let alone love, any of them, but then she doubted that her mother loved her father when they got married. "Marrying out," which meant to an Ashkenazi boy, was considered in her community a proverbial fate worse than death. In fact, some parents rent their clothes and sat in mourning when this happened. It was all so claustrophobic, Serena thought, and quite different from this Russian/South African family, whose mother was a Boer converted to Judaism – converted by the Chief Rabbi of South Africa, albeit he was Ashkenazi.

She had never met a man like Max before. He was quiet and solid, with a mathematical brain that was in constant motion, and a quirky sense of humour. He seemed to like her. He held her hand last night and again this morning, which surely meant something.

Just then Alison slid down the grassy slope, ending up next to Serena. Closing her eyes, she lay on her back, letting her body process the Vitamin D from the sun's rays. Serena was itching to ask Alison a question, and eventually she plucked up the courage to do so.

"Does Max have a girlfriend?" she asked shyly.

"Hell, no," Alison said. "He hasn't got time for girlfriends."

"Is he queer?" Serena said, saying a silent prayer that he wasn't.

"He had a girlfriend a few years ago who was mad about him. For a while they got on well together, but then he outgrew her. My brother has all the equipment, and he knows how to use it, Jeanette told me. She was his girlfriend."

"He certainly is different from the boys l know," Serena admitted.

'The guy is a genius. When still at school he was lecturing to final-year applied maths students at university. As sharp as his mind is, he is soft and gentle inside. Whoever pushes his button will have the most wonderful husband."

Serena wanted to know what that meant, but Maimon's and Max's return (both excited at the instruments they had seen) prevented her from doing so. Hopefully, she would have an opportunity to find out when they got to Kew.

On the way downriver to Greenwich, Max had asked Serena about London. Upriver to Kew he wanted to know about her. What made Serena laugh and what made her cry? What did she like doing, and what did she hate doing? The quicker she answered, the quicker more questions came. No one had ever asked her what she was scared of, or if she wanted to go to the Amazon jungle. What was she reading, and did she write poetry or prose, and if so in what language? Did she have a horse and did she like dogs? The one question she didn't answer was, 'Do you think it is a problem being an only child?' When he stopped for a breath, Serena slipped in a question of her own.

"Why the interrogation?"

Max looked at her as if she had asked the most unnecessary question, but as she was waiting for the answer, he told her: "Because I think you are a terrific girl. I don't often meet terrific girls." Then, more to himself than to Serena, "Actually, I don't ever meet terrific girls."

As if some proof of his statement was necessary, he picked up Serena's hand and gently kissed the back of it, before replacing it on her lap. With his hand gone, she moved it onto his leg, where he let it rest while he smiled at her. Serena squeezed his leg and winked at him, and he winked back.

At Kew they split up again, agreeing to meet in an hour at the Great Pagoda. After a while Max and Serena sat down, Max with his back against the trunk of an oak tree, and Serena with her head on his thigh. She could see he was wrestling with something, but if he wasn't going to tell her what it was, she wasn't going to ask. Then it came out.

"Will you come round the world with me. I mean with my family?"

It was the question Serena hoped he would ask, and at the same time feared he would ask. She knew about the trip from Jenna, but really didn't know what to say.

"You are coming to Paris with us" Max reminded her, then adding the logic, "It is just a longer trip."

More silence. Realizing that this wasn't getting him the answer he wanted, Max changed tack.

"You said you liked to travel and that you hadn't been to Hong Kong or Jerusalem. We would look after you, you wouldn't have to worry." And then, the parting shot from his heart, Max said quietly, "If you don't like me now, you might grow to like me."

Max saw the tears welling up in her eyes and realized he had said the wrong thing. "I am sorry," he said, "I really didn't mean to upset you." And in reply he heard just two words, "Kiss me."

"Now?" Max asked, not sure how this affection tied in with her tears.

Serena didn't answer the question, at least not with words. She got up, put her knees on either side of Max's thighs, and kissed him like she had never kissed any man in her life. Then they got up, and kissed again, and wordlessly headed to the Great Pagoda, hands clasped together. For Max this was a done deal; for Serena, the beginning of a mighty battle, and the sooner she started the fight, the better the chance she thought she would have of winning it.

By the time the family got back to the hotel, they were all exhausted. Serena excused herself from dinner and Max saw her into a cab, kissed her goodnight, and pointed out it was only nine hours till they would be at breakfast together.

Serena had her parents' permission to go to Paris for a couple of days with the whole Sokolovski family, and so in a way the ice was broken, or at least severely cracked. As usual her parents wanted to know what Serena had done every single minute of the time she had been away, and as usual she didn't tell them. She did say that Maimon and Elize were going to Buckingham Palace on Wednesday to be knighted, which reminded her father what a wonderful family they were, and how nice it was that they had taken Serena into their bosom, so to speak. Serena kissed her parents goodnight, and as she turned to go to her room, motioned her mother to follow her.

Malka closed the door of Serena's room and sat down on one of the two chairs. Serena took the other one.

"I have met the man I am going to marry," Serena told her mother.

"Which of the three is the lucky one?" Malka asked, smiling, grateful that at last her daughter had made up her mind.

"None of them. It is Max Sokolovski."

Her mother looked at her as if she had been told that her daughter was going to marry one of Mohammed's great grandsons. Then she said slowly, "Doing that will kill me."

Serena was used to this Sephardic emotional blackmail. "I will come to the funeral."

"It will kill your father, too," Malka said adding another layer of guilt.

"I am sure it will be a big funeral," Serena said. "He has many friends."

"How can you do this?" Malka asked, still not believing what she had been told.

"Very easily," Serena said. "I am twenty-two years old, and in this country, where I live and am a citizen, I don't need your or Father's permission."

"I think I am going to faint," Malka said melodramatically. "Don't faint yet. There is one other thing."

Malka looked at her daughter in horror. What else could there possibly be that might be worse than this?

"Two weeks from today I am getting on a train to Southampton with the Sokolovski family, to catch a boat to New York."

Malka fell on the floor, and Serena made a half-hearted effort to help her up.

"Don't touch me," her mother cried, obviously fully conscious. "What shall I tell your father?" Serena accepted that this was a very real question.

"Why not start with the truth?" Serena said. "It is always easiest to remember."

Malka stormed out of her daughter's room and slammed the door.

"Round one," Serena muttered to herself. Serena was under no illusion that this was a serious social problem. Her father, one of Aleppo's most successful carpet dealers, had been thrown out of the country for either bribing the wrong people, or not bribing the right people enough. Everyone knew he had started in London without a Dinar, but no one knew how well he had done. His daughter's wedding was the one, and only, chance he would have to show the Morenos and the Neris and the Abreus and the Amarals that Alberto Alfombra was back.

It is going to be an interesting two weeks, Serena realized as she got into bed and switched off the light.

Monday morning saw Serena back at the Savoy Hotel for breakfast – no need for an extra place to be laid, the staff were quick to adapt to the Sokolovskis requirements. News of Maimon's impending knighthood might have had something to do with their increased attention. Max walked in, saw Serena, and his face lit up like Mr Edison's electric bulb factory.

"Alison is going up to Cambridge shortly, and asked if we would like to join her," Max said.

Still feeling her way, Serena said, "Would we?"

Max smiled, which Serena wasn't sure how to interpret. Was he smiling because of her, or because of their going to Cambridge, or for some other totally different reason? He wasn't easy to read.

"We are meeting Alison in the lobby in three minutes," Max announced, which answered that question. Gathering up her bag and umbrella, Serena made sure not to be late.

CHAPTER 55

CAMBRIDGE DEVELOPMENTS

Alison didn't take any papers out of her leather briefcase on the train up to Cambridge, which gave Serena an opportunity to ask about life in Johannesburg. The answer she got was, "It is like asking, 'What do you think of this or that lecturer?' The reply obviously depends on 'compared to whom?'"

Her enquiries about the South African Jewish community didn't elicit much more information, nor did Serena's question about the Governments "Native Policy." Serena did strike gold when she asked about Alison's hopes for the year ahead.

"For years I set my sights on reading law at Oxford or Cambridge," Alison began, "and focussed on nothing else. Right up to a few days ago, in fact. Then I heard about Solomon Schechter and his plans to collect documents from the Genizah and bring them to Cambridge to study."

Noticing no recognition on Serena's part, Alison explained, "Solomon Schechter is a Hungarian-trained rabbi-turned-Hebraist, and the Genizah is a stash of Jewish documents that had been hidden in a Cairo synagogue for centuries. I am going to meet him today to discuss being his personal assistant on this venture. He leaves for Egypt on Thursday, so there isn't a lot of time."

From reading law at Cambridge to digging about in a Cairo synagogue for ancient manuscripts was a leap even Serena's imagination had difficulty making.

"What did your parents say about that?" Serena asked, expecting that her father would have had her confined to an asylum for the insane, had she asked his blessing for such a trip.

"They are totally supportive," Alison replied. "My father suggested

449

I kick in some mizuma to evidence my enthusiasm." Noticing the blank look on Serenas face, Alison explained, "It is Yiddish, from the Hebrew word, m'zuman, for money."

Serena was battling to get her parents approval to join a family of seven on a trip to New York, and here was Alison going off to Egypt with a man more than twice her age whom she had never met, the parental approval for which she seemed to have obtained in less than twenty-four hours. What a breath of fresh air the Sokolovskis were, compared with her conventional constrained Sephardic Jewish upbringing. Could she jump ship? Serena wondered. Did she want to jump ship was really the question, Serena realized, the answer to which she needed in the next day or so. She looked across at Max, who winked at her, as if knowing the question, she was wrestling with.

"I am on the noon train back to London," Alison said as she jumped out of the still-moving coach as it slowed into Cambridge Station. "See you then, if it works for you," she turned round to say, before jogging off to her appointment.

Serena shouted "Good Luck," which Alison acknowledged by waving her arm. Then she was gone.

With the university colleges a mile away, Max picked up a taxi and Serena told the driver to drop them at Newnham College.

"You have a friend there?" Max asked.

The way Serena shook her head, Max realized there was more to this than she was saying, so he squeezed her hand, which was unresponsive. The driver dropped them outside the college, and Serena walked slowly round to the front of the largest red brick building Max had ever seen. Stopping, she stared up at it.

"Looks old," Max said, feeling he needed to get involved in whatever was going on in this wonderful woman's mind.

Serena turned away, and looking down at the grass, slowly walked toward a round pond in the middle of the college's grounds.

"Hey, hey, hey!" Max called after her, and when Serena turned round, "What's the story?"

"No story," she replied, obviously lying.

"Here comes a rugby tackle," Max called out, gently catching Serena by the waist as she half-turned round, the two of them tumbling onto the soft green grass together. With Serena on her back and Max sitting next to her, he said, "Newnham College. Sad girl. No story. Really?"

"It is not important," Serena told him, keen to move on.

"Secrets already?" Max asked, which didn't elicit a response, so he continued, "I will tell you my secret, if you tell me yours."

Serena propped herself up on her elbows, now curious. "Alright. You go first."

So he did.

"When you go home this afternoon, you will find an arrangement of sixty red roses. I would have sent more, but that is all the florist had. There isn't a card because I didn't want anyone to read the note. I don't know about your parents, but some can be nosey."

No one had ever sent Serena roses before, and for a second, she was quite overwhelmed. The next second was occupied imagining her mother's reaction to the giant arrangement that would surely be put in the middle of their sitting room – just in case any of their family friends dropped by.

"Go on. It is your turn now," he said, smiling.

Her defences down, Serena told him, "After high school I applied to this college to study ancient French. It is the language they spoke in northern France from the eighth to the fourteenth centuries."

"You didn't get in?" Max asked, surprised.

"I got accepted alright. My parents wouldn't let me go."

"Couldn't you borrow the cost of the fees from one of your friend's parents?" Max asked, hardly believing that this was an insurmountable hurdle.

Serena smiled, "It wasn't the money. They wouldn't let me leave home."

For Max this was like someone telling him the earth was flat. "Do you still want to study this old French?" he asked.

Serena shook her head sadly, knowing it was not possible.

"In that case," Max said, "we will buy or rent a house here. You can go to school, and I will take the train to London when I need to." In Max's eyes, problem solved.

Serena looked at him, clear what she had heard, but wondering if her understanding of these words was the same as Max's.

"Did I say something wrong?" he asked, suspecting he might have.

"Will we be married then?" Serena asked, thinking this was not the kind of thing one joked about.

"Yes," Max told her, in response to another "flat earth" question.

"Are you proposing to me?" she asked, realizing that Max was deadly serious about this whole thing.

"No. I will do that in some romantic place. Maybe Paris next week."

"But we are going to get married?" Serena asked, just to be 100% sure. As a little girl she had fantasized about who would ask her to be his wife, and how he would do it, and where he would do it, and none of her imaginative situations were anything like this.

"Yes," Max answered. "Don't you want to marry me?"

By way of reply, Serena pulled Max down to the ground and kissed him first gently and then sensuously. This is what she had imagined.

Realizing this marriage thing was now sorted out, Max lay on his back and said, "Why do your parents still live in the Middle Ages? I thought everybody had moved on."

"They are a bit old-fashioned," Serena said, not wanting to break the spell and tell Max of her battle that lay ahead.

They lay on the grass and discussed what kind of a house they should look for. Serena wanted a thatch-roofed cottage on the banks of the river. Max remembered reading that thatch roofs were the homes to a lot of crawling insects. Also, he had seen a sign – "Danger: River Flooding" – but if that made Serena happy, he was fine with it, and he told her so. She kissed him, pulled him to his feet, and together they went to look for a taxi.

"I think we should keep this to ourselves for the time being," Serena told Max, who replied that was OK with him.

They met Alison on the station platform just before noon. She had had a good meeting with Professor Schechter, who had offered her the job, which Alison had accepted. He was coming down to London on Wednesday afternoon with his wife to have dinner with her parents, and if Serena and Max wanted to join them, that would be fine. The three of them – the third being Mrs. Schechter – would leave together by train on Thursday morning for Marseille, from where they would catch a boat to Alexandria. Serena considered telling her parents about this, but on second thoughts decided against it.

CHAPTER 56

A NIGHT AT THE OPERA

Monday night being *La Traviata* at Covent Garden, Serena didn't have time to dawdle. Back at her parent's apartment, she breezed in, kissed her mother, who, as Serena knew she would, had placed the sixty red roses in full view of anyone entering their apartment.

"There wasn't a card," her mother said.

"Yes, I know that," Serena answered as she disappeared into her bedroom to shower and change into an emerald-green satin dress that her mother had bought from a shop in Sloane Street. The justification for doing so, her mother had pointed out, was that Serena could wear it at one of her friend's weddings. Unusually, none of her friends' status had moved from "single" to "married" since the purchase, and as a result it was the first time Serena had worn the dress.

Getting dressed, Serena noticed something was different. She couldn't put her finger on it, but she felt a sort of inner glow that coursed through her whole body. Like a flower's anthesis, in the last few days her life had opened up. The sun that had done this was the Sokolovski family, and Max in particular. They had enveloped her in what felt like a giant roll of warm cotton wool.

And then there was Max. Unlike any man that she had ever met, not that she had been introduced to that many but, by any standard he was different. Different considerate, different kind, different very clever and different … she didn't know the word for it. Unconventional and sort of quirky. But whatever the word, different nice. Even though he hadn't said the three words that she wanted to hear, she knew he loved her.

By this time Serena was dressed, and her bedroom's full length mirror confirmed her mother's choice of dress, she looked stunning. Her father had come in from his shop minutes before and was being told about the flowers when Serena flitted in and out, kissing him on the way. Not usually speechless, he was then.

By arrangement they met in the foyer of the Opera House, and when the Sokolovski party arrived, they were not the only people struck by a beautiful-looking Serena. Her off-the-shoulder dress showed off to dramatic effect the twenty-first-birthday-present diamond necklace from her parents. Maimon automatically did a quick calculation on the value of Kimberley stones being worn around Max's date's beautiful neck.

"How much?" Elize asked, knowing her husband well.

"A lot of money," he replied.

The opulence of red velvet cladding in the auditorium, and the hundreds of tastefully shaded electric candelabras, took the Sokolovski children's breath away. No sooner had they reached their seats than the lights dimmed, the orchestra conductor appeared, and the overture began.

At the first intermission, sipping glasses of champagne, the younger Sokolovskis looked at a world they didn't know existed. Serena pointed out that, except for the penniless artists and poets, it could easily have been a scene from the opera *La Bohème*. All the men were in dinner jackets, and the women in elegant flowing long dresses. Maimon and Elize, enjoying their children's wonderment, winked at one another.

"What happens after the opera?" Max asked.

"There is 'Stompin at the Savoy,'" Serena told the family, explaining that their hotel hosted a famous dance band that usually played till in the early hours of the morning.

"Then it is 'a stompin' we will go," Morrie announced, as the bell sounded, announcing the commencement of the final act. Even though the op- era was sung in Italian, the story was easy to follow, and walking back to the hotel they all agreed on the selflessness of Violetta and the terrible choice that society placed on her. Serena thought to herself that it wasn't all that different in London's Syrian Jewish community.

Back at the hotel, Serena, Jenna, and Alison took turns dancing with Morrie, Max, and Ari. Towards the end of the orchestra's blocks, Maimon and Elize joined them on the dance floor, and together with Ari/ Jenna and Max/Serena danced the new "foxtrot". It was the only dance step where the partners held each other really close, the three in-love couples having eyes only for one another.

The band stopped playing at one o'clock, at which point the waiters brought out mini-sandwiches and took drinks orders, and the family agreed what a wonderful day it had been. They were all excited for Alison about her new job, and though none of them had been to Cairo, Egypt had recently been in the news because of Howard Carter's discovery of Tutankhamun's intact tomb. None of the family noticed that Max and Serena were particularly silent, holding hands as young lovers do, happy to be alone in their own special bubble.

Around one-thirty, the party broke up, Max taking Serena home and the rest making their way upstairs, thankful that their beds were in the same building.

Instead of getting in to bed, Serena went and lay on the La Corbusier Chaise Longue that her father bought, because the Amarals had done so, and reflected on the just passed day, and night. Max was special, of course, but so was his family. Half Russian half Afrikaner, but totally Jewish, and not at all embarrassed to tell anyone who needed to know. So different from the community in which she grew up, where the people Serena had come to realize were 20th century Muranos. Jewish at home, but outside their homes, typically English, which, of course, they patently were not. Not for the first time Serena realized what she had missed being an only child; but for the first time she appreciated how much she had missed.

The interaction between Max and his brother and sisters was wonderful to see, and Serena decided then and there that if she could, she too would have four children. Max would surely agree. Later she would reflect, Serena decided, on why she went to synagogue last Saturday, but to do so she needed to consult her stars, and she was too tired to do that now. Tomorrow promised to be another wonderful three-dimensional day, her life up to the minute she met Max was if it was just up and down and left and right.

On her pillow Serena found a note from her mother suggesting that the three of them meet at nine the following morning. At other times Serena might have dreaded another intergenerational argument, but as she lay in bed reflecting on the most momentous day of her life, she realized she was looking forward to whatever lay in store. As usual, the conversation started off-low key with her father asking about the opera. Then things got serious.

"Do you realize you are playing with fire?" her mother asked, getting to the point.

"It doesn't seem like a fire to me," Serena told her quietly.

"The pain, which comes from the burns, lives for a long time afterwards," her father said.

"I won't have pain, and if there is pain, it will be you, not me, who feel it," Serena told them. Then realizing neither of her parents understood what she was saying, Serena explained.

"I need to tell you about this man I love – the good points and the bad point of our relationship as seen through your eyes. The good points first. He is Jewish, comes from a rich family, and his parents will be knighted this week. Of possibly lesser importance to you, we love one another; he is very clever, kind, and considerate, educated, reasonably religiously observant, has a good relationship with his parents and siblings, healthy, not bad-looking, and has an open mind about more or less everything.

"And now for the bad point, as you see it – he doesn't come from the inbred Syrian Jewish community, whose main, and seemingly only, interest in life is money, not only how much they have, but how much everyone else in the ghetto has."

"What about Elazar Marcos?" his mother asked.

"Elazar Marcos is an overgrown schoolboy with an ego the size of Buckingham Palace, and a brain smaller than a lentil. He never sent me a daisy, not that his father can't afford to buy a whole flower farm, as you often tell me. Sure, he can tell you how many knots per square centimetre there are on an Aleppo rug, but ask him about Chopin or Galileo or Rembrandt and he looks at you blankly. And you know what? He tried to put his hand on my private parts, which Max hasn't."

Alberto and Malka looked at one another. They had only one shot left, and it wasn't a very powerful one, but when your back is against the wall ...

"Your father will cut you off. He won't leave you a penny," Malka told her daughter.

Whatever reaction Serena's parents expected, it wasn't mirth. Serena started laughing, because, in the circumstances, it was really funny. And then Serena stopped laughing, because she realized how pathetic it was.

A sharp knock on the door brought everyone back to reality. They looked at one another. No one they knew would visit at 9:30 in the morning. Tightening the belt of her dressing gown, Serena opened the door to find Max.

"You weren't at breakfast. I was worried about you. Are you alright?"

Serena kissed Max, smiled, and pulled him into the room. Malka, without makeup, disappeared to do the best she could in the limited time available. Serena introduced Max to her father, adding that she would get them coffee.

Except for their love of Serena, Max and Alberto didn't have much in common, but in the five minutes they were alone they managed with the weather and other banalities. Malka and Serena returned, served coffee, and sat down.

"I understand you have a problem," Max started, addressing Alberto and Malka, "with Serena coming round the world with me and not being married. I went to see Westminster Council, and they told me that they can marry us next week."

Serena started giggling, went and sat next to Max on the settee, kissed him on the cheek, held his arm, and smiled at her parents. Max thought the problem was solved. Serena knew it wasn't. No one said anything.

"There is a problem?" Max asked Serena, who nodded, confirming this was so. "Don't they want me to marry you?"

"You had better ask them," Serena said.

Max looked at her parents for an answer. For a long time no one spoke.

"We need a bit of time to think about it," Alberto said finally.

"That's alright," Max told them, getting up. "I will wait outside."

"I think they need a bit more time than that," Serena told him. "OK. We will come back after lunch."

Max and Serena had lunch on a floating restaurant on the Maida Vale Canal. Again, the weather god shone on them, and helped by a bottle of white wine that they finished, the two young lovers arrived back at the Alfombra's apartment in a happy mood. As soon as Serena opened the door, she knew her parent's decision wasn't the one she desperately wanted. Her father simply shook his head.

Mathematicians need clarity. More than a headshake, so Max asked for a specific response.

"We would not like you to marry our daughter," Alberto said. This was specific enough for Max, who strode over to Serena's father, his eyes shooting daggers, the index finger of his right hand pointing at Alberto's throat. When he was just inches away, Max dropped his arm, smiled, shook Alberto's hand, said "Goodbye, sir," and walked out of the apartment door.

Over tea in a Lyons Corner House some minutes later, Max explained his position.

"Your father is silly. One day we will have babies and he will want to come and visit them, and every time I see him, I will be reminded of this man who said he didn't want me to marry his daughter. No man is good enough for a father's daughter, but if that man makes his daughter happy, then the father should withdraw his opposition."

"What will happen to us?" Serena asked, this bittersweet day, with all of its twists and turns, becoming more and more confusing.

"You will come with our family," Max said, "and we will get married on a Hawaiian beach, or in Palestine, and we will live happily ever after."

That sent a shot of adrenalin coursing through Serena's veins.

"Will that happen? Will it really?" Serena asked, and Max assured her it would.

Things didn't go well for Alberto. First of all, Serena went back to the flat and told her father he was a fool. Stupid people usually knew that they were stupid, she said, but he was so stupid he didn't even know his degree of stupidity. Then, in Paris, Max formally proposed to Serena on a romantic bridge over the river Seine one moonlit night.

The next day the two of them, together with Maimon, went to Maison Chaumet, where Maimon bought Max a four-carat blue-white pear-shaped diamond, surrounded by sparkling baguettes, set in a simple platinum ring, which Max put on Serena's finger. As fate would have it, back in London, Serena bumped into one of her girlfriends while wearing her new ring, and in minutes the news roared through the Syrian Jewish community like an out-of-control bush fire. Neither Serena nor her parents would confirm or deny that she was engaged, and if so who to, which only raised the temperature of the rumour to white-hot.

These kind of secrets are always difficult to keep, and a picture in the London Jewish Chronicle of the Sokolovski family, including Serena, outside Buckingham Palace narrowed the lucky man down to three. Jenna and Ari were photographed walking arm-in-arm, so it had to be Morrie or Max. The two brothers thought it was a load of fun, each of them looking deeply into Serena's eyes from time to time and the ring-wearer was so cross with her father, that she was happy to see him squirm for a while longer. Uninvited, most of the Syrian Jewish community descended on the Alfombra's flat, bearing sweet meats and other delicacies, and being indiscreet enough to ask which of the Sokolovski brothers was the lucky one. Alberto should have met Max and welcomed him into their family, but humble pie was rarely eaten by anyone in the Syrian Jewish community at that time, and sadly Serena's father was not one to break ranks. Only when boarding the train for Southampton a week later was Max unmasked as the fortunate man.

CHAPTER 57
COUNT SOKOLOVSKI RETURNS

The main reason for the Sokolovskis visit to London was for Maimon to introduce his children to their family's three custodial bankers. Even without Alison, there were effectively five people, whom Maimon considered too many to be included at each visit. After careful consideration, he took Morrie to meet Seligman Brothers, Ari and Max to accompany him to Rothschilds, and Jenna and Max to join him at Barings and then onto the Bank of England. Each visit was an eyeopener for the younger generation, none more so than when they called upon Barings and the Bank of England, also known as "The Old Lady of Threadneedle Street."

During his first visit, more out of boredom than anything else, Maimon had adopted his Russo-English accent, and for old time's sake, he decided to do so again.

His geopolitical sweep had so impressed the government's bankers last time, that Maimon, Jenna, and Max found themselves shown into a considerably larger conference room than the one used for their previous meeting. Maimon counted fourteen chairs, and to his surprise, a few minutes later, almost all of them were filled. Happily, he noted that the head of the table was occupied by the same man with whom he had negotiated his previous £5 million loan. Pretending to suddenly recognize him, Maimon ran across and kissed the banker fully on both cheeks.

"My friend," Maimon beamed, "I am good to be seeing you again. You are many people, but I am justly three. Daughter Jenna and son Max came to be sure that I borrow money to you, not the other way round, ha."

Before being asked to do so, Maimon gave the assembled company his views on the current world situation. "Big war coming. Keiser Schmeiser building ships and army to fight England, also France. Very stupid. Many killed both sides."

Maimon stopped for a theatrical pause, and then continued. "Uncle Samuel – you know I am meaning? – will come flumph Germany. Be careful Japan. Many little yellow men on islands with lots high mountains so need more space. Little men look through binoculars and see pretty girls – 'pretty girls' Japanese code for iron ores and black coal. Korea, Mongolia, many pretty girls."

Suitably impressed, the chairman asked Maimon about Africa.

"Rich continent, wonderful people. One problem. People sleeping long time. White man, also yellow man, work hard many years. Discover wheel, to write, earth run round sun, world not flat. Now black man wake up. See very small white man, yellow man, because far away. Black man start running, but long road many bumpings." Maimon slipped in another dramatic pause, and then, "Now we speak money."

The table head said he was happy to do so, but that Count Sokolovski's terms were too onerous. Maimon smiled broadly.

"Me own-yer-ous, you own-yer-ous, together we two-yer-ous. Good."

The table head looked to Jenna and Max for help. Jenna got up and beckoned her father to the corner of the room, where she whispered, "Stop messing around."

While nodding energetically, indicating he understood what she was saying, Maimon said, "Leave me alone. I am having fun."

Jenna and her father returned to the table, where Jenna told the senior Bank of England man that her father now understood. English was not his first language, she pointed out, and sometimes he got confused. All the while Maimon smiled. When Jenna had finished Maimon slipped in, "What are bank's proposiliations?"

They would take his £40 million, or more or less, the table head advised, but with interest compounding annually.

"No good," the Count informed them. "But OK for me. I go to New York on Lusitania. See Federal Reserve. Also, good bank."

With no movement from the bank man, Maimon continued.

"Before I go I tell you two importants. Number-one important: Balkan people crazy. Serbs, Croats, Herzegovinians, Bosnians, Montenegronians, all crazy. If they want fight, say OK. England no fight for

Transylvania or other joking country. Number-two important. Big war coming. Big war costing big money. War Office lie if say not so. On money, here last words. Count Sokolovski OK to lend Bank of England £40 million for four years at four percent with interest compounding every four months. No handeling. You know *handeling?* Dutch people always handeling. Dutch cheeses more better than Dutch handeling. You think under or over, whichever right one, Count's proposiliation. After decide, sent letter to count at Savoy Hotel."

At which point, Maimon stood up, shook hands with everyone in the room except his children, whom he then kissed, explaining, "Always kissing children. Good for children, also for kissinger."

Walking back to the hotel they debated whether the Bank of England would accept their terms. Maimon was convinced, absolutely, that they would. Max believed there was no chance, and Jenna was on the fence. Maimon was right.

CHAPTER 58

SOLOMON SCHECHTER

Looking back later, they all agreed that the highlight of their London visit was the dinner with Solomon Schechter. While researching her future employer, Alison noted that he had learned to read Hebrew by the age of three, and at five spent hours studying the Chumash.[138]

Maimon had reserved a private dining room at the hotel, and from the moment the rabbi (for he was so qualified) walked in the door, he held the family spellbound. His face was framed with white hair, which was complemented by a foot-long white beard. A pair of delicate glasses remained balanced on his nose throughout the evening, as if by magic.

With regard to the Genizah, Rabbi Schechter told the family that he was alerted to the existence of the papers by two Scottish sisters, Mrs. Gibson and Mrs. Lewis, who showed him some leaves that contained the Hebrew texts of Sirah,[139] which for centuries had only been known in the Greek and Latin translations. The sisters had bought them in the Cairo bazaar during their visit to Egypt the year before.

"So I went and found this amazing treasure," the Rabbi said. "These archives, containing hundreds of thousands of pages, originating mainly from the eleventh to the thirteenth centuries, offer a detailed picture of the spiritual and material aspects of medieval Jewry. They contain rabbinical responsa and rare formulas of prayer, trial protocols and instructions of community authorities, books and linguistics, collections of

---

138 Genesis, Exodus, Leviticus, Numbers, and Deuteronomy

139 *The Book of Sirach is a Jewish work, originally in Hebrew, of ethical teachings, from approximately 200 to 175 BCE, written by a Jewish scribe, Ben Sira of Jerusalem*

poetry, treatises of Halakhah[140], science, philosophy, and history, registers of merchants, books that had been in private and public libraries and portray the cultural profile of the community, bills of sale, letters, private notes, and other assorted papers."

"How many are there?" Max asked, trying to get his head around this amazing source.

"I think about 300,000, but most of them shouldn't be there at all."

"Why do you say that?" Serena queried, wondering if any of her ancestors might have contributed to this amazing archive.

"According to Jewish law," Solomon explained, "objects containing the name of God cannot be destroyed, and therefore have to be preserved, even when unusable. Alternatively, they can be ritually buried. Almost all of these documents have one trait in common, no matter what language they use – Hebrew, Arabic, Persian, Spanish, Greek, and even Yiddish – they are written with Hebrew letters. Fortunately for us, the men responsible for the Genizah extended the definition of 'sacred' to all works that were written in Hebrew script, regardless of its content."

"Why do you think they did that?" Serena asked, never realizing that while she was interested in France during this period, Alison would be delving into Jewish life at the same time.

"This was probably due to the decline in the use of Hebrew in everyday life," Solomon went on, "a process that turned it into a holy language and hallowed the letters themselves."

"Amazing," Elize commented, "and all this without pogroms or anti-Semitic actions."

"Sadly not," Solomon replied. "The custom of concealing texts may have been the result of mob attacks on Jewish funeral ceremonies. At the beginning of the eleventh century, a wave of anti-Jewish and anti-Christian riots swept through Palestine and Egypt. Churches and synagogues, including the great synagogue of Cairo, were desecrated. The Jews, therefore, preferred to avoid burial ceremonies, and while waiting for better times, regarded the Geniza as a temporary solution. Reconstructed in the 1030s, the synagogue continued to house this treasury of documents in its attic."

"Are you going to take all 300,000?" Maimon asked, thinking of

---

140 Halakha is the collective body of Jewish religious laws derived from the written
and oral Torah. Halakha is based on biblical commandments, subsequent
Talmudic and rabbinic law, and the customs and traditions compiled in many
books such as the Shulchan Aruch

what would be involved in documenting, packing, and shipping this number of papers. "Also, will they let you take them?"

"I have a letter from the British Chief Rabbi, Herman Adler, to the Chief Rabbi of Cairo, Aaron Raphael Ben Shim'on," Solomon explained, "and with Alison's help, I plan to select the most important papers and bring them to Cambridge for scholars to study."

The conversation then drifted into life in Cairo today, its Jewish community, and how soon they could expect a photograph of Alison on a camel.

Reflecting on the evening after Rabbi Schechter had left, they all admitted that after initially feeling sorry for Alison (as she would be missing out on a big part of the trip), they now felt almost envious of the satisfaction she would derive from working with Rabbi Schechter on this once-in-a-lifetime discovery.

CHAPTER 59

"EVIL EYE" BLOCKER

The family all spent their last few days in London differently. Maimon had to be ushered out of the Science Museum at closing time on two occasions, so engrossed was he on the workings of this machine or that one. Elize's days were unstructured, which was how she liked them. After seeing Maimon and the children off in the morning, she wandered round the West End of London, in and out of shops and galleries, revelling in the fact that her time was entirely her own. Unlike those in Johannesburg (and she suspected in New York), shop-owners were happy to discuss their wares with her, even though Elize had made it clear that it was unlikely she would buy anything from them.

Morrie, who held a degree in Mining Engineering, became interested in the minerology of America's mid-western region, and discovered books on this area in the British Library, which he spent hours poring over.

Serena delighted in showing Max corners of London not usually visited by tourists. Her favorite was the Portobello Road Market, which specialized in just about everything old, from suits of armor to silver toothpicks. There was only one thing that Serena wanted to take from London to her new home, wherever that was going to be, and that was a pair of Georgian silver candlesticks. These were to be found, Max was told, in the Silver Vaults, an underground complex of shops selling only silver and sliver-plated items. Max would have bought the first pair they were shown in the first shop, but in view of the amount of money involved, Serena insisted on comparing pair "A" in shop "B" with pair "C" in shop "D" with pair "E" in shop "F," which was how a whole morning came to be spent.

Ari and Jenna decided to stay on in Paris, the city of lovers. Rising late, they either had picnic lunches in the Tuileries Garden, or they ate at one of the many bistros on the Seine's left bank. The rest of their days were spent ambling about, enjoying the wide range of art in galleries too numerous to count. Tired by late afternoon they took a nap, and then after dark went up to Montmartre to eat at one of the many restaurants, while watching the world stroll past. As they had promised Maimon they would be back in London the day before their ship sailed for New York, Jenna and Ari boarded a train at the Gare du Nord, wondering when they would return to Paris. If anyone had told Jenna it would be with their daughter in a couple of decades, she would have burst out laughing.

In expectation of a form of appreciation from the now "Sir Maimonides Sokolovski," the hotel manager made sure to be on hand when the family left for the station. He was not disappointed with the financial reward, and was surely relieved that the Count did not kiss him goodbye, for which he had Elize to thank. It was she who extracted a promise that the Count would remain out of sight until they left London. Maimon agreed, but gave no such undertaking with regard to the Count's activities on the *SS Lusitania*.

The family's departure from the station to Southampton should have been entirely unremarkable. As it happened, it was anything but. Waiting patiently next to the door of their coach were Alberto and Malka. The atmosphere at home was so bad that Serena had moved into the Savoy Hotel and had accepted that she might never see her parents again.

Serena was wrong. In seconds, Serena and her parents were hugging each other, and when Alberto saw Max respectfully standing aside, Max was engulfed as well. Not many words were exchanged; so overwhelmed were all of the women and Alberto that Morrie noted four women and one man openly weeping. Then Malka pinned a little bit of coral on the inner lining of Max's coat, and Alberto did the same to his daughter's. Handing a small white envelope marked "Para el/ la Familia"[141] to Maimon, saying only "Serena will explain," Alberto did something he had never done in his life. Remembering it from his parents' home, the man who understood he might never see his daughter again put one hand each on the heads of both his daughter and future son-in-law, and blessed them.

"May the Lord bless you and keep you," Alberto started. "May the

---

141   *For the family*

Lord make his face to shine upon you and be gracious to you." And then in a quivering voice, just holding back his tears, he concluded "And may He look after you on your travels, and bring you safely to your home, wherever that might be."

The train's whistle sounded, the family scrambled aboard, and Max and Serena leaned out of the window to see her parents holding hands, waving with their other arms, and smiling. It was those smiles that Serena would remember for the rest of her days.

Expecting a letter he couldn't read, Maimon handed the envelope to Serena, who smiled. She knew what was inside. Five little bits of pink coral clipped onto five safety pins. Attaching one to the coat of each member of her almost family, Serena explained smiling, "It is to keep the evil eye away."

CHAPTER 60
CHARITABLE PROPOSALS

As Jenna pointed out, being on the Lusitania was like living in the Champagne Bar of the Covent Garden Opera House, in that everybody, men and women – and she admitted that she was talking only about the 1st-class passengers – looked like they had been dressed by Central Casting at the Warner Brothers Studio. No matter what time of the day, or night, all the men and women were impeccably dressed for whatever activity took their fancy. This ranged from meal times to recreation to sporting activities. One man, she noted, had different outfits for deck quoits and shuffleboard. The record, Jenna advised, was held by a lady with an American accent, who wore eight different outfits in one day.

Shortly after boarding, and before the ship had even left the quay, Mai- mon had called the family, and Ari and Serena, into his suite to tell them that, the morning after next, they would be meeting in one of the ship's conference rooms to discuss the family's approach to charity – basically, how much they should give, and to whom. Each of them, and this included Ari and Serena, were to set out on a piece of paper their suggestions and be prepared to defend them.

Maimon wanted to have the family round a formal table, as opposed to lounging on easy chairs in his suite, as he felt it vital that they understood the subject's importance.

Forty-eight hours later they reconvened in the George Washington Conference Room. Maimon had put seven little pieces of folded paper in a glass, and when everyone was settled, he upended the glass on a piece of white cardboard with a little circle drawn at its center.

"Each of the pieces of paper has one of your names on them,"

Maimon explained. "The one closest to the circle goes first. The second closest second, and so on."

Picking up the closest, Maimon handed it to his wife, who unfolded it, and read, "Alison." He then took an envelope from his pocket, and gave it, to Elize, who opened it and read, "'I feel a bit uncomfortable about being asked to suggest beneficiaries for money I had no part in earning. This I told Dad, who said that having money carried with it a responsibility, and that when he and Mom were gone, we children would have to do this, which is why he has asked us to give him our suggestions now. Fortunately, or unfortunately, he didn't tell me how much is available for distribution – I don't know if any of you are aware of the quantum – and so my suggestions are in percentages.

"'I feel very strongly that our charitable donations should not go to the SOBs (symphony, opera, and ballet), but to organizations where, if it wasn't for our help, their situations would be seriously worse. So, I would like to see 50% of my allotted funds to be used for building, and maintaining, a home in Johannesburg for mistreated horses and donkeys. Time and again I have seen the pitiful state of these animals pulling native carts, and I fear they will continue to do so till they drop down dead. As for the other 50%, I would like to see it divided three ways equally: between Rabbi Schechter's Cambridge Genizah Resource Center, helping with the native's health and education in South Africa, and to assist Jewish people living in Palestine.'"

Elize's name was the next closest to the circle. She put a folded piece of paper in front of her but did not open it. Instead, looking round at her children, she said, "Before I give you my suggestions, I want to say something. None of you will ever go to bed hungry, as your father and I did when we were children, and for that I thank God in my prayers every night. We ran around barefoot because we didn't have shoes. It wasn't what we wanted – our parents not being able to go to the doctor or pay for medicine – but we survived. And here we are today so blessed, as it says in the Bible, 'our cup runneth over.' Money not only brings responsibilities, but is also a burden because it puts temptation in one's way. I have heard of families destroyed by money, and I pray it does not happen to ours.

"That is the end of my speech. Now for my suggestion. I think that all of the money should go to help the poor Jewish communities in Russia. You have not seen, as I have, how these people live in abject poverty. Their clothes are threadbare, they are all as thin as sticks, Cossacks come and rape and kill them, but still they believe in God, and if they have a few coins, they give one or two to charity. They are the people who really need it."

Next closest was Serena's paper. Like Elize she left her suggestions folded unseen and spoke without notes.

"We are all hostages in a way to our backgrounds, and mine is quite different to yours. The Syrian Jewish community in London is rich, extraordinarily rich, not that you would know it. They behave as if they are still in Aleppo or Damascus, with all the good and bad that involves. I grew up believing that the highest form of charity is giving a lot of money to already overfunded art galleries.

"But Max told me that the highest form of Jewish charity is giving someone a job, which of course makes sense, but was not something that anyone ever mentioned to me. When I suggested to one of my rich uncles that we should give money to homeless people, he said that we needed to look after our own, because if we didn't, who would? Other communities should look after their people, he told me, making clear to me that that closed the subject.

"Because of this, I am ashamed to say that I don't even know what charities need money, and, therefore, without percentages, I think money should go to the following deserving causes. In the East End of London, there are a lot of extremely poor Jews, mainly from Russia, I have been told. They should be helped. Also, old people. I see extremely poor old people. Do they have enough food? What about single mothers whose husbands died or left them for other women? They can't work and look after their children at the same time, so how do they get food? Lastly, orphanages. I would think that there are never enough toys or books or cuddly animals. That is all."

Morrie's piece of paper was the next closest, and he too spoke without notes, leaving his paper folded on the table.

"Like Alison, I felt a bit uncomfortable giving away Dad's money, but then I realized that someone has to, and it needs to be us. There is an organization in Russia called ORT, which trains Jewish boys, and maybe even girls, to be blacksmiths and carpenters and tailors and so on, so that they can earn money, which they can't do by studying all day with their rabbis. I would give at least 50% to those people. Then, in South Africa, there are St Helena boys."

Turning to Serena he explained, "That is what the people in South Africa who are not white or black are called. Originally they came from that little island halfway to South America, but now they include the children of whites who marry blacks, or just have children with them. People look after the natives and most whites are OK, but nobody cares about these coffee-colored people." But he wasn't finished yet.

"Also, I read about the Jews in Palestine. They are working in the fields, draining swamps, and removing stones so crops can be planted. To do so they need equipment, so I think money should be given to them."

Jenna was chomping at the bit, but Max's paper was next.

"Dad hasn't told me either how much money we will be giving away, but however much or little it is, I believe it needs to be managed and disbursed in a professional and responsible manner. I would give it all to medical research. The human body is the most complex machine ever constructed, and we know so little about it. The Science Museum in London has working models of internal combustion engines, water mills, and other energy-related machines; but what about blood circulating round the body? Why do people die from heart attacks? Are their hearts intrinsically weak, or are we interfering with nature by what we eat and drink, or even smoke? And illnesses. There must be a cure for tuberculosis. And malaria, too. That is my call."

At last, Jenna's name was next.

"I would like to see," she began excitedly, "lots and lots of farm schools, for the white children, and also for the native children, and for the St. Helena children as well. Not only must we build schools, but also pay for the children's uniforms and give them two meals a day. The government must pay for the teachers. We have to educate them – boys *and* girls – because there isn't enough farm work for them now, and there certainly won't be in the future. When they come to town, as inevitably they will, they must be qualified to do something, otherwise they will steal things to sell to get food."

Then it was Ari's turn.

"Sir, my allocation, please, I would like to go 100% to Betar."

Maimon saw Serena look at Max for clarification, so he explained. "A man called Ze'ev Jabotinsky was in Odessa, where he saw Jews being attacked while the city police stood by and did nothing to protect them. Then and there he realized that Jews had to defend themselves, and in Riga he formed a Revisionist Jewish Youth Movement called Betar."

"And you, Dad?" Jenna asked. "Where are your pennies going, and by the way, how many are we talking about?"

"Betar for me, too," Maimon answered. And then, doing a quick calculation in his head, said, "Two hundred and forty million."

They all looked at Max as he was the only one of the children who was their father's equal at mental arithmetic. In response he gave a low whistle, which didn't answer the question, so he said, "One million pounds."

The children and Elize sat in shocked silence.

"Over two thousand years ago a man called Plato lived in Athens," Maimon began, breaking the silence, "and during his lifetime – he lived to 80, which was very old in those days – he said many wise things. One of them was 'Virtue does not come from money, but from virtue comes money, and all other good things to man.'" And then to lighten things up, looking at Elize and Jenna and Serena, he added, "I am sure he meant women, too."

"How does he know this?" Jenna asked, amazed at her illiterate father's knowledge.

"Don't ask," her mother told her quickly.

Absorbing the magnitude of what they had just heard, the children slowly got to their feet and filed out of the room, leaving Maimon and Elize alone.

"You just gave away a million pounds," Elize told Maimon, as if he needed to be reminded of what had just happened.

"No, I didn't," he contradicted her. "*We* just gave away a million pounds. And for me the unbelievable thing is, neither you nor I, nor our children, will be any poorer for it. In fact, we will all be richer."

Elize didn't understand the last statement, but this wasn't the time for an interrogation. It was the time to think about all the people, and Alison's animals, who would benefit from Maimon's generosity, and that left a warm feeling in her body that she wanted to enjoy for as long as possible. It did prompt her to write Maimon letter # 9, which she left on his pillow. It didn't stay there long.

My Darling "give it away" Husband,

Every now and again, after having lived with you for all these years, I think I know you, and then ... along comes another wonderful surprise.

You will never know how proud I was this morning, listening

477

to our children's suggestions with regard to charities they would like to see funded by our family. They certainly didn't get that from their du Toit genes. As you know, my parents never had any money that they didn't need for food and clothes or necessary farm maintenance; but there were a few rich farmers in our community, and I never heard of them giving money to charity.

We Jewish people, and I get a wonderful warm feeling when I say that, or even remember that I am part of Jacob's family – did you know that Jacob's name can be used to describe the Jewish people? – are so different in ways y ou don't even think about. Charity is one, of course. Another is the way you look after your parents and grandparents. The Afrikaners put them in old-aged homes, and I think the English do as well.

Old people need love and human contact as much as children do, and from what I have seen, that is one of the things Jewish people do better than anyone else, or any nation I have observed. I was thinking the other day, when we are old and not able to get around the way we do now, our children and grandchildren, please God, will come and visit us. I read somewhere that old people need things to look forward to – can you imagine anything nicer than seeing our children driving up the gravel road at See Da View, coming to visit us? I can't.

Do you know what I am most looking forward to on this trip? Not the skyscrapers in New York, or the floating villages in Siam, but observing our children's excitement when they see those things. Thank you again for taking a year out of your life to give the children, and me, what is sure to be not one unforgettable experience, but hundreds of them.

We are so blessed to have you, and we all know it. Your ever-grateful life partner,

Lady Maimonides Sokolovski

The remainder of the voyage was a blur for the family, each one remembering a different specific event.

For Serena, it was dancing on the deck with Max under the moonlight and saying, "We have the most back-to-front romance. You asked my father if you could marry me, he said no, so we didn't, and then we went on our honeymoon, except it isn't a honeymoon because we are not married."

For Max it was having Serena's parents' permission to marry this most special, exciting, caring, considerate, loving girl, whom he couldn't believe was as deeply in love with him, as he was with her.

For Ari it was a double whammy. Not only did the most wonderful girl in the world want to spend the rest of her life with him, but in addition, Betar had been given a quarter of a million pounds.

For Jenna it was spending every one of her waking moments (well, not exactly every one of them, because she shared a girl's-only suite with Serena) with the only man she had ever loved.

For Morrie it was striking up a friendship with Isaac Newton Seligman, the managing partner of J.W. Seligman & Company, one of New York's major investment banks. Jenna, ever on the lookout for her brother, asked Isaac if he had any sisters, and was amazed to be told not, as Seligmans only produce boys. In his generation there were 36 of them from his father and his seven brothers.

For Maimon and Elize it was just being together, doing whatever they wanted, whenever they wanted. Sometimes they played bridge, other times deck sports, and what Maimon enjoyed most of all, Elize reading Joseph Conrad's novels to him, particularly *Outpost of Progress* and then *Heart of Darkness*, both of which were set in the Belgian Congo.

CHAPTER 61

TEXAN BLACK GOLD

At a very formal dinner in New York hosted by Isaac Seligman, Morrie found himself sitting next to Pattillo Higgins.

Pattillo Higgins and his partner, Captain Anthony Lucas, who was a specialist in salt-dome geological formations, told Maimon that at Beaumont in Texas such conditions existed and that there should be a significant quantity of crude oil beneath the formations. The problem was they didn't have the money to rent a drill rig, nor the finance to pay the crew team to operate it. Maimon and Morrie, knowing nothing about oil drilling, had a breakfast meeting with Higgins and Lucas. Maimon believed that the two men were honest, and agreed to put up $100,000 for a third interest in the venture.

Leaving the rest of the family to explore New York, Maimon, Morrie, Pattillo, and Anthony took a train to New Orleans, and then a coach to Beaumont, where Anthony contracted with the Hamill Brothers to drill on land he had leased from the Beaumont Pasture Company. At 1,139 feet the well "came in" gushing 100,000 barrels a day 150 feet into the air. It took the Hammill Brothers nine days to cap the well.

As soon as they saw the crude oil fountain, Maimon and Morrie headed back to New York, where they arrived just after the newspapers had pictures and reports of the blowout. Elize wanted to know why the site was called "Spindletop," which Morrie thought was because of a nearby copse. The press was full of "Who is Sokolindustries, Inc.?" and Maimon was tempted to call on Count Sokolovski to tell them of his oil-drilling experiences in Baku, the capital of Azerbaijan, but Elize pointed out that this was New York and so it might not be the wisest thing to do. Elize did tell Maimon of a problem Jenna had informed her about yesterday.

"It is sensitive," Elize warned Maimon.

"I am ready," he replied, remembering how many problems could be solved by what someone in the Bible said was "the root of all evil". He had lived much of his short life desperately poor, and now that he was thankfully no longer in that camp, Maimon realized that for him any problem that could be solved by money, wasn't a problem at all.

"Jenna and Ari are going to get married."

"That is a problem?" Maimon asked, hoping that nothing had derailed the young couple's affection for each other while he was away.

"The problem is that Serena has an engagement ring and Jenna hasn't."

A money problem. Maimon breathed with relief.

"Ari hasn't asked you if he can marry Jenna, because he thinks you will say yes; and if you do, he will have to buy Jenna a diamond ring, and as he has hardly got two brass farthings to rub together ... you get the picture?"

"So, I will lend Ari some money, as I did to Max." Problem solved.

"You know it is not the same," Elize pointed out. "I am embarrassed for him."

"If his skin is so thin that he also feels embarrassed, then he should go and live on an ashram in India, where nobody has any money and every- body loves everybody else."

"That is not fair."

"Maybe it is, and maybe it isn't. Let me tell you what happened in Texas. Pattillo and Anthony had done all the work, and the only missing piece in the puzzle was money, which they didn't have. What would Rockefeller have done, I asked myself? He would have given them two percent each, maybe, and he would have taken 96%. Would that have been fair? I don't know, but Rockefeller works on the golden rule – he who has the gold, makes the rule.

"What did Morrie and I do? We said we would give them the money for thirty-three percent of the equity, which would be sufficient to pay for the drilling program. Was that fair? Maybe yes, maybe not. Rock-efeller would have thought we were crazy. Some socialist would have said we squeezed their kishkes – testicles – which we did. Was it fair that you and your mother spent years in a concentration camp? Was it fair that I was railed out of Saratov, relieving my family of any further embarrassment? Life is like a native's left leg, it is neither right nor fair. If Ari doesn't get that, he is marrying into the wrong family."

"I will tell him," Elize said quietly, not having expected this lecture.

"Good. Tell him everything," Maimon said, wondering if he and Elize had made life too easy for their children. Before the expected knock on his door, Maimon had a chance to reflect on this question, and reached a decision that would have far-reaching consequences.

The family, Maimon and Morrie excepted, had been in New York for ten days, and with shopping done, galleries visited, and shows taken in by everyone, they were ready to move on. That was fine with Maimon and Morrie; what was not fine with some in the family was that instead of heading to San Francisco as scheduled, Maimon told them that the next stop would be in Boulder in Colorado. Jenna was not sure if this was some kind of a joke, and asked if Maimon had considered going to Little Rock in Arkansas instead. Most of the party hadn't heard of either.

CHAPTER 62

BOULDER ACCIDENT

On the long train ride heading west, Maimon pointed out that the schedule he had drawn up featured only cities, and as cities occupied an exceedingly small percentage of the earth's land mass, they should not overlook the planet's rural areas. Boulder was in Colorado, at the foot of the Rocky Mountains, which were quite different from the Magaliesberg, where the children had scrambled when growing up. Also, the animals were different. Bison instead of Wildebeest; and in the mountains, black bears and bobcats as well as coyote and elk. To keep away from were rattlesnakes and striped skunks, Maimon pointed out. To the children's credit, the more they thought about it, the more excited they were; and when the train finally pulled into Boulder's Downtown Station after thirty-nine hours of traveling, no one wanted to stay on the Union Pacific to San Francisco.

Boulder was a breath of fresh air in more ways than one. It didn't take long for the family to explore the town, and, as Maimon expected, the snow-covered mountains had a magnetic effect on the children. None of them had seen snow before, and they all wanted to try the quite-new sport called "skiing." The helpful receptionist at the Boulderado Hotel pointed out that it was cold in the snow and people skiing needed warm clothes as well as gloves and hats. Forty minutes and almost $50 later, the Sokolovskis extended family returned to the hotel, laden with clothes they hadn't known existed. The closest ski area was at Eldora, and seven excited, overgrown children set off laughing and joking the next morning.

At Maimon's request the coach driver stopped as soon as they crossed the snow line, when they all tumbled out of the wagon and started throwing snowballs at one another. A little out-of-breath because of the altitude, and wet from some of the snow balls that weren't successfully dodged, they climbed back into the coach for the last big uphill stretch to Eldora. There they had to rent skis and poles and boots. Parties of seven rarely came to Eldora midweek, and word had got around that there could be work for a ski instructor.

While they were struggling into their ski boots, which everyone agreed were the most uncomfortable footwear ever invented, a tall – about 6'4" – cowboy sauntered into the store. Stick-thin, with a drooping moustache and leather leggings, he introduced himself as A. Kito. Around these parts, he told the first Africans he had ever met, everyone called him Kito.

Skiing, they all found out, looked easier than it was. As expected, Ari had little difficulty putting into practice Kito's complicated instructions. Serena had the most difficulty. She seemed to spend more time on her bottom than standing up on the skis, but she was a good sport and laughed a lot. The others coped with greater or lesser success. They stopped at noon for a bison burger and ice cream washed down with a beer for the girls, and two for the boys, made by a local brewery.

After lunch, and not yet on the main ski run, the family were standing listening to Kito's instructions about weight transfers for parallel turns, when suddenly they heard a woman scream "LOOK OUT!" followed by her crashing headlong into the Sokolovski party. Morrie took the main impact, and then the skier knocked down Jenna, Max and Maimon, who fell over like dominoes. Slowly everyone got to their feet, except Morrie, who remained prone in the snow.

Elize kicked off her skis, in her cumbersome ski-boots stumbled over to Morrie, dropped to her knees, and then with her face just inches away from his, cried out, "Morrie! Wake up! Talk to me!"

He didn't wake up and he didn't talk, but lay dead still.

"He is dead!" Elize screamed, and then turning to the skier shouted, "Look what you've done." You killed him."

"I am most terribly sorry," the woman said. "I was going too fast and couldn't stop. I really do apologize."

The woman, who was about 5'8", in her mid-twenties, and spoke with an Irish accent, told the shocked family that her name was Colleen McGuire and that she was a doctor.

Bending over the unconscious Morrie, she felt his pulse, pulled down the lower lids of both his eyes, and looked into them. Then she put her hand under Morrie's nose to make sure he was breathing.

"He is probably concussed," she said, looking up. "We should take him to the hospital for a check-up. I really am so terribly sorry," she said again, and then turning to the ski instructor, "Amos. Get ski patrol with a sled and a neck brace."

"He has broken his neck!" Elize shrieked and then burst into tears. The doctor told Maimon, who was comforting Elize, that this was most unlikely, and the neck brace was merely a precaution. Furthermore, she informed them that she would accompany the patient to the Foothills Hospital Emergency Department, where she suggested they all meet in an hour.

Spot on time, six very worried family members filed into a new and bright hospital, where they were shown to Morrie's private room. Lying on his back under the covers, he looked to all the world that he was fast asleep. Sadly, he wasn't. Professor Crainy Lukeson, the resident neurologist, explained that Morrie was not concussed but had suffered some brain injury. X-rays had confirmed that none of his bones were cracked or broken, and a lumbar puncture indicated that there was no pressure build-up in Morrie's brain. As to when he would regain consciousness, it might be today or tomorrow or next week.

"Or next month or next year or never?" Maimon asked.

"That is a possibility, but a rare one," the professor replied. "Patients often respond to verbal stimulation, so it is important that you talk to your son, remind him of things you did together. Sing songs. Retell jokes he may remember, anything that might jog him back to consciousness. I am here every morning and afternoon, and the hospital knows how to get hold of me over the weekend and at night. Dr. McGuire has requested to be your son's designated doctor, which I was delighted to hear as she has extensive experience with patients suffering from head injuries."

It was then that they noticed Dr. McGuire standing quietly in the corner. The professor departed and Dr. McGuire apologized again to Maimon and Elize. Possibly not yet realizing the implications of Maimon's predicament, Elize reminded her that it was an accident. Maimon said nothing, knowing well that it had been a very avoidable accident. Maimon and Elize decided to stay with Morrie, and the children walked slowly back to their hotel, largely in silence.

Morrie didn't wake up that day, or the next, or the next, or that week or the next or the next. Every time one of the family arrived the doctor was talking to Morrie. Telling him about growing up in Ireland and how she got to be in Boulder. What they didn't see, or hear, was Dr. McGuire playing her guitar and singing to Morrie, which she did early every morning.

She rose at five and was in his room less than an hour later. People can be creative in different ways, some paint, others write, a few tell stories. Colleen sang. People who heard her sing said her voice didn't come from her throat, it came from her soul. It was pure and it was honest, and it pleaded for this man she didn't know, and somehow she felt that she did know. Surely God would hear her this time. They were not normal prayers but prayers that God would understand, and then He would give Morrie his life back, his life that she had taken away.

Modern medicine had done all it could, now it was up to her, Colleen knew. God hadn't always listened to her prayers. But it was not for herself that Colleen was now pleading, and so maybe this time ....

When the family visited, she did other duties in the hospital, and as soon as they left, she returned. Elize and the children came to really like the doctor who said she would be happy if they called her Colleen and so they were all on first name terms except Maimon who remained Mr. Sokolovski.

The split second Morrie had crashed into the snow changed all of their lives. Elize knew that only the Almighty could return to her the charming extrovert character they all remembered, and she made sure that He knew this was something that needed to be done. Serena, admitting only to herself that she was being horribly selfish, was thankful that Colleen had crashed into Morrie and not into Max.

Jenna was beside herself. Their family of four, already down to three with Alison's departure, was now two. Morrie and Max were the two pillars on which she had leant for her entire life, and she honestly did not know if, and how, she would hold herself together with one of them gone. Ari, the salaried employee, and very much the outsider, wondered how the family dynamics would change with Morrie absent, and particularly what extra responsibilities might now devolve on his shoulders.

Max, the fellow twin that he had grown up with, his alter ego, who complemented his introvert character, felt the loss more deeply than any of the other family members. Maimon, with everything seemingly under control, had compartmentalised the issue. Dealing with the challenge of getting Morrie home gave him a hands-on, but detached, view of the problem. He was affected, more seriously than he appreciated, as for the first time in his life, wires went unanswered and important decisions postponed.

After two months, when it was increasingly apparent that Morrie was unlikely to regain consciousness in the foreseeable future, if at all, Maimon set the wheels in motion to transfer him back to Johannesburg. A hospital rail coach was booked to transport Morrie to San Francisco, where he would be loaded into the infirmary of a large passenger liner. There he would remain till the ship arrived at Durban. After that he would be transferred to a special hospital coach for the last leg to Johannesburg. All the while he would be monitored twenty-four hours a day, seven days a week, as he needed to be fed continually with saline liquid into one arm and protein nourishment into the other.

Instead of gallivanting around, Elize and the children wrote letters. All of them wrote to Alison, who wired back immediately requesting bi-weekly cabled reports on Morrie's condition. Elize wrote to her mother and two of her school friends; Serena to her parents daily; Ari to his parents and sister; Max for technical books; and Jenna lots of letters to no one in particular. Maimon spent his writing time walking, thinking of how he could upscale his businesses to increase their profitability.

One Friday evening the whole family was chatting in Maimon's room, when Colleen entered carrying a tray with two lit candles, a glass of red wine, two slices of bread, and a salt cellar. The children looked at each other, which Colleen noticed, and putting the tray on a table, she said nervously, "I know Russian Orthodox Church people hate Jews. I am only doing this for Morrie, and as we all believe in the same God, I hope you won't be angry with me."

The family being too shocked to speak, Colleen continued. "This is for our Friday night service. We say a blessing over the wine, and we drink a bit, and we dip a piece of bread in the salt and eat it, also after having said a blessing."

One by one broad smiles broke out over the children's faces. "It is not a joke," Colleen said angrily.

Then Jenna said "Shmah Yisroel," and Ari added "Ador-nai Elorheinu," and Serena finished the sentence, "Ador-nai Echad."[142]

Colleen half-raised her hands in the air and shouted, "No, no, no," and ran out of the room crying. Serena chased after her into the Ladies

---

142   *"Hear O Israel, The Lord Our God, The Lord Is One"*

Toilet, where she found Colleen had locked herself in a cubicle and was sobbing uncontrollably. When the sobbing had died down, but not stopped, Serena knocked quietly on the cubicle door.

"Go Away! Please, go away," Colleen's distraught voice sounded emotion al and angry.

"Why are you cross with me?" Serena asked, not being able to make head or tail of Colleen's reaction.

"Because I killed your brother," came through the door. "And he is Jewish."

"You haven't killed him," Serena half-lied. "And we are all waiting for you to say Kiddush."

Slowly the door opened, the girls hugged, and a few minutes later walked hand in hand down the passage to Morrie's room.

"Is Maimon really Jewish?" Colleen asked, and when Serena assured her that there was absolutely no doubt, Colleen added, "But I heard him talking Russian, or Russian English, to Morrie one afternoon. I wasn't listening, but Maimon said he was a Russian Count."

"Count Maimonides. Do you really think so?" Serena told Colleen, and then they both smiled, walking through the door into Morrie's room.

After prayers Colleen told her story. Her mother, Chaya Cohen, came from Lithuania, and for a number of complicated reasons gave birth to Colleen in Ireland. Her father, who was supposed to follow a week later, was killed in a pogrom. Destitute, Chaya was taken in by a family called McGuire, with whose son she fell in love and married.

Colleen started Hebrew lessons with a wonderful man called Isaac Herzog, who later helped her get into Trinity College medical school at Dublin University. In her final year, Chaya and her husband moved to Boulder, where he had been promised a job. When Colleen graduated, she came to Boulder, only to learn that the company that had offered her step-father a job didn't exist. Colleen didn't have the money to look for her mother, and even if she had the money wouldn't have known where to start the search, so she applied for and got a job at the hospital. As to why she was Dr. McGuire and not Dr. Cohen, that was the name she had used at university and that was the name on her medical certificate. Her story finished, Colleen looked around to gauge the family's reaction, and what she saw were sympathetic smiles on the faces of all the family, except for Maimon.

CHAPTER 63

LAST-RESORT PROCEDURE

The hospital arranged for a barber to shave Morrie every day, and to cut his hair every third Monday; this was more for his parents, Professor Lukeson explained to Max and Jenna, as they might have more faith in their son recovering were he to look presentable. On these third Mondays the family came to visit a little later, and Colleen had Morrie to herself for longer. Speaking to herself while straightening the bed she said,

"Professor Kali Petersen told us that when we have tried absolutely every other course of action known to medical science, it is in order to activate the 'last-resort procedure,' and now, my girl, we are at that point. Colleen, you are a lucky lass, having such a good-looking man on whom to implement 'the last-resort procedure.' Should I do it from the left or the right side of the bed? Professor Petersen never told us, but he did tell us to close, and if possible to lock, the door, so that is what I had better do. Am I ready? Yes, I am. Do I have the necessary equipment? Yes, I do. Then go to it, girl."

Colleen bent over Morrie and kissed him gently on the lips. She thought his lips might have moved, so she kissed him slightly more passionately, and his lips definitely moved, so she French kissed him as she did a boy in school, and he kissed her right back. Mystified, she lifted her head and saw Morrie's eyes wide open, and then one of them winked at her. Shell-shocked, she didn't know what to do.

"Why did you wait so long to kiss me?" Morrie asked.

Surely, she was dreaming, Colleen realized, so she said to her smiling patient, "Please pinch me?"

"After you have given me another kiss."

So she did, and then he did. In silence, they just looked at one another.

"I have some bad news for you," Morrie told Colleen. "It wasn't the kiss that did it. Last night I found I could move my fingers and toes, and then my hands and feet; and then this morning my arms and legs. I can swallow, blink, and wink, blow my nose and cough, but there is one thing I am afraid I can't do."

"What is that?" Colleen asked, worried that she had missed an important anatomical function.

"I can't move my ears. As I couldn't move them before you crashed in to me, I suppose that is not too serious. You had better unlock that door, Or some people will get the wrong idea."

Laughing and crying Colleen ran out of Morrie's room, down the passage, through the lobby to the hospital's forecourt, where she saw a saddled horse eating some grass. Forgetting that under her hospital white coat she had only a bra and undies, Colleen jumped on the horse and galloped to the hotel. Running into the dining room she found the family at breakfast. Crying and laughing, all she could do was nod her head.

"He's awake!" Jenna cried, and when Colleen nodded again, she rushed outside, found Colleen's horse, that wasn't Colleen's horse, jumped on it and galloped to the hospital.

Maimon got up, gave Colleen his handkerchief, and asked quietly, "Do his arms and legs work?"

"He says they do."

"He's speaking?" Elize asked not really believing what she was hearing.

"And coughing and blowing his nose and making jokes."

Later that morning it was as if someone had opened a cylinder of laughing gas in Morrie's room. The patient, with both drips removed, was slowly eating a soft-boiled egg followed by a half a glass of warm milk, while the family looked on in wonder. Morrie explained that from the moment of impact he could hear and understand everything that was being said – he glanced at Colleen, who looked at the ceiling – and was so grateful for the chats and songs and jokes that he so looked forward to every day.

Professor Lukeson explained that a minutely small blood vessel might have ruptured when Morrie's head hit the snow, and it took the weeks in hospital for it to repair itself. Dr Lukeson added that because Morrie had lain in bed for so long, it would take him a month, or maybe two, to regain his strength. He might even have to learn to walk again. Twice daily physiotherapist sessions would be arranged, and the harder Morrie worked, the sooner he would be allowed to leave hospital.

"Hospital is for sick people," Morrie pointed out. "I should move back to the hotel."

No one took that seriously. Prof Lukeson added that he would need to examine Morrie as soon as possible, and that it would not be necessary for the family to be in attendance. They all got the message. One by one they took their leave, until just Maimon and Elize remained.

"I knew you would be alright," Elize told her son.

"I remember you saying that," Morrie told his mother, who, having lost her first son, had prayed to God every morning and every evening not to take her second one as well. "I am a little tired now. Maybe you could come and see me this evening."

Maimon and Elize got up, kissed their son, and, mentally exhausted, walked slowly hand-in-hand back to the hotel.

The hour-long examination undertaken by Professor Lukeson and assisted by Dr. McGuire could find nothing wrong with Morrie that gentle exercise, sunshine, and a healthy diet couldn't fix. Dr. McGuire undertook the responsibility of ensuring that their patient neither over-exerted himself, nor shirked any of the scheduled physio sessions. The extensively planned programme was scheduled to start at nine a.m. the following morning.

On the chime of nine Colleen walked into Morrie's room to find him dressed (in clothes Jenna had brought him earlier and helped him get into) sitting in the armchair reading a book entitled Plasmonic Resonators: Fundamentals, Advances and Applications.

"Top of the morning to Morrie, me patient," Colleen said smiling.

"Sure, and Begorrah, if it's not me darlin' doctor from County Tipperary?"

"Actually, it is Yerr darlin' doctor from Omagh in County Tyrone."

"Give me yer goitar, doctor," Morrie said; and when she did he broke into a song from that part of Ireland:

> *"There's a pretty little girl I call my own She's*
> *the sweetest rose Ireland's ever grown*
> *And sure as the moon and stars above*
> *I'm falling head over heels in love With a pretty lit-*
> *tle girl from Omagh In the county of Tyrone."*

Colleen stood with her hands on her hips, smiling, not quite sure what to say. That was fine with Morrie, who had an important announcement.

"And Doctor Nightingale, I am not getting into that four-wheeled contraption of yours."

"And what might I know is wrong with it?" Colleen asked.

"Nothing for anyone who wants a four wheel Heath-Robinson wheelchair, with a ship's bell to frighten pedestrians, a too-big steering wheel, too-small brakes, and lights for night-time operation. Either my horse, or I walk." Saying which, Morrie stood up, and if Colleen hadn't caught him, he would have crashed to the floor.

"You play goalie in lacrosse?" Morrie asked, regaining his balance. When Colleen shook her head, Morrie replied in his best imitation of an American gangster accent, "Let's get outta here, baby."

He held her tightly round the waist and headed for the door. Like a Siamese twin they marched, step in step, down the passage, through the lobby, onto the grass to the closest bench on which they gratefully sat down.

"Well done, you were great," Colleen told Morrie encouragingly.

"It wasn't well done, and I wasn't great. *We* were great, which is what we need to talk about. Do you believe in bashert?"

Never having heard of bashert, Colleen shook her head, leaving Morrie no option but to start down a different road.

"Colleen McGuire, do you know why I am here, sitting on the bench with you at 9:20 this sunny morning?"

Colleen knew a smart answer wasn't called for, so she kept quiet.

"Because we are marionettes, you and me, and someone is pulling our strings. You are a good skier, so why did you crash into me. You said seven times in my room, when you thought I couldn't hear, that you didn't know. And why did you kiss me yesterday morning, just hours after I found out I could move my arms and feet, and not a week or two before? And why did whoever put a beautiful, smart, intelligent girl inches in front of me, so that even a dumbo like me couldn't miss her?"

"Can I ask a question?"

"Sure," Morrie said.

"To how many girls have you given your above questionnaire?"

"Good question. Just one."

"And what did she say?" Colleen asked, now interested.

"I am waiting to hear."

"Morrie, you are a good-looking man. You come from a great family. Everyone is strong and healthy, or soon will be. Money doesn't seem to be a problem. You must be the catch of Johannesburg."

"So?"

"So what are you doing messing with an Irish girl in the shadow of the Rockies far away from both of our homes?"

"I am trying to woo you, and you are not making it easy for me. Do you hate me?"

"No."

"Do you dislike me?"

"No."

"Do you like me?"

"Yes."

"Do you love me?"

"I don't know."

"If I killed a bull, would you love me?"

"No."

"How about a chicken?"

They both burst out laughing.

"Have you been married, engaged, or in love?" Colleen asked, now getting into the spirit of it.

"No, no, and no."

"And you?"

"No, no, and maybe once."

"If I killed him would that improve my chances? I have never killed anyone, but how hard can it be?"

"Do you joke about everything?"

"Only important things."

"What do you like about me?"

"You want the truth?"

"Of course."

"Then we will be late for supper."

"Give me the top ten."

"Elevator style?"

"Any style you like."

"I think your toes are cute. So many women have ugly toes. Your legs are unbelievable. If I ever lost my money you could model your legs in stockings. I think they call it hose here. The next bit I don't know about, but you have a cute navel."

"When did you see my navel?"

"The other morning before you kissed me, you were explaining the umbilical cord to one of the students and you showed her your navel."

"I thought you couldn't see!"

"I peeked."

"Horrible man."

"Am I allowed to say nice things about your breasts?"

"No."

"Your neck has the grace of a swan's."

"Used before?"

"Never. I once told a girl she had a neck like a chicken. It is not a smart thing to do."

Morrie then kissed Colleen as she had kissed him in bed the day before.

"Why did you do that?" Colleen asked, not expecting the answer she got.

"Because I owed you one. 'Neither a borrower nor a lender be.'"

Impressed by his *Hamlet* quote, Colleen responded with one from *Romeo and Juliet*.

"'It is too rash, to unadvised, too sudden.'"

"'Tempt not a desperate man.'" Morrie reminded Colleen, also from *Romeo and Juliet*.

"'How beauteous mankind is! O brave new world. That has such people in it.' *The Tempest*," Colleen told him.

"How thou tempteth me with thy knowledge and beauty. My heart is full of love for thee, as sure as the cock crows at day's first light."

"William Shakespeare?" Colleen asked, not recognizing the quote.

"Morrie Sokolovski," he told her honestly.

They walked back to Morrie's room, again holding each other tightly by their waists; but on the return there was a degree of tenderness and affection in each of their hands. Back in his room Morrie collapsed onto his bed. Colleen removed his shoes, covered him with a rug, and before she closed the blinds, Morrie was fast asleep.

Doctor Lukeson and Colleen met with Maimon later that day and told him that Morrie should be well enough to travel in two weeks. Following this news Maimon booked berths for four couples on a boat leaving for Hong Kong eighteen days later. When Jenna pointed out that this gave them no time in San Francisco, Maimon said they were weeks behind schedule and needed to do some catching up. He ignored Jenna's response that they didn't have a schedule, nor did he tell her that he was not prepared to put his family at risk in a city that was prone to earthquakes.

The last two weeks flew by, so much more so than the previous seven had, when Morrie was in hospital. Except for one day when Maimon and Morrie went to Denver on business, the family remained in Boulder "enjoying the nature," as Max put it.

Morrie and Colleen spent more and more time together, and the family were considerate enough to remain at least a double arm's length away from them. Three days before the family's booking on the Pullman coach to San Francisco, Morrie took Colleen to the Waterwise Garden in Chautauqua, where they found a bench in the shade at the water's edge with a large "Reserved" sign on it. They sat down close together, as Morrie folded up the sign and put it in his pocket. Colleen smiled. They held hands, neither saying anything. After a while Morrie spoke.

"It comes down to two questions."

"I think I know the first, but what is the second?"

"Will you make my family happy or sad?"

"Doesn't that depend on the first?"

"Not necessarily. I ask you to marry me – you say yes or no. Second question. If you say no, you stay in Boulder, as do I, and my family and I are sad. If you say yes, but want to stay in Boulder, I am happy, and my family is sad. If you say yes and agree to marry me in a civil ceremony on the beach in Hawaii, and formally in Jerusalem, then I am happy, and my family are happy, and you are happy."

"Anything else?"

Morrie pulled a black velvet ring-box from his pocket, opened it to reveal a platinum ring with a four-carat, heart-shaped blue diamond in a slightly raised setting. Morrie had practiced saying, 'What shall I do with this?' but he didn't have to. Colleen held out her left hand and Morrie slipped the ring onto her fourth finger.

The family who knew about the ring agreed that if the answer was "no," Morrie would drop Colleen at her apartment, and if it was "yes" they would come to the hotel. Jenna and Serena borrowed two pairs of binoculars and set themselves up on the hotel roof, with a table, umbrella, and cool drinks. At about 3:30 everyone within ten miles of the Boulderado taking a nap was woken by the screams from the top of the hotel building. Five minutes later a coach pulled up at the hotel, where the family, and a waiter with two bottles of champagne, were waiting for them.

Colleen's last two days were hectic and exciting. Despite Maimon pointing out that the shops in San Francisco probably had a wider range of ladies clothes and accessories than those in Denver, Colleen, Jenna, and Serena spent the whole of one day, and a fair amount of Maimon's money, kitting Colleen up for San Francisco and their trip to Johannesburg. The second day was spent preparing and enjoying the young lover's engagement party.

"I have never seen a heart-shaped diamond as an engagement ring," one of the nurses remarked to Colleen, who replied, "You have never met a man like my fiancée."

A good third of the hospital staff came to the station to say goodbye to the Sokolovski family that now included Colleen, whom they had unofficially adopted.

Tears were shed both on the train and on the platform, and as the wood-burning engine slowly got up speed, the only people not waving from the open observation car at the train's rear were Maimon and Elize, who were quietly grieving together over a chocolate cupcake, remembering little Adam, whose birthday it was.

Returning to their compartment, Maimon found an envelope with "#10" beautifully printed on its outside. Without saying a word, he opened it and handed the pages it contained to Elize, who began to read.

My Dearest Maimon, who does so many things, sometimes not even knowing why?

When trying on wedding dresses in Johannesburg, I overheard the girls in the adjacent dressing room talking about what was or wasn't Bashert. Not knowing what this meant, I asked Rabbi Hertz, who told me the closest English word to it is "destined." You and I were definitely Bashert, as were Max and Serena, as well as Morrie and Colleen. I am not sure about Jenna and Ari. Don't ask me why I feel this way, I don't know myself.

I dare not mention this to Jenna, but I feel I must do something, but I don't know what. Do you have the same feeling? Whether you do or not, what should I do? You who are so wise, please tell me.

After God gave us Morrie back, I feel we owe Him something. It can't be money, because you have just given away a million pounds to various charities. I feel He expects us to do something good. Do you know what that might be? I have been racking my brain trying to think of something relevant, and all I have come up with is a ward in a hospital for people with brain injuries, which probably isn't practical. If there is a Neurological Unit at Johannesburg General Hospital, we could ask the professor there when we get back what his unit needs.

You have always got such wonderful ideas – what do you suggest?

I miss Alison so much. When we go to Palestine, could we please take a few days off to visit her in Cairo? It would be so wonderful for all of us to be together again.

Thank you again for this wonderful trip, which I know is not even halfway through. I will never forget it and I am sure neither will our children. Sometimes old people forget things, so I am keeping a diary of what happens every day. When we are old, I will read it to you, then both of us will remember these wonderful days, weeks, and months.

Your ever-loving, ever everything good, life partner, who thanks God every night for telling me to sit on the wall where you could see me.

Elize

CHAPTER 64

HO'AO[143]

After the helter-skelter of their last days in Boulder, the rhythmic chuff-chuffing of the train's engine through the breath-taking Rockies provided a welcome relief for the whole family. Morrie's illness had taken its toll on Elize in particular, and for her to sit quietly opposite her so happily recovered son, and his ever-smiling fiancée, was as good a therapy session as could ever be provided by the most experienced psychologist.

One afternoon Morrie asked Colleen to give him her guitar, and when she did he started strumming it and sang the second verse of what he had begun to refer to as "our song."

> *"Well, I don't know what she's done to me*
> *There's nothing else my eyes can see*
> *My pretty little girl from Omagh*
> *In the county of Tyrone.*
>
> *She wears my ring and tells her friends*
> *She going to marry me*
> *Best of all she tells them all*
> *She's going to marry me, oh lucky me."*

By the time the train pulled into San Francisco's railroad station, all their batteries had been recharged, and the YPs were ready to explore the city's attractions. Unfortunately, it was pouring with rain, and so

---

143   *Hawaiian wedding*

they all went along with Maimon's suggestion that they board the boat, hoping the weather would improve later. Maimon had booked them on the American-Hawaiian Steamship Company's latest launching, whose engines were oil- (instead of coal-)burning, with the whole ship lit by electricity. It was as if the weather gods waited for the Sokolovski family to board before opening the heavenly flood gates again, and almost washing all San Fran-cisco into the bay.

Sightseeing was ditched, and after unpacking they met for cocktails, dinner, and an early night. The rain continued for the entire duration of their stay in San Francisco, which they all agreed was a good reason for them to come back another time. When Elize quietly pointed out that their children were no longer children, "old-fashioned" Maimon capitulated and changed their bookings to cabins for people who loved each other unconditionally. It was the natural progression of life, Maimon reflected, and reminded him of his blissfully happy months with Elize at her parents farm. Noting that this was one of the first steps in the inevitable generational hand over, Maimon realized for the first time that he was truly the paterfamilias, a word he remembered Ayna teaching him."

At lunch on their third travel day out of San Francisco, Jenna brought up the subject of weddings. Morrie and Colleen were getting married on the beach in Hawaii, and also in Palestine, and Jenna and Ari would also like to do so. "So would we!" said Max. That sounded great, Maimon responded, and as beach weddings, at least in his family, were a novelty, he suggested that the Hawaiian one be a combined event (which he would organize), while in Palestine each of the couples should have their own ceremony. They all agreed with that, Elize realizing that as mother of one of the brides, and probably stand-in mother for the other two, her work would be cut out in the Holy Land.

While the children were discussing the advantages of getting married in Jerusalem, on the top of Masada or in the vineyards of the Rothschild estate, Maimon's imagination was working overtime thinking how special he could make the Hawaiian event. He had twenty-seven days to organize it, and as the boat sailed serenely into Honolulu harbour, Maimon was given his telegraphic bill, which he noted was for thirty-four intercontinental transmissions. If the Palestine weddings would be memorable, his Hawaiian one would be unforgettable.

Maimon had commissioned a chupa[144] to be constructed, which,

---

144   *A fabric-covered construction held aloft by poles at each of its four corners*

he said, had to be large enough for twelve people to stand underneath without touching one another. The four poles had to be heavily garlanded with flowers, as was the roof. That was the easy part. More difficult was finding a ten-strong choir who could sing Baruch Ha Ba from the Hallel prayer. For money and kind words Maimon believed one could get most things in life, and that included native Hawaiians learning to sing a Hebrew prayer.

At 4:50, almost an hour later than the scheduled start (which didn't bother any of the wedding party, or their guests, of which there were none), Maimon and Elize walked down an elongated tatami mat on Waikiki Beach, to the much-rehearsed Baruch Ha Ba.

Like the three brides, who were to amble down on the mat arm-in-arm a minute or so later, Elize was dressed in a short-sleeved, floral-patterned brilliantly colored muumuu. Maimon and the three grooms all wore buttoned-down white shirts, with a colorful bow tie and braces to match. All the men had calf-length white pants and were shoeless.

Waiting under the chupa was a grossly overweight Hawaiian priest, known locally as a "kahuna" – this particular official correctly as the "Big Kahuna" – as well as the three grooms.

"You were amazing," Serena said to Maimon afterwards, giving him a kiss on the cheek.

"Amazing or not," Elize commented, "it is a good thing your parents weren't here to witness it."

"Hopefully, they will come to the Palestine one, even though I suspect the count won't be officiating next time."

"He won't be allowed into the country," Elize assured Serena.

They strolled over to the bar, where Maimon picked up a drink and accepted compliments from the six YPs and the Big Kahuna, who made it clear it was time for the exchange: Maimon's money for three beautifully colored wedding certificates. The caterers had set up a table on the beach, lit by candles, and passed round poi, lomi salmon, and haupia, together with salads made up of fruits not seen in western countries. This was followed by pineapple flambé.

Back on the boat Maimon and Elize took a shower, and then in their night attire lay on their bed reflecting on the afternoon's weddings.

"How do you think our grandchildren will get married?" Maimon asked.

"That is making two assumptions. That we have grandchildren and that they will want to get married."

"I will give you odds," Elize said, "that by the time we get to Palestine, at least two, and probably all three, of the girls will be pregnant."

"How do you think the Syrians will take that?"

"In their stride, as long as Serena isn't the only one with child, and none of their friends come to Palestine for the wedding," Elize answered confidently.

"Sad to say," Maimon reflected, "that there are more communities ruled by convention across the globe than there are free thinkers like us."

"Convention has some good things going for it."

"Like female genital mutilation and honor killings," Maimon said. "Living in an emancipated world isn't good enough. The Syrian Jewish community has to move with the times as well."

Elize thought of the society in which she grew up, and how everything in it was so regimented. She hoped it wouldn't be to their detriment, but she feared it would. Largely cut off from the scientific advances that were pouring out of Europe and the United States, she worried about the Transvaal and Orange Free State farmers, and if Maimon was right about the natives taking over… A shudder went down her back. Consoling herself that this was not her problem, and furthermore that there was nothing she could do about it anyway, Elize stretched out next to Maimon, who had dozed off while she was contemplating the future of the Afrikaner nation.

When Maimon woke the following morning, Elize was in the bathroom and letter "#11" was on his bedside table. While he was getting dressed Elize read it to him.

My Darling Count Sokolovski, aka Sir Maimonides Sokolovski, aka the Most Wonderful Man in my life,

I wanted this letter to be all about today's weddings, which none of us will ever forget. Thank you for arranging it all. I still can't believe that you got the Pacific Islanders to sing that song in Hebrew – how did you do it without even being in Hawaii? And that Calypso band – where did you find them? You are really amazing.

But that is looking back, and you tell me it is more important to look ahead.

After you went to sleep last night, I started thinking about how different life is going to be when we get back to Johannesburg. We left with children who did what we told them to, or largely did, or mostly did; and are returning with adults who will want to make their own way in life, with input from us only when requested. I am sure you will handle the introduction of Morrie and Max in to your company with your usual aplomb. When it comes to where they live, no matter what we think, and would like, it is their decision, which we will have to respect. Enough of this.

I too am getting tired so will end now. You look so handsome in the bed – I would like to pour a bucket of plaster of Paris all over you, well just the top part, and then make a bronze bust of you. I do think of some silly things, but they are only because I love you so much.

Sleep well my darling.

Yours for ever,
Elize

CHAPTER 65

JACK DEMPSEY'S RHUC

Before Maimon had a chance to comment on the letter, there was a sound like half a dozen simultaneous thunder-claps, the boat rocked in the calm sea, and the sun disappeared behind clouds that suddenly came from nowhere.

Maimon threw on a robe, ran outside, and saw that the mountain closest to the town had an open gash in its side, out of which poured black smoke ascending to the heavens, and molten red magma oozing down into the sugar cane plantation below. Running back to call Elize, Maimon noticed an envelope on the carpet addressed to Elize and him.

MORNING MOM AND DAD – IT IS SUCH A LOVELY DAY WE HAVE TAKEN A GUIDE AND GONE FOR A WALK. DON'T WAIT FOR US FOR BREAKFAST. WE SHOULD BE BACK AT ABOUT 11 – THE BOAT ONLY SAILS AT ONE. MUCH LOVE – THE YOUNG MARRIEDS

Throwing on some clothes Maimon rushed up to the boat's Customer Relations desk to find out about his children's tour. One of the tour group's reliable and careful shore-based guides, Bennie-Ho, had taken the six youngsters on a circular walk from which they should return soon. Elize joined Maimon, heard the news, and climbed to the observation deck to try and spot their returning family members.

If all was calm on the boat, it was exactly the opposite on shore, where Benni-Ho, aware of the damage a lateral eruption could cause, abandoned his charges and ran as fast as his little legs would carry him, to a village four miles away where his family lived. Morrie and Max shouting after him had no effect on his trajectory. Serena and Jenna, unused to nature's pyrotechnic exhibition, began sobbing.

507

"We will be running, with me in front and Max at the back," Morrie instructed. "Any questions?"

There weren't any, so Morrie set off at an above-average speed down a path through the cane fields with the girls bunched up behind him, followed by Ari and Max. Serena's legs were pumping faster than they possibly ever had, made possible by adrenalin coursing through her veins. For about three miles they kept up this pace until Morrie raised his arm, slowed, and stopped. Ten foot in front of him was a six-foot wide, four-hundred-feet deep gash in the earth that ran from the top of the mountain down to the sea.

Looking round for any planks or uprooted tree trunks to make a bridge, and not seeing any, Morrie called out, "Watch me."

Taking a twenty-five-foot run as fast as he could, Morrie launched himself in the air and landed a good four- feet beyond the far-side edge of the crevice.

"You saw it wasn't hard," he called out. "Colleen, you are next. Run as fast as you can."

She did, and landed next to Morrie, as did Serena, whose short legs pumped like pistons in one of the latest motor cars and landed further on the other side than her taller in-laws.

"Ari, you're next," Morrie called, and instead of seeing the most athletic of them all soar over the crevice, they watched a man, white as a sheet, rooted to the ground.

"I am scared of heights" a little voice croaked, "I can't do it."

Initially Morrie, and then the girls, encouraged, implored, begged, and screamed at Ari to jump, which, for a man of his athleticism, should have been a stroll in the park. It wasn't because he was petrified of heights. With the rolling magma getting closer – they could now all feel it's heat – and Ari immovable, Jenna suddenly realized the seriousness of her husband's predicament, and started screaming hysterically. This did nothing for the party's peace of mind.

Summing up the situation, Morrie realized there was only one pos-sible solution. Instructing the girls to stand shoulder-to-shoulder facing away from the crevice, with Jenna in the center, he made the three of them grip each other, like front row forwards in a rugby tight scrum. They were not to move an inch, until instructed by him to do so. This they promised to do, despite Jenna's now incessant wailing, which, for everyone's morale, had to be stopped. Morrie first asked her to stop, then told her to stop, then shouted at her to stop – all of which had no effect – so he slapped her hard across the face. More out of shock than pain, it shut Jenna up.

Morrie then jumped back to the fire side, and beckoning Max to join him, said calmly to Ari, "It is all going to be alright. You won't have to jump over the crack in the ground. No one is going to make you do that. Now breathe deeply, that is right, and again, very good, now close your eyes and raise your chin a little bit, and breathe again and lift your chin a little higher still."

When Ari was as relaxed as he was ever going to be, Morrie, with the knuckles of his right hand encased in a handkerchief, half-turned away, and then like an uncoiled spring, landed a right-hand uppercut on Ari's jaw that knocked him out stone-cold. Max removed Ari's shoes and socks and threw them to the girls. After that he picked Ari up by his ankles, Morrie did the same to his wrists, and moving as close as they dared to the edge, began swinging him. First little swings, each one getting higher, until on nine, Morrie said, "On twelve we let him go."

They did. Ari landed on the harbour side, the red-hot, slow-moving magma wall now less than 50 feet away from Morrie and Max.

"Colleen," Morrie called out, "faiceallach gu bheil giallan briste aige,"[145] using the Gaelic she had taught him in the weeks since they left Boulder.

"Girls, OK to turn round now" Morrie shouted; and when Jenna did, she saw Colleen ministering to Ari. She rushed to help. They couldn't slap his face in case his jaw was broken (it was) so they had to resort to what Colleen said is known in Irish rugby circles as "The Welsh Resuscitator."

The twins had never heard of that, so Colleen explained: "The two of you urinate in his face at the same time. Always works."

"Kindly remove the young ladies," Max requested. "I am unaware of the protocol with regard to their viewing grown men's privates."

Colleen carried out Max's request, and Morrie and Max carried out their doctor's instruction, and in seconds Ari was staggering to his feet.

Retaining control of the situation, Morrie said, "Jenna. Please put on your husband's shoes and socks," which she did, and at a somewhat slower pace, they made their way back to the boat. The harbor master, concerned that the magma might fill the harbour, trapping the ships anchored there, instructed the captains of all the boats to leave port at once.

---

145 *"Careful, he has a broken jaw"*

Colleen went with Ari and Jenna to see the ship's doctor, pointing out that Ari might need to have his jaw wired, which, upon inspection, proved to be necessary. When asked how Ari had crossed the narrow deep ravine, both Max and Morrie advised it was by utilising the earth's magnetic field, including induced levitation. Jenna knew this not to be true, but did not want to reopen this painful wound; she knew she had been within inches of losing Ari to a massive crack in the earth's crust.

The Gold Medal, everyone agreed, needed to be shared by Colleen for prescribing the Welsh Resuscitator, and to Morrie and Max for administering it.

CHAPTER 66

MAIMON LOSES A NEGOTIATION

Always in control Maimon, was reminded that he wasn't, when his much looked forward to visit to Hong Kong was cancelled. It was partly his fault, as he had not taken into account that his family's planed stay in this Chinese outpost coincided with their Typhoon Season. With gale force winds measuring 130 miles an hour forecast, the captain explained to Maimon that under no circumstances would he venture anywhere near Hong Kong where the typhoon was expected to make landfall in the next twenty-four hours. Appreciating that this time his "money and kind words" strategy would not work, Maimon reluctantly told the family the sad news. To his surprise, none of them appeared particularly disappointed, telling him that as with their trip to San Francisco, they hoped to return sometime soon.

As Rangoon, Bangkok, Singapore and the sub-continent Indian ports were all in the paths of other typhoons, to Maimon's further disappointment, the captain decided to sail directly to Aden. This didn't bother the YP, as Elize reminded Maimon they needed to be called, who spent their days and nights blissfully happy in their inter-marriage honeymoons. Steering well clear of the typhoons, the captain virtually guaranteed his passengers calm seas and clear skies, and so the Sokolovski party's days revolved around late breakfasts, light mainly alcoholic lunches followed by inevitable naps. Post-tea, their afternoons were the most active part of their days, when they chatted, played cards and reflected on the trip so far. Cocktails at six was followed by dinner and early nights.

Aden was known as the British Government's Near Eastern Supply and Maintenance Station, and so Maimon wasn't surprised to count nine Royal Navy ships as the *MV Colchester* tied up to the big cast-iron bollards set in to the harbour's concrete quay.

Back in a British Colony, where his knighthood carried some weight, Maimon was easily able to secure a British Army truck, with driver and two armed guards, to take them up to Sanaa, the capital of Yemen.

Both commercial and residential houses in Sanaa were constructed entirely of mud, with one or two religious and government buildings being the exceptions. Its population of over three million people included about 50,000 Jews, and it was this community that Maimon sought. Without an army driver it might have taken the family hours to find the city's Jews, but with corporal "Cobra" Calloway, once they arrived in Saana it took just minutes.

From the synagogue's furniture, or lack of it, it was obviously a poor community, but rich in at least one sense, that of the beadle, who introduced himself as David ben Abraham, a man who said he was fluent in many languages including English. Fluency, the Sokolovski family was to learn, had a different meaning in Sanaa than elsewhere in the world. While DbA's English had a similar grammatical make-up to that of Count Sokolovski's, his self-constructed vocabulary way exceeded that of the Count's. Also, from his energy level, Ari and Morrie believed he was on some natural product that gave him a high.

It took David a whole three minutes to explain when, and where Jews had lived in Sanaa continually for the last 2,500 years.

In/out, in/out was not a procreative explanation, but David's apparently accurate itinerary of Sanaa's Jewish population.

"In citadel, out citadel, in Ghumdan Palace, out Ghumdan Palace, in Falayhi Quarter, out Falayhi Quarter. Now 6th Century. You understandable? In al-Quzali out al-Quzali, in al-Sa'ilah, out al-Sa'ilah. Now 1679. Then able build New Jewish quarter. Right? Should be quarter or half? No mattering, in al-'Ulufi and out to Jerusalem. You Jerusalem?" Jenna answered this with a nod, thus opening up the proverbial 4th dimension.

Imploring the family to "wait" about fifteen times, David ran out of the synagogue, returning shortly with a woman a little younger than him and four children aged between two and six. Three of them went one each to the girls, raised their arms, and said "Up," which got the required response. The fourth went to Elize, who also got the message.

"My families," David said proudly, ushering Maimon's out of the synagogue and back onto their army truck. David, his wife and children joined the Sokolovski family on the British Government property.

"We decendations from mighty Jehonadab," David announced, expecting this information to open whatever doors needed to be opened.

Maimon leaned into the driver's cab and told "Cobra" not to start the engine until instructed by him. Then Maimon reclaimed his seat.

David mimicked starting the engine, with appropriate noises for a four-cylinder Austin, and turned an imaginary steering wheel this way and that, pointing ahead and shouting "Jerusalem" to the driver. No one moved for ten minutes, including the children, who were obviously well-schooled in this act.

"You no Americanos. Americanos much shouting and jumpable up, jump- able down."

Wondering how much ransom he would have to pay to release his family, Maimon explained with many hand signals that their boat was full. David said OK, his family would sleep on deck. Maimon mimicked being handcuffed and David lay on the floor of the truck with his hands together, snoring.

Having enough of this charade, Maimon said "How much?" which David immediately understood and answered, "£1,000." After a lengthy negotiation they agreed on £5, which Maimon gave David, who jumped off the truck and waved goodbye to his wife and children. The Sokolovski family burst out laughing.

"What is your freedom worth?" Max asked his father, and by way of reply was given £30, which Max put in his pocket before hopping down onto the dusty road and going to stand in the shade of a large mud wall. David joined him, and in due course was followed by his wife and children. The money handed over, Max climbed back onto the truck, whose driver got the OK to start the engine.

"How much do you think the woman got?" Colleen asked Morrie.

"You mean his wife?"

"That wasn't his wife. Maybe his unmarried sister," Colleen replied, and then answering the next question before it was asked, said, "No rings."

"That doesn't happen very often, Dad," Morrie pointed out.

"Not very often," Maimon said, still smiling at the successful sting.

Back on the boat the three girls excused themselves from dinner, and when Maimon mentioned something about "Gypo tummy" caused by the water in these parts, Max and Morrie exchanged glances. Later that night Maimon found letter "#12" waiting on his pillow, which Elize happily read to him.

My Dear worldly naïve man of my dreams, both those when I am asleep and also those when I am awake.

Today is one of the happiest days of your life, and amazingly you don't know it, or won't until you have read this letter.

For the past couple of weeks, you have been, and still are, a ZTB. Mazal Tov.[146]

Your ever-loving OTB,
Elize

Maimon, lying on the bed, looked up at Elize smiling. For one of the few times in their married lives, and even before that, Elize knew something that her encyclopaedic husband didn't, and she was going to enjoy the moment.

"Alright O. What is the 'TB'?"

"Why don't you think about it overnight?" Elize said, still smiling, knowing that Maimon wouldn't get a minute's sleep until he knew what the letters stood for.

"Fine," he said picking up a magazine, turning the pages without looking at the pictures.

"I'll go to sleep," he heard from the other side of the bed as Elize switched off her table-light. "Goodnight. Sleep well."

The silence didn't last very long. "You can't do this to me," he said.

More silence.

"I'll give you a Zelda lesson."

"I have got a headache," Elize told him.

Then Maimon remembered the two words that he used many years ago to pry a secret out of Elize.

"Here comes the tickle monster," he growled, ripping the covers off her bed.

That did the trick. "OK. OK. I will tell you." Elize blurted out,

---

146 Congratulations

laughing already. "O is for 'Ouma.' Three times, or maybe more, if the du Toit genes are working."

It took Maimon a few seconds to digest this news, and while he did Elize added, "Zaida,[147] give me a kiss."

He did, and held her tightly. It was a day neither of them would ever forget.

---

147 *Grandpa in Yiddish*

CHAPTER 67

SOME PALESTINIAN SURPRISES

The *MV Colchester* made her way so slowly up the Red Sea that Maimon wondered if her fuel tanks were virtually empty, requiring the Chief Engineer to run the engines on an economy setting. On the one hand, Maimon was in no hurry; on the other, he was impatient to set foot on the Holy Land. The boat was scheduled to stop at Aqaba, the most northern port of the Red Sea, captured by the British towards the end of the Great War.

Eventually they docked. Customs and Immigration Port officials swarmed aboard to inspect the passenger list, the ship's cargo and manifest, Health Papers, and the Main Ship's Log. Duly satisfied, the passengers were permitted to disembark, and board a coach on the railway built by the Saudis and paid for by the Ottoman Empire. Maimon had been in many trains during the past few years, and this one came closest to the Russian coach that first carried him out of Saratov.

Half the journey would be through the Sinai Desert, and while none of the family had been in a desert before, it was as dry and stony as they were warned would be the case. The distance to Jerusalem was about 150 miles, and when they finally arrived just after six p.m., no one was disappointed at having to get off the train. Jenna and Serena were concerned that the shaking and jolting might be bad for their babies, but Colleen assured them to the contrary, that babies like movement.

The American Colony Hotel had sent a bus to collect the family, and as it wound its way through Jerusalem's little streets, none of them actually believed that they were, at last, in the city where the two temples once stood. Jews, Christians, and Arabs thronged the streets, and Maimon even saw what he later learned were about fifteen Tibetan monks down a little side alley. After about twenty minutes they arrived at the hotel, where Serena was first out of the bus and into the lobby. There she spotted her parents reading. Walking over quietly, she said, "Hello Mom, hello Dad."

Alberto and Malka jumped up as one and hugged their daughter, who they had missed much more than they believed was possible. So happy that their London arguments about Max were now forgotten, Serena joined her parents, crying tears of happiness.

By this time Jenna, who knew Serena's parents, and Colleen, who didn't, as well as Elize, had joined the little Alfombra family.

"Have you heard the wonderful news?" Elize asked Malka, and as it was apparent that she hadn't, Elize added, "We are going to be grandmothers."

That brought more hugs and tears, not only from Elize, but from Colleen and Jenna as well.

Alberto went over to the reception counter, where Maimon and the boys were checking in, and gave him a hug and a "Mazaltov" kiss on both cheeks.

Colleen caught Maimon's eye, and with a nod of her head indicated that she would like him to join her at a table in the corner of the room. At first Colleen didn't say anything. Maimon waited until she did.

"I am sorry to ask you this now – I have tried to find a quiet moment, but in our family they don't happen very often – so I hope this is OK."

"Of course, it is," Maimon assured her, apologizing for his unavailability, and offering her an orange juice.

Coming straight to the point, Colleen said, "As you know, my father is dead, and in his absence, I need someone to give me away. I know it doesn't make sense for you to do so, being Morrie's father, but there is no one else I can ask."

Maimon quickly realized that there were times for jokes and time for surprises, and a woman's wedding day was neither of them. Taking Colleen's hand in his, he said, "You and I have been thinking about this problem for a long time. I have a solution, which I should have mentioned to you when I thought of it. And then I should have asked your permission to invite this man, and for not doing so, I also apologize. Had you not told me of the high regard in which you hold him, I would never have done so.

Colleen looked at Maimon, smiling gratefully.

"Rabbi Herzog from Ireland," Maimon said.

Colleen dropped her head so that Maimon couldn't see her tears of gratitude, but when they splashed onto the glass tabletop, he knew he had done the right thing. Unobtrusively, he pulled a handkerchief out of his pocket and slipped it into her hand.

The tears wiped away, Maimon was told, "You are an amazing man. I don't know whether your children appreciate what they have, but I do, and I pray that in some way I can repay some of the many kindnesses you and Elize have extended to me. I don't know what I have done to deserve them, but every night I thank God for Morrie and his family."

"The rabbi is in his room. Number 232. Why don't you go up and see him."

Colleen squeezed Maimon's hand, kissed him on the cheek, and then ran to the stairwell, bounding up the steps two at a time.

In room 242 Serena was not convinced that her parents were as excited about her pregnancy as she was. The Pintos were not coming to her wedding, in fact none of her parent's friends were, but word would get back about her condition, and that would be embarrassing. Serena tried to get her parents to see her pregnancy in perspective, but they were immovable.

"You must understand Serena, it is difficult for me," Alberto said.

"It is only difficult because you make it so. It is your call, Dad. You don't need any of those bozos you call your friends. You tell me you have enough money. Come to Africa. You have worked hard enough for long enough. Please tell me that you will think about it."

In the absence of any response at all, Serena continued.

"Let's talk about the wedding. Where would you like it held? The options include on the beach, on top of Masada, in Jerusalem, at the Rothschild Wine Estate, or wherever else works for you. We are all going out for dinner tonight to some Arab restaurant that is reputedly particularly good, and it would be great if you came along, especially as we are short of parents."

Later that night the extended family met at the restaurant for what turned out to be an outstanding meal. Unfortunately, the Count was refused entry to the country, and in his absence Maimon made a short speech.

"Relations and friend – and what a friend he is: the Chief Rabbi of Ireland, no less. If someone had told me twenty-five years ago that I would be having dinner in Jerusalem with my amazing wife and three of our four wonderful children, and their spouses, I would have asked if the sun was also rising in the west. Sadly, Alison ..."

Maimon's speech was interrupted by the family chanting, "Bring her in, clap, bring her in, clap, bring her in, clap," each stanza being louder than the one before. After stanza number ten, when the whole restaurant had joined in, Morrie put his hand up for silence, and after the room eventually quietened down, he stood on a chair and shouted out, "Ladies and Gentlemen, I have great pleasure in presenting... Mr. and Mrs. Daniel Rackson."

Maimon and Elize looked at each other frowning, and then saw Alison carried into the room on Max's shoulders, and Daniel on Ari's. From that moment on, and for the next forty minutes, chaos reigned. Alison, happily back on terra firma, made her way to her parents, kissed and hugged them both, introduced Daniel, and then got pulled away to meet Colleen. Speaking was out of the question, and shouting wasn't much better, so Maimon gesticulated for Elize to sit on his lap, and that is where she stayed for the next hour or so, their faces stuck in permanent smiles. With both Maimon and Elize suffering from noise-induced headaches, Maimon handed Alison a note reading: *We are going back to room 440 at the hotel. When you return, knock loudly on our door no matter what the time. XXX.*

Out in the street Maimon and Elize kissed, hugged, and got into a taxi, both insisting that they had no idea Alison was coming to Jerusalem, let alone married. At 7:45 the next morning, a rather tired knock, knock was heard in the senior Sokolovskis' room, and when Maimon opened the door, an exhausted Alison collapsed into his arms. Daniel was just behind her and made it to a big armchair, into which he crashed and fell asleep.

Leaving Alison on their bed and Daniel in the armchair, Maimon and Elize showered, dressed, and went down to the dining room, where Serena's parents and Rabbi Herzog were enjoying a typical Jewish Palestine breakfast.

Two by two the children came down, and when all except Daniel and Alison had arrived, the story came out. Sabra Daniel was a professor of Jewish Antiquities at The Hebrew University – "so young and already a professor," Malka commented – and had visited Rabbi Schechter at the Gezina in Cairo for a week. Two months later, working closely with Alison, and apparently more closely as time elapsed, Daniel returned to the university because had he not done so, he would have been let go.

A few weeks after that, Alison resigned her job with Rabbi Schechter, enrolled for a course in Jewish Antiquities at the university, and at Daniel's parents' insistence, moved into their large apartment. Married? No one thought so, largely because Alison wasn't wearing any rings, but with Sabras[148], who knows? Later it transpired they weren't married, but as her siblings were doing so, she and Daniel decided they might as well also tie the knot.

Maimon asked those who were getting married to come to the café on the corner at five that afternoon, in a position to tell him and Elize when and where their ceremony, and the subsequent reception, would take place. That said, he left for a meeting with Meir Dizengoff. When the last of her family finished breakfast, just after one o' clock, Elize went upstairs and wrote a somewhat belated letter "#12."

> *My Dearest unforeseeable Maimon,*
>
> *I don't think "unforeseeable" is the right word, what I mean is a person whose actions cannot be foreseen. Every now and then I pinch myself just to make sure I am not in one giant expandable dream. You said last night, in your interrupted speech, that you would never have thought as a teenager in Saratov you would one day be dining with your wife and four children, and their husbands and wives, in Jerusalem.*
>
> *I never expected to get out of the Orange Free State, and here I am, with a wonderful family, a husband whom I don't have words to describe, in Jerusalem, having almost sailed right around the world. Many years ago, you taught me to be observant, and it is one of the greatest lessons one can learn. Had you not mentioned it, I would have missed so much in life.*
>
> *The other big lesson for which I have you to thank, is to be generous of spirit. It is what you call the half-empty/ half-full glass – which I must admit I didn't understand when first you used that saying. I have tried, and largely*

---

succeeded, in impressing on the children how important this is.

On the subject of children, I am worried about Colleen. She is the only one who doesn't have parents here. I know it was wonderful of you to have brought Rabbi Herzog to give her away, but as great as it is to have him here, he is a poor substitute for her own parents. Sometimes I notice Colleen looking into space, with a sad mournful expression, and so I decided to make an extra special effort with her, and it would be nice if you did, too.

I set aside some time to speak to Serena's parents, and for people who live in the center of London, they are very insular. I always thought that a ghetto was where poor people lived, but they live in a rich ghetto. The Syrian Jewish community is very inward-looking, and Malka mentioned that some of its members would go into mourning if one of their children married outside it. I am sure she was referring to Max. I had it on the tip of my tongue to say that instead of sitting shiva they should go into a madhouse – there is a nicer way of saying that – a lunatic asylum.

Have you come to a decision about Ari and the business? He gets on well with the boys, but I wonder sometimes if it is an act. What do you think? He dotes on Jenna, and she on him, but man cannot live on love alone. He is lucky to be alive, and if our boys hadn't tossed him over that crack in the ground, he would have been burnt to a cinder. Max mentioned that Ari never thanked him, and Morrie voiced similar sentiments, not that they wanted thanks, but Morrie said it just seemed strange. We were going to dine at his parents' house, but that fell through. Perhaps we should get off the boat in Cape Town instead of Durban and accept their invitation if it is still extended. We could go out to the farm and see if everything is alright there. What do you think?

We must also make an effort to see Daniel's parents, not only because it is the right thing to do, but because doing so one gets a good idea about the home Daniel comes from. I don't mean if they have expensive furniture or not, but how they relate to one another.

Time marches on – what a stupid expression, time doesn't march anywhere, it just ticks, but that wouldn't have sounded so good, would it? – and Colleen and I have some shopping to do. By this I mean Colleen needs some dresses, and I am going to say if they make her look good or not. Remember that Jewish custom you told me about, which has the father of the bride putting some money under his daughter's pillow. Rabbi Herzog said he had never heard of it. If it wasn't a custom then, it is now, and when I told Colleen about it, she was bowled over.

So, my lover, and inventor of customs, I must end off. I hope your meeting with Meir D. went well, and if you bought some more land here without asking me, that is OK. I am sure you remember how you wound me up in the old Hights Hotel in your negotiations with M.D. last time.

I do love you so much, and am counting the hours till we are together again. I wonder how many couples who have been married for as long as we have, are as in love with one another as we are.

Take care.

Your loving partner,
Elize

Maimon made it back in time for the meeting at five o'clock, where he found Elize waiting for him. The two of them being the only ones in the coffee house, their children on holiday time. Half an hour later they had all arrived, and while Maimon found their disregard for his time annoying, he decided not to mention it. In the scheme of four weddings, it was small potatoes.

After their children had told Maimon and Elize where they would like to get married – Morrie and Colleen at sunset at the top of Masada, Max and Serena at the Rothschild Wine Estate, Daniel and Alison at the kibbutz where he grew up, and Ari and Jenna in a floodlit quarry outside Jerusalem at midnight – Maimon had something to say.

"Your mother and I wish and pray that your marriages are as happy as ours are, and that all last for many, many decades. While we are told that marriages are made in heaven, the facts of life are that they are lived on earth. Sadly, as we have all observed, for one reason or another, they don't all last.

"With this in mind, we have decided that both parties to all our children's marriages need to sign a pre-chupa prenup, which is the legal shorthand for an agreement that states that should a marriage break up, each party takes out of it whatever financially they have contributed, both before the wedding and after it. Should either party fail to sign this agreement, then together they will not get one penny from your mother and from me. This is not something that has to be discussed, it is a black-and-white yes or no. Going round the table, Serena, yes or no?"

"I think it is fair" she said. "I have no problem signing such an agreement."

"Nor do I," Colleen added quickly.

"And neither do I," Daniel said.

Everyone looked at Ari, who advised Maimon that he would like to think about it.

Maimon said to Jenna, "In the business world that is a polite way of saying no."

Not wishing to air their dirty washing in public, Jenna hissed at Ari, "Come up to the room now" as she ran upstairs. Ari followed a few yards behind, and as soon as their bedroom door was closed, Jenna rounded on him.

"What exactly do you mean 'think about it'?"

"Just that. It is a big decision that shouldn't be taken lightly."

"Is there anything else you are thinking about, that I should know?" Jenna asked, looking her fiancé straight in the eye.

"No, nothing," Ari replied, concerned where this conversation was leading.

"Not even using our family money to bail out your bankrupt father?"

"How can you say a thing like that?" Ari asked, acting all hurt. "My father isn't bankrupt."

"What about the £50,000 he owes the bookies that he can't pay?"

"Who told you that? It isn't true!"

"Ari, I want a yes or no on the prenup in ten seconds, starting now," Jenna said, looking at her watch.

"Come on, sweetheart. This isn't how we discuss things," Ari said, forcing a smile. No longer the smooth-talking. confident young man, he reached out to Jenna, and then realizing that, like his face, the palm of his hand was wet with nervous sweat, he quickly withdrew it. His father's battle lost, Ari realized he was now fighting to save his marriage, his career and possibly his future. Pleading, he said with false bravado, "We haven't got that kind of relationship. Let's talk about it."

Looking daggers at Ari, Jenna said, "Your time is up, and our engagement is off. When I come back here in fifteen minutes, I want you and all your clothes out of here."

Saying which, she walked out of their bedroom, closing the door quietly behind her. What Jenna didn't say was that if she found any of Ari's possessions in what was now her room, she would throw them out of the window. Smiling, she rejoined the table, taking the seat that she had vacated next to her mother a few minutes earlier.

The conversation was about the "after-the-weddings' party," and the thinking was that they would have a combined festivity on the Tel Aviv beach with a live band, finger food, and free drinks.

"You OK with that?" Morrie asked Jenna.

"Absolutely," she replied smiling, taking a folded piece of paper out of her handbag, and handing it to her mother. Elize read the cable that had inadvertently been handed to Jenna by one of the bellmen:

FURTHER EARLIER ADVICE ACS FATHER DECLARED BANKRUPT ALLEGEDLY OWING BOOKIES FIFTY THOUSAND POUNDS REGRET BUT THOUGHT YOU SHOULD KNOW REGARDS CHARLES

Elize winked at her daughter, who winked back, whispering, "Like rotten meat, it is off."

A few minutes later Elize said quietly, "Stay here, I am going to tell your father."

Elize squeezed Maimon's shoulder, which was their code for "Get up. I want to tell you something," and when he did, and out of sight of the YPs, Elize read Maimon the cable. Back at the table they noticed Jenna had left.

"We should go and check that she is alright," Elize said anxiously, worried that her emotionally pummelled daughter might be in tears.

Thankfully Jenna wasn't crying, instead she was happily cutting the trouser legs and jacket arms off Ari's blazer, trousers, and two suits, and then tossing all the parts out the window, together with his circumcised ties. This was followed by all of his left shoes, the right ones being stashed in a laundry bag, ready to be thrown out with the garbage overnight.

"You want to talk about it?" Maimon asked.

"Not really. I knew there was something wrong when, as soon as I told him I was pregnant, his attitude changed towards me when just the two of us were together. He was uncaring and indifferent towards me and lately cruel. Not physically, but in some of the things he said were really horrible. Of course, I am sorry," Jenna continued, "But better I found out about it now, rather than after the wedding."

Colleen, Serena, and Alison, leaving the hotel for a girls' walk, witnessed an amazing sight: Ari searching frantically for a right shoe, any right shoe, in the hotel's car park, finding instead many clothes' arms and legs, to the amusement of a growing crowd of spectators.

Later that night Maimon visited him in the windowless room he was sharing with three Arab kitchen staff, who fortunately were on duty, so the two of them had the privacy their discussion warranted.

"What is this?" Ari asked, looking at a piece of paper Maimon handed him. "I don't owe Jenna £100,000."

"Actually, you do. It is called alimony."

Ari looked at Maimon for an escape route, not finding one.

"Let me explain. Alimony is the screwing you get for the screwing you gave. Either you sign this document right now, or it will be replaced by one for £200,000 tomorrow, or one for £300,000 the day after, and so on, and so on."

"You have got no proof," Ari shot back "And anyway we aren't married."

"I have an affidavit from your wife, Dafna, so among your other problems, you will also be charged with bigamy."

Now visibly squirming, Ari clenched both his fists and lowered his head, so that all he could see was the room's almost worn out dirty brown linoleum floor covering. Like a boxer in his corner waiting for the bell to herald a further onslaught, Ari braced himself for what he knew was coming.

"Your other problems are that you have been kiting checks, which you surely know is a criminal offence. And if that isn't bad enough, after getting Dafna's sister drunk, you took advantage of her sexually."

Ari turned a paler shade of white. He tried to speak, but the fight had gone out of his voice.

"As for your marriage to Jenna in Hawaii," Maimon continued "I have the official certificate from the Big Kahuna, who I am sure you remember. So, are you going to sign the £100,000 agreement tonight, or the £200,000 one tomorrow? Or do I get a judgement for a million pounds enforced against you when I get back to South Africa? I understand you know that we Sokolovskis are a ten-second-decision family. Sign it in ten seconds and I will be gone. Leave it until tomorrow and it is £200,000. I have the higher value contract in my pocket."

Maimon waited the agreed time and then took the contract back.

"Give it to me. I will sign it," Ari said, grabbing the divorce paper.

"Not so fast, Harold Abrahams," Maimon reminded him. "We need two witnesses."

Maimon stuck his head round the door, holding two £5 notes, and in minutes the document was signed and witnessed. "I will pay for your share of this room tonight, but from tomorrow you are on your own," Maimon said, getting up. Just before walking out he said to Ari, "Good luck. You are going to need it."

CHAPTER 68

THE WEDDINGS

Relating his evening's discussions to Jenna and Elize, Maimon had some questions to answer. How did he know Dafna, and how much did he have to pay her to sign the affidavit?

"I don't know her and I didn't pay her anything. She came to the office looking for Ari, and when she learned that he was overseas, she told Saul her story. Wisely, he took her to Edward's office, where she signed an affidavit setting out all the sordid details, which Saul cabled to me this morning."

"One last question. Who read the cable to you?" Elize asked.

"The girl cleaning our room. She thanked me not only for the tip I gave her, but also for the opportunity to improve her English."

"I must hand it to you," Elize said to Jenna, "you did a good job on his pants and jackets, and also on all the ties that he bought in New York. I wouldn't have thought of that."

The other YPs, particularly the girls, were characteristically supportive of Jenna, especially when Colleen mentioned that Ari had made a pass at her. She had slapped him as hard as she could on the side of his face whose jaw was broken, necessitating another visit to the doctor to rewire it. Unfortunately, the doctor had given away his last bottle of pain killers.

The weddings went off largely as planned, with everyone attending all three riding from one to another singing songs in between. Alberto and Malka got a lesson in Zionism from Daniel's parents, who told them that they also had Syrian relations, most of them living in New York and Los Angeles. Rabbi Herzog and Colleen reminisced about growing up in Ireland, and the boys about their years at See Da View. Inevitably, the girls got on to the subject of babies, and Colleen, Jenna, and Alison were amazed to hear that Serena's parents had not yet booked a cabin on a boat to South Africa. How could they miss their grandchild's bris or baby-naming? Even thinking of doing so was heresy. Once again, Serena realized what a wonderful family she was marrying into.

The beach party was even better than expected with uninvited sabras joining in, helping to ensure that the caterers took away as little food as possible. Word of the party got out to the Charedi community, who came in their droves, and in doing so brought their own special vibe and action, including those of their wives and daughters, who organized separate horas[149] and other dances. "Not quite London, old chap," one of their senior community leaders, dressed as an aristocratic Pole from times long gone, said to Alberto. This was lost on the Syrian Jew who was concentrating so hard on maintaining his grip on the shoulders of the man in front of him, that he missed making an appropriate response.

Just after midnight, when the band was taking a break, Daniel helped Colleen onto one of the trestle tables and handed her a microphone. On an evening devoid of speeches, one of the brides about to make one resulted in a hush overcoming the almost 150 revellers.

Colleen looked down at her new family bunched around Maimon, smiled, and took a deep breath. She knew it wouldn't be easy, but she had rehearsed it well, and if nothing else, she knew the words.

"A few of us got married in Hawaii last month," Colleen began. "It was not your usual Jewish wedding. In fact, it was hardly Jewish at all. There was just one thing Jewish about it, apart from our family, and that was a Polynesian male choir singing Baruch Haba."

Knowing what was coming, Elize and the children moved closer to Maimon.

"After the wedding, when we were back on the boat, I went looking for Maimon, to thank him for the most wonderful day he had given Elize and us children. Unusually, I found him in the bar, and more unusually on his third vodka. Unbeknownst to me, he had told the others he wanted to be alone."

The guests, those invited and uninvited, realized this was not going to be a humorous speech.

"I thanked Maimon, and he smiled, and … and he started to tell me

---

149   *A single-gender circular dance that originated in the Balkans*

something, and then he stopped. I asked him if he wanted me to leave, and he shook his head."

Elize hugged one of Maimon's arms and Jenna the other one.

"We sat together, in silence, for about ten minutes, till he was ready. Then he told me. It was something I realized he had not told another human being."

The waves quietened down, seemingly in respect to this man who had overcome so many hardships in life.

"The Jewish community, where Maimon grew up, is desperately poor. Children don't have shoes, adults don't have coats, and rarely do they have enough to eat. Except on wedding nights. Then everyone, young and old, poor and poorer, sing together Baruch HaBa, and there is enough food for everyone."

The guests looked at Colleen as if hypnotized.

"One day, when Maimon was five years old, he asked a little girl to marry him. He was hungry, had practiced Baruch Haba, he told her, and was ready to be her husband."

Colleen swallowed. This was the hard part. She had practised it, but …

"Little Rochi told him she wouldn't marry him, and neither would any girl in Saratov, because he was stupid. Her mother told her that."

Elize and Alison and Jenna held Maimon tightly, as if to stop a giant wave carrying him away to the land where no one got married.

"Maimon has known for the past thirty five years that no one would sing Baruch Haba for him, and no one has. And that is why," Colleen continued, tears now streaming down her face, "Maimon organized a choir of Polynesians to sing it for Jenna and Ari, and for Max and Serena, and for Morrie and me."

Almost finished, in more ways than one, Colleen continued, "Just because no one would sing it for me, Maimon had said, doesn't mean they couldn't sing it for my children, which is why he went to the trouble he did to get a crowd of South Sea Islanders, who had never heard a word of Hebrew in their lives, to sing Baruch Haba. For us."

Maimon smiled, having no idea what was coming.

"God sometimes gives us a second chance," Colleen said, smiling through her tears at the man she had come to love as her father. "And tonight he has."

From behind the bandstand, firstly very softly, and then a bit louder, and then louder still, Maimon heard the voices of the Polynesian Minyan, as he called it, led by the Big Kahuna.

Two wooden chairs appeared. Maimon was seated on one and Elize on the other. Then both chairs were lifted, one corner of a man's handkerchief held by Maimon, and the other by Elize, while all the guests sung Baruch Haba at the tops of their voices.

Still today, over 100 years later, they tell the story of that night on the Tel Aviv beach when Baruch Haba was sung for a man who couldn't read or write, and his wife who loved him as Juliet loved Romeo.

Every hour Maimon kicked in another two hundred shekels to keep the band playing, until at four a.m. the band, dancers, guests, married couples and two British policemen who had been sent to quieten things down, all collapsed close to exhaustion. Rather than face the long ride back to Jerusalem or to the kibbutz, Maimon had booked some rooms in a beachside hotel, making a note to find out if they were paying him rent, as they should have been doing.

Next morning the family surfaced for brunch and the inevitable post-mortems on the truly unforgettable triple wedding-day before. Was David Ben Gurion really at Max's and Serena's wedding? And Ze'ev Jabotinsky at Morrie's and Colleens? They must have been, because who else was Maimon talking to for such extended periods?

CHAPTER 69

GOING HOME

Meeting up with the family for sundowner drinks, Maimon told them that he had booked berths on the *Oriental Star* leaving from Aqaba on Sunday a week.

"Your mother's and my plans are to spend some time in the north," Maimon informed the younger generation, "visit the Kineret lake – the Sea of Galilee, to those who haven't bought an atlas recently – take in some beach time in Tel Aviv, do some walking tours of Jerusalem, visit Petra with Daniel and Alison, and end up in Aqaba in time to catch the boat on the twelfth."

"Did you know about this?" Alison asked Daniel, still getting used to being married. She and Daniel had discussed and agreed months ago, that in the years ahead they would have children and get married, and at the time Alison was too busy to think about either. Not that she was thinking now about having children, but being married to Daniel gave her a nice warm feeling inside. She couldn't really explain it, and so didn't feel comfortable telling Jenna or her sisters-in-law, but it did make her feel good, really good. Alison smiled and squeezed Daniel's hand, and held it against her heart, so that some of her overflowing love could get into his body, by a kind of osmosis.

"No, but any excuse to go to Petra is fine with me."

The family then entered into a general and wide-ranging discussion on who wanted to go where when, and as Maimon and Elize had decided to join whichever tours appealed to them, they excused themselves and quietly set off to find one of the restaurants their hotel had recommended.

With only one or two exceptions, the family spent all nine days touring together, Maimon and Elize passing up the opportunity of climbing Masada in the dark to see the sun rising behind the Judean mountains.

Sitting on the beach and wondering how long it would take man to convert the sun's light into energy, Maimon was delighted when Alison and Daniel plopped themselves down on the sand next to him and Elize.

"I am so excited to show Daniel South Africa," Alison said. "The Hebrew University gave him compassionate leave for a honeymoon."

"My parents are quite jealous," Daniel told Maimon and Elize. "My moth- er asked me to look down when I walk, and to give her any diamonds I find. My father said a baby lion cub would be a nice present, which he would give to the zoo when it grew up."

Elize realized that once back in Johannesburg, she would be full-on, first getting the house straight, and then helping with three nurseries; and after the babies were born, she would be a triple Ouma. It still wasn't clear if Serena's parents would come out, and if so when, and anyway Elize couldn't imagine Malka changing nappies, let alone getting down on all fours looking for some colored wooden toy that had rolled under the couch. Jenna would need a good dollop of TLC, and Elize wanted Colleen to feel special and cherished. For this she had inspanned Maimon, who was only too happy to help, especially because he was particularly fond of Colleen. Picking up on Elize's suggestion, he found some special time for her every day on the boat.

At dinner on the first night, the YPs had agreed that they would go ashore at every port, as who knew when they would be in a position to do so again. After the first port of call this decision was reversed, it being agreed that their time could more enjoyably be spent at, and in, the boat's swimming pool, napping, and washing their "smalls," which, because of the babies, Maimon pointed out, should more correctly be called their "bigs."

One evening at sunset, when the boat was anchored off the Eritrean port of Mitsiwa, and the family sipping Singapore Slings were watching the crew hoisting fresh vegetables and fruit aboard, Alison quietly slipped away. Minutes later she returned smiling, carrying a large, thinnish, brown paper parcel which she put on her father's lap. Maimon looked up at her waiting for an explanation.

"It is for the man who has everything." Alison told him. "For whom it is near impossible to find a present he will treasure."

Intrigued, Maimon unwrapped the gift to find a double sided framed document, one side of which contained an old letter written in Hebrew, and the other, a typed paragraph of Roman letters. Knowing he could read neither, Alison explained.

"Among the documents we found in the Genizah was this letter," she said, pointing to the Hebrew side, and then waiting dramatically for a couple of seconds, added, "From Moses ben Maimon."

"Maimonides himself?" Morrie asked, realizing how rare it must be.

Alison nodded, took it back from her father, and read the Roman letter sentences.

"The greatest misfortune that has befallen me during my entire life – worse than anything else – was the demise of the saint, may his memory be blessed, who drowned in the Indian sea, carrying much money belonging to me, to him, and to others, and left with me a little daughter and a widow. On the day I received that terrible news I fell ill and remained in bed for about a year, suffering from a sore boil, fever, and depression, and was almost given up. About eight years have passed, but I am still mourning and unable to accept consolation. And how should I console myself? He grew up on my knees, he was my brother, and he was my student."

"He was writing about his brother," Alison explained, "who was drowned when the ship he was on from Egypt to India, sank en route.

"That was tragic," Serena remarked, imagining what it must have been like bringing up his dead brother's daughter.

"We also know about tragic" Elize said, looking at Maimon, who swallowed, cleared his throat and said, "Maybe it would be wise if you and your children and grandchildren did not burden any of our descendants with my name." And then to brighten things up he added, "Like hemispheres, two are enough."

Remembering from cheder all those years ago that Moses came down from Mount Sinai with two tablets, he was going to use that instead of the hemispheres, but as the tablets got smashed, he decided not to.

Intrigued by what else Alison might have found, Morrie said, "Alison, tell us about the Geniza. Was it what you expected?"

"Nothing about the Geniza was what I expected. Before we were allowed within five miles of the Ben Ezra synagogue, where the Geniza was, Solomon had to earn the confidence of Cairo's chief rabbi."

"Didn't you have a letter of introduction from the Chief Rabbi of London to his Cairo counterpart?" Colleen asked.

"We did, and that got us in the proverbial door," Alison started, "to the library of the Rabbi himself, Aaron Raphael Ben Shim'on. There we spent many hours that stretched into days, smoking cigarettes and drinking coffee, until Solomon's patient naturing won the rabbi's trust. Only then he summoned his carriage and took us to one of Cairo's oldest synagogues."

"Was there a secret trapdoor?" Serena asked, imagining how excited Alison and Solomon must have been, about to see the thousands of documents they had heard about for so long.

"Exactly the opposite," Alison told her. "At the end of one of the galleries was an opening high in the wall, accessible only by ladder. Solomon climbed up with a lamp and peered into a windowless and doorless room. When his eyes got accustomed to the dim light, he made out stacks of books and papers, manuscripts, and printed texts tossed in at random. This had been done for over 800 years. I also had a lamp and climbed up behind him, wanting to get in and see this unique treasure trove."

"What did it look like?" Serena wanted to know, thinking that perhaps some of her ancestors' documents might be stored there.

"Piles and piles of dusty papers. Slowly, we started taking them down, and only then did we realize what a treasure chest it was. We found a letter to Dad's namesake, Moses Maimonides, from his brother, written in a Sudanese port, describing the caravan trip across from the Nile, and telling Moses not to worry about him, and that he intended to sail to India on business. That was the last that was heard of him."

"I thought you would only find prayer books," Max said, appreciating how exciting it must have been for his sister.

Remembering those wonderfully exciting days, Alison's eyes came alight, as she continued. "There was a letter from a school master about a child's bad behavior, always cursing his sister and fighting with her, and suggesting to his father that a little spanking might be a good idea. There was also a letter in Yiddish, written in 1567, from a woman in Jerusalem, to her son in Cairo, asking him to bring the grandchildren and come to see her."

"Did he?" Elize asked, looking at three bulging tummies and feeling for the unknown grandmother.

Alison's reply was drowned out by the combined noise of the *Oriental Star's* anchor being raised, and the ship's bell summoning them to dinner.

When the *MV Oriental Star* docked in *Lourenço* Marques, the largest port in Mozambique, it was pouring with rain, and Inhaca Island could not be seen, so Maimon and Elize decided it was far better to be left with their memories, and instead went to the bar at the Polana Hotel and had a drink, remembering those wonderful times they had spent on the island together.

Eventually they docked in Durban, the cold front having moved up the coast and left the city sparkling clean. Once again "first-class magic" ensured that the family were processed seamlessly through Immigration and Customs, and escorted onto the train that was awaiting all Transvaal-bound disembarking passengers. Bypassing the city, the double-coupled locomotives pulled fourteen coaches through the Valley of a Thousand Hills, up to the Natal Midlands, on to the Highveld, and finally to Johannesburg. Two little buses organized by Kris met the family on the platform, and before Colleen and Serena realized what was happening, they were pulling into the drive of See Da View.

"It is not a hotel," Max explained to his similar-aged in-laws. "Even though some people think it looks like one."

While the girls gazed up in amazement, the archaeologist wondered what researchers in a thousand years' time would make of this wedding cake-like structure.

CHAPTER 70

A DARK HORSE

Kaylah rushed out to see them, as did the staff. Eva was first to arrive, then Alpheus, followed by Daniel the driver, two gardeners, and finally Perdman, who looked after the horses. Even though Sarah had outgrown Katya, Maimon had agreed to keep her for the babies, in appreciation of which Sarah promised to teach them to ride.

Max's and Morrie's homecoming was another step in their evolving lives and already on the boat the brothers and their wives had discussed the pros and cons of buying a house as opposed to building a custom-designed one, and in either event, where, and on what sized piece of land.

For Jenna it was hugely different. With a heavy heart she made her way to the suite that Maimon had ensured was as big, and identically furnished, as those of her brothers, but there was no escaping the fact that they were couples, and she wasn't. She had left with such high hopes. With a man she loved, or thought she did, and had come home an about to be unmarried mother. Without a father her baby might grow up to be a monster. She was sure her brothers would involve her child in all the activities they organized for theirs. That gave her a glimmer of hope, until she realized that at six o'clock she and her child would come back to an empty house, or flat, or wherever they were living. Jenna sat on her bed and wept.

At first, she didn't see it. Taking in the Swedish-design, built-in, light-colored wood cupboards, matching table and chairs, vanity unit … then she did.

On the bedside table was a crystal vase with a dozen deep red roses. For a fleeting second Jenna speculated that they might be from Ari, but quickly discarded that idea. Under the vase was an envelope with her name on it, and inside a note in handwriting she recognized but could not identify. It read, "A new dawn is breaking on the most wonderful time of your life." No signature. Jenna looked at the flowers and tried to work it out. Her parents wouldn't have done this, and neither would her brothers, or Alison. One person would know. Eva.

"It was Mr Joshua," she told Jenna.

Of all the people … Jenna's mind scrolled back to her earliest memory. She must have been about three of four, and desperate for a ride on Sarah's pony. Joshua had picked her up, put her in the saddle, made sure her little feet reached the stirrups and then held her tight while leading Katya round the paddock. Joshua had pulled out of his school's football team to take her home after her first day at school. She didn't think about it at the time, but why would a fifteen-year-old boy do that? There were other occasions, too. Joshua always looked out for her. Once or twice, Jenna wondered if he fancied her, but Joshua never indicated that he did … and now the flowers.

"Does he still live with his mother, and Sarah?" Jenna blurted out, the first of a million questions that were flying round in her head.

"Miss Sarah married a doctor, Larry Kalishnikovsky. He only looks at people who are sick in their noses or ears. Also their throats. They are going to live in Australia."

"And Sarah's mother?"

"Miss Francine also got married. To Mr. Hymie Komorovsky. He is the man who owns the petrol station next to the Sai Woo restaurant. On my day off I sometimes see them in the shops, holding hands. They are always laughing and happy."

Eva waited to be asked about Joshua, but she wasn't, because Jenna was remembering the many times that, it seemed almost by coincidence, Joshua was there for her. The first time she swam without inflatable water wings he was poolside to make sure she didn't get into difficulties. When she fell out of a tree and broke her leg, it was Joshua who carried her to the doctor. It was always Joshua, Jenna now remembered, who picked her up after midnight from teenage parties. Other girls were collected by their parents, but Joshua insisted on taking her home. "Some of them drink on Saturday nights and shouldn't be driving," she remembered him saying.

"He is a good man," Eva said, bringing Jenna back to the present.

"Where does he live?"

"In a cottage in somebody's garden. There is always girls there cooking for him and bringing him wine. One even let the air out of her car's tyres so she had to stay in his cottage the whole night."

"How do you know all this?"

"When you and Mr. Ari went overseas, Mr. Joshua got very sick. Not in his body, in his head. He stayed in bed for weeks and weeks. I used to take him food from the big house. Only when Miss Sarah's husband gave him pills did he get better and go back to work."

"Thank you for telling me all of that."

Jenna didn't sleep well and was up early the next morning and first down for breakfast, except she wasn't the first. Sitting at the table, as if he belonged there, drinking freshly squeezed orange juice, and reading the newspaper, was Joshua. Seeing Jenna, he put the paper down, got up, and smiling, said, "Welcome home."

The boy she had grown up with, taken for granted as an older brother, was a good-looking, mature man, obviously confident with his position in life, and self-invited to breakfast.

"Thanks for the flowers," Jenna said quietly, feeling a little embarrassed. There was no reason for her to be so, she had known Joshua all her life. He was the first man to send her flowers, Jenna realized, so maybe that was why she felt as she did.

Joshua smiled by way of a reply.

In the highly specialized engineering works that Joshua built, owned, and ran, he was confident. Dealing with the banks he was confident. Negotiating with the buyers of the big mining houses he was confident, but alone with the only girl he had ever loved, it was a different story. It wasn't that he didn't enjoy the company and attractions of the fairer sex. Many girls had passed through his life, a few through his bed, and two had asked him to marry them. He fenced them all off, as nicely as he could, explaining that he wasn't ready.

Word around Johannesburg was that he couldn't commit, which was fine with him. One of the many things he had learned from Maimon was not to make the same mistake twice, and if it was the last thing he ever did, he would never let another Ari get ahead of him in the race for Jenna's heart. He had it all planned out, but would it work? Logically, he knew it should, but women didn't always react logically.

"I have planned a 'Eerooah Meyoochad' for us," Joshua said softly.

It was a long time since Jenna attended Hebrew School, and her brain frantically scrambled to remember .... Then she got it – "A Special Event."

"Us?" she said.

"You and me."

"When?"

"Tomorrow morning."

Not that Jenna knew what to expect, but if she had, this was way faster than anything she imagined. In other circumstances she might play a little hard to get. "Sorry, but I am busy tomorrow and in fact all this week. How about next Thursday?" But these weren't other circumstances, and it seemed this man loved her, possibly the first man who had truly loved her, and, after all, she wasn't sixteen anymore.

"Sure."

"You want to ride or drive there?"

"What do you recommend?"

"Riding. I'll pick you up at ten. Please apologize to your parents for my rushing away now, but I have a meeting. See you tomorrow."

One minute he was there, the next he was gone. Jenna decided not to tell anyone about her special event.

Joshua arrived the following morning in an Armstrong Sidley open-top sports model, whose engine was longer than the rest of the car.

"You don't see many of these around," Jenna shouted to make herself heard above the engine's deep-throated rumble and the air rushing through the not-very-well insulated passenger seats.

"I think it is the only one in Africa. I imported it a couple of years ago," Joshua shouted back as the speedometer touched 58 miles an hour, which felt like double that speed to Jenna.

A few minutes later Joshua pulled into the Kyalami Stables, parked his car under a lean-to, and was greeted by a smiling jockey holding the reins of two well-groomed, saddled, and bridled horses, a black one about sixteen hands tall, and a brown horse a hand or so smaller.

"Take your pick," Joshua said, climbing out of the 1920s car that was a bit of a challenge for anyone over six foot.

By way of reply, Jenna mounted the brown horse, adjusted the stirrup lengths, and began to realize that whatever Joshua had planned, it certainly was going to be a special event. He hadn't told her what lay in store, and she hadn't asked.

Across the grasslands they galloped, Joshua guiding his horse effortlessly this way and that, until the Jukskei River was in sight, when he slowed to a canter, a trot, and then a walk as they reached a large shade-providing willow tree. The day had started with a clear blue sky, but in the course of the morning, clouds had built up, as they often did in hot highveld summers.

Under the tree a large blanket had been spread, and on it a number of cushions. A few yards away was a small table with a bottle of champagne submerged in an ice bucket, a plate of cut-up raw vegetables, and a few dips to accompany them.

Joshua dismounted, tied his horse to a fallen tree, and said to the man who Jenna realized had set it all up, "Thanks, Hendrik. I will whistle when we are done." And then to Jenna, "There is a portable toilet and washing facilities behind that big termite mound."

This is really a special event, Jenna realized, wondering if some musicians were about to appear. "I'll try the washroom" she said, disappearing behind the ant heap that hid it. A minute later there was a clap of thunder.

"You alright?" Joshua called out.

Very funny, Jenna thought, combing her hair in front of the mirror next to the wash-stand. Ready for whatever Joshua had planned next, Jenna walked back to the willow tree to see him loosening the cork of a champagne bottle. The cork flew out and Joshua poured two glasses of bubbly handing one to Jenna.

"You want to propose a toast?"

"I'd rather make a wish," Jenna replied diplomatically, thinking all of this can only be heading in one direction.

"I'll make a wish, too," Joshua said. "To our wishes coming true."

Another clap of thunder, this time louder, accompanied their toast. The sky had darkened, and the distant lightening had moved closer.

"Pleased to be home?"

"It is too early to tell."

Another clap of thunder persuaded Joshua that whatever he had planned, he and Jenna had better find some shelter from what was about to be a donner-en-blitzen[150] thunderstorm, accompanied by buckets of rain. Between the thunder claps he let out a piercing whistle, untied the horses, and said, "We passed a farmhouse half a mile back. I'll race you there."

They got to the farmhouse, but not before the storm broke, drenching them from top to toe. Next to the main building were some stables, into one of which they led both horses. Standing on straw, wet and

---

150 *Thunder and lightning*

bedraggled, Jenna said, "It certainly is a eerooah meyoochad. This is the first time I go home from a date soaked to the skin."

Joshua had spent so much time and energy arranging every last detail of Plan A, that he never even considered the necessity of a Plan B. Now he had to. Joshua couldn't think of anything witty or clever to say which didn't surprise him as he wasn't very good at thinking on his feet.

"You OK?" he asked.

Jenna giggled. She knew what was coming, and she wanted to make it easier for this man who had put so many hours of planning into a day that was supposed to be perfect in every way. Instead, here they were, like two drowned rats, in a smelly horse's stable, one of the least romantic settings in the whole Transvaal. So she kissed him, not like brother and sister do, and not like cousins would, but like a lover who has been pining for her soul mate.

Joshua knew he hadn't died and gone to heaven, but after "that kiss" he would happily have flown up to meet his maker. Except that wasn't one of his options. One of them was to take out of his pocket the little jewelry box that hadn't left his possession for five days, open it up, remove the ring, and slip it onto Jenna's finger. Was that presumptuous? Yes, it was. Was he being arrogant assuming that this woman he loved wouldn't give the ring right back? Probably, yes. Was this the best shot he would have? Possibly, yes. So very slowly, without saying a word, that is what he did.

Jenna looked at the white-gold ring and the not-small diamond in its clasp, and then up at Joshua. "Why didn't you tell me? All those years ago, why didn't you say so?" Tears welling up in her eyes.

The truth was he was too shy, but that wasn't the thing to say. What he did say was, "I was waiting for the right moment, but it never came."

"You could have pulled me into a shower with some horse droppings."

"Funny. I never thought of that," Joshua said, now totally relaxed. Of course, he wanted to know if Jenna would marry him, but he didn't have to ask her. She would tell him in good time. Between now and "good time" he had to make sure the answer would be yes.

"Can I keep it and tell you later?"

"For as long as you like."

Jenna kept it for 52 years, the first two days in her underwear drawer, and the rest of the time on the fourth finger of her left hand

CHAPTER 71

THE DRIVE-INN

On the third day of his new life, the day Jenna phoned him at the office to say that she was now wearing his ring, Joshua asked her out to lunch. Jenna wanted to know what she should wear, expecting her now fiancé to have somewhere special in mind, probably one of Johannesburg's five-star hotels, she thought; but to be safe, she asked him. It was just as well.

Collecting her from See Da View in his Armstrong Sidley – Jenna told him that the two things he loved most in life were her and his car, and she hoped in that order – Joshua refused to disclose their lunch venue. He had said that unsmart clothes would be fine, and while he refused to provide the restaurant's name, he did give Jenna a clue – it was for little people, he told her. That didn't help her at all. Up Empire Place and down Louis Botha Avenue they motored, and the further they got from town, the more mystified Jenna became. Then she burst out laughing and gave Joshua a kiss as he carefully manoeuvred his beloved car over a storm drain, into the parking lot of the Doll's House. As soon as Joshua had switched off the engine, and the noise that prevented a normal conversation disappeared, a smartly dressed native appeared with a big smile and two menus.

"It's the car," Joshua said, explaining the smile. "It happens all the time."

"We eat in the car?" Jenna asked, not having seen or even heard of this kind of thing before.

"It's only been open a month or so, and as you can see it is very popular. Rumour has it the next thing will be drive-in bioscopes."

"You don't do *popular*," Jenna reminded Joshua. "So why are we here?"

"Because it is the only eating place where one can be assured of not being overheard."

Jenna realized that there was only one subject that fell into this category, and so she raised it. "Our wedding."

Joshua smiled, not quite believing the day was actually turning out the way he had hoped, and in fact had prayed for. "Let's do something different," he said, hoping Jenna would go for his unconventional idea. With a bit of luck, it wouldn't rain on his parade, as happened to his last one.

"It is going to be different already," Jenna replied smiling, looking down at her ever-growing tummy.

"I was thinking about God's Window." Joshua said; and then, seeing that Jenna was trying to work out what, in fact, he meant by this, he added, "Blyde River Canyon in the Eastern Transvaal. I gather you have never been there."

Jenna's reply was interrupted by the returning waiter, who Jenna told, "A boerewors roll and a Coke, please."

"Make that two," Joshua said. And then turning back to Jenna, "It would be small, and afterwards we can honeymoon down in Pilgrim's Rest."

"You think you have everything worked out, but you haven't," Jenna said firmly, but not angrily.

Not sure what was coming, Joshua waited to hear what he hadn't got worked out.

"Go and find our waiter, pay him for the lunch we are not waiting for, give him a good tip, and then come back to the car."

Joshua did what he was told, and as soon as he had shoehorned himself back next to her, Jenna added, "Now find a hotel not more than five minutes from here, and book a room for the afternoon." Again Joshua did as instructed.

Ari was Jenna's first, and only, man, and she had done whatever he wanted. She didn't always enjoy all those things, but as he was more experienced than she was, she imagined that the things she didn't like, other girls did, and because she loved him, she did them. Joshua didn't love any of the girls who relieved him of his pent-up sexual drive, but they did whatever he asked of them, and two considerably more.

Joshua found a hotel, recently built, and clean, whose receptionist was not at all surprised by the fact that Jenna and Joshua had no luggage, and only wanted the room for a few hours.

Expecting a repetition of Ari's domineering requirements, Jenna was amazed by Joshua's so different approach.

Very slowly and carefully he took off her skirt and blouse, and then led her to the bed where he let her down so she lay on her back. Gently, he kissed her neck, and the side of her nose, one of her ears, and then her lips, his tongue tentatively looking for hers. After that, Jenna sat up, took off her bra and removed Joshua's shirt, before throwing the bed's thin brown blanket onto a chair, kicking off her shoes, and unwinding back onto the bed. Siting on its edge, Joshua kissed her breasts, licked her navel (which gave her a funny feeling), and carefully scratched both her thighs until she wanted him in a way she had never wanted Ari.

Discarding her panties and opening her legs told Joshua she was ready. He wasn't. Instead, lying on top of her, he first caressed and then kissed her breasts, and when she started moaning quietly, he went in gently. Very slowly, Joshua pushed as far as he could, and when he and Jenna were as one, he started moving. First little nudges, then slightly longer pushes, and when Jenna was hot and wet and calling his name over and over, and gripping his back, and saying yes loudly and often, Joshua pushed long and hard.

After it was over, neither of them said anything. Instead of getting up and going for a shower (as Ari used to do), Joshua stayed where he was, and kissed Jenna again, gently, here and there. Tears welled up in Jenna's eyes, tears not of sadness but of happiness, and Joshua knew this, so he wiped them away gently and kissed her damp cheeks. When her body was still, Joshua withdrew, pulled Jenna on top of him, alternatively caressing her back and scratching it gently.

"Can you reach the phone," Jenna said, "and ask them to extend our booking here?."

"Till the morning?" Joshua asked.

"For two or three weeks." Jenna told him.

At dusk they showered together, kissed some more, washed and then dried each other, both feeling, but neither saying, that they felt reborn, thankfully as adults.

Driving back to See Da View, Jenna left her hand resting on Joshua's thigh, not in a sexual way, but because she felt that was where it belonged.

CHAPTER 72

ELI'S SURPRISE VISIT

Back at the office a couple of days later, Roisin told Maimon that a Mr. Eli Sokolovski had arrived to see him.

Maimon knew that one day this would happen and from time to time he wondered how he would handle it. He realized in a few minutes he would know.

"Appointment?" Maimon asked, and when Roisin shook her head negatively, Maimon instructed his secretary of many decades to "Show him in and close the door."

A tall, bedraggled fellow ambled into Maimon's office and, before being invited to take a seat, slouched down in the chair across from the managing director. Quite a difference, Maimon thought, from the last youngster who came to see him.

Taller than Maimon, he looked like his mother, and acted like her, too, Maimon noted, searching for some similarity with this overgrown boy who, after all, had 50% of his blood. Visually he saw none, maybe verbally he would identify something.

"I am Eli Sokolovski I have come for a job," Maimon was told.

A chip off his mother's block, Maimon realized, before saying, "We have a Personnel Department. If you would like a job with one of our companies, they are the people to see."

"You are the boss. You can tell them what to do."

"I can, but I don't."

"In this case you should," Maimon was told.

"There is a book called *How to Make Friends and Influence People* by Dale Carnegie. You might read it."

"I didn't come here for a reading list, but for a job," Eli said in a voice that indicated he really had no interest in anything else.

It is time to tell this ungrateful son of a bitch some home truths, Maimon told himself.

"Tell me, Eli, how old are you?"

"You know, you fucked my mother."

Maimon went to his office door, opened it, and said, "If you are not out of my office in ten seconds, I will have the security people remove you from these premises."

"Perhaps that wasn't the smartest answer," Eli said, making no move from his chosen chair.

Maimon walked to his secretary, and said in a loud enough voice for Eli to hear, "Tell the security detail to come to my office right away. There is a man to be removed from our property."

"I am sure that won't be necessary," Eli said. "Let's talk about my job."

Maimon didn't say a word, just watched as two uniformed, very big black men lifted Eli up, with one hand under each of his arms, making sure that his feet did not touch any of Prestige Milling's property.

"What an unpleasant young man," Roisin said.

CHAPTER 73

AT LONG LAST

As if it was a competition, Colleen, Serena, and Jenna compared tummy size, weight increase, number of hours slept/not slept, swollen ankles, etc., ad nauseum, which interest was further ratcheted up by the arrival of Alberto and Malka from London. At first, the Alfombras were afraid that Serena's baby would be born before they arrived, and then they were worried why it appeared reluctant to be born at all. The atmosphere became so highly charged that Maimon started planning a business trip to Tsumeb, from which he was saved by the popping out of first one baby and then another and then another. A visitor from Mars could easily have been convinced that these were the first babies ever born. All Sokolovskis, Martin belonged to Colleen, Matiyahu to Serena, and Dalia to Jenna.

Maimon felt that after about six years they reached the age of two, when they and their Johannesburg resident grandfather could begin to appreciate one another. Alberto and Malka returned to safer London, not prepared to believe Maimon that the ten hippopotami about to crash through the wall of their See Da View bedroom at night were in fact bullfrogs.

CHAPTER 74

TWO PRIME MINISTERS AND
THE FUTURE HEAD OF THE ANC

Holding the unshakeable view that the future of South Africa would be determined by the education of its citizens, and having read the election manifestos of the main political parties, Maimon felt it imperative that Jannie Smuts and Barry Hertzog understand the folly of their stated policies. To this end he invited the above gentlemen, plus the future leader of the African National Congress, Albert Luthuli, to a discreet dinner at See Da View.

Albert and Nokukhanya Luthuli had an uneventful drive to Maimon's and Elize's home from their house in the Orange Free State the day before the dinner. They were to stay at See Da View for two nights, and ahead of the get-together with Smuts and Hertzog, Maimon took the opportunity of having an in-depth conversation with Albert, then a schoolteacher.

Prime Minister Hertzog and Leader of the Opposition Smuts arrived in unofficial cars within minutes of one another. Maimon was at the front door to meet them, and ushered the two parliamentarians into the small dining room where Mvumbi was waiting.

"If you don't know each other, you know of each other, so introductions are unnecessary. In fact, I would like this supper to be as informal as possible, so I suggest that we take off our jackets and waistcoats, and also our ties."

This was the first time that the two generals had been invited to remove their jackets at a dinner, let alone their ties, and somewhat hesitantly they waited for their host to do so first.

"Then I think we should get on to first name terms. You might not know that to his friends, Mr. Albert Luthuli is known as Mvumbi. Jan Christiaan is Jannie, James Barry Munnik is Barry, and I am Maimon. I think each of us should propose a toast. Barry, as you are closest to the bar, actually to the Bar, you should kick off."

"To the Springbok Rugby Team," the wily politician said.

Jannie said, "To an unforgettable evening," and more whiskey was downed.

Mvumbi's toast was "To education," at which point Maimon refilled everyone's glass.

"What is yours?" Barry asked Maimon, who answered, "To the four of us."

"I understand that you have just been round the world, Maimon," Barry said. "What did you learn?"

Before Maimon could respond, one of the domestics brought in four servings of Avocado Ritz and filled four glasses with white wine.

"Probably the most significant was the imminent implosion of the British Empire. Not many people appreciate the body-blows Great Britain took in the Great War. Jannie probably knows, but not many other people do."

"So this is the American century?" Barry asked.

"I suppose so," Jannie answered, "but whose is the twenty-first?"

Not the Russian, they all agreed.

"Maybe the Chinese or the Brazilian," Mvumbi suggested.

"For that to happen, there has to be a lot of catching up," Maimon pointed out, "and America will need to fall asleep and be overtaken."

The fish plates and white wine glasses were removed, replaced by large carpet bag steaks and vegetables, and KWV's best Roodeberg blended red wine.

"What about India?" Barry asked. "They are well-educated, speak English, and there are many of them."

Everyone agreed they couldn't be written off.

"And our little Japanese friends? Is it worth putting a pound or two on them?" Mvumbi enquired.

"They finished off the Russians when no one expected them to," Maimon observed, "but their problem is too many people and not enough land."

"So we should expect some belligerence from them, probably in the Far East," Jannie observed.

The meat course was replaced by ramekins of apple crumble and chilled late-harvest wine.

"What about the Mexicans?" Mvumbi asked.

This question developed into one about the Spanish-speaking world, the outcome of which was the unanimous view that there was little likelihood of them becoming a world power again.

During the discussion, the dessert plates were removed and replaced by coffee and Cuban Montecristo cigars. Being the first to finish lighting his, Barry asked, "So, tell us, Maimon, why did you get us together?"

Maimon swallowed what was left of his brandy, cleared his throat, and began.

"In the twenty-first and twenty-second centuries," Maimon started, "the difference between winning and losing nations will be education. Education for all its citizens, men as well as women."

"Theoretically, you are right," Barry said, and then the politics kicked in, "but remember, turkeys don't vote for Christmas."

"Unless there are jobs for everyone who wants to work," Mvumbi said, "there will be rioting, wealth destruction, and your voters will vote with their feet, Barry."

"What do you think, Jannie?" Maimon asked.

"If either of us came out with that now, we would be kicked out, and Creswell's Labor Party would get a majority, and then the country would really be … err, in a very bad way."

"Couldn't you do it on the QT?" Mvumbi asked. "Get everybody up to standard six, and then, a few years later, to standard eight, and have one national set of exams, not each province setting its own."

"Jannie and I know we have to get there. The problem is that all the roads leading to that destination take one over a cliff," Barry pointed out.

Realizing no breakthrough was possible, Maimon suggested that the four of them meet again twelve months hence, during which time hopefully a crack might appear in the country's political wall. The two politicians and one school teacher all agreed that that was a good idea, and like so many good ideas, it ended up in the wastepaper basket.

There was no follow up dinner, the next year, or ever.

CHAPTER 75

AYNA

If Maimon was a gambler he would have laid a bet with himself as to how long it would be before the cavalry rode to Eli's rescue. A week after Eli's visit, Roisin told him that an Ayna Cassaro was in her office asking to see him. Maimon let her wait for twenty minutes; and when he did see her, he pointed out that if she wanted to do so in the future, it was better to make an appointment. For a minute or two they just looked at one another.

"It has been a long time," Ayna said, which Maimon acknowledged with a nod. The years, he noticed, had not been kind to her. The bright floral dress usually sold in one of the bazaar chains she was wearing, and scuffed, well- worn leather sandals, made her unrecognizable as the pretty girl he had last seen in East London. Ayna's thinning, streaky brown/gray hair did little to complement her lined face, and her glove-less hands evidenced signs of aggressive nail biting. All in all, not a pretty sight.

"You have done well," she said.

"All that maintenance and child support had to come from somewhere."

"You paid it because you had to," Ayna told him.

"I paid it out of the goodness of my heart. You know that, just as you know you seduced me. And you also know that neither you nor your son ever had the decency to drop me a note of thanks for the thousands of pounds you two have had. If you are here about a job for your son, I told him what to do."

"*Our* son, actually."

This was the opening Maimon was waiting for. He knew Eli was his son, but that didn't stop Maimon from saying, "Are you sure?"

Speechless, Ayna looked as though she was going to have a heart attack. Responding to her silence, Maimon rubbed in a bit of salt.

"Are you?"

To her credit Ayna got up and walked out of his office.

CHAPTER 76

A POLICE MATTER

A few weeks later Maimon had a visit from the head of his Personnel Department. Eli had applied for a job. He had no references, not even from his school, and schools gave letters of recommendation to even their worst students, the personnel man pointed out. There was a job available as an assistant storekeeper at Thabazimbi, the man added, but it only paid £2,000 a year. Maimon told the man to offer it to Eli, and somewhat to Maimon's pleasant surprise, Eli accepted it. Perhaps Eli wasn't as bad as the first impression he created. Sadly, as Maimon would learn, he was worse.

The rest of the story came to Maimon in a curious way. One of the mine workers was in hospital, having been shot in the foot by Eli. On that detail everyone agreed, but from that point onwards the story went off in different directions. From past experience, Maimon knew that the only way to ascertain what really happened was to visit the mine and speak to everyone who claimed to have some knowledge of the incident. It was a trip he welcomed, as every waking hour at See Da View was devoted to discussions about infants' feeding schedules, a subject that Maimon felt had been debated to death.

While he had not heard Eli's version – the young man having been suspended on full pay and now living with his mother in Barberton – what seemed clear was that Eli had regularly lain in wait for miners returning to Basutoland with the money they had saved during the past twelve months, and that he had robbed them of their entire savings. It was a pastime that Eli had apparently perfected, as seven other miners maintained that he had similarly robbed them. To their credit, the police had obtained signed affidavits attesting to these incidents.

This whole matter had only come to light because, when one of the miners refused to hand over his savings, Eli had threatened to shoot him. Whatever Eli's intentions were, four witnesses corroborated the story of the miner recovering in hospital. Armed with these documents, Maimon retuned to Johannesburg, getting word to Eli that he should come to the office next Tuesday morning at eleven a.m. Not only did Eli come, and on time, but he brought his mother along – or, more likely, it was the other way round, Maimon decided. So that there was no doubt that the minutes of the meeting correctly reflected what took place, Maimon inspanned his efficient secretary to record the proceedings.

Asked to give his version of events, Eli said that he was out hunting. He confirmed that the incident took place at eight o'clock at night, when it was pitch-dark, and the reason he shot the native was because he mistook him for a warthog. Eli admitted that he was unaware that warthogs slept at night in underground burrows.

Maimon then had Roisin read aloud all the affidavits, after which Eli said that as they were from natives they should be discarded.

Maimon pointed out that the police, following discussions with the public prosecutor, held a different view, and in fact were on the premises to arrest him.

Eli jumped up, ran to the door of Maimon's office, opened it … to find a policeman holding a warrant for his arrest. Realizing that escape was not an option, Eli surrendered quietly.

His mother did the opposite. Shouting and swearing like a fish wife, she cursed Maimon, his wife and children, as well as all of his relations in South Africa and elsewhere. Unfortunately, the curses were wasted on Maimon as he didn't understand Spanish, but his secretary, Roisin, did, and even though she was not in Maimon's office, she blushed to the roots of her hair upon hearing them. Unseen, Maimon pushed a button under his desk, which summoned the same two big native security guards who had elevated Eli off the premises a few weeks earlier, and who this time afforded his mother the same treatment. All that remained was Roisin's comment, "Mr. Sokolovski, I have never heard such terrible language in my life. I know it is none of my business, but if I were you, I would never see that woman ever again."

Maimon smiled, realizing that, like his keenly awaited Butchers' Hall meeting in London, his long put-off reunion with Ayna had been a damp squib. It was quick, and from his point of view, painless, neither of which he regretted.

CHAPTER 77

ANNUS HORRIBILIS

"It looks like a lost little cloud," Elize said in a tone that Maimon knew did not need a reply.

He had been married to this wonderful woman for fifty years and there were things about her that he still found perplexing. They had come down to Cape Town for the week Maimon had promised Elize, which, for one good reason or another, had never happened. So he had re-promised her that when he turned 70, if they had not already done so, they would spend a week together in Cape Town, no matter what.

Most of December had been taken up with parties, all because the Good Lord, or whoever, got Maimon to the Biblical three score years and ten. Elize turned their house into an Italian villa with its own piazza, having many of the walls painted with scenes from the Amalfi Coast, and gave him the most wonderful party. An Italian band played mainly Neapolitan music, to which people danced on the boarded-over swimming pool, and when those Italians rested, a fiddler, accordionist, and singer from the land that gave the world lasagna, osso bucco and Tiramisu serenaded whichever couples they came across. All this was atmospherically enhanced by 285 strategically placed candles on the large party-occupied patio and throughout the garden. Colleen found a Jewish male choir to sing "Baruch Haba" at midnight, having first explained to the 450 guests the song's significance.

Separately, their children gave Maimon a barbeque party under the stars in a game reserve, the latter part of which was watched by a pack of hyenas that reminded Maimon how far he had come since their ancestors sized him up for a lunchtime meal all those years ago. Back in Johannesburg his younger grandchildren hosted a birthday tea party with home-made indigestion-guaranteeing cupcakes.

In between, three companies in their group, and nine charities, managed to fit in parties to celebrate what everyone involved called a "momentous event." As wonderful as all these parties were, for Maimon the most momentous event was he and Elize getting on the recently introduced Blue Train to Cape Town.

Ensconced in one of the Mount Nelson Hotel's luxurious Garden Suites, they had filled their week doing whatever Elize wanted. Remembering their first visit to Thabazimbi, Maimon wasn't surprised that initially she was scared of the many gray squirrels in the Company's Garden, and that a few days later she was feeding them monkey nuts out of her hands. Together they ate in a wonderful Malay restaurant up in the area above the city where descendants of the Batavian slaves lived, and spent hours in Kirstenbosch Botanical Gardens, where Elize threw coins into Major Bird's bird-shaped pond, making wishes she refused to tell Maimon.

Less happily they remembered their Koos and Elna meeting, how initially unhappy and overwhelmed Anshul and Gittel were by the hotel's magnificence, and comforting Rochel Gottelbaum on the white marble steps of the recently completed 550-seat Gardens Synagogue. The day they visited the shul (as it was called) happened to be the anniversary of the death of Rochel's late husband, Julian, a dentist who was killed in France during the Great War. While numerically South Africa did not suffer as many deaths as France and Great Britain, those that never came back caused no less painful emotional wounds, in Rochel's case leaving her with two young children, Nathan and Janit.

Elderly people enjoy looking forward to events, and for Maimon and Elize their Cape Town stay was the hors d'oeuvres to a magnificent main course, a month with their children and grandchildren in Muizenberg.

"What do you think that cloud means?" Elize asked a somewhat mystified Maimon, who knew very well clouds did not mean anything.

They were sitting on the patio of their Garden Cottage, enjoying a breakfast of orange juice, fruit salad, and yogurt, and the "full English breakfast" that Maimon didn't get at home. Maimon knew about clouds, and he realized that the little white ball seemingly suspended above Robben Island in an otherwise cloudless sky was probably a puff of smoke from an ocean liner.

"I hope it doesn't mean there is a storm coming. Not a hail-and-rain storm, but another kind that will hurt us badly," she said.

Maimon was about to explain the atmospheric conditions that cause storms, but he stopped when he realized this "another kind" of storm was beyond his understanding. What other kind of storm could there be? He and Elize were in good health, as were all their children and grandchildren; their businesses were all doing well, and their overseas money was invested in a variety of industries, some of which were performing outstandingly. There was no reason to believe that 1929 would not be even better than the just-ended 1928.

Maimon had reserved all twelve ocean-facing rooms with their own balconies at the Alexander Hotel in Muizenberg for his three-generational family, their spouses, and assorted white and native nannies. Realizing that his promotion to senior professorship at the Hebrew University was blocked, Daniel and Alison had moved to Hebron with their children, so that he could be closer to the archaeological excavations that were the basis of the book he was writing.

No longer tied down by university responsibilities, Daniel gladly accepted Maimon's invitation to bring his family to South Africa for an extended holiday. It also gave the fourteen first cousins, as well as Kaylah's children and grandchildren, the opportunity to get to know one another, and in the process have the most wonderful time together. Apart from morning and afternoon swimming, there were donkey rides on the beach for the children and sailing on Seekoei Vlei for the adults.

The Sokolovskis were not the only Johannesburg family holidaying at Muizenberg, and had he been so inclined, Maimon could have spent all four weeks chatting to his Newtown business friends and enemies. Instead, he chose to spend it all with his family, having told Kris Skot not to disturb him with anything that didn't put one of his businesses at risk of insolvency. Morrie and Max had daily phone calls with the office, which Maimon was happy to note were not important enough to disturb his holiday.

Walking on the beach one morning soon after their arrival, Maimon and Elize bumped into Rochel and her children, and Rochel's acceptance of Maimon's invitation to join them for their lunchtime beach picnic resulted in Nathan and Janit being included in all their gender-common activities over the following four weeks. These included watermelon-peel skirmishes among the boys, and dressing up in assorted borrowed clothes by the girls.

Most nights they all went to the newly reconstructed Muizenberg Pavilion, where comedians, magicians, hypnotists, ventriloquists, and bands of Cape Coloreds and Malays, in multi-colored silk costumes, from the recently concluded Coon Carnival, played Cape Town music to packed audiences.

Tragically, Elize's little white cloud soon turned big and black, and driving home at the beginning of February, Saul and Kaylah were involved in a horrendous car crash. Their children, extending their family-friendly holiday time, were training back to Johannesburg with Maimon and Elize. Kaylah was killed, and Saul sustained multiple and serious injuries, necessitating lengthy hospital stays, first in Beaufort West, and when he had recovered sufficiently to travel by ambulance, in Johannesburg's General Hospital. Worse was to follow.

In the middle of the year Wall Street crashed, which was followed by stock markets around the world, and then financial markets of any kind, imploding. Simultaneously tens of thousands of companies went out of business, and hundreds of thousands of individuals were made bankrupt by banks closing their doors.

Unfortunately, Maimon had signed unlimited personal guarantees, and when called upon to meet these obligations, was unable to do so. The South Britannic insurance money he had invested mainly in Ivar Kreuger's International Match Company, which despite, or because of, controlling 75% of the world's match production, went out of business. Maimon's 6.5% Convertible Gold Debentures, with interest payable in gold or US Dollars at the holder's option, were worthless. His sterling London balances had been invested in many blue chip, now valueless, British and American companies. Furthermore, he lost all of his American money, having put the income from the Spindletop oil field in the Bank of The United States. It was the largest bank insolvency in American history, taking with it $200 million of customers' deposits, much of it Maimon's.

Only Maimon's courage and confidence – some people said chutzpah – stopped him losing all of his South African assets as well. Called to a bank meeting to sign away his factories to meet his personal guarantee obligations, Maimon put all of their keys (and there were about sixty) on the table and told the bankers, "I am going for a walk. When I come back, you tell me whether I will continue to operate the factories and use their profits to pay off my debts, or whether you run the factories into the ground and get no money at all." The bankers buried their egos and got their money back over the next six years.

There was still worse to come. Much worse. On a cold and bright Monday morning in late August, the 26th to be exact, Roisin opened a cable addressed to Maimon, read it, went white, and burst into uncontrollable tears. Not able to speak, she ran to Max and handed the cable to him. Max read it, and for the first time in his life his legs gave way under him and he fell to the floor.

Stumbling back to his feet, Max instructed Roisin to phone Elize and tell her to come to the office right away. This done, as if in a trance, Max walked into Morrie's office and showed him the wire. Assured by Roisin that Maimon, Max, and Morrie were all fine, Elize drove into town wondering what news, good or bad, couldn't wait till the evening. When she saw her boys she knew that whatever it was, it was worse than terrible. They sat her down, and then one on each side handed their mother the cable that none of them would ever forget

TRAGICALLY SORRY TO ADVISE DANIEL ALISON AND CHILDREN MASACRED YESTERDAY BY ARABS WHO KILLED 67 JEWS INJURED MANY OTHERS SINCERE CONDOLENCES RAYMOND CAFFTERTA CHIEF OF POLICE HEBRON

In shock, absorbing this unspeakable horror – neither Max, Morrie nor Elize had spoken a word – they all looked up to see the door flung open. It was Colleen, who ran to the couch, dropped to her knees, buried her head in Elize's lap, and burst into tears.

Then Maimon walked into the room.

Max and Morrie, both with blood-shot eyes, stood up and went to their father, who said "Alison?" and they nodded. "And Daniel?" and they nodded again. "And the children?" and they nodded again. Maimon's eyes glazed over, his legs gave way, Morrie and Max catching him as he crumpled to the floor. Gently, they picked up their unconscious father and placed him on the now vacated settee. Colleen and Elize clasped together, both sobbing.

Roisin, ashen-faced, standing at the door, later told Serena what happened next. Colleen, whom she had phoned, examined Maimon, said he was having a heart attack, and that there was no time to wait for an ambulance. She instructed Max and Morrie to bundle him into her car, which she drove at breakneck speed to the Johannesburg General Hospital. Morrie went with her, Roisin said, and the last thing she heard was Colleen telling him to make sure Maimon didn't swallow his tongue. Then Kris Skot drove Elize and Max to the hospital.

In Maimon's office Roisin saw the morning newspaper open at the Foreign News page, whose main article was about the Hebron Massacre.

Maimon survived, and putting the pieces together a year later, he realized that it was due to a combination of Colleen's speedy intervention; the dedicated, mainly Afrikaans, female nursing staff at Johannesburg's General Hospital; syringes full of Epinephrine that fooled his body into producing large amount of adrenaline; constant badgering of the Almighty by Elize; and probably some good luck, too.

The young heart specialist, Manny Klug-Leon (unusually for those days, his mother insisted on the inclusion of her family's name on Manny's birth certificate), was also due some credit, Maimon admitted, with the imposition of his unusual diet and exercise regime. Maimon was instructed to chew through a handful of biltong each day, partake of a whiskey around sunset, and for the rest, to eat as much fruit, nuts, and vegetables as he wanted. Nothing else was permitted.

Equally unusually, because heart attack victims were universally instructed to rest in those days, Manny K-L prescribed a walking regime that Maimon followed religiously, because if he didn't the good doctor wouldn't allow him back to Cape Town in December. Starting with 50 yards on the flat a day, accompanied by Elize and his driver, Casper Daniel, over the next few months Maimon built it up to a mile a day, also accompanied by his driver but now following five yards behind at the wheel of Maimon's new big black Cadillac.

Getting over Alison's death was more difficult. In the first few months the pain was acute, incessant, and almost unbearable. Slowly the wound began to heal, covered over by the routine of everyday life, and then reopened again by memories of the wonderful times they had spent together. Maimon doubted that the wound would ever close, but eventually it did, leaving a scar evidencing the deep wound it covered. Unlike a duelling scar, no one could see it, but Maimon felt it deeply and did so for the rest of his living days.

The end of December saw Maimon and Elize back in a Garden Suite at the Mount Nelson Hotel, thankfully for a happy occasion. Rochel had visited Saul, first in the Beaufort West Hospital, and then in Johannesburg. Over the months that followed, and as a result of the time they spent together, Saul had realized the gaping hole that Julian's death, now over ten years ago, had left in her life.

In the hope that it would help Rochel come to terms with her loss, Saul suggested that they visit Julian's grave in France, something

Rochel had refused to do. Reluctantly, and somewhat scared, Rochel agreed, which turned out to be a wonderful, liberating event. While in Europe they traveled throughout Italy, which Rochel loved so much that Saul came to calling her "Roma." Consoling each other over their tragic losses, and deeply in love, they returned to South Africa and asked their children for permission to marry. With the chupa in the garden of the hotel, it wasn't a big wedding, but it was a happy one and an antidote to a truly horrible year.

CHAPTER 78

ALIYAH

On the business front activity was low. No sooner had the northern hemisphere consumers recovered their confidence following the Great War than they were metaphorically hit in the solar plexus by the 1929-1933 recession. It took armament orders in Britain, Japan, America, and on the European continent for their economies to recover.

Maimon used this period to consolidate his position in the food industry, buying up competitors when doing so made sense, and purchasing empty land adjacent to his factories for possible expansion.

In 1930 Ze'ev Jabotinsky paid a visit to South Africa, and Maimon took the opportunity of inviting him for dinner one Sunday evening, primarily to give the family an opportunity of learning first-hand of developments in Palestine, and also of the Zionist movement in Europe. As Monday was a working day, Maimon asked Z.J. to come at six, expecting everyone to be on their way home by ten. When the hall clock struck two the following morning, and the family were still listening in rapt attention to Ze'ev's plans to create a Jewish state in what was Palestine, Maimon could not be happier. The reasons for this were twofold, their justifications intertwined.

From a South African perspective, Maimon was convinced that it was only a matter of time before the natives were once again in charge of the country. Having been dispossessed of their land over the past 300 years, it was not unreasonable to expect that they would want it back. Furthermore, as the Boers hadn't paid the natives for it, there was no reason to expect that the natives would buy it back. Most of the people with whom Maimon discussed this shared Elize's view on this matter, being that his sanity should be questioned, and anyway, "They can't run the country," he was told many times. That it was the white man's fault that this was the case cut no ice at all with these naysayers.

From a Jewish perspective, and sharing similar experiences with Z.J. in Russia, there was no doubt in Maimon's mind that until the Jewish people had their own country, they were vulnerable in the extreme.

This would be difficult to achieve, Z.J. admitted, but nothing worthwhile, he pointed out, comes easily. There was the Balfour Declaration that gave Jews a foot in the door, but it also caused a lot of animosity, and some embarrassment to the British Jewish community, quite a few of whom wanted to be English with a greater or lesser amount of Jewish identification.

After Z.J. was driven back to his hotel by Daniel, the six "middle-generation" family members discussed possible Aliyah[151] up hill and down dale, and only agreed to go home at 4:30 in the morning, on the understanding that they would regroup next weekend to progress this subject. Maimon didn't have to wait that long, Joshua and Jenna informing Elize and him the following evening that they proposed making Aliyah in the next twelve months.

---

151 Literally "going up," originally to Jerusalem from other parts of the country, "making Aliyah" has come to mean immigrating to Palestine/Israel

CHAPTER 79

WAR CLOUDS GATHER

In Europe, the situation for Jews was deteriorating almost by the day. Ninety thirty-three brought Hitler to power in Germany, through the ballot box rather than the barrel of a gun. Immediately thereafter a set of draconian anti-Semitic laws was passed, the most dramatic of which was the firing of all Jews employed by the government or any of its agencies.

In 1938 Germany marched into Austria to cement an Anschluss (union) with its neighbors, and a few months later, with no opposition from Britain, France, or America, Hitler invaded Czechoslovakia to "free" the three million Germans living in the Sudetenland part of that country.

Also in 1938, synagogues were torched in Germany, Jewish-owned businesses vandalised, and almost all the Jews remaining in Germany were desperate to get out. While "getting out" could often be purchased, "getting in" to other countries was more problematic. As Chaim Weitzman noted at the time, "The world is full of countries in which Jews either cannot live or cannot enter."

Maimon was careful to keep his business activity and charity work at the office, well away from his precious family time, and so it was with a little surprise that Elize answered the front door to find a middle-aged, heavy-set man asking to see her husband.

"Do you have an appointment?" Elize asked as the first step to sending this man away.

"When the Nazis came to collect Jews for their labor camps, they didn't first phone to make an appointment," she was told.

That knocked Elize back, and asking the man to sit down, she went to find her husband. Maimon came down the stairs, smiling, saying, "Leo,

I was expecting you. I hear you and Gitlin are chartering a boat to bring about 700 German Jews to Cape Town."

Leo Raphaely, who had worked tirelessly to bring German Jews to South Africa from 1935 onwards, didn't deny this. Instead, he hauled a pile of papers out of his battered brown briefcase, and wordlessly handed them to Maimon.

"You want me to sign ten £50 guarantees," Maimon said, counting the papers Leo had handed him, "so that these people are not a burden on the Union. I am afraid that is not possible."

Leo looked at Maimon, the friend with whom he had fought many battles in the past, winning most of them.

"Today is Tuesday, and on Tuesday I only sign twenty guarantees. My wife and daughter-in-law will sign ten each, though, if we ask them nicely, and they could probably be persuaded to increase that to fifteen each. How bad is the situation?"

"As bad as I believe it is, it is probably worse," Leo began. "To think that a civilized nation like the Germans would behave like this. From the Poles or the Russians, one might expect such things, but from the country of Schiller and Heine, I would never have thought."

"I hear you got in your car in Cape Town and drove up the Garden Route, collecting guarantee signatures all the way. Is that right?"

"More or less. I started with the Jewish hotel owners in all the country towns, and they gave me the names and addresses of Jewish farmers in the district. I got two guarantees from each man and his wife. With yours I am nearly up to one thousand."

"From only Jewish people?" Maimon asked.

"I never ask non-Jews, but in Riversdale, when I was telling the garage owner whose boy was fixing my puncture what I was doing, he insisted on signing one himself. It is from a Mr van der Merwe. I won't use it unless I have to."

"Why do you think he wanted to sign it?" Maimon asked curiously.

"It seems that his father had an ostrich farm in Oudtshoorn, and when the price of feathers collapsed, his family were wiped out and starving. A smous in the district gave his parents money to buy milk and eggs, even though the smous was as broke as everyone else in the southern Cape. Apparently, many farmers owed the smous money that they could not repay."

Leo refused the coffee and food offered, advising that he still had a number of people to call on.

Whilst it seemed that the 1930s brought peace and prosperity to South Africa, under the surface the political situation was far from calm.

Hertzog and Smuts combined to form the United Party, and then proceeded to legislate who could live where, or more accurately, who couldn't live where. Natives were moved out of Johannesburg and into their now empty dwellings, Colored and Tamil people were relocated. The first legislation restricting the residence of black women was introduced, and people of Indian descent were prevented from owning land. The very few natives who had been given the vote were transferred to a separate voter's roll, and henceforth were represented in parliament by four white senators.

While politically impotent, various groups comprised of non-white sectors of the country's population formed entities representing their interests. The Indian sector was the most active and organized, while what was to become the mighty African National Congress was slowly stirring. The Communist Party, later to be outlawed, was also building a solid base.

None of this went unnoticed by Maimon, who was also aware of the undertones emanating from the Afrikaner sector, who spoke of themselves as a chosen people ordained by God to rule South Africa. They established their own cultural organizations and secret societies, and argued that South Africa should be ruled in the interests of Afrikaners, rather than English businessmen or African workers. Throughout the 1930s the Afrikaner nationalist movement grew in strength, fuelled by fears of black competition for jobs. They also openly showed antipathy toward the English-speaking mining magnates, reminding their supporters of past suffering. This fear was compounded by the impact that massive black urbanisation was having on the white population.

While other people may have missed it, or chosen not to acknowledge it, in Maimon's mind there was no doubt that South Africa was to be governed by a party that planned to shape its policies to work in favor of whites in general, and Afrikaners in particular. Furthermore, the purified National Party denied that Africans, Asians, or coloreds could ever be citizens or full participants in the country's political process. At the same time, Johannesburg's Afrikaans newspaper, *Die Transvaaler*, edited by young Hendrik Verwoerd, was spewing out anti-Semitic vitriol on almost a daily basis. For Maimon, all this was the beginning of the end for South Africa as he knew it.

CHAPTER 80

AN OLD PROBLEM RESURRECTED

Lying in bed that night, Elize knew that something was bothering Maimon. If she waited, he usually told her what it was, but tonight it seemed he wasn't going to.

"What is on your mind?"

"Nothing," Maimon lied.

"Nothing is bothering you a great deal," Elize said.

"We can talk about it in the morning," Maimon told her.

"Sure we can. But I know you, Maimon Sokolovski, you are like a dog with a bone, and you are not going to let that bone alone, at least until you have told me what is bothering you."

"It is my brother, Zelig," Maimon admitted.

"I think we last discussed Zelig ten years ago. Is this the same anniversary conversation that we had twenty and thirty years ago?"

"This time it is different. There is going to be a war, and unless I do something, Zelig and his whole family might be killed."

"God told you this?" Elize asked.

"I need to go and rescue him," Maimon replied.

"You need to get a good night's rest, that is what you need," Elize told him, switching off the light.

Elize noticed that the following morning Maimon was still chewing on his bone. Maimon didn't talk when he was thinking, and the only way Elize knew if he had a solution to whatever was bothering him was when a little smile played across his mouth. Sure enough, at about 10.30, she saw the smile.

"I need to talk to the children," Maimon said. "Let's have lunch together."

Elize and the YP knew this wasn't a suggestion, it was an instruction, and in a couple of hours she had conjured up more than enough food for all of them. Whatever appointments anyone had were cancelled, and at one o'clock all six of them were at the table.

"There is going to be another war in Europe," Maimon started, "and once again millions of people are going to be killed. In all likelihood, they will include your uncle and aunt, your cousins and their children, and your great nephews and nieces or whatever they are called."

Elize and the YP knew there was a detailed plan coming, and any questions would have to wait till afterwards.

"If this happens without my making whatever effort I can to remove them from this war theater, I would never be able to live with myself. So, this is what is going to happen."

Colleen loved Maimon for a hundred reasons, one of them was his ability to identify a problem, and then it's solution.

"This afternoon I am seeing General Smuts about chartering one of the Airforce's Douglas DC4 airplanes. Then next week I am going to fly to Saratov to rescue as many of our relations as possible and bring them to South Africa."

That was the plan, and in Maimon's mind it was a done deal. He knew there were other hurdles that would have to be overcome, but they would be, as they always were.

"What makes you think they will agree to leave this time, when they refused so many times in the past?" Morrie asked.

"I haven't thought that through yet, but I do have some ideas," Maimon replied. "Your mother and I will work something out on the plane."

Which is how the YP knew that Elize was also going to Russia.

They had spent hours arguing long and hard about it. Elize had insisted that she come along, and Maimon had refused to even consider it, until Elize pointed out two inescapable facts.

"Right now, the party consists of five men – the crew and Maimon," Elize pointed out. "Whatever chance 'Operation Magic Carpet' has of succeeding would surely be increased if there was a woman in the party."

Maimon wasn't sure about that, but waited for the second reason.

"If you get killed and I was left in South Africa, I will commit suicide."

That was a risk Maimon was not prepared to take.

"Now if you will excuse me," he said, "I don't want to keep General Smuts waiting."

At Smuts' office in the Union Buildings in Pretoria, Maimon got straight to the point.

"I must apologize for not seeing you sooner, but I know you are very busy, and I don't like to trouble you with trivial matters."

Jannie smiled. Whatever it was Maimon wanted, it surely wasn't trivial.

"First of all, please accept this small donation to the United Party," Maimon said, handing an envelope to his long-time friend. Jannie knew it wasn't a small donation, and as he considered it discourteous to look at the check in a donor's presence, he put the envelope in the top drawer of his desk. Later, after Maimon had left, he saw the largest single donation ever received by the United Party.

Maimon gave his friend the outline of his plan, plus a few important details.

"The only thing I can't help you with is permission for one of our planes to land in Russia," General Smuts said, not using it as an excuse to refuse Maimon his request.

"I have an appointment with Sam Khan and Harry Snitcher, senior members of the South African Communist Party, whom I am sure will help me with that permission," Maimon replied.

"I am sure they will," Jannie said smiling, knowing that if they wouldn't, his old nemesis, James la Guma, surely would.

" 'n Boer maak 'n plan,"[152] Maimon said rising to leave.

"Maar 'n Jood maak 'n plan wat werk,"[153] General Smuts replied, smiling.

"Come and see me on Monday morning. My secretary will find some time for us."

Three days later Maimon came back home with a letter from the General Secretariat of the South African Communist Party, encouraging the Russian Government to grant permission for a South African Airforce DC4 to land three times in Saratov.

Without fanfare, the DC4 took off at dawn the following Saturday, first to Nairobi to refuel, and then to Cairo to overnight, top up the four engines' oil and Avgas, as well as to give the crew a good night's sleep. It also enabled Maimon to buy a tin of silver metallic paint and a brush to apply it. Up till then everyone on board had been relaxed, but once

---

152 *"A farmer makes a plan"*

153 *"But a Jew makes a plan that works"*

they crossed first into Turkish airspace, and then over the Black Sea to Russian-controlled airways, all the crew members were fully focussed on their tasks.

On Sunday at 12:26, dead on schedule, ZS BIH did two low, slow fly pasts over Saratov town center, before touching down at its little-used airport. The captain had hardly switched off the last of the four Pratt & Whitney radial engines before Maimon was out with his paint and brush, changing one of the plane's registration marks from "BIH" to "B'H." When Maimon explained to the captain that this stood for "Bless the Almighty," he was told that he could change the other ground-level markings as well if he wanted to.

With the wheels chocked, and doors locked, the crew joined Maimon and Elize on the ride into town in a 1920s bus that had miraculously appeared in the parking lot of the abandoned terminal building. In ten minutes the six unexpected visitors were deposited at the school building that Maimon remembered so well, if not so fondly. A "reception committee" of half-a-dozen rabbis greeted them suspiciously; the uniformed airmen looked much more impressive than did Maimon and Elize.

After extending greetings from the South African Jewish community, Maimon explained that as a major war was imminent, it might be wise for some members of the Jewish community in Saratov to consider moving to where there was less chance of fighting taking place.

The most senior rabbi thanked Maimon for his consideration, adding that if there was a war, he was sure the Almighty would look after Saratov's resident Jews.

Maimon didn't question that, but pointed out that if Saratov was fought over, the Torah scrolls might get damaged or – perish the thought – destroyed; and if the community leaders would like, he would be prepared to instruct the pilot to deliver the scrolls to any Jewish community of their choice.

Whatever the rabbis were expecting, this wasn't it, and to discuss this offer they requested a thirty-minute recess. This Maimon readily granted.

Captain "Sailor" Malan came over to Maimon and reminded him that, Russia apart, they did not have permission to fly over, or land, in any European country.

Maimon nodded in acknowledgement.

Elize pulled him to one side and asked, "Do you think it is going to work?"

Maimon nodded to her as well.

The meeting reconvened a little later than planned, when the senior rabbi thanked Maimon for his most generous offer and asked if it might be possible to include the Torah scrolls of the neighboring villages as well, which would make fourteen in all. Maimon went over to the pilot, pretended to consult with him, and then confirmed with the rabbi that would be in order, which resulted in more consultations.

"Would it be further possible," the senior rabbi asked, "for the congregation to have a farewell party for the Torah Scrolls tonight, and for them to be flown away in the morning?"

"No problem," Maimon assured them.

"You are truly blessed," the rabbi told him, with tears in his eyes.

You don't know how truly blessed he is, Elize thought to herself, knowing what was coming.

Maimon had specifically not visited Zelig ahead of his meeting with the rabbis, as he did not want to put his brother under pressure. But as soon as the meeting was over, he and Elize rushed to his parents' old home, where about twenty-five people awaited them. Elize had bought an album of photographs, which showed not only pictures of the family but of See Da View as well, which no one could believe was Maimon's and Elize's home.

As forewarned, that night there was a "going away" party for the fourteen Torah scrolls, which Maimonides explained to the captain and his crew was a sort of "We will meet again" celebration.

The next morning the whole Jewish community serenaded the fourteen scrolls out of town to the airport, and with the crew's assistance, the rabbis strapped each of them into their own seats before the plane's doors were closed.

Maimon had placed the red refuelling ladder next to the plane's left wing, and he climbed onto it holding a little canvas bag. Lifting his hand up for silence and speaking through a battery-operated megaphone, Mai mon began, "Learned rabbis, fellow Saratovniks, and my beautiful wife. I am not here to debate the value of the Torah, or that of man and woman that God created in his image. Both are important, and in times of peril, both must be saved. Neither one over the other."

Elize held her breath, knowing what was coming and how difficult it was for her non-religiously observant husband to carry it off convincingly.

"It seems that this both-must-be-saved principle is not shared by all your religious leaders," Maimon continued. A murmur of discontent rippled through the crowd.

"You know as well as I do that each Torah has 54 portions." Maimon took a deep breath and looked down at Elize, who smiled up at him.

"If you want me to save a Torah, then you must give the pilot of this airplane 54 souls to fly away with it.'

Male voices of antagonism started to be heard, for which Maimon was ready. Reaching into his canvas bag, Maimon removed a pair of empty Torah scrolls that he had brought from Johannesburg. Showing the crowd that they contained no parchment writing, Maimon said, "Kindly note this little demonstration I am about to perform. I am going to get into the plane, taking with me these wooden scrolls. The pilot will take the plane up to one thousand feet, and then I am going to throw these two empty wooden scrolls out of the airplane's door onto this concrete here. You will see them shatter into a million pieces."

For all their insularity, the rabbis were far from stupid, and realized at once what was coming. Some of them started wailing.

"If you want fourteen Torahs saved, I want at least 756 men, women, and children saved as well. If not, I will drop every single one of the fourteen Torahs from the plane, so that they smash in front of your very eyes." After stopping for dramatic effect, Maimon added what he hoped would be the knock-out blow. "It is you who will decide whether these sacred words are destroyed or saved for future generations to learn from."

The demonstration was more successful than even Maimon expected, and when the plane's engines were switched off after landing and taxiing to the crowd, the senior rabbi was waiting for him. Seven hundred and fifty- six men, woman, and children would make themselves available, Maimon was told.

The captain did have a problem with regard to the plane being loaded over gross. Fortunately, it was a cool day, the passengers had little luggage, and Saratov's elevation was only 150 feet. Additionally, most of the passengers were children or thin adults, and a ten-knot headwind was blowing that assisted the plane's take-off. Furthermore, thanks to Pratt & Whitney building a large safety margin into their engine's capacity, and with God's help, 756 souls and fourteen Torahs were safely flown to Cyprus. It took four days, and more Avgas than Captain "Sailor" Malan had bargained for, but they made it. Most of the 756 went to America, all but a few of the remainder to Palestine, and not one came to South Africa.

After hours of soul-searching, and without consulting anyone, Zelig decided to board the plane, accompanied by Rivka and their nine children and fifty-seven grandchildren.

Shortly after returning to South Africa, Maimon went to see General Smuts, to thank him once again for his support, without which OMC would not have happened.

"OMC?" Jannie asked.

"Operation Magic Carpet."

"Where did you get the idea from?" Jannie asked.

"Mr." Prime Minister, Albert Luthuli once said to me 'You have to learn the rules of the game. And then you have to play better than anyone else'. That is what I did."

Jannie smiled and asked, "Maimon, tell me, do you believe in divine intervention?"

"A month ago, I would have said absolutely not; but now, I am not so sure."

"Why the doubt?" the more devout man in the room asked.

"First of all, my changing BIH to B'H. Why did you send that plane and not another? And then Gematria."

"You mean the numbers?" Jannie asked.

"The alphabetic value of 756 is 'ving,' which is only one letter away from 'wing.' If there had been fifteen Torahs or thirteen Torahs, it wouldn't have worked out."

"Did you tell the Saratov people that?" Jannie asked, now caught up in this mystic numerical science.

"I didn't have to. It was my fall-back position."

Pity there are not more Maimons in South Africa, the Prime Minister thought, getting to his feet and saying goodbye.

Following this episode, there were two unexpected developments.

Firstly, on every one of Maimon's remaining birthdays, he received hundreds of cards, letters, and good wishes from OMC passengers. And secondly, after the carnage of the Second World War finally ended, someone erected a plaque at Saratov Airport, reading, "Here in 1938 two Jews and four Goyim saved fourteen Torahs and 756 Jewish men, women, and children who, without such assistance, would have been murdered in Auschwitz." Only the Almighty knows the number of descendants from these 756 souls, and where they live today.

CHAPTER 81

PASSING THE BATON

Suspecting that, the Balfour Declaration notwithstanding, Britain would not hand Palestine over to the Jews, Maimon hatched a plan which would work to the sabras' advantage in the seemingly inevitable Middle East war.

In 1938 Kris was given the task of undertaking a market survey on machine guns, and in four weeks produced an exhaustive report indicating that the fastest, most reliable armament in this category was the German MG42. Count Frederick von Schullenbach, a long-time friend of Maimon's, was inspanned to contact the German Commercial Attaché to ascertain whether he could facilitate a contract enabling the manufacture of this gun in South Africa under license. The civil servant doubted that this was possible, until Frederick made some conveniently derogatory remarks about Jews and blacks. Two weeks later, a contract was signed between Krupp and Seebaccam (Pty) Ltd., whereby Krupp would supply the machinery for Seebaccam to manufacture guns and bullets in South Africa.

Maimon met with General Smuts and offered him the MG42's manufacturing output of guns and bullets. These were to be used by loyal members of the police force in case there was an insurrection by South Africans opposed to the country's likely alliance with Britain in the forthcoming war. Maimon undertook to export at the end of the war the machinery as well as the guns and bullets it had produced. Furthermore, Maimon offered to store the armaments produced at the General's house in Irene until then. General Smuts was extremely grateful for Maimon's generous offer, especially as it required no government funding.

Fortunately, the guns were not required by the South African police force, and in 1948 Maimon reclaimed them, and the 5000 bullets stored in the basement of the General's house. He then persuaded Kurt Hellerowitz, the owner of Kenilworth Canners, to give him a whole load of obsolete fruit-canning machinery, which Maimon placed on top of Krupp's equipment, and its armaments production, and shipped the whole consignment to David Ben Gurion, clearly marked as "fruit-canning machinery."

The first and subsequent licensing fee payments to Krupp fell due after war was declared, and thus any such funds were not transferrable till after the cessation of hostilities. When this happened in 1945, Krupp was in such bad odor that Max successfully persuaded them to waive the licensing fee due, on the condition that Seebaccam paid an identical amount of money to Jewish relief charities. Surprisingly, they agreed.

In September 1939, the first shots were fired in what became known as the Second World War. Six years later, those left alive looked at the carnage and devastation created in Europe and the Far East and mourned the millions who had died in battle, in the Nazis' extermination camps, in labor camps in Germany and elsewhere in Europe, constructing a railway line in Burma for the Japanese, and the unknown number who died of starvation on both continents.

Morrie and Max signed up, as did Joshua. Maimon tried to as well but was rejected on account of his age. The government refused to permit Morrie or Max to leave the country as they were both considered strategically vital to the country's food production.

The family's businesses had done well during the war, and continued to do so in the years immediately thereafter. Increasingly, Morrie and Max made the important decisions, which Maimon was happy to rubberstamp.

One Tuesday morning Maimon didn't go to the office. He went instead and sat in the far corner of their Parktown property, on an old wooden bench under a giant magenta bougainvillea bush. There, as he had done in the past, he reflected on his life to date, and mapped out his plans for the years that God had left for him. Maimon must have been in that quiet corner of their grounds for over an hour when Elize came to look for him.

Getting down on her haunches, holding Maimon's two hands in hers, and looking him in the eye, she said, "It's alright. I am ready to go."

"This is your country," Maimon began in his rusty Yiddish. "Your family have been here for hundreds of years. We have two farms. Can you leave them and start again?"

"We go down to the bush at Passover every year. We can still do that. And I can start an orange farm in Palestine. I know it will be different from farming sheep and cattle and grapes, but it will be a challenge, and you know I like challenges."

"And we have our children and grandchildren to look after us when we get old," Maimon pointed out.

"And you know I will have a problem living under a native government."

"The boys don't need me to run the businesses here. It is their time now." Maimon paused for a moment, and then, reflecting on reality, added, "They are already running them."

Then, as in years gone by, Maimon and Elize were drawn together like two ever-powerful magnets, and though their arms were no longer young and strong, no one could have pried them apart. Elize kissed Maimon in a way that he knew there was something else important.

"What is it?" Maimon asked quietly.

Elize took an envelope – letter "#13" – out of her pocket and handed it to him. He opened it, removed the sheets inside, and gave them back to the woman he loved no less now than he did in East London all those decades ago.

My most wonderful man, without whom I would be a pale shadow of myself,

Thank you for everything you have done for me, from turning round the upside--down Jewish Siddur prayerbook, to telling me without words where in our garden I could go to find you this morning.

I know what you are thinking, and it is the right time to be thinking it. It is time that we moved on. We have done what we can here. Now it is up to other people to pick up the "baton," as little Ben told me yesterday the cardboard cylinder is called that the children use in running races.

I have one favor to ask of you, please. Let's not have any announcements, or farewell dinners – offhand, I can think of nine charities who would insist on hosting one – thank-fully, it is not your style, as it isn't mine.

Let's agree on a day and then fly out. Not too soon, so we are not in a panic about getting everything finished, and not too distant, so we are waiting and waiting. How about two weeks from now?

I have found this little book that I used, to write down all the things that needed to be done after we bought "Kom Weer Terug." It has still got lots of unused pages. We should work on it together, so nothing gets left off, though if it does, that won't be a "train smash," as Max says.

I am so excited about the next chapter in our lives together.

I love you more than words can say, or the words that I know anyway.

Take care.

All my love
Elize

On the way back to the house they bumped into Perdman, and asked him to tell Daniel to get the car ready. Twenty minutes later, Maimon was in Max's office, waiting for him to finish discussing the purchase of a thousand beehives. That done, Maimon and Max went to the meeting room between the two boy's offices, beckoning Morrie to join them.

"Anything interesting going on?" Maimon asked.

"We settled the strike at the oil mill, and the negotiations to sell our stake in Union Steel continues. Bread prices are up a little more than the cost of wheat, so those margins are expanding. Garfunkel Easton is sniffing round our business again. They talk about buying us out, but Morrie and I think it is just a fishing expedition. Also, Abe Shapkatz told us we should buy his fishmeal factories, which probably means that the sardines are moving offshore again. I think that's about it."

"And I think it is time you gave me a non," Maimon said.

"*Non* meaning 'no' in French?" Morrie asked.

"*Non* as in non-executive chairman. In fact, on reflection, you don't need a chairman at all."

"Aliyah?" Max said.

Maimon nodded. "It is time for your mother and I – and me, sorry – to move on. Time to start an orange farm."

"Any time soon?" Morrie asked with mixed emotions. While he expected to be sad not to see his parents a few times a week, Morrie felt increasingly uncomfortable having his father constantly looking over his shoulder. He welcomed constructive criticism, but those from his father were not always in this category. Furthermore, Maimon was increasingly yesterday's man. The men he had worked with for the past thirty years had all died or retired, and while "old-fashioned" was often good, it didn't sit comfortably in the modern business world.

"Not really. About two weeks. No farewell parties or dinners. We will be back for Passover, so it is just another trip."

"Just another trip, indeed. The man who built this empire is leaving, on just another trip," Max said.

"King Solomon said there is a time for this and a time for that. A time to get into the animal feed business and a time to get out of the peanut butter one."

"That wasn't exactly what he said," Morrie pointed out.

"Maybe not. But that is what he would have said with feed lots developing and Black Cat squeezing peanut butter margins."

"We will survive, Dad, but it won't be easy," Max said softly.

"Easy or not, please tell Roisin to send all my files home, and then we can have a big bonfire."

"Sure. We will schedule that for three weeks' time," Morrie said, having no intention of doing so.

Maimon ruffled the hair of his two boys, beginning to realize how much he was going to miss them, and the food conglomerate that they had expanded on the back of his reverse-takeover of alcoholic Bellingham's Prestige Milling Company all those years ago.

"Don't forget to send me the management accounts every month," Maimon reminded them as he walked out. "Your mother is beginning to understand them at last."

Taking two envelopes out of his pocket, Maimon handed one each to his sons, then he walked out and into the car, whose door Daniel held open for him. In their office, the boys opened the envelopes that had identical letters in them.

My Dear Sons,

This wonderful country, which has been so good to all of us, is, it pains me to write, on a slippery slope. Like a glacier, it moves so slowly that one hardly notices the changes, but moving it is every day.

In your lifetimes, or maybe in those of your children or grandchildren, the natives will take over this country, and because the whites have been too near-sighted to educate them, they will be ill-equipped to run what could be the United States of Africa. Could be, but tragically will never be a country rivalling the USA.

The natives will take over our assets, which are our businesses and our factories, and they will either pay us nothing for them, or will do so in a currency that will probably be next to worthless.

I know it is not for me to tell you how, or where, to live your lives, but I leave these thoughts with you for your consideration.

You should both have homes in Palestine, which I sincerely believe will flower and become our long-awaited, prosperous homeland. As I write this, the United States is seen by many as Utopia, and so for some people it might be. Should you decide to live there you might consider Colorado.

Sometime in the future, a significant portion of the Canary Islands are going to slip into the Atlantic Ocean, which will create a tidal wave that will kill hundreds of millions of people on the Eastern Seaboard of the United States and Canada. I have been told that California has a pleasant climate, but it is also susceptible to forest fires, particularly in the south of the state, and earthquakes in the north. You know, of course, about the San Francisco earthquake of 1906 when over 3000 people died.

As important as it is to cater for the welfare of our descendants, and by "welfare," I mean Education and Healthcare, it is no less important that we do the same for those of our fellow dwellers on this planet, to the extent that our relatively meagre resources permit. I have set up an international version of the DAG Foundation, into which I will put 10% of our offshore assets, and each year we will supplement them by adding 10% of our profits, so the three of us (you two and I) had better ensure that there are sufficient profits to do so.

Towards the end of his life, Paul Kruger told me, "Seek all that is to be found good and fair in the past, shape your ideal accordingly, and try to realize that ideal for the future."

If you two can do that you will be contented, and I will be immensely proud of you.

Affectionately,

Your father,
Maimon

CHAPTER 82

BACK AT THE RANCH

Just after one, Morrie and Max walked into the meeting room between their offices that also served as a mini-canteen, where they and their father had eaten lunch together for the past twelve years. There were still three chairs, but places set for only two meals. The boys, who were approaching forty, sat in their usual places but said nothing, silently aware that their father was no longer there to guide and advise them.

A double knock on the door was followed by Roisin rushing into the room towards the now unoccupied chair, which she picked up and was about to carry out, when Morrie stopped her doing so.

"What's going on here?" he asked the woman who had worked in the company longer than he had.

By way of reply, Roisin took a piece of paper out of her pocket, which she handed to Morrie. Dictated by Maimon, it read,

> *Don't give Roisin a hard time, my chair doesn't belong here anymore. As we had a rather good year, we can afford to get this room redecorated, and you should do so. A new wall-to-wall carpet, table, and chairs. Also, the lighting is old-fashioned. Fluorescent is all the rage now, as you know, and getting the tubes recessed so that they can't be seen is very attractive. Don't use that crook Lewis unless you want to be robbed. When I come back, I expect not to recognize this room.*

> *Love*
> *Dad*

P.S. If you don't want to be thought of as Victorian businessmen, you might as well get your offices redecorated as well.

Morrie handed the note to Max and smiled as Roisin carried Maimon's chair out of the room.

"It is our business now to fuck up or build up," Morrie said reflectively.

"And if we want to increase the chances of the latter happening, we need to make some changes."

"Like?" Morrie asked, knowing as well as Max did what needed to be done.

"Solidifying the board. This business is too big to run as a two-man partnership. There are people smarter than we are, from whose knowledge we could benefit. Edward Nathan has exposure to many industries and could be of inestimable worth. Also, the accountant, Sonny Fisher."

The first Sokolovindustries Limited's board meeting was unconventional by contemporary corporate standards. Roisin was called in to keep the minutes, which proved to be impossible; it was finally decided that if she recorded what was agreed that would be sufficient.

At the outset Max pointed out that discussing the last year's results wasn't the best use of his fellow board member's time. He and Morrie knew what needed to be done – allocating more resources to their thriving businesses and selling or closing down those whose future seemed questionable – and they were in the process of implementing these necessary actions. The main question facing them, he believed, was where the company should be in ten and twenty and thirty years' time.

All agreed that the group was too agriculturally focussed, and while South Africans would continue eating, and more people needed more food, Sokolovindustries should also be active in fields that were not subject to droughts, locusts, and the rinderpest.

Max pointed out that sugar cane was not affected by any of these misfortunes, and with its big volumes, there should be significant profits to warrant their involvement. After two and a half hours of many interrupted suggestions, Roisin recorded two decisions.

Sonny Fisher suggested, and everyone agreed, that Max and Morrie meet with Hans Merensky, probably the most competent geologist in South Africa, to learn about the country's geology with a view to possibly buying deposits that could be sold or developed later.

Furthermore, they all agreed that Max would meet Hugh Kela-Ushu, chairman of the largest sugar-producing company in South Africa, with a view to possible cooperation with them in the feed industry.

Over the next few weeks Morrie and Max held several meetings with Hans Merensky, in the course of which he convinced them that a gold-bearing reef at deep levels occurred in the northern Orange Free State. Persuading them wasn't very difficult, as neither Max nor Morrie had any South African geological knowledge, and they decided to buy the farms under which the gold-bearing ore allegedly lay. Their rationale for doing so was that, at worst, they would have productive farms. Realizing that Hans Merensky was almost certainly telling other people of his deep gold ore theory, Morrie and Max moved into action.

Checking with the Bloemfontein deeds office, they ascertained the registered owners of the eight farms in question, and then each of the brothers visited four of them, explaining that they were looking to buy corn- and sunflower-producing properties. The conversations therefore revolved around crop yields and average rainfall statistics. Having done so, Max and Morrie then sat down with two local real estate brokers, whom they commissioned to work in tandem to secure offers for all eight properties. Max came up with a complicated but ingenious formulae, whereby the lower the price at which they bought the farms, the higher commission the agents would make. Neither of the brokers had ever worked under conditions such as this, but they set about it with a will, the result of which was that three weeks later the family owned eight Orange Free State farms, and the two brokers took their wives on holidays to Europe, something they never imagined they would ever be able to afford.

There was the fury in the boardrooms of Rand Mines, the Corner House, General Mining, and Central Mining when they realized that the farms they wanted to buy had been purchased by the Sokolovski brothers. Not years before as farming investments, but just a few weeks earlier, surely because of the brothers' accepting Hans Merensky's view on the northern Orange Free State's geological make-up. Anglo American's Ernest and Harry Oppenheimer approached this setback differently.

At Ernest's request, the lawyers Walter Webber and Charles Wentzel hosted a lunch to which Morrie and Max were invited, as were the Anglo's father and son. The outcome of this lunch was a confidential agreement that should the Sokolovskis decide to sell their farms, Anglo American would be given the opportunity of buying them at a price 3.625% higher than the most attractive bid received by the brothers.

Some years later the drilling company, Shaft Sinkers, confirmed Hans Merensky's views, and the family sold all eight farms to Anglo American, who developed their deposits as Western Holdings, Presidents Brand, and Steyn mines, as well as those of Free State Geduld, St. Helena, and Welkom. As a result of this transaction, the Sokolovski family became the largest shareholders in Anglo American after the Oppenheimers.

Hugh Kela-Ushu, the doyen of the Natal sugar industry and the chairman of the largest cane-growing and sugar-producing company in South Africa, advised that he saw no purpose in meeting with Max or hearing what he had in mind. What Max and Morrie wanted to do was to buy from all the sugar producers their total molasses output, for which the sugar refineries presently had no use. Unknown to the South African cane farmers, molasses was an important cattle feed supplement, the use of which was being pioneered in Holland.

Keeping their ears to the ground, Morrie and Max heard that the Cookson family were looking to sell their plantation and sugar-refinery interests, but did not want to do so to the sugar barons. Chris Cookson felt that following his sister's rejection of Hugh's marriage proposal, his vow "to bury the Cookson family financially" was still in force. Proof of this was the insulting price they had been offered for their properties and refinery, by a consortium representing the industry. In five working days, Morrie and Max had bought control of the company, and six weeks later turned up as bone fide sugar producers at the industry's next quarterly meeting.

Discussing their reception afterwards, Morrie said he was not sure if a native or a coolie would have been more warmly welcomed. At the outset, very subtly but unmistakably it was made clear to the brothers that Jews, and particularly Russian Jews, were not wanted or needed by the sugar producers.

The rules of the association included one that required all members to preadvise their fellow producers of any factory expansion plans, which is what Morrie did. To stunned silence, he announced that Cookson Brothers would be building a state-of-the-art refinery, which, when he gave its capacity, all present realized was bigger than Kela-Ushu's largest unit. Max mentioned that they had options on sufficient cane lands to feed their planned refinery.

Morrie didn't tell them that the cost of the Cookson Brothers factory, and the cane lands they had bought to supply it, was totally funded by the profit on a large parcel of Kela-Ushu shares they had bought and sold on the Johannesburg Stock Exchange a month or so earlier. At that time there were very few secrets on the trading floor, and when word got out that the Sokolovski brothers were accumulating Kela-Ushu shares, the price quickly ran up.

CHAPTER 83

A FATALITY

At noon on a late summer day when Morrie should have been gently pointing out to the largest sunflower farmer in the northern Orange Free State that his price ideas were unrealistic, he was instead slouched on a hard wooden chair in a police station not ten miles away.

"Are you sure you killed him?" the earnest officer asked Morrie, who nodded affirmatively, looking up for some sympathy from the youngster questioning him, if not sympathy for the dead black man, then at least for him, Just out of Police Training College, the white, clean-shaven, dark-haired, Afrikaans constable with a spotless uniform and mirror-shiny shoes was doing what he had been taught – taking a detailed statement. Morrie dropped his head into his hands and sighed deeply.

"Did you inspect the victim? Did you feel his pulse? Did you check if he was breathing?"

"Officer, I told you. I hit him at 80 miles an hour. His head smashed into the windscreen divider and split open. Look at my car. It is covered in blood and brains."

"What kind of a car is it?" the officer asked, having come upon that part of the form requiring this information.

"A Studebaker Champion. I told you," Morrie said again.

"Ja. But that was earlier. You hit him instead of the pig?"

"The pig was in the road. The man came out of the mielie field and ran into the road after the pig. When I swerved to miss the pig … I told you all of this already," Morrie said, now sweating profusely. It wasn't hot, but looking at his now-shaking hands, Morrie realized that he was falling apart. In the office and at home he was in control. Now he wasn't, and it petrified him.

"Ja. And you didn't stop because you were afraid of being killed by other natives?"

"I drove straight here. Have you sent an ambulance?"

"You said he is dead. An ambulance won't help him. We will send a kaffir truck for the body."

Having convinced the policeman, with some difficulty, that the man he had hit was dead, Morrie didn't have the energy to fight for an unnecessary ambulance. His head was clearing, and apart from realizing the magnitude of what he had done, Morrie now knew that he needed his brother and also a good lawyer. With difficulty he persuaded the policeman to let him use the telephone.

Now sweating so much that he almost dropped the black Bakelite telephone handset, Morrie croaked, "Roisin, give me Max."

His father's PA knew the brothers so well that those four words, and the tone in which they were said, left her in no doubt that whatever the reason, this was a matter of utmost importance and urgency.

"Morrie, you OK?" was Max's response to Roisin having handed him a note in big black letters saying: END THIS CALL NOW. MR. MORRIE NEEDS TO SPEAK TO YOU.

"I just killed a man."

"Where are you?"

"In the police station."

"Let me speak to the policeman."

As if in a trance Morrie handed the receiver to the policeman. "Here is Konstabel van Vuuren."

"Good morning, Constable. I am Max Sokolovski, the brother of the man in front of you. Is he alright?"

"Ja. He is unharmed."

"Constable, please tell me what happened?"

"He was driving, and he hit a kaffir and killed him."

"In which police station are you?"

"Viljoenskroon,"

"Please give my brother black coffee and keep him there for two hours. I am coming down now."

"The magistrate goes home at four o'clock. I will book him in at 3:45. Do you want the case number?"

"Not now. Thank you, Officer. I will see you soon."

Thirty minutes later, Morrie and the Sokolovski family lawyer, Edward Nathan, were speeding through the southern Transvaal as fast as Max's car would go, which was something over 110 miles an hour. Just under three hours later, a dust-covered Willys-Overland car pulled into the police station car park, its water temperature gauge well into the red part of the "Warning Overheating" section.

Leaving Edward Nathan to switch off the engine and close the car's doors, Max ran into the police station, where waiting for him, was Constable van Vuuren, who led him to the cells under the building. In one of them Morrie was sitting alone on a wooden bench, his head in his hands. Hearing the steel gate being unlocked, Morrie looked up, saw Max, and, bewildered, shook his head. Then the brothers embraced, and for the first time in thirty-five years they both cried.

After a minute or so the brothers separated, and Morrie saw his always-in-control brother, who had ridden to his rescue like John Wayne in a western movie. Max, on the other hand, saw a man he hardly recognized. Disorientated, with a forlorn haunted look, almost like a fugitive, his confident "can-do" brother was gone. Forcing a smile, Max gripped his brother's shoulders and told him "It's going to be alright," knowing that, in fact, it would. Morrie heard the words but couldn't comprehend them.

Thanks to Edward Nathan and a thick wad of pound notes that Max had farsightedly brought along to pay for Morrie's bail, twenty minutes later the brothers and their lawyer were driving back to Johannesburg.

"The case will be transferred to Bloemfontein," Edward Nathan explained, "and there is every chance that the manslaughter charge will either be withdrawn, or, if it comes to court, the judge will direct the jury to find Morrie not guilty."

"When is that likely to be?" Max asked.

"In about six months," their now-gray-haired family lawyer, who had seen their father through many rough seas, replied.

The first thing Colleen knew of the day's events was when Max's dust- coated car drove up their drive and a haggard Morrie and an exhausted Max got out. Taking his brother's arm, Max said, "Let's go and sit down quietly."

It was as well that Max did, as walking to their garden chairs, Morrie tripped twice. Drooling and slurring his speech, he was obviously more affected by the day's events than Max originally realized.

Over the next twenty minutes, Morrie and Max, mainly Max, told Colleen – who sat holding Morrie's hand in her two – of the day's events. Having experienced traumatic events herself, as well as in her medical career witnessing many similar cases, Colleen took control of the situation. First, she covered Morrie in a thick blanket, then sent one of the domestic servants with a prescription to the chemist for some tranquilizers, after which she phoned a psychological counsellor to come and see Morrie in the morning, After that, she went off to tell their children. As a result of Colleen's quick action, and Morrie's resilient make-up, he was back in the office the following afternoon.

With the help of the local farmers, Morrie learned the name and address of the deceased's widow and arranged for her to have a pension for the remainder of her life.

Months later, Edward Nathan told Morrie that the Department of Justice had decided not to prosecute him for the native's death.

CHAPTER 84

BAD NEWS SELLS NEWSPAPERS

Of the things the boys had learned from their father, the importance of having connections up and down the social scale and across the racial and financial spectrum could not be overestimated.

One morning Roisin handed Max a large sealed white envelope. It had no mention of the sender or the intended recipient.

"A man I had never seen before gave it to me a few minutes ago, insisting that I hand it to you personally."

Max opened the envelope and removed the single sheet of paper it contained: the front page of the *Sunday Leien* newspaper to be published in four days' time. Emblazoned across the top of the page, in three-inch black headlines, were two words SOKOLOVSKI MURDERER. Underneath it was a picture of the man Morrie had hit lying in the middle of the road, and next to it a photograph taken at a charity fundraising dinner of a tuxedo-clad Morrie smiling.

"That anti-Semitic son of a bitch," Max spat out. "We are going to squeeze his balls till tears run down his bloated red alcoholic cheeks. That God- given misery is going to remember for the rest of his miserable days this hornet's nest he has kicked open."

With almost messianic fervour the brothers swung into action. Morrie called Edward Nathan and instructed him to get an interdict forbidding the Sunday Leien from printing any article of this nature. Max called the manager of Sokolovindustries' media department and told him to pull every advertisement they had booked in the *Sunday Leien* as well as in all the magazines in the Deitado Group's stable. Finally, Max instructed the company's treasurer not to pay any money owing for past advertisements.

"Today, tomorrow, never? When do you think we will hear from these mamzayrim?"[154] Morrie asked.

"Hours," Max replied, "and not too many of those. Let's go and have a good lunch. Chez Andre do a very decent duck à l'orange and their crêpe Montmorency is the best way of getting 1,000 calories into one's body in less than five minutes."

As they drove through their office-complex gates on the way back to the Sokol Building, the security guard handed Max an envelope. Inside was a note from Roisin advising that a director of Deitado Publishing was waiting to see them. Max handed the letter to Morrie, saying, "I should have bet you on this."

Morrie and Max walked into the reception area where Roisin stood – or, more accurately, sat – guard. Wishing Max and Morrie good afternoon, she handed Morrie the card of the visitor, a 50-year-old man in a dark suit, white shirt, and Rand Club tie. Morrie looked at the card, dropped it, picked it up, and passed it to Max, who read aloud, "Constantine Heathstone-Fotheringham – Commercial Director, Deitado Publishing."

Addressing Roisin, Max said, "Please tell this gentleman that if a representative of his company wishes to see us, it should be their managing director, and he should make an appointment, not assume, as this commercial fellow has, that we see any Tom, Dick, or Harry who happens to wander into our premises. Thank you." Saying which, Max and Morrie walked into their offices.

"Shall we disturb his drinking or his sleeping hours – 6:30 this evening or 6:30 tomorrow morning?" Morrie asked.

"Getting up early is good for the soul. Let's do it tomorrow morning."

When Deitado's managing director's PA duly called an hour or so later, she was given the good news. To his credit, Sir Ponsonby McAucliffe arrived spot on time and was shown to the meeting room, where Morrie and Max awaited him. Around the table were three chairs, two of which were occupied, and in front of the third was the *Sunday Leien's* proposed front page mock-up that Max had received anonymously. Max motioned their visitor to the empty chair.

"Sir Ponsonby," Max began, "both my brother and I, as well as our families, were appalled at this proposed front page of your newspaper. So was the judge who issued the interdict, forbidding you to publish it."

---

154   *Originally people born as a result of incest or from a forbidden relationship, but today considered a deliberate insult*

"A most unfortunate situation," Sir Ponsonby admitted. "It should never have been produced."

"Actions have consequences," Morrie pointed out, "and your proposed front page is no exception. My brother and I have discussed it, and we believe the following would be appropriate under the circumstances."

"Going forward," Max continued, "it will no longer be necessary for you to mention the religion of any person appearing in your newspaper, or in any of your group's magazines."

"That will be no problem," Sir Ponsonby conceded.

"For the next four weeks your newspaper will publish articles on the creches run free of charge by every one of our eleven factories countrywide"

"Count that as done," Sir Ponsonby responded, grateful that he not been called upon to bear a financial penalty – yet.

"Additionally," Morrie told Sir Ponsonby, "before the end this month the Deitado Publishing Group will make a £25,000 donation to the Johannesburg Jewish Helping Hand & Burial Society."

"That is a lot of money," the managing director pointed out, the blood temporarily drained from his alcoholic face.

"Not such a lot spread over five years. Later this morning, one of your people will deliver to this office five checks for £5,000 each. One dated today, and the other four a year ahead of one another."

"Don't you trust our group to pay the money each year?" Sir Ponsonby asked offended. When the brothers ignored his question, he added, "Are post-dated checks really necessary?"

Both Max and Morrie ignored the question.

"Lastly," Max added, "your sports editor seems to be a bit understaffed. No matches in which the Balfour Park football team play are ever reported. That needs to be changed."

"Of course it will. There is one matter I would like to raise. It seems that your account is somewhat overdue. If this can be looked into, I would appreciate it."

By way of reply Max and Morrie stood up, indicating the meeting had ended. The unsubtle message got through to Sir Ponsonby, who walked to the door, through it, and down to his car.

"The son of a bitch didn't even apologize," Morrie pointed out.

"I was going to make it £15,000, but in the absence of , 'I am really sorry,' increased it to £25,000'," Max explained.

CHAPTER 85

A NEW GOVERNMENT

In 1948 white South Africans voted the National Party into power for the first time and continued to do so uninterruptedly for the next forty-six years. It was this political party that brought in a number of race-orientated bills, which resulted in them being known as the "Apartheid Regime."

In the period between the election and the National Party taking power, Philip Rahmen, the owner and managing director of the country's largest textile company, convened a meeting attended by the prime minister-to-be, Dr. Malan, and his designate minister of Finance, NC Havenga, together with the leaders of South African industry. The purpose of the get-together was to give the industrialists an opportunity to learn what legislation the government-in-waiting proposed tabling in the months ahead. As few of the attendees knew Dr. Malan; all were requested to introduce themselves when asking a question. Out of deference, Mr. Oppenheimer was given the opportunity of framing the first question.

"In the last decade, your party made it abundantly clear, Doctor, that should it come to power, all new legislation would benefit the Afrikaner sector, with little regard for other population groups. Is this still the case?"

"Yes," Dr. Malan responded to the apparent surprise of some of the meeting's attendees.

"William Scawman – Steel Industry. Doctor, you will shortly be the prime minister of all South Africans. Do you not consider you have a responsibility to look after citizens of all colors?"

"Mr. Scawman, you and the other people in this room are well able to look after yourselves," Dr. Malan began. "As for the blacks, we have plans that will restore them to their historical position in South Africa."

"In the rural areas? Stanley Michael – Fishing Industry" asked.

"Yes. That is where they came from and that is where they belong," the doctor added, leaving none of the captains of industry in any doubt about the legislation they faced in the weeks and months ahead.

"Max Sokolovski, the Food Industry. One of your members of Parliament recently said that black people would not be permitted to drive trucks. Is that correct?"

"If trucks have to be driven in the rural areas, blacks can drive them there. In the urban areas, whites will do that job."

"Philip Rahman – Textile Industry. If the blacks are going to be living in the rural areas, then who is going to work our factories in the Pretoria-Johannesburg-Vereeniging industrial complex?"

"Philip Rahman," Dr. Malan began, "you should move your factories to the black areas. We are going to call them Bantustans. The mines obviously can't move, so we will continue to allow blacks to work for them on a contract basis."

"Zalman Ziegel, representing the Building Industry. Dr. Malan, should a white person have sexual relations with a black or a colored person, would you designate a special part of the country for their offspring to live in?" he asked somewhat tongue-in-cheek.

"Any such person will go to the devil when he dies. Until then, he will sit in jail," the prime minister designate told him.

"And if such a person is a woman?" Morrie asked.

Dr. Malan looked at Morrie in disgust, as if he was advocating such practices.

"Mr. Sokolovski, no white woman would do such a thing, unless she was mentally unbalanced, and if she was, there are homes for such people."

The meeting broke up shortly thereafter, with the industrialists agreeing amongst themselves that, the moral issue aside, economically what the government-in-waiting had in mind was unworkable and unaffordable.

CHAPTER 86

THE CURTAIN COMES DOWN

Away from their Johannesburg responsibilities, Maimon and Elize had the most wonderful time. Living in a modest wooden beach house on one of their sand dunes, the two of them walked on the beach every morning. Around noon assorted visitors dropped in, and after lunch their house was invaded by Jenna's and Joshua's children, David and Arielle and later the twins Matias and Mikayla, sometimes with one or both of their patents, often without them.

One morning Golda Meier arrived, unannounced. The three of them chatted for about an hour, and then Maimon asked, "How much?"

"One million dollars," his incorrigible guest answered.

"And from Elize?" Maimon asked. "She should not be left out."

They agreed on three million dollars from the family, after which Maimon had a request.

"We are desperately short of fighting men," Maimon reminded Golda. "As they come off the boats, we put them in uniforms and send them to one of the fronts."

"That is sadly so. But what choice do we have?" Golda asked more to herself than to Maimon and Elize.

"I am going to fight with them," Maimon told Golda. "I could do with a bit of training. Not much, though."

Elize, beside herself with fear, looked at Maimon in horror. As soon as the door behind Golda closed, she exploded.

"Are you stark raving mad? You are old. Really old. Wars are for young people. How could you ask Golda without our discussing it first?"

Elize continued with a list of relevant and well-thought-out questions and statements. When she stopped for air, Maimon put his hand on Elize's and said quietly.

"I am almost 90 years old – or '90 years young,' as little David says. You and I have done everything we want to do, and more – much, much more. What better way is there of saying thank you for all the blessings God has given us than to fight for what we believe in."

"*Us?*" Elize asked.

"I wouldn't go without you. Unless you agreed to come with me, I couldn't go. We have done so many things together, we should do this, too."

Elize wasn't sure about this. Her father's and brother's deaths were seared in her mind, and she had never forgotten Maimon's statement on the way back to the hotel from Dr. Storkman's rooms in London, wishing that none of their children would ever have to fight a war. This was different, of course, and maybe she owed it to Alison and Daniel. In fact, she decided, because of them, and their children, she did, Elize told Maimon.

Elize admitted to herself that this threw a completely different slant on the whole subject. Sitting all day in their beach house, with occasional trips to the orange farm to see how the South African citrus was taking to Palestine's climatic conditions, was very boring. Helping fight for the nation you love was the ultimate joy, she admitted to herself. She also knew that a bigger problem would be the children, but together they had fought, and won, more important battles.

"You are right. We should do it," she said.

Maimon told Golda, and Elize mentioned it to the children, both with correctly anticipated responses. Golda said she would see what she could do, and the children and grandchildren said absolutely not. When Elize and Maimon pointed out that they had discharged all of their responsibilities, and then some, and was it not selfish for their children to prevent them spending the rest of their lives as they wished to, the opposition largely fell away. The following morning, on returning to their bedroom from his shower, Maimon found a numbered envelope on his pillow. He handed it to Elize, who smiled, removed the pages, and began reading letter "#13."

My Diamond Jubilee Husband, Partner in Life, Lover, and Soul Mate,

Today it is sixty years since our wedding in Johannesburg, and what a wonderful almost 22,000 days they have been.

So much of our lives together have been upside-down or back-to-front. Firstly, the Siddur, then you asking my father for permission to marry me, and only doing so years later, and now we are going to fight for our country, which is usually done by people sixty years younger than we are.

Last night after you fell asleep, I started thinking about the wonderful times we have had together, there are so many of them. When my father brought you to the farm, and that wonderful Friday night at the concentration camp, the night in Jerusalem when Alison and Daniel were carried in, sitting in Morrie's hospital room and hearing him talk again, the two of us playing with our grandchildren, there are so many.

For me one stands out head and shoulders above all the others, and that was when you gave Koos another chance.

I was so proud of you that morning at the Mount Nelson Hotel. There was no advantage to you for helping him. You could have given him £20 and sent him on his way. I do not know one man in the whole world who would have done what you did.

You know I say my prayers every night. I pray to God to look after our children and grandchildren, and I name every one of them every night, and then, before I go to sleep, I thank God for putting me on that wall in East London where you would see me.

Tonight I am going to ask God to please answer just one more prayer for me, and that is if you get killed, would he please kill me at the same time.

Life without you would be worse than death for me.

Your ever-loving, always loving,
Elize

As Maimon and Elize expected he would, Joshua made sure that his parents-in-law were drafted to a lower risk theater of war, which was being fought by professional Israeli soldiers, specifically the army's 8th and Givati brigades, and not by refugees just off the boat. They were battling the Egyptians in an area known as the Falouja Pocket. In central Sinai, its main feature was the Suwaydan Police Fort, which the British had handed over to the Muslim Brotherhood. Due to its strategic position Israel had to capture it, which they eventually did, at their eighth attempt.

Despite the couple's protestations, the Israel Defence Force refused to let their two elderly, enthusiastic volunteers into a fighting unit, offering them instead kitchen duties. Not entirely happily, Maimon and Elize accepted, and were instructed to collect their fatigues, some underwear and toiletries from the army's Tel Aviv stores. Then they were shipped off to Falouja in a US Army Jeep driven by a recently arrived teenager from Hungary. When Maimon learned the young man had never had a driving lesson, he swapped seats with the soldier. The trip took most of the day, but that was OK because driving in an open Jeep with your wife alongside you, through your new country, Israel, what more could one hope for?

That evening they sat on camp chairs outside their tent, looked up at the millions of stars, and reminisced about when and where they had done this in the past. Starting with their trip to the Thabazimbi iron mountain, their freezing nights in the Yorkshire Dales, and numerous visits to game farms, and ending with the night they had recently spent at the Dead Sea. Holding hands, they shared these wonderful memories.

As it came from over their right shoulders, neither Maimon nor Elize saw the mortar shell arcing towards them, nor could they have felt for longer than a mini-second the searing heat that engulfed them, their tent, and its contents.

Memorial services for Maimon and Elize were held in Johannesburg and Tel Aviv, and, at their workers' insistence, at every one of the group's seventeen industrial plants scattered around South Africa.

Towards the end of the service at the company's Idutywa factory, one of the workers stood up. He didn't say anything, he just stood looking at the priest. The room fell silent, as it did every year when the manager was going to make the Christmas bonus announcements.

"Our Father who art in heaven," L'wazi began. But instead of continuing with The Lord's prayer, he said, "I am not referring to Jesus

610

Christ, but to Mr. Maimonides Sokolovski, who was truly a father to all of us." A murmur of agreement came out of three hundred throats, as it was not only the workers who were present, but also their wives and girlfriends.

"You all know my boy Dumisa, the one who was born a cripple. From a little boy he had to walk with a stick. The doctors called it a club foot. You know Mr. Maimon took Dumisa and his mother to Johannesburg. You know he had three operations and was in hospital for many months. In Johannesburg he was nearly one year. You saw Dumisa when he came back, that he could walk and run, and even play football, and that was thanks to the Lord and Mr. Maimon."

A round of applause went round the hall. When it stopped, L'wazi held up a letter.

"What you don't know is this letter I received today. From Johannesburg. From Kaiser Chiefs. They have given my Dumisa a contract. For three years. To play football. For three years Kaiser Chiefs are going to pay my Dumisa to play football. Praise the Lord for this miracle and for his disciple, Mr Maimon, for making it possible."

The hall broke into wild applause, the letter being passed from hand to hand for all to see what truly was a miracle.

Tributes poured in from all over the world, almost all expressing in their own words those that Field Marshall Smuts quoted from *Hamlet* in his address at the Johannesburg memorial service.

"He was a man. Take him for all in all. I shall not look upon his like again."

ABOUT THE AUTHOR

Aaron Di Dertseyler was born in Cape Town, South Africa, where his education was interrupted first by junior school, and then by high school in Grahamstown. Unhappy with many aspects of South African society, at eighteen he boarded a boat for London, where, after a brief foray into the medical world, he joined a city merchant bank. In addition to financing, his business career took in resource commercialization in North and South America, the Middle and Far East, in the course of which he spent extended periods of time in Peru, Iran and Hong Kong. Passing through London on one of his trips he met and subsequently married the girl of his dreams. In Africa Aaron flew his own plane on business and to game reserves, and in Papua New Guinea and French Polynesia he scuba-dived among hammer-head sharks. Aaron and his wife live in London, from where they visit their children and grandchildren in the United Kingdom, America, and Australia. For over twenty years he has run a colour-blind charitable trust financing "bright and broke" students studying practical degrees at South African universities. During this period, over 1,000 students have graduated, most of whom would not have been able to attend university without his trust's support .

Printed in Great Britain
by Amazon

80522083R00356